For Them

To Ellen

FINAL TRUMPET

A Novel of Rescue, Romance and Revenge

Karl Lenker

ENJOY THE RIDE!

FINAL TRUMPET is a work of fiction. Names, characters, places and incidents are either products of the author's imagination or used fictitiously and are not intended to reflect in any way on actual events or actual organizations or persons, living or dead. Any opinions of the characters are theirs alone and do not necessarily reflect those of the author or publisher.

The plight of the African elephant is, regrettably, all too real and worthy of our intervention.

Library of Congress Cataloging-in-Publication Data

Final Trumpet, Karl Lenker
Second Edition, First Printing
10 9 8 7 6 5 4 3 2 1
Published in Boca Raton, Florida, by Trimark Press, Inc.

ISBN: 978-0-9816092-0-1

2500 North Military Trail
Suite 260
Boca Raton, FL 33431
800.889.0693
trimarkpress.com
publisher@trimarkpress.com

TaleWinds Press, LLC
author@Talewindspress.com

Printed and bound in the United States of America.

AUTHOR'S NOTES

My favorite works of fiction are those wherein I learn new facts, enjoy new experiences and travel instantly to real places on the wings of the written word. FINAL TRUMPET is as real as fiction gets. The primary plot and main characters are a product of my imagination. The technology, methodology and weaponry is dead-on accurate circa the early 1990s. The happiest 1,800 hours of my life were spent with the world's most destructive attack jet strapped to my butt—a pilot's, shooter's and pyromaniac's wildest dream. The finest, closest and most trusted friends I have ever had are my fellow civilian pilots and those with whom I proudly served for 25 years in the Maryland Air National Guard. I hope to honor all of them by including portraits of a select few in this story.

I have witnessed the endearing elephant behaviors portrayed in this book with my own eyes, on video, or through the eyes of actual researchers as reported in their journals and documentaries. The illegal ivory trail is fact. I have changed or modified player's names just enough to keep me out of court. The mysterious man encountered by John Forrest is, amazingly enough, an actual person. If, after this writing, his magic hasn't failed him and he hasn't become dinner for the crocodiles who contribute to his livelihood, he is a living, breathing, human being.

In 1981, an unknown writer visited my fighter squadron to supposedly conduct research for an article on the A-10. To my knowledge, no such article ever materialized. However, in late 1984, my unit, the 175th Fighter Group, appeared on page 251 of The Hunt for Red October. That brilliant, blockbuster book and my conversations with its author were the inspiration for my own. Thank you, Tom Clancy.

ACKNOWLEDGMENTS

No one ever creates anything without the help and inspiration of others. This work is no exception.

First and foremost, thanks to the African elephant and the despicable scum who kill them for profit. Dear elephants, you are the noblest of beasts and above any accolades I could bestow. Poachers, your incredible vacuum of compassion, humanity and anything decent makes you the best of antagonists and the worst of villains, far better bad-guys than anything I could create.

Many thanks to all those who have provided me with research material, technical facts and suggestions. You have helped me put the "real" in realism.

Special thanks to Betty Reed, my first manuscript editor, for the hours of dedication, corrections, scolding and encouragement.

A thousand thanks to Elizabeth Hickman and the team at TriMark Press for their hard work in making this book a reality.

Heartfelt thanks go to my son John Lenker for your common sense approach to editing and to my talented wife Laurel Wood. Laurel, your ability to catch the most subtle of errors is amazing. Your unwillingness to patronize me and say "it's good" when it wasn't, is most appreciated. Diplomacy may be the art of compromise—good work, isn't.

Eternal thanks to almighty God for creating it all and forgiving me for my mishandling of it.

Any mistakes, errors or misrepresentations are all mine. I, alone, accept responsibility for them.

Certainly, there is no hunting like the hunting of a man.
And those who have hunted armed men long enough
and like it never care for anything else.

Ernest Hemingway

And the fear of you and the dread of you shall be
upon every beast of the earth, and upon every fowl of the air,
upon all that moveth upon the earth, and upon all the fishes of the sea;
into your hand they are delivered.

GENESIS 9:2

He who sets out for revenge should first dig two graves.

Chinese Proverb

PROLOGUE

"I'VE GOT A very bad feeling about this, Nat," Amy Lee uttered anxiously, trembling in the predawn chill.

"About what, honey?" her husband of three weeks asked over his shoulder, only half paying attention as he made a few last-minute adjustments to their video camera's tripod.

"Remember what that brochure said: 'Tsavo means a place of slaughter.'" She turned up the collar of her thin, hot-pink jacket and leaned over to hold the flashlight on his hands. "Maybe we shouldn't be here."

"Mmm hmm," Nathan murmured as he pointed the camera's lens—a wedding gift from her father—vaguely toward the waterhole which spread before them in the darkness. "I'm sure that means animals, babe, not humans. It seemed safe enough the other day. Every lion we saw was sleeping, remember?" He leaned forward to check the switchology. "Move the light to the buttons."

She did as he asked, trying her best to hold the light steady. "Yeah. But we were with ten other tour busses and it was broad daylight. The safari guide warned us not to come out here by ourselves," she continued, thinking about the safety of their rented Land Rover which was hidden in the thick brush a hundred meters to their rear—much too far away for her liking.

Nathan checked his watch and set the camera to begin recording with the touch of a single button. He would do so at the first sign of their quarry's arrival. "Well, it'll be daylight soon," he said, dismissing her fear while going over a mental checklist: *Full tape...full battery...*

spare's in my pocket. Then, realizing some reassurance was in order, he turned and surrounded his new bride in his arms. "Don't worry, babe. Those guys always make it sound more dangerous than it is. It makes the whole thing seem more dramatic—more adventurous." He squeezed her until she groaned. "That's all showbiz! Besides, if everyone came out here by themselves, think of all the tourist revenue they'd lose."

Amy shuddered and pushed him away. "Think of all the *tourists* they'd lose."

Nathan snorted a laugh. "Aren't you the one who fell in love with the elephant family; you know, all the babies they have, 'n stuff?"

"Hmm. Yeah," she responded, looking away for a moment.

"Hmm. Yeah," he mimicked. "Was there another beautiful blonde who suggested that we get away by ourselves and come back out here or could that have been you?" Nathan questioned further, lowering his head for emphasis.

Amy drew back with a mock indignant look. "There'd better *not* be another beautiful blonde asking you a question like that."

They exchanged smiles.

Amy folded her arms across her chest and shivered again.

"Are you cold?" he asked, immediately realizing she wasn't.

Her answer came after a minute's hesitation. "Sort of."

"I know a good way to warm you up," he teased. "Guaranteed or your money back."

Although she could barely make out the outline of his face, she could feel the glow of his lecherous smile. "Yeah, right," she replied with a mirthless laugh. "There's probably a big lion out there watching us, right this minute, just waiting for us to get naked so he won't have to bother with our clothes."

Nathan laughed. He loved her dry humor along with everything else about her—her long blond hair, her big brown doe-like eyes, her wonderful body. Visions of their wedding night played in his head on fast-forward, a night he was sure he would never forget as long as he lived. Their honeymoon, courtesy of their parents, had been a dream come true. And now it was almost over. They were scheduled to leave Nairobi the next morning. "It'll only take a minute," he continued, feeling for her jacket's zipper. "And it won't hurt a bit."

She slapped his hand away. "Cut it out." She scolded, wrestling herself out of his arms. "Besides, my father's probably watching us right now." She looked up at the East African sky. A zillion stars sparkled before the magenta edge of dawn's first glow. Some of them, she knew only too well, were man-made.

"Oh yeah?" Nathan laughed dismissively. "Watch this!"

Her body trembled, this time with a silent chuckle. Barely twenty-one, Nat was full of youth's piss and vinegar, just like his father, she thought, shaking her head. Making her laugh was one of his sexiest and most endearing qualities. She recalled what her father had said about him at their wedding as Nathan danced with his new mother-in-law. "The apple never falls far from the tree," he'd whispered in her ear. "God help us, honey."

"I'll give him something to photograph." Nathan quickly unzipped his fly and pulled his Levis and briefs down around his ankles. "How 'bout a moon shot?" Grabbing his ankles, he arched his back sticking his bare butt high in the air, cackling a defiant laugh as he did. "That ought'a give the CIA something to talk about."

In the brilliant first light of dawn, the snow-capped peak of Mount Kilimanjaro glimmered majestic and aloof under its crown of white. Dominating the southwestern horizon, the crest shone like a beacon above the shadow blanketing the surrounding savanna. In the waning darkness, massive gray forms drifted silently eastward into the sunrise. Africa's gentle giants had begun their morning commute.

It was late November and although the end of the dry season approached, drought tenaciously gripped the land. For the third time in as many years the merciful, rain-bearing monsoon clouds were late for their annual appointment.

As sunlight gradually evicted the stubborn darkness, the dim figures acquired the unmistakable shape of the world's largest land animal—*loxodonta africana*—the African elephant. A few meters in front of the herd, a large female led the way. When she paused to check on her plodding followers, she noticed that, occasionally, some of the calves had to be spurred on by their mothers. They were tired and hungry and wanted to stop to nurse. But she knew that there would be plenty of time for that later. First, they had to find water.

In all, there were eight elephants in the family group. The matriarch, the largest and oldest, presided over three females who each had one calf. An adolescent male brought up the rear of the procession, ambling along at his own pace. Playful and easily distracted, the young bull stopped to watch a small flock of guinea fowl flutter through the brush.

The matriarch stopped for a moment and looked back to assess the situation. Assured that everyone was more or less in line, she turned and headed on. For thirty years, the majestic lady had used her experience and instincts to protect her family from a host of dangers. Today would be no exception.

In the distance, a throaty roar reminded her that the big cats still owned the night. As they neared the water hole it became increasingly important for her to keep the family together and avoid leaving vulnerable stragglers. During the dry season water holes were precious, life-saving features of the savanna. But, during any season, they were also fraught with perils. And, like other "watering holes" all over the world, the rough crowd usually showed up later at night.

The family moved ponderously through the brush and dry grass, periodically pausing to sniff the air and listen. Good security was a must for any wild creature, even those as large as a bulldozer. Adult elephants, with their tremendous bulk and brute strength, could fend off even the most formidable attackers. Calves, however, were an entirely different matter. Constant vigilance was required so that no predator could approach them unnoticed for, in nature, almost all surprises are bad surprises.

The family rounded two large, flat-topped acacia trees and entered a huge expanse of open grassland. One hundred meters ahead, the matriarch sighted the muddy banks that marked the edges of the water hole. She brought the group to a halt while she studied the situation.

Three hundred meters to the east, a dozen zebras and a small herd of Thompson's gazelles eyed the scene. Warily keeping their distance, they scrutinized the approaching elephants. The matriarch's experience told her that their alert posture was a signal that something was amiss. Normally, the approaching behemoths would have to make room for themselves in the pond or along its crowded edge as other thirsty creatures begrudgingly moved out of their way. This day, however, aside from a few doves, sand grouse and marabou storks drinking from the mocha-colored water, the water hole appeared to be empty.

The matriarch sniffed the air, nervously urinating onto the dusty soil. There was a lot wrong with this picture and all those wrongs spelled warning. She gave a low rumble, communicating her uneasiness to the rest of the group.

Mirroring their leader's example, the other elephants lifted their trunks and spread their ears. The calves mimicked the adults. Their immature yet animated nose-hoses stretched and twisted to sample the airborne soup of scents. One scent the calves did recognize was the unmistakable smell of the muddy water. Oblivious to the rising apprehension among the adults, they began to push ahead toward their favorite playground.

Off to her right, the matriarch noticed a sudden movement in the brush and turned to face it. She lifted her trunk and sniffed in that direction. The dead calm of morning had given way to a slight breeze that blew from her left rear quarter. Whatever it was, it would be difficult to detect downwind.

Suddenly, there was another quick movement in the brush. With growing anxiety, she sniffed more vigorously. She took a few tentative steps toward the area of the last movement. Her ears spread wide as she strained to detect any sounds which might identify the intruder.

As she listened, one of the calves bolted off in a trot toward the water. Instantly, his mother, grunting in protest, charged after him. Before she could turn her head to investigate the commotion, the matriarch caught several more quick movements off to her right front. She didn't have to see the objects clearly to know that they were sizable and threatening.

The matriarch wheeled one hundred eighty degrees to her left, reversing course, her eyes wide with alarm. Responding to her about-face signal, the column turned around and hurried back the way they had come. Instinctively, the adults gathered around the calves pushing them to the center of the gray fortress they created with their massive bodies. As they moved to regroup in the concealment of the thorny brush, the cloud of dust they created blew ahead of them, obscuring their vision. The young male now found himself in front of the formation, driven along by the momentum of the group. Unable to see ahead, he held his trunk and head high to shield his eyes from the needle-covered branches.

"What do you think scared them? Us?" Amy suggested, answering her own question with a fallen face.

Nathan moved forward to the edge of the brush, watching the elephant's speedy withdrawal, his brow knitted with concern. "Beats me, babe," he responded with a shrug. "It's not like they've never seen tourists before."

Suddenly, the young male elephant saw them just twenty meters ahead—the most dangerous and feared predators on the planet. Half hidden in the brush and swirling dust, their appearance halted him so abruptly that the cow following just behind rammed her tusks into his hindquarters.

Sandwiched between his mother and his older brother, a small calf bumped into the teenager's rear legs just as two assault rifles began firing in short, three-round bursts. The metallic chatter punctured the morning serenity.

As the first bullets tore through his forehead and widespread ears, the young male stumbled backward, tripping on his little brother. His hind legs collapsed bringing his massive rump down like a falling boulder, crushing the baby's head against the ground. The calf's muffled cries were scarcely noticed by his mother who was being torn apart by another volley of fire from the automatic weapons. One round penetrated her right eye, ricocheted off hard bone and exited through her forehead covering her face with a soupy mixture of blood, bone fragments and soft tissue. A second and third round ripped into her neck, cutting her windpipe and exiting through the lower part of her left ear. Even before she hit the ground, the mother of two was struck by two more rounds in the neck and shoulder. Her fall was broken by the body of her calf and the rear legs of the juvenile male—her first-born offspring.

"My God!" Amy Lee gasped, bringing her trembling hands to her ears. Though utterly frightened, she had no idea of the situation's true gravity. She saw the color suck from Nathan's face.

"Go! Go! Go!" he hissed, his eyes wild with fear. "Get the hell outta here!" Nathan spun around and lunged toward his wife, tripping on a leg of their camera's tripod, toppling it into a nearby thorn bush.

Needing no further encouragement, she waited not a second. She was already ten paces in front of him when, remembering the camera, he pivoted about to retrieve it.

Amy dug her Nikes in hard then suddenly slid to a stop. "Aaaahhhh," she screamed. Five feet separated them when a man's opaque white eye met hers for a terrifying instant. His face was gruesome. A hideous, pink scar lined his forehead, skipped over his dead, opal-like eyeball to bite deeply into his coal-black cheek. His good eye was wide with shock—apparently as surprised by the encounter as she. Stunned by his appearance, she hardly noticed as he brought his rifle to his hip.

Amy lunged to her right just as the Cyclops-come-to-life yanked back hard on the trigger. The muzzle of his AK-47 rode up cutting thorny branches above the new bride's back as she dove into the shadow beneath.

"Amy!" Nathan bellowed. He abandoned the camera and took off toward the sound of his wife's cries. Just as he was about to round a bush, a hail of bullets cut through its branches driving him into the dirt. Nathan went down on his face, then scrambled for cover on his belly as still more bullets whizzed through the branches above his head.

The remaining elephants were stunned by the deafening cacophony of gunfire. Unable to react in time, the second female in the herd was assaulted from her right by another pair of men who expended half of their thirty-round magazines into her side. Several bullets tore through her rib cage. Shattering bone, they careened through her lungs and heart stealing her last breath. She lay down slowly and, like a capsizing battleship, rolled over onto her side. Her young calf stood paralyzed with terror in the U shaped area formed by his mother's belly and her front and rear legs.

Desperate to defend her family, the matriarch charged in front of the remaining female and her calf. Her head lowered and ears spread wide, she propelled herself toward the two nearest attackers.

Caught off-guard and stumbling backwards, the men fired the last two-or-three rounds in their magazines. One of them quickly fingered his magazine release and removed the empty. Hurriedly, without wasting motion, he flipped it over and reinserted another one which was conveniently taped side-by-side to the first.

His diminutive partner turned to run as the mountain of fury closed the distance between them to a mere twenty meters. With the bearing and nerve of a combat veteran, the first man brought his rifle up digging the butt into his shoulder. The matriarch charged ahead. Ten meters—he could feel the ground shake. At that range there was no need to use the sights. He steadied the muzzle on the center of the matriarch's face and pulled the trigger. Six rounds ripped into her head forming a dotted line which arched upward from just below her left eye and ended just above the right.

Despite the mortal wounds, her momentum carried her forward. The tall man lunged to avoid the ivory spears then shoulder-rolled to a kneeling position. As the huge beast thundered past, he emptied the magazine into her left side beginning just behind her shoulder. The bullets, stinging like hot copper hornets, cut through her thick hide as if it were foam rubber. Puffs of dust marked their entry points. Her front legs collapsed and she slid several feet on her knees, her tusks plowing through the loose soil. Unable to move, yet unwilling to let herself fall, the old lady remained motionless, gasping for breath.

The second man, recovering from his momentary loss of control, moved ahead cautiously. He emptied his entire magazine in the direction of the struggling beast. Though the 7.62mm projectiles were designed for killing humans rather than large animals, the sheer number of rounds fired compensated for their ballistic unsuitability. The few that found their mark were enough. At the remarkable age of sixty-one, the family's matriarch took her last painful breath.

The group's leader looked around to recover his black hat. As he dusted it off on his trousers, he shouted for the little man to follow him. Though Black Hat suffered with a noticeable limp, the second, much shorter man, struggled to keep up with him as they headed off in the direction of their partner's gunfire.

Nathan lay on his belly under a huge bush, firmly gripped in panic. He wanted desperately to scream his wife's name but feared the shout would help their assailants target both of them. After what seemed the longest, most anguished wait of his life, he heard a distant man shout something in Swahili which brought two others running from a position of concealment just in front of him. Nathan heard more shouting and the roar of gunfire as the screaming elephants finally fell silent.

"Amy," he gasped, crawling frantically through the brush. "Amy! It's me!" young Nathan whispered hoarsely as he slid along on his belly from bush to bush. The only elements to meet his senses were the odors of dust and gun smoke and the occasional voices of his assailants. His bride was no where to be seen. The anxiety of not knowing her situation crushed his lungs.

"Oh God. Oh God," he moaned, "Please help us!" His chest heaved as he sank further into the depths of despair.

Nathan's prayers were answered immediately though not with divine intervention as he had hoped. Instead, his back was pounded with a short burst from a Russian-made assault rifle which drove him forward to breathe his last, his head lying in an expanding pool of his own dark blood.

Faint traces of smoke drifted out of his Kalashnikov's barrel as Black Hat raised the weapon and turned to locate the other men in the dense thicket. He motioned to the Little Man who lingered for a long hard look at the white man his boss had just slaughtered. He was stunned, but an angry shout turned him around to follow Black Hat into the dense brush.

Amy lay motionless beneath a huge acacia bush like a petrified rabbit. Thoughts bounced around in her pounding head alternating between escaping in their Land Rover, locating her husband and trying to evade these monsters and their guns.

She allowed herself another thought: how like this awful moment, a quarter century ago, it must have been for a frightened soldier—just a kid like her, really—to be concealed in a jungle thicket while eluding a deadly enemy.

A snapping twig and the rustle of boots against branches startled her back to the present day. Her eyes searched frantically for signs of movement.

Nat? Is that Nat?

She crawled to the edge of the shadows for a better view. The appearance of boots, well worn military boots beneath branches some feet away dashed her desperate hopes. Trembling, she slowly turned around and crawled the other way, snapping a dead twig.

A shout! Behind her!

Amy came up on her knees, crawled faster, as fast as she could—right into another pair of dirty boots planted inches from her nose.

"Oh God," she whimpered.

A powerful hand grabbed her hair and lifted her to her feet; her face, streaming with tears, was brought level with another, a very dark one, wearing a toothy, sinister sneer.

Black Hat bellowed something indecipherable bringing the man with the horribly disfigured face to grasp her bicep from behind. Struggling was futile as she was dragged between the bushes toward an unknown destination.

"God no!" Her startled shriek was answered with raucous laughter. Her sudden struggle to free herself was met with a back hand across her face and nose. Blood splattered into her dirty blond hair and began pouring down the front of her pink, Speedo jacket as she was dragged past the body of her dead husband and pulled along several meters into a small clearing littered with the bodies of dead or dying elephants.

Amy collapsed to her knees in heaving sobs as Black Hat surveyed the scene. His men had just completed their grisly work. The third cow and her calf lay dead on the ground. Streams of blood flowed in all directions—the thick liquid fading from bright red to dark brown as it soaked into the parched earth.

CHAPTER-ONE

SCOURGE *a: an instrument of punishment or criticism*
b: a cause of widespread or great affliction

THE PRATT AND WHITNEY turbofans rumbled like distant thunder propelling the airliner ever-higher into the sparkling clear air. Leaving faint trails of black exhaust in its wake, the silver-blue and white Boeing 727 climbed effortlessly into a sky as blue as it was cold.

Southeastern Flight 106 had just taken off from the SEATAC International Airport in Seattle, Washington. At the controls was veteran Captain John Ruger Forrest. It was his turn to fly, or, in airline jargon, his "leg." His medium-built, six-foot frame sat comfortably in the left seat; the seat traditionally occupied by the pilot-in-command. Dark brown hair, trimmed to military standards, framed his clean-shaven yet mildly rugged face. A touch of gray frosting at his temples betrayed forty-odd birthdays and, like his logbook, attested to years of experience. The First Officer, a quiet but instantly likeable man of forty, was George Simpson. It was customary at Southeastern Airlines, as with most airlines, for the captain and copilot to alternate flying duties while the other assisted and handled the radio communications.

Rounding out the cockpit-crew was the flight engineer, Second Officer Glen Forsyth. He sat behind the other pilots, at the "panel," operating the aircraft's systems. "Skin," an Air Force nickname derived from changing Forsyth to Foreskin and then dropping the "Fore," busily scanned the instruments at his station to insure the cabin was pressurizing and climbing on schedule.

"Southeast, one-oh-six, Seattle Center."

"Southeast, 106, go ahead," George replied.

"Southeast, 106," the air traffic control center instructed, "turn left heading one-one-zero, intercept the Olympia zero-nine-seven-degree radial and resume the Summa Four departure."

"Southeast, 106, one-ten heading, join the SID," Simpson responded. He reached up to the autopilot heading control and rotated the knob to the appropriate setting. This action moved a heading marker, or "bug," around the edge of his and the captain's compasses to mark the desired heading.

Captain Forrest banked the jet to the left until the turn brought the airliner's nose around to a heading twenty degrees south of east.

Summa Four was the name of the standard instrument departure route that would take them just to the south of Mount Rainier on their way eastbound, passing a few miles to the north of Mount St. Helens. After that, the flight plan called for them to cruise over the northern tier of the United States enroute to New York's LaGuardia Airport or "LaGarbage," as the crews refer to it since it was built on a landfill. There the crew would overnight.

A strong arctic cold front had passed through the region forty-eight hours earlier removing the haze-producing pollutants from the air and taking all the rain clouds endemic to the Pacific Northwest along with it. For the passengers and crew, the exceptional visibility was a spectacular treat.

With the snow-capped summit of Mount Rainier passing well below the airliner and off to its left side, flight 106 was cleared to climb to thirty-three thousand feet. Surrounding the inactive volcano for as far as the eye could see were the Snoqualmie National Forest to the north and east and the Gifford Pinchot National Forest to the south. Beyond the vast mountain forests to the east lay the semi-desert areas encompassing Yakima, Washington, and the Columbia River.

"Beautiful country," Captain Forrest commented into the thick glass of the L-2 window.

"That it is, boss," Simpson remarked with a long breath.

"How late is 'late' going to be tonight, Skin?" the captain asked the flight engineer without turning his head.

"Well, sir, depends on your definition of late."

Forrest, turned in his seat, half smiled and gave Forsyth a look comprised of anticipation, frustration and amusement. After all, this was his favorite flight crew and he allowed a lot of levity as long as professional standards were never compromised.

"If you're thinking you're pregnant, late is a month. To a creditor, late is 10 days. If you're the FAA," Forsyth continued with a smirk, "it's fifteen minutes. At the Zoo, it was anything that wasn't early. To the average woman ..."

Forrest turned back to the side window view. "Just tell me what it would be if you were a watch."

"Well, the high altitude winds are strong on the tail. But the New York weather is going to be dog shit. We might pick up a little boost of jet stream component over South Dakota..."

Forrest interrupted with a tight-lipped smile: "I didn't ask how to *build* a watch, dammit, just where the big hand and the little hand are going to be when we arrive."

Forsyth dropped the weather print-out to his lap and mocked a dramatic frown.

"So I guess we're pregnant...again," the captain concluded with a knowing glance and smile at the first officer who answered it in kind.

Forrest motioned for Simpson to take the controls. "Time to talk to the people who're paying our bills."

Simpson took the controls as Captain Forrest lifted the PA microphone from its cradle at the rear of the center console.

"Remember, boss," Forsyth goaded, still enjoying the banter with his favorite captain. "Don't say fire, fuck or fog on the PA."

Forrest chuckled quietly and took the microphone away from his lips. "I really appreciate that twenty-four-karat nugget of wisdom, Skin. I don't know what we would do without that Air Force Academy professionalism."

Pumping with rhythmic urgency, his short legs carried his stocky frame along the west colonnade's covered walkway that led from the main mansion of the White House, past the Rose Garden, to the Executive Offices of the west wing. Preoccupied with four surprise changes to an already impossible schedule, the man hardly noticed the autumn leaves sailing obliquely on a cold, wind-driven rain. Their silent, soggy landings on the plush, green carpet of the west lawn contrasted sharply with his crisp, leather-against-concrete footsteps. His breath came in faint puffs as he hurried along toward his office and the beginning of another thirteen-hour day.

After checking his in-box for messages and faxes, Hodding Schnaffhorst strode down the corridor and entered the Oval Office to join the president's first meeting already in progress and slightly ahead of schedule. He knew another twenty-four hours would pass before that would happen again.

Secretary of State Samuel Cook and retired Rear Admiral Walter J. Small, the National Security Advisor, had been called in along with a man from the CIA to counsel the president in dealing with the ever-growing famine in eastern Africa. Wilcox was too preoccupied with his reelection problems to be very concerned about small things like two million people facing imminent starvation. He had privately confided in his Chief of Staff that, "None of them can vote for me anyway, so what does it matter?"

But then there was the president's wife. She had other ideas on the subject and the power to put them in play. She had made the famine a top priority for the president. Hopeless people always got her attention and consequently, his. Besides, these desperate Africans were fleeing all over the continent in search of food. As they did, they resorted to killing any wild game that was edible, including her beloved elephants. Of all the endangered animals in the world, elephants had a particular appeal for Mrs. Wilcox. She was practically obsessed with them. Her love of elephants had been the subject of a significant amount of media attention. It was well known that she had a collection of elephant porcelains and china figurines from all over the world. Even the elephant exhibit at Baltimore's Druid Hill Park Zoo had been renamed in her honor after she had raised considerable funds for its renovation. Some privately joked that it was a fitting namesake for a woman whose own physical proportions resembled those of the creatures she so admired. Few Democrats, however, were amused when "60 Minutes" aired a story illustrating the irony of a high-profile party member who chose to glorify the trademark of their archrival.

None of that mattered a whit to Abby Wilcox. In the course of events she had come by her own form of political leverage. When faced with the prospect of an election-year scandal involving his seven-year adulterous affair with an aide, President Wilcox discretely brokered a great deal of indirect power to the first lady in exchange for her silence and cooperation. Paybacks are a bitch, as the adage goes, and in the president's case, it was true—figuratively *and* literally.

To her credit, the first lady was careful not to abuse her power and push her husband too far—at least not in public. Behind the scenes, however, she manipulated and coerced the president to her heart's content. For the time being, she was satisfied with the novel and ironic ability to control the "world's most powerful man." Using her considerable influence, she championed her favorite causes: feeding the world's starving children and saving endangered species. She gave little thought to the fact that sometimes the simultaneous pursuit of these two goals was counteractive.

Schnaffhorst and the first lady were not on the best of terms. Theirs was a relationship of tolerance. At her convenience, she manipulated the president through his Chief of Staff by simply making "suggestions" which the staff implemented. For Schnaffhorst, referred to as SNAFU by some of the less-than-kind White House underlings, cooperation meant survival. It would have been most unwise for the Chief of Staff to go up against the president's wife. The first lady, he knew, had much more power and influence over his boss than he did. After all, the *real* Vice President of the United States was Abby Wilcox.

Schnaffhorst noticed that the tall CIA man, with salt-and-pepper hair and deep-set, brown eyes had just started his briefing. Dressed in a dark gray, double-breasted suit, Steven Henry Henderson opened a file folder marked, SECRET, WNINTEL, NOFORN and began to read.

"Mr. President; Mrs. Wilcox; Gentlemen. This briefing is classified, secret. The information contained in this file is not particularly sensitive. However, the dissemination of this material could compromise our sources. Therefore, it is not releasable to foreign nationals."

The president slowly and deliberately closed his eyelids and nodded his head in acknowledgement as if anything else was beneath a man of his stature. Besides, Wilcox had heard this statement before. It was required by regulations.

After a pause, Henderson continued, "The country of Somalia is situated on the Horn of Africa." Henderson pointed to a map of the African continent. "From a strategic standpoint, its location at the southern approaches to the Red Sea and the Suez Canal have, in the past, made it of some interest to the former Soviet Union and Warsaw Pact member nations.

"Geographically…"

"Mr. Henderson," Schnarfhorst interrupted, looking at his watch as a signal. "I believe everyone present is generally familiar with the topic and the background, especially after last month."

Henderson smiled with a nod. "Of course. I'll move it along." He cleared his throat and continued, "With your permission, Mr. President."

Wilcox issued a patronizing smile.

"Thank you, sir," Henderson replied.

"Bottom line, sir, the root problem persists. The Somalis can barely grow enough food to support their population in the prevailing extreme drought conditions and what they do grow is usually stolen or confiscated by the clans. Furthermore, they can't sell enough of their natural resources to feed themselves. As for a prognosis, the population growth has far exceeded the ability of the land and the ecosystem to sustain it. Continued relief will provide only short term results." Henderson noticed the look of concern on the first lady's face.

"But it *will* make *some* difference, will it not?" Mrs. Wilcox asked to cement a point.

"Yes, ma'am. Of course." Henderson responded, remembering he had received something of a mandate from the first lady.

Henderson continued: "This fact is a very telling one, sir: Even under severe stress, the population growth rate has continued at over three-point-three percent. This is among the world's highest growth rates. Compare that with a growth rate of point-eight percent for the United States. The infant mortality rate, by contrast, is thirteen times what it is in this country. Those people are starving and reproducing at an alarming rate. The figures haven't changed much since Operation Restore Hope began nor have they changed significantly from a political perspective. And since last month's debacle, the warlords have resumed their turf wars with renewed ferocity. There's nothing like a victory against the west to make despots feel invincible."

While Henderson flipped to another chart, Schnaffhorst refilled Wilcox's coffee cup before pouring one for himself. The next graphic displayed an organizational chart of blocks connected by lines of subordination. Photographs appeared inside most of the blocks along with the individual's name and title. Some of the blocks contained only names.

"These are the major political players in Somalia as of last month. There have been very few additions to, or deletions from, this rogue's gallery since 1992. The government is largely impotent and superficial. They have three branches of government, similar to ours. There is a president, two vice presidents, a prime minister and a Council of Ministers which functions much like our presidential cabinet. At any given moment, there are roughly fourteen clans or tribes which are struggling for a preponderance of power and another half-dozen or so splinter groups. On the chart you will notice that each clan is represented by a photo of its warlord. Some of the faces have changed in the last year or so due to some untimely deaths. The untimely aspect, I suppose, would depend on one's point of view." Henderson paused for a moment to punctuate the dry humor with a wry smile. It was difficult for him to conceal his conservative leanings and warrior's heart in a room full of liberals.

"These warlords represent the *de facto* power of the country simply because they out-gun the legitimate government's military structure."

Admiral Small interrupted: "What do the clans have in the way of weaponry?" the Admiral asked as the first lady took a sip of her coffee during what she assumed was going to be the boring part of the briefing.

Henderson flipped two charts ahead to one labeled, SOMALI ORDER OF BATTLE.

"Most of the weapons are old and have largely Soviet origins. It is interesting to note that some of their equipment was originally manufactured in the U.S. and was sold to them by some of our closest allies. They have some light armor, light trucks and jeep-type vehicles. Just how many are operational at any given time is anyone's guess. Practically all of the equipment is over twenty years old and replacement parts are hard to come by. Most of the trucks, called "technicals," and jeeps have 12.7mm and 14.5mm machine guns mounted on them. Some sport light, anti-tank weapons and 23mm anti-aircraft artillery. Quite a few of these weapons were seized by U.S. Marines in the last several months, but quite a few more were hidden in the countryside or driven across the border into Kenya and Ethiopia for safe keeping until the Marines withdrew. There are some unconfirmed reports, rumor mostly, of MANPADs—shoulder-fired surface-to-air missiles being smuggled in from Iraq. Most likely, they are few in number and are old, Soviet SA-7s.

"Their tactics and methods have not changed due, primarily, to the fact that their weapons and opponents have not changed," Henderson concluded.

"Mr. Henderson," Mrs. Wilcox interjected, "how does the Agency go about collecting information in a place like Somalia?"

"We employ standard NSA, ELINT and SIGINT methods..." Henderson paused. He noticed a puzzled look in the first lady's eyes. "Pardon me, Ma'am. That's electronic intelligence and signals intelligence."

Mrs. Wilcox nodded and mouthed a silent thank you.

Henderson continued. "In addition, we have several assets located throughout the country who engage in HUMINT activities." Henderson, catching himself, paused again, "Spies, ma'am."

The president's thin smile, Henderson noticed, failed to completely hide his annoyance with his wife's presence.

"Some are even recruited among employees of the International Red Cross, CARE, Save the Children, UNICEF and any of a number of relief organizations," Henderson added.

"How do you get those kinds of groups to allow CIA agents to work out of their storefronts?" asked Samuel Cook, somewhat astonished.

The first lady's eyes widened with new interest as she brought her coffee cup to her lips.

"They don't *allow* anything of the sort, Mr. Secretary. They simply don't have any idea that some of their top field people are moonlighting for the Agency. One or two of them are doctors!" Henderson smiled thinly.

"Doctors?" Cook repeated, unable to mask his surprise.

Mrs. Wilcox halted in mid sip.

"Yes sir. Doctors. The Company has found some creative ways to allow these young physicians to repay their government-backed student loans."

Admiral Small chuckled and shook his head. He was amused by the shocked looks on the faces of the president and his Secretary of State. These men were academics. Neither of them had ever served in the military and neither of them had any sort of intelligence background. The first lady, he sensed, was really nonplussed that some of her favorite charities had been invaded by "spies." He almost laughed out loud.

"Our agents are trained to extract information from the locals using many, seemingly innocent, techniques. They also have their regular informants and some are even paid. Most are motivated by their gratitude for the aid or by their hatred of rival clans. None realize they are being interrogated when they bring their children to the medical clinics or feeding stations for treatment or food. The questions they are asked are all very benign so as not to arouse suspicion. Agents are trained not to ask too many interconnected questions. By asking various people different questions, they get a collection of data and build it into something significant. The method also insures accuracy by way of corroboration. The agents can collate and correlate the information later and get a pretty fair picture of what is going on. All intelligence work boils down to collating facts or strings of facts from bits and pieces of innocuous and seemingly insignificant information. Rarely do we get the whole package delivered to us intact like we did with the MIG-25 that a Soviet defector flew to Japan in the late seventies."

"Even *I* remember that one." Wilcox smiled like a schoolboy whose dog *hadn't* eaten his homework.

Henderson tipped his head to the president in a salutary manner. "We also have high-tech methods for tracking some of the groups and the larger weapons. Some of the airplanes that fly the food stuffs in are rigged with gear that can detect nitrates and explosives and large ferrous masses. Conveniently enough, we have a Keyhole KH-12 satellite and one of its advanced follow-ons doing double-duty in the area. While its primary mission is to keep an eye on Iraq, its elliptical orbital track takes it directly over Somalia and several other east African countries providing some excellent imagery.

"I think I can safely state that The Agency is pretty much on top of things, gentlemen," Henderson added with a confident note of professional pride.

"Thank you, Steve." Admiral Small used Henderson's military lead-in as a prologue to his briefing about the military options available to them. For the next several minutes, the Admiral listed the units, facilities, and equipment that could be made available to support another relief effort. President Wilcox listened quietly while some discussion followed the presentation of each military option. An astute man, he made notes when key points were made. The Secretary of State voiced diplomatic concerns about another large military presence in eastern Africa and southwest Asia.

Mrs. Wilcox occupied herself with the pastries during the discussion. She was trying to be polite, but Henderson could see that she was uncomfortable with her husband and his cronies. The only person she seemed to genuinely like was Admiral Small.

"Gentlemen," the president concluded. "I don't want to put any more U.S. troops on the ground to police a foreign country if I don't have to. We've lost quite enough of our brave, young men already. This administration took a lot of heat after our soldier's naked bodies were dragged through the streets of Mogadishu. It's very difficult to explain to the mother of a dead soldier why her son or daughter was killed while trying to save the life of a Somali child. I'd like to avoid sending any additional ground troops. I *am*, however, under a lot of political pressure to provide some continued relief." Although he tried not to look, the president let his eyes catch his wife's glare. He immediately looked away.

"I'll go along with some airlift, but I'm reluctant to put more troops on the ground without compelling justification." The president was clearly uncomfortable with the entire situation. "I'd like you gentlemen to come up with a minimum-risk plan for airlift. I want minimum involvement of U.S. personnel. I'll be going out to California in a week or so and I'd like to hear your plan then. I'd also like General Clark to be in on the meeting. We'll need his input if we are to come up with a workable plan."

Henderson nodded in acknowledgement. "Very well, Mr. President."

Schnaffhorst made several notes on his legal pad as the president talked. He looked at his watch and realized that they had run ten minutes over the time he had allotted. He stood and opened the door that led to the corridor. A Secret Service agent appeared just outside holding the president's Kevlar-lined raincoat. With a torrential rain blowing against the bullet-proof Lexan windows, the raincoat would serve both of its intended purposes.

"Mr. President, we must be going," Schnaffhorst reminded.

Wilcox acknowledged by nodding his head as he shook hands with his advisors.

Mrs. Wilcox stopped to thank Henderson on her way back to the residence. "Very interesting briefing, Mr. Henderson."

"Thank you, ma'am."

"In case your mother failed to mention it, the plight of those people is high on my list of priorities. I'm also *very* concerned about Africa's wildlife. And since I am the one who invited you here for this briefing, they are now high on *your* list of priorities, as well. Please don't forget that."

Henderson politely smiled and nodded, noting the look of conviction in the first lady's eyes. There was a lot of sand and steel in this woman, he thought—the sort of woman who was used to getting her own way.

"Give my best to Margaret. And please do let me know if there is anything we can do to help each other," she concluded with a wry smile and a knowing look.

"I will." Henderson smiled back, noticing the sterling silver elephant pin on her red blazer.

The first lady then turned to say good-bye to Admiral Small.

Schnaffhorst signaled the agents that the president was coming and rechecked his appointment roster.

"RINGMASTER is coming out. PACHYDERM is returning to the residence," Henderson heard a Secret Service agent say into his radio. The names, he knew, were the president's and first lady's Secret Service call-signs.

Schnaffhorst motioned for the president to hurry. He had less than thirty minutes to prepare Wilcox for his luncheon with key members of Congress. His reelection campaign had begun and they had to do their best to keep their friends close. Even so, it was more important to keep their enemies even closer.

Carrying their Kalashnikov assault rifles casually over their shoulders, two ebony figures walked south through the brush, smoking and talking. In the lead, the tallest man, wearing a black, broad-brimmed hat with a leopard-skin band, limped along scanning the open areas for soldiers or game wardens. Just behind, dressed in a dirty white shirt and faded blue trousers, a man, shorter by a foot than his comrade, quickened his pace to keep up.

An old, Mercedes, flat-bed truck waited for them just ahead, well hidden under a small cluster of trees. Remnants of a small fire marked the spot where the gang had spent the previous night. As they approached, particles of cold, gray ash fluttered across the ground in the soft morning breeze.

The leader climbed into the driver's seat as the other man pulled away the branches that camouflaged the truck's hiding place. Slowly, so as not to kick up a telltale cloud of dust, he drove back to the killing ground.

Already, a dozen vultures were tearing at the edges of the wounds made by the automatic rifles. Half a dozen more spiraled overhead looking for a place to alight. Even before they sighted the carcasses, the flying butcher shops knew that the carrion market was open for business. For the winged meat-cleavers, the sound of gunfire was a call to dinner.

As the truck approached, the ugly, bald-headed birds fought among each other for the best feeding spots. Only after the truck pulled within ten meters of the carcasses did the vultures finally yield their positions and take off.

Amy Lee Henderson-Forrest sat red-eyed in the shade of an over-hanging, whistling thorn acacia branch. Her face flushed from the effects of heat and stress, she seemed oblivious to the squadron of flies harassing her head. Her blood-spattered, pink jacket had been cut and torn from her body by her captors in order that they may better assess the quality of their prize. An active defense was impossible with her wrists bound tightly behind her back. Cyclops knelt next to her leaning on his weapon, the muzzle poking into his filthy green T-shirt as a certain discouragement to any escape attempts.

One man, wearing a cotton bandanna with a faded red print, walked up to the three elephants that had been the first to die. He judged the juvenile male's tusks to be just under a meter in length. Their alabaster luster was undiminished by the ugliness of age or death.

The man lowered a chain saw from his shoulders and tossed his cigarette on the ground. After several quick pulls at the recoil starter rope the machine roared to life, its blue smoke engulfing the operator.

The short man watched as the man with the chain saw repeatedly revved it up while positioning himself to the side of the male elephant's head. As he steadied himself, the saw man lowered the buzzing blade into the elephant's face just below his right eye. As he did, a hundred dung flies dispersed in all directions. The whirring chain of steel teeth had no trouble penetrating the skin and bone that held the base of the tusks. After several strokes with the saw and a little judicious working of the blade, the top tusk began to sag under its own weight. Slowly, the front of the elephant's face came away from its head.

The spinning chain spattered blood on his arms and legs as Red Bandanna used the tip of the vicious blade to slice through the last strings of sinew and muscle. Sensing it was free, the fourth man dragged the tusk and severed trunk off to the side. The saw operator yelled at the short man to hurry back and get a grip on the remaining lower tusk. He warned him not to let the ivory pinch the blade. Red Bandanna positioned himself and went to work. Once the saw broke through the tissue and bone, it dug into the dirt and was quickly withdrawn. As the saw-man held his machine clear, the man in the faded green shirt delivered a few deft whacks with his machete to free the last clinging pieces of flesh.

For the next few minutes, the men worked with finesse to cut away the surrounding skull structure. Once this was accomplished, they used their sheath knives and an old bayonet to dig the nerve pulp out of the tusks' hollow bases.

Shortman, who wore an old game ranger's uniform shirt owing to the fact that he had once been a ranger and fired for misconduct, was enlisted to help. He and Red Bandanna loaded each tusk onto the back of the truck before the latter returned to work on the other two elephants with the growling saw.

The baby elephant's ears were cut off along with his tail and the tails of the other two. They would bring a few dollars for their souvenir value. The ears of the larger animals were also removed. Later, at the campsite, they would be painstakingly skinned. The thin skin of the ears would be worked into a moderately high grade of leather suitable for boots or a satchel. The men sawed off all of the elephants' feet as well. They would make garish trash baskets for a rich man's office. Unfazed by the ghastliness of the task, the men labored at their gruesome work well into the afternoon.

Red Bandanna, wearing a sheen of spattered blood spewed from the chainsaw, took on the look of a gruesome ghoul. As they went from animal to animal, cutting away what they could sell, the men developed a rhythm for their work. Only the staggering size of the matriarch's one hundred pound tusks slowed them down. Gradually, like stolen cars being stripped of their parts in a vacant lot, the gentle monarchs were systematically reduced to pathetic piles of meat and bone.

Although the meat from one of these animals could feed an entire village for many months, the robbers took only the most valuable portions. The rest they left for a scavengers' market where there was no shortage of shoppers. Many were lurking just a few meters away, waiting for the men to leave. Hoards of vultures perched in the branches of nearby trees whose canopies assumed the appearance of macabre Christmas trees decorated with dozens of grotesque, black ornaments. Other winged scavengers continued to circle overhead in a foreboding holding pattern. Hyenas, attracted by commotion and scent, paced nervously near the edge of the clearings.

As they came upon the last two elephants, the short man noticed the calf's tail and ear twitching, reacting to the bites of the relentless flies. When the baby elephant involuntarily jerked its front leg, the short man jumped back drawing another round of laughter from his heckling cronies. Since he was no more than a year old, the calf bore no tusks and was, therefore, of no value.

Though numb with shock, Amy watched the men in utter disgust and barely concealed fury. There was no sympathy among these men for animals whose only purpose was to grow ivory—white gold that they would harvest with their guns. This subspecies of the earth's most evolved creature had no room in their hearts for compassion and no thoughts in their minds for tomorrow. They lived for today and killed for today. Slaughtering for profit, they looted Africa's natural treasury. They were the scourge of the land. They were poachers.

Baring rotten teeth and a peculiar snake-like, bifid tongue, Black Hat shouted to Red Bandanna: "See that the wazungu boy is definitely dead." To the cyclops he said: "Matwana." (Truck).

The man pulled the bandanna from his head and wiped the blood from his face before entering the brush to do as he was ordered. Upon reaching the murdered groom, he prodded his head with the toe of his filthy boot. A thousand flies and a dozen vultures already knew what he'd just confirmed. Satisfied, he returned to the clearing where Black Hat was waiting in the driver's seat.

Their leader's hand went up for a moment to halt Cyclops and the girl while he studied her. His black eyes bored holes into her from top to bottom as he considered his options: kill a witness or keep a useful asset.

She may be more useful if not valuable alive. Perhaps Captain Abu can find a buyer for fine, white flesh in Yemen.

With a directive wave of Black Hat's hand, Cyclops pulled the sullen and seething young woman to the back of the truck where she was half encouraged and half dragged onto the back to join Red Bandanna, their tools and the grizzly harvest. The American was shoved onto her stomach next to a pile of meal bags.

As the truck lumbered along through the brush, Cyclops caught a glint from Amy's hand, the one-carat, brilliant cut diamond Nathan had lovingly placed on her finger only months before. Checking to verify that Red Bandanna had instantly fallen soundly asleep following a hard day's labor, he reached down to seize it. Despite Amy's resistance he had it off in a matter of seconds after placing his knife against her neck. Once the ring was free, she heard him lay his blade down with a clunk before examining it up close. From the corner of her eye she watched him slip it onto his pinky and hold it up for an admiring glance. A moment later he turned his eyes toward her with a taunting smile. Amy rolled over on to her back and kicked her left Nike at him in defiance. It bounced off his shoulder and went over the side. His defiant smile cut even deeper across his face as he looked his victim hard in the eye, relished in her anger then roared a laugh before lighting a cigarette. When she kicked the other shoe at him, he ducked it completely and belched a burst of sardonic laughter and smoke. As they bounced along, Amy rolled onto her side, buried her face in a meal bag and began to sob in silent despair.

It was late afternoon as the poachers drove across the savanna to the south leaving the place of slaughter to nature's clean-up crew. In the fading light of the dying day, something moved in the thorny bushes fifty meters from the mutilated carcasses. Emerging from his hiding place, the baby elephant sniffed the air searching for his mother's scent. He smelled something familiar and moved toward its source.

As the vague smell of his mother grew stronger, he picked up his pace, startling dozens of vultures who flapped wildly in an attempt to flee. For a moment, even the hyenas backed off while they assessed the new arrival.

Slowly, the baby walked around the torn and mutilated form. Only her familiar scent enabled him to identify her remains. The once doting mother who had tirelessly provided for his every need was now reduced to a pile of raw meat lying in a foul-smelling mud of dirt and bodily fluids. What was left of her gray skin was streaked by white trails of vulture urea and covered with swirling flies.

The baby walked around to his mother's head sniffing and probing her body with his trunk. Protesting and squealing in utter despair, he nudged her and prodded her to get up. He found her severed trunk and wrapped the end of his little trunk around it not realizing that it was no longer connected to anything. He pulled at the tip and lifted it in an attempt to get a response. Without his mother and the protection of his family group, the young calf's life expectancy would be measured in days, if not hours. Dozens of eyes were fixed on the bewildered calf as darkness found him still clinging to his mother's trunk.

CHAPTER-TWO

EMERGENCY *a: an unforeseen combination of circumstances or the resulting state that calls for immediate action*
b: a pressing need

LEAD FORECASTER JIM JOHNSON stood at a long gray Formica counter examining the most current GOES-8 (Geostationary Orbital Environ- mental Satellite) imagery under the antiseptic glow of fluorescent lights. Cocooned within the windowless room of the National Meteorological Center in Camp Springs Maryland, he ignored the idle banter of his colleagues, ringing telephones and the monotonous whisper of several computer-cooling fans. What he saw had captured his full attention. A tremendous counter-clockwise spiral of clouds, something resembling a tropical storm, was invading the United States—not from the south, but from the north.

In all his years as a meteorologist, Johnson had never seen such a deep low-pressure system developing over the eastern Great Lakes this early in the winter season. The graceful, curving arm of a cold front extended southwesterly from the swirling low sweeping the length of the Appalachian mountain train and penetrating deep into the South.

Johnson's alert, green eyes scanned the latest surface analysis with an unconscious shake of his head. November had never before seen temperatures this low—not since his department had been keeping records, anyway.

Johnson moved to a computer terminal and, with a few keystrokes, brought up another high-tech product regurgitated from the innards of the government's largest non-military supercomputer, a hundred-million-dollar Cray YMP. Unlike previous machines which took over 90 minutes to formulate predictions, the Department of Agriculture's latest liquid-cooled, number-cruncher could churn out forecast models every 67 seconds when it wasn't at work doing the Federal payroll.

Johnson didn't like what the mind-boggling speed and power of his favorite toy was telling him. Sometimes the slim 40-year-old had been fooled by the weather gods, but not often. He concluded that Atlanta and Augusta would be pounded by violent thunderstorms. One or two would probably be level five monsters ready to spawn evil tornadoes. New York, Philadelphia and Boston would get a mix of rain, snow, sleet and enough wind to blow down small trees. For commercial air traffic operating along the eastern seaboard, there would be icing in the clouds and moderate- to-severe turbulence.

Johnson rubbed his chin and sighed. "Tonight ought to be a 'bumpy night' for everybody," he muttered to the CRT screen. "Glad I'm not flying anywhere."

"Well gentlemen, there's good news and there's bad news," Captain Forrest announced, as he switched his audio selector button back to the number one comm. "This front we've been following across the country is developing into one big mess!" Forrest grumbled. "You name it, and this beauty's got it. Thunderstorms, sleet, freezing rain, high winds, moderate-to-severe turbulence—all thirty-one flavors."

"So what's the good news?" George Simpson asked, wearing his trademark incredulous smirk. His dark brown hair, slightly darker than Forrest's, matched his brown eyes.

Forrest smiled. "The good news...well...the good news is there's no more bad news."

"Not so fast, boss." Forsyth said ominously, an easy grin on his handsome face. "Remember the maintenance write-ups we're carrying on this piece'a junk?" He turned in his seat and retrieved the ship's logbook from his tiny gray desk.

"Yeah. I was trying to forget." Forrest grimaced as Forsyth opened the log. "Alright. Let's have it one more time from the top," he groused.

Forrest glanced at Simpson whose smirk faded a bit as Forsyth began to read.

"Well, for starters, the left inboard landing light is INOP as is the right turn-off light." He cleared his voice and continued. "The number two generator is INOP and the CSD is disconnected," Forsyth announced as he pointed to the second of three red cover-guarded switches at the top left of his panel. "Number one fuel flow is tits-up as is the ADF receiver."

"Jesus Tecumseh Sherman. Doesn't this airline know they occasionally have to *maintain* their equipment? You know, as in the laying of greasy hands," Forrest groused rhetorically. "Could be worse," he added with a barely audible grumble.

"Oh, but there's more, Herr Flugkapitan," the flight engineer taunted with mock amusement.

"Jesus Tecumseh Sherman," Forrest exclaimed. "What *else*?"
Simpson laughed quietly. "Looks like we're in for one of those 'fun' evenings, boss—the kind management says we get paid too much for."

"From what you said, icing is a definite possibility in the New York area tonight," Forsyth said, matter-of-factly.

"More like a *probability*," Forrest confirmed with a grim look.

"That brings us to one last item," Forsyth continued, "the pneumatic system." A graduate of the United States Air Force Academy, he was a fastidious man in his early thirties whose thick blonde hair had begun an early transition to silver. "I was looking back through the log book and I discovered this bird has a history of intermittent bleed air leaks. Most of 'em have been signed off as 'could not duplicate' or 'system checks OK.'" Forsyth looked at the captain with a knowing smile. "You know what that means."

"Yeah," Simpson interjected sarcastically. "They didn't do shit. They just keep pencil-whipping it."

Captain Forrest looked straight ahead through the windshield. "Yeah, but it's all quite legal, isn't it?" he muttered in disgust, a facetious statement—not a question. Forsyth nodded in agreement. Since most of the systems on a modern commercial airliner had some type of redundancy or backup system for critical functions, some of the equipment did not necessarily have to be functioning properly for the aircraft to be safely dispatched.

Forsyth knew all too well that maintenance was only as good as the company's willingness to invest in it. Trouble was Southeastern's management was no longer willing to do so. Two years before, the company had been acquired by the notorious corporate raider Frank Lawrence when Lawrence's holding company, Air Intercontinental, had swallowed up Southeastern in a hostile takeover.

Lawrence had immediately begun selling off the useful parts of the airline, like its excellent computer reservations system, to Air Intercontinental for pennies-on-the-dollar. To add insult to injury, the holding company then leased the same reservations system back to Southeastern at ridiculous rates. In the process, Lawrence's company, and Lawrence himself, became very wealthy at the expense of the acquired airlines as the predator sucked the life out of his victims like a spider does the juices of its prey.

Forrest considered all the angles as they flew east—the politics, the FAA, the union. His license, not to mention his butt, along with one hundred twenty-four other butts were on the line. As the pilot in command, he had the ultimate responsibility for everyone's safety. And irresponsible was something John Ruger Forrest wasn't. "Anybody uncomfortable with continuing?" He looked at each of their faces in turn.

Forsyth gave a small shrug indicating that there really wasn't much choice since all the sign-offs were legal—at least on paper.

"If we divert *before* we have an actual problem," Simpson added, "some management stooge will likely try to fire us."

A moment of silent consideration passed.

"Alright then," Forrest said. "It might not be a piece-of-cake, but it seems we agree it's worst-case, legal and best-case, safe. Lets press on."

One hour later Southeastern flight 106 was handed off from Washington Center to New York Center as the 727 began its long descent.

Ahead, marking the backside of the cold front, cloud tops glowed blue-white under a full moon. Lightening flashed sporadically like artillery in a distant battle. Captain Forrest leaned forward and switched on the Bendix, color, weather radar. He tilted the antenna sweep down so that, at the range of 80 miles, ground returns emerged at the outer fringe of the scope. Green and yellow splotches materialized on the screen 60 miles ahead followed by some that were more well-defined. Irregular red blobs were encased by bands of yellow which, in turn, were surrounded by bands of light green. Individually, they resembled the cells a biologist might see through a microscope and hence their common name. The radar return revealed half-a-dozen cells along their route with more emerging as they proceeded. Cells represented areas of moisture, usually in the form of rain. Green indicated light precipitation, yellow moderate, and red a downpour heavy enough to overpower an automobile's highest wiper setting. Heavy areas of precipitation were usually accompanied by wind shears and turbulence which, in mature storms, were capable of tearing an airliner apart. Professional pilots knew to respect their terrible destructive power and went well out of their way to avoid them.

"Looks like the easy part's over," Simpson commented as he watched lines of weather take shape on the radar screen.

Captain Forrest managed a tight smile as he reached overhead and turned on the seat belt sign. He monitored through his headset as the flight attendant in charge completed her obligatory PA reminding the passengers to return to their seats.

As the jet descended through twenty-four thousand feet, Simpson pointed his flashlight beam through the windshield illuminating his wiper blade. "Looks like we're starting to pick up a little of that advertised ice, Boss." Super-cooled water droplets suspended in the clouds instantaneously completed the change of state from liquid to solid as they attached themselves to the protruding parts of the airplane. Fine, white ice crystals appeared under the wiper blades and frosted the windshields.

"Okay, Skin," the captain commanded, "lets have that anti ice on now, please—engine and airframe."

Forsyth had all the switches turned on before Forrest could finish.

"Washington Center, Southeast 106. What kind of delays are you showing tonight for New York?" Forrest queried the air traffic control center as they passed to the east of Baltimore.

"About what you'd expect on a night like this, sir. You can start slowing to 250 knots now. Expect additional speed adjustments, maybe a turn or two in holding. Kennedy traffic is moving okay, but La Guardia is experiencing some delays because of the wind." The busy controller's voice carried a tone of frustration and fatigue as he radioed the news.

"Well, he ain't lying," Simpson added to the report. "Information Charlie has measured three hundred overcast, one mile in rain, thirty-three degrees. The wind is kicking butt—three six zero at twenty, gusts to twenty seven. ILS to runway four." Simpson's smile contained an evil gleam. "Glad it's not *my* leg."

Ice crystals made a hissing noise as they impacted the windshield. Simpson checked the windshield wiper bolt every few minutes to see how rapidly the ice was accumulating. If ice was allowed to build up on certain parts of the aircraft, it could seriously affect the machine's ability to fly. Only a small accumulation of ice was required to disrupt the smooth, laminar flow of air over the wings. A serious disruption could prevent an airfoil from producing enough lift to support the weight of the airplane, resulting in a stall. Chunks of ice could occasionally come loose and fly into the engines, damaging their delicate blades. If a blade were to break off, it would smash into other blades in a chain reaction of shattering metal—fatal to the engine.

Most jet-powered airliners had no problem flying in icing conditions. The windshields are electrically heated as are pitot probes, drains, antennas and vents. The leading edges of the wings, tail, and engine nacelles can be heated with bleed air extracted from the compressor sections of the turbofan engines then plumbed to the air foils and engine cowlings through a network of valves and pipes. As air is drawn into the engines, it passes several rows of spinning blades which pack air molecules closer and closer together increasing pressure and temperature. Depending on RPM and from what stage of the compressor it is bled, the air can be 400-600 degrees Celsius—hot enough to melt aluminum and start fires.

"Uh-oh, Houston," Forsyth announced, calmly. "We've got a problem."

Forrest glanced back at the engineer.

"Duct overheat," Forsyth clarified, a trace of urgency in his voice.

Forrest looked up to see the glowing amber light over Simpson's head.

"Probably a leak in the wing anti-ice ducting," Forsyth added as he reached for his abnormals manual.

Forrest frowned. "You've got the jet, George." He looked at his engineer. "Looks like you were right about the pencil whipping."

"We're probably going to have to shut down the airframe anti-ice," Forsyth predicted while he thumbed the pages to the proper procedure.

Forrest had learned long ago to trust his crew, especially when he knew they were right. "George, see if you can find a clear layer."

Simpson made inquiries with air traffic control while Forrest turned his attention to the bleed air problem. "Go ahead with the procedure, Skin."

For the next few minutes, the captain and the engineer went through the recommended procedure, step-by-step. Glen read the abnormal checklist aloud so the captain could stay with him without having to read over his engineer's shoulder. Finally after exhausting options, they switched off the wing anti-icing system.

"We need that layer now, George. We're going to plan B," Forrest said facing forward in his seat.

"Doesn't seem to be one, Boss." Simpson explained. "They just switched us to New York Center. Maybe they've got better info.

"Center, Southeast 106, two four zero and we've got a problem," Simpson announced calmly.

The "P-word" got the controller's attention. "Go ahead, Southeast 106."

"Are you getting ice at all the lower altitudes tonight?"

"Yes sir. Several aircraft, a Mad Dog, a DC-9 and a 757 all reported icing, on and off, almost all the way to the surface. We've had the same all the way up to two four oh, as well. Light to moderate rime." The Center controller responded.

"Okay, great," came the sarcastic reply from Forrest who jumped in on the conversation. "We had to shut down our airframe anti-ice due to a leak. Looks like we'll have to declare an emergency. We need to get this thing on the ground in a hurry." Forrest's voice was very even considering recent developments. "If we find an altitude that's relatively ice free, we'd like to level off there until we can be cleared for the approach."

"Understand, you are declaring an emergency, Southeast 106. Turn right heading zero-four-zero. This will be vectors for the descent. Expect the ILS to runway four at La Guardia. Pilot's discretion, descend and maintain, one zero thousand. You will be number one for the approach. Say fuel and souls on board." The controller wasted no time getting the flight headed in the right direction.

"I'll take the jet back now, George. Let's have the descent and approach checklist. Skin, give the Company a call and tell them what's going on. Tell 'em were about fifteen minutes out."

Simpson told the controller what he needed to know.

As the airplane leveled off at ten thousand feet, the clouds cleared away. They were between layers. There were clouds above and below them and the ice stopped accumulating. However, the ride became quite rough.

Forrest checked the wiper bolt, again and was pleased it had stopped growing. "Could be worse," he grumbled to no one in particular.

"Center, Southeast 106. We're level at one-zero-thousand. We've stopped picking up ice, for now, but at least we've got white caps on the coffee. How soon can we expect approach clearance?" Simpson inquired.

"Standby, Delta four-fifty-four. Southeastern 106, descend maintain six thousand. Contact New York approach, 120.8." The controller was obviously under some strain as he tried to rearrange his traffic to accommodate the flight with the emergency.

The copilot changed frequencies while Forsyth and Forrest completed the approach checklist. Forrest started the airplane down very slowly.

Simpson informed the controller they were starting down. "Southeastern 106's taking it down slow to stay out of the ice as long as possible."

"Roger that, Southeast 106, expect approach clearance in one minute." Only thirty seconds had ticked by when approach control gave them a heading to intercept the final approach course and cleared them to commence the approach.

The Instrument Landing System, or ILS, is the primary form of electronic guidance airliners use for approach and landing. Pilots relied on their instrument's guidance to make constant subtle control inputs to stay on course and on glide-path all the way down to an altitude where the crew could pick the runway lights out of the gloom. Once they sighted the runway, they would have to make the landing visually.

When they entered the clouds again, at seven thousand feet, Forrest noticed ice crystals building on the wiper bolt just outside his windshield. Once only the diameter of a pencil, the bolt was the now the size of his thumb. His eyes went back to the instruments. There was nothing more he could do about it anyway. The engine anti-ice was still working, he reminded himself. It was on a separate, though similar, system. The captain called for increasing amounts of flaps as he slowed the 130,000 pound machine to its computed approach speed. Groaning and rumbling sounded through the fuselage as hydraulic machinery moved the huge metal slabs into the wind.

At seven miles from the runway, Forrest called for the landing gear to be lowered. "Throw out the Goodyears, George."

"Gear down." Simpson repeated. He moved the large handle up from the "off" position, then lowered it all the way to the "down" position with a heavy clunk.

A red light in the handle's clear plastic tip stayed illuminated any time the landing gear position did not agree with the position of the handle. Most of the time, the light would stay on a few seconds while the various landing gear doors opened and the gear lowered into position. This time it stayed on.

"Well, boss. It's worse," Simpson announced through clenched teeth.

Forrest glanced at the landing gear handle and then at the landing gear indicator lights. Two green lights were illuminated for the left main and nose gears. The right main, green position light remained out and, in its place, a red gear door warning light gleamed in the dim cockpit.

"Want me to recycle it?" Simpson asked, moving his hand toward the handle.

"Hold it, George, no!" Forrest blurted out. "Not with a gear door light."

Simpson quickly withdrew his hand as if he had touched something hot. He knew that moving the handle was not a good idea but, for a moment, his hand had been quicker than his brain. While retracting the gear and re-extending it might cure a dirty indicator switch, moving the landing gear in a situation like this might make the problem worse. It could become hopelessly jammed in the up position. In the time it had taken to ascertain the new problem they had traveled almost three miles. The 727 was on course and on glide slope only twelve hundred feet above the ground.

Forrest punched the Go Around button while simultaneously advancing the throttles. "Tell 'em were missed approach."

"Southeast 106 is missed approach," Simpson told the tower. "Requesting ten thousand," he radioed in a calm voice which belied his uneasiness. What had begun as a routine flight was now anything but.

"Southeast 106, New York Center. Understand you are missed approach," the nonplussed controller responded. "Climb maintain three thousand. Maintain present heading. Say your intentions." Just a few minutes before, those guys had declared an emergency in order to get their aircraft on the ground, he thought. Now they were going around. It didn't compute.

Simpson could hear the confusion in the controller's voice. "We've got a gear problem, sir. Southeastern 106 is climbing to three thousand, zero-three-zero's the heading," he confirmed. "We need to get back to ten thousand, ASAP to get out of this ice!"

"Okay, Southeast 106. Understand," the controller said, wishing that they still allowed them to smoke at their stations like the old days. "Turn left to two-four-zero, climb, maintain one zero thousand. Say your intentions, let me know what you want to do." While he was waiting for Southeast 106 to respond, the controller issued instructions to some of the other aircraft on the frequency. For the second time in the last twenty minutes, Southeast 106 had trashed his game plan.

As Forrest put the 727 in a climbing left turn, his mind raced ahead of the jet. Training and experience kicked in along with a mild dose of adrenalin. First things first, he thought. Certain priorities must be followed. *Before we do anything else, we've got to get clear of this ice.*

Climbing through 8,500 feet, the Boeing popped out of the clouds into the clear layer they had found previously. That took care of the icing problem...for the time being. The next order of business was to find a place to hold so they could analyze the problem.

Simpson coordinated a holding pattern while Forsyth pulled the emergency procedures manual out for the second time. Most crews didn't have to use "the book" twice in as many years, much less the same flight.

The copilot guided the 727 around the holding pattern while the captain worked with the second officer to compute their fuel reserves and assess how much time and gas could be spent dealing with their new problem.

Forsyth came up with some new figures for time and burn to the various suitable airports within their limited range.

Using the number 2 VHF transceiver, Forrest talked to the company dispatcher in Miami making notes on the latest weather observations for La Guardia, JFK and other airports further south. The Philadelphia weather was bad, at the moment, with heavy rain. The Baltimore weather was better. But, they had already consumed a lot of fuel on their initial approach to New York. If they diverted to Baltimore now, they would have barely enough fuel to do one approach. And, he remembered a second later, their fuel burn computations were figured on a clean airplane, not a sick one with its feet dangling in the breeze. If they couldn't get the right main to come down, Forrest wanted to be able to make as many attempts as it took to set up the approach as close to perfect as he could. He knew it might take more than one attempt to get the plane on the ground. Forrest had already decided not to make another approach to LGA. It was not the kind of airport that he wanted to deal with under the circumstances. An inquiry about the JFK weather brought good news: it had improved a bit. After a few minutes thought, Forrest told the dispatcher he'd decided to go to Kennedy and asked him to make arrangements to receive the passengers there. That would give them a little more time and fuel to deal with the landing gear problem.

"George, tell 'em we want to go to Kennedy."

Simpson smiled. "Sure you don't want to go to Palm Beach, instead, boss?"

Forrest huffed a mirthless laugh and glanced at the fuel gauges on the engineer's panel. Based on their present rate of burn, they had less than an hour to get the jet on the ground. Forrest told Forsyth to start the alternate gear extension procedure. Then, last but not least, it was time to let the passengers and the flight attendants know what was going on. Understandably, their apprehension would be high. The passengers, he knew, would be asking a lot of questions for which the flight attendants would have few answers. He was surprised they hadn't called before this. But, patient or not, they could only deal with a bunch of nervous New Yorkers for so long before things got ugly.

"Ladies and Gentlemen, This is Captain Forrest." He spoke slowly and calmly as if this sort of thing happened every day.

"I apologize for not making this announcement sooner, but we've been a little busy for the past few minutes. As we attempted to lower the landing gear, we encountered a problem." No point telling them about the ice or running out of gas, he thought. TMI. There was, after all, such a thing as being too honest.

Forrest continued. "The wheels on the right side of the airplane failed to extend into the landing position. While I'm speaking, the crew is working on an alternate procedure designed to extend it. In a few minutes you will probably see the second officer in the passenger cabin looking through a viewing port in the floor. He will be checking to see if the gear is up or down, or someplace in between. If it won't cooperate, we will have to land with the gear where it is—meaning we will have to land with the gear up. While that may sound ominous, there's really no cause for alarm.

"I'll be sure to keep you informed. For now, I can tell you that we are diverting to JFK where the runways are much longer. Arrangements have been made to receive you there. We appreciate your patience. In the meantime, please follow your flight attendant's instructions."

"John," Forsyth said. "I'm ready to crank down the right main if that's okay." He was out of his seat, kneeling over a small compartment in the cockpit floor. He had opened the cover, exposing the end of a shaft about the same diameter as a roll of quarters.

Forrest held his flashlight on the opening. "Go ahead." Forsyth inserted the gear crank over the end of the shaft and started rotating it in a clockwise direction. By turning the shaft, he hoped to manually release the large hooks that held the landing gear in the up position. Theoretically, gravity would do the rest...theoretically.

"Almost done," Forsyth said with a slight grunt. "That should do it."

All eyes went to the landing gear lights on the center of the forward instrument panel. Nothing —no green light.

Forrest scowled. "Go check it visually, Skin." He reached up and turned on the wheel well lights. "Something tells me we're not going to like what you see."

Forsyth took his flashlight with him as he headed for the main cabin. A hundred pairs of anxious eyeballs fixed on the man in the crisp, white uniform shirt, black tie and black slacks as he strolled calmly down the aisle. Four rows aft of the wings, he kneeled down on the blue carpet. Pulling it apart at a VELCRO seam, he exposed a round panel in the floor. Removing the cover, Forsyth peered inside. One look was all it took to confirm what the captain had predicted. He closed the cover, replaced the carpet and walked back to the flight deck—the same hundred eyeballs burning anxious holes in his back.

"Just like you said it would be, boss." Forsyth said with characteristic calm and clarity. "From what little I can see, the door is partially open and the gear is resting against it. I don't think it's going anywhere tonight," Forsyth reported.

"Okay, then. No sense fooling around with it any longer. Let's get this thing on the ground. We're running out of time." The captain turned in his seat as Forsyth strapped in. "How much fuel left now, Skin?"

"7,000 pounds. About to start burning our reserves."

"Alright, George," Forrest sighed. "Tell 'em we'd like to head for Kennedy." Forrest picked up the interphone to talk to the lead flight attendant.

"Animal Control, Cynthia speaking!" she announced as she answered the chime.

"Hate to tell you this Cynthia, but you're going to get to practice your emergency evacuation tonight. The gear won't budge so we're going to do a little asphalt surfing." Forrest briefed her on what to expect. "I'll give you about five minutes to brief the other flight attendants on the emergency landing and evacuation procedures and then I'll make a PA to the folks. After that, the PA will be all yours. I suggest you have them put their coats on, now. It's going to be chilly when they evacuate. Let me know when you're ready. Don't rush it, but don't fool around, either. We don't have a lot of fuel to play with," he warned.

"We've done most of it, already." Her voice trailed off nervously. "I'll call you back in a few minutes." CLICK.

"Southeast 106, Kennedy Approach, you are cleared to JFK via radar vectors. Turn left, heading one-four-zero. Will you be coming in right now, or do you need a little more time?" Kennedy approach was all set for them.

Forrest smiled. *Gotta love those New York controllers!*

Simpson looked over at the captain who nodded and pointed into the darkness in the general direction of the airport. "The boss says we're going to bring it straight in," he answered.

"Roger, Southeast 106, the winds are now three-three-zero at two one. Would you like to have runway three one left? It's our longest one, fourteen thousand, five hundred feet and change." Forrest nodded, again, as Simpson confirmed the choice. "That's affirmative, Kennedy. We'd like to turn on to the approach just outside ZACHS for a long final."

"You can expect that, Southeast 106. We've got all the equipment standing by on thirty-one left. We're ready when you are. I show you twenty-five miles from ZACHS. Turn left to three four zero. Maintain two thousand feet until established on the localizer. You're cleared for the ILS approach to runway three-one-left. Weather is four hundred overcast, two miles in light rain. You are cleared to land."

These guys had their act together, Forrest thought as he switched on the PA. *Let's hope we can do as well.* "Ladies and gentlemen, we are beginning our approach to the Kennedy airport. We should be landing in about seven minutes. The flight attendants have briefed you on the emergency landing procedures. Please do exactly as they say. I'm sure many of you are nervous about this little adventure.

There is very little to be worried about. The landing shouldn't be very much rougher than normal. It will, however, take us a lot more power to taxi to the terminal than usual," he joked with a laugh in his voice. He thought a little gallows humor might be appropriate at this point. "Your biggest concern will be not skinning your knees or twisting an ankle as you slide down the chutes. Once again, there will be no need for you to push or shove. Just take your time and follow the instructions of the flight attendants. Once you're at the bottom of the chute, quickly get up and walk to an area about fifty feet away from the airplane. If you take too long to get up, someone will, most likely, slide down on top of you. Once you're clear, just stand by for the ground people to help you. Please do not wander off on your own. We don't want anyone to get lost. The Second Officer will get back to you when we're two or three minutes from touchdown."

As he switched off the PA, Cynthia called him on the interphone. "Captain, a lady in the back wants to know if she has time to go to the bathroom...wait a minute...hold on...whoops...never mind.... I think we're going to need a replacement seat cushion for 25C, though."

"Mine too," laughed Forrest, glad to know that their humor was still intact. "See you on the ground."

Three minutes later, Forrest turned the Boeing onto the localizer lining the jet up with an invisible runway. The crew ran through the checklists one more time and went over their evacuation procedures. Seven miles from the runway, Forrest had the 727 slowed down to its final approach speed. Everything was just as it should be...almost.

Four-and-a-half miles from the end of the runway, they were still in the clouds. An eerie glow from the anti-collision and navigation lights made it seem as if they were driving through a black foggy tunnel. Rain mixed with snow streaked horizontally into the powerful landing lights. Descending through seventeen hundred feet, a flashing blue light on the instrument panel announced their passage over the MEALS outer marker.

"Southeast 106, passing the marker. Wind check, please," Simpson called.

"Three three zero at two zero. The equipment is standing by." The tower controller's voice was calm, steady and distinctly New York.

Forsyth picked up the cockpit handset and selected PA. "Ladies and gentlemen, we're one minute from touchdown. Please assume your brace position. Brace. Brace. Brace." He hung up the receiver and directed his attention to the approach.

"Okay, George. Cover me on the rudders. I may need some help keeping this thing on the runway. Skin, call the radar altitudes, every ten feet starting at a hundred, all the way down to touchdown, please."

"You got it, Boss. Thousand above minimums. On course on glide path." Simpson checked his instruments against the captain's. They each received their information from separate sources.

"Well," Forrest said wryly, "if I get this right, we'll probably get the rest of the month off. If I don't, we'll probably get the rest of our careers off."

Nervous snickers.

"If I *really* screw it up, we'll get the rest of our *lives* off."

Silence.

Twenty seconds later, Simpson announced, "Approaching two hundred above. I've got intermittent ground contact." Lights reflected off wet streets through gaps in the clouds.

"One hundred above..."

Forrest scanned his instruments. *A little right rudder. Just a tad of power. Where's the stinking...?"*

"Approach lights in sight just to the left of the nose!" Simpson called out.

Forrest looked up to verify the copilot's call. In order to stay lined up with the runway centerline, he had to steer a heading about ten degrees to the right of centerline, compensating for the crosswind. "Runway in sight. Give me the rest of the lights and the wipers."

Simpson reached overhead and turned on the nose gear lights. Cycling the wiper switch to the medium position produced a loud annoying whir as blades slapped water off the thick glass.

Forrest lowered the right wing a few degrees and fed in some left rudder to bring the fuselage into alignment with the runway. A small power adjustment compensated for the extra drag and anticipated sink rate.

"One hundred feet. Ninety feet. Eighty feet," Forsyth read as the radar altimeter tape scrolled toward the ground. "Speed's good. Sink rate is good. Seventy feet."

Forrest and Simpson saw the green runway end lights pass beneath the nose. Lights everywhere—presumptuous—adamant—intrusive—invaded their periphery. Dozens of fire trucks, ambulances and other emergency vehicles attached themselves to the distracting glitter before smearing into wet blurs near the edges of the windshields.

"Thirty feet."

Forrest eased the nose up slightly and nudged the big bird toward the left half of the runway to compensate for the unavoidable tendency of the ship to swerve right once the right wing made contact with the surface.

"Twenty...Fifteen...

Back gently on the yoke.

Ten...Five..."

The left main tire touched the runway.

Forrest tightened his grip. Reflexes put in a sudden twist of left aileron to hold up the right wing.

"Hundred and twenty knots," Forsyth called.

Forrest gently lowered the nose wheel to the pavement, constantly working the ailerons to keep the right wing from dropping too soon.

"One hundred knots."

Forrest fought the gusts for control. Sooner or later that wing would have to come down.

"Ninety."

Forrest had the ailerons at full deflection. The controls felt heavy as they lost speed.

As aerodynamic forces yielded to gravity, the edges of the right wing flaps started digging into the concrete. A tremendous shower of sparks spewed from the dragging metal, suppressed somewhat by the numerous puddles.

Forrest shoved in some left rudder to compensate for the right pull. The drag increased as more wing came in contact with the wet pavement demanding more brake and rudder. Forrest's left leg began to protest. "Get on the rudder, George," he grunted.

Both pilots applied all their strength to the brakes and rudder as the jet drifted further and further toward the north edge of the runway.

"All the way to the stop."

One after another, the lights marking the edge of the runway snapped off amidst a flash of arching electricity and shattering glass as the 65-ton machine ground to a halt. Well before it came to a complete stop, the fire trucks stationed at the east end of the runway roared to full speed in a spectacular chase. In less than a minute, the firemen were shooting the smoldering right wing with truck-mounted foam cannons.

The captain shut off the engines and gave the evacuation order over the public address system while Forsyth and Simpson ran the EVAC checklist.

Water and blowing mist flowed over the top of the fuselage as the first escape slides inflated from the door and window exits. Firemen and arriving medical workers grabbed emerging passengers by the arms and lifted them quickly to their feet and out of the way.

Flight attendants sent passengers down the chutes at two-second intervals. It took some longer to sit and slide when they saw the long drop. Most who hesitated were pushed by the anxious passenger just behind. Abrasions and twisted ankles were inevitable. "Sit and slide! Sit and slide!" they shouted in their loudest, most authoritative voices. Training and temper overcame sympathy. Frustration invaded their commands as many had to be disarmed of their brief cases and personal computers when they arrived at the emergency exits. A small pile of confiscated paraphernalia grew by the door. Initially, some passengers reacted like they were being mugged until someone behind them threatened to do far worse if they didn't get moving.

No doubt about it, Cynthia mused, New York was full of warm and caring people. She glanced inside the cabin. Aside from a little human friction, the evacuation was going pretty smoothly.

Forrest reached up and turned on the emergency lights just as Forsyth and Simpson opened the cockpit door and headed for their evacuation stations.

Forrest followed them out. He was glad to see that less than a third of the people remained on board. Because the aircraft listed to the right, people were walking awkwardly, holding on to seat backs and overhead luggage racks as they made their way to the nearest exit. Picking up the command cadence of, "Sit and slide!" from Cynthia, the captain directed her to the middle of the plane to help the people at the over-wing exits. When the last of the forward passengers went down the slide, Forrest headed to the back of the plane checking between seats to see that no one remained on board.

"I'm the last one. Let's go." Taking Cynthia by the arm, the captain collected the two flight attendants at the rear doors. "Well ladies, there's a hundred and twenty-four people who'll never fly Southeastern, again," he said sarcastically as he sent them on their way. A minute later, Forrest followed them down the R2 chute into the biting rain and wind. At that moment, Captain John Ruger Forrest had no way of realizing the true irony imbedded in his quip: though most of these people would indeed never fly a Southeastern jet again, neither would he.

CHAPTER-THREE

MOTIVE *a: an emotion, desire, physiological need, or similar impulse that acts as an incitement to action*

AMY LEE'S EYES SNAPPED OPEN. A subtle change in her environment was enough to bring her out of an exhausted but fitful sleep. Slowly, she rolled onto her back to take stock of the situation. It was nearly dark and the truck had stopped, its diesel engine rumbling at idle. Cyclops and Red Bandanna were still asleep. In the background there was a new sound–the faint whisper of a river moving between its banks.

Amy sat up slowly so as not to arouse the two sleeping monsters. Deftly and silently she inched her calves and ankles around the truck bed feeling for the knife Cyclops had dropped and, amazingly enough, forgotten in his excitement with his new found prize. Her eyes went to the filthy, weathered finger which had become her precious engagement ring's new home. A surge of hot anger shot down her spine and grounded itself in the pit of her stomach.

You bastard!

At that instant her left ankle found the knife Cyclops had set down and forgotten—her anger now somewhat mitigated by elation.

Careless bastard, too.

Voices to her left made her freeze. She eased her head and eyes in their direction to see the long shadows of Black Hat and that pathetic little pygmy walking back from the river's edge.

Amy focused her attention on the blade trapped under her ankle and slowly slid it toward her bound hands. Her eyes remained locked on the two poachers slumped against the blue plastic canvass covering the pile of fresh ivory. She froze for a moment when she felt Black Hat climb into the driver's seat and slam the door. Cyclops shifted a little in his sleep then settled as the truck moved forward. Sensing the fleeting opportunity, Amy slid the knife quickly under her lower back and fumbled for a grip on the handle.

Just then she felt the front of the truck tilt abruptly downward, creep down the steep bank and rock from side to side as the vehicle entered the swift brown water, its musty smell assaulting her nostrils. Cyclops and Red Bandanna startled awake and sat up to orient themselves. With their attention diverted to the river crossing, Amy used this second diversion to slide the knife into her waistband and pull her shirt out to conceal it.

She watched as the truck came to a stop mid-river and a shout from the front passenger seat brought Red Bandanna over to Cyclops' side of the truck to watch an unfolding spectacle upstream. A struggling wildebeest was at the center of a tug-of-war between two huge crocodiles. The beast's last stand brought a pang of empathy from deep within a young woman who could identify with its pathetic plight only too well.

"Mamba watashiba leo usiku," Cyclops said with a sinister laugh. (The crocs will eat well tonight)

"Ninanjaa kubwa kuwaliko," (I am hungrier than them) Black Hat snarled, failing to appreciate the humor of the situation. "Twende haraka!" (Let's get out of here fast) he shouted, turning to gesture angrily at the driver with a finger pointed at the far bank.

Amy used the sad spectacle as an invitation to gather her legs under her as she rose to a kneeling position to observe the death struggle 50 meters upriver. This maneuver brought another laugh from her captors.

Apparently, she thought, they're not too worried about me trying to escape in the middle of a croc infested river with my hands tied behind my back.

Most women, hell, most anybody would be too frightened and too sensible to try a stunt like that. With good reason.

Then she remembered her father telling a story of how at least one soldier in Vietnam had escaped the VC by being just brazen enough to surprise the Gomers by overturning a dugout in which he was being transported at night with his hands tied behind his back. She'd also heard him talk about how the best time for a POW to escape was as soon as possible after capture.

Amy felt the truck begin moving again as the wildebeest went under for the final time. A glance at Cyclops assured her that he and his buddy were still watching the crocs fighting over choice cuts as the sun settled into the far horizon. Darkness was quickly swallowing the sunken riverbed.

Suddenly she said a short, silent prayer, took a deep breath and held it then came to her feet and threw herself over the side. The muddy water engulfed her in a splash as she sank to the bottom, pushed off with her feet, broke the surface and dove again kicking with the swift current.

Bedlam erupted in the truck. Cyclops and Red Bandanna grabbed their rifles and fired wildly into the water, brilliant muzzle flashes strobing in the near darkness. Black Hat stopped the truck at the bottom of the far bank and scrambled out to join the search.

Amy felt her forehead brush the muddy bottom as her body was bumped along with the current. Her lungs burned for a breath. She felt the buoyancy of a full chest of air lifting her slowly to the surface. Enthralled by the POW story as a child, she had practiced with her Dad in the pool the drown-proofing technique taught to every special-forces soldier since Vietnam. In seconds that felt like hours she felt the back of her head and upper back break the surface.

Now!

Amy threw her head back, exhaled explosively and sucked in a full breath before sinking back to the bottom. A basketball-size rock caught her right kneecap, the sharp pain almost causing her to lose her breath. She gritted through it and held on. Then, ten meters later, she felt her shoulder bump into something big and hard. *Oh God. Croc!*

Then she realized it was nothing more threatening than a submerged log. Still, aching lungs drove her to the surface. Once again, she broke the surface without benefit of her hands, gulped a lungful of life and submerged.

On shore in the gathering darkness the poachers searched the river surface as best they could. They were astonished that a young girl would have the grit to throw herself into a river full of monstrous carnivores. But it was those same prevalent perils that allowed them to give their prisoner up for dead. If she miraculously hadn't drowned, sooner or later she would make a tender and tasty meal for something.

The fabric of Buddy "Norman" Bates' clothes flapped in the slipstream as the Bell JetRanger made its way to the scene of the riot in downtown Mogadishu. In order to create an unobstructed field of view for his camera, he and the CNN helicopter pilot, Tony Assaf, had removed the starboard passenger door. A safety harness allowed Bates to hang out of the machine to tape the action, his feet resting on the external step rail.

Assaf had laughed at Brooks McKewen, the tall, handsome, onboard "talent," when he expressed some concern that, with the door removed, Bates would have no protection against the prevalent small arms threat—not to mention the bumper crop of RPGs the Somalis had used to bring down 2 Black Hawks the month before.

"Doors don't stop bullets," he'd chuckled, shaking his head at McKewen's naivete. The Irishman, Assaf, a talented pilot with curly dark hair and brilliant blue eyes knew the high-speed projectiles would easily pierce the chopper's aluminum skin like needles through a toy balloon.

As a precaution, all of the crew members wore bullet-resistant vests constructed with DuPont's Kevlar; a synthetic fiber that had many times the tensile strength of steel. Although the body armor was effective against low-energy pistol bullets, the so-called "bullet-proof" vests would offer little protection from a high-velocity rifle round. The crew's only real protection was to stay in the hotel. But then, as Boots Blesse once said, no guts—no glory and more importantly—no story.

Bates, a skinny University of Georgia grad who most of the time looked like an un-made bed, watched as their residence, the old no-star Sahafi Hotel, and architecture which reflected both Italian colonization and third-world decadence drifted by under the skids. His youth belied his worldliness for his young eyes had seen their share of the world's horrors. Somalia was just one of many hellish assignments for a man who possessed the innate talent to see things just as a lens would see them and the tenacity to be in the right place at the right time for that Pulitzer-winning shot.

That morning, the CNN news crew's scanners had picked up the military radio traffic associated with an emergency. An angry mob was threatening a military checkpoint manned by a rifle platoon of Italian nationals. Two squads of troops, one Nigerian and one American, were being mobilized to respond to the disturbance. They were ordered to reinforce the Italians who were outnumbered at least a hundred to one. Brooks McKewen wanted to be there to capture the event on tape, especially if the demonstration turned ugly.

Above the roofs and trees in the northern part of the city, Assaf could see a column of foreboding black smoke. It was a perfect guide-post to the scene of the riot. Ever mindful of the loss of two U.S. Army Black Hawks and 18 American soldiers the previous month, he was determined not to be the news, just to film it.

In the back seat, Bates leaned out into the hundred-knot relative-wind and took a few seconds of tape to test the camera and to enter the time and date onto the leader.

Arriving directly over the mob, Assaf put the machine into a hard right turn to give Bates the best camera angle. A mile to the west on the paved street leading from the U.N. headquarters, the crew could see two white Saracen armored cars bearing the U.N. insignia approaching at high speed. Mounted in the cupola of the lead vehicle was a .30 caliber machine gun manned and ready for action.

Below them, they could see the upturned faces of several people in the crowd. Some shook their fists in angry defiance. The Italians kept their rifles pointed at the crowd. They held their fire while waiting to be rescued. Bates counted ten of them crouching behind the walls of a sandbag bunker. He taped a few seconds of the milling crowd as they pelted the soldiers' position with debris they found on the street. He guesstimated the number of Somalis to be several hundred. Some were throwing sticks and boards on a burning car causing the flames to reach ever-higher into an otherwise clear morning sky.

Women and children were encouraged to go to the front of the mob. Bates knew the Italians would not fire their weapons unless their lives were directly threatened. Living, fighting and sometimes dying by civilized rules put the soldiers at a distinct disadvantage in a situation where their enemies had no such compunctions. Bates struggled to hold the heavy Sony videocam steady as the pilot held the JetRanger in a tight turn over the crowd. G-forces generated by the constant maneuvering often doubled the camera's weight, compounding the difficulty. Assaf could have put the helicopter into a hover but that would have made them a stationary target for anyone looking for an easy shot at Americans. Also, orbiting as they were, it made it easier for him to keep an eye on the Black Hawks and Little Birds which were holding in the area below them to provide air support. Assaf's intense blue eyes scanned furiously over the cityscape looking for the telltale smoke and dust plume of an RPG launch.

Bates filmed the convoy of armored cars as they came within two blocks of their position. He was standing on the right skid, leaning against the door frame when it happened. He didn't hear it at first. The sound would not arrive for another second.

God-*damn!*

A derelict bus and an old truck parked along the side of the street blew apart in a tremendous ball of fire and flying steel. Their chassis were lifted into the air by what Bates guessed must have been at least two thousand pounds of high explosives. Awestruck, he watched the shock wave from the blast as it kicked up dust and debris from the street and hurled it against the side of the U.N. vehicles. Most of the people on the street within a block of the blast were knocked off their feet. The armored cars were blown over onto their sides, their huge rubber tires spinning uselessly in the air. The lead vehicle rolled over twice, crushing the gunner whose upper body was hanging out of the cupola like a rag doll dangling from a toy baby carriage.

Arriving simultaneously with the concussion of the blast, a strong shock wave rocked the helicopter. Assaf fought to keep the craft righted. The pressure wave knocked Bates' headset and Georgia Bulldogs cap off and sent it tumbling to the streets below. He watched the red and black cap drift to the street like a falling leaf. Before it landed it was snatched up by a teenage boy who defended his prize against the assault of two others who arrived a second too late. All three ran off in the direction of the explosion where they joined a group of armed men and other opportunists who grabbed anything of value.

Though the chopper pitched and yawed violently, Bates kept the camera reasonably steady on the burning U.N. vehicles and the gun battle that erupted on the street below. He continued to tape as the few survivors of the remotely-detonated explosion were systematically located and shot by the marauding gang of ebony bushwhackers.

As two more U.N. vehicles roared down the street toward the ambush site, the Somalis scrambled to gather whatever weapons and equipment they could. They brazenly lingered as long as they dared before running down the side streets and back alleys between the dilapidated buildings.

Bates leaned inside the chopper for a moment and tapped Assaf on the shoulder. He pointed at the fleeing bandits.

"Follow them," he urged above the noise.

Assaf instantly understood what Bates wanted. He dumped the nose of the helicopter and hauled up on the collective propelling the shuddering machine in their direction. Bates caught the boy who had taken his cap and some of the other clansmen on tape as they jumped into an old black Toyota pickup truck and spun out, heading north along one of the intersecting streets.

They pursued the Somalis for three minutes before Assaf swung the helicopter around and headed back to the ambush site. He knew that further pursuit would serve no practical purpose and the helicopter would eventually draw their fire.

Bates grabbed the edge of the doorframe as the centrifugal force threatened to throw him out. That was the last he saw of the Bulldogs hat and its new owner.

Two AH-1 Cobra helicopter gunships appeared over the tops of buildings to the south and began circling the ambush site, firing on Somali gunmen who exposed themselves. Assaf headed the JetRanger toward the burning vehicles and arrived just in time to see some troops deploying out of the back of their APCs.

The troops hurriedly set up a defensive perimeter around the site and fired at anyone who did not flee. Two-man medical teams scurried about checking the bodies of the U.N. soldiers.

Bates realized that only one warranted some desperate life saving measures. The cameraman watched as the medics quickly bypassed anyone who was beyond saving. He could tell by the unique "chocolate chip" desert camouflage pattern of the uniforms that the soldiers who had borne the brunt of the blast were Americans.

The Cobras made several threatening passes over the retreating mob and dispersed them into the expanses of the city. All was chaos below. Bates and the crew could hear the Army pilots talking among themselves, coordinating their maneuvers.

They ordered the CNN crew to leave the area immediately.

Hesitant at first, Assaf thought better of continuing the mission when a rifle round penetrated the Plexiglass chin-bubble at his feet and shattered the lizard-belly-green housing of his headphones.

"Aaallll righty, then!" Assaf sighed into his microphone. "I think that's our cue to leave, guys!"

* * * *

"Does anybody here think I, or anyone on my crew, did anything wrong?" Forrest asked the three middle aged men with blue plastic FAA name tags clipped to the breast pockets of their cheap sport jackets. In fact, he noticed, their entire collective wardrobe was "designer" stuff for sure—Salvation Army or Good Will. Forrest filled the uncomfortable void in the conversation with another question: "You guys all shop at the same place?"

The response was blank looks times three.

Forrest glared up at them from the corner seat of his hotel room sofa. *Typical government drones. They don't get it.* "So, I say again, would you gentlemen have done things any differently?"

Two of them mumbled something negative and one remained silent—the one who Forrest watched closely. For the last hour, Inspector Rick Shepard, the most arrogant and condescending one, had been countering Forrest's every statement with sarcastic, second-guess objections and petty, Monday morning quarterback criticisms. Forrest had had quite enough of FAA losers in his 12 years with the airline. With few exceptions, the feds were mostly second-rate pilots whose dubious flying skills and personality difficulties had prevented them from getting "real" jobs in the private sector. One of Forrest's famous adages: Those who can't do, teach. Those who can't teach become critics. And those qualified to do none of the above, regulate. Predictably, this team of government-issue toads was no exception.

His previous visitors, the NTSB team, was far sharper, much more polite and had been only interested in determining the cause of the accident. The FAA, by contrast, was on a witch-hunt. They were looking for someone to blame.

"Well then, you've already got the only statement I'm prepared to give at the moment," Forrest responded firmly with a contemptuous politeness as he clicked on the room's TV. Forrest's tone let them know that he'd reached the end of his patience, and by standing, the end of the interview.

Two new men, dressed in business suits, looked in as the FAA team was leaving. "Everything okay, John?" the tallest man asked. They were from the Air Line Pilots Association. The night before, the ALPA team had been among the first to arrive on the scene to ensure that Captain Forrest and his crew were well cared for and had proper representation. Southeastern management, true to form, had done nothing.

"Yeah, fine, now that these pukes are leaving," Forrest said, flipping through the channels until he spotted a story, in progress, on the evening news.

The three men watched quietly as WABC played videotape of the aircraft recovery crew lifting the right wing of the airliner with a crane. Another segment, taken several minutes later, showed mechanics lowering the landing gear and subsequently towing the wounded bird away to a hangar. Additional shots showed footage, taken the night before, of the jet's spectacular landing, sparks showering the runway for half a mile.

"Helluva show, John!" exclaimed the tall man. "And, by the way, helluva good job!"

Forrest deflected the praise with a thin smile. "Flight attendants got 'em all out pretty quickly, didn't they?"

"In a New York minute," one laughed.

"Any more word on injuries?"

"So far, we've only got two passengers with sprained ankles and three or four skinned knees and elbows," the other answered.

Forrest nodded. "Well, we haven't heard from the lawyers, yet. That number will probably triple."

"No shit," was the cynical but honest reply.

The morning news went on to show clips of the interviews with the passengers, all of whom praised the pilot for the wonderful job he did getting the airplane on the ground. Some commented that the landing was smoother than most of the normal landings they had experienced. They used the word "hero" several times.

"Makes you wonder, doesn't it? These people think I'm some kind of hero or something and our friends from Federal Aviation Assholes treat me like a criminal," the captain muttered, not taking his eyes off the TV screen.

"Mmm."

The news anchor came back on with the words: "In a related story, Judge Marcus Nelson, presiding jurist in Southeastern Airlines' bankruptcy proceedings, denied management's motion to extend the company's loans for another 60 days. The judge cited creditor's growing skepticism toward management's business plan and poor advanced bookings for the holiday season. According to reliable sources, creditors saw last night's accident as a bad omen. That leaves the airline until the end of the month to come up with other capital.

"Wall Street reacted harshly, as well. Southeastern stock is down three and an eighth as of..." CLICK.

Forrest sighed, throwing the remote onto the bed. "Anyone care to wager whether or not we'll still be in business next week?"

Amy Lee's feet found the sandy bottom as she tentatively brought her head above the water near the edge of the river. She froze and listened in the darkness for any sign of the poachers. She eyed a vague dark shape on the bank warily, wondering if it were an inanimate object or a prehistoric meat grinder. Slowly and deliberately, so as to draw no attention, she decided to wade a few more meters downriver before moving closer to the bank. Her hands lifted her shirt and felt for the knife still tucked into her waistband. Although she decided to wait until she had reached dry land to extract it lest she lose it in the water, its presence was somehow reassuring.

Steven Henderson watched President Wilcox calmly pace the carpet on long, stiff legs, asking questions and allowing his staff and advisors to free wheel. A wayward strand of sandy-gray hair hung away from the side of his head as he tracked a path around the carpet's presidential seal.

The mood inside the Oval Office wasn't nearly as relaxed as it was the first time he'd visited. News from Somalia was as objective and dispassionate as a police accident report: vehicles were damaged or destroyed, and there were casualties—American casualties. The Secretary of Defense, a short, deliberate man with a white bristle-brush crew-cut, had arrived only moments before reporting that the Naval amphibious taskforce had been moved closer to shore and that all wounded personnel had been med-evaced. "Seven dead, eleven wounded," he added, grimly.

Mrs. Wilcox, Henderson noticed, sat on one of the sofas, a cup and saucer clutched in short freckled fingers, her wide blue eyes taking it all in. The Secretary of State was mostly silent as was the Chief of Staff.

"What now?" the President asked calmly, brushing his hair back in place with bony fingers.

Admiral Small answered. "It's mostly wait and see, at this point. First we assess the scope of the threat, determine their objectives, then take measures to ensure the threat is negated before continuing the mission—that is, *if* you think the mission should be continued, sir."

The Admiral and the first lady exchanged looks which, in an instant, reiterated their opposing positions.

Having no answers and no solutions, Henderson felt frustrated. Satellites were of little use in situations like this and NSA, not for lack of trying, hadn't come up with much, either.

The president stroked his chin and shot the Admiral a look, which he quickly shifted to his wife.

The message in her eyes was clear.

"Hodding," the President said.

"Yes, sir."

"Set up a meeting for later—all the key players. Invite the Armed Services Chairman and the majority leaders so they don't feel like they've been left out."

"Mr. Henderson," the president continued. "I want you to find out who was behind this. Priority one, understand?"

"Yes, sir."

The president's eyes went to the Secretary of State and then to the National Security Advisor. "I think we need to take another look at things before we commit to a continued humanitarian airlift." *I don't know why in God's name we continue to feed people who love to kill Americans.*

Henderson saw the president's eyes go back to the first lady as he dismissed the meeting. He read no conciliation in them. The CIA man was standing close enough to hear the Chief of Staff whispering to one of the president's aides. "Jesus Christ," he snapped, looking at the daily schedule. "Just when in hell am I supposed to do all that?"

Fewer than ten alabaster tusks remained in a pile that had, just hours ago, been waist high. Not so many years before, the master poacher remembered bitterly, the piles in his camp had risen above a man's head. But that was another time, a time when great herds of elephants had darkened the forests and grasslands.

Black Hat leaned against the truck. A cigarette dangled from his bottom lip dripping ashes onto arms folded across his chest. His dark eyes followed the workers as they finished the loading. They had saved the smallest pieces for last, when space would be tight.

The old British-built tanker truck was the perfect transport for these products, especially after its considerable, yet invisible modifications. Streaked with rust and coated with dirt, the truck was the second vehicle in a fleet of three. The first had departed with its load for Dar es Salam a few days earlier. The third, its hood agape like the jaws of a yawning hippo, sat parked under the trees near the edge of his camp awaiting parts. Even in their less-than-roadworthy condition, the tankers were Black Hat's most valuable pieces of equipment.

Capturing his driver's attention, Black Hat gestured toward the hood of the truck. "Test the oil and see that the radiator is full," he ordered. He couldn't afford to have the truck break down enroute for want of basic service.

He turned his attention to the opposite end of the truck, where his men were inserting the last few pieces of ivory. Its tank had been completely rebuilt from the inside out. A second tank was constructed inside the original shell creating a hidden compartment almost six meters in length. The outer tank held several hundred gallons of gasoline. The inner compartment, accessible only through cleverly hidden hatches built into the rear end, held the contraband. Two vertical cylinders, welded into place below the filler hatches, formed wells which extended to the bottom of the tank. These were filled with fuel for the benefit of any official who might inspect or "stick" the truck's cargo. Measuring sticks dipped into the tank would always indicate the same quantity indicated on the driver's bogus shipping documents.

Black Hat stepped away from the truck to insure that the hatch was properly closed and bolted down. The driver stopped briefly to receive last-minute instructions from his employer before sliding in behind the steering wheel. After a few turns from a tired electric starter, the old engine came alive. A ton of ivory, rhino horn, and other animal products, representing months of work, lumbered off on the second leg of a journey that would ultimately take it half way around the world.

Bad news travels fast. Terrible news sometimes takes a little longer, Steve Henderson realized as he read the telegram from the American ambassador to Kenya for the eleventh time. Apparently Amy and Nathan had been dead for days and he was only learning about it... *now*? His fingers tingled as if he had stuck them into an electrical outlet. "Holy mother of God," the CIA officer gasped as his executive assistant slumped into an overstuffed office chair and began to sob.

Amy and Nat...dead. Murdered. It *had* been days since he'd heard from them but then international phone calls weren't exactly cheap nor were they to be expected from a young couple on their honeymoon. *But killed?* His mind struggled to comprehend the incomprehensible. *No way. Couldn't be.* He'd even checked the current intel files himself before OK'ing their trip. No demonstrations, the government was relatively stable for Africa, nothing unusual.

Shit! What the hell could have happened to them?

He took a deep breath and held it, then realized he hadn't breathed for at least a minute. It was only then that he noticed Roselle's sobs. Henderson laid the telegram on his desk, lifted himself out of his leather chair onto wobbly legs and went to the woman who'd been his right arm for seven years. "Roselle." He reached out and took one of her hands. "Roselle."

The woman shuddered and sobbed even harder. "Oh Steve," she wailed. She avoided his eyes, instead burying her face in her boss' shoulder. "I'm so sorry. I'm so sorry."

Henderson wrapped his trembling arms around his assistant's shoulders, patted her back and looked down at the floor. "Maybe it's a mistake," he heard himself saying to the back of her head. "Maybe the police made a mistake." He said it again hoping he could make himself believe it. He felt her shuddering in another spasm of tears, waited for it to pass, then pulled her face away from his shirt. "Roselle… Roselle." He gripped her very gently by the shoulders and looked her squarely in the eyes. "I'm going to need your help. I'm going to need you to get it together. You can't help me like this." Henderson choked and swallowed, his own emotions barely under control. Helping her, he realized, was actually helping him to be strong. Roselle was more than a co-worker and an assistant, she was a friend of the family. She, her husband and three children were frequent guests in his home for one occasion or another, special or not.

"Roselle." He squeezed her shoulders. "First, see if you can get the Kenyan police on the phone. Then get in touch with someone down at the East African desk. Maybe someone at Foggy Bottom can help, too."

Roselle sniffled and took a deep breath. Her eyes found his to be clear, resolute, and calming. "Do you want me to call John and... and…" She felt her bottom lip curling up then fought to control it. "... and Marie?"

The mere mention of his wife's name nearly pushed him over the edge. He'd deliberately avoided thinking about her. Henderson looked away. "No," he whispered, his voice as heavy as a wet mattress. "That I'll have to do myself."

CHAPTER-FOUR

PRESSURES *a: the burden of physical or mental distress*
b: the action of a force against an opposing one
c: the force of selection that results from one or more agents and tends to reduce a population of organisms
d: the stress or urgency of matters demanding attention

THE ATLANTIC OCEAN LAY AHEAD like a sparkling azure ribbon stretched between a clear subtropical sky and the green continuum of palms and oaks that defined the barrier island. Viewed from the high arch of the Wabasso bridge, it was always a welcome sight—a proper finish line for the weekly rat-race.

John Forrest felt the tightness in his chest ease perceptibly as his arrest-me-red 930 Turbo Porsche turned south onto Florida's scenic A1A. Two miles later, it squirted past electronic security gates into the soothing shade beneath the stately live oaks lining his street.

After stopping at the Sub-Zero for a tall glass of iced tea, Forrest entered his spacious office at the front of the house. The answering machine held a short message from Southeastern crew scheduling letting him know that all of his November trips had been removed from his schedule.

Forrest's Caller ID indicated he'd received eight calls in addition to the one from scheduling. Four had been from Steve Henderson. Had to be him. Calls from his CIA office always displayed: ANONYMOUS CALL. And, Forrest remembered, he had a serious aversion to leaving messages. One call had been from the Grizz, one from the FAA and two had been from his attorney, Allen Meadors. Like his friend Steve Henderson, Meadors deliberately avoided conversations with "machines."

Forrest set the glass down on a coaster and began reviewing six days' mail. The fat envelope from Meadors was opened quickly with the polished blade of a Soviet infantry officer's dress dagger. His eyes rapidly scanned the double-spaced lines of legalese.

"You're a real piece'a work, Gloria," he exasperated, re-reading his ex-wife's petition for an increase in alimony. The snotty cover letter from her attorney rankled him even more. "Who said prostitution isn't legal?" he muttered to the antique photograph of his great-great-great uncle, the Civil War Confederate General Nathan Bedford Forrest, hanging in a gilded frame over his oak desk. He tossed the papers in with the rest of the trash.

"Hello!...Hello!" echoed a high pitched, raspy voice from the glass-enclosed lanai at the back of the house.

Forrest smiled. At least someone was glad to see that he was home. Forrest peeked around the corner to see Ralph, his blue-and-gold macaw, pumping his head affectionately. Forrest laughed at his attention-getting antics. Puffing his gold chest and flushing his white leathery cheeks, he paced back and forth on his perch, muttering and flexing long blue wings.

"Okay, Okay. Let me change clothes and then we'll go outside," Forrest said in a special voice reserved for beloved pets.

After a quick change into navy blue shorts and a striped polo shirt, Forrest took Ralph outside where they "talked" on the screen-enclosed patio. Sitting on Forrest's knee having his back and head scratched was easily the comical psittacine's favorite activity. Compelled by habit, Forrest clicked on the television, set the channel to CNN Headline News and hit the mute button.

Once again, Forrest's tension began to melt away as they sat by the pool under a warm afternoon sun and left his mind to freewheel over the incident in New York and items on his "things to do" list. "Ow, dammit!" Forrest scolded, realizing Ralph was biting his thumb. It wasn't really a hard bite, not a skin-breaker, anyway. It was just the bird's way of reminding him he had stopped scratching. Forrest smiled. "Okay. Sorry."

Forrest stopped stroking the bird's head for a moment when he saw his airline's logo flash onto the TV screen. He pressed the remote's volume button to hear what the CNN announcer had to say: "... in late breaking news, Southeastern Airlines has announced that it will cease operations as of midnight tonight due to lack of cash, poor holiday bookings and the court's failure to grant further relief from its creditors."

CLICK.

"Jesus Tecumseh Sherman," Forrest gasped, feeling his jaw drop. The company's fate shouldn't have surprised him, but to hear it on the news... "What else could possibly go wrong, Ralph?"

The portable phone warbled gently.

"Hello," said Ralph.

"Thanks, pal. I'll get it if you don't mind." Forrest held the phone with one hand while scratching the top of the bird's head with the other.

"Hello."

Ralph looked at him as if to say, "I already said that, stupid," while Forrest listened to the caller's voice.

"Now that you asked, not all that wonderful, Steve. How's everybody up there...?"

Perspiration dripped off of William Temba Yumba's chin as he sat in the cab of the tank truck. Dark, wet patches stained the armpits of his light blue cotton shirt, the byproduct of heat, humidity and nerves. Three vehicles filled the space between his truck's front bumper and the gate-pole the Kenyan customs inspectors routinely lowered between each vehicle that passed through their checkpoint on the Kenya-Tanzania border.

The inspectors always made him nervous. There was always risk. Customs inspectors could be unpredictable. Sometimes they just waved him through after checking his papers and sometimes they checked his truck over front-to-back. Usually, suspicions and officials' pretensions evaporated when they found a few hundred shillings among his documents. But, he observed with a twinge, these faces were unfamiliar—a thought that brought new beads of sweat to his ebony forehead.

It took ten minutes for the preceding vehicles to clear customs, moving Yumba to the front of the line.

"Your documents, please," the inspector asked ever-so-politely. The extended hand and the accompanying look told Yumba it wasn't a request.

Yumba retrieved the papers from the dashboard and handed them to the official. As if the whole world ran on his schedule, the inspector methodically shuffled through them, his bureaucratic eyes scanning the forms for pertinent information. All of the documents were in order and most were legitimate. Passport, truck registration, tax receipt, his identity papers; all were accurate and all would hold up under routine inspection. It was an in-depth inspection that worried him. Yumba gave the inspector a broad, yet tentative smile and lit a cigarette trying his best to look unconcerned.

Without explanation, the inspector summoned his assistant and walked alongside the truck eyeing it suspiciously. Yumba watched them in the cracked side-view mirror as they disappeared to the rear.

BONG!

A nervous pang shot through him, tingling the skin along the backs of his hands.

BONG!

BONG!

Yumba's eyes narrowed at their reflected image as the inspectors made their way back to the cab.

BONG! Yumba's breathing froze when he saw the assistant strike the side of the tank with a stick. The sound had a nice ring to it, just as a steel tank full of gasoline should.

The inspector reappeared at the window and returned his documents while the other official raised the gate.

Yumba sucked his lungs full of tobacco smoke, revved the engine and moved the shift lever into low gear. With a protestant creak from its burdened suspension, the truck crossed into Kenya.

"It's true, John. I talked to the Police Commissioner just an hour ago." Henderson told his longtime best friend. "They have their IDs, suitcases, passports, everything. It's them."

"Everything?" John Forrest asked, his tone suggesting a meaning too sensitive to utter. He couldn't bring himself to say: "bodies."

A long silence met the question. "I suppose," finally came across a thousand miles of wires and microwave towers. "The Commissioner asked what we wanted him to do with..." Henderson's voice trailed off.

Forrest listened to the pained silence a while before speaking. "What do you want to do?" He felt as if someone were dragging a dull hacksaw blade down his chest from his throat to his groin. His eyes filled with hot stinging liquid.

Henderson hesitated. "Same thing you do."

"When do we leave?"

"Wait 'til Weight Watchers hears about this diet," Amy Lee thought out loud wondering just how much weight she'd really lost on her trek. Her progress was slow, owing to the heat and lack of shoes. Her soles were already blistered and sore.

"Every fat-body in America could use a trip like this." *But I'd give almost anything for a good sloppy burger, fries and a shake right now.* She wouldn't allow herself to speak that thought for fear she would hear herself and make the hunger pangs even worse. Like any survivor in an arid environment, lack of water was her worst problem and most immediate concern. A healthy human could go without food for over a week. Water had to be obtained every 48-72 hours. She had managed to eat the base of some palm fronds and extract a little moisture from that. Cactus was another source. But it wasn't enough. River water was dangerous—too many diseases resided there and she had no fire to boil it pure.

Oh, dear God. Please send a shower!

Amy Lee figured she was south of C103 and north of A109, the main road that connected Mombasa and Nairobi. But where, exactly? She thought of the map they'd left in the Land Rover. A lot of good it's doing me now.

If I continue north or south I'll cross a road sooner or later. But roads might be dangerous, as would be the rivers. They might be there—waiting. They would expect me there. Avoid lines of communication, Dad's Army friends always said.

Must get some help somewhere! I can't last much longer out here. But outside the parks and tourist areas who could you trust? One of those murdering bastards was wearing a uniform!

Neither man spoke very much on the long trip to Nairobi. Each chose instead to escape their pain by sleeping as much as possible on two uneventful connecting flights.

As they descended over the Great Rift Valley and the mountains to the west of the city, Henderson gazed through the Plexiglass windows at the unchanging sameness of the Kenyan bush. It was a featureless sea of the browns and greens where areas of trees stippled miles of expansive grassland. The Masai people had a word for its spotted appearance and had bestowed it upon their world-famous wildlife reserve: the Masai Mara. In preparation for landing at the Jomo Kenyatta airport, the 767 arced the mile-high city whose name had also been given by the Masai tribe. Uasu Nyrobe, "place of cold water," had actually been founded in 1899 as a headquarters camp in the midst of a level swampy area along Britain's Uganda Railway. Ironic, he thought, recalling that the historical material from the CIA country study file had mentioned that the railroad project had been engineered by none other than Colonel J. H. Patterson, a man who knew a lot about tragedy. As one of the colony's founding builders, Patterson had faced the unenviable task of eradicating a pair of vicious lions who were, for months, daily decimating the mostly Indian construction crew laboring on the bridge spanning the Tsavo River gorge. His 1907 memoirs, The Man-Eaters of Tsavo, had depicted the marauding lions as super-intelligent and fearless; seemingly possessed. *Tsavo—the place where Amy and Nat had been murdered. Maybe it was damned.*

Time flashed by as the rest of the day was devoted to the numbing chores associated with international travel. Baggage claim, customs, the taxi ride, the hotel check-in conducted by a young girl who was more cheerful and charming than anyone had a right to be all went by in a blur of depression and jet-lag.

Morning would bring a visit to the police station where he and his best friend would, once again, come face-to-face with searing reality and every parent's worst nightmare.

They hadn't felt much like eating breakfast, though the Hilton's sumptuous buffet would have tempted even the most anorexia-prone guest. Rather, Forrest and Henderson hailed a taxi for the short ride to the central police station so as not to arrive late for their appointment. Their driver dropped them off at the police station situated on Harry Thuku Road.

Initially hopeful, their optimism soon evaporated as they absorbed the station's atmosphere of indolence. Officers and clerks loitered about the station's long wooden counter apparently indifferent to the most adamant complaints from the occasional tourist reporting the theft of passports, money, or both. Henderson noticed that few if any of the complainants were citizens or residents. Evidently they knew how fruitless a police report would be and didn't bother. As they waited well past their appointed time, Forrest and Henderson shared looks with others who, after enduring long waits themselves, would be met by an officer who might agree to take a statement on whatever scrap of paper presented itself. On more than one occasion they watched as a policeman wrote names and particulars in the margins of newspapers found strewn about the waiting area then stuffed it in a breast pocket.

It took some doing, but they finally got an officer's attention. After discovering that they had an appointment with the Police Commissioner, he handed them several forms to fill out and instructed them to wait in an area designated with an apathetic nod.

Nearly an hour later, the Police Commissioner, apparently perturbed by a small group of reporters gathering outside the station, arrived dressed in a military-style uniform complete with garlanded epaulets. "Get a load of this," Forrest grumbled as Kenya's top policeman walked right past them without so much as a look. Two officers, their deportment seemingly transfused with enthusiasm at their superior's arrival, quickly followed him into an office where they adjourned behind closed doors. A full fifteen minutes later, one reemerged to summon the grim-faced Americans inside while the other assembled a team of officers to keep the press outside. Unbeknownst to the two Americans, the story of a honeymooning couple brutally murdered in a national park had become big news and the reporters were eager to talk to their fathers. The press and the parents soon became aware of the other's presence and both parties quickly grasped the potential value in exploiting the other's needs.

Commissioner Afande, a portly Kikuyu with a round face and onyx-black eyes, stood stiff with self importance at the front of his desk to offer his sincere condolences.

Forrest watched through hard eyes as Henderson did all the talking: "We've come a long way Commissioner. You'll forgive us if we're abrupt. But, we'd like to get right down to business."

Afande nodded graciously as he returned to his seat behind his desk and motioned them toward chairs.

Henderson had just started to speak when a new face appeared in the room, a small Kamba man who was introduced as David Kaviti, the head of the CID or Criminal Investigation Division. Pleasantries were exchanged before Henderson pressed ahead. "Gentlemen, what more can you tell us about the circumstances surrounding the deaths of our children?"

"The investigation is still ongoing." It was Kaviti. His tone indicated that that would be the extent of his statement.

Forrest and the CID man exchanged looks. Why does that sound like bullshit? thought the former.

Kaviti read his mind. "We have reassigned three CID officers to Tsavo to help in the investigation. We will leave no stone unturned."

And no patent lie untold, Forrest thought. He'd already been warned by his CIA friend not to expect much and so far he hadn't been disappointed. "Do you have any suspects?" He looked at the Commissioner who referred his eyes back to Kaviti.

The CID man started to shift his eyes to the floor—the best polygraph ever invented—then caught himself. He looked to the Commissioner for support then back to Henderson, deliberately avoiding Forrest's probing glare. "None at this time. But we are optimistic," he offered, evasively.

"Optimistic about what?" Forrest's tone had an edge to it.

Henderson took a deep, impatient breath as he sat, silently biting his tongue. He knew what to expect. He'd been warned by his intelligence experts during a thorough briefing conducted at Langley before his departure. Only a few years before, he'd been told, a German businessman had been jailed for two weeks by the Kenyan authorities for complaining too directly about African inefficiency.

Sensing the building tension, the Commissioner interrupted with a shred of truth. "Gentlemen, Mr. Kaviti and his people may have no suspects for the present but they do have the best of intentions. And I'm confident that they will do their best to find the men who killed your children. For now, suspects are many and resources are few. There is a lot of territory to cover out there along the border and I'm afraid there is no shortage of crime. Nevertheless, we have given this case the highest priority."

Henderson, sensing his partner's rising temperature, decided to intervene. "Commissioner, we appreciate your efforts thus far, but you can understand that we are more than a little upset." Though he'd been carefully coached in the business of Kenyan culture, he was fast running out of patience. Still, if either of them were to maintain control of the situation it would have to be him given his best friend's proclivity for direct, decisive, unbridled action—read; extreme violence.

Afande nodded sympathetically. It seemed sincere enough.

Kaviti's face remained impassive.

Patience. Patience, he told himself. Henderson brought the conversation back on track. "We came here to recover our children's remains, find out who killed them and, if possible, see to it that they are justly punished. What can you tell us about the case?"

After first taking a deep breath, the CID man fielded the question by first deflecting blame. "You see, your son and daughter were warned not to go off by themselves into the bush. It is very dangerous even for the most experienced guides. As I said, I am very sorry for your loss. But your children were simply in the wrong place at the wrong time and stumbled into a gang of poachers it would seem. And, as poachers are prone to do, they left no witnesses. In fact, we did not know they were missing until their Land Rover was reported stolen by the rental agency. Then their tour group manager reported that they did not turn up at the airport for their flight home. However, none of these occurrences are at all unusual. Tourists are frequently tardy and sometimes decide to extend their visits with little or no notice, especially the younger set." Kaviti attempted to solicit an understanding smile from Henderson with one of his own. He failed.

"Did you begin a search at that point?" Henderson asked, already anticipating the answer.

"No, we decided it was better to give it a few days, first. As the Commissioner has said, we do not have the manpower to waste on frivolous searches."

Nor the willpower, Forrest thought, his blood pressure rising at the last remark. "Frivolous? He snapped. "What if it were *your* children who were missing, Mr. Kaviti? Just how fucking frivolous would it be if *your* kids were missing?"

Henderson grimaced.

Afande held his hands up apologetically. "I understand your feelings, gentlemen. Truly I do," the Commissioner conceded with a patronizing tone and a wave of his hand. "You have to understand that the Kenyan police are on this case and will conduct a full and proper investigation. Leave this one to us."

Forrest began with a growl—low, controlled and understated, but a growl nevertheless. "Well Commissioner, let me tell you what we understand. We understand that our children—our children are dead—fucking dead! We also understand that they were here enjoying their honeymoon when some low-life dirt-bags, good citizens of your country, slaughtered them. And now we are beginning to understand that Hell will be selling frozen holy water on a stick before your police department arrests its first suspect."

Forrest took a deep breath to clear the stress from his lungs. "Now *you* need to understand something," he continued. "We're not here on safari. We're not on vacation. We're not your average dumb-shit tourists. We came here to bring our children back home. When we do, we're going to have to explain to their mothers how their babies were reduced to vulture-food. And they're going to want to know what you people are doing about it. So far, the only thing we've heard are bullshit excuses, however eloquent. Now unless we get your complete cooperation we're going outside and hold the first of many press conferences. And in a country that depends so heavily on tourism, bad press is bad business.

"Let me make this simple. We want our kids or whatever's left of them returned to us. We want to be taken to the place where they were discovered. And we want the bastards who did this brought to justice."

The CID officer bristled at the tongue lashing. Like most Kenyans, he took a raised voice and aggressive demeanor as a personal insult. But there was something in this wazungu's delivery—no, his eyes—which unnerved him.

Commissioner William Afande, who was more of a practiced politician than his subordinate, tried to defuse the situation. "Gentlemen. Gentlemen. Please. There is no need to become upset. We want what you want. We want this case to be solved just as much as you. After all, this sort of tragedy is bad for my country, bad for our reputation and, as you implied, bad for tourism. Please, let us handle the press. And I promise you we will arrange for you to visit Tsavo in a day or so."

"The sooner the better, Commissioner," Forrest warned, calming down a bit, though his eyes were still blazing. "'Cause we're not leaving until we do."

It had taken two days—two days of frustrating visits and unanswered phone calls followed by a brief press conference in their hotel meeting room to get the police to arrange a visit to Tsavo National Park. The third day's afternoon sun bathed the shrunken water hole in white-hot light as Forrest and Henderson walked its perimeter trying to grasp a sense of what had happened to their kids.

Henderson came across the first of many elephant skeletons and froze, the bleached white bones driving home the terrible finality of death.

Forrest bent down to retrieve one of dozens of brass cartridge casings ejected from an AK-47. He showed it to Henderson who nodded grimly then moved ahead.

Two policemen, dressed in white cotton shirts soaked through with perspiration, followed at a distance as the two Americans were left to "satisfy their curiosity."

Henderson felt a twinge as he rounded a large thorny bush. A crumpled wad of hot-pink cotton cloth lay crammed beneath its ground-hugging branches. He bent on one knee and pulled the soiled fragment free of its thorny entanglement. His fingers went cold as they unfolded material stiff with dried blood, vulture feces and dirt. A plastic zipper emerged from the folds then an embroidered SPEEDO logo. "Oh God," he breathed. It was a piece of Amy's jacket–the dark brown stains he recognized as blood. He had given it to her three Christmases ago. He remembered it because he had kidded her about driving too fast in the family car and cautioned her not to live up to the logo's name. He closed his eyes and sighed, letting the cloth drop to the ground. He felt strong fingers clamp down on the top of his shoulder and squeeze sympathetically.

"Amy's?" It was his best friend's voice.

Henderson nodded, his eyes still closed against the ugly images the garment brought forth from the recesses of his imagination.

"You wanna leave?"

Henderson let out a deep breath before answering. "No. I want to look around a bit first." In truth, he would just as soon depart but he sensed his friend was not yet satisfied. He lifted himself to his feet and shared a pained look with Forrest.

"You handling this?" Forrest asked, doubt and empathy coating his words.

Henderson's eyes were equivocal. "I'm trying."

Forrest squeezed Henderson's upper arm, "We'll go soon."

Forrest gestured at the tire tracks and started following them to the south for a few meters. It wasn't long before they came across the first of Amy's pink Nikes.

Henderson's eyes grew wide as he snatched it off the ground, examined it and clutched it to his chest. He and Forrest exchanged glances as Henderson jogged ahead searching the track for more remnants. Soon they came upon the other shoe.

"She's alive, John," he said with a breathy heave.

Forrest's face read no agreement.

"No, man. I know her. She's alive or at least was." His eyes were almost pleading with his best friend for agreement. "They haven't found any of her remains." As they had Nathan's, he didn't say. "She kicked her shoes off to let us know the direction they took when they left."

Forrest's eyes locked onto his buddy's. He began a series of slight nods. "Maybe."

"No maybe. Fact. I can feel it." Henderson looked longingly down the trail to the south.

Forrest squeezed his shoulder. "Let's go back and see if there's anything else these dipshits missed."

They turned and walked ahead into the brush, Forrest in the

lead. He hadn't gone far when something caught his eye—a straight line in a bush. There are no straight lines in nature. He looked harder and walked closer. It was the black metallic leg of a camera tripod. Then he saw another leg hanging askew among the thorny branches, converging with the others near the top of the bush. Forrest stopped and looked around to see if he was being observed. He leaned into the bush and stopped breathing. *Nat's camera!*

"Steve," he whispered.

Henderson jumped, his attention coming back from a mental tangent.

Forrest waved him over dramatically while looking over his shoulder to see if the police were watching.

Henderson walked closer. "What?"

"Nat's camera."

"What? No shit?"

"Keep an eye out for those Bozos while I get it."

Henderson turned to peer over the brush while his friend pulled the tripod and attached camcorder past the thorns.

"Battery's dead," Forrest whispered as he examined the dusty instrument. He wiped the grime off the tape compartment door and peered inside. "Tape's at the end of the reel."

"What?"

"The tape is full!"

"Jesus." Henderson's eyes went wide.

They heard voices approaching.

Forrest quickly unscrewed the mounting bolt and shoved the tripod back into the bush. As the police approached their position he shoved the camera into Henderson's camera bag with the rest of the lenses and accessories.

"Gentlemen!" a voice called from a few meters away.

Forrest grabbed Henderson by the arm and led him in their direction. "Let's go."

The two Americans stumbled into the Kenyans as they rounded a bush.

"Here we are," Henderson announced.

"How much longer?" the inspector asked politely, looking at his watch.

Forrest looked at Henderson then back to the policeman. "I think we've seen enough."

Yumba backed off on the gas as the truck entered the outskirts of the port city of Mombasa, Kenya. His first stop would be a gas station located on the city's west side where he would off-load the legitimate portion of his cargo. Profits from the sale, Yumba calculated, would more than cover his costs. The contraband money would be pure profit. He smiled to himself at the thought. Smuggling was a very good business, indeed. As long as you didn't get caught, he wouldn't let himself think.

An hour later, after the orange glow of sunset had faded behind the warehouses that lined the concrete piers, Yumba watched as five laborers removed the ivory, animal skins and rhino horn from the truck's inner compartments and loaded them onto a wooden dhow. Triangular lateen sails hung like heavy furled curtains from two sloping yards, each supported by its own mast.

A brisk on-shore breeze, pungent with the smell of salt and rotting fish, blew against his back bringing relief from the day's heat. It had been a good day, he happily assessed. Another successful trip. The thick wad of shillings in his shirt pocket pressed warmly against his skin adding to his contentment. He thought about the evening ahead of him, looking forward to several bottles of Tusker, the favorite local beer, and the company of one of the women that inhabited the waterfront bars. Better to hide most of the money in the truck, he reminded himself. It wouldn't be smart to let the whores see so much cash.

Shallow waves slapped rhythmically against the side of their craft as the Arab crew impatiently directed the placement of the last few pieces. When loading was complete, two canvas tarps were stretched over the cargo and lashed down with ropes. The Arabs and their valuable cargo would sail with the morning tide.

* * * *

Steven Henry Henderson and John Ruger Forrest had survived the funeral, though Henderson refused to acknowledge his daughter's demise. It was, without a doubt, the most difficult ceremony of its kind they had ever experienced. After all, there was nothing more tragic than a young person's funeral and nothing more heart-wrenching than the sight of other young people, classmates, bridesmaids, and friends sobbing uncontrollably at the side of a double grave—the graves of their own newly-wed children.

While most of the other relatives, friends and well-wishers commiserated in the kitchen and living room of the large, red brick Colonial, a select few men excused themselves to Steve Henderson's spacious, walnut paneled study. Their absence was conspicuous enough to raise questions among the many guests. Marie Henderson and the other "team wives," though used to their husbands' "bonding behavior," apologized for them but answered almost invariably with a dismissive: "If you have to ask you wouldn't understand."

Behind closed doors, each man was handling his individual pain in a different way, though dozens of empty beer bottles attested to their preference for one of the more traditional methods.

The five, most still wearing long sleeved dress shirts and ties, somberly watched as Henderson played the 8mm video tape on a camcorder which he had connected to his 32-inch Sony television. It had begun happily enough; laughing Amy and smart-ass Nathan clowning in front the camera for what was to have been part of a video album of the most exciting time of their lives. Then there was the footage of the water hole, the adorable elephants and finally the terrifying poacher's attack—every bit as violent as anything they had seen in Vietnam.

"Jesus, Mary and Joseph," Zito breathed, his fingers pulling his skin back from his forehead as he heard the first staccato pops and Amy's scream. His fingers fell to his chest, then clenched at his sides. "What possessed those kids to go out there by themselves?" he pleaded with the TV in anguish.

Forrest shared a look with his friend before turning his gaze back to the television just in time to see the screen twist askew as the camera tumbled into a thorn bush.

"Look," Henderson exclaimed unnecessarily as the figure of a tall man limped past the camera's lens. He and Forrest had seen the tape many times before. But now, they felt the need to share its horrific contents with their comrades if for no other reason than to avoid the inevitable questions being asked and answered multiple times. That was pain best endured only once.

Everyone got a good look at Black Hat's taught face as he paused, crouched, listened, then moved ahead followed by a man of smaller stature. Seconds later they heard Nathan's muffled voice...pleading?

All present viewed the rest of the tape in utter silence as each of the four poachers eventually unknowingly walked in view of the camera's lens. Each poacher's face became an image indelibly seared into their memories.

The tape ended with a rush of static and a screen full of electronic snow. Henderson set the camera to rewind. A full five minutes of heavy silence passed before anyone spoke.

"So what are we going to do about it?" It was Frank Zito, senior with more of a demand than a question.

"What can we do? It's out of our hands now," Henderson answered, ruefully. "We have to rely on the Kenyans to avenge her… or find her." The last remark came under his breath.

Forrest looked at Henderson then down at the floor. Like his friend, he was long on pain and short on answers but he had been working on a plan ever since they had left Kenya. "Do we?"

"I'll ask some of my friends at Foggy Bottom to see if they can lean on the Kenyan police through diplomatic channels," Henderson offered though he knew it was a hollow, feel-good statement.

"Yeah. Right," Forrest sneered. "The U.S. government to the rescue. That makes me feel a lot better, almost as satisfying as the Kenyans. Even if they gave a shit, and they don't, the Kenyan police couldn't catch the clap in a Mexican cathouse."

Henderson didn't respond. Absolute truth was unassailable.

Zito rose and opened the study's door and paused, gesturing with his own long-neck empty. "More pain killers, gentlemen?"

When Frank Zito returned to the den with a tray stacked full of fresh Budweisers, he was glad to see that someone had loaded another tape into the VCR. Images of last year's combined annual hunting trip and team reunion filled the screen allowing some semblance of laughter to return to the room. As he passed the tray around, Zito watched a scene of animated faces glowing red-amber in the light of their campfire, their laughter visible in the chilly Montana air. What an ironic contrast, he thought as his friends told jokes and stories with wild gestures that sloshed beverages onto hands gloved against last November's cold.

Henderson paused for a moment in front of one of his leather wing chairs. A symbolic beer was set on the seat left empty in honor of missing Nathan. As Henderson took a seat in a matching chair, bottles were raised to the vacant seat in silent salute to Forrest's son before their attention returned to the TV.

"Hope you're better with that new rifle than you were with your new shotgun, Zit," Steve Henderson taunted from the opposite side of the roaring campfire.

"How 'bout I stick it where the sun don't shine...don't miss much at that range," Frank Zito growled over the hilarity of his closest friends. He took a defiant swig from a coffee mug containing two fingers of Jack Daniels.

"LZ, ask your Dad to 'splain you how he, and his 'perty' new shotgun, missed four pheasants last year," Jim "Grizzly" Adams taunted from the young man's immediate right.

Frank Zito's youngest son, Frank, Jr. just smiled and shifted a knowing look to his father who sat on a camp stool to his left. It had been his first invitation to the sacred annual pilgrimage of his father's Ranger team to an outdoors destination for a little hunting or fishing and a lot of camaraderie.

"I got one...finally," his father grumbled before spitting a soggy piece of cigar into the fire.

"Three shots later," John Forrest reminded him, concealing a sly smile with a mug lifted to his lips at just the right moment. Having Frank junior present at the gathering reminded him of his own son whose initiation to the "men only" affair had occurred just three years before. He shot a grin and a wink at Nathan who was taping the whole thing for the first time.

"Three shots, Pop?" Little Zit asked with an innocent tone that unleashed another round of laughter.

"Damn thing was brand new—wasn't even broke in, yet," Zito protested, avoiding his son's gaze. "Might'a been a little hung over, too," Zito admitted, looking into his mug, a faint smile cracking his cheeks. "That might've been part of it."

"The guide was so worried about his dog," Forrest chuckled over the campfire, "I thought he was gonna put a flak jacket on him."

A new wave of laughter drowned out the crackling flames. Young Frank joined in the laughter. He had known these men his whole life. He heard many of their stories and was familiar with the rudimentary biographies—the versions appropriate for youngsters, at least. Although this outing was an annual male bonding ritual none of them would dare miss, it was an event exclusive to adults—for years, restricted to members of his father's Ranger team.

Every year, since they served together in Vietnam, the four men had faithfully rendezvoused somewhere in the world for a hunting or fishing trip. Fate and the Vietnam War had brought this group together when they were assigned to the Special Forces school in Ft. Benning, Georgia, in the early spring of 1967. Training school hardships and tough discipline had taught them the value of teamwork and trust and had forged a lasting bond. The shared stresses of combat soldiers had fused them into something much closer. The men in this group were more than best friends. They were brothers.

At the beginning of their tour, the group had numbered eight; seven of them being bewildered young kids who had volunteered for one of the United States Army's most elite forces: the Airborne Rangers. After attending the MACV Recondo school at La Trang, they traded their green berets for black ones and were assigned to the

1st Battalion, 8th Infantry Division as Long Range Reconnaissance Patrollers or "Lurps." When Neil Armstrong was making permanent footprints in lunar dust, these men were leaving theirs in Vietnamese mud.

The final member of this small fraternity was, at the ripe old age of 23, their boss, his father, buck Sergeant Francis Ignacious Zito. The young sergeant had received Forrest, Adams, Henderson, and four others as replacements after the 1968 Tet Offensive. Many of the men in his platoon had either been killed or severely wounded in the fiercest fighting of the war leaving the platoon well under strength. Zito's team had stumbled across the southward movement of an entire battalion of NVA and had been pinned down for three days before they could make their way to a landing zone for extraction. As team leader, his father had been wounded while saving the lives of two of his team members and, for his actions, awarded the Purple Heart and the Silver Star.

After Tet, Sergeant Zito became the platoon's senior NCO. As such, he had been assigned to break in the new guys and acquaint them with the requirements of surviving, "in country." His school was tough. It had to be. Only two grades were given: life and death. Four of them eventually failed the course.

"Whereas this is Little Zit's first elk hunt," Forrest announced from the screen. "I move we let him have the first shot." The gesture had become something of a tradition begining with his son. So it was only right that he make the motion.

Murmurs of agreement went around the fire.

"You ladies might change your minds after you hear the news," Zito countered.

"What's that, Zit?" Adams asked in a pleasant, Burl Ives voice.

"My youngest son...my namesake...my baby-fucking-boy, here, has shamed me greatly. I may never recover from such a dastardly blow. Little shit, here, up and joined the goddamn Navy last summer; just graduated from swabee basic."

Eyes went to Frank, Jr. who rolled his eyes and smiled.

"He's already been accepted into SEAL training," Zito continued, with disgust, "so maybe he ain't totally worthless." There was a begrudging trace of pride in his voice.

The others, however, were unequivocally impressed. "Shit hot, LZ!" Forrest commended, lifting his mug in salute.

"Why'd you choose the Navy?" Henderson asked.

The youngest among them responded with a sheepish smile. "Mostly, to piss my Pop off," he said in a bashful yet resolute voice. Amidst the laughter, he quickly ducked when his father raised his arm in a feigned backhand.

Frank Zito, Jr. hesitated for a moment before continuing. "You guys have always been my heroes, I guess." His smile faded. "All my life, I've heard Vietnam stories, seen your photos and mementos, admired and sometimes even envied your friendship. I guess I've always wanted to be a soldier...just like you guys...I wanna have what you guys have."

The men were quiet now—listening. They understood full well what he was talking about.

"But I wanted to be more than just Little Zit...Frank Zito, Junior." The young man's eyes fell to the glowing embers. "I guess I wanted my own identity, too."

"Understandable." Henderson said simply, noticing anew the remark-able resemblance between father and son.

"Understandable? Understandable is nuking the fucking Japs in 1945. Understandable is being scared shitless coming ashore at Omaha Beach on D-day. Understandable is wanting to screw Marilyn Monroe or Raquel Welch senseless. What's so fucking understandable about joining the goddamn Navy?" Zito shouted, his pronounced black eyebrows raised high with excitement. "This is an Army family! Always been an Army family. The U.S. Army's always put a roof over your head and food in your belly and you have'ta go and sign on with the fish-fucking, rust-pickin' squids. It don't figure." Zito paused, pensively wiping his nose between thumb and index finger. Besides," Zito said, his tone softening a bit, "I just wanted him to go to college like the rest of my worthless offspring."

Young Zito turned to look at his father. "You can't afford that right now, Pop. You got three other kids in school and the Army isn't paying for that. You told me, yourself, you can't even think about retiring until all the tuition is paid for. I don't want to add to that burden. Besides, this way I can get out on my own and let Uncle help me through college."

"You'll never get around to it," Zito mumbled, followed by another swig from his "coffee" mug.

"Pop, if I can get through SEAL training, I can get through anything. You said yourself, it just takes a positive mental attitude."

"He's right, Zit. That's how we all did it," Henderson reminded. The others nodded. "Tell him, man."

"I want you to have a good future, son, better'n this bunch'a yuppie, drippy-dick, degenerates." He gestured around the circle with his empty mug. As always, the insult brought smiles or jeers.

"That extinguished looking dweeb over there, Peeper; we call him that cause he likes poking his nose where it don't belong; is a professional spook. Couldn't get a real job. Has to go peeping in windows and keyholes 'n shit for a living. Back in 'Nam, he was Zulu team's S-2 specialist; goddamn intel puke. Counted trucks, gooks, and their weapons all up and down Uncle Ho's trail. After the war, he got a college degree in...some damn thing I can't remember... interracial masturbation and polygamous science or some damn shit."

"International Studies and Political Science," Henderson corrected with curious amusement.

"That's what I said, goddammit!...Pay attention," Zito rasped with an intimidating yet good-natured sneer.

Henderson smiled, pretending not to hear. "Zit, you are absolutely, positively the crudest, most vulgar individual I've ever met."

Zito beamed at Henderson. "Why thank you, Peeper, you limp-dick, pussy-whipped, geek-ass, intel-puke. Comin' from a toad like you, I take that as a condiment."

Henderson looked at Zito's son and laughed. "How does your mom stand it?"

Little Zit smiled and shrugged. "I think she drinks a lot more'n she used to."

Intense laughter on tape was echoed in the room.

"Before, I was so rudely interrupted..." Henderson continued, waiting for the laughter to subside. "As I was saying: Later, I received a commission and went to Army Intelligence Officer School at Ft. Holabird, Maryland and worked various jobs for Army Intelligence. Then I went to DIA as a photo/image interpreter as they're now called. I attended night school, actually day school since I worked at night, and received an MBA. CIA recruited me after that and I started with them as an analyst in the Intelligence Directorate."

"Now he's some kind'a big shot who spends most of his time bullshitting the world's biggest bullshitters over at the White House," Zito concluded with a sarcastic laugh.

Zito cut Adam's hearty laugh short as he shifted his attack. "That overgrown, ham-fisted dipshit over there with the stupid I-just-swallowed-a-tampon grin smeared all over his face, has destroyed more U.S. Government property in his time than the entire Japa-fucking-nese Empire. Just how many choppers have you crashed, Grizz?"

Jim "Grizzly" Adams, snorted a defensive laugh. "Eleven. Eight shot out from under me, two came apart all by themselves, and one a student rolled over before I could get him off the controls. Broke my back in that one." Adams looked at Zito with narrowing eyes. "And for the record, I never 'crashed' a helicopter, they all crashed me."

Adams was an Army helicopter pilot during the war, serving a remarkable three tours; remarkable because quite a few helicopter pilots never lived long enough to complete three months much less three tours. Wounded twice in combat, he had a box full of medals and accompanying citations about which he never talked.

After his third tour, Adams returned to the States under protest. To his mind, however, he wasn't as useful "back in the world" as he could be in Vietnam. The Army thought otherwise. They also knew he had pushed his luck about as far as mortal man could expect. Consequently, he had been assigned to the helicopter training school at Fort Rucker, Alabama. Adams considered the year he spent instructing new students more dangerous than his three combat tours in Vietnam. But that wasn't the only thing he didn't like about the new assignment. The stateside Army was completely different from the one fighting in Southeast Asia. And Adams, despite his good nature, found it difficult to make the adjustment. Ultimately, a timely job offer from Southern Air Transport rescued him from certain self destruction.

"You still work for that cargo outfit, Uncle Jim?"

"Yep, 'fraid so."

"I thought I read someplace that Southern Air Transport was the official airline of the CIA," Little Zit commented.

"Oh, I don't know about that. We do lots'a different stuff. The airline was started, way back when, by a former CIA lawyer and we've flown our share of interesting missions, some for government agencies, but I wouldn't know about a CIA connection." Adams smiled and cast a knowing look at Henderson.

"That sinister looking bastard over there with the wanted-poster face," Zito chided as he threw some fresh wood on the fire, "has killed more people with a rifle than John Wayne and made more women cry than Elvis-fuckin'-Presley. Must run in the family or somethin' 'cause his great-great-great uncle; was that enough 'greats?'" Zito paused and looked at Forrest who smiled and nodded. "Okay, shut-the-fuck-up and stop interrupting me, then...Where was I?...Oh yeah, his bunch'a-greats uncle Nathan Bedford Forrest was a famous Civil War Confederate general who personally killed thirty-one Yankees and had about the same number of horses shot out from under him. Balls and brains run in that fucker's family, although I think 'ol Thumper got shorted a little in the brains department...can't shoot worth a shit either, though he does get lucky, now and then."

Everyone laughed which again blended with the laughter in Henderson's study.

"Now," Zito continued, "he's just another glorified bus driver."

As if on cue from a hidden director Little Zit's voice broke the ice. "Where'd you get the name, Thumper, Uncle John?"

Forrest smiled. "Oh, I don't know. Your Pop's responsible for all the nicknames around here."

Young Zito turned to his father. "Pop?"

"One day, up near the Plain of Jars, Zulu team was crossing a rice paddy when we came under fire from a VC sniper."

All eyes turned to Zito, senior.

"He was way out there, too. Damn near a click. But he couldn't hit shit at that range. Took us a while to get a line on his position. 'Ol Forrest, over there, kept listening to the bullets crack over the dike we was hidin' behind. I watched him count the seconds until he heard the 'thump' of the muzzle blast. When I asked him what he was doing, he said in sniper school they taught him how to calculate the approximate range by using the 'crack and thump method.' Well after a while, your Uncle John decided the shooter was far enough away that it might be safe for him and his spotter to di-di-mau outta there and find the fucker. So they did. 'Bout an hour later we hear a shot. 'Bout an hour after that, Forrest shows up and says it's okay to move. One of the boys asked him what happened to the sniper. John said: 'I thumped him.' Just like that," Zito laughed. "The rest is legend."

"Cool," said young Zito, with a laugh. Yet another reason to respect these men he so admired.

Henderson picked up the narration: "After a few months in Vietnam," he went on to say, "Forrest had become the battalion's top sniper. By the end of his tour, Forrest had taken top honors with 38 confirmed kills. There had been several other kills that he was sure of but, the bodies had been removed by their comrades and thus, could not be included in the official tally."

"So why don't we let Uncle John take the first shot? Why take a chance?" young Zito asked from his seat at the fire.

Forrest spoke before the others could answer. "These guys are good shots, too. Besides, we're not really here for trophies. It's more about camaraderie—old friends, clean air and good times. I don't think any of us give a damn one way or the other if we get a shot or not."

"I just like being in the great outdoors with my old buddies," Adams picked up. "Thumper's right. We get just as big a charge out of seeing an eagle or a moose as we do from the hunt."

"If we go home empty-handed, that's fine," Henderson echoed. "That's not what we came for."

Young Frank Zito, seated on the floor next to his father's chair, reflected on that wonderful trip. In those few days he had achieved a much more intimate understanding of his father and his friends and their "secret" world—a world they only shared among themselves or others like them.

"Here's to LZ's becoming a SEAL!" Adams voice roared from the TV, raising his mug in a toast.

"Here-here," Henderson and Forrest echoed.

Eyes went to Zito, Senior who scowled.

"Get that mug in the air, Sergeant," Forrest ordered.

Zito's eyes went to Forrest, Henderson and Adams, and then his son. "To another SPECOPS warrior in the family!" he roared, lofting his freshly filled mug.

The men gulped their mugs dry, tuned them upside down and balanced them on top of their heads.

Famous for timing, good and bad, Zito picked that exact moment to break wind. It was a trophy winner, measuring about 7.5 on the Richter scale. Cracking up with laughter, Henderson and Adams fell off their camp stools as if they had been hit by a tidal wave. Mugs went tumbling into the dirt.

"Jesus Christ, Zit! You probably scared every elk for a hundred miles back up into Canada!" Adams roared painfully as he held his sides and rolled on the ground.

"I hope you don't do that stuff at home," Henderson remarked, still laughing.

"Mom would kick his ass," Little Zit snickered.

Forrest laughed. "Must'a been your chili, Zit. What the hell's in that stuff, anyway? Anything we should report to the EPA?"

Zito grinned. "Same stuff I put in my spaghetti sauce: ten cans of Mighty Dog, and equal parts green peppers, pinto beans, panther piss, goat shit, and gasoline."

"Good thing we got fireproof sleeping bags," Adams laughed.

Henderson stopped the tape when he heard his wife knocking on the study door.

Marie heard the laughter stop and wisely waited a moment before sticking her head inside. “Honey, I know how important this is to you—all of you—especially right now. But we have quite a few guests that would like some of your time.”

The faces in the room went respectfully somber.

“You’re right, honey,” Henderson said, sharing a look with Forrest. We’ll be right out...”

“Uh,” Forrest interrupted politely, “can we have just a few more minutes? I have some unfinished business to discuss with these guys.”

Marie Henderson gave Forrest a look and a knowing smile then glanced at her watch before closing the door behind her.

CHAPTER-FIVE

BACKER *a: a partner taking no active part in the conduct of the enterprise*
b: one that supports

AMY LEE CHEWED VORACIOUSLY on the piece of bush-meat, an unfortunate antelope she had found in a poacher's snare. Wisely, she'd followed circling vultures to their diner and arrived before the meat had had a chance to spoil. Screaming and wielding a stick scared them off long enough to secure her share of the freshly killed prize. She used the bayonet to cut away as much of a hind leg as she could carry and skinned enough hide to cover her feet.

Making a fire had been easier than she first thought. A smoldering clump of grass left from a brush fire had proved to be an excellent lighter. Better than Ruth's Chris, she thought, tearing another bite off with her teeth, not to mention a lot cheaper, too.

Obtaining water had been a little harder. From a place of concealment Amy had watched a family of elephants digging in a dry river bed for water. After they had left, she duplicated their effort with her knife and enjoyed her first direct water source in days.

A pair of moccasins had been fashioned out of the skin carved from the antelope and lashed to her ankles with strips of rawhide cured over the fire. They weren't Nike Airs but they decreased the pain of walking by orders of magnitude.

Now that shoes, food and water had been handled—at least temporarily—she had to do something about the chronic lack of sleep. Burrowing beneath thorny clumps of spiny palms growing in acacia thickets had given her some protection from animals at night. Nonetheless, she had taken to sleeping with one eye open or not at all.

"Hello," Forrest, said picking up his office phone on the second ring.

"It's Peeper. Go secure."

Forrest pushed the secure button on the new STU (secure telephone unit) III telephone. After a second, SECURE appeared in the unit's liquid crystal display indicating their conversation was now scrambled, courtesy of Motorola and the CIA.

"Looks like my early Christmas present works pretty good," Forrest remarked at the remarkable clarity. The phone contained a microprocessor that digitized the analog signals coming in over the phone line, deciphered the encryption code, and then converted the message back to an analog signal which powered the ear-piece. When the caller spoke, the chip reversed the process, transmitting electronic noise to the other party's instrument. Transparent to the callers, it all happened in milliseconds.

"From this moment on, there's no such thing as being too careful, buddy. There's too much at stake, here," Henderson cautioned in a voice clouded with worry. "All our conversations, from here on, must be conducted as if everyone in the whole world were listening."

"If you say so," he sighed, well past caring a great deal about such things given the unimaginable events of late.

Henderson bristled slightly. "No shit, man. You'd be surprised at the amount of comm traffic that's exploited by any number of government and law enforcement agencies. These gimmicks provide a layer of security in our overall COMSEC plan. But, there's no such thing as totally secure voice. If they wanted to, the 'crypto-knights' at 'No Such Agency' could crack this little toy like a made-in-Taiwan piggy bank."

"Hey, man. Look," Forrest interrupted in a burst of temper, "I'm down to one good nerve left and that mother-hen security shit is stepping all over it with golf shoes. In the last few years, my lazy whore of a wife, who did nothing but play with her cats or her face and nails all day when she wasn't fucking her tennis pro and *screwing* me, divorced me and took a ton of money she neither earned nor deserved. Then, to add injury to insult, the goddamn, bleeding-heart judge threw out our prenuptial agreement leaving me up to my neck in financial quicksand. And now, in the last few *days*, I've lost my career and my only child, the last person on this earth that I truly loved. So, air-off with the preaching. At this point I really don't give a shit. I really don't. Fuck NSA, the CIA and, if need be, the *U-SA!"*

Henderson listened to his best friend's uncommon yet understandable diatribe, waited for his emotional propellant to burn out then waited a long, pregnant moment before responding. "John…John…What can I say?" he asked in his softest, most non-confrontational tone. "I hear you five-by five. I really do. Try to remember who you're talking to. I've lost a child, too." Henderson summoned all of his emotional self-control. "I totally support our plan. I want the bastards as much as you do. Trust me. But, I've got the rest of my family to think about. Losing my job and maybe my freedom will not bring Amy back. I can't take stupid chances with our future no matter how I feel. So don't you go kamikaze on me. Okay? Be the calculating, cold-blooded professional I know you to be. And let's get the rat-shit, dirt-bags that did this thing to us without self-destructing in the process…Agree?"

A tense silence spanned the many seconds while blood pressures came back down to normal.

"Okay, pal. Okay." Forrest let out a heavy audible breath.

"Also, beginning with the next call, we'll start using an authenticator system so we can verify identities and ensure that neither party is operating under duress. It's just like the one you used in the Air Force. By the way, did you find the code generator in the package I sent?"

"Got it right here," Forrest responded. "Where's the decoder ring?" he quipped, using his dry humor to help get a grip on himself.

Henderson cleared his throat and smiled into the mouthpiece. "As you can see, it's a simple system. Don't lose it," he instructed.

Forrest chuckled. "I'm starting to feel like James Bond, already."

"Well, don't forget, James," Henderson chided, "if we get snagged on this little caper, there'll be second marriages in both our futures. Only this time some 300 pound, iron-pumping dope dealers at Ft. Leavenworth will be the husbands and we'll be the wives."

Forrest smiled. "I'm definitely not interested in doing the 'M-word,' again."

"Okay. Day after tomorrow we're going to see Santa. So, I'm making a list and checking it twice and then I'm sending a copy to you. We'll need some expensive toys this year. When you get it, look it over and add anything I've left out. Plane tickets will be in the same package."

"What if he doesn't want to play?"

"Then we'll have to go to plan B."

"Government money?"

"No way. I might be able to call in some favors, find some surplus equipment here and there and a little satellite and computer time won't be missed. But I can't misappropriate Government funds," Henderson declared, resolutely. "There are lines I won't cross."

Not even for Amy? Forrest thought but didn't say. *Well, that makes one of us, then. Peeper, you were always a little too much of a Boy Scout.*

"Okay. I'll see you then." Forrest hung up and sighed. There would be more to this adventure than he thought. Piled on his desk top were stacks of books about Africa; its history, politics, ecology, and its wildlife. There were several volumes about elephants.

He leaned back in his leather chair and returned to his reading. A few minutes later, Forrest was lost in a chapter having to do with elephant communications when his eyelids slammed shut.

****

People working at the dock paid little attention to the procession of Pakistanis carrying ivory into the warehouse. Ivory shipments were commonplace in the United Arab Emirates and, as in most other Arab countries, cheap labor from India and Asia performed most of the menial tasks.

Although there was nothing extraordinary about the flat-roofed, cement-block building, "shed 65A" was an infamous address. Situated on the docks of Abu Dhabi's Free Trade Zone, it was well known to conservation groups around the world. Its owner, Henry Poon, a Chinese businessman and prominent member of the Hong Kong ivory syndicates, was equally notorious. He alone was responsible for as much as a third of the world's trade in illegal animal products—a business that generated as much as a million U.S. dollars per week.

Inside, thirty skilled craftsmen went about their work in the heat and humidity endemic to the shores of the Persian Gulf. Laborers distributed elephant tusks to semi-skilled men who ran the band-saws. Ivory dust floated to the floor as thin steel blades whined, slicing the ivory into long rectangular blocks that met the minimum standards necessary to satisfy the "readily recognizable parts and derivatives" clause Chinese customs inspectors applied to imported goods. If it looked like an animal part, Chinese law forbade entry. But, if the product was not readily recognizable as such, it was allowed. Just as heroin and cocaine is poured, cast and molded into legitimate looking objects, the gracefully curved elephant teeth were systematically reduced to blocks suitable for shipping and carving.

After the tusks were cut, workers picked up the finished product and delivered it to packers who crated it. Some, oddly enough, would be shipped back to Africa, flown to Zaire where it was given CITES certification and re-exported as legal ivory. Some would be shipped to Poon's Hing Lin jewelry boutique in Paris. Most however, would be loaded into shipping containers bound for distant ports in the Far East—Hong Kong and Japan.

Poon, wearing a gray-green silk suit, white shirt and black silk tie and a solid gold, Rolex Presidential wristwatch encrusted with diamonds, stood at the entrance carefully eyeing his latest shipment. Although this delivery would generate thousands of dollars in profits, his face wore a grave look. There were very few large tusks. Nothing like it had been twenty years ago. And, to his disdain, he watched as two boxes of hippopotamus teeth were carried into his warehouse. Too bad it is getting down to this, he thought, a sour knot growing in his stomach. Hippo teeth were a poor substitute for ivory. But, he reminded himself, the damned environmentalists were making life difficult and a man did what he had to do to stay in business.

"Get away from me, dammit!" Amy screamed in frustration and an attempt at intimidation. A small pride of lions had cornered her for the last two days in a tiny but dense cluster of thorny palms which she employed as a makeshift fortress. Although extremely thirsty and exhausted from lack of sleep, she held them at bay with an eight-foot wooden spear she had carved from a sapling. As distraught as she was, she sensed the lions were losing patience with this worthier-than-expected adversary. At the moment, survival had come down to which opponent would give up first. Two hours later, a combination of boredom and hunger drove them off in search of less difficult prey.

"Would you gentlemen like a drink?" The Colonel asked.

"Maybe some iced tea, thank you," Henderson replied.

Henderson, Forrest and Colonel Grant were seated in Grant's labyrinth private study. Forrest scanned the room, admiring its many framed oils including a famous, original Frederick Remmington. Within arm's reach a full scale, museum quality Gatling gun, mounted on a period wheeled gun carriage, stood on the room's dark oak floors. Lining the 16 foot high walls, shelves of books alternated with glass-enclosed gun cases containing everything from fabulously expensive antique rifles and pistols to modern day sport and military firearms of all descriptions.

Forrest smiled and shook his head with a mixture of appreciation and envy before turning his attention back to their host.

At five feet, six inches, Colonel Maxwell T. Grant was shorter than Forrest remembered, but projected a very big presence even for a Texan, just as he had when he was their battalion commander in Vietnam. Snow-white hair capped a rugged face with a square chin and muscular body for a man in his late sixties. And although the Colonel appeared to be in generally good shape, affluence had left him a bit of a belly held in restraint by a Texas-size silver rodeo belt buckle. Grant wore a light blue cotton shirt beneath a tan leather vest. His blue denim jeans rode up revealing alligator cowboy boots.

The conversation had come back to small talk once Henderson had been up front about what they needed and the urgency if Amy was, in fact, still alive. "I saw the piece 'Dateline' did on you a couple of years ago along with some of your magazine articles. It's all very impressive. Few other people in the world have the resources and the conviction to go as far as you have to protect threatened species. I understand you have a large population of African elephants on your ranch and even some black rhinoceros?"

"That's right, Steve," the Colonel said, beaming. "I've got seven black rhino—two adult males and five females. That's more than there are in some African countries, you know. One of my girls is due to pop, here in about a month," Grant announced proudly.

"Congratulations, sir. That's wonderful." Henderson grinned weakly, wondering if his daughter would ever have that option.

"As for white rhino, I've got a few more of them—seven females and three males. The white rhino seems to have fared a little better in the wild than the black. Even so, there's only a few of them left. Goddamn poachers have killed so many for their horns, you know. They sell 'em to the goddamn gooks so they can grind 'em up and eat the powder to make their pathetic little gerbil-dicks hard." Grant shook his head in disgust. "You know, you'd think that with over a billion of the little, zipper-head assholes multiplying like mosquitoes, the last thing they'd need is a god-damn a-phro-di-siac."

Forrest and Henderson shared a glance, a laugh and an insight.

The Colonel went on, oblivious to his guests' reading-between-the-lines. "I've also got twenty-seven elephants. Can't remember just now how many of each, though," Grant continued. He looked up at the high-beamed ceiling, attempting to run a mental tally. "Well, anyway, the breeding program is going quite well. We've had two new calves in the last four years." The Colonel, suddenly struck with an idea, leaned forward and slapped his legs but the thought was interrupted by the butler.

"Colonel, there is an urgent fax arriving from Kenya."

"Thank you, Marshall." Grant addressed his guests. "Excuse me, boys. I'll be right back."

While the colonel went to an ante-room which contained various office machines and their supplies, Forrest and Henderson talked among themselves.

"Where did you say he got all his money?" It was Forrest.

"Most of it—the old family money—is from oil, cattle and shipping. After Vietnam, he retired from the Army, lost an election for the U.S. Congress and became something of an international arms dealer and a manufacturer's rep for several defense contractors. He's got his fingers into just about everything and knows everybody worth knowing. He's on the Fortune 50 list."

Forrest raised his eyebrows. "Think he'll help us?"

"Hard to say. He has a lot more at stake than we do and less motive. But he seemed moved by what happened to Amy and Nat."

Forrest nodded. "Sure as hell can't do it without him."

"Mmm."

Fifteen minutes later, Grant entered the room. Forrest was the first to notice the pained look on Grant's face. He was obviously very distressed and preoccupied—even more preoccupied than before.

Grant lowered himself slowly into a leather, winged chair near the door—seemingly unable to make it back to his massive desk. His left hand and papers flopped in his lap as if they were too heavy to lift.

Marshall entered a moment later and stood patiently off to the side. After a moment, Grant looked up as if returning from a place very far away. "My usual," he said lifelessly to his butler. "Make 'em doubles and keep 'em coming."

Henderson noticed that Marshall regarded his boss oddly for a moment before disappearing to fill the order. Something was definitely amiss, he thought.

Silence hung in the air like a cloud of frozen fog. Forrest and Henderson both sensed it was best to wait for Grant to initiate any conversation. A full five minutes passed without a word.

Henderson looked at Forrest then at Grant who sat perfectly still, staring unfocused into a pistol case.

Finally, the arrival of his drink shattered the trance. "You mind if I tell you boys a little story?" he started, almost inaudibly.

There was another long pause as if Grant were struggling with the words. "Years ago, when I first got interested in saving endangered animals, I learned that doing so was going to take more than determination, more than money. It was going to take dedication and education. So, I started a foundation to provide scholarships for promising young people all over the world who were willing to dedicate themselves to that cause. Since then, I've sent dozens of youngsters to the best colleges in Europe and America with the understanding that each one had to return to their native country and establish conservation programs or improve existing ones. They also had to teach their peers how important it was to protect the environment and in so doing, their heritage." Grant took a healthy swallow from his second drink. "Overall, the foundation's done pretty damn well. We have quite a few PhDs to our credit now, and dozens of devoted environmental stewards. One of the most promising to date came to me from northern Kenya. He was tall, thin, and dirt-poor, but very eager and very bright. I could see, right off, that he was an animal lover and wanted to save his country's treasures." Grant stopped for a while and fortified himself with another slug of bourbon-and-branch. He waited for it to settle before proceeding.

Henderson sensed tragedy waiting on Grant's lips.

The Colonel took another long swallow and continued. "Young David Nchoko, his name was..." Grant halted once again. "...earned a PhD from Cambridge University just two years ago. I had high hopes for that boy. I really did. I intended to make him the head of my East African projects, all of 'em. He was the brightest star in my conservation constellation. We had become very close. Practically speaking, I regarded him as a son."

Forrest saw the Colonel's eyes glisten.

"Well, today I get this FAX." Grant lifted his hand limply then let it flop. "David Nchoko, was killed today, shot dead by a group of poachers he'd been harassing for some time near Meru National Park, not far from the Somali border." Grant let the papers drop to the floor. "Right near the spot another bunch of bastards murdered George Adamson...you know, the 'Born Free' guy."

Henderson and Forrest nodded.

"He'd told me he was having trouble with those people, but said it wasn't anything he couldn't handle." Grant made a weak smile, his eyes red with grief. "Guess he was wrong. Well...I should have sent him some protection...Now, it's too late."

Forrest let a respectable amount of time go by before commenting. "It's not your fault, Colonel."

Grant looked at him.

"We understand your pain, sir. We really do. More than you realize," Henderson offered, sympathetically. Henderson paused to share a look with Grant.

"Of course you do," the Colonel said apologetically. "I've been thinking about your proposal, gentlemen." His eyes went to Forrest. "Do you know the kind of risks you'll be taking, alone, out in the bush? Even if you don't get yourself killed by the bad guys, there are plenty of dangerous animals and diseases, any of which could finish the job." Grant's eyes found Henderson's. He caught himself slipping into an unacceptable display of emotion and checked it by biting his lower lip.

"I have some idea, sir. I've never been to Africa before but it shouldn't take me long to get a feel for things. As far as risks go, Steve and I…and you…and a few hundred thousand other guys, were thrown waist-deep into a world full of risks when we were just kids—young, dumb, and full of cum—just like the Army likes 'em. The way I see it, Colonel, 'Nam was a lot more risky than this little venture. Plus, I'm a lot older and a little wiser, now. I think I can handle it."

"Maybe—maybe not." Grant said, ominously. "How much money do you think you'll need, Steve?"

"Three- to-four hundred thousand to start, sir."

Marshall returned with another round of drinks on a silver tray. After everyone had been served, Colonel Grant stood and raised his glass in a toast, "Gentlemen, let's drink to a just and noble enterprise."

Forrest and Henderson pushed back in their chairs and stood, glasses high. Grant put his glass to his lips and emptied its amber contents. Forrest and Henderson stood there for a moment looking at each other in astonishment.

"Come on gentlemen, drink up! It's not every day I get a chance to take on partners in such a great cause! The Colonel's weak smile waned completely as his thoughts turned to his late protégée. "John. You said, no prisoners, right?"

"That's right, sir. No prisoners."

"Then I'll accept that as your personal pledge." The Colonel stared Forrest straight in the eye. After a meaningful pause, Grant raised his second glass. "Come on, gentlemen! I'm already one ahead of you."

Henderson stared at the NEC computer monitor, his heart pounding in sync with the pulsing cursor as he waited for the distant modem to complete the "hand shake." Although he had previously been involved with covert operations where funds were laundered in order to protect agents, assets or entire operations, he had always been doing so with the blessings of the "Company." Tonight, he was on his own—performing without a net. And though he was putting money *into* a bank—legal money transferred legally—guilt nagged at him, nevertheless. His tongue felt like a wool sock clogging his dry throat.

Colonel Grant's "donation" had been transferred to a shell corporation without a hitch. The next step would be to move the money, in small increments, from the corporate account to an account in the First Cayman Bank, Ltd. in the Cayman Islands.

The answering modem raised a chorus of squeals and static. He was in—two CPUs chatting with each other as if exchanging the latest cyber-gossip over the back fence. Menus danced onto the screen building fields whose hungry squares demanded to be filled with the appropriate keystrokes. Account numbers, PIN, transaction amount, test keys, authorization number, beneficiary names, all rolled off Henderson's moist finger tips in under a minute. He typed fast, abandoning his normal methodical pace to get this job behind him before he could change his mind. His right middle finger came down hard on the ENTER key, sealing the deal and, he noted with no small amount of trepidation, possibly his fate. Ironic, he thought, how CIA, DIA, and the DEA used the same offshore banks as drug smugglers and other criminals. Criminals, he repeated mentally, though he dare not speak it. How far could he go before he became one himself?

While he awaited confirmation, he glanced through his half-lens reading glasses at a note he'd received from Grant the day before:

> PEEPER:
> DISPERSAL COMPLETE. MORE WHEN NECESSARY.
> KEEP ME POSTED. GOOD LUCK. GOOD HUNTING.
> MIDAS

Movement on the monitor caught his eye. The cursor raced across the screen leaving time, date, and transaction numbers in its wake. A few keystrokes later, he had backed out of the program and returned to the familiar *Windows* main menu screen.

Henderson pulled the top left drawer open and withdrew a black vinyl pouch. Its plastic zipper slid silently in his fingers. He read through several letters of introduction from Colonel Grant to the African Wildlife Fund and two other conservation groups active in

East Africa. Clipped to the back of the letters were replies offering sponsorship to John Forrest and his research project. Another letter from Texas A & M University attested to the fact that John Ruger Forrest had been enrolled in the University's Masters Program. Having Colonel Grant on A & M's Board of Regents didn't hurt a bit, he thought, with a weak smile. Henderson inspected the passport, visas, and various ID cards for accuracy. Last, and perhaps the most difficult to come by as far as Forrest's arms were concerned, was a record of inoculation from the Surgeon General's office indicating Forrest had received all of the required immunizations for typhoid, yellow fever, hepatitis B, and the like. Henderson slid all the documents back into the pouch and zipped it closed.

His eyes drifted to a photo of himself and Forrest in Vietnam. "I wonder how his refresher course is going. Gotta be more fun than this," he mused aloud.

He rechecked his list of things to do. Normally, he would designate members of his staff to complete most of the tasks. This time, however, that would be out of the question given the enormous security concerns. This op would definitely be a do-it-yourself affair.

A combination of foam earplugs and sound-suppressing headphones reduced the rifle's sharp report to a dull thud. The faint smell of burned powder drifted over the men as the silhouette target disappeared below a long earthen berm 600 yards in front of them. Forrest opened the rifle's bolt and ejected the still smoking, brass casing onto his shooter's mat. He rose up on his elbows and moved his right eye to a twenty-power spotter's scope and waited. To his left and right, other shooters fired at individual targets down range. After thirty-seconds, Forrest's target reappeared from behind the berm with a large white dot pasted on its face marking his last round's point of impact. Forrest noted the score and recorded it in his shooter's book then settled back to the mat.

He took a deep breath to clear his head and resumed his prone firing position, the most stable of all the shooting positions. Ignoring the noise and activity going on all around him, he took up the slack on his leather sling, tightened his position, and concentrated on target and sight-picture. A tight, stable firing platform was a must for competition shooting. At distances over 200 yards, the act of breathing and even a shooter's heartbeat could significantly affect the accuracy of a shot. In an effort to keep the number of human tremors and twitches to an absolute minimum, smoking and caffeine intake was discouraged while a shooter attended the course. Serious professionals, they were told, disposed of those habits entirely. That wasn't a problem for Forrest. He had never smoked—not even one. Sucking your chest full of noxious gas had never made an ounce of sense to a young man ruled by common sense. But the java...well, he did enjoy a hot cup once in a while. So, he'd again taken the common sense approach—he'd compromised and switched to decaf.

Forrest let the Leupold Ultra M3A scope's mil dot reticle stabilize over the center of the target and looked for shifts in the light breeze. Magnified by the scope's optics, the subtle variances in air density down range appeared as ghostly mirages like those rising from the pavement on a hot summer day. He watched patiently as they shimmered in his field of view. By watching the shimmer's trends of movement, a shooter could estimate wind velocity and make the appropriate adjustments in his sight. Judging there to be a five knot breeze from right to left, Forrest moved the reticle slightly less than one mil to the right. Theoretically, in the seven tenths of a second it would take the bullet to make the flight from the end of the barrel to the target, a breeze of that velocity would move the point of impact an equal and compensating distance to the left. The result should be a dead-center hit—theoretically. Satisfied that all was ready, he took a shallow breath and let some out allowing his mass to come to rest on partially deflated lungs. He concentrated on keeping the crosshairs steady until his finger had applied slightly less than three pounds of pressure to the trigger.

Boom!

The rifle spoke, driving the recoil pad into his right shoulder.

As it should have, the shot had taken him almost by surprise. With another quick throw of the bolt, another spent cartridge joined a growing pile on the mat.

"Bullseye!" Zito shouted over the din. Through his huge, tripod-mounted, sixty-power scope, Zito could see the hole that the bullet cut in the paper before it was pulled down out of sight. "Looks like you've got that baby pretty well sighted in, pal!"

"We're getting there," Forrest muttered, still mired in concentration; "we" being a subconscious reference to man and weapon as a single entity. "I'm still not as comfortable as I remember being with my Model 70, but this ERMA SR100 definitely has some advantages over the old technology," Forrest shouted to overcome the dual acoustic obstacles of loud noise and redundant ear protection.

Zito, the NCOIC of the U.S. Army Sniper School at Ft. Benning, patted his friend on the back as the senior marksmanship instructor kneeled down to give Forrest a few pointers while Sgt. Eber Samples watched quietly a few paces away.

Forrest nodded, resumed his firing position and fired several more rounds, his last shots consistently piercing the X-ring.

"Cease fire! Cease fire! Clear and ground all weapons," the range safety officer commanded through the loudspeaker system. Forrest opened the bolt on his new ERMA SR100 and laid it on the mat with the barrel pointing down range. He took a second to admire the weapon. It was as mean as it looked—a fifteen pound, all black, death delivery system. The stock was laminated wood and composite with a fore-stock that extended two-thirds the length of the 29.5 inch barrel before terminating in an integral bipod.

"Looking good, man!" Zito exclaimed in a near normal voice as Forrest pulled the foam plugs out of his ears.

"I can feel it starting to come together," Forrest almost whispered, dismissing the praise. "A few thousand more rounds and I ought to be able to hit a cement truck about half the time."

"Repetition is the mother of all skills," Zito postulated.

"In my opinion, sir, it won't take nearly that much work. You've got the best scores I've seen on the range today," the instructor observed.

"Well, if you say so, Sergeant. I appreciate that," Forrest said with genuine humility. "But don't forget, I've also got a twelve-thousand-dollar, high-tech, man-popper, here".

"Impressive, sure enough. But, it wouldn't matter a lick if you couldn't hold true," the instructor offered.

Forrest raised his eyebrows slightly and nodded.

"That .338 Lapua is a better round than I thought—a good sniper load," the marksmanship instructor continued. "The flight path is a little flatter than the match-grade .308 we use but a lot more expensive. I had my doubts about it. I thought the magnum load might be harder to control but you seem to have a pretty good handle on it."

Zito began collecting his friend's gear. "Tomorrow, we'll fire a hundred rounds at a thousand yards. That'll be a good test."

Forrest rolled his eyes. His shoulder was already sore from the battering delivered by the magnum loads.

"When I opened the box on this little beauty, I must admit I had my doubts about it. It doesn't have the charm of my Weatherby and it's not as comfortable as my old Model 70 Winchester, but it sure puts the lead where you want it—250 grains of it at 3,000 feet per second. A nice little punch," Forrest admitted.

"Midas comes up with some pretty good shit," Zito affirmed with a smile. Just 2 days prior, Forrest had received the ERMA drop-shipped from Germany's Steyr-Mannlicher firm and a thousand custom-loaded rounds from Colonel Grant through Forrest's local gun dealer, Florida Firepower. An accompanying note explained that the presentation was partly business since he was lobbying on behalf of the manufacturer for the Army to procure it as their issue sniper weapon. Forrest, being somewhat of a legend at the sniper school, would serve as a good endorsement.

Zito and Forrest gathered up the gear and loaded it in Zito's Ford Explorer. Twenty minutes later they arrived at the modest but homey Zito hacienda in plenty of time to have a few beers before dinner. He handed Forrest an icy bottle from the fridge and the two men settled into a cozy den decorated in early *Field and Stream.*

"Only one more training day left, pal," Zito announced, raising his brown bottle in salute. "You haven't lost your touch after all these years." Zito guzzled half the bottle and belched. "Just as pathetic as ever."

Forrest looked sideways at his friend. "Getting back into shape will be the hardest part for me. I've spent too many years sitting on my ass in airplanes. Those young kids run rings around me," Forrest admitted after taking a long pull.

"Maybe, but you've got something most of 'em will never have—the hunter's eye and the patience of a rock. You see things they don't see and you have the maturity not to rush your shots. Some of that will come with experience. But most of 'em'll never be more than just average." Frank Zito found himself developing a new respect for his friend's courage as he considered all of the possible situations that Forrest might face. Forrest would be completely alone and cut off from virtually every kind of support available to most conventional two-man sniper teams. There would be no MEDEVAC to pick him up if he suffered a wound or injury. If bad guys tried to rush him or flank his position, there would be no means of calling for indirect fire support from a mortar or artillery battery. Granted, the enemy would be for the most part, poorly trained and poorly equipped and suffer similar disadvantages. But, they would be working in familiar territory, operating on *their* schedule, and would almost always outnumber and out-gun him—very big advantages.

"You want to go through the jump course, again?" Zito asked. "You think the mini-sniper course kicked your ass, wait till..."

Forrest put up his hands. "No thanks. No time. And I'm actually fairly current."

Zito gave him an incredulous grin.

"I do a little jumping every now and then in Sebastian, Florida," Forrest explained. "Got my own rig and everything."

"By the way," Zito remembered at the last minute. "Peeper sent you airline tickets to Baltimore."

Forrest raised his eyebrows as Zito retrieved an envelope from a shelf near the doorway. "He made hotel reservations and sent directions to Edgewood Arsenal. Said he's arranged for you to get a little hands-on explosives and demolition training at Aberdeen Proving Ground. He said to call this number and coordinate with a character by the name of 'Doctor Pyro' for a short Boom-Boom 101 refresher course."

Forrest looked the note over and chuckled. "Cool."

"Between me, Peeper, and the U.S. fuckin' Army, you'll be the best trained poacher-poacher in the *en*tire world. And that's a fact." Zito raised his nearly dead long-neck in salute. Zito had made sure his friend received training above and beyond that offered in the standard syllabus as if he were personally responsible for Forrest's safety. They had spent considerable time together, after the few but very long days at the range, brainstorming tactical scenarios and their probable outcomes. Zito was able to borrow several of the weapons to which poachers might have access from the post museum so that he could familiarize his friend with their operation and limitations. A thorough knowledge of the enemy, and his weapons and tactics was essential for any mission.

Forrest had spent several hours in a survival refresher and field craft training to review the tricks of stealth and woodsmanship. At first, the training was exhausting for a man approaching middle age. However, what Forrest lacked in youth and stamina, he made up for with dogged determination and force of will. It usually took him longer than the younger students to move into position for a shot. But, not once, had he been detected by instructors ever-so-eager to ruin a student's day. After observing a student's approach to their assigned targets the instructors would gleefully pounce on them. The youngsters, impatient to get the mission "over with" usually moved too fast for too long and were seen by the "enemy." Once discovered, the instructors employed counter-sniper tactics against them with embarrassing results. Humiliation, however, was better than the alternatives.

Forrest knew that in order to use his shortcomings to his advantage he had to make maximum use of patience. It was, after all, more about willpower than firepower. He played a mental game with himself and the instructors and projected himself inside their heads.

He constantly asked himself: "If I were a bad guy, where would I be? What would I be afraid of? What are my weaknesses? What do I do to minimize my exposure? What are they expecting me to do?" By placing himself inside his enemy's skin he was usually able to put himself in the right place at the right time. The mental exercises provided the additional benefit of helping him kill time while waiting out his opponents. For brash young men, used to instant gratification in a fast-food, video-game society, lack of patience and intolerance for discomfort proved to be a fatal flaw. Only when the hare spooked and flushed would the hunter have a shot, he reminded himself. The most important tool in a sniper's bag of tricks was the ability to blend into the surroundings, become invisible and wait as long as it took.

It was one thing to be out in the savanna during the day and another thing altogether at night. Darkness magnified all the growls, howls and animal sounds and increased their perceived proximity. Paranoia convinced her that the subject of all those animal communications *had* to be her. Absent the horrifying poacher experience, nights alone in the savanna were the most terrifying experiences of her young life. Amy Lee was lost, hungry and thirsty. And this night's only safe haven was an umbrella tree she had barely been able to climb. But she knew only too well there were predators out there in the darkness who were also excellent climbers. Perched as high up in the small limbs as she could get, she clung to her make-shift spear. A leopard would only be able to get at her one way and it would have to get past its sharp point…if only she could manage to stay awake.

CHAPTER-SIX

DEPLOYMENT *a: movement of a military force to its area of operation*
b: placement in battle formation or appropriate positions

A US AIR FORCE C-141 STARLIFTER, a C-5A Galaxy and two C-130s, all painted overcast gray, were parked on the military ramp across from the airline terminal of the huge Frankfurt-Main airport. Near them sat a Lockheed L-100 (the civilian version of the C-130 Hercules) painted glossy white with a light gray top and underbelly and black trim—the trademark colors of Southern Air Transport. SAT had long been a contractor for the U. S. Government and other customers requiring reliable nonscheduled air transportation. After a stop and obligatory inspection at the base security checkpoint, Forrest's German driver pulled the van onto the ramp and up to the waiting civilian cargo plane. A familiar face emerged from the L-100's forward personnel door.

"It's about time you got here!" Adams smiled, extending his hand. Aside from a black leather nametag with wings affixed above his left breast pocket, his Nomex flight suit was void of patches or other insignia normally worn by military personnel.

Forrest was surprised and delighted to see his good friend. "I didn't know you'd be driving this thing, today, Grizz!"

"You expecting somebody else?"

Forrest shrugged and smiled.

"Well, I managed to swap the trip with another captain so I could fly you down for your safari vacation." Adams looked Forrest over admiringly. "I see Zit whipped your ass into shape."

Forrest's smile turned to a grimace. "Damn near killed me."

"Old fart disease."

"You should know." Forrest slapped the big man on the back.

As the two friends climbed up the steps into the cargo bay, Forrest saw an unmarked Ford van pull up to the rear cargo ramp. Two men emerged and boarded a gray plastic container about the size and shape of a large ice chest. The loadmaster slid the container onto a pallet and lashed it down after signing for it.

"Looks like you've got a full load today, Grizz."

"You've got that right. Just about all of it's your stuff. Your friend, 'Midas,' contracted for most of the load. One entire pallet is your shit." Adams raised his voice as the ground crew cranked up the external generator cart parked on the ramp next to the plane. Its long electrical cord supplied the power needed to raise the cargo ramp and power the L-100's systems until it was time to start the engines. "The White House is cranking up the Somali and Ethiopian airlift again so some of the cargo is gonna be used in support of that operation. But the Land Rover and those three big crates in the back are yours, too."

"Land Rover?"

"Yep. A brand new one. Midas and Peeper made sure you got what you requested—the best equipment money can buy. You and the spook must have done quite a sales job on him. Whose idea was the ultra-light?"

"Mine."

"Glad you'll be flying that thing instead of me," Adams commented, shaking his head. "I can't keep supplying you with rubber bands for it, you know," he added with a grin.

Forrest smiled. "It's the only thing that'll do the job most of the time."

"Let's go up on the flight deck. I'll show you a real airplane. Besides, we need to get this party started pretty soon. We've got a firm departure slot and we don't want to miss it. And," he added with his best German accent, "you know how ze Krauts are when it comes to doing zings in ze proper order."

Vultures circled the prey as if it were simply a matter of time. But Amy Lee Forrest was far from dead. She lay on her back in the dry grass looking up at them.

"I wish that was Uncle John searching in his plane," she muttered to herself. "But everyone must think I'm dead by now. It's been a long time."

Dad wouldn't give up on me. He told me many times: 'never give up.' A survivor's best asset is their attitude—their will to survive. If only I could send an e-mail or a text message or something.

Amy's eyes went to the small dry lake bed shimmering to her left, her brain chewing on a seed of inspiration.

Text message. Hmmmm!

"Come *on*, Margaret," implored a voice graveled by years of cigar smoking. "Just *one* more." Robert Poisall, a retired U.S. Marine Corps infantry officer, glared impatiently at his reticent wife. His hairless scalp and pale face flushed with barely contained frustration.

Margaret Poisall turned away searching the narrow traffic-choked street for something more appealing—shoes, garments, china—anything other than the weird stuff that fascinated her husband. She had seen enough for one day. Garish signs replete with golden dragons advertised dozens of the 3,000 shops selling ivory products in greater Hong Kong. Her feet hurt as though they'd visited 2,000 of them already. With few exceptions, they were all the same; like T-shirt shops at American tourist resorts. One more, she thought, and I'll lose my mind.

IVORY...IVORY...IVORY... flashed in storefront windows alongside neon elephants and other electronic displays adamantly promoting gold jewelry and jade. She was numb to it. Her silence reflected her mood. Traipsing from one ivory shop to another in Kowloon's Shamshuipo district was definitely not her idea of a good time. Although an admitted QVC shopping addict, the 66-year-old woman had not traveled to the opposite side of the planet to lose herself in local tourist traps. Restaurants, museums, palaces, The Great Wall—those were the things he'd promised—not souvenir shops.

"You go," she said flatly without turning around. She hailed one of the taxis drifting closer in an endless stream of moving vehicles and bicycles. "I'll meet you back at the hotel." The cab stopped. Before he could protest, she inserted herself in the back seat and slammed the door.

Poisall stuffed his Cuban cigar between clenched teeth attempting a quick puff. Nothing. It had gone out two stores ago. Frustrated, he flung it to the side walk and turned to the ornate door pushing past the gold-leaf letters painted on the glass:

NATHAN SHING FINE JEWELRY
GOLD, IVORY, JADE
MAGIC BALLS OUR SPECIALTY

A tinkling bell summoned the proprietor. A slight Chinese gentleman in his late fifties emerged through a beaded curtain peering at his customer through dust-coated eyeglasses. He removed them quickly, wiping the ivory dust on his white smock. A polite bow accompanied his equally polite greeting. "Good, kind sir. Most pleased to show you something." Shing's smile was thin and tentative, his enthusiasm offset by suspicion. This man was American. In recent years he had experienced many Americans more interested in protests than purchases. Some just came to look. Others bought a few inexpensive items. Some even scoffed at his treasures. Most were difficult to deal with, rudely bargaining as if they were in a Mexican border town. But this man was different, he saw, his expression one of genuine admiration.

Poisall moved directly to a glass display case stocked with dozens of intricately carved ivory spheres. "Very nice," he growled, without acknowledging the shopkeeper's presence. He didn't want to appear too eager. During his many military tours in the Far East, he had developed a taste for oriental art forms while harboring an acquired distaste for the people. Never liked any of 'em. Never would, he often exclaimed. But, he loved their stuff. And he was particularly fascinated by Chinese magic balls.

"Ah, so. You appreciate magic ball." Shing said wiping dust-coated fingers on his trousers.

"How much for this one?" Poisall asked, poking a finger at the glass.

"Very good deal for Americans," Shing replied, opening the case. "Excellent choice. Very good taste." His smiled broadened instantly. "Twenty-four ball. Very good price."

Poisall took the piece, cradling it in loving fingers. It was magnificent. About the size of a softball, its entire surface was a continuum of intricate carvings. Through decorative holes in the outer ball, he examined subsequently smaller inner balls each decorated with highly detailed carvings. Like a Rubic's Cube, he thought, hardly able to contain his wonder. *I don't know how they do it.* But then, he *did* know. At least he understood the process. Three men were usually involved. The first converted an ivory block into a sphere. The second man etched a pattern of familiar Chinese figures into the surface of the outermost ball. The third artist, carved out the internal balls with a specially designed, L-shaped tool, cutting each new ball through the holes made in the one above it. Each piece took several days to complete. Poisall marveled at the craftsmanship without so much as a thought for the animal to whom it once belonged.

Strategy time, he decided. Time to chip away at the price. Step one: rejection. Poisall handed the ball back to Shing. "It's a nice piece, but I'll never get it back into the States," he replied forlornly, noticing for the first time a sign that said: BUY IVORY—HELP SAVE ELEPHANTS. Smaller print just below explained further: "Elephants in Zimbabwe and South Africa are overcrowded to the point that they must be culled to protect their habitat. The ivory sold here helps to support conservation work."

"Oh, not so," Shing proclaimed in his most solemn voice. "No problem. Only large pieces a problem." Shing gestured to a framed notice printed on official U.S. Fish and Wildlife letterhead.

Poisall stepped up to the frame tilting his head back slightly to better view it through his lower lenses. An adhesive label, obviously printed in Shing's own hand, announced in bold print that ivory import was permitted into the U.S. But he saw, almost hidden underneath Shing's statement, there was a catch. Poisall frowned at the small print. Ivory was only permitted into the United States *if* it was a hunting trophy or included in the shipment of household goods. He smiled inwardly. Leverage. He was returning home, space available, on an Air Force C-5A. Customs inspectors were generally "courteous" to vacationing officers and their families. Inspections were usually cursory, at best. It would be worth the risk, he considered *if* he could get the piece for the right price.

"I think you misinterpret the regulations, sir." Poisall countered, tapping the glass. "Magic balls don't fall into these categories, I'm afraid." He put on his sad face.

Shing's smile fell away. He shifted gears. "Ah, may be true now. I do not keep up with the regulations as well as I should."

Nice try, pal. You save face—I'll save some cash, Poisall thought, drifting toward the door. He'd heard it all before. Few dealers were willing to let on that it *might* be illegal to take ivory back to the USA. Sales were weak since the '89 ivory ban and the little slanty-eyed bastards were hard up for cash. Most, he knew, were betting on the come, sitting on their stockpiles hoping for the day when the ban might be lifted, if ever. "Oh well. Sorry. Maybe they'll change the rules some day." *Step two: Leave.* He placed his hand on the handle.

"For you, sir, thirty percent off."

The bell tinkled.

"Okay. Okay," came a voice tainted with a trace of desperation. "Fifty percent!"

Poisall hesitated.

"Sixty percent."

The door closed. Another tinkle.

"Seventy," the Marine countered, lighting another cigar.

"Sixty-five."

"Okay, Hop Sing," Poisall said, a sinister grin growing at the corners of his mouth. "You takey Amelican Expless?"

The first thing Forrest noticed about Kenya was the stifling heat. It was almost liquid and it hit him like a tsunami as he emerged from the air conditioned aircraft. Even for a man who had lived in South Florida for many summers, it would take some getting used to.

The workers unloading the aircraft had already sweat through the bandannas they wore under their baseball hats. Dressed only in worn trousers and cotton shirts, the laborers moved about carrying the supplies from the airplane to two ladder-back trucks parked near the tail. The workers were well organized and completed the loading very efficiently under the supervision of a native foreman. Even as the last of the supplies and equipment were being unloaded from the big Lockheed transport other workers arrived in trucks loaded with medical supplies destined for Mogadishu, Somalia.

Despite the deafening roar of engines and airframe noise in the back of the big transport, Forrest had slept for much of the long flight from Frankfurt to Nairobi on a bed of tarps and sleeping bags the crew kept aboard.

He gathered up his small bags and prepared to load them in the new, dark green Land Rover which the crew had backed off the plane and parked near by. Two uniformed Kenyan customs officials stood near the vehicle checking the declaration against the items listed on the shipping manifest. They asked to see the contents of Forrest's trunks and looked through the Land Rover for any contraband. The inspectors displayed no emotions as they asked their questions.

They dealt with shipments to scientific research groups routinely and the sort of equipment Forrest was bringing in was not out of the ordinary.

"Very well then, sah. Our inspection is nearly complete," the lead inspector said holding out his hand, with the light colored palm facing up. For a moment, Forrest just looked at it quizzically.

"He's expecting a gratuity, man," Grizz whispered coming up behind his friend.

"What the hell for? He's just doing his job!"

"Hey pal, remember where you are. It's SOP in the Turd World," Adams reminded him. "You wouldn't want to stand out, would you?" The big man gave his friend a knowing look. Forrest considered his friend's wisdom for a moment and reached into his pocket for some cash. He gave the man a crisp American ten dollar bill.

"Ah, but you see, sah, this was a very big shipment." The inspector's hand remained extended, his forced smile bright.

Forrest gave the inspector another look and then looked over at Adams who was now grinning. He took the hint. He produced two fifties and handed them to the inspector who seemed satisfied enough to withdraw his hand. The inspector gave him a slip of paper and a carbon copy of the manifest and walked off toward the terminal.

"Buncha goddamn thieves," Forrest muttered under his breath as they walked out of earshot.

"Payola, my friend. Payola. Almost all African governments are kleptocracies. You might as well get used to it." Adams chuckled at his friend's disgusted look. "It's how the rest of the world does business." Adams laughed. "Well pal, looks like this is it, for a while," Grizz said, extending his hand. Forrest clasped his friend's big paw with two hands for a warm, lingering hand shake.

"If you see me pop red smoke, come and get me."

"Right." Just be extra careful out there," Grizz cautioned.

"Just make sure you don't miss the drop zone."

"Yeah, Yeah. Don't forget to duck. We're gonna lay your shit right in your lap!" Grizz's eyes twinkled as he laughed. "Just call us, collect, on your 'Batphone' when you're ready for your toys."

Forrest waved and turned to see if his caravan was ready. The loaders and drivers from the camp stood on the shady side of the trucks smoking cigarettes and waiting for the new arrival to say his good-byes. A tall, lean Kenyan, in his thirties, leaned against the side of the Land Rover waiting for Forrest.

Forrest walked over to introduce himself. "Jambo. I'm John Forrest," he said, extending his hand.

"Jambo. I am Joseph," the Kenyan said with a cautious but friendly smile. He was one of the darkest men Forrest had ever seen. The lead driver climbed behind the steering wheel as Forrest settled into the passenger seat. "I will be taking you to the camp."

"Good. I'm ready to be there."

The long ride to the research camp took the rest of the day. It was nearly sunset when the small caravan pulled in. Joseph barked an order in Swahili and two young Kenyans ran to the back of the new Rover. Before Forrest could climb out, they were busy carrying his belongings into one of the huts. This guy runs a tight ship, Forrest thought as he surveyed his new home.

Forrest stretched his cramped muscles as he looked around the research center. It was more like a small village. Several huts were more-or-less neatly arranged among thick clusters of wild date palms and graceful yellow-barked acacias. Some of the huts or bandas were more traditional structures with stick-reinforced mud walls and thatched roofs. Others, like the one to which he had apparently been assigned, employed more conventional materials and modern construction. It even had a small porch and glass windows.

A small murmuring crowd gathered around Forrest, expressions ranging from toothy smiles to fearful withdrawal. Youngsters fidgeted nervously, cautiously regarding the new white man. Men of all ages smiled broadly talking among themselves in their native tongue. Most hung back at a comfortable distance, too shy to move closer. Forrest smiled tentatively and nodded a greeting to his new neighbors.

After a few awkward moments, the crowd began to part at the rear as people made way for someone's approach. The tan crown of a safari hat came into view followed by white hair and the glint of thick eyeglasses. A white, close-cropped beard and mustache framed the man's face. Whiskers gave way to a merry smile as he stepped clear of the villagers and presented his hand.

"Based on Colonel Grant's description, you would appear'ta be Captain Forrest," the short, elderly man said in a thick Scottish brogue, extending his hand.

"Doctor McCullen, I presume," Forrest said with a grin. The Stanley-Livingston cliché was irresistible under the circumstances but it went right over McCullen's head. The Scotsman was a Norman Rockwell painting of Santa Clause on safari. The two men shook hands vigorously.

"Please, call me Malcolm," he said, turning to face the gathering like a minister about to deliver a benediction to his flock. He gave a short speech introducing Forrest as a new researcher from America.

Forrest followed up with a brief biography at McCullen's insistence after which the doctor made several personal introductions to the camp's company.

"Let's go over to my place and have a drink, lad," McCullen offered. "Joseph will stow your personal gear in your hut and the bulk of it we'll put in the storage shed until tomorrow," he added leading the way to his hut. As they walked, McCullen explained that the camp was sponsored in part by the African Wildlife Fund but was funded almost exclusively by the Grant Foundation. "Tomorrow, I'll give'ya a proper tour," he promised. "After you get organized and catch up on your sleep, that is."

The two men entered McCullen's hut. "Your choices are Scotch and Scotch," he offered while closing the mosquito netting behind them. "Please, take my chair," he insisted, dragging it out from under his old wooden desk.

"I think I'll have a Scotch, then," Forrest responded dryly. "A small one." He could tell instantly that McCullen was a man he was going to like. He noticed there wasn't another chair in the room and remained standing.

"Have a seat, Cap..."

"John, please," Forrest interrupted.

"Very well then, John it is. But please," McCullen motioned toward the chair, "I insist. I'll use the end of me cot."

Forrest sat while McCullen poured two glasses of amber liquid, two fingers deep, from an emerald-green bottle of Glenlivet, 12 year old, single-malt scotch. The doctor handed one over to the tired traveler who really didn't care for Scotch but wouldn't think of being impolite. "To a successful project, John." Doctor McCullen said raising his glass in a toast.

Forrest clinked the edge of his glass against the doctor's. "Thanks, Malcolm. I hope it has quite an impact on my subjects."

Traditions: age-old practices handed down from one generation to the next. And of all the countries in the world, no culture is more centered in tradition than Japan's. Whether simple or elaborate, traditions are often rituals based in religious beliefs. Less often, traditions find their roots in practical need. Sometimes they make perfect sense, and sometimes absolutely none at all. "Time-honored" traditions—the hardest ones to change—are very often neither timely nor honored but rather petrified habits—anachronisms in conflict with contemporary politics and conventional wisdom. Such was the nature of Tamotsu Murasaki's dilemma as he emerged from the elevator to find himself in the outer offices of the Tokunaga Ivory Company, Ltd.

Of late, the short, plump artisan with a pleasant round face and built-in smile had become a man attempting to live simultaneously on opposite sides of a great dichotomy—the traditional Japanese reverence for nature and their modern-day rape of it.

A waist-high glass case positioned against the room's longest wall exhibited the company's most lucrative product: *hanko*—Japanese signature seals—commonly called chops. Tokunaga Ivory was their largest manufacturer.

In Japan, written signatures have little or no meaning with respect to official documents. A tradition predating the kimono has it that bills of sale, business and legal contracts, certificates of birth and death, and every document in between, are invalid unless stamped with a personal seal dipped in ink.

To acquire his own seal, each person selects an individual chop pattern which is carved into the head of a *hanko.* A representative print is then registered with a central office, whereupon it becomes that person's legal mark. Corporations follow a similar process to register logos and trademarks.

Traditionally speaking, *hanko* used to be made of common substances such as ebony, boxwood, jade, malachite or buffalo horn. More recently, plastic and ceramics had been used. But, commensurate with Japan's exploding wealth in the 1970s, *hanko* became status symbols. Once the soaring price of elephant teeth put them beyond the reach of the average salary man, ivory *hanko* became all the rage among the well-to-do. And, to compound the situation, a super-heated economy built on high technology made for ever-increasing numbers of the well-to-do.

Murasaki had recently read that, during the 1980s, an estimated 700,000 elephants had been slaughtered. Seventy percent of the ivory had been imported to his country and of that, 70 percent had been used for *hanko.* It had alarmed him to learn of the elephant's drastic decline especially when he discovered that 80-90 percent of the great beasts had been poached. The tusks had not been taken from animals found dead of natural causes as he had once believed. His beloved country, he was ashamed to admit, for all of its reputed appreciation for nature, had become the world's true elephant graveyard.

While he stood in the climate-controlled room, the temperature and humidity held constant to prevent the ivory from drying out and cracking, workers, four floors below, went about the task of converting elephant teeth into products identical to the ones he was admiring. Dozens of band saw operators carefully cut the tusks across the grain into blocks three inches long. Another group of workers ground the blanks down on a wheel until they were perfectly cylindrical and ready for polishing. White powdered tooth dentine, like flour, thickened the air coating everyone and everything as if they were standing in a driving snow. More workers dusted and swept the dust and chips into bags to be sold as a highly prized fertilizer and ingredients in new folk medicines. Throughout the Far East, many believed that ivory purified the blood and served as a general tonic. Some believed that, boiled with meat in a soup, ivory was a remedy for irritated eyes.

Murasaki came across a small collection of beautifully carved ivory rings, proudly recognizing some of his own work. Netsuke were Murasaki's specialty. Historically, the ornaments, something like napkin rings, were used to prevent *inro* cords from slipping off kimono sashes. In more recent times, after kimonos had gone the way of the samurai, the toggles had become collectable objects *de art.* The best *netsuke* were not just gloriously carved but an embodiment of style and wit. Classical *netsuke* reflected the virtues of *wabi* (serenity) and *sabi* (elegant simplicity). His father and *sensei* (master) had once told him: "Art can only be made by understanding the spirit of nature and becoming one with its essence." Dark contrast, he reflected with a shudder, to the screaming death throws of an animal violently forced to surrender its body parts.

Before investigation had stirred his conscience, Japan's premier carver of the traditional adornment had also preferred ivory. Elephant teeth (he had never before stopped to think of them as such) were the perfect medium for his art. Wood was both too soft and porous to hold the intricate detail for which his work was so highly acclaimed. And, unlike ceramic, jade, or onyx, ivory wasn't so brittle that it would snap under the blade of his tool. The milky substance had a sort of magic elasticity that held great detail while forgiving an artist's mistakes. If only nature, he hoped, could be as forgiving.

Murasaki mumbled to himself, "I must persuade Tokunaga-san to..."

"Persuade me to what, Tomatsu?" the deep voice resonated in the tomb-like quiet of the room.

Murasaki spun around. Lost in thought, he hadn't heard

Tokunaga's approach. He smiled nervously, embarrassed at being overheard, bowing politely at the waist. "Good morning, Tokunaga-san. I did not hear footsteps. You move like a shadow."

Tokunaga loomed over his colleague. Nearly a foot taller and several years older, the man cut an imposing figure. Gray temples crowned his ears, blending in sharp contrast to thick black hair gelled straight back from his forehead. His warm smile accentuated the lines of his face, mitigating the intensity of his coal-black eyes. As president of the company, Katsutoshi Tokunaga was one of the richest men in a country with no shortage of rich men, a fact that made him all-the-more intimidating. "Your family is well, Tomatsu?" he continued, ushering his visitor into the long dark hall that led to his private office. Tokunaga did not pursue Murasaki's unfinished comment despite his growing curiosity. Customarily, Japanese avoid direct discussion of delicate matters. Instead, they prefer to talk around issues. Bluntness is considered to be in poor taste.

"Yes, quite well, thank you. And yours?"

The two men moved effortlessly through Tokunaga's hallway galleries exchanging pleasantries and catching up on recent events.

Murasaki began to move as if in slow-motion, distracted by the incredible treasures on display.

Tokunaga smiled knowingly at his countryman's preoccupation with his collection. He was proud of his family's treasures. Murasaki-sensei, he knew, was the best ivory carver in Japan and Tokunaga was only too happy to accommodate such a qualified and appreciative admirer.

Large alcoves lined the hallway, each filled to capacity with ivory pieces from all over the world. There were antique, child-size figures from India and China, flocks of ivory birds, sprays of ivory flowers, and nests of ivory dragons. Many figurines were inlaid with jewels and covered with gold and silver. Some, his host explained, were worth half-a-million dollars, each.

Murasaki was practically limp with awe when they entered the office, itself. There he was stunned to realize that Tokunaga had saved the best for last. Magnificent pieces, beyond appreciation, stood around the room, their value impossible to estimate. The master carver was sure that his feet were no longer touching the floor.

Murasaki felt faint, as though he had been about to reach sexual climax only to awaken from a dream. "May I sit, Tokunaga-san?" he asked politely, leaning toward a black leather chair. The short, round man retrieved a handkerchief from his pocket and mopped his pudgy face.

"I was about to take tea, Tomatsu. Would you join me?" Tokunaga took a seat opposite his colleague, separated by yet another ivory-inlaid antique table.

"Domo, Tokunaga-san." Murasaki smiled nervously. He took a deep breath to calm himself. The act amused his host. "I have never seen such wonderful..." Another deep breath.

Tokunaga simply smiled.

Murasaki gave a conciliatory nod, closing his eyes momentarily. His thin smile faded as he summoned the courage to speak. "Tokunaga-san...," he said, then hesitated. This would be more difficult than he thought.

Tokunaga, still smiling warmly, gestured for him to continue. His executive assistant entered the office, bowed politely and served tea. Then, just as politely, the young woman bowed again before leaving them. She came and went as quietly as a ghost. Tokunaga sipped his tea as Murasaki began to speak.

"For generations, our families have passed on a legacy founded in the appreciation of fine art. My life's work has been carving ivory just as yours has been the production of ivory products. I would like to continue my work just as you would like to see your fine company grow and prosper." Murasaki paused to sip his tea. The warm liquid helped sooth his nerves.

Tokunaga nodded to support his guest's last point.

Murasaki continued. "But, I fear for both of our futures. Ivory is becoming more difficult to obtain. My supplies are very short."

"As are mine, Murasaki-sensei," Tokunaga added.

"When I first experienced difficulty in obtaining the high quality, hard ivory, I decided to learn more about the ivory and the elephants that produced it. I knew I was ignorant as to its origins but I never knew just how naive I was until I began my studies. I was not alone. Most of my clients, I discovered, were more ignorant than I. Most were not sure just what ivory was. They were simply in love with its smooth feel and warmness—its balanced heaviness. Not too light, like wood; not too heavy, like metal. A good heaviness. A quality especially important with *netsuke.* The best ivory for my work—the hard ivory—comes from the forest elephant, the one that lives in the great rain forests of Zaire, Gabon and the Congo." Murasaki took another sip of tea to wet his dry throat. He was gaining confidence as he spoke.

"Some of my clients believed that ivory is a substance mined from the earth like jade. Others thought that it is a tree, like ebony. Still others imagined it to be something that grew on trees, perhaps confused with something called "vegetable ivory," a hard white product made from the nut of a plant that grows in South America. But sadly, none of these things are true."

Tokunaga nodded in agreement. But Murasaki thought it a token gesture.

"If it is ivory you need, Tomatsu, I have enough to donate to art such as yours."

"You are most generous, Tokunaga-san. But that is not the solution I seek. Art is important, but nature is more important. The elephants are disappearing in great numbers. We must not allow that to continue."

"I see," Tokunaga replied, looking down at the reflections in the shiny black tile. "Our art—our traditions too would disappear. My business would suffer greatly."

"That is true. And I fear that my tradition may never return. There are almost no apprentice carvers these days. Young people see my art as a dying trade. They see no future in it. I am among the last of my kind. Not being able to pass on what I have learned from my father and his father is among my greatest sorrows. But I have learned there is a greater sorrow; the sorrow that comes from watching the death of a great species and the knowledge that I have helped cause it.

"Those great beasts have traditions much like our own. But for them, traditions mean survival. The traditions the old mothers pass along to their offspring teach them how to live in their world. Where to find food and water during times of drought. What foods to eat when they are sick. The migration routes they must follow when the weather changes from dry to wet. Their babies cannot learn these lessons any other way. They are not instincts. They must be taught. And when the old are killed, cut down by the rifle, their traditions die with them. The families are leaderless and the young often do not survive. They fare no better than would a five year old human child." Murasaki paused and looked directly into Tokunaga's eyes.

"What do you propose, Tomatsu?"

"The great beasts are endangered, Tokunaga-san. We cannot let them disappear. We must stop using ivory."

Tokunaga drew in a deep breath, his smile long since departed. "It is we who are endangered, Tomatsu. You and I. I have a business, a family. I have employees and *they* have families. What will become of them?" His volume rose. "Would you have me close my factory? Tell all my people that I no longer have a job for them? My products are an essential part of this country's business. There are over 12,000 hanko shops in Japan, each with several employees, Tomatsu! What of *them*?" Tokunaga slammed his fist down on the table, emphasizing his last word. The china rattled. His whole body began to tremble with anger.

Murasaki drew back slightly, but maintained his resolve. "The world is changing, Tokunaga-san. And so must we change. So must our traditions. Your product can be made with other substances as can mine."

"I sell over 2 million hanko per year, most of them ivory. Would you have me cheapen my product, my reputation, my very name by switching to...to *plastic?*" Saliva flew out of Tokunaga's mouth spraying the table and his guest. His brow narrowed above eyes dark with anger.

"We must. Soon there will no more elephants left. And then what? The change will come either way. If we stop the slaughter now, while there is still time, perhaps some day we will find a way to control the ivory trade so that it is obtained only from animals that have died a natural death. But that will require international cooperation. And it will require something else."

The two men stared at each other intensely. Their eyes locked like the arms of two wrestlers.

Murasaki rose to leave. "It will require that there be some animals left to die those natural deaths."

"Nice set-up, Doc." Forrest said after the tour. "I expected to see more animals, though."

"Most people do, lad. But I'm afraid it's not like it used to be. Not like the movies, anyways. The few that are left rarely venture outside the parks durin' the dry season," McCullen explained. "There's not enough water this time 'o year outside Tsavo, Amboseli and the Mara. And by the end of the dry season, most of the vegetation's been chomped down'ta the roots by the ungulates and the Masai cattle. This past season's been especially bad—the worst I've seen in quite a time."

"Any problem with water at the camp?" Forrest asked, noticing that the trees and vegetation around the camp seemed pretty healthy.

"Not yet, at least. We're pretty lucky, usually. Two good wells. Plenty 'o water from the mountain," McCullen said nodding his head toward Kilimanjaro.

Forrest eyed the hazy snow-capped summit of the distant volcano as McCullen continued.

"Water from the snowfields and glaciers percolates down through the volcanic ash and cinder to resurface as dozens of springs on the Kenya side. Swamps of various sizes have formed in the flatlands around most of the springs." McCullen used his hands frequently to illustrate his points.

"Usually, there's plenty 'o plant life to take care 'o most of the animals. And that's where you'll find most of them on a scorcher like t'day." McCullen removed his hat long enough to wipe his brow with a handkerchief. "In other places, like here, the springs go a little further underground. That's where the trees take hold—the palms and the fever trees."

"Fever trees?"

McCullen squinted a smile in Forrest's direction while he used his damp handkerchief to clean his glasses. "An old African name for the yellow acacias. One of those names that sticks even though it doesn't make any sense." The doctor put his glasses back on his nose and continued. "The trees were once thought to harbor malaria. Today, we know that isn't true, o'course. Turns out that the same periodically flooded ground where the Acacia xanthophloea flourish makes good breeding area for Anopheles—the mosquitoes that transmit the disease."

"Hmm. Like this one, you mean," Forrest said, slapping at his arm. He was suddenly glad he had taken the medication program seriously. There would be many dangers facing him in the bush, he knew, not the least of which would be microscopic. Threats didn't have to be large, armed or carnivorous to be deadly.

Birds chattered in the treetops and a light breeze washed through rustling leaves. Forrest took a deep breath and let it out. The jet lag was beginning to abate. Now, he was only two or three time zones behind. "Does your camp have a name?"

"Indeed." McCullen looked to the top of Kilimanjaro—the "Roof of Africa." "Uhura. The name's Uhura. Swahili for peace."

"Fitting."

McCullen smiled. "So, what's the subject of your thesis or have ya decided?" he asked as they passed stockades whose vertical timbers had seen better days.

Forrest thought about his answer as they walked back to their huts. He saw the facilities were in general disrepair. Brush had grown up in some of the corrals. They obviously hadn't contained any animals in a few years. "I'd like to work with elephants. I'm considering an investigative study on how human populations affect elephant populations—a correlation in population dynamics. Something like that."

McCullen stroked his chin whiskers thoughtfully, his gaze fixed at the ground.

"Colonel Grant said you're the world's foremost expert on

rhinoceros," Forrest continued.

"I don't know 'bout that, lad. But I've been studyin' them for a few years, I guess. If I'm the 'foremost expert' in the field—and that's doubtful—then it's because I've out-lived the others, not because I'm some great authority er' anythin." McCullen chuckled quietly. "If I was that good at what I do then these pens would be full of study animals." He gave the great stockades a forlorn look. "If things keep goin' the way they are, my work will be left to the paleontologists. The only thing left to study'll be bones and fossils. Mine along with theirs," he added, only half joking.

Forrest felt a great empathy for the old gentleman. He responded with a sympathetic smile. He watched as McCullen lit up a cigarette, inhaled, and coughed violently, mucus rumbling like a flushing toilet. He started to say something, then decided against it. *What good would it do now?*

The men came to a stop in front of Dr. McCullen's hut.

"I've got an idea, lad," McCullen said, perking up, suddenly. "We need'ta get your research off on the right foot. How 'bout I take'ya down to Amboseli tomorrow and introduce you to Mama Tembo and the First Lady of the elephants—Cynthia Marsh and her assistant, Diane Chernik. Talk about 'foremost experts.' Aside from one other person I know, those two know more about the great beasts than anyone in the world."

"Sounds good, Doc. But can it wait a few days?"

"I suppose. Why?"

"I've got to go into Nairobi soon and see about my airplanes. The Cessna's due in tomorrow and the little one just cleared customs. Now I've got to get 'em both inspected and registered. The ultralight has to be flight tested." Forrest's expression turned angry. "Knowing the way these bureaucrats operate, it'll most likely take a few days."

"It might at that," McCullen said, rolling his eyes. "Don't let 'em see that anger, John. Impatience only slows 'em down. And, no matter, it can wait. Anyways, Cynthia would like it better if I gave her a little more notice."

Forrest didn't hear the last remark. He was still thinking about his planes, specifically, how to wrest them from the bureaucrat's clutches and get them to camp. "Doc, do you think you could get Joseph and some of the men to work on the airstrip while I'm gone—knock down some of the weeds and fill some of the ruts?"

McCullen nodded and turned to go inside. "Consider it done, lad."

"Okay, good," Forrest said, starting toward his own hut. "The ultralight can land just about anywhere there's a hundred-foot patch of open ground. But the Cessna needs more of a runway." Just then he stopped in his tracks with another thought. "Doc. Who's that third elephant expert you were talking about?"

"Aye, that would be Dr. Sargent," the faint voice called from the dark interior. "Don't worry, you'll get to meet the good doctor soon enough."

Forrest turned to go and paused. "Hmm," he said to himself, thoughtfully, "that sounded like a warning."

Steven Henry Henderson pushed the remnants of his salad around its clear glass plate, his mind far away. Mixed greens and iceberg lettuce, propelled by a salad fork, chased pine nuts into a celery crescent which captured the remaining cherry tomato squeezing it until it ruptured. Henderson focused on a tiny seed as it slid slowly around the red orb like an orbiting moon.

His thoughts went to another "moon" orbiting unseen and unacknow-ledged hundreds of miles above his favorite restaurant. When the waiter removed his salad plate, he ordered another coffee and thought about the fruitful NFIB meeting. Until a new Director of Central Intelligence could be nominated and confirmed, various deputies had shared the duties of chairing the National Foreign Intelligence Board's weekly meetings. Months ago, Henderson had volunteered to represent CIA at the meeting his boss, the Deputy Director of Intelligence, currently chaired. With the blessings of the White House and the SECDEF, Henderson had successfully negotiated with other COMIREX (Committee on Imagery Requirements and Exploitation) members for a small portion of the DOD's immensely expensive satellite time.

Henderson leaned back as his waiter placed his entree on the table. Once in a while he enjoyed eating alone. No forced conversations. No small talk. No distractions. It gave him time to take a breath and sort things out.

"Will there be anything else, sir?" the waiter asked with strained politeness. The Hawk and Dove was a popular spot for Washington power lunches and at 11:10 AM, there was already a line forming at the "reservations only" establishment.

Henderson smiled. "No, thank you. Everything's fine."

And everything was fine—so far. The National Reconnaissance Office (NRO) had executed the committee's requests flawlessly. As he lay watching Nightline two nights before, a KH-12 reconnaissance satellite, about the size of a tractor-trailer truck, responded to encrypted commands originally uplinked from Fort Belvoir, Virginia, then relayed through a higher flying SDS platform. Right on cue, state of the art optical technology went to work focusing multispectral scanners and telescopic cameras capable of "reading" newspaper headlines over a hundred miles below. Normally tasked to track events in Iraq, Iran and other high-interest areas, the latest marvel in the extraordinary Keyhole program had received its "wake-up call" earlier than usual and had begun relaying real time imagery of Tanzania, Kenya and Somalia to monster computers at the National Photographic Interpretation Center (NPIC) in Washington, DC.

Henderson smiled at a thought. Like most photographers, he couldn't wait to get his pictures back from the developer. But even pros who processed their own negatives and prints couldn't get that kind of service. Without a doubt, the NRO and NPIC could beat any "one hour" photo processor in town.

"Well, Cap'n. That oughta do it. The breaker was too small for the load. New one should bloody well take care of it." The short Brit mechanic with powerful arms, large dark eyes and a bulbous nose wiped the grime off his hands with a rag.

"Any other problems?" Forrest asked as walked around the Cessna 185. He ran his hand admiringly along the worn but sound aluminum skin.

"I replaced the number one cylinder. Did a valve and ring job on the rest." The mechanic wiped his face with the rag then jammed it into a back pocket. "Whatta'ya plan on using that thing for, anyway, mate?" he asked, nodding to the round black pod he had mounted beneath the left wing.

"It's a FLIR pod. Forward Looking Infra Red. I need it to see things in the dark."

"What sort'a things?"

"Animals, mostly. I do animal research," Forrest said, matter of factly. "I need to be able to track them at night." He stopped when he came to the engine cowling and ran his hand over a decal bearing the airplane's name. IMMACULATE CONTRAPTION, it read in two-inch red script. Forrest smiled.

The mechanic anticipated the American's question. "Used to belong to a Catholic missionary. Had a heart attack, he did. Can't fly no more."

Forrest nodded. "When's the paint job gonna be finished?

"'Bout a week, Cap'n." The mechanic eyed the decal. "I was plannin'ta leave it."

Forrest smiled. "Religious?"

"No. Superstitious, about some things. It's bad luck to change a ship's name."

Forrest considered the thinly veiled advice with an understanding smile. "Well, I need all the luck I can get. Leave it."

"What ever you say, Cap'n."

"You said the Zenair was ready?"

"It's in the hangar. Good'ta go."

They walked into shade that, absent a breeze, seemed hotter than direct sunlight. Forrest climbed into the tiny plane newly painted a dull flat green and tan camouflage pattern. His hands moved over the controls as he familiarized himself with the simple cockpit.

"I'll get the bill."

"Okay. Bring the one for the Cessna while you're at it. I'll take care of 'em both."

When the mechanic returned, Forrest climbed out and looked at the handwritten statements. "You don't come cheap," he commented with a thin smile.

"Ya get what'ya pay for, mate."

Federal Building 213 is a perfect example of hiding something in plain sight. Painted an unobtrusive beige, only the Cyclone fence topped with coils of razor wire would give one the impression that anything of value was stored in a building designed to look like any other government warehouse.

Henderson pulled up to the M Street entrance and showed his CIA ID to the Federal Protection Service guard. "I have an appointment to see Ms. Goetz."

The guard checked Henderson's ID and his Social Security number against his visitor list and glanced at his watch. "You can park over there, sir, next to the air conditioners."

Henderson nodded and pulled into the parking lot. Air conditioning units big enough to cool a battleship boiler room droned a dull roar cooling the huge bank of Cray Research supercomputers he knew to be on the other side of the windowless walls. He extracted his briefcase, locked his car and walked quickly to an entrance topped by a blue sign. White letters announced the building's name: National Photographic Interpretation Center.

Henderson walked inside, happy to be out of the cold. A quick inquiry with yet another guard led him past offices to the clearing house where all military satellite imagery was collected and stored. The air still carried the faint odor of photo processing chemicals even though virtually all imagery was now retained as billions of bits of data in scores of computer disk drives.

A bright smile and extended hand greeted him as he rounded the corner of one of the many cubicles containing computer monitor workstations. "Hey, big shot. Glad to see you're not above visiting the trenches."

"From what I've heard, you're a pretty big shot, yourself. How've you been, Kris?" Henderson took her hand then gave her a quick hug appropriate for old friends of the opposite sex.

"Not bad for a girl who works the night shift." Kristine Goetz said with an easy smile. Bright green eyes accented by conservative make up and red lips gleamed upon seeing an old friend and colleague. Brunette hair pulled into a long pony tail hung down her back. "What brings you down to the 'Nit-pick Center?'"

"Well..." he said looking around at the few people working in the building.

"Come on. We can talk in my office." Goetz was used to people who looked over their shoulder as a matter of habit.

Henderson followed her down a narrow hallway and into a private office. He went to a chair set up for guests and waited for her to take a seat. He opened his briefcase and produced a letter on White House stationery.

"Well, well. You're a bigger shot than I thought," she said handing the letter back to her friend. "What can I do?"

"A favor."

Goetz, an attractive woman with a quick wit, chuckled and nodded. "You can't sleep here. My husband wouldn't like it. Short of that, I'm listening."

A grin tugged at the corners of Henderson's mouth. "I need a good PI to do first-look exploitation of all imagery collected over Tanzania, Kenya and Somalia. This is code-word stuff and I'm to be the only person contacted."

Goetz raised an eyebrow. "What are you looking for?"

"I'm tracking bad guys. The ones that did the ambush in Mogadishu a while back. The President wants 'em." He looked Goetz in the eye. "So do I."

"Why Tanzania and Kenya, then?" intellect and innate curiosity compelled her to ask.

Henderson let out a breath and let his eyes drop. He knew she'd ask and he knew he'd have to lie to an old friend—something he was doing a lot, lately. He decided on a more comfortable answer, an old cover-all: "Sorry. Can't tell you that."

She looked at him. Her smile dissolved. "You're not about to pay cash for a Jaguar and a new house in Arlington, are you?"

Henderson gave a weak laugh. "My wife likes the one we've got, thank you." His expression became more serious. "You'll have to trust me on this one."

Goetz shrugged. "Okay. Let me see the imagery request. I have to know where to look."

Henderson gave her the forms from his briefcase. "I'm looking for guerilla camps and/or hunting camps." His hands trembled slightly as he handed them over. "The bad guys also moonlight in the poaching business—elephants and rhino, mainly. It helps fund their political action committees."

She looked the forms over. "I hate 'em already." Goetz smiled and looked up. "I like animals."

"Good," Henderson noticed a picture of a pampered golden retriever on her credenza and breathed a little easier. "Look for everything from skins to ivory. They have to cure bush meat before they transport it, so you might want to crosscheck infra red for large or numerous fires."

Goetz didn't write anything down. She didn't have to. Her memory was superb. And she didn't like paperwork.

Henderson looked at his watch and rose. "By the way, when you find something, don't send it over the net. Save it on disk and I'll come down and review it...or send a courier."

"Okay." She smiled. "Might cost you a few lunches, though.

Henderson turned. "Do this well, and you'll be buying *me* dinner when you get promoted."

She wasn't sure what he meant by that, but she liked the way it sounded. "When do you want this?"

"Yesterday, of course."

CHAPTER-SEVEN

ORIENTATION *a: the act of turning to or determining direction*
b: sense of direction
c: establishing one's position
d: initial briefing

AT 4:30 IN THE AFTERNOON, most government employees in Washington D.C. were well on their way out of the office in a futile attempt to beat the rush hour traffic. CIA employees were no exception being eager participants in the evening migration to destinations beyond the Washington Beltway. Steve Henderson welcomed the early exodus. Fewer people at work meant fewer distractions and interruptions.

As an Assistant Deputy Director, Henderson rated a nice seventh-floor office with a view. To the north, across the Potomac River, he eyed the woods surrounding the bedroom community of Cabin John Creek as he buzzed his executive assistant of seven years. "Roselle, after you return the classified to the vault, you can head home if you like," her boss offered.

"Thanks, Steve. Have a nice weekend."

"You too," he said to the intercom.

Henderson returned objects from the top of his desk to their drawers and packed his briefcase in preparation to leave. After he locked his credenza, he exited through the outer office and walked down the hallway to the elevator. He punched the down button and did a quick inventory of his belongings while he waited. The shiny stainless steel doors parted with a rumble and he stepped inside. He swiped his ID badge through a cipher-lock and pressed the button marked B3. All levels below B1 had restricted access and a special code was required to select any of the basement floors. A minute later the elevator doors opened into another hallway. Ten meters down the hall on the left, Henderson stopped and swiped his security badge through another card reader. Henderson's badge was one of the few that allowed access to virtually every room in the Langley complex—except, of course, the women's bathrooms. He waited for the red LED to turn green. As it did, he heard the electronic lock's distinct click. He put his overcoat over his left arm as pushed through the door. There was nothing outside the room to indicate that he had just entered the highly-secure digital wonderland of the CIA's Office of Imagery Analysis.

Details about the technology used to produce the imagery were more highly classified than the imagery itself. The true capabilities of the cameras and enhancement systems were, by themselves, extremely sensitive and closely guarded secrets. The few intelligence photographs made available to the public were carefully screened or degraded to insure that they did not reveal a system's true performance parameters. In most instances, it was better for potential adversaries to overestimate intelligence gathering capabilities and in some instances it was better for them to underestimate them. In almost all instances, it was better to keep everybody guessing. Such was the nature of the business. At the end of the day, it all came down to intelligent guesses.

Henderson was greeted at a glass inner door by a familiar face. "How ya doing, Mr. Henderson? Working late again I see." A man in his late sixties smiled broadly as he let the Assistant Deputy Director inside his little world. The room carried the moderate odor of the developers, fixers, washes and other chemicals used to process film and print photographs. After all, some photographs were still produced the old fashioned way—taken up close and personal by people who risked their lives to snap a shutter.

"Yeah, Bill." Henderson replied, dismissively. "Some things you've just got to do yourself."

"I know what you mean, Mr. Henderson. Nothing like the personal touch when it has to be right the first time." Bill Masters' black suspenders clashed with his thin red bow tie and light blue cotton shirt. A black vinyl eyeglass case was clipped inside his shirt pocket keeping company with a plethora of pens. Masters was the Agency's top technical expert on image enhancement techniques. He was a plank holder. Masters had been at CIA since the Kennedy administration, and was one of the fathers of satellite imagery. Much of the equipment at OIC and NPIC was a product of his fertile mind. "Let me know if you need anything. I'll be in the shop working on one of my problem children."

"Okay, thanks. And Bill..."

"Yes sir."

"What do I have to do to get you to call me Steve? You were analyzing world-famous recce photos that were published in Life magazine when I was still in grade school, for Chrissakes!"

Masters lowered his head and gave a bashful grin, before walking off down the hall to leave Mr...Steve to his work.

Henderson entered one of the cubicles used by the imagery analysts during the day and closed the door behind him. He lay his briefcase on a table and extracted several removable hard disks he'd received by courier from Kristine Goetz at NPIC. Yellow Post-It notes gave him frame index numbers, lat-longs, and a brief description of what she had found. He flipped on the monitor and loaded the first disk.

"Well now. Let's see what Kris got from the crystal ball," he muttered with a long anxious sigh.

For the next two hours, Henderson examined image after image. He made notes in a Sharp Wizard pocket database whose memory could be erased at the push of a button. Images taken over Tanzania and Kenya received special attention. Aside from the suspected camps

Goetz had indicated, he was looking for elephant herds and dead animals. Bipedal predators were easy to spot. They made fires, built huts and other structures. They stored their trophies and sometimes drove vehicles.

Goetz's infra red analysis had turned up a few fire pits and drying racks where illegal meat was hung to cure. Henderson smiled at his next discovery: Kris had done him one better. She'd told the computer's spectralanalysis software to examine smoke for fat residue and other organic chemicals and, as a result, discovered four additional sites. The infra red camera had even located what she believed to be patches of "freshly turned" soil; an indication that something had recently been buried. The same technique had been used to locate mass graves in Rwanda and Bosnia-Herzegovina.

Henderson marveled at the computer's capabilities. The system had come a long way since his days at DIA. Phenomenal technology lay at his fingertips. Tell the computer what you were looking for and it could find it for you by circling or highlighting it. It could also salvage what used to be utterly hopeless images by correcting atmospheric distortion, mirror distortion and eliminate sun glint and shadow. A keystroke and subtle tracing with the track-ball allowed him to change contrast, color and aspect using techniques he'd learned from his daughters' desk-top publishing programs. And just like his home computer, it could play Einstein by distorting time.

"You going home tonight?" Masters asked.

"Hmm?" Henderson looked at his watch. "Oh man!" He removed his reading glasses and rubbed his eyes. "I'm outta here or I'm divorced." He pushed his chair back and stood up and scanned the screen one more time before performing a save and shut down. As his eyes focused on the image of a dry lake bed near Tsavo National Park, Henderson sat back down.

"Don't forget to close out and lock up," Masters cautioned as he left.

Holy Jesus! Henderson was completely focused on an image, not quite believing what he saw.

"Mr. Henderson…" Masters reminded, hesitating at the door.

"Hmmm? The experienced photo analyst commanded the

computer to zoom in on the lake bed at the highest resolution. "Ahh… sure, Bill…. I've got it. You're covered," Henderson added without looking up. Fingers trembling with excitement clicked on some of the icons at the edge of the screen to improve the contrast. *Oh please, Lord. Don't let this be anything other than what I think it is.*

After saving the data he had collected in his Wizard, Henderson took all of his paper notes and ran them through the shredder in the corner of the work room. Then he emptied the basket of spaghetti-thin strips into the burn bag sitting against the wall.

Henderson looked at his watch mentally calculating the time difference in Kenya. *I've got to get a message to Thumper!*

Dark, soulful eyes, round with wonderment, followed each article out of the foot locker and onto the front porch of Forrest's "hootch." When he turned to look at them, the camp's children drew back apprehensively. Forrest smiled at them. He turned back to the trunk and watched out of the corner of his eye as ten dark faces leaned in, eager to see the next bit of treasure emerge from the chest. It was all he could do to restrain a laugh. They were like dogs tracking table scraps as they watched him unpack his gear.

"You guys think this is Christmas, or something?" he commented with amusement.

The children pulled away, murmuring among themselves nervously. Forrest had no idea what they were saying. When he brought out a Sony Discman and a stack of colorful CD jewel boxes, their eyes lit up.

"Mmm. You guys like oldies?" He pulled out a pair of mini-speakers and plugged them in. "Let's see. How 'bout a little *Isley Brothers.* Slap this baby in here—like this. Close the top...and...fire!" *You know you make me wanna SHOUT*, split the air. Forrest danced, throwing his hands into the air at the appropriate times.

The kids laughed and giggled and started to dance, imitating the crazy American.

"Makin' some new friends, I see," McCullen's brogue announced above the din.

"Yeah. They're helping me unpack," Forrest said, rolling his eyes and making quotes with his fingers.

"Indeed. Mind they don't 'unpack' anything else." McCullen raised an eyebrow in warning.

Forrest smiled and took several items inside. When he emerged he found a young boy handling his Gerber survival knife. He was older than the rest, about 10 or 12 years old. "That's a little big for you, isn't it?"

The boy thought he was being scolded, dropped the knife and ran off.

Forrest looked at McCullen and shrugged. "How 'bout I take everybody for an airplane ride?"

McCullen's eyes twinkled. "I think they'd like that."

"Okay." Forrest turned off the music. "You handle the boarding passes."

Forrest waited until the camp settled down for the night before testing his most sophisticated piece of equipment. The kids were all asleep, worn out from the day's excitement. Most of the adults, it seemed, had joined them.

Forrest glanced at his watch. In half an hour, the diesel generator would be shut down for the evening and the camp would revert back to a time when life was simpler and a camp fire was the highest level of technology known to man.

He went back into his hut, sat on his bunk, and spread his legs wide apart, grunting slightly as he reached between his legs and slid the heavy fiberglass box from beneath his cot. Grasping both fold-out handles firmly, he stood up and took the chest outside, walking silently through the darkness to a small clearing behind his hut.

Kneeling, Forrest popped the fasteners that held the lid in place. Carefully, just as he'd been shown, he opened the leaves of the parabolic antenna and attached it to a small tripod stand. Forrest took out his lensatic pocket compass and took a bearing to the southwest. He carefully aimed the dish toward a bright star that conveniently lined up with the bearing. An invisible satellite, hanging 22,300 miles above the planet in geosynchronous orbit, was the target.

Forrest uncoiled a five foot coaxial connector cable and attached the end to a socket in the base of the antenna. He plugged the other end into the antenna receptacle in the control panel. Next, he removed a Dell notebook computer from its slot and placed it on top of the chest. A serial cable connected it to an encryption-capable field satcom unit housed in the bowels of the chest next to a signal scrambler. He rechecked the connections and pushed the plastic-coated power button and the notebook's power switch in rapid succession. The screen flickered to life as it booted.

Forrest typed a standard command into the keyboard to load the communications program. At the prompt, he entered his six-digit password. Another set of keystrokes selected "data" and instructed the system to sign on. After a 60 second delay, the unit displayed a message indicating it had accessed the satellite's transponder.

Forrest typed:

> DEAR SANTA - I'VE BEEN A VERY GOOD BOY.
> PLEASE SEND ALL THE TOYS I ASKED FOR.
> THUMPER

He pushed the "Enter" key and waited for a reply.

Three minutes later the "stand by" message was replaced by a new message that scrolled across the screen:

> AUTHENTICATE A A N.

After referring to an authenticator code-card to which only he and Henderson had access, Forrest typed:

> BRAVO.

He hit "Enter" and waited.

WHAT IS YOUR BIRD'S NAME?

"Ha! Well I'll be damned! This thing really DOES work!" Forrest remarked out loud to himself. He was still smiling as he typed: R-A-L-P-H.

It took less than a minute for the reply:

> AUTHENTICATION RECEIVED. TOYS READY FOR SHIPMENT. DELIVERY SET FOR BASE DATE PLUS SEVEN, BASE TIME PLUS TWO HOURS AND THREE ZERO MINUTES. SEND LAT-LONGS - SAME TIME - BASE DATE PLUS TWO. ABORT CODE MUST BE RECEIVED NLT DELIVERY DAY MINUS ONE - BASE TIME. SEVERAL POINTS OF INTEREST ON NEXT CONTACT. REMOVE SATCOM FROM ITS CASE TO FIND EQUALIZER UNIT.
>
> ALL SEND OUR BEST.
>
> SANTA.

Forrest was about to sign off when another message floated across the screen:

> THUMPER – SPEEDO IS ALIVE – REPEAT ALIVE! THIS IS NOW A RESCUE MISSION. PROCEED WITH ALL HASTE TO THE FOLLOWING COORDINATES. SEARCH THE AREA AROUND A DRY LAKE APROXIMATELY 500M IN DIAMETER.

Seconds later the screen displayed the coded lat-longs.

Forrest acknowledged the message, signed off the satellite and shut the unit down. It took five minutes to disassemble the rig and return it to its container. He carefully looked around the camp before emerging from the shadows and reentering his hut.

The next few minutes were spent deciphering the information with a cipher he had worked out with Henderson. The base date was the tenth of the month so the target date would be the seventeenth.

The base time was twelve, noon which made the pick-up time 14:30, local.

I can't believe Amy is alive. What does Peeper know? *How* does he know? His mind couldn't help but turn to his own child in an attempt to reconcile his best friend's joy against his own searing anguish. Forrest sat lost in his thoughts for a time then startled.

Almost forgot!

Forrest retrieved a screwdriver from a canvass tool bag he kept in the corner of his hut. He sat down on the edge of his cot and slid the satcom container between his feet. Seconds later he laid the top of the unit on the floor and studied the face of the control panel. Four Phillips-head screws fastened the panel to the edge of the fiberglass housing. He quickly loosened them and lifted the guts of the device out of its protective container. Secured to the bottom of the fiberglass chest next to the lithium battery pack was a black plastic box surrounded in black neoprene foam. He poked his fingers into the foam, lifted the heavy box out and placed it next to him on the bed. Using his thumbs, he snapped the plastic latch open and lifted the lid.

A grin spread over his face. A big stainless steel revolver bearing Sam Colt's trademark logo glowed in the lamplight. Engraved along the six inch barrel under the words: 'Colt Anaconda' was the inscription:

CAPTAIN JOHN RUGER FORREST
CHAMPION - MARKSMAN - FRIEND

"You wonderful bastards!" he whispered to himself, admiring the satin luster of the .44 magnum, hand-cannon. "'Equalizer unit,' indeed."

"Holy shit!" Forrest gasped. The letters A – M – Y were gouged in the dry, gray-white mud of the lakebed. Forrest banked the Cessna hard for another pass, then a third before expanding his orbit in search of the graffiti artist, herself. He patrolled the surrounding area for an hour searching for his daughter-in-law, her tracks, or any other sign.

A glance at his watch and the fuel gauges told him it was time to go.

"Hang in there, honey," Forrest called out to the terrain moving under the aircraft. "I'll be back."

Sobs rippled through her body in waves. The little plane had gone right by her. It had circled in the distance and passed directly over her head. *Why hadn't they seen me? Does anyone know I'm here?*

Having flown in light aircraft with her "uncles" in the past, it occurred to her that she had to be positioned off to the side in order for a pilot to see an object on the ground. *If only I had some sort of signal device, a mirror… a fire. Something!*

Her meager subsistence had left her gaunt and lethargic. Though water had been obtained in various forms, thirst stalked her every waking moment. She was so dry she was surprised she had enough water for tears. Still, frustrated and despondent, she had not been able to hold them back.

Once back at Camp Uhura, Forrest hurried to get an update to his friend at CIA:

> LETTERS CONFIRMED. SHOULD WE INFORM THE POLICE?

Forrest hit the send key on the SATCOM and waited.

> I DON'T TRUST THEM. AND IT WILL COMPROMISE TOO MUCH IF WE DO. NEGATIVE.

He shut down and disassembled the unit, locked the container and slid it under his cot.

Forrest rose and rubbed his tired dry eyes. "I guess I'm still on my own." As he walked over to his sink he looked at himself in the mirror. *If that girl is out there, I'll find her. Failure is unacceptable.*

It was a new day. And Forrest was flying the *Immaculate Contraption* with a new co-pilot. Forrest glanced at the Cessna's fuel gauges and checked his watch. At a consumption rate of eleven gallons per hour, he had enough time left for one more pass over the Masai Mara before turning toward Lake Magadi and Camp Uhura.

"It's a beautiful day, isn't it now, lad?" McCullen asked, a cheery smile splitting his gray whiskers.

"That it is Doc. That—it—is."

"Lovely country, too. God's country."

"The real Holy Land, Doc—the cradle of mankind."

McCullen nodded and looked out across the vast savanna. Hundreds of animals drifted through miles of dry grass on an endless migration. "The world's largest gathering of land mammals." He noticed many were dead—victims of the long drought. "And I don't know how much longer they can go without rain."

Forrest, succumbing to the power of suggestion, took a swig from a canteen then passed it to McCullen. He noticed McCullen's melancholy had abated somewhat at the prospect of an airplane ride. The scientist wasn't particularly keen on flying, but with the courage found in a generous dose of Glenlivet, he had decided he just might be able to trust an ex-airline captain with 11,000 hours of flying time. Besides, it was a nice change of pace and Forrest had been careful to emphasize how much he needed the elder man's expertise. Forrest was pleased to see that a renewed sense of purpose had brought him around.

"The Masai patrol the Mara," McCullen explained. "It's the only place in the country where the Kenya Wildlife Service's authority is superseded. The Masai think they do a better job. And now that Leakey's gone, they're probably right."

"Who's in charge, now?"

"Allen Windridge. A Brit." McCullen screwed the top back on the canteen and laid it on the floor behind Forrest's seat. He longed for a cigarette, but Forrest wouldn't let him smoke in the plane. "He's been Director for a few years. And, I'm afraid, he's a better politician than he is a steward. He's managed to keep his job, at least."

Forrest nodded but said nothing. Something caught his attention and he banked the Cessna sharply to the right to give the Doctor the best view. "Ladies and gentlemen, a little slice of life coming up on the right side."

They watched as two lions brought down a wildebeest too weakened by the drought to put up an adequate defense. One huge female clamped down on the beast's windpipe while another dug her claws and canines into its haunches.

Forrest leveled the airplane and plotted their position on an Operational Navigation Chart, checking the landmarks depicted on the chart against the bends in the Mara River and the configuration of the hills and mountains in the distance. Dead reckoning was the oldest and, depending on the navigator, most reliable method of getting an airplane from point A to point B. Still, experienced pilots knew it was best to use all the aids available to them. Forrest cross checked his position with a Garmin 195Map GPS strapped to his left leg. Receiving distance information from as many as eight of the 24 Global Positioning Satellites, the hand-held unit determined its position by calculating the common intersection of several spheres, the largest being the Earth's surface.

McCullen watched the exercise with great interest, oblivious to its ultimate purpose.

In the distance, Forrest noticed several columns of gray smoke which towered to the bottom of an inversion layer then trailed off laterally on the wind.

"Quite a few fires, t'day," McCullen commented. "Durin' the rainy season most of 'em are caused by lightening. All of these were started by man."

"Carelessness?"

McCullen looked at him, shaking his head. "Intentional."

Forrest raised an eyebrow.

"They use 'em to drive game."

When McCullen turned his head, Forrest marked the locations on his chart.

"Can't the game wardens go to the fires and stake out the bad guys?" Forrest asked.

McCullen looked back. "How many fires do'ya see out there?"

Forrest shrugged. "A bunch."

"How many wardens do'ya think are available to patrol this area?"

Forrest looked at the fires and nodded his understanding. He rolled the airplane into an easy turn to the east and descended. Just ahead, he spotted a small herd of elephants. He made a mark on his chart indicating their location and number. Startled by the engine noise, a herd of gazelle bounded away to the north. Some of the smaller elephants spread their ears, broke and ran. The adults stopped short and turned to look before trotting off.

"All the animals outside the parks spook pretty easily," McCullen commented. "They associate man and his noisy machines with grief."

"Me too," Forrest said dryly, watching the animals disappear behind the plane. He toggled the GPS to a page displaying bearing, distance and time enroute to Camp Uhura's tiny airstrip.

McCullen watched and smiled. "How much longer?" he asked, dying for a smoke.

Forrest grinned. "About thirty-five minutes."

"Make it in under thirty and I'll grill you a big steak."

"Deal." *But first I want to search for Amy a little on the way home.*

The next day Forrest's new Land Rover left a long billow of dust in its wake as it sped along the unpaved roads of Kenya's Amboseli National Park.

"Look! Over there!" Forrest exclaimed with child-like enthusiasm, his finger pointing at the huge animals emerging from the brush. "Mag-*ni*-fi-cent," he exclaimed in an awed whisper. "Posilutely magnificent."

McCullen beamed.

Elephants! The first they had seen since leaving their camp; the first Forrest had ever seen on the ground. His excitement was barely contained. He brought the Rover to a halt as the first animals crossed the road 100 meters ahead. A large female, probably the matriarch, crossed first followed by lesser females and their calves. He counted twelve in all. The matriarch hesitated for a moment, ears and trunk extended, checking out the humans and their contraption before moving on. A young female, the gray train's caboose, flanked what must have been her year-old sibling. She became nervous as they came to the center of the road and urged her small charge across. After a moment, only the tops of heads, rumps and snow-white egrets hitching a ride remained visible above the thorny brush.

McCullen's twinkling gray eyes shifted from the animals to his new American friend. The Scotsman could see Forrest genuinely admired the elephants. A smile spread through his whiskers. "Once you're hooked, you never wiggle off, you know. Every time I get close to 'em, I still feel the excitement," McCullen continued.

"Yeah?" Forrest, preoccupied, turned back for another look. Too late. They were gone. He eased the Rover back to cruise speed, a slower one this time, anticipating another encounter. "How long have you been doing this kind of work, Doc?" he asked, his eyes scanning the brush ahead. His were hunter's eyes, the product of thousands of years of evolution and a boyhood spent hunting small game on his father's farm. But he was not hunting today, at least not animals. He was looking for friends.

"Oh, I don't know. Thirty-odd years, I guess."

"What ever brought you here from Scotland? Somehow you don't fit this place." Forrest hit the brakes hard as they rounded a curve and bounced over a deep hole in the road.

McCullen chuckled. "I might say the same about you, lad. You don't seem the type to be lecturin' in a university amphitheater in a tweed jacket 'n bow tie. I picture you in a uniform of some sort." His comment drew a sideways look and an odd smile from the man behind the wheel. McCullen continued. "I got bored doctorin' sheep in Scotland. So one year I got an invitation from one of me college friends to come to Africa for a few months to help him on a field project. He'd been hired by the Kenyan government to prevent the spread of anthrax in the cattle population. I gave it some thought and finally talked me wife into comin' though she was never quite taken by the idea. She was pregnant at the time, ya'see." McCullen paused for a moment at the thought of his wife.

"I fell in love with the place when I first laid eyes on it—the same as me darlin' wife, it was—beautiful—enchantin'. I never went back."

There was a long silence.

Forrest turned to look at the doctor. McCullen had a far away look in his eyes. "Where's your wife, now?" he asked, impulsively; sorry he had the instant he uttered the words.

"She died a few months after we arrived. Complications with the pregnancy. May have been due to a tropical disease. Don't know for sure." Tears welled up in his eyes. "Medical treatment here's not up to European standards and she got too sick too fast to fly her home."

Forrest looked ahead, at a loss for something to say. He felt stupid for asking the question. "I'm sorry, Doc. I really am." He looked back over at the doctor again. "Hell, Doc. I'm even sorrier for asking."

McCullen simply nodded, staring straight ahead, his thoughts for the moment, a prisoner of the past.

The terrain was changing ahead. The road curved around a huge alkali pan that measured more than two miles across. Forrest watched a pair of dust devils whirling above the baked white surface. Born of the sun's blistering rays and a rising breeze, they were like spiraling columns supporting an azure ceiling. In a moment they had dissipated into fleeing ghosts whisking across the ground. In the distance, a mirage of legless elephants floated above the shimmering surface. Behind them, giraffe's long necks jutted skyward, rocking back and forth lazily like the masts of sailing vessels adrift on a pale, green sea. Here, the sun-scorched lakebed yielded to grassy plains, or what the drought had left of them.

Hundreds of gazelles, zebra, and wildebeest moved across the sparse grasses in an organized hierarchy. Their disparate digestive systems dictated the order of file. First, the zebras clipped off the coarse upper stalks, exposing the lower grasses for the wildebeests whose four-chambered ruminant stomachs extracted nutrients from the mid and lower portions. Finally, the diminutive Thompson's gazelles moved in behind munching the tender new shoots that emerged in the swath. The procession, Forrest had learned, was a perfect example of how species compliment each other in nature's grand plan.

Suddenly they were among the elephants, surrounded on all sides by giants. Forrest brought the Rover to a crawl. "Damn they're big!" he gasped. The vehicle had become another member of the herd as it moved along the edges of a large marshy area. The road bent to the left and the elephants continued right before immersing themselves up to their bellies in water thick with vegetation.

"We're almost there, laddy." McCullen announced, coming most of the way back to his usual cheery humor. "Another kilometer or so."

The road curved and twisted among thickets of date palms and passed through stands of acacias. Just ahead, Forrest saw the smoke from two camp fires and several *bandas*. He brought the Rover to a stop under a tree and shut the engine down.

A blond-haired woman dressed in cut-off jeans and a white cotton T-shirt emerged from a tent erected beneath a shelter of poles and thatched palm fronds. Forrest noticed several similar shelters among the trees.

"Morning, Dr. McCullen," the woman called out as she approached. Her hair, uncombed and pulled back into a hastily fashioned pony tail, was the color of new straw. Reading glasses hung on the end of a white cord suspended around her neck. Her outdoorsy, almost mannish face, appeared tired, her pace very slow.

"And a good mornin' ta' you, lassy!" McCullen squeezed her extended hand then stepped closer to give her a friendly hug. "And how are ya this fine day?"

"As well as can be expected," she said, her forced smile waning instantly. Forrest thought he noticed a trace of New York accent.

McCullen noticed her melancholy but ignored it for the moment. "I brought someone who needs to meet you," McCullen gestured toward Forrest. "Doctor Cynthia Marsh—John Forrest, Kenya's newest wildlife researcher."

Forrest smiled and extended his hand. "John Forrest. Pleased to meet you."

"If there's anyone who knows more 'bout pachyderms than Cynthia, I'd like to meet her." McCullen added, as proudly as if she was his own daughter. "She's mama tembo—mother of the elephants."

Marsh flashed an embarrassed smile at the newcomer.

Her handshake was very limp, Forrest noticed, even for a woman.

"Are you sure you're alright, Cyn? You don't seem at all well." McCullen's smile faded to a look of concern.

"Well..." she started reluctantly. "You could've picked a better day to come, frankly." She was friendly but preoccupied. She regarded the concerned stares from the two men for a moment before offering more. "Well...if you must know, I just learned that three of my bulls, three of the best breeders in Amboseli, were killed yesterday afternoon across the border." She tilted her head to the south toward Mt. Kilimanjaro and Tanzania. "Sorry." Her chin quivered "It's hard for me to talk about it." Her voice wavered at the verge of breaking.

"Poachers?" McCullen asked in a concerned, almost fatherly tone.

"Not this time. Trophy hunters. Morgan Richards, again; he and two wealthy American clients." Marsh looked down at the ground and towed the dirt with her boot. "Friends of mine, two baboon researchers, found one of the bodies just two miles from the Kenyan border; a clear violation of the formal agreement that puts elephants roaming the border area off limits."

Forrest made a mental note of the name. "Who's Richards?"

"A big game hunter, a damnable Brit who runs a safari company in Tanzania," McCullen answered, a mixture of pain and anger in his voice. "Charges $20,000 for a 21 day hunting safari." He turned back to Marsh. "I'm terribly sorry, lassy." He put his hand on her shoulder.

"*Legal* hunters?" Forrest asked, incredulously.

"Legal enough. They buy the permits in Tanzania." Marsh drew her fingers into angry fists and jammed them down into her pockets.

"I didn't think big game hunting was legal anymore."

"The government allows it because they can charge huge fees. They claim they use it to fund their conservation programs." They get $4,000 each for the 50 permits they allocate each year. That's $200,000 per year for 50 dead animals when *one* live animal can generate *twice* that amount as a tourist attraction." Marsh paused and sighed in frustration. "Some conservation program," she groaned, sarcastically. "The weasels would let them shoot their own mothers if there was enough money in it." Marsh muttered the bitter words under her breath. "I registered a formal protest with the Tanzanian government but I'm sure this one will be ignored just like the rest. If I make too much trouble for them, they'll restrict my access, maybe even revoke my visa. Anyway, they won't do anything about it. No one will."

"Maybe not," Forrest said quietly to no one in particular, his gaze fixed on the big mountain looming to the south.

"Nobody'll do anything about it 'til it's too late," Marsh repeated. There was desperation in her voice. "Who'll stop it if the government won't?"

"You never know," Forrest turned and looked her straight in the eye. "You never know."

An elephant trumpeted in the marsh and everyone turned to look.

At first Forrest wasn't sure but they seemed to be drifting in their general direction. "Are we standing in the middle of the expressway here, or what?" he asked, feigning a twinge of trepidation.

"Not exactly," Marsh answered with her best attempt at a chuckle. "We're coming up on the heat of the day and sometimes they like to hang out under the trees around my camp until evening."

Forrest smiled. "Cool."

"Cool, indeed." Marsh smiled back weakly.

As they stood watching the approaching herd, Marsh invited them to have lunch. The hungry men gratefully accepted.

"Hello Malcolm, my love," another feminine voice came from behind.

"Diane, darlin'. Glad you could join us!" McCullen responded before he turned around. When he did, he gave the woman a hug and a whiskery kiss on the cheek.

She drew her face back, feigning pain. "Ooh, Dr. McCullen, you old rogue. I told you before, I don't like beards."

"Alright then," McCullen laughed, "I'll shave it straight away."

"I've heard that before," Diane said with a sarcastic laugh.

McCullen introduced Forrest to the new arrival. "John, meet Dr. Diane Chernik, our lady of the elephants." As casually dressed as her colleague, Chernik stood five-foot-seven under a pageboy-cut of light brown hair. Pale blue eyes shone bright beneath the large round lenses of her eyeglasses.

They shook hands and exchanged pleasantries.

"Doctors, doctors everywhere, and not *one* can treat a paper cut," Forrest joked.

"Malcolm can, but you've got to have wool or a horn to be a patient."

More laughter.

Forrest, who stood facing the other three, was puzzled by the mischievous grins on everyone's face. Something was up, but he had no idea what. His eyes searched their faces for a clue.

Spissssh!

A strong blast of air sounded just behind him. Forrest jumped, startled by the noise. Before he could turn to see what it was, he felt a nudge against his back. Something big and powerful shoved hard between his shoulder blades driving him forward two steps. He turned just in time to come face to face with a writhing muscular appendage attached to a curious young elephant. Rough yet pliable, it wrapped around his head, the moist tip probing vigorously for scents.

"Jesus Tecumseh Sherman!" he gasped, at once shocked and amused. He was astonished that such a huge creature could have approached so quietly. He hadn't heard a sound. Pads of thick fibrous tissue cushioning their huge round feet made them as stealthy as a cat wearing Nike-Airs.

McCullen and the ladies burst into laughter.

"I think she likes you," Marsh laughed. "Or maybe it's your aftershave."

"Just plain nosy, I'd say," he grunted, wincing as the cold wet tip slid across his eyes and nose.

The young elephant knocked Forrest's brown felt hat off as she uncoiled her trunk and sniffed about his head and shoulders. Her big brown eyes were bright with curiosity. Her victim cooperated, standing still with his hands at his sides. He cast a nervous glance and an uneasy smile at the three scientists prompting another wave of laughter.

Chernik came to Forrest's rescue even though she could see he was enjoying the experience. She patted the elephant's face affectionately. "Ella's my sweetie," she cooed. "Aren't ya, baby?"

A moment later the young female moved aside as another, much bigger, female approached. A trunk, three times the size of the youngster's, probed Forrest's clothing with loud hisses of sucking air.

"I've been frisked before, but this is the first time I've ever been *vacuumed*," he laughed.

"This is Emma, Ella's mother," Chernik explained. "Actually she's Ella's adopted mother. Ella's an orphan. In fact almost all the elephants in Emma's family are orphans—even Emma."

"She's beautiful." Forrest touched the huge hose probing at his clothes, slowly running his hand over its course surface. Emma, he noticed, didn't seem to mind at all. She was friendly and curious, like a four-ton golden retriever. He could feel the organ's mass. It had to weigh several hundred pounds, he figured, yet she wielded it as if it was nothing. He respected its tremendous power. Used as a weapon, he realized, the trunk could easily have broken him in half. Yet she examined him with a tenderness and dexterity he wouldn't have thought possible.

Marsh moved to join them. She spoke melodious words to the huge beast and received a gentle rumble in return. Forrest could feel it in his chest. The gray lady was obviously enjoying the attention as much as the humans.

After a few minutes, curiosity satisfied, Ella followed Emma as she joined the rest of her family in the shade of the trees.

"Man!" Forrest whispered. "I don't know what a religious experience is supposed to feel like but that's got to be close."

Chernik smiled at him. "Mmm. For sure."

Forrest was entranced, for a time disconnected from the rest of the world. He stood motionless watching two elephant mothers pull down palm fronds for calves too small to reach them.

"If I can tear you away for a while, John," Chernik said with a knowing smile, "lunch is ready."

"Hmmm? Oh yeah. Sure." He smiled sheepishly as if he'd been caught sleeping in a high school English class. "Sounds good."

The four spent the next hour and a half dining on the salad and fruit Diane and the camp cook had prepared for their guests. Marsh explained that they had become vegetarians since they started their animal research. There wasn't a scrap of meat to be found at the table. "It seemed incongruous to us that we were trying to save animals only to turn around and eat them."

"Besides," Chernik chimed in, "as a trained biologist, I can tell you that human teeth were not designed to eat flesh."

Forrest and McCullen shared a guilty look for a second. Both loved their charbroiled steaks.

While they ate, they took turns giving brief biographical sketches of themselves—small talk mostly. The women were fascinated by Forrest's airline career; a fact that struck him as rather odd in perspective to their careers working in the wilds of Africa. Grass is greener syndrome, he thought with an inward smile. Chernik had once worked for the Kenyan government's ministry of Wildlife and Tourism. Frustrated with bureaucracy and politics, she had joined

Marsh's long-term elephant study seven years before. Marsh, he was surprised to hear, was once a journalist, a reporter for U.S. News and World Report magazine.

As the cook removed the empty plates, there was a commotion in a grove of date palms just behind the dining area. The sharp crack of tusks clacking together like two giants fencing with telephone poles carried across the clearing. Two young males, locked in mock combat, crashed through the thicket onto an area where mowed grass carpeted the ground. Immediately, two of the camp's Kenyan workers emerged from the cook shack beating on pots and pans and shouting at the top of their lungs. The elephants disengaged their tusks and intertwined trunks and stared at the noise makers. Their expressions seemed to be saying, "What? Who, *me*?" Other members of the family, alerted by the noise, entered the clearing to see what was going on. The mowed grass, Marsh explained, was a territory marker of sorts and the elephants had been conditioned to respect it.

"Well," she qualified with a dry laugh, "as much as you could expect from *any* ten thousand pound animal."

"Uh oh," Marsh said in a tone that was at once annoyed and amused. "It's Elmo and Eddie, again." She got up from the table and walked slowly in the intruder's direction. Everyone else followed a few paces behind.

"Ma'am," the cook said, warily, "they were about to trample the garden."

Rows of vegetables grew in parallel furrows only 20 paces from the closest elephant. Lengths of string stretched between wooden stakes marked the garden's perimeter.

With a wave of her hand, Marsh gestured for them to relax and back away. "It's okay, Jim. I'll take care of it."

Forrest and McCullen looked on in silence. Emma, they noticed, had come to the edge of the camp and stopped to tear off a clump of high grass near the base of a tree. She chewed contemplatively as she watched the proceedings.

"I don't know what's gotten into these two, lately," Marsh said over her shoulder. "They're just like ten year olds looking for trouble.

But then," she caught herself with a chuckle, "they are ten year olds. You two get away from the garden," she scolded loud enough that they knew she meant business but not loud enough to frighten them.

"Go on, now," Marsh commanded with a wave of her hand. "Git!" She turned around and covertly smiled at her guests as if she didn't want the bad children to see her amusement; like they wouldn't take her seriously if they did.

For a few seconds the two males just stared.

"Oh," Chernik exasperated, "would you look at that." Then she stifled a laugh.

"That's it," Marsh shouted, sternly. "I'm telling your mother."

Elmo waggled his head from side to side. Eddie, the co-conspirator, Forrest saw, followed suit. The two seemed to be laughing at the blonde-haired woman who took a demonstrative step forward and clamped her hands on her hips.

After a moment, Elmo, the instigator, lumbered over to the garden, seized a long length of string and made off for the cover of the brush. He waggled his head the whole way as if intensely pleased with himself. Eddie blasted an excited trumpet which was echoed by several others. Extended trunks sought the string from all directions as everyone attempted to check out the stolen treasure. All seemed to be delighted with the captured prize.

Forrest crossed his arms over his chest as the elephants trumpeted and screamed with joy. They raced around kicking up a cloud of dust. 'Wow!' they seemed to be saying, 'check this out, dude. *String!*'

Marsh and Chernik burst into laughter at the antics. McCullen and Forrest joined them.

Trumpets intermixed with rumbles and grunts as the elephants seemed to have to "talk" about this new thing they had discovered. Eddie wound several feet of string around his trunk. A young female straddled the opposite end then whirled in circles, winding it around all four legs. Emma casually sniffed at it with her trunk satisfying her own curiosity. The entwined female shrieked in delight, stepped free and ran off into the bush dragging the entire length of string behind her. Their sounds faded with them.

"That's the damndest thing I ever saw," Forrest gasped, his words garnished with laughter. "Any other animal would have taken one sniff, declared it inedible or non-threatening, and moved along. Not these guys, though. Amazing!"

"Not so amazing, really," Chernik replied, thoughtfully. "Not for a species as intelligent as they are."

Marsh walked over to join them. "And to think," she added, "all *that* over something as innocuous as a piece of string."

More chuckles.

"They're such wonderful creatures," Chernik exclaimed with an adoring sigh. "Nothing they do surprises me anymore." She looked at Marsh who shook her head in agreement. "We've seen them amuse themselves for hours with a stick or a bone. I've even played catch with a stolen shoe. One little male, Elias I think," Marsh nodded in confirmation as Chernik continued, "ran off with one of my sandals then tossed it back to me. I picked it up, threw it back, and he repeated the action several more times. When I got tired of playing the game and kept the sandal, he tossed half a dozen more things at me before he gave up. I know this is blatant anthropomorphism," she said, holding her hands up defensively, "but I *know* he enjoyed it. The same way a dog enjoys fetching a stick; only dogs can't throw it back."

"They make the smallest thing a big deal." Marsh explained. "But then *everything* elephants do is a big deal," she said laughing at her own pun. "For animals so big, they have an amazing regard for the smallest things. I've seen them step around tiny animals that cross their path. Or give wide birth to unusual things encountered in their environment like a discarded drinking cup."

"*If* they've been raised well by their mothers," Chernik added.

"Mothers *are* important," Forrest commented in a dismissive, patronizing way.

"No kidding," Chernik corrected, dropping her smile. "There is growing evidence of a serious problem because so many mothers have been killed."

Forrest gave her a quizzical look.

"In the last few years we've seen more juveniles attacking other animals for sport, usually orphans in fractured families where the senior leadership has been eliminated."

"Oh yeah? How come?"

"Their moms and the rest of the adult supervision have been lost to poachers or other causes.. That leaves no adults left to monitor their behavior and teach them the difference between right and wrong."

"We've found several rhinos that were gored to death by young, out-of-control males—juvenile delinquents." It was Marsh. "Poaching has more of a ripple effect than any of us imagined."

"I never would have guessed," Forrest responded with a grim look. His face shifted to a look of puzzlement as he formulated a question: "I'm new at this stuff. What is anthro...?"

Chernik answered. "An-thro-po-mor-phism, a no-no in the scientific community. That's when observers attribute human thoughts and feelings to non-human subjects. No matter how sure you are that an animal is feeling or thinking something, you can't state it in a scientific context. If you can't prove it empirically, it isn't science."

Forrest nodded. "Just because it can't be measured, doesn't mean it doesn't exist."

"True enough, lad," said McCullen. "But we have to be careful not to lose our objectivity. If we do, we'll lose our credibility along with it.

"Not with me, you won't," Forrest said. "I'm a believer, now." He looked back to the bare stakes surrounding the garden. "Three hours ago, I thought they were magnificent. Now, I think they're fantastic. Absolutely incredible."

"Now you know why Cynthia's been doin' it for twenty years," McCullen added. "These two recognize over seven hundred animals on sight."

"I've just never gotten tired of it," Marsh explained. "I forget they're animals sometimes. It's just like studying people, only more gratifying."

Forrest raised his eyebrows. "I can understand why."

Chernik's eyes caught a new guest emerging from the shade.

"It seems everyone is coming to camp today." A knowing smile of admiration crept across her face.

The humans all turned to look.

An immense bull had drifted to the edge of the camp, his movement very slow and labored. In contrast to his height it was immediately obvious that he was very old. Resembling a giant piece of leather luggage long abandoned in a dusty attic, the old man's lower left ear was shredded, his tusks broken and battered, his shoulder and rump bones protruding like poles supporting a large gray tent. Forrest noted he bore his years with great dignity like a distinguished public figure. The younger elephants, previously full of mischief, respectfully kept their distance.

Chernik made the introduction: "That's Elder. He's the oldest male I've ever seen—probably in his seventies."

Everyone's eyes remained on the aged bull as Chernik spoke.

"Usually bulls maintain an almost solitary life. It seems that since he's too old to cause problems, Emma and the senior females allow him to tag along with the family. Normally they wouldn't tolerate it."

As she spoke, Emma approached Elder and sniffed his head with her trunk. The tip of Elder's trunk seemed to be too heavy for him to lift, the lower half of it making feeble attempts to capture the kigelia tree branches suspended above his head.

When Emma twisted her trunk around a branch and pulled it down for Elder to reach, a collective "aawwwww" came from the human audience.

Forrest smiled in appreciation for an act most of his own kind would not commit for a stranger. He was sure no poacher would do it in any case.

"And to think men kill them for their teeth," Forrest muttered to no one in particular.

"Indeed," McCullen acknowledged almost under his breath.

"Or for bragging rights," Chernik added, an acerbic reference to the big game hunters she despised.

As Elder slowly chewed his lunch Forrest came back to a question which had come to mind after hearing all of the elephant names being tossed around. "How do you keep track of that many animals? How can you tell who's who?"

"We have a photo catalog and card file," Marsh answered. "Every elephant has distinguishing characteristics. Body size, shape, tusks—they're all different. We mostly use the irregular patterns of tears and scars in their ears to identify them. They're almost as good as fingerprints."

"And a wee bit more practical, I might add," McCullen chuckled, pointing to a large round footprint in the soil.

"Our file has been immensely helpful over the years, John," Chernik added. "If you intend to do any type of inventory, I suggest you make one too. We'll be happy to show you ours if you like."

"Sure, that would be..."

"John," McCullen interrupted. He noticed the sun was getting low and looked at his watch. "We really should be gettin' along, lad. It's not good ta be out in the bush after dark."

"Animals?" Forrest asked.

"Human animals, lad. *Shiftas.*"

Forrest made a puzzled frown.

"Bandits," Marsh chimed in. "There's been a rash of tourist robberies since the drought. A lot of them are Somalis. A bad bunch," she added, ruefully. "They're favorite M.O. is ambushing tourists in shiny new Land Rovers."

Forrest raised an eyebrow. He could see McCullen was genuinely concerned. "Okay, Doc. I'm ready to leave."

McCullen turned to the ladies and said his good-byes.

"Cynthia. Diane. Nice to meet you," Forrest said shaking their hands in turn. "I know where to come if I need help with my thesis."

"Anytime," Chernik offered. "Please don't feel shy about asking."

"I appreciate that."

"I mean it. Maybe you can return the favor one of these days." Marsh noted the cryptic smile that spread over his face—that same odd expression she'd noticed before.

"Maybe I can, at that."

****

The next day, another aerial search in the Cessna revealed nothing of Amy's whereabouts. He flew over additional lakebeds and every wisp of smoke within range hoping it was a signal fire.

"Zippo," he groused out loud. "I sure hope Peeper has a new hit, soon…for both their sakes."

Two days later, Forrest circled the edge of a large, dry lakebed several times looking for the best place to set the Cessna down. The surface had to be firm enough to support the weight of the plane. It also had to be clear of any obstacles that might damage the plane's balloon tires. Skeletal remains of a dozen antelope lay scattered over the basin. Forty meters from the edge, the color of the earth changed from greenish brown to chalky gray indicating a hard-baked surface. As good a runway as I'm likely to find, Forrest thought. He circled the basin twice more, trying to get a feel for the wind. Judging from the movement of the blowing dust and the plane's drift, Forrest set up his approach to the south. A minute later the little plane shuddered and rattled like a tin can as its wheels rolled over the cracked surface.

Forrest had spotted a huge baobab tree from the air and taxied the plane toward it, off the lake bed and into the dry grass. He taxied slowly to avoid hitting anything hidden among the weeds and grass. The undergrowth thinned out as he approached the shade of the one-tree forest. Venturing as far as he dared, Forrest revved the engine, locked the left brake and ground-looped the machine 180 degrees to point it back toward the lake. Dust and blades of dry grass swirled around the plane as he pulled out the red mixture knob, shutting the engine down. A quick glance at his watch: 14:24. He had made the trip with a little over 30 minutes to spare.

Forrest popped the door open and stepped onto the ground. He retrieved his Colt Anaconda from a zippered case which lay on the front seat and inserted it in a pouch slung across his chest. He patted his top shirt pocket, checking his signal mirror. After retrieving his binoculars from a pocket behind the right seat, he strode a few paces toward the lake and paused, watching the sky to the west and northwest. Forrest glassed the area, checking for any humans not visible from the air. With the exception of a few birds, nothing moved in the shimmering brush.

Twenty minutes later, Forrest turned his eyes back to the western horizon. Just above the hills to the west northwest, an object appeared trailing a faint stream of black smoke. It grew in size without changing its bearing—an indication it was coming straight for him. He looked at his watch. Right on time, Grizz, he thought as he reached for the signal mirror. Forrest smiled. He admired people of honor; dependable people who kept their word.

Peering through the aiming hole in the center of the mirror, Forrest flashed the oncoming plane to confirm the drop zone's location. The signal also told Adams the drop zone was cold—clear to drop. Forrest had chosen the site for its remote location and geographical features. The lake was surrounded on all sides by the Chyulu hills.

The gray Hercules descended to a hundred feet above the ground. The low altitude would hide the drop and prevent the chute from drifting. As it passed, a five foot long cylinder, about the size and shape of an oversized golf bag, tumbled out of the rear cargo door. A parachute inflated slowing the container from 150 knots to under 30 knots in less than a second. Four seconds later, it bounced onto the dry lake with a faint but audible thud. The chute stayed partially inflated for a moment in the 12 knot breeze before collapsing in a crumpled pile of olive drab nylon. Forrest waved as the L-100 continued off to the east toward Mogadishu, climbing into the afternoon sky.

Forrest walked out to retrieve the package, pausing to watch the plane disappear beyond the hills. He released the shroud lines and rolled the chute into a ball. The cylinder weighed over a hundred pounds and he had to alternately roll and drag it back to the baobab. After ten minutes of shirt-soaking work, Forrest and the container lay at the base of the tree.

Forrest retrieved an orange plastic chainsaw case and a jug of water from the back of the plane. He sat on the former and took a long drink from the latter, contemplating his next task. He retrieved two coils of climber's rope and a nylon-webbed climber's seat from the floor behind the front seats and tossed them on the ground under the base of the massive tree. He started the saw and let it run for a moment before shutting it down. Then, he tied the end of one of the ropes through the saw's handle and tied the other end to his climbing harness.

"Well, let's see what Santa brought me," he wondered out loud. Forrest released fasteners which held the container's lid in place. Next, he spread the parachute canopy on the ground like a picnic blanket. Carefully, he pulled a 10 inch foam plug from the end of the PVC container then methodically pulled the contents out of the end, one item at a time. He laid each piece of equipment out on the chute, checking for damage.

Twenty minutes later, Forrest took inventory. His ERMA sniper rifle lay next to ten, 50-round boxes of hand-loaded match grade ammunition. He counted ten fragmentation grenades and ten flash-bang grenades—the type used by SWAT teams to stun criminals. There were ten, 20-round boxes of .44 magnum hollow point ammunition and six Claymore antipersonnel mines. Included with the mines were trigger switches and arming wire. Wrapped around the rifle were four complete sets of tri-color desert cammo fatigues, a slouch hat and two dozen tubes of face paint crayons. Also in the assortment was a roll of olive drab cloth tape, two rolls of steel wire, two rolls of OD (olive drab) nylon parachute shroud line and a rifle cleaning kit. Among the last items in the container was a Heckler and Koch, MP-5 SD, submachine gun—the Mercedes of automatic weapons. The SD suffix indicated it had an integrated suppressor. Quiet as an old lady's fart, he thought with a smile. The weapon came with ten 30 round magazines and 500 rounds of subsonic 9mm ammunition. It did no good to silence the gun if the bullets created noisy shock waves as they broke the sound barrier. Peeper and Midas, he thought with a satisfied smile, had thought of just about everything.

"Looks like a World War III starter kit to me," he commented to himself. "Oughtta make a good first impression on some very bad bad-guys," he muttered, walking over to the solitary baobab.

For a moment Forrest stood with his head back and studied the immense example of botany run amok. The tree's size was staggering. It was over fifty feet tall and had a trunk that was nearly twenty five feet in diameter. The purplish-gray bark looked more like the skin of some mammoth animal than the bark of a tree. More than likely, he observed, it was several hundred years old. Some baobabs, he had read, lived for a thousand years, ranking them among the oldest living things on Earth. He could see at a glance why the native Africans had bestowed such mythical characteristics upon the trees. Called the "tree of life" by the natives, the baobab did have a wondrous and mystical presence about it. One of the native legends held that the Great Spirit gave each animal a tree to plant. Due to his late arrival, the hyena was last in line to receive its tree. And since the hyena was a none-too-fastidious animal, he mistakenly planted the tree upside down. Some of the natives even referred to it as the "upside down tree." Its twisted arboreal architecture did, indeed, look more like roots than limbs and branches.

Forrest unraveled the climber's rope and tossed a length of it over a limb nearly 15 feet above his head. He retrieved the end of the line and made a double loop. Taking a strain on the rope, he used it to walk up the side of the tree which felt more like walking up the side of a small building. He climbed onto a limb that was easily two feet in diameter. Another ten feet up in the tree, Forrest spotted a crevice which appeared to be suitable for his purpose. He flung the rope over another large limb and continued climbing. Since the immense trunk of the baobab was formed by several new trunks fusing together over many dozens of years, many crevices and compartments formed in between. He found one with an opening that was almost a foot in diameter and appeared to be several feet deep.

"Perfect."

Forrest secured the rope to his Swedish sling and tested it for

CHAPTER-EIGHT

PROMISE *a: an undertaking to do or not do something*
b: to give one's word
c: cause or grounds for hope

RAYBAN AVIATOR SUNGLASSES shielded Forrest's eyes from the harsh glare reflecting off the savanna haze. A molten-white sun beat down on scores of antelope and buffalo drifting under the Zenair's wings as Forrest steered a course to the west-southwest toward Lake Natron, just across the Kenyan border in Tanzania.

Henderson had plotted three camps occupied by poachers and transmitted the lat-longs. A week before, Kristine Goetz had seen no sign of activity in the area. In the last two days, however, the satellite imagery showed several fires at night where none had appeared previously. The fires were bigger than would be required for ordinary Africans to cook and boil water. And there were more fires than should be required for the number of people present in the camps. Daylight photography showed considerable signs of human activity along with the arrival of some trucks. Henderson wasn't certain, but the images indicated the presence of large lattices constructed with long wooden poles, the same type structures Forrest had said were used to cure "bush meat." A particularly well-timed image showed men carrying ivory into the largest of the three camps. In another, several tusks were clearly visible lying on the ground. Any doubts Henderson may have had evaporated in light of this unequivocal evidence.

Equipped with Henderson's intel, Forrest assessed his options. First, scout the area for any sign of Amy. She was apparently keen enough and in good enough shape to leave sign. The shoes dropped next to the tire tracks were strong evidence she'd been abducted, but the letters in the lake bed were too bold to have been made by a captive. Until Amy left another clue, Forrest had decided stalking poachers was the best bet. Taking on an entire camp full of armed men would be out of the question. Instead, Forrest elected to guard elephant herds most vulnerable to attack. He would use the elephants as bait and let the predators come to him.

Four miles from the nearest herd and a long mile from the most active village where ivory had been seen, a low, slow pass over the grass yielded a safe place to set down. Forrest found a spot near a large cluster of scrubby trees to hide the ZenAir. It took over an hour to hack enough thorny brush to build an all but impenetrable barrier around his plane, eat a sandwich and drink a quart of water.

Forrest donned his camouflaged fatigues and painted his face with the tan, green and black makeup sticks he carried in his pack. Checking to see that he hadn't forgotten anything, he took a compass bearing toward the elephant herds and started off in their direction.

He carried the ERMA in a camouflaged rifle case called a drag bag that hung over his shoulder next to his pack. For immediate access to firepower, if the need arose, he carried the H&K MP-5SD on a short sling across his chest.

Over the course of the next hour Forrest made his way to a place from which he could watch the camp for any evidence of Amy. His Zeiss binoculars made for good detailed viewing as he scanned the camp for telltale sign. A small party of armed men departed the camp, walking right past his position in the direction of his hidden plane. Though none resembled the faces from Nathan's video tape Forrest smelled poacher on them, nonetheless. He waited a few minutes then abandoned his position in an effort to get to the herd before they did.

At a brisk yet stealthy pace it would take him two hours to reach the herds. Haste would both tire him out and make him more visible. But he wanted to get to the target area ahead of them. And if anybody stumbled onto anybody, Forrest wanted to see them first.

Griffin vultures circling overhead were a sure sign that something on the ground was dead or at least, spinning around the drain. Forrest stood for a moment partially concealed in a thicket. He took a few sips of water from one of four canteens fastened to his web belt. It was stale and warm and carried the taste of its plastic container. But at least it was wet.

Although the sight of massing vultures was certainly not an uncommon sight in East Africa, something told him to check it out. Wherever there was a dead animal there might also be the predator which brought it down—a thought which gave him pause. Forrest thumbed the MP-5's selector switch from safe to full auto before venturing on. There was only one predator he had come to hunt. The others he would just as soon avoid.

Moving cautiously from thicket to thicket, it took 15 minutes to cover the distance to the vulture's anchor point. Several of the bald-headed birds leaped into the air as he approached. He moved the last few yards very slowly, careful to make no sound. Forrest had circled the area to approach with the breeze at his back. Unlike the hunters of animals, he wanted the diners to catch his scent and vacate the carcass as he approached. He was hoping the scent of man would make even the most tenacious scavengers think twice about a confrontation.

Through a thin spot in the leafy brush,. he caught the first glimpse of a young bull elephant carcass. He lay on his stomach, resting on his knees. Where its ears and tusks had been there were now only gaping holes and raw meat. Flies attracted by putrid juices buzzed around the body, clinging in thick clusters to exposed flesh. Nature assigned many agents to the grim business of reducing dead animals to bleached bones. Everything from lions to ants had evolved a niche in the food chain. And when their work was long finished, microorganisms living in the soil completed the nitrogen cycle begun by plants.

Forrest shook his head. Life, it seemed, was one big chemistry set. Elements became chemicals, which became organic chemicals, which became organisms, which evolved into fantastic creatures capable of almost anything. Then it would all collapse, coming full circle. It seemed ironic that species which once dined at the bottom of the food chain would find sustenance at the expense of an animal which existed near the top.

In life, adult elephants had no enemies except man. Plants, on the other hand, had many. Death had reversed that. It had a way of changing the rules. Death was the ultimate equalizer.

Forrest looked around the small clearing to size up the situation. Four spotted hyenas glared from the far edge of the clearing. They had retreated to cover when he approached, their ghoulish muzzles covered with a thick coating of fresh blood. Forrest tore at a Velcro fastener, lifting a flap covering one of four flash-bang grenades stored in his vest—just in case.

Although it appeared the elephant had only been dead a few hours, there were almost no signs of the humans who had butchered him. Any footprints had been obliterated by hordes of scavengers. A metallic glint caught his eye—brass casings, 39mm in length and necked to an opening of 7.62mm—AK-47 rounds.

Forrest stood quietly studying the dead elephant. Even lying on its belly, the animal dwarfed him, a mountain of flesh and bone. Its wrinkled skin was covered with flies and bird droppings, his flanks and rump coated with the same color dirt as the area's termite mounds.

He was most disturbed by the sight of the huge brown eye, frozen and glassy like a prized marble. It got to him, brought hot blood to his face. The size of a tennis ball, its edge was coated with a ring of busy flies. It was a cloudy window through which he was certain he could see the darkest side of man.

Forrest reached out and touched the elephant's forehead, gingerly at first, just with the tips of his fingers. After a moment, he laid the palm of his hand gently on the top of the animal's head, almost caressing it. There was something about touching that completed the connection, conveying more than sights or sounds. Even in death, Forrest could feel his strength. To look at, the animal was just... big. But to touch...he was immense. Solid. Powerful. Like touching the hull of a battleship and feeling its might in the steel. And even though the spark of life had left him, his presence still inspired awe. That such a treasure had been destroyed was unthinkable. That it might happen again, unacceptable.

Forrest patted the elephant's head gently. "It may be too late to save you, my friend. But, I promise you this: When I find the bastards that did this—and I will—I'll deal them the same hand they dealt you."

Forrest stopped to take a drink. He estimated he had traveled three miles in an hour, the terrain becoming more uneven in the last two. A mound rose 75 feet or more over the surrounding gullies and flat plain, a perfect spot from which to survey the surrounding landscape and get a fix on the elephants. Forrest crouched low as he climbed, careful not to silhouette himself against the sky. No matter how effective his camouflage, it would do no good against a brilliant blue background.

Upon reaching the top, Forrest dropped his pack and took a seat on the ground between two large boulders. He retrieved his powerful Zeiss binoculars from his backpack and scanned the area. None of the men he had spotted leaving the camp were visible. Four hundred meters to his 11 o'clock, a small group of elephants, or jumbos as the Africans called them, grazed peacefully on grass shoots and tender leaves. They had not moved very far in the last two hours. Grazing animals followed food and water, moving only when they ran out of one or the other. Unless they're threatened, he thought.

Forrest put the glasses down for a moment and leaned his tired back against the boulders. It was well past 3:00 PM and he didn't hold out much hope for an encounter before dark. Pleased to have found such an ideal set up on his first "combat mission," he prepared himself for the possibility anyway. He slid the ERMA out of the drag-bag and loaded five rounds, careful not to damage the yellow plastic tips. The hard plastic helped insure that the tip of the bullet would not be deformed during loading or chambering and thus, affect its aerodynamics. Even a tiny dent or deformity could throw the projectile's flight off by an inch or more at long ranges. After checking the rifle over, he laid it out on a neoprene mat. He took another, smaller piece of heavy canvass out of his back pack and laid it out on the ground below the point where he estimated the end of the rifle barrel would be when it was shouldered and ready to fire. Left uncovered, fine particles of dust would be sucked up from the ground by the low pressure area created by the expanding, then collapsing sphere of gases. The canvass would prevent a telltale dust cloud from forming when he fired, revealing his position.

After all of his gear was arranged to his satisfaction, he unrolled another essential piece of equipment. Forrest had constructed a ghillie suit, a lighter version of the ones worn by military snipers. He had woven a patchwork of green, tan, brown, and olive drab fabric strips into a backing of quarter-inch fishing net. Mop-like tufts of twine varied the texture and filled gaps. He had no idea when the poachers might show so he pulled the "tree tux" on as a precaution.

Forrest placed his pack so it could double as a pillow and a shooting rest. Preparations complete, he made a few touch ups to his face paint and settled down for dinner. The evening's entrée: saltines, peanut butter and water. His appetite satisfied, he evaluated his position, looking for ways to improve it. As an extra measure, Forrest spent some time cutting thorny brush to pile around his hide. Like natural barbed wire, it would offer more concealment and provide a barrier to animals with the soft noses and sharp teeth.

Though disappointed his quarry had not appeared, he knew that humans could be as unpredictable as animals. It was almost dark when he finished his preparations. Thoroughly exhausted from the long hike and work on his "hide," Forrest pulled out a roll of camouflaged mosquito netting and hung it tent-like from the thorny branches. Carefully, he crawled inside and stretched out for the night. Sleep did not come easily. But after a several false starts, he drifted off, his submachine gun clutched in his arms like a black steel Teddy Bear.

Forrest was awake before dawn, startled back to consciousness by a large agama lizard skittering across his legs. He sat up groggy and stiff, at first not quite remembering just where he was. His sleep had been tormented at best. It had been years since he had slept on the ground under the stars. Annoying insects, muscle cramps and recurring dreams filled with blood and bugs had made for a fitful night.

Forrest rubbed his eyes and yawned. "What have you gotten yourself into, here?" he asked himself under his breath. He stretched and worked the knots out of his aching limbs. He reached into his backpack for his binoculars and rolled over onto his stomach. Careful not to tear the netting on the thorns, he pulled it away from the top of his head and rose up for a look. The rising sun highlighted thin wisps of ground fog which had formed during the night over the marsh. Through the mist, he could see the elephants moving toward a large muddy pond. Four groups congregated within 200 meters of his hide. He watched for a while in fascination as the gray giants greeted each other with grumbles and probing trunks. Mothers attended to calves, two of which were nursing hungrily. The females stood patiently while the youngsters drank the rich, fatty milk. The babies worked their mouths rhythmically at their mother's breast, their trunks tucked back over their heads to keep them out of the way.

Satisfied that he had considered all contingencies, Forrest returned to observing the elephants and other animals which were beginning their day on the plain below. Although the animals regarded each other warily, they showed little concern for species they knew to be non-threatening. Gazelles followed zebra as they moved along, slowly grazing on what grasses remained on the plain.

For the most part, species stayed together in small herds or groups of their own kind. Herding behavior in mammals evolved in much the same way schooling behavior evolved in fish. Both relied on the "safety in numbers" principle for protection from predators. Zebras were perhaps the most effective at the "numbers" defense, using the confusion of a fleeing mass to deny attacking lions a single victim. They had also evolved an added twist in a world of camouflage: stripes. Stripes offered no camouflage against the surrounding terrain but was quite effective at blending one animal into a dynamic background of many others. A swirling black-and-white kaleidoscope overwhelmed a predator's optical processing capacity frustrating the target selection process. To observers outside the struggle, the defensive strategy might not appear to be very effective. But from a pursuing lion's point of view, it was like trying to tackle a single football player amidst a moving mass of bodies, all wearing the same uniforms and colors and all moving in different directions. A millisecond of confusion often made the difference between a narrow escape and a clean kill.

For over an hour Forrest watched wildlife following daily routines. Dining alternated with vigilance. But the elephants were the first to notice them as they approached. Forrest was alerted by their body language as raised trunks sniffed the morning breeze. A light wind blew from his right front so he was certain that the animals had not detected his scent. Some of the animals spread their ears and turned to face the breeze. Mothers with small calves decided not to wait. Taking no chances, they hurried their calves into the cover of thorny thickets. Forrest noticed that the elephants seemed to sense the alarm almost simultaneously. They seemed to be communicating with each other, spreading the word as it were, that something dangerous had entered their area.

Forrest picked up on signs of anxiety. Like the creatures below, he prepared himself for whatever had cast its scent on the morning breeze. Carefully, he laid the ERMA down on the mat and crawled into position. Propped up on his elbows, Forrest traversed his powerful binoculars back and forth looking for a sign. Some of the gazelles and zebras moved off to his left, down wind, increasing the amount of open ground between themselves and the thickets.

A flock of doves bursting skyward gave Forrest his first clue as to their whereabouts. He let the binoculars drop to the mat and reached for the rifle. He worked the bolt, chambering a round. Forrest substituted the rifle's optical sight for the binoculars, panning to acquire the target. Movement caught his attention. He steadied the rifle on the spot and froze, his heart raced at the prospect of firing his first shot.

Another shadow spirited through the brush. He lost track of the other animals as he concentrated on the quarry. If they continued on their present course, he predicted they would emerge in a small clearing 450 meters in front of him. Forrest snugged the rifle into his shoulder and waited. Another movement at the edge of the scope's field of view broke his concentration. He moved the crosshairs. Forrest held them steady over a vague object half hidden at the edge of the brush. A bead of sweat trickled down his left temple. Ignoring the discomfort, he tightened his position and waited, bracing himself for the recoil.

There! Three men were making their way toward the elephants. Through the scope, it was easy to see their rifles. Two of them were armed. His mouth suddenly went dry. The targets were dressed in well worn civilian clothes, not uniforms. Shooting game wardens by mistake would be unacceptable.

Forrest followed their approach and tried to predict the path they would take.

The elephants had grown wary of human scent. They had lost members of their family to poacher's guns before and were doing their best to put some cover between themselves and the approaching humans.

Forrest studied the men through the scope. Any doubts about their intentions vanished when one pointed toward the elephants and signaled a split. Then he disappeared into the brush. The other two started a flanking maneuver, attempting to stay on the elephant's down wind side. Forrest tracked them. One carried a rifle he had not seen too often, an FN-FAL. It had open sights and a large magazine to hold its .308 cal ammunition. It was capable of fully automatic fire and Forrest knew it had enough range to reach his position. The weapon presented his biggest threat therefore Forrest decided to take the man with the Belgian-made assault rifle out first. He lowered the rifle and brought the binoculars to his eyes. He steadied them on the quarry and pressed a button. An invisible laser measured the range and produced a readout in his field of view: 380 meters. When the first shot had to be a hit, accurate range was essential. Forrest factored in wind velocity and made the appropriate windage and elevation adjustments to his scope. This would be a "cold bore" shot which would always be a factor for the first 2 rounds fired. The rifle was, by necessity, sighted in for a warm barrel after firing 5-10 rounds. The temperature of the steel barrel affected the metallurgy and shifted the point of aim a measurable amount. For long shots it could be a significant consideration. But, for a 380 meter shot it would not be something to worry about. The rifle's cold bore would not be nearly as important a factor as the shooter's cold blood.

The two men paused for a moment, assessing their position relative to the elephants. They peered around the bushes to get a look, planning their attack.

He had to make quick work of them, he thought, as he tightened the rifle's black composite stock against his shoulder. It had been 24 years since he had laid crosshairs over a man and fired a shot in anger. Back then it was just business—survival. This time it was personal. And anger, he decided, was reason enough. His blood boiled with the vision of Nathan's grave—of the tatters of Amy's little pink jacket—the heartbreak in his best friend's eyes. And he remembered yesterday's promise to that elephant and Colonel Grant before that. When Forrest pulled the trigger, the bullet he unleashed would be propelled down the barrel as much by his simmering rage as by the expanding gases of burning powder.

He could feel the adrenalin pumping, his pulse pounding in his ears. Forrest took a deep breath and let it out. A flick of his right thumb removed the safety.

The two men crouched for a moment to discuss their approach to the elephants. *Thank you gentlemen. You just made this job a little easier.* If I do this right, he reasoned, I'll drop the first one and knock the second one off balance long enough to get off a second shot.

Like a billiard player, Forrest wanted his first shot to leave him an easy second. He drew the sight to the right and centered the crosshairs on the man's spine. His back was almost perpendicular to Forrest's line of fire. Squeezing the trigger slowly, he waited for...

BOOM!

Forrest ignored the sound and the recoil. Through the scope, he watched the bullet tear into the man's khaki shirt just to the left of his spine. The poacher went down in a heap, face first, knocking the other man back on his hands and butt. In less than a second, Forrest cycled the bolt and shifted the scope to his stunned companion who presented a sideways aspect. Correcting a little to the right, he lined up on his left breast pocket and squeezed the trigger.

BOOM!

A split-second later, the bullet ripped through the upper torso, exploding tissue and bone. Human anatomy offered little resistance to the devastating energy carried by the high-speed projectile. Both lungs collapsed. His arms folded at the elbows dropping him onto his back like a sack of fertilizer.

Satisfied that the first two targets were no longer a consideration, Forrest quickly shifted his scope, searching for the third. He panned the rifle around slowly stopping briefly at likely places of concealment.

The shots had panicked the nervous elephants. They screamed in terror and stampeded into the thickest brush they could find. Zebra and gazelles bounded in all directions into the open savanna.

Judging from the way the third man popped up from his hiding place, Forrest could tell that he didn't have a clue as to what was happening. He thought his friends had fired the shots. A frightened elephant ran through the brush right in front of him, not ten meters distant. The third man stood frozen for a moment not sure what had happened or what he should do. That moment's hesitation was all Forrest needed. He steadied his sights on the target's chest and squeezed off another round. The bullet cut through the sternum, severing the major arteries at the top of the heart. His back exploded as the projectile exited between two ribs. His assault rifle tumbled out of his hands as the man slumped into the thorn bush to his left. His limbs twitched with spasms triggered by a blood-starved brain and severed spinal chord. A minute later, he was still.

Forrest was confident all of his shots had hit their mark. All were well-placed to destroy vital cardiopulmonary systems. He studied the bodies for several minutes through the scope. No movement. He knew that shot through the torso, the average man would bleed to death in 4 to 5 minutes. Forrest looked at his watch and decided he would wait thirty. He couldn't afford to approach a wounded man who still had the capability to do him harm. And, he reminded himself, there was also the possibility that there might be more.

He leaned back against the rocks and sipped from a canteen. Then he packed his gear to pass the time. He slid the ERMA back into its case and picked up the three spent casings. No clues, no signs, no evidence. It took another five minutes to cover his gear with brush. A final scan of the area with the binoculars revealed nothing new. The animals were settling down again, a sure sign that he was, once again, alone.

Forrest left his pack and rifle and worked his way down the hill, taking only the MP-5, his machete, and a black plastic garbage bag. The veteran sniper took a slow and circuitous route to examine his victims. It took 15 minutes, moving from one patch of brush to another, to reach the first two men. Forrest stood a few paces away for a moment, looking for signs of life. No movement. No respiration. Appropriately enough, he noted, they lay among fresh, grapefruit-size elephant droppings. Moving closer, covering them with MP-5, he prodded the bodies with the toe of his boot. They were as dead as they were going to get.

Forrest went through the men's pockets. There wasn't much to find. The man with the FN-FAL had a few shillings in his pocket which Forrest took and stuck into his own. He went over the bodies turning their pockets inside out. Poor men who poached animals for a living would not leave anything of value on their victim's bodies.

He picked up the FN and leaned it against the stout trunk of a nearby bush.

Minutes later, he found the third poacher. Forrest dragged the body out of the bush by his feet and repeated the routine, rummaging through his pockets, turning them inside out. The men carried no food and very little water. Apparently, they had planned to make it a short trip and live off the land—then make a quick return to their village. *Well, you bastards are gonna do just that...in a manner of speaking.*

He stood for a moment looking at the poacher. A coating of flies buzzed over his blood saturated T-shirt. Lifeless eyes, glazed and fixed, stared into infinity. They weren't the faces he was looking for but they were probably the ones who'd killed the elephant he had found, he told himself.

Forrest drew his machete from its scabbard and raised it over his head. With all of his strength, he brought the well-honed blade down on the dead man's wrist. A second deft whack severed the bone. Forrest scooped the hand up in the plastic garbage bag and twisted it closed. Then he removed the other hand in a similar fashion. He picked up the AK-47 and fired a burst into the corpse, leaving the spent casings where they fell. With the garbage bag slung over his shoulder, he returned to the first two bodies where he repeated the surgical procedure and the fireworks, riddling the bodies with bullets, depositing hands in the plastic bag.

Using lengths of the parachute shroud line he carried in his pack, Forrest fashioned slings for the poacher's rifles and slung them over his shoulder. He didn't have much use for the AK-47 but he didn't want it to find its way into another poacher's hands. In any case, no bandit would leave the valuable weapon behind. If the police found the bodies, however unlikely, the evidence would have to be consistent with a bandit attack or a firefight with another gang of poachers. Better still, he thought, I could play both ends against the middle, pitting one gang against another. He left the bodies for the vultures and jackals; a fitting method of disposal. After all, that's what his son's murderers had done, wasn't it?

* * * *

The gunshots had startled her awake from a badly needed nap. A twinge of panic shot through her. *Could it be them?*

Instantly, Amy's fingers went to the spear as she strained to determine the direction from which they came. Wedged for protection into a crevice between boulders at the base of a rocky outcropping, distant sound was difficult to track—especially through the thorny branches she'd piled in front of the opening to deter carnivores. But the shots sounded fairly close—perhaps less than a mile away. Under other circumstances her instincts would have drawn her toward the gunfire in order to find help. Human contact, after all, would be wonderful after days and days alone in the bush. And they could well have food and water. What she wouldn't give for something more substantial than the sun-dried lizard meat she'd consumed earlier that afternoon. And even that had left her stomach churning. *Sure as hell didn't taste like chicken.*

After considerable deliberation, Amy decided to avoid the gunmen altogether. Just can't take the chance, she decided. The next time I see a poacher I want to be carrying a gun of my own.

It had taken nearly five minutes to climb to 6,000 feet after a lengthy yet fruitless air search for his daughter-in-law. Forrest adjusted the throttle and stared past the glow of instrument lights into the growing darkness. No moon and a smooth ride made the sky seem like a sheet of black satin. Stars twinkled like distant buoys on an endless sea. The pulsating glow of widely scattered fires merged with the bright stars, all but eliminating the horizon. A few miles ahead—4.7 according to the GPS receiver—Forrest could see several large fires marking the camps he had located the previous day. According to Henderson's intelligence, at least two of them were definitely poacher's camps and the other two were probables. Forrest steered a heading for the closest cluster of light. It didn't really matter which ones were which, he reasoned. They would all get the message sooner or later.

Confederate General Nathan Bedford Forrest's words came back to him: "Put the skeer into 'em and keep the skeer in 'em."—his infamous ancestor's description of psychological warfare.

"That's exactly what I'm going to do, General," he said to the instruments.

Before breaking camp and uncovering the Zenair, Forrest had prepared his "psyops package" for delivery. Included with the container Adams delivered, Henderson had provided a deck of cards; special cards. The size of regular business cards, the word "poacher" was printed on plastic card stock in five different languages. Forrest had placed a card into each of the six hands, closed the fingers over it, and bound the fingers in place with a piece of string. The message was simple and direct: anyone caught killing endangered animals would meet a swift and horrible end.

Forrest rolled out on a heading which would take him directly over the first camp. He set the autopilot for "Heading Hold" and throttled back to begin a descent, freeing both hands for the delivery.

Forrest opened the pop-out side window. Rushing wind doubled the noise level as he set the garbage bag in the other seat and opened the top. A foul odor poured out of the bag, filling the plane's interior—a stench that made the task even more disagreeable than he first imagined.

The descent bottomed out at 2,000 feet directly over the camp. He released the severed hands.

He glided two miles before easing the power up, initiating an easy climb. Forrest left the windows open for a few minutes to blow out lingering fetor. Once he leveled off at altitude, Forrest banked the Zenair toward Camp Uhura and closed the window. It would be good to get some sleep, he thought, now that he didn't have to worry about animals with big teeth and bad attitudes. The best part was he had taken out his first poachers and, better still: he'd kept his promise.

CHAPTER-NINE

BUREAUCRAT *a: an official of a bureaucracy*
b: an official who works by fixed routine without exercising intelligent judgment

ALMOST FORGOTTEN WHAT a luxury warm lather can be, he thought. John Forrest, clad only in BVDs and hot foam, stood shaving over a porcelain bowl—the blade of his disposable BIC whisking off the last of three day's growth.

"Who are you and what are you doing in my hut?" The heavily accented female voice came from behind, dripping with acid.

Forrest turned slowly to face its source. A tall woman dressed in a military-like KWS uniform complete with epaulettes stood five feet from him, her arms folded across her chest. Her green eyes blazed with annoyance.

Forrest's only immediate response was an incredulous stare.

Her eyes went to the lather dripping off his chin and then back to his half-shaved cheeks.

"Sorry lady, I ordered a blonde, not a brunette. But the cop outfit's a nice touch." Forrest went back to shaving—his eyes watching the intruder in his mirror. "Very kinky, by the way. Did you bring cuffs?" he added with as much disinterest as he could feign. She had a plain but mildly attractive face. Her hair was pulled up into a uniform baseball cap concealing whatever femininity she may have possessed. A smile crept across his face when he saw her eyes go to his butt for a second before she turned on a heel and left.

Forrest shook his head and laughed to himself silently. He finished shaving, dressed in his usual Polo shirt, shorts and Docksiders then went outside to investigate.

A light green Land Rover with Kenyan government signage on its doors was parked beneath the sausage tree next to the picnic table, its driver nowhere to be seen.

"John. John. Come over here." It was McCullen.

He turned to see the flustered lady storm trooper and the Doc standing on the latter's porch.

McCullen waived. "John, there is someone I'd like you to meet."

Forrest felt a wave of dread pass over him. *This oughtta be interesting.* He stepped off his own porch and strode over to McCullen's.

"Anne, I'd like to introduce you to John Forrest. John, Dr. Anne Sargent-Windridge, Field Inspector for the Kenyan Wildlife Service. She's here to check on the camp and see how our research projects are coming along."

Forrest extended his hand but his eyes went to McCullen. "We've already met."

McCullen wore a nonplussed look.

Sargent frowned, turned her eyes to McCullen and started to speak.

Forrest cut her off with a contemptuous laugh. "I believe Dr. Sargent was trying to have me evicted—something about her hut."

"Oh, dear. Yes, quite." McCullen, flustered, cleared his throat and turned from Forrest to Anne, his face turning three-drink crimson. "My apologies, dear. I forgot to tell you. We've moved your things to the guest hut. Since John's going to be with us for a while, I thought it best if he used the permanent-party facility. It's a bit bigger and he has quite a lot of equipment."

She started a second protest but Forrest interrupted: "Right, Doc," he taunted with a smirk. "And I believe she's already seen the best of it."

Sargent glared at the American, on the edge of losing her composure.

McCullen was clueless. "Am I missing something?"

Anne gave a huff of exasperation, clearly frustrated and embarrassed with the fun Forrest was having at her expense.

Noting her discomfort, Dr. McCullen intervened, "I've brewed up some tea. Why don't we go over to the picnic table and have some?" He motioned for the lady inspector to proceed ahead. As she turned to lead the way, McCullen glared at Forrest. Grabbing the American by the upper arm, he detained him for a moment, "Really, John!" he hissed through clenched teeth. "Lighten up a little." McCullen dug his fingers into Forrest's arm to emphasize his point. "This lady is a dear, close friend of mine."

Forrest looked at McCullen with softening eyes, sorry he had angered his friend. It was the first time Forrest had seen Malcolm lose his temper. "Sorry Mal, but she started in with *me!* I was just standing there in my skivvies, shaving, minding my own damn business, and she pounced on me like some wet cat with PMS."

"Oh dear," the elderly Scotsman sighed.

"Besides, I just have a thing for bureaucrats, especially bossy, *female* bureaucrats," Forrest muttered.

"Now see here, my chauvinist, American friend," McCullen glared up at Forrest. "I don't know what your problem is, but you *will* be polite and cooperative with *this* lady bureaucrat as long as you are working out of this camp. Lord knows she can be trying at times. She has personal problems at home. But astonishing as it may seem, Dr. Sargent is an excellent field researcher and can be a great deal of help to you in your work. She is well known and well respected by the faculty at Texas A & M, our sponsor, and many other universities throughout the world. It would do you a lot of good to listen very carefully to everything she has to say." McCullen gave Forrest a friendly slap on the back and broke into a warm smile. "Come on, now. Let's go mend a few damaged first impressions."

"I'm not much good at mending things, Malcolm."

"Well, you'll just have to learn how."

"We'll see."

The lady inspector sat across the table from him, leafing through a file folder, Forrest's name penned in longhand on the tab. The manila folder showed little wear. A good sign, he thought. The less they knew the better.

She had not spoken a word since they had started their "audit." Judging by the look on her face, the silence wasn't accidental. You had to work at it to be that quiet. She was a stoic one, this lady inspector. Her annoyance was palpable and, try as she might, she wasn't very good at hiding it.

Forrest studied her poker face with inward amusement. He didn't like "officials" and never had. And lady officials particularly annoyed him. They had a way of being especially rigid and condescending in their adherence to regulations and procedures—void of common sense. Usually, there was no dealing with them. Men, on balance, were a little more reasonable, though; perhaps a little more corruptible and therefore more malleable. At least they could tell the difference between pepper and fly shit and were willing to make adjustments.

Forrest waited, outwardly patient, doing his best to control his temper. He didn't like wasting time; being held hostage by people bestowed with limited amounts of power and possessed of unlimited self-importance. Time was life's only irreplaceable commodity. *I'm sitting here killing time when I should be out there searching for Amy and hunting poachers!*

Offending this lady might work, he reasoned—get her to go away. After all, the best defense might be to be as offensive as possible. *If so, I'm off to a good start.* She certainly seemed thin-skinned enough. *If so, she's going to be easy—just like playing with a cat's tail.*

The silent treatment continued for several more minutes as she shifted through his papers. Maybe she was just trying to regain her composure before she continued the interview. Maybe she was just playing mind games. Probably. Maybe she simply wanted to review his file completely before she went on to something else. Probably not. Making him wait demonstrated control—power. And, for the moment, his time was her time.

Her eyes moved behind her horn-rimmed glasses scanning the various documents, the reflections of which he could see on the surface of her lenses. Occasionally she stopped reading long enough to make a note somewhere within the layers of officialdom. *That's it. Take as long as you want. I can wait as long as you can.*

He passed the minutes assessing the woman sitting across from him at the picnic table. She was as plain as a sheet of typing paper. If she had a personality it definitely didn't reflect in her appearance. Like himself, she appeared to be in her early forties—old enough to be past playing games. Overall, he noticed, the years had been kind to the inspector. There were a few lines here and there—a smidge too much exposure to the African sun. Makeup was nonexistent, no eyes, no lips, no cheeks. Her fingernails were neatly clipped but no longer than a man's. Aside from her plain silver wedding band she wore no jewelry whatsoever. Unless, of course, you would consider the waterproof, black plastic, man's wristwatch to be jewelry. The clothing, or uniform, was pure L.L. Bean—very androgynous. Definitely a plain-brown wrapper, he judged. Was it a requirement, a functional necessity, or a fashion statement—an extension of her personality?

"Your research permit says you have been here for two weeks," she stated, shattering his musings. "Is that correct?"

"Hmm?"

"I said, your work permit indicates your date of entry to be almost two weeks ago." Her tone was short and curt. The British accent gave it an additional edge.

"That's right." He was on guard now. This was an interrogation.

"My records indicate your project has to do with effects of human population on elephant populations, birth rates and mating behavior. Is that correct?" Dr. Sargent spoke like a prosecuting attorney.

"Isn't that what it says?"

"*I'll* ask the questions, thank you," she snapped, peering over the top of her glasses.

Forrest stared her down until she looked away. “There’s a copy of a letter in there from Texas A and M. It explains, in English by the way, my thesis and research.”

Her nostrils flared slightly. “How long do you anticipate the project will take to complete?”

“Don’t know for sure.”

“How long do you plan to stay here? Your permit is only good for a year.”

“As long as it takes.”

Dr. Sargent was becoming frustrated. The interview wasn’t going well. Most researchers were only too happy to share their projects with her. This man was being deliberately evasive. Why? She sighed, exasperated. She stared at the American for a moment, sizing him up. He was a handsome man, not a lady killer by any stretch, but ruggedly handsome, nevertheless. He didn’t have the refinement typical of a college professor or academian. She detected something dark and brooding in this man. He was curt and edgy and something in his eyes was even a little frightening. Again, why? Never in her life had she encountered anyone that she had so instantly disliked. Yet, for all of his unpleasant aspects—and there were an abundance of them—there was something intriguing about him.

Amy Lee was near the end of her endurance. What was left of her clothes barely grasped her dangerously narrow waist. Heat, stress and hunger were fast grinding her down, literally to the bone. Her ribs felt as though they would poke through her skin. She trudged along to the west, mechanically putting one foot in front of the other, telling herself rescue in the form of a human structure of some kind was just a few miles away and each step put her that much closer to food and water.

Ahead in the brush, just 200 meters distant, Amy spotted a small family group of elephants. They were eyeing her warily as she plodded toward them occasionally stumbling on rubber legs. She was trying to decide which way she would circumnavigate them when she thought she heard a rumble from behind. She wondered for a moment if it was her stomach.

No. That was a growl!

The weary figure stopped and slowly turned in the direction of the sound, her senses now on red alert. She scanned the high grass, her forearms tingling with tension. Her hand felt for the knife she kept tucked in her waistband, the other tightened around the spear's shaft. Then she heard it again and caught a glimpse of a large straw-colored cat, moving in the grass.

"Oh God," she gasped. *Lions!*

She turned back on course, walking fast, holding back the urge to run. That would for sure trigger their pursuit instinct, she reminded herself. *Dad said 'never run from a predatory animal.'* But these were lions, for God's sake! *He never said anything about freakin' LIONS!*

Amy breathed hard as she put as much distance between her and the carnivores as she could at an Olympic fast-walk pace. A look back over her shoulder told her it wasn't working. Three lions were intermittently visible and moving stealthily yet deftly in her direction.

The elephants were watching the unfolding drama with increased tension. Their trunks rose in the air to sniff for scents.

Amy was a mere hundred meters from the elephants when the lions began to trot, their ears now turned and tuned ahead along with their rapt focus.

"Oh shit, shit, shit!" she screeched as she broke into a run.

She stumbled, fell and instantly caught herself with her hands then lunged ahead without noticing that her knife had slipped out of her pants and fallen silently into the grass.

The young widow glanced back, almost running sideways as the lions closed on her.

Amy uttered a desperate gasp and stumbled forward into a hard run. She eyed the elephants, wondering if they would turn and run or hold their ground given the mixed bag of danger coming at them through the crisp grass. She considered her options frantically—the conclusion awful: there was not a tree anywhere and no cover. She would have to stand and fight when the animals got close enough.

Her hand instinctively went for her knife.

"Oh Jesus," she cried breathlessly, when neither hand could find the handle.

The lions were only ten meters behind her pumping legs. She abruptly halted, wheeled, then flung the spear at the closest cat, which halted and defensively reversed course for a moment. All stood still for a bit, considering their next move, panting in the intense heat.

Amy used their hesitation to put some distance between herself and the stalkers. As she ran, she took a long, hard look at the elephants standing their ground in front of her. The adults' ears were spread wide as they formed a semicircular line between the approaching predators and their two young calves. They too, knew that running was not a good option. It would only make their calves more vulnerable.

Amy made a quick situational assessment. *Only two options on the menu: get trampled or eaten.*

The lions were nearly at her heels when she threw herself on the ground only five meters in front of the largest elephant. She tucked into a ball and waited for the inevitable.

Instantly, the matriarch sensed that the human in a defensive posture was no longer a threat. She charged at the lions, tusks down-trunk up, swinging her head and ivory from side to side like huge clubs.

The lions halted in their tracks and turned hard away. A coordinated second charge from the matriarch's sister sent them reeling back into the grass for cover.

Amy lay as still as she could, much too frightened and exhausted to move. Without turning her head, even a millimeter, she strained to see what was happening. A spasm shot through her body when the matriarch let out a huge blast of air as a show of strength and defiance. Her sister charged into the grass a few meters sending the lions back in broken formation. Sensing that the attack's momentum had been quashed and their advantage gone, the most feared of Africa's capital predators retreated from sight.

Amy lay shaking as she felt a huge trunk pass over her; puffs of air that smelled of digested grass and leaves wafted past her nostrils. A fearful spasm shot through her as a cold drop of mucus fell on her cheek.

What will it feel like to be crushed beneath one of those huge feet?

After what seemed like an eternity she found the courage to slowly turn her head and assess the situation. The elephants, with amazing silence, had vanished into the brush.

It was the quiet time before the coming of dawn, the coolest part of the day. Forrest took the pot of boiling water off the camp stove and poured it into a cup containing freeze-dried coffee crystals. The savory aroma carried to his nose on the rising steam. After adding liberal doses of powdered cream and sugar, he took his first sip. The hot liquid bit him back. Grimacing, he looked up at the reddish-gold cumulus floating overhead and fondly remembered the countless morning flights when a smiling face had brought the captain his first cup of the day. He always enjoyed sipping at a hot cup while layers of clouds drift lazily under his airliner's nose. *If I had it to do all over again I'd never complain about another cup of airplane coffee. Well, almost never.* Forrest smiled at the thought. Funny thing, memories, he mused. The mind had a marvelous way of selectively recalling the best and the worst of the past. Interesting, he thought, how a song or an aroma can conjure up recollections from the dustiest parts of the brain.

Back to reality. Today was to be a research day and today he had to make notes—eyewash for a lady inspector who wanted to check his homework. And, she had told him in no uncertain terms, he was also going to have company on some of his future outings. Not good, he decided, definitely not good. He was already trying to think of ways to put her off, or better, scare her off completely.

After securing most of his equipment in the Land Rover to protect it from marauding bands of baboons and other thieves, Forrest grabbed his 35mm camera, note pad and "tool kit" and set off to find the herd he and McCullen had spotted earlier.

Forrest made no effort to be stealthy as he worked his way through the brush growing along the river. He didn't want to surprise anyone and, more importantly, he didn't want anything to surprise him. A few minutes later, he made his way through an opening in the vines which covered thorny bushes at the water's edge. A large, fallen tree jutted out into the river, presenting him with an opportune vantage point from which to survey the herd. Walking on the upper surface of the thick tree trunk proved to be easy. After a moment of maneuvering, Forrest sat with his legs dangling a few feet above the murky waters of the Ewaso Ng'iro River.

The elephants watched Forrest with cautious interest as he took photographs and made notes detailing their family tree. Several of the mature females lifted their trunks to sample his scent. After a half hour had passed, the elephants settled down and resumed their bathing.

He counted 16 elephants in the group, seven adult cows including a large, older female whose right tusk was broken off a foot from the end. The exposed dentine's concave shape gave it a spoon-like appearance. Judging from the way the other animals regarded her, Forrest inferred that she must be the matriarch. In addition to four juveniles whose sex he couldn't determine at a distance, there were five younger calves, two of which appeared to be less than a year old.

Near the far bank, he noticed a very large animal who pensively kept his distance. He was a large bull with a pair of huge tusks that crossed in front of his trunk. Standing alert, the bull sniffed the air, assessing the reproductive status of the cows. Normally loners, the bulls rarely came into contact with the female groups unless they were in a reproductive condition called musth. The word, a corruption of the Urdu word "mast," translated as intoxicated or angry and described the aggressive behavior of mature males during their period of physiological change. It also gave rise to the western expression: rogue elephant. The bull's presence was noticed by the group but, aside from some of the females inquisitively extending their trunks in his direction, he was given little attention. For now, the "girls" were simply enjoying their bath. The dating game would have to wait.

Forrest changed his observation position several times in order to keep up with the group. He followed the herd at a safe distance, paralleling their line of movement. On several occasions, the matriarch, whom he had named Roseanne, approached him and twice advanced on him in mock charge. Flapping ears the size of car doors, the lady in charge of the family group established her proximity limits for humans, a limit Forrest had no difficulty learning to respect.

Aside from the occasional charge, the elephants paid him less and less attention as they became accustomed to his presence. They seemed to know he wasn't a threat.

As they moved from the river to feeding areas and back again, the elephants covered several square miles in search of food. Forrest moved his camp several times to keep up with the group and at the end of the third day, he found himself back at the spot where he had first found them. At dinner that evening, he reviewed his notes. He had filled several pages mostly with names, physical characteristics, gender and approximate ages. Firelight reflected off of his face as he perused the data. He had named over half of his subjects and, by now, recognized several of them on sight. Roseanne was the matriarch, the leader of the female group. The largest of the bulls was the impressive fellow he had seen on the first day out. He had an imposing presence and all of the younger bulls gave way when he approached. The first name Forrest thought of was "The General" but by the third day he had changed it to "Schwarzkopf." He was aggressive and imposing yet amiable and gentle despite his size. He was also a lady's man who took his time investigating all of the females for signs of ovulation—all except Roseanne. Occasionally rebuffed, Schwarzkopf took it all in stride. He was never pushy and never violent. In the elephant world, Schwarzkopf was a gentleman if there ever was one.

On the morning of the last day out, Forrest made a disturbing observation. One of the young females limped noticeably. A closer look through his powerful binoculars revealed the problem. Trailing her left hind leg was a length of rope. After an hour of observing her movements, Forrest realized that it was not rope at all but a seven-foot piece of wire. Blood and raw tissue marked the spot where the wire had cut into her ankle. Although the little lady continued to feed and keep up with the group, she often stood for several minutes at a time with her leg off the ground, obviously in a great deal of pain. Sympathetically, some of the other cows in the group probed her injury with the tips of their trunks as if to diagnose and treat it. In time, Forrest realized, the injury could make her vulnerable to predators or lead to septicemia. Either could prove fatal. It pained Forrest to see her discomfort. It bothered him even more that, at least for the time being, he would be unable to do anything about it. Thoughts of McCullen's empty rhino pens crossed his mind as he took several photos of the limping cow. Although, since his divorce, he usually considered women to be more of a pain in the ass than they were worth, he never could resist coming to the aid of a lady in distress.

"I don't think it would be a good idea to bring her here, lad. Treatin' her where she is would be a lot less stressful for her and us. 'Course that depends on her condition. Blood poison is nasty stuff."

"I don't care if we treat her here or there, Doc, but let's do *something*!" Forrest urged.

"Alright then. Have Joseph bring my field kit and load it in your airplane. We'll need the dart gun and some overnight supplies just in case it takes a few days to tag her."

"How soon can you be ready, Doc?"

"Before you can, probably."

"Don't count on it. Joseph and I have already gassed the Cessna. We're waiting for *you.* Meet you at the plane." Forrest turned and headed for the airstrip. Fifteen minutes later, the little plane and its three occupants were moving across the African landscape toward the Ewaso Ng'iro.

****

Two days of elephant tracking had turned into three. Forrest was surprised to find that darting and treating animals was far more difficult and time consuming than photographing them. Unlike using a rifle to kill prey, even human prey, the task of taking animals alive was proving to be a much more complicated affair than he originally thought. Forrest regarded McCullen's unexpected tactical competence with combined admiration and amusement. The doctor was amazingly adept at the art of stalking and tracking and equally deft at predicting animal behavior. Separated from his Glenlivet and chronic depression, McCullen had proved to be a more-than-worthy accomplice. The doctor was an excellent teacher and Forrest had become a willing student of the master's art.

As he quickly discovered, there were several important safety factors that had to be considered. First and foremost, in an area that was often very thick with brush, the three men had to work themselves into a position from which they could get a clear shot. The dart they would fire could do as much harm as good if not carefully placed. As McCullen pointed out, a missile deflected by a branch could hit an animal in the eye or other vital areas. McCullen explained that they would shoot for the rump. It made a large muscular target that would cause the animal no harm yet allow maximum effectiveness of the drug.

Secondly, there were animal welfare considerations. Although sodium secobarbital is a potent and fast-acting barbiturate, it would take several minutes for the drug to totally incapacitate an animal the size of an elephant. During that time, an animal could fall victim to any number of perils to include degraded judgment, lack of motor coordination and panic.

McCullen pointed out that shooting the injured female anywhere near water was completely out of the question. If she managed to make it to the river or even a shallow pond before the drug took effect she could easily drown when she became unconscious. Groggy and stupefied while both succumbing to and recovering from the effects of the sedative, she could easily stumble down a steep gully or embankment and injure herself. It was also possible for her to fall on her trunk in such a way as to block her air passages. Since it would be impossible for the team to move three tons of snoozing pachyderm, any combination of these circumstances would most certainly prove fatal.

During the first two days of tracking her family group, an opportune moment had eluded the team. Each time they thought they might have a shot one factor or another had presented an unacceptable risk. Persistence and patience finally paid off. After two-and-a-half days of meandering about through unsuitable terrain, the elephants worked their way into an open grassy area far away from water hazards and relatively free of dense brush. Finally, following two hours of flanking, stalking, approaching, and occasionally retreating, the team realized their chance. Under McCullen's direction, Forrest made a shot that placed the barbed end of a tranquilizer dart in the cow's left hindquarters. Minutes later, her rubbery legs folded and she slumped to the ground in the middle of a large clearing. For a moment, the gray lady rested on her belly rapidly blinking her eyes before rolling over on her side. As McCullen and Forrest approached the sedated pachyderm, Joseph kept a watchful eye on the rest of the elephants who maintained their distance, nervously watching the team's every move. Roseanne, Forrest noticed, stood as close as she dared. Although wary of humans, she seemed to sense that they were trying to help.

McCullen glanced at his watch and activated the stop-watch feature. "We've got about thirteen minutes to attend to her leg. I don't want to keep her down any longer than that."

He noticed Forrest's quizzical stare. "She's got three tons of dead weight pressing down on her heart and lungs. That's pretty stressful. Thirteen minutes is as long as I think she can stand."

Forrest nodded, fascinated by the whole procedure.

The doctor coated her eyes with an ointment to keep them from drying out. Next, he doused a hand towel with water from his canteen and laid it over her eye to shield it from the sun.

"Joseph, bring those jugs of water and wet her down." McCullen moved quickly and expertly like he had done this sort of things many times before.

"I'd say, off hand, she's about ten years old and aside from her injured leg, she's in pretty good shape," McCullen observed as he examined her teeth.

"How can you tell her age?" Forrest asked, watching over McCullen's shoulder.

"Look here, lad. I'll show ya."

Both men knelt down in the dirt as McCullen forced her mouth open far enough for them to inspect her molars.

"As you can see, she's got some whoppers," McCullen chuckled affectionately, probing her soft cheeks with his fingers. Forrest leaned in close, intent on learning everything he could about their patient and her kind. "Elephants have molars and premolars which increase in size as they get older and their jaws grow larger. When they're very young, their upper deciduous incisors fall out and the teeth that grow in behind them become tusks which grow for the rest of their lives. Over the course of their lifetime, they wear out their chewing teeth and replace them sort of like we do, with one difference: Unlike most other mammals whose teeth are replaced vertically, elephants' teeth grow in from back to front like a conveyor belt. The process is repeated six times in sixty- to-seventy years. After the last tooth is lost, the animal cannot feed properly and normally dies from malnutrition."

"So if we got her some dentures she might live longer?" Forrest's asked with a coy grin.

"It's possible," McCullen chuckled. "Disease and drought take quite a few of the young and sick and predators take a few calves here and there, but aside from man, they have no natural enemies."

"Man is more than enough, it would seem," Forrest replied, ruefully. His grin departed as quickly as it came.

"Aye lad, that he is."

After closing her jaws, the two men worked their way back toward the young female's injured leg.

"She's a fine specimen," McCullen commented, examining her for other maladies. "Interesting," he muttered, checking her chest and foreleg. "She's got unusually large breasts for a non-lactating cow."

Forrest made note of his observations. Everything the doctor said would be useful in his "research." If he wanted to maintain his cover under Anne's scrutiny he had to be able to walk-the-walk and talk-the-talk. What better way to get an education, he thought, than to observe the bedside manner of one of the world's foremost authorities on African wildlife.

McCullen paused for a moment to pull the tranquilizer dart out of her rump and rub a little antiseptic ointment into the tiny wound. A moment later, they arrived at her hind legs.

"Bloody bastards," McCullen muttered in disgust.

"Do I take that remark to mean that somebody did this deliberately, Doc?"

"That ya do, lad. This is no fence wire. And looping it around her leg was no accident. This is a bloody snare. The bastards use 'em to catch all sorts 'o animals—even elephants." McCullen picked up the end of the wire and showed it to Forrest. "Here's the loop they made in the end—like a slip knot. You can see where the wire stretched a bit before it snapped. But not before diggin' itself into her leg a good ways. Looks like we've got a little infection brewing here, as well."

Snares, Forrest thought. *Of course. I should have known. This close to two major parks you don't want to make too much noise, do you? Well, I can play quietly, too.*

McCullen took a jumbo syringe from his field kit and drew a measured amount of antibiotic from a bottle. After clearing it of air, he plunged it into her shoulder and completely dispensed its contents.

McCullen continued talking as he worked. It pleased him that Forrest was taking so much interest in his work. "I saw an elephant last year who had torn a hole in the side of his trunk trying to pull it out of a snare like this. Poor thing had a terrible time drinking. Every time he drew water into his trunk it gushed out of the hole. He was only able to get a liter or so at a time. But to give you an idea how smart these animals are, somehow he learned to press his trunk against the side of his leg to stop up the hole a bit as he drew water."

Forrest smiled and shook his head in admiration.

Drawing another dose of liquid from a different vial, McCullen repeated the injection.

"What's that stuff, Doc?" Forrest asked, engrossed in the process.

"First, I hit her with a good dose of broad-spectrum antibiotics. The second needle was a vitamin shot. Hand me those dykes out of the bag, please."

McCullen used the pliers to cut the wire and remove it from the wound. It had cut all the way through the skin and underlying muscle exposing a small area of bone. The two men used water from their canteens to wash the gash as clean as possible. Forrest fanned the insects away while the doctor applied a liberal dose of antibiotic ointment to the raw tissue. Finally, McCullen wrapped the wound with a roll of gauze.

"That oughta hold 'er awhile," McCullen remarked as he repacked his kit.

"The gauze won't stay on very long but it'll keep the dirt out long enough for it to scab over."

Joseph gathered up the equipment and backed off several meters. He knew what came next. Forrest noticed a twinge of fear in Joseph's eyes. When he saw the syringe in McCullen's hand he understood why.

"Hold her ear, John while I administer the antidote."

Forrest pulled the huge flap forward, over her eye, and held it steady. It reminded him of the plastic kiddie-pool he used to keep in the yard for his childhood dog.

McCullen inserted the needle into a large vein in the back of her ear and injected the drug. "All we have to do now is wait for the Mickey Finn to wear off and make sure she finds 'er feet."

"How long will that take?"

"Oh, not too much longer I should think. About two minutes. She's startin' to change her breathing rate a little, already."

Sensing the opportunity would soon be lost, Forrest ran his hand over her ribs and felt them rise as she inhaled. It was an awe-inspiring moment. To have the opportunity to feel the power in a living creature of this enormity—an animal which could, under other circumstances, easily kill him with one swipe of her powerful trunk was exhilarating. He ran his fingers over the course skin of her face and upper trunk. Forrest realized that performing this simple act with a conscious animal would be as impossible as touching the surface of Jupiter. "You think Dolly will be okay, Doc?" he asked, without looking up.

"Dolly?"

"That's her name...er, ah...the name I've given her for my research project."

Malcolm looked at him curiously.

"You know, Dolly," Forrest explained, "after the American country singer with the legendary bazookas."

"Bazookas?" McCullen's slate eyes, magnified by his thick glasses, stared back blankly.

"Yeah. You know, Doc. Bazookas," Forrest explained using his hands to cup imaginary breasts, "tits, boobs, knockers! You said she's got the biggest set you ever saw—right?"

"Oh, right," Malcolm flustered, finally catching on, "I did, indeed." He chuckled.

"Besides, it beats calling her something like R-21 like some of the other researchers do."

"Indeed." McCullen smiled, shaking his head.

"She'll be okay, right?" Forrest repeated, more insisting than asking.

"You really *care* about these animals don't ya, John?" McCullen observed as they walked to the cover of some nearby brush where they would await Dolly's recovery.

Forrest, somewhat amused, noticed that Joseph had doubled the size of his buffer zone. He was taking no chances.

"That's why I'm here, Doc." *Well, partially.* Forrest sat on a nearby log and stretched his legs out in front of him.

McCullen sat and lit a cigarette. He was glad the chase was over. Some of the elephants approached Dolly cautiously, investigating her with their trunks. Her sisters, Oprah and Liz helped to steady her as she struggled to rise to her feet. They rumbled with nervous excitement.

Dolly was still wobbly as she attempted to take a few tentative steps. Her siblings stayed close to her in a poignant display of compassion and concern.

"Touching isn't it?" McCullen observed. Smoke flowed with his words. "I've been at this game for more years than I care to count and I have never encountered a species more noble, or more sentient. They are among the most intelligent of beasts. Sometimes, I think they're smarter than we are."

"You just might be right about that, Doc. They're smarter than a lot of the people *I've* met, anyway. And they certainly have better character than a lot of the humans I've run across."

McCullen noticed Forrest scribbling a few notes on a small pad. "How's the thesis coming along?"

"It's coming. My data isn't ready to stand '*inspection*' by any standards, yet. But, it's coming along."

McCullen gave the American a look but let the reference to Anne lay without comment.

They watched as the matriarch moved closer to Dolly to make her own assessment of her niece's condition. She probed Dolly's mouth with the end of her trunk and sniffed her body like a doctor with a five-foot stethoscope. After assuring herself that her niece was no worse off for her encounter with the humans, the matriarch turned and stared at the men for a long moment. Forrest allowed himself the thought that she might be saying "thank you" as she rumbled and flapped her ears. After a time, she rumbled again and moved to lead the group slowly toward the river.

McCullen looked at the low sun and then at his watch. "How 'bout we turn in early?"

"Sounds good to me," Forrest responded as the trio gathered the rest of their gear and moved off through the tall grass, turned golden by the setting sun. "Uh, by the way, Doc. In the morning, after we check on Dolly, I want you to show me how those poacher bastards rig snares."

The trip to Camp Uhura to drop off Doc McCullen, then to the cache and then back to the river took longer than he thought. It was 11 o'clock before Forrest set out from his new camp, anxious to get down to business.

Hoof-prints and dung marked a well-used antelope thoroughfare. The spoor was fresh and abundant. Forrest knelt next to a bush and rested his MP-5 across his knee.

He rose slowly, taking it all in. The chatty birds were unwitting parts of his security system. Their uninhibited communications told him all was well. Stillness, although subtle, meant danger. Silent creatures were frightened creatures. To be quiet was to be invisible to the ear—to be still was to go unnoticed by eyes attracted to movement.

After a moment, he moved off down the trail, his submachine gun at the ready. Eighty meters further on, he came upon an intersection. Forrest looked around, examining the details. His scan stopped when he noticed them. They were the first ones he had seen that day. The prints were new and sizeable—five toes on each foot—eleven inches long from the tip of the largest toe to the back of the heel. Forrest followed them for a hundred meters learning what he could from the sign. There were three of them, one missing a toe. Heavy at the ball and light at the heel, the prints indicated they were moving quickly—deliberately—as stealthy as he. The footprints were fresh—immaculate. No hooves had marred them. The humans had been the last to traverse the path.

Forrest continued down the trail, a little slower than before. Bending slightly at the waist, he moved ahead in a crouch to diminish his profile. The silenced muzzle of his MP-5SD pointed ahead of him, its fire selector switch set on full-auto. His right index finger embraced the trigger. Any sudden movement would meet with a spray of 9 millimeter.

The trail passed through what Malcolm called a bogani, an

opening in the forest. Then it turned dark under a canopy of acacias and mopane trees. The footprints clustered together and overlapped. They had stopped here for a while, he thought, trying to understand why. And then he knew. His eyes came across their handiwork.

The dull sheen of the steel wire was all but invisible concealed in thorny branches; a sinister noose erected in an innocent looking gallows. It hung like a hoop, two feet in diameter, the bottom suspended four feet above the trail. Portions of the wire not hidden in the brush were disguised in a wrapping of vines. Forrest saw that the end of the wire had been wrapped several times around the trunk of a young tree to anchor it. The snare was just where McCullen had said it would be, suspended between two substantial trees at a narrow point in the trail, a natural funnel for game.

Forrest glanced warily down the trail in both directions. Nothing. The birds were still chirping away.

He reached up and pulled the loop closed. Bending it aside, he wrapped it around the trunk of the tree so it would no longer pose a threat to hapless animals.

Twisting a little to his right, Forrest reached into his rucksack and pulled out an empty coffee can. It made a hollow clunk as it fell to the dirt. Dropping to his knees, Forrest unwound the snare's anchor and let the end dangle on the ground. He used his survival knife to dig a hole eight inches deep and four inches in diameter and placed the can inside. Its open top pointed upward, its rim resting just below the level of the surrounding soil. Like a kid building a sand castle, he used his hands to push dirt around the outside.

Forrest brought his rucksack alongside and felt around the bottom. The M-67 grenade felt heavy and solid in his hands as he lifted it out. His hand trembled a little as he pulled the pin and lowered the grenade into the can until it rested on the bottom. Ever so carefully, Forrest let the spring-loaded safety handle expand against the side of the can which held it in place. Even with a five-second fuse, there would be no time for his enemies to react to its presence—no time to escape the blast and flying shrapnel. They would never know what hit them. And, he thought ruefully, neither would he if he slipped.

He looped the free end of the snare wire around the top of the grenade's neck and twisted it tight. Dust filled his nose as he scraped the remaining dirt into the can, covering it completely. He snapped his hands away quickly as he convulsed in a series of sneezes.

"Steady, John. You don't want this martini shaken *or* stirred."

He backed away, examining the deadly device. When greedy fingers pulled at the wire, the device would be lifted out of the can. Free to move, the grenade's handle would fly off allowing the firing pin to slam against the primer, lighting its fuse.

Satisfied that it was well camouflaged, he obliterated his tracks with the leafy end of a branch. The job was complete. The trap had been turned against the trappers.

Forrest backed down the trail smoothing the dirt as he went. When he reached the intersection, he veered off into the grass and knelt down to assess his work. So far, so good, he thought as he rose to his feet. Three more to go before dark.

It sounded like thunder; so much so that Forrest expected to see threatening clouds as he awoke with a start. The sound still echoed through the river valley as his eyes adjusted to the dim light.

After he had collected his wits he realized what it was. "You guys start early!" he muttered to himself, pulling on his boots and gathering his gear. The sun was barely above the horizon. Tree shadows seemed infinitely long, weaving and crossing like city streets.

Didn't expect results this soon.

Two minutes later he was moving through the brush in the direction of the sound. His pulse pounded in his ears as he picked up his pace.

In a moment he found himself on the trail. His pace slowed as he passed the intersection, his breathing labored when he paused at the edge of the brush to scan the shadows under the trees on the far side of the bogani.

Nothing.

He listened.

Nothing.

The silence was ominous. Aside from their initial cries of alarm, bird chatter was now conspicuously absent. A thin cloud of dust and smoke hung like a veil in the still air just above the trees.

"Gotcha!" he hissed under his breath. Instincts urged him to rush to the scene. But training dictated patience. Zito's words whispered to him from the past: *Stop, look and listen. Don't be in a hurry to die.*

Forrest waited five full minutes. He timed it on his watch just to be sure. In his excitement he knew he couldn't trust his sense of time.

With a minute to go, Forrest eased the MP-5's bolt back, checking to see that a round was chambered. A nudge of his thumb assured him the fire selector switch rested on the full auto position.

He sprinted the short distance across the glade and fell to his knees at the base of a tree. Again, he waited—listening. There was a rustle in the brush a few meters ahead. His ears picked up a low faint sound. At least he thought so.

A moan?

He waited for the sound to repeat itself.

It didn't.

Forrest moved forward crouching low, hugging the brush and shadows for concealment.

There it was again. *Definitely a moan.*

Forrest brought the MP-5 up to a firing position and crept ahead. Feet and breathing froze when he saw them lying in the dirt. He pulled back into the shadows and crouched, surveying the situation. Two men lay on the ground at the base of a slender tree, the site of his first boobytrap. One of them lay on his back. His eyes, fixed and blank, stared up into the tops of the trees. His legs were bent 170 degrees at the knees, his feet pinned beneath his buttocks, a bloody stub was all that remained of a left arm.

The other man lay face down in the dirt, his feet twitching spasmodically.

Forrest watched the second man intently. *Still alive.* A low moan followed by a rising chest confirmed it. Forrest saw his fingers contract into an agonized fist.

Satisfied that the two poachers posed no immediate threat,

Forrest turned his attention to the surrounding brush. Yesterday, he had seen sign of three poachers. One was unaccounted for.

Forrest moved toward the two men, his eyes ever moving, looking, searching. He merely kept them in his peripheral vision. If they moved he would see it in time to react. The real threat was elsewhere, somewhere out there in the shadows and leaves; invisible. *It's the one you don't see who gets ya.*

He crouched next to the man with the missing arm. A quick glance was all he needed to see he was dead. Forrest noticed that the opposite hand had been blown away, as well. Forrest rolled him over on his belly and glanced at his feet. All of his toes were present and accounted for.

Forrest moved to the other man and squatted. He was still alive—just barely, bleeding from several wounds, mostly to his legs and lower torso. The man was in deep shock. Forrest checked his feet. Ten toes.

Forrest rose, moving tentatively, scanning the ground for other signs. Two metal-tipped spears and a machete lay in the dirt. Anachronisms, he thought, in a world of machine guns and lasers. He noticed marks in the dirt where someone had fallen then struggled to get up. Footprints, the distorted prints of a man staggering and falling, covered the ground. Upon closer examination, Forrest noticed one or two of the tracks had been made by a foot with four toes. The prints, punctuated with an occasional pool of blood, led off down the trail.

Forrest felt a chill surge down his spine. *The third one got away!*

Instinctively, he lowered himself to a defensive crouch and leaned against the base of a tree. His mind raced. At first he thought to track the man; hunt him down and finish him. Then he thought better of it.

No. He'll tell his friends what happened here. Maybe they'll think twice before they set any more of those goddamn snares.

Then another thought struck him:

If he makes it to his village, his friends will come back looking for the others! Finish up here, John and get the hell outta Dodge!

Forrest backed away from the tree and moved back to the two

men. The live one began making gurgling sounds—the death rattle of people whose lungs were filling with fluid. Forrest moved to the dead one and, after slinging his MP-5 over his shoulder, drew his machete and pulled a plastic garbage bag out of his back pocket. As he moved around the site, Forrest came across one of the missing hands. It lay not far from the shallow crater created by the exploding grenade. He opened the bag and dropped it inside.

Setting the plastic bag aside, Forrest shot the other poacher in the head. Better than you deserve, he thought, as he cut the poacher's hands off with the machete and dropped them into the plastic bag.

Forrest found the snare wire and cut it into two equal lengths. One piece of wire was wrapped around each man's ankles.

"Now for the most important part," he thought aloud as he wedged a "poacher" card between each man's toes. Sweat trickled through his eyebrows into his eyes as he dragged the bodies down the trail. Adjusting their position directly under an overhanging tree limb, Forrest contem-plated his next task.

He attached his plastic canteen to the end of a length of nylon shroud-line and, using it as a weight, tossed it over the limb. After two attempts, Forrest duplicated the maneuver with a second length of line. Double half-hitches secured the end of each line to the wires binding the poacher's ankles. The cord dug into his fingers as he took a strain on the first line, hoisting a body into the air, feet first. After resting a moment, Forrest lifted the second body to the same height as the first. The poachers' arms dangled like bologna links three meters above the ground; well out of the reach of scavengers. The limb, Forrest noticed, sagged dramatically under the weight. Its leafy branches drooped five feet into the tops of the thorny brush.

As Forrest studied the new configuration, another idea came to him. *One final touch.*

Forrest lashed another length of parachute cord to the sagging branches and routed it through the bushes to the ground. There, he dug a shallow hole and reburied the coffee can used for the original boobytrap. He reached into his survival vest pocket and took out yet another explosive device which he inserted in the can. The grenade's pin was pulled, the parachute cord tied to the fuse cap, and the entire apparatus covered over with dirt and dry leaves. Forrest stepped back and surveyed the new setup. "That oughta liquify their Levis," he muttered to himself with something approaching a satisfied smile. Its function was simple, yet completely dependant upon human predictability. When villagers returned to retrieve their comrades they would almost certainly cut them down. Suddenly relieved of its load, the limb would snap upward, plucking the flash-bang grenade out of the ground. And although they would, no doubt, suffer a few missing heartbeats, they would live to tell about it—which was the whole point. Psychological warfare was about hearts and minds—changing behavior—largely a game of negative reinforcements. And you couldn't get much more negative than dead.

It was just after sunset. The western horizon still glowed with the faint indigo of twilight. Forrest throttled back the Zenair's engine and nosed the craft into a shallow dive. Flickering amber light from village cook fires reflected in the Plexiglass windshield as they disappeared under the nose.

Without taking his eyes off the ground, Forrest dumped the contents of the plastic bag overboard through the open door. The propeller buzzed as he pulled the ultralight out of the dive and applied power to sustain the climb.

Three human hands fell to the ground with hardly a sound, each bound with a length of string which held its fingers closed over one of Forrest's special "calling cards."

"Sooner or later these people are gonna learn rule number one," he muttered to himself as he turned the plane toward Camp Uhura: "Hands off the elephants."

CHAPTER-TEN

ORPHAN

a: a child who has lost both parents through death
b: a young animal that has been deserted by or lost its mother
c: one who or that which is without protection

FORREST PANNED HIS ZEISS BINOCULARS across the water holes one more time. There were two of them, a large shallow one and a smaller one with high banks. Two families of elephants shared the residual water with a small herd of impala and three warthogs; a sow and two tiny babies. Everyone was having a nice day until a small calf, less than a year old, unwittingly placed himself squarely in harm's way. Following the adults' lead, he slid down the steep muddy bank to stay close to his mother. After a while, everyone climbed out and moved over to the larger pond, everyone except the small calf who struggled to climb out but couldn't. His terrified squeals brought an immediate response from the rest of the family. While the others nervously milled around the top of the high bank, the matriarch and the calf's mother climbed back into the hole to assess the situation. Clearly, everyone was upset over the baby's predicament.

Initially, the adults' approach was logical and methodical. They did what any human would do; they tried the easiest and most obvious methods first. Under the supervision of the matriarch, the calf's mother used her trunk to push the baby up the steep bank. It didn't work. The bank was too slippery and the calf too clumsy to assist in the effort. Next, the mother and then the matriarch used their tusks like a forklift to raise the youngster to the top of the bank. Those attempts also failed. The bank was too high and too steep.

Forrest could see growing concern in the animals' body-language. The longer the process took, the higher the level of anxiety. Two more adults slid down the muddy bank to offer their assistance. They touched the baby with their trunks as if to reassure him, letting him know there was plenty of help and he would soon be rescued. Several other trunks were extended by those standing at the top of the bank.

The matriarch stood quietly for a moment, studying the embankment. Forrest was certain he could see the gears turning inside her head.

The baby was becoming panicky. He rocked back and forth and paced around, unable to stand still. Even his mother's presence failed to calm him.

For a fleeting second, Forrest thought of the length of climbing rope he carried in his field pack. Just as quickly, he dismissed the idea. The elephants would never allow him to get close enough and, even if he could, there was little he could do to help a calf that easily weighed 400 pounds. For the moment, frustration was his only option.

Just then, Forrest saw the matriarch go into action. As the others stood by watching, the huge animal went to a low point in the bank and began digging her tusks into the soft, damp earth. As she pushed her tusks into the dirt, huge chunks fell away landing at her feet.

"I'll be damned," Forrest muttered behind his binoculars. He grinned. "She figured it out!" He suddenly felt as proud of them as a father would a child who had finally figured out how to ride a bicycle.

The other adults caught on quickly. Some assisted the matriarch with her pick-and-shovel work while two others used their front feet to scrape earth into a growing pile at the water's edge. It was a clumsy, disjointed effort by human standards. But, by anyone's standards, they were clearly working as a team. A remarkable feat, Forrest thought. In less than an hour, the bank had been broken down far enough for the forklift method to succeed in putting the calf over the top.

As the adults emerged from the hole a spontaneous celebration, of sorts, erupted among the family members. Elephants trumpeted their exhilaration. Forrest watched as other youngsters ran in circles with their ears and trunks extended. Waiting adults sniffed and greeted the calf and her mother as if they hadn't seen them for days. Shrieks of joy split the air. Temporal glands at the sides of their heads oozed copious amounts of fluid in the excitement.

Forrest laughed and shook his head. You'd think their team had just won the World Series or something, he thought. After ten minutes of pachyderm pandemonium, they settled down and moved into the shallow water of the larger pond. Other animals gave way as the advancing gray armored division approached. The stranded baby, Forrest noticed with a chuckle, hesitated for several minutes before wading in up to his belly.

Elephants, he saw, were the undisputed rulers of the water hole. They dominated all who came to drink or bathe. But then, again, they had created many of the ponds so it was only fair that they had something to say about their use. Dr. McCullen had explained that a surprising number of ponds were unwittingly created, expanded and maintained by elephants. In the course of rolling and playing in what may have begun as a large puddle left by a passing shower, water holes grew bigger with each visit. Each time the titanic bathers covered themselves with mud or departed with a coating of dirt clinging to their creased hides, they took pounds of earth with them. Over time, they carried away tons of dirt and sand leaving the water hole wider and deeper. Constant tamping from huge, flat feet packed the bottom as solid as concrete preventing the water from leeching into the soil. With each passing day, murky pools were transformed into sizable reservoirs which served the needs of many. Elephants, it seemed, certainly got the most pleasure from the water but all animals derived benefit.

Forrest thought about nature's plan—nature's order of business, Doc McCullen had called it. Every creature had their own special function—their own particular "job." None of them, however, were intelligent enough to understand their contribution to the greater good. Only an organism capable of abstract thought could understand that. But then, he thought with a shake of his head, why were they always the ones to screw it up? *Homo sapiens* translated to "man, the wise," he remembered reading somewhere. *Was he, really?*

Forrest returned to his sentinel duties. He had positioned himself on the highest portion of a bank overlooking a lugga or dry river bed. From his elevated position, he was able to see over a mile across the grass and brush. There had been no signs of poachers during the last four days—very few signs of humans, at all—a situation that both frustrated and pleased him. He worried he was in the wrong place at the wrong time. Near the end of his field rations and water supply, he knew he would have to leave soon. He thought he'd chosen an ideal location for this sortie. Just outside the parks near the Tanzanian border, it seemed like a logical choice for poachers. But, just like fish, they didn't always bite according to the Field and Stream forecast. And, he reminded himself, fish didn't read magazines or listen to CIA analysts. Peeper wasn't far off with his site selection, though. Poachers had been here before. He'd seen the bones to prove it. Skulls with small round holes in them littered the ground near the river bed. Spent brass was abundant.

"Fear not the gun, but the hole it makes," he recalled hearing in conversation at one time or another. A lot of truth in that. Nice, neat little openings in the sun-bleached bones. They looked so innocuous; so harmless. Who could have inferred the pain and terror inflicted by things that made such neat little holes? The torn flesh, shattered brains, ruptured organs, lacerated vessels hemorrhaging life itself into terrible wounds.

Forrest's thoughts went back to the poachers. They may have skunked him on this trip but sooner or later they'd be back. It was just a matter of time. Hunters, he knew, liked to revisit the sites of past successes—a habit he hoped would contribute to his own success.

Forrest rolled up his mat and secured it to his pack. Cumulonimbus clouds were building over the rift mountains to the west. He thought he heard the faint rumble of thunder. He listened again before he turned to leave. There it was again. Or was it? He cocked his head and closed his eyes to better concentrate on the faint sound.

Gunfire...to the south. "Son of a bitch!"

Traces of blood mixed with perspiration trickled down Forrest's face as he turned the Zenair south. Thorns from the brush he had used to hide the aircraft had extracted payment for his haste. He was just starting to catch his breath as the little plane climbed through a thousand feet.

After he had traveled three miles without spotting anything, Forrest snapped the stick hard to the left setting the ultralight's wings in tight turn. After each circle, he shallowed the bank slightly to widen his search pattern. The sun had changed color from white to yellow on its way to orange. Only a few hours of daylight left, he reminded himself. His face wrinkled in frustration. "Nothing!" he shouted out loud above the noise of the engine.

Something caught his eye—large rounded objects in a vast area of dead trees. Forrest reversed the turn. Stark jagged skeletons of an extinct forest pivoted beneath the right wing tip. He relaxed the back pressure on the stick, leveled the wings, and the objects drifted back into view.

Carcasses! Four...no five. Sonofabitch!

His fingers poked the keys on the GPS receiver marking the location. Reflexively, he ducked his head as a dark object blurred past the windshield. His head came back up. Another one. One o'clock. Vulture.

Forrest yanked the stick to the right as the huge bird folded its wings and dropped. "That was close!" he muttered, as he snapped his head around to watch it sail past the tail. There was no time to consider what such a large bird could do to a tiny plane. Forrest tugged at the fasteners of his parachute harness just in case.

Forrest had a good visual fix on the location so he decided to expand his search pattern in hopes of catching a glimpse of the poachers. Fifteen minutes went by and he was about to give up when movement caught his eye.

Gotcha!

A man darted across an open area and slid in under a black log. Forrest pulled the Zenair up in a wifferdill, a steep climbing turn reversal, then pointed the nose down at the log as the speed bled off rapidly. Forrest swooped in low hoping to flush them. As he racked the tiny craft around in a tight left turn, he saw muzzle flashes at his eight o'clock. "Hope you fuckers don't know how to lead a moving target."

He grabbed the MP-5SD to return fire then thought better of it. Might hit the prop or saw through the strut! On his next pass, Forrest dropped two hand grenades to see one explode in the air and the second impact far from its target. When a second burst of muzzle flashes appeared 20 meters from the first, Forrest realized he was out gunned and a tactical withdrawal was his only sound move. Wishing he had something more effective to fire, he turned away from the fight. At least I scared them off, he thought.

Careful to avoid the circling vultures, Forrest brought the Zenair back to the carcasses. He orbited for a few minutes in order to get an accurate count. Three...four...five. One of them moved. His heart raced. A calf. "Jesus Tecumseh Sherman! He's alive!"

Forrest banked the plane hard to the left letting the nose drop for a closer look. "Sure as hell is! Poor little sucker. Can't be more than a year old." The little animal turned and ran at the sound of the plane then trotted back to what must have been his mother's body.

"Motherfuckers!" he growled, giving no thought to the expletive's ironic double meaning. Immediately, Forrest's thought processor went into the rescue mode. His mind raced with possible scenarios. Landing was out. The terrain was too rough. And besides, he thought, what would he do even if he could land? He checked the GPS for the distance back to Camp Uhura. 26 miles. "Hang tight, buddy," he heard himself shouting toward the ground. "The cavalry is coming!"

Anxious minutes later, the Zenair bounced along the runway as Forrest throttled the Rotax engine back to idle and applied the brakes. Before the propeller spun to a stop, he was already unstrapped and climbing out. McCullen and Joseph were there to meet him as he had requested via radio. Actually, there was a small reception party. Some of the workers and their wives had come to see what the excitement was all about.

Then, he noticed someone else at the back of the group.

"Oh man! What's *she* doing here?" he growled to himself before McCullen came within earshot.

McCullen and Joseph walked up briskly, both wearing a look of concern. "What's up, lad?"

"Baby elephant. Orphan. His whole family's just been massacred," Forrest explained in clipped phrases as he hurried to his Land Rover. "You gas the Rover like I requested, Joseph?"

"Yes, bwana." The placid Kenyan was running to keep up.

"Good man. You take the Doc with you in the truck and follow me."

Anne Sargent intercepted the trio enroute to their vehicles. "What's going on?" she asked the group, Forrest in particular.

Ignoring her, Forrest quickened his pace.

Malcolm McCullen answered for him. "John just flew over an elephant family. They've all been killed, save one—a baby."

"What are you going to do?" she asked.

"Find him and bring him back," Forrest answered over his shoulder, annoyed that this government bureaucrat was becoming a pest.

"Can I help?"

"I don't know. Can you?" Forrest snapped, frustration coating the question.

Sargent shot McCullen a look of indignant exasperation.

"Indeed you can, lass," McCullen contradicted with a half smile, half disdainful look. "We can use all the help we can get."

Forrest circled the Rover and yanked the driver's door open. "You got everything you need, Doc?"

"It's already in the truck."

"Lets get moving, then." Forrest paused to look at Sargent who stood trying to decide whether or not she'd officially been invited. "Are you coming or are you just here to check my paperwork?"

"I'm coming, I suppose," she said tentatively, glancing at McCullen for further approval.

"Well then, get your little pink ass in the truck with the Doc."

"She'll have to ride with you, John. There's no room for three people in the front of the truck."

Forrest looked at McCullen. His jaw tightened. He started to protest but checked himself. There wasn't time. "Okay, come on," he growled, jerking his head toward the passenger seat.

"How far did you say it was, John?" McCullen asked.

"Twenty-six miles, southwest.

"We'll never make it. Not before dark," the old Scotsman warned as he walked toward the big truck they had once used to transport captured rhinos.

Forrest ignored the assessment as he climbed in behind the Rover's steering wheel and slammed the door. Anne Sargent quickly closed hers as he started the engine. "If we don't make it," he called toward the truck, "then neither will that calf."

"Can you read a map?" Forrest demanded as they turned onto the first decent road that led anywhere west.

Sargent answered with a glare.

He tossed the chart he had brought from the ultralight onto her lap. "Good. Plot this position." He read a set of coordinates off the GPS screen. The liquid crystal display (LCD) also gave him distance and magnetic bearing to the orphan's position. They had 20 miles to go. He noted the dash-mounted compass and looked for distant landmarks.

Sargent fumbled with the chart to find the grid lines. After a few minutes, her finger marked the spot where the latitude and longitude lines intersected. "Here," she announced, tilting the chart slightly so Forrest could see.

"You sure?" he asked, dismissing her with a doubtful look.

Sargent frowned and replotted the position he had given her. "If your numbers are right, then this is the place."

"You know where you are?" he asked.

Another glare. It sounded more like needling than a question. "I bloody well do—seated right beside a bloody arse."

Forrest looked at her and grinned.

"Here," she replied, acerbically stabbing her index finger into the map.

"Good. Not bad for a girl." The grin dissolved somewhat. "Now, see if you can get us from here to there. That calf won't last long out there by himself," he added looking first at his watch and then at the orange sun.

"Oh dear Lord," Amy moaned. "Thank you." Like an angel from heaven a helicopter was landing less than 2 football-fields distance in front of her. A cloud of swirling dust billowed as it touched down. Not taking any chances on it taking off again without her, Amy used the last of her strength to push ahead on legs as wobbly as warm taffy.

Amy had just finished scraping her name in another small dry lake bed. Her mind was wandering, unable to focus. *Maybe it's dad! Maybe he saw my messages!*

A warm feeling of exhilaration washed over her when she made-out the Kenya Wildlife Service logo on its white fuselage.

Government. I'm safe! I made it!

New energy found its way into her painful feet as she trudged weakly around the nose of the helicopter in time to see the pilot collecting a small package from a very small man. Through her mental fog, it didn't register at first. The small man's face was one she should never have forgotten.

He hadn't forgotten hers.

Amy collapsed to her knees at the chopper's door at the same instant the little man lunged to catch her under the arm pits. As the little man struggled with the nearly limp torso of the girl, he exchanged a knowing yet shocked look with the pilot.

The pilot nodded and motioned with his head to put her in the back seat. Once she was positioned inside the aft passenger compartment the pilot shouted a single word over the noise, gesturing with his fists joined together wrist-against-wrist. The little man nodded, bounded back to his truck and returned with a length of heavy cord with which he bound her wrists and ankles. Then he looped the seat belt through Amy's arms before buckling her in. The pilot, watching over his shoulder, nodded approval then motioned for the little man to close the door and stand clear. Too weak and wrung out to put up any resistance, Amy Lee Henderson-Forrest slumped to her left and passed out on the bench seat.

Forrest braked the Rover to a stop and checked the rear-view mirror. McCullen's big capture truck, 500 meters behind, lumbered along just ahead of a column of dust. He looked down at the GPS receiver which lay on the seat next to his leg. It showed less than 10 miles to go. 9.67 to be exact. That was the good news. The bad news was that they would have to leave the road, poor as it was, and make their way through the bush. They had made good time so far, he judged. And, there was still plenty of daylight left; well, enough hopefully.

"You've been pushing them pretty hard." Sargent broke the icy silence, turning in her seat to check on the truck's progress. "I don't think..."

"You want to make it in time, don't you?" Forrest cut her short without taking his eyes off the mirror. When he thought he had waited long enough, he started the Rover forward with a jerk.

It took another hour to reach their objective. The drive had been tough on both vehicles and occupants. At times their pace had been a slow walk. Hundreds of dark, jagged tree trunks protruded from the grass and brush-covered landscape like markers in a forgotten cemetery. Tattered bark, black from the effects of a devastating fire, told the tale of the woodland's demise. To Forrest, it had a foreboding look about it, like the haunted forest in the Wizard of Oz. Fittingly, a dozen vultures circled overhead, silhouetted against a magenta sky.

Sargent laid the map down. It was no longer necessary.

Forrest set his jaw and steered the Rover around a fallen log. Sargent ducked toward him as thorny branches slapped at the side of the Rover, raking across her open window.

Branches scraped at the undercarriage as the Rover slammed through a thick patch of low thorn bushes. Twigs, dirt and leaves obscured their vision momentarily as the vehicle bounced and came down with a crunch.

"Shit!" Suddenly, as the windshield cleared, two dozen vultures leaped into the air uncovering a mound of elephant remains.

"Oh God," Anne gasped.

Forrest grunted, turning the wheel violently to the left. The lateral G-forces generated by the turn threw his passenger against her door.

Another mound of flesh and bone loomed just ahead.

"Watch out!" Anne cried as she ducked her head and reflexively brought her hands over her face. A flailing vulture careened into the windshield and bounced into the air leaving a feathery imprint on the dust-coated glass.

Forrest twisted the wheel back to the right as fast as he could and slammed on the brakes. The trailing dust cloud caught up with them engulfing the Rover and four fleeing hyenas.

"Let's go!" Forrest barked, before the Rover had come to a complete stop. "Stay close or stay here."

Sargent hesitated, giving some thought to the second option before leaping out, then running to catch up. "Slow down. I'm coming."

"You speed it up." Forrest jogged ahead working his way around stumps, carcasses and fallen logs. Most of the animals, he noticed, still had their ivory. Only one's face had been hacked away by the poachers.

Movement off to his left caught his eye. He turned. Two hyenas jousted with a small pack of wild dogs as they circled a gray mound of wrinkled skin. Forrest reached into the bottom-right pouch of his survival vest and brought out what looked to Anne like a tall can of shaving cream.

Four vultures flapped into the air leaving a shower of feathers and down.

Forrest was the first to spot the calf. "There!"

Snarls punctuated high-pitched hyena "laughs" as the hungry animals circled the cornered calf. Forrest was glad to see that the calf had maneuvered himself against his mother's belly. He was using her body and legs as a protective revetment.

The hyenas froze for a moment then backed off before baring their teeth in a threatening snarl. They would not be denied their prize.

Forrest pulled the ring at the top of the flash-bang grenade and lobbed it onto the ground in front of the menacing animals. He grabbed Sargent by the arm and jerked her to the ground.

A thunderous concussion rocked the air accompanied by a blinding burst of light. When the dust cleared, Forrest saw the predators were in full retreat. Anne, he noticed, had eyes the size of grapefruits. Cringing, she held her hands protectively near her face in a look of astonishment.

"Sorry," he said, insincerely. "Those things are great for getting rid of unwanted party guests, aren't they?"

Sargent's look was anything but amused.

A raspy squeal brought Forrest's eyes back to the left. The baby elephant paced and squirmed with fear. Forrest heard the screech of dusty brakes yards behind him.

"Hold your ears," he warned. He drew his Colt Anaconda revolver, held it over his head, and fired two quick shots into the air.

Sargent uncupped her ears and eyed him angrily. "Where did you get that?"

"What? This? It was a gift...you like it?"

"I don't remember seeing a gun permit in your file."

Forrest looked at her contemptuously. Spoken like a true bureaucrat, he thought. "Probably because I don't have one."

"Then, that gun's illegal."

"No shit?" he replied with mocking innocence. He alternately watched for McCullen and kept a wary eye on the hyenas who circled a comfortable distance away. "Look, Sarge. Spare me the Sarah Brady bullshit right now. If you don't like it, arrest me."

"I don't like guns. They kill things."

"Mostly things that need killing." He extracted the empty brass and inserted two new cartridges.

"They're the devil's invention—evil."

"Now there's an objective, scientific observation," Forrest snorted sarcastically.

Joseph and two camp boys came running, holding a pair of struggling baby warthogs. Joseph responded to the quizzical stares. "We found them along the road. Their mother is dead."

Forrest smiled. "Put 'em in the Rover."

After a few minutes, a white-faced Malcolm McCullen marched up. "What's all the commotion about?" he shouted, moving as fast as he could.

"Hurry up, Doc!" Forrest urged. "He's alive!"

"Well, glory be," McCullen flustered. "I never thought..."

"Let's 'thought,' Forrest interrupted, "about how we're gonna get'im outta here, Doc. We're running out of daylight. And," he added, nodding toward the growing number of predators pacing their perimeter, "the night shift is just punching in."

The helicopter landed in a small clearing surrounded by trees and huts. The aircraft's approach had surprised the inhabitants and no one approached until the pilot waived his arms dramatically.

After a few minutes, two men, one with a ghoulish face and opaque eye, the other wearing a black safari hat and walking with a limp moved up to the still running chopper and opened the back door.

The two men shared looks and wide grins as they reached inside and extracted the limp body of the young wazungu girl. After vigorously patting the uniformed pilot on the shoulder, Black Hat closed the back door and waived the pilot off.

"Careful now, lads. Don't let'im hurt himself." McCullen leaned against a tree as Forrest and Joseph eased the calf into a long-abandoned holding pen back at the camp. McCullen was unusually cheery, especially at this late hour. It was after midnight. It had been years since any of his pens had held any "guests" as he liked to call them. And this one, a particularly adorable baby elephant, brought him a chest full of mixed emotions. Every family in the camp, from the oldest woman to the smallest child, had come to watch.

He was elated to feel the excitement generated by the rescued calf. McCullen savored the good feeling one gets when one does a particularly good deed. But his elation was offset by worry. Saving the little bugger would be no easy feat.

Anne saw his face fall at the thought. "What is it, Malcolm?" she asked, laying her arm affectionately across his shoulders.

"I was so happy to get him here, Anne..." he stopped short, choking on a bitter thought. "Now..." he paused again. "Now, I'm afraid I won't be able to keep 'im alive."

"He'll be alright, I should think," she said, rubbing his upper back with the palm of her hand. "He doesn't appear to be injured. That's a good sign, at least."

"Aye, but he's in shock, ya know."

"I know."

"And..." McCullen hesitated again, "well, you know how difficult it is to get them to eat. And even if we do, it's near impossible to duplicate their mother's milk."

Anne nodded and patted his shoulder reassuringly. "It's been done before." She smiled as she watched Forrest and Joseph pile some dry grass they had cut to make the calf a bed. "Cynthia and Diane will help us. And there's always Daphne Sheldrich."

"Even they can't save them all," he reminded her.

"He's over a year old, though. That's in his favor."

"I guess."

"I'm exhausted," she said with a sigh. "Can I stay the night?"

McCullen turned and flashed her a tired smile. "O'course ya can, dear. I'll walk'ya to your room."

The morning was delightfully cool and, except for the singing insects, peacefully quiet. A few women were busy making their morning fires and attending to other chores. Faint stars faded in the gathering blue as Anne Sargent stepped off the porch and started in the direction of the animal pens.

Sargent slowed her pace as she approached the holding pen, trying to keep her footfalls as quiet as possible. It took a minute for her eyes to adjust to the deep shadows cast by the high walls. The sound of labored breathing came from a vague dark lump at the far end of the pen. Short gasps and tormented groans occasionally broke the rhythm. Hoover, the name John had given the baby elephant, was asleep. But she realized, it was a fitful sleep. And she could only imagine the nightmares that would come from seeing his family murdered before his eyes. *Poor little bugger.*

Anne climbed through the poles the boys had pulled across the entrance. The pen smelled of damp earth and dry grass; that unmistakable barn smell that permeates large herbivores and their facilities. She leaned against the tall, log walls and listened, wondering what would happen to this pathetic little orphan. Most didn't survive. Usually because they wouldn't eat. Even if they would, no one had yet found a way to duplicate an elephant's rich milk. Synthetic formulas weren't sweet enough. Elephant milk is the second sweetest milk produced by any mammal. Only human milk was sweeter.

The sleeping calf moaned and stopped breathing for a moment, then inhaled in quick sharp breaths. Tortured dreams played in his head. Anne's breathing rhythm changed sympathetically as she listened. She knew of several calves that had literally died of a broken heart after losing their families. There was simply no other explanation, scientific or otherwise.

Her mind wandered to her husband. Her own nightmare was never far from her mind. She reflected on the long drive through the bush with a stone-faced American more rude and enigmatic than any man she had ever met. So different from Allen, she thought. Yet, there was something about this strange man that fascinated her—challenged her in a way. John Forrest was a matrix of inconsistencies and contradictions. He seemed the born leader type; strong and certain of himself. He'd certainly taken charge of the rescue operation in fine style. If he hadn't intervened, the young elephant would now almost certainly be a side dish at a scavenger's banquet.

She admired him for that. How could she not? Even Malcolm respected him. She could sense it—see it in the way Malcolm dealt with him. But he had, after all, been an airline captain. All that responsibility for huge, expensive, complicated machines and peoples' lives. Weren't they supposed to be competent leaders? Didn't they *have* to be?

There was power in this man, too. Purpose. And, she felt, something else. Pain. Maybe. No, probably. Something or someone had hurt this man. Maybe a lot of somethings or someones. Maybe that insane Vietnam war. Maybe a woman. Probably both. There was nothing like war or a woman, she knew, to tear at a man's insides; make his soul bleed. The same thing had driven her brother to drugs then suicide only ten years ago.

The American was hiding something, perhaps protecting something. She sensed he didn't like her meddling, but that was her job. And doing her job—the right way—was important to her. It had become her whole life now that her marriage was a shambles she hesitated to admit, even to herself.

Hoover murmured a faint cry.

It was getting lighter inside the pen. She could see the calf clearly, now. His chest heaved and ears twitched in concert with his dreams. Looking up she could see the stars were almost gone.

Something stirred behind her. A pang of fear went through her like a lance. She froze. It moved again. Another jolt tingled down her spine. She turned her head to look, very slowly at first. A man's form lay slumped against the log wall. *John! What on Earth?* He was asleep, she saw, and next to him on the ground, what was that? Her eyes strained. *A bottle?* It was a baby's bottle, fashioned from one of Malcolm's whiskey bottles and a rubber glove. She caught herself smiling in the fading darkness.

Zeiss makes some damn fine optics, Forrest thought as he followed the graceful flight of a pair of crowned cranes over the long wide lugga. Sunlight glinted off their exquisite gold crests as they turned north in tight formation. Probably heading toward the water hole, he reasoned, turning the binoculars back to the elephant carcasses. Stiff, gray skin lay like rumpled tar paper blankets over newly exposed bone.

Even at a distance of three hundred meters, the 10 X 50s revealed the grisly remnants of the orphan's mother and her family in vivid detail. Wild dogs and hyenas had abandoned the carcasses to the lesser scavengers. What remained of the elephants was of no interest to them. The left-over scraps of skin and bone were no longer worth their time. Birds, maggots and ants would clean up after the previous diners. Nothing would be wasted; a fact that was little solace to the man whose cold eyes watched and waited through expensive, coated lenses.

Greed, he thought, grimly. Greed was responsible for this. In that regard, he thought, poachers are no different than stock market investors. The real driving forces for both are fear and greed. The strategy, then, is simple: fear must win. Period. But sometimes greed is good. It makes people predictable. And predictable people make good targets. He turned the glasses back to the ivory. "Some nice specimens out there," he commented to himself. "They'll be back for those." He was surprised that they hadn't come back for them already. Forrest thought about the roaring fire he'd built near the carcasses before they had left with the orphan. He'd hoped to make it seem as if a ranger patrol had made camp for the night. Rangers often seized ivory left behind by poachers to deny them the fruits of their labor. "Fire must have spooked 'em," he muttered. And the chase, he reminded himself. "Bought a little time, anyway." Then he had an after- thought. "Not too much, I hope."

Forrest set the binoculars down and rubbed his eyes. His sixth sense nagged at him. He wasn't very happy with his position. But, it was the best one in an area that offered little other cover. The dilapidated termite mound gave him a stable shooting platform, but provided little height and even less concealment. He looked around at some of the dead snags and fallen logs. Nope. There wasn't anything he liked better with a good view of the dead elephants. Nothing in sure range, anyway.

Forrest checked his watch and stretched his cramped muscles. It was getting late. "Looks like another night at the Thornbush Inn."

Forrest had been awake for a while before he realized what had stirred him. A horrific stench wafted over his position, carried on a whisper of a breeze that flowed from the killing ground toward the sun rising at his back. Any desire he may have had for breakfast went along with it.

A quick scan with the binoculars assured him the area was still clear. A movement caught his eye, then another. One minute there had been nothing but bones and brush out there and the next...

He almost smiled. "I knew you'd come," he hissed like a coiled snake as he settled in behind his rifle. Then, his cold emotionless expression gave way to one of alarm. "Holy shit," he whispered, his adrenalin surging as he played the scope over the area. "You people brought the whole stinking tribe!"

At first, five armed men emerged from the brush warily checking the area for threats. They fanned out in a circle around the killing ground checking their perimeter. After a moment, five more men appeared, beckoned on by the leader of the first group. They carried axes and machetes in lieu of firearms. Shooters and butchers, Forrest noted, sarcastically. The shooters will have to go first.

He brought the rifle down from his shoulder as he weighed the risks. There was no particular urgency, he reminded himself. The elephants were already dead. Pressing this situation wouldn't save any lives, but a more cautious approach just might save his own. On the other hand, the sun was at his back, now. That meant it was in their faces. And what little wind there was blew straight across the target over the top of his mound—a direct head wind. An ideal situation that wouldn't last very long. The higher the sun got, the more visible his position would become.

What's it gonna be, John? Shoot or watch? Are these bastards gonna die or walk?

A smart sniper would wait for a more tactically sound situation, he reminded himself. He smiled as he remembered his friend Zito's words across thousands of miles and dozens of years: "That's one of your many and most serious faults, Thumper. You were always too goddamned smart to be a good sniper. Sometimes you just gotta spit in death's face." The smile faded a bit. "Just hope it don't spit back."

Forrest took a deep breath and brought the scope back to his eye. The butchers were hard at work now, hacking away at bone which stubbornly clung to its white treasure. The shooters had relaxed a bit, he noticed. Three of the five had set their weapons down on the ground while they relaxed and enjoyed a smoke. The remaining two cradled their guns in their arms, watching the butcher's progress. Forrest thought about Hoover, the little orphaned calf with the vacuum-cleaner nose. His mother's skull was now being smashed apart by two flying axes.

"You're right, Zit." Forrest collected a mouthful of bitter saliva on his tongue. A sharp blast of air deposited it on the rusty-red termite mound.

Forrest pulled the rifle into his shoulder and rested his cheek against the stock's adjustable cheek rest. A football-field away, he watched a thin blue cloud of cigarette smoke disperse giving him a clear picture of the first target's face. The cross hairs settled on the glowing ember as his trigger-finger applied pressure to the curved piece of steel resting beneath its tip.

BOOM!

The cigarette exploded as the bullet shattered the poacher's upper incisors before boring itself into his brain stem and blowing out the back of his skull. He was dead before he hit the ground.

For a second, Forrest's field of view blurred as he swung the rifle a few degrees to his next target. He settled the crosshairs on a startled man's chest and fired. Forrest pulled his eye away from the scope as the target dropped from view. A third round nestled snugly in the chamber waiting for its turn to fly. Five seconds had elapsed—two men down.

Forrest swung the barrel toward the next target. His eye found only a shimmery field of dry grass and bare dirt. Nothing. Then he slowly panned the scope over the entire kill zone. Still nothing. The remaining men had gone to ground.

Silence hung over the area like a bad mood. This part of an engagement was always a test of nerves, he thought. Nine times out of ten, the enemy would dive for cover and freeze while they tried to figure out what was happening. If his primary targets had been eliminated by then, it was also the best time for a sniper to withdraw—when confusion in the enemy's ranks was at its maximum. This situation was different. Every poacher was a primary target. Withdrawal was an option but not a desirable one.

Forrest scanned the area slowly through the telescopic sight. The next move was theirs. All he could do was wait. Invariably, someone would poke his head up for a look. Curiosity, absent training and discipline, very often overcame patience. And everyone knew what curiosity did to cats. Forrest panned and paused—panned and paused. *There! A face. Gone. He'll look again.* He held the crosshairs over the spot previously occupied by a human head, waiting for the void to be filled one last time.

Up it came.

BOOM!

Forrest saw the top of the man's head explode.

Now there would be more paranoia than curiosity, he knew, as fear tightened its grip. The enemy would find it increasingly difficult to believe that a sniper could not see their every move. Things would be less predictable, now. Individual personalities would determine individual fates.

An alarm sounded in the back of his mind. His instructor's words shouted at him from the past. There were some things you just never forgot. "Three shots. No more than three shots from any one position. The first shot alerts the enemy to your presence. The second gives him approximate direction. The third, if the enemy's any good at all, gives him refined direction and approximate distance. And, if he spots your smoke...well then, son...your ass is his."

Forrest looked around for another position. He felt compelled to move. Rules were made for a reason, his training told him; usually the result of lessons learned. To ignore a rule was foolish but then, there were exceptions to every rule. It depended on the circumstances. That's where experience and judgment came in. An experienced sniper knew when to play by the rules and when to ignore them. And snipers, like pilots, either became experienced after a time or they became extinct. The learning curve in both professions was either straight up or straight down.

Anxiety gnawed at him. There was really no other place to go. And even if there was, there was too much open ground to cross.

Bullets cracked over his head bringing his head down in a snap. A second burst flew by well off to his right. Wild fire, he realized. That was a relief. They didn't have him spotted. Not yet, anyway.

Forrest swung the scope around just in time to catch a lingering puff of smoke and dust. He centered the cross hairs on the spot and waited.

The poacher rose quickly and fired off an unaimed burst. Before Forrest could draw down and hold steady, his target disappeared. His trigger-finger relaxed. He waited.

The poacher came up again, this time at the other end of the log he was using for cover. He fired and dropped. Again, there wasn't enough time for a clear shot.

"Ssshhit!"

A long silence filled the interval between waves of noise as both sides played the waiting game. Forrest took the time to reload.

A movement to the left of his primary target caught his eye. Another head came up and went down fast. Forrest noted the spot and turned his attention back to the log. Nothing.

"That guy's making like a door mat," he muttered in frustration.

The target to his left moved again. Forrest aimed the rifle at the spot and waited. The head came up again.

Forrest squeezed the trigger.

The butcher's left hand came up reflexively holding the side of his head. Forrest wasn't happy with the shot. He'd rushed it. But the round, he saw, had taken the man's left ear off. And, if I'm lucky, he thought, I shaved enough skull to put him out of the fight. Either way he'll have one helluva headache.

He made a mental inventory of his targets. Six guys left. Three with AKs.

His eyes moved back to the log. He thought he saw a slight movement. He couldn't be sure. Nerves and eyes could play tricks under stress.

A flock of sand grouse exploded into the air at Forrest's four o'clock. Their rapid wingbeat startled him. They were less than 50 meters away.

Brripp! Bullets smacked into the front of his termite mound. From the log, again. They had him now, he knew. He gave some additional thought to moving. Another sound, a faint one, interrupted the thought. Four o'clock, again. Too much of a coincidence. He'd lost track of two of the shooters—an ominous development. His mind raced. The hair stood up on the back of his neck as his fingers moved to one of the pouches on his survival vest.

Off to his right, his comrade crouched behind a thorn bush. Their tense fingers choked the grips of their AK-47 assault rifles. Their dark eyes, wild with fear and adrenalin, met and locked. His signal to move ahead was answered with a nod. They rose on bent knees peering around the foliage at the termite mound just a few meters ahead. Their keen noses, used to tracking animals scents, noticed it right away—the odor of human urine. Their anxiety grew as it rose in their nostrils.

The first man saw their quarry lying on his belly at the back of the mound. He nodded to the second man and held his rifle up to a firing position. Sweat trickled down his face. A second later, he charged ahead, emptying his magazine into the prone figure. His partner did likewise, spraying over 20 rounds in three long bursts.

The mound was obliterated, covered in the red dust kicked up by the impacting bullets. The men fell to their bellies, lying there for a long time, panting; quelling their nerves.

After what seemed like an endless wait, they rose slowly and advanced. The form lay there, deathly still, covered by the muzzles of their Kalashnikovs. It looked strange, they noticed, as they crept closer. The figure was dressed in a curious suit; some sort of camouflage costume. His rifle, also a curiosity with its unusual stock and telescopic sight lay on its side under his chest.

They exchanged a wary look and moved ahead. Tension tightened their chests as they neared their victim. Whoever he was, he couldn't have survived the fusillade they'd unleashed. Could he? At least a third of their rounds had to have hit home at that range.

As one shooter rolled the body over with the toe of his boot, the other man stood off to the side covering it, just in case. It was surprisingly light and limp. It rolled quite easily—too easily. At first their eyes went to the rifle; a fine prize that would serve them well on future hunts. But…

Human cognitive processes require a few seconds to comprehend the unexpected. At first, people tend to see what they expect to see. What should have been a shattered torso was, instead...what? A back pack? Fear swelled in their throats.

Their eyes found another object. Round and dark, about the size of an orange, it didn't register at first. It lay in a small depression under what should have been the man's belly. They had only two seconds to realize what it was.

An M-67 fragmentation grenade contains a half pound of Comp B high-explosive encased in a 13 ounce steel ball. Once initiated, the fuse burns 4-to-5 seconds before unleashing an explosion with a lethal radius of 5 meters.

It functioned as advertised.

Forrest ducked behind the log as steel shards buzzed through the air, propelled outward by the sharp explosion.

At least now he knew where the other two gunners were. He rose up and pumped a short burst into each body just to be sure. A trickle of smoke poured out of the stubby suppressor as he crouched low and moved back to the base of the mound. Keeping his head low, he dragged the bodies out of his way.

Forrest resumed his position and checked his gear. Everything seemed serviceable except one of his plastic canteens, which he had positioned inside the suit's hood to make a "head." It had a clean round hole in it. He removed the cap and poured what was left of the water down his parched throat.

He resumed his prone position and peered through the sight. All was quiet. It wouldn't be for long.

First one head, then another popped up near the elephant remains. The poachers couldn't stand not knowing the outcome of their gambit. A quick swing of the rifle caught the remaining gunner gesturing for his men to keep down.

"So you're the brains of the outfit," Forrest muttered, as he aligned the sight with the leader's left temple. Taking out the leader, he realized, would completely unnerve the remaining two. Then they would be easy pickins. He took a breath and let it out, slowly. All the while "talking" to the poachers down range under his breath.

"The following is a public service announcement..."

Forrest steadied the crosshairs just above the target's ear.

"This is your brain..."

His finger pressed down on the trigger.

"This is your brain on slugs..."

When Forrest returned to camp he found Doc McCullen already asleep, his hut dark and quiet. Just as well, he thought. I've got things to do and the old guy needs his rest. Before returning to his own hootch, Forrest wandered down to the holding pens to check on Hoover. As he rounded a sharp corner, he startled, nearly running into Joseph in the dark. "Damn, Joseph, I almost knocked you down."

"Excuse me, bwana."

Forrest smiled. "No. Excuse *me*. I'm the one who ran into you." Forrest patted him on the back. "How's Hoover doing?"

"Good, I think. My oldest son Isaac is with him now. Dey are bot asleep."

Forrest loved listening to the man's melodious tenor high voice and Caribbean English. He sounded like a reggae singer. "Has he been eating?"

"Ah yes. Isaac and me, we visit Mrs. Sheldrick with da Doctor. She show us how to make de milk. She use palm oil and cow's milk wit lott'a vitamin. Da Doctor, he make it. Isaac and I, we take turn feeding. Dr. Sargent come by and help us, too."

"Dr. Sargent?"

"Yes. She good lady. Help us a lot."

"She still here?" Forrest asked, thinking he hadn't noticed her Rover near McCullen's hootch.

"No. She stay two days den go back to Nairobi."

Good.

It took 12 minutes for him to set up the "Batphone" and sign on to the satellite. Forrest plugged in the voice headset and adjusted the boom mike.

"Peeper. Thumper."

Static.

"Peeper. Thumper."

"Afternoon, Thumper. Good to hear your voice."

Forrest smiled. "Same here." Forrest could hear a fresh sense of urgency in his best friend's voice.

"I got another one," Henderson said almost before his friend could finish.

"Another what?

"An Amy-gram." A short pause. "She's alive, man. Definitely alive!"

"Where?

"Ready to copy?"

Forrest readied a small pad of paper and pen. "Go."

Henderson rattled the encoded lat-longs then added: "Another small dry lake bed."

Forrest scribbled while Henderson spoke. "Got it. By the way, your last info package was good. Real good. But no primary."

"You surprised?" Henderson asked, feigning insult.

Forrest laughed. "You ready for my shopping list?"

"Go ahead."

Forrest explained that he'd been flanked on the previous sortie and that he needed a "power tool" with longer reach.

"Sounds like a job for Midas to handle."

"Roger that."

"Thumper. She's alive, man."

Forrest felt his friend's desperation. "I know."

"Find her, man. Find her."

"I will."

The Masai ranger team leader stood frozen in his tracks at the sight. A human head sat eyelevel atop a blackened tree stump, the neck impaled on a vertical splinter of charred wood.

"Over here, sir! We've found others!" one of the men shouted.

The leader, Ben Otieno, walked over to the base of another tree stump left in the wake of the fire that had scorched the area two years before. His men led him from find to find. Seven more heads, in various stages of decomposition, were found hanging from or resting on the stumps. He saw that the ivory was still intact. Most unusual, he thought. He had never seen anything like it before.

"Who could have done this, sir?"

The leader dismissed the question with an incredulous look. He had no idea. "Take one of them down," he ordered.

Nobody on the five-man team moved. The ranger team fearfully clung to their guns. No one wanted to touch ghastly objects that crawled with flies and maggots. Remnants of human bodies and tattered clothing lay scattered about intermixed with the bones and hard skin of several elephants. Fear and death hung in the air. The men could sense it. Even under the hot sun their blood ran cold. It was an evil place. Bad magic. Bad juju.

Finally, after a full minute of waiting, Otieno stuck the muzzle of his rifle into one of the gaping mouths and coaxed the head off the stump. It slipped off the barrel and fell to the ground with a sickening thud. The two closest men jumped back as if evading a striking cobra.

"What's that?" he asked, pointing to the mouth. A couple of nervous shrugs were his only response. He reached down and retrieved an object from the open mouth. Two of his men took a step back as he brought it up for a closer look. With a sharp breath, the team leader blew a dozen writhing maggots away. It was a white plastic card, he saw, streaked with dried blood. There were many words printed on either side. He only recognized two of them: Poacher.

"What is it?" one man asked in a whisper.

The question drew another annoyed look from the leader. He didn't have an answer for that question, either. Besides, the whole situation was making him nervous, too. The team leader stuck the card under the flap of his shirt pocket and looked around. He had a bad feeling about this place. Definitely bad juju. Things he didn't understand frightened him as much as it did his men. But he couldn't let them know it.

CHAPTER-ELEVEN

INTERCEPTION *a: the act of intercepting*
b: to stop, seize or interrupt in progress
c: to interrupt or gain possession of communications or connections

CHIEF MASTER SERGEANT DAVE CRAMER rotated his stiff neck and closed his weary eyes to his console's CRT monitor. Everything was nominal anyway, he thought with a yawn. Momentarily hanging his headset around his neck, Cramer stood up and massaged the hot spots beneath his light brown hair with his fingertips. He didn't know which was worse, the hot spots, the chronic dull pain in his butt or the ambient noise of the EC-130E's cargo bay. Well, he reasoned, if I want to be able to hear anything when I retire, I'd better keep wearing these friggin' things.

After a few minutes, Cramer slipped the headset back on and remained standing. Tones generated by the ELINT equipment chirped in his ears. He looked at his Air Force issue watch. Three more hours and the Commando Solo variant of the Lockheed Hercules aircraft would be touching down in Riyadh, Saudi Arabia. Four more hours and he would be buried between the sheets in his air conditioned trailer. Three more weeks and a detachment from the 343rd Reconnaissance Squadron out of Offutt Air Force Base was slated to relieve them. RC-135 crews would take over the ongoing ELectronic and SIGnals INTelligence mission from his unit: the 193rd Special Operations Group, Pennsylvania Air National Guard.

It'll sure be good to see the U.S.A, again, Cramer thought with another yawn. He'd had enough of the ragheads and their cultural Twilight Zone. And, he thought longingly, he was more than ready to be back in Harrisburg sucking down copious quantities of ice-cold Rolling Rock.

Chief Cramer sat, reattached his seatbelt and leaned back in his crew seat. He looked down the console at the other Electronic Combat Specialists. Eight hours into the mission, their "fun-meter" had long ago pegged. Eavesdropping on the Somalis' radio and telephone traffic was only slightly more interesting than listening to the Iraqis' indecipherable jabbering which was only slightly more interesting than watching earthworms fuck.

Advanced technology was a double-edged sword for the senior ECS technician. Digital electronics had made his job a hundred times easier at the cost of making it a thousand times more boring. Most of the equipment's operation was automatic—transparent to the operators. Multiple, quick-sweep RF scanners filled out his panel. Each band had a series of light-emitting diodes (LED) which flickered in sequence as the program selected various frequencies in rapid succession. When electromagnetic energy was picked up by the multitude of antennas that studded the specially modified aircraft, the unit would lock on the active frequency and automatically begin recording. Although human intervention wasn't necessary, Cramer could select and monitor any band with the push of a button. Whether he chose to listen or not, the electronic goings-on were recorded on magnetic tape for analysis by people he would never meet in a government building he would never visit and be used for purposes he would never completely understand. "Maybe we really are just 'self-loading baggage,'" Cramer muttered to himself, referring to the designation the flight crew used for his technicians. "Could be worse, I guess. Somebody—CIA, NSA, DIA—would have to listen to all this garbage and try to make sense of it all."

Cramer felt the EC-130 enter a gentle bank to the right as it reached the southern end of its hundred-mile orbital race track pattern over the Indian Ocean. The borders of Somalia and Kenya lay unseen, 12 miles to the west. Two minutes later, he felt the wings level off on a heading that ran parallel to the coast. Their mission was to gather as much of Somalia's electronic emissions as they could during their hours aloft, a difficult assignment given their target's relatively low-tech infrastructure.

Two stations down, another ECS tech readied equipment which would broadcast the TV and audio tapes they'd received from the 4th Psychological Warfare Battalion based at Fort Bragg, North Carolina. The ship's transmitters were so powerful they could burn through the regular radio or television broadcasts of any network in the world.

"Oh, I bet they *do* love their *M*-TV, don't they, Boomer?" Cramer exclaimed spontaneously, arching his eyebrows as he did. "E.C...M-TV, that is."

The other tech responded with a smile. "Right, Chief, especially that psyops channel. Were running a free promo this month. If they sign up today, we throw in C-SPAM and Skin-e-Max. No extra charge."

The techs shared a laugh at their consoles.

"Why don't you guys just hit 'em with 12 hours of the TV FOOD NETWORK," Cramer suggested with an evil laugh that sounded like a lawn mower engine that wouldn't quite start. "Now *that'd* bring the skinnies to their bony fuckin' knees."

"Aw *man*, Chief!" the man at the next console exclaimed. "Cold, man. Really cold!"

The Chief and the psyops tech shared a devilish look. "Comin' right up," the man replied with a mock gesture at his controls.

Cramer snickered and closed his eyes again, lost in boredom. He would never know about the encrypted conversation the super-sensitive satellite receiver had intercepted at the southern end of the track. Even if he had been monitoring the band, he would only have heard faint bursts of static. And for all of its sophistication, the equipment had only recorded half of the message—the downlinked portion. The other half, the uplink from the ground station to the satellite, was highly directional and narrow therefore, undetectable to the plane's gear. To receive both sides of the conversation, the aircraft would have to fly directly between the satellite and the parabolic ground antenna. And to accomplish that, the pilots would have to ignore their standing orders against violating the airspace of a friendly foreign nation.

"Atta boy, Hoover. Feels good, doesn't it, pal," Forrest laughed. He and Joseph splashed in the "bathtub" they'd dug for the young elephant 20 meters from the camp's well pump. The baby elephant rolled onto his side, immersing himself in the cool, slippery mud.

Forrest looked on with a wide smile. He was relieved to see the calf had lost much of his initial fear. Hoover was clearly enjoying the attention and companionship.

Forrest picked up the running garden hose and squirted it in Hoover's face. Squealing and grunting, the elephant climbed to his feet. He gulped down a mouthful of the clear water, joyously waggling his head from side to side. The whites of his eyes grew wide as he grabbed the end of the hose with his trunk and tugged with all his might.

Forrest's feet started to slip. "Oh no!" Mud splattered everywhere as he fell flat on his back with a wet, sloppy smack.

Joseph howled with laughter, leading a chorus of squeals and giggles from the camp's children who had come to watch.

McCullen chuckled heartily from a chair he had set up in the shade.

Forrest's eyes, the only uncoated part of his anatomy, shot them a mean scowl as he rose from the mud like a swamp-monster. He was only kidding but they didn't know it. He crouched and growled at the kids, menacingly holding his arms in the air. Then he advanced toward them, legs stiff and rigid like the marauding creature from the brown lagoon.

The laughter came to an abrupt halt. In unison, the children backed away from the edge of the wallow, their eyes frozen in terror. One tiny shriek precipitated several others. A little girl burst into tears and ran.

Joseph gave Forrest a puzzled look. His smile faded. He'd never seen anything quite like it before.

"Leave it to *you* to frighten innocent children," a familiar female voice called out of nowhere.

Forrest halted. He turned, the mock scowl still fixed on his face.

Anne Sargent stood at the edge of the mud hole looking down at him. Her arms were folded across her chest, a disapproving look in her eyes.

Forrest hands slapped against his sopping shorts as he dropped his arms dejectedly to his sides. "Leave it to you to ruin the party." *The last time I passed over the Ewaso Ng'iro River I couldn't find Roseanne, Dolly and the herd. Why don't you make yourself useful and go look for them.*

Hoover, impatient to continue the hose game, came up behind Forrest and nudged him hard. Forrest again struggled to catch himself. His feet couldn't find traction and he went down face-first in the mud.

The children were delighted to see the baby elephant had so easily "slain" the monster. They squealed with laughter as Forrest pulled himself out of the mud and wiped it from his eyes and mouth.

Joseph rejoined the laughter, hosing Hoover down as a reward.

Anne restrained a laugh. "Aren't you three a sight? Children playing in the muck like mud men from Borneo. What do you think you're doing?"

"Well," Forrest said, laboriously climbing out of the hole, "we were having a good time until *you* showed up."

Anne's smile collapsed into a thin-lipped frown.

"Come on, Hoover," Forrest coaxed, ignoring the intruder. "Feeding time."

Forrest pulled the hose out of the mud hole and ran the water over his head, face and arms. Hoover joined him in the shower, tugging at the hose. After a minute, most of the mud had been washed into a brown puddle at their feet, the monster transformed into a human clad in swim shorts.

"Okay, Joseph. Let's see if we can get him back to the pen."

They had to turn the water off before the young elephant would move. His little snout probed at the end of the hose trying to get the water to flow. He squealed and grunted in protest, eventually giving it up.

Sargent tagged along behind as the three men led Hoover back to the pen. "Did you get my note?"

"Yeah," Forrest grunted, his attention fixed on Hoover.

"Well."

"Well, what?"

"When are you going out again?"

"When are you gonna get a life and go bother somebody else?"

Anne stopped short for a moment.

The men kept going straight into the pen.

Forrest didn't know it but his rebuke had touched a nerve.

Anne slowly peered around the edge of the doorway as the two men tried to get the playful baby to settle down. Forrest steadied the baby's head while Joseph held a blanket over Hoover's face to simulate his mother's belly as Daphne Sheldrick had suggested.

Forrest shot an irritated glance at Anne who had stepped inside the pen and now stood next to Dr. McCullen. "Don't just stand there," he demanded. "Hand me that bottle."

He took the bottle abruptly without noticing the hurt look in her eyes.

"Macrocanthorinchus haeroudinaceous," she blurted as she turned, ducked through the gate and left.

Hoover took a few disinterested sips from the nipple then opted to probe Forrest's clothes with his trunk. Forrest turned to see that she was gone. His eyes went to McCullen to find a shaking head and disapproving frown. "What did she say?"

"My Latin is a little stale but I believe she called you a giant kidney worm of swine."

* * * *

"The program flagged a few transmissions last night, Kathy," the NSA analyst announced as he laid the printouts on his boss' desk. The 47-year-old mother of three hardly looked up from the pile of papers already threatening her desk's structural integrity.

National Security Agency's bank of Cray supercomputers always gleaned a few suspicious tidbits from the endless stream of world communications selectively melted down and dissected at the super-secret facility at Ft. Meade, Maryland. "So what else is new?" the senior analyst for East Africa inaudibly asked herself with a quiet sigh. "Anything in particular grab your attention?" she asked the back of the young man's wrinkled white shirt as he turned to leave.

The analyst hesitated just short of closing the office door. His head came back inside. "One of 'em might be interesting," he added as an after thought. "It was encrypted. Looked like some of our stuff. Pretty clean product. Langley people, I'd say from the routing and the conversation's guarded wording. Although, I'm not aware of any EastAF ops."

"Neither am I," she added curiously as she reached for the new stack of folded paper. "That doesn't mean there *aren't* any."

Her office door clunked shut as she took a gulp of cold coffee. The bitter taste made her wince as much as the thought of working late yet another evening. "And, just 'cause they have U.S. Government ID cards hanging around their necks," she reminded herself, "doesn't mean they're all good guys."

"You've been spending quite a lot of time with that old man, lately," said Anne's husband, Allen Windridge, Director of the Kenya Wildlife Service. His words had a harsh edge to them. Pointed and accusatory, they pierced the dining room's icy silence and penetrated his wife's onion-thin skin.

Anne Sargent-Windridge, not one to let well enough alone, fired back instantly. "How would you know? You're never home anymore."

Thank God.

His nostrils flared as their Kenyan cook cleared his plate from the table then escaped to the safety of the home's spacious kitchen. His pale blue eyes narrowed into a glare. Biting his tongue until the servant moved out of earshot, Windridge lifted his glass, pouring its amber contents down his long thin neck.

Anne regarded him cautiously. Her eyes tracked his movements, looking for warning signs. Usually, she could tell when she had pushed him too far. She studied the features she had once so admired; the lean athletic build of a marathon runner; the chiseled face with its sharp handsome lines; thin blonde hair—almost white, now gelled and spiked, combed back at the sides accentuating a face reddened by sun and alcohol. She wondered what she ever saw in this man who now looked more like a Griffin vulture than the man she had married 11 years before. She went back to the eyes, once clear and bright, now sometimes bloodshot and blurry, cold and angry, pale and dead. There was a certain meanness in them, the frightening look of a cornered leopard. His ambition had once attracted her—his recklessness even aroused her. Allen was so unlike her father, an Episcopalian Missionary, a gentle man of the cloth. He was exciting—a go-getter who aspired to lofty office and all the trappings of power. Her father had read something in the young man, something that had made him uneasy. And he had told her so. He had even forbidden her to see him at one point. But, headstrong as she was, she would hear none of it. Allen was everything—handsome and thrilling. And at age 33, she had listened to her father's rigid "advice" long enough. They had been married within the year and both had gotten jobs working for the Kenyan government in wildlife management. It was just as well that the jobs had paid almost nothing. Their needs were simple, just the necessities: food, shelter, and a minimum of clothing. That plus an endless supply of animals to study and photograph, an old Land Rover and timeless days and nights to fill with their work and each other. That was more than enough. Who could want more? Allen, apparently.

Anne folded her linen napkin and laid it on the table's dark, shiny veneer. During the last five years her husband had become restless and edgy. He wanted more; more money, more power, more status. The more he got the more he wanted. And advancement meant politicking and politicking meant socializing.

Enter alcohol.

Allen had changed. And alcohol was responsible. He'd taken to dulling the pain of constant frustration in a political system driven by corruption and tribalism, a system where being white meant exclusion from top government jobs and political office. Despite his education and obsessive drive, he would never rise higher than Director, Kenya Wildlife Service. And, when his rage had not been sufficiently anesthetized by liquor, he had taken to venting it on his wife.

Allen Windridge sensed her mood and decided to change the subject.

"Her husband is her boss," McCullen explained, chewing his vegetables slowly, wishing they were steak.

"Convenient," Forrest replied smugly.

"Not so convenient as'ya might think, lad. He's a bastard, that one. Mad-dog mean when'e drinks."

Forrest glanced at McCullen then put his eyes back on his plate. "He beat her?" Forrest asked his vegetables.

"I'm not sure. I've noticed a few bruises from time to time. But she always has a ready excuse for 'em. Fell against this. Knocked into that. She'll not admit'ta anythin'." McCullen sat for a moment, his empty fork poised in mid air.

"Well, that would explain why she always acts like her tampon is screwed in a little too tight."

"Aye, lad." McCullen allowed himself a chuckle. "Women can certainly try one's patience, at times."

"Yeah, the times when they're not asleep." Forrest returned the smile and took a long drink of tea. He wished it had ice in it, but ice was a luxury in a camp that generated its own electricity. "The only thing more frustrating than women is golf...and occasionally, I actually do pretty *well* with golf."

"Did you hear the latest from the field?" Anne's husband mumbled from behind his newspaper, his question prompted by an article concerning a series of murders in Mombasa. "Seems some bloke is bashing the hell out of the natives. Killed quite a number of them near the border."

"What?" she asked, her thoughts interrupted.

"Haven't you heard? Someone's killed quite a few hunters during the last couple of months."

"How dreadful," Anne said, tentatively. It wasn't like Allen to spontaneously initiate conversations anymore. Both the story and his telling of it took her by surprise. She gave him a puzzled look. "I didn't see that article. What page is it on?" she asked, partly to encourage the conversation and partly out of genuine curiosity.

"It's not in the paper. They've been instructed to keep the story quiet. Don't want to alarm the tourists and all that."

"How did you hear of it, then?"

"Ben Otieno told me his boys found some corpses strung up in a tree. Nine or ten more several miles away." He lowered the paper to savor the look on her face. "Decapitated corpses."

She started to blanch, noticed his expression then, with a surge of will, wiped her face clean denying him any pleasure he might attain at her expense.

A sadistic smile grew across his face as he reached for his drink. "Want to know what happened to the heads?"

"No!"

"I thought you might. Oddly enough, they turned up, speared on shards of burned out trees. And human hands have been found in some of the nearby villages."

"That's really more information than I require, Allen."

"Aren't you the one who always wants to know everything?"

Silence.

"Oh forgive, me. That's right. You *already* know everything."

The room temperature dropped five degrees.

"Now for the really curious part," he taunted.

"Please..."

"The severed hands had cards in them."

Anne let out a breath. "Cards?"

"Rather like business cards—calling cards. Same size. But more like a warning."

"How so."

"They had the word 'poacher' printed on them."

"Poacher?" She paused to consider the implications. "Were they?"

"Seems our mystery assassin thinks so. And there were slaughtered elephants near the last find. Everyone is quite terrified, actually. The Masai have taken to calling him Baba Tembo."

Father of the Elephants. Another thought flashed through her head. Forrest had found the little orphaned elephant near the Mara. "Rather gruesome. Are you sure it's one man?"

"Actually, there is evidence which would lead one to conclude it was the work of a rival poaching gang. Perhaps a territorial dispute of some sort."

"Poachers or not, they are human beings. What's being done about it?"

"I've asked Luther Mkumbe to increase patrols along the border. The Tanzanian police have been alerted, as well. The Masai aren't too enthused about it, however. So we're keeping the patrols out of the Mara, proper, leaving that area under their jurisdiction. Politics, you know."

"How well I know," she said, her voice heavy with disgust. She watched as her husband poured himself another drink. She longed for the days when they barely eked by. Back then they couldn't afford enough spirits to get a man drunk. The only alcohol they had then was in their medical kit. She resented her husband's habits of late. And his undisciplined spending made her very insecure. Her thoughts went back to Camp Uhura and Dr. McCullen. Drinking was killing him, as well—not to mention the cigarettes. Although he did have more of an excuse. Curiously enough, Forrest didn't drink very much. Odd, she mused. He seems like the macho straight-down-the-hatch type. He certainly had that effect on Malcolm. He was more reckless since the American arrived. Must be a testosterone thing, she thought with a grimace, or the same effect a pack of dogs have on each other. Other thoughts nagged at her. Things just didn't add up. Forrest was a man of contradictions—and so secretive. He was intelligent but he was no scientist—not like any she had ever met, at least. He was banal and brutish, certainly no gentleman. Yet he had the kindest, softest heart when it came to the animals, Malcolm and the children. And he was dashing—an untamed beast—either brave or crazy. He hadn't hesitated to take on a pack of hyenas with only a pistol to save a baby elephant. Intriguing.

She watched her husband reading; ignoring her. Perhaps he could offer an opinion. "A new researcher has taken up residence in Malcolm's camp. An American."

She saw the top of her husband's head move behind the pages of his newspaper. She heard his teeth crunching on ice. "Mm hmm."

She hated that sound. It was quite like the sound of fingernails on a chalk board. "He's doing a study on elephants."

"That so?"

"He seems quite wealthy or at least well funded. But he's really quite odd. And there's something disturbing about him."

Windridge laid the paper on the long table and stared at her blankly before pouring himself another drink from a crystal decanter. "Sounds like someone else I know," he said flatly while looking her straight in the eye. "Nothing you can't handle, I'm sure."

Anne felt her face burn. Father was right about you, she thought. She hated to admit being wrong about anything. *Probably something I got from Mum.*

"...Irish mother. Immensely stubborn woman, she was," McCullen explained. "Outlived her father by five years. That must be where Anne gets it."

"She's definitely got it," Forrest grimaced, shaking his head. He was working on another thought. "That why she hangs around here so much; to get away from her husband?"

"Perhaps." McCullen looked off into space to complete the answer. "I suppose I'm something of a father figure for her now that her real father is gone."

Forrest sipped his tea, listening thoughtfully. "She could do worse."

McCullen smiled at the compliment. "I feel sorry for her. She's a good lass. And she means well. She just has a problem warmin' up'ta people, especially men."

"She needs to get a life—get rid of that asshole, too."

McCullen looked at him. "Her *work* is her life. And her husband controls her job."

"Like I said, Doc. Maybe she needs to have something more. Then she won't need him or his abuse."

McCullen thought about Forrest's comment. "We could all use a life. I don't see you havin' too many extracurricular activities."

Forrest gave McCullen a knowing smile. "Oh, I wouldn't be too sure about that, Doc."

"Right on time, Grizz." Forrest smiled and rose to his feet as the gray and white L-100 droned overhead. A small white, cargo chute blossomed atop its container and drifted quickly to the chalky lake bed. Adams waved hello and good-bye with the plane's wings before banking into a gentle turn to the east.

Fifteen minutes later, Forrest had the contents of his latest package spread out on the parachute like a picnic lunch. He sat in the shade under the baobab taking stock of his latest shipment. Claymore anti-personnel mines, M-67 fragmentation grenades and ammo cans contrasted sharply with first-aid kits, batteries, sun screen, and packets of grape Koolaid for his canteens.

The most interesting item, by far, was the imposing rifle which rested on its butt-stock and fold-out bipod legs—a Barrett Light Fifty. Two heavy metal olive-drab cans full of .50 caliber ammunition sat next to the rifle. One contained special copper-jacketed ball rounds and in the other, rounds tipped with high-explosive projectiles. Also included were a cammo Cordura drag-bag, ammo pouches and other accessories.

Forrest picked up the U.S. Army operating manual titled M-82-A1 and pulled out the laser-printed letter inserted between the pages:

> RECEIVED YOUR REQUEST. IS THIS WHAT YOU HAD IN MIND WHEN YOU SAID "POWER TOOL?"
> ENJOY — MIDAS

"Enjoy, indeed."

It took Forrest another hour to store the new equipment inside the giant tree cache. After that chore was complete, he sat down next to his new man-portable cannon, took a tasty grape-flavored swig from his canteen and started to read. Like all boys, he couldn't wait to play with his new toy.

This had to be Amy's work, Forrest thought. A-M-Y was carved into the dry lake bed, sure enough. Who else could it be? And there were tracks, small feet in soft soles, on the lake's edges. *No well defined toes. Maybe she's wearing some sort of moccasins. Why no directional pointer to let us know her direction of travel? C'mon girl. You've gotta help me out. In any case, Peeper will be happy with the latest update.*

"You haven't been making very much progress on this project. What have you been doing with yourself?" Anne Sargent-Windridge plucked her glasses off of her nose and laid them on the picnic table.

Forrest, his right elbow already resting on the table, planted his chin in his hand, closed his eyes and let out a long exasperated breath. The whereabouts of Roseanne's herd weighed heavily on his mind and he had less patience than usual for bureaucratic crap.

"Well?"

Forrest opened his eyes and returned her stare. "You've been all over my ass like a bad case of diaper rash for weeks. So why don't you make yourself useful for a change? Some friends of mine are missing. And you've been pestering the piss out of me to join me in the field. So, maybe you can help me find them."

"Friends?" she asked, a look of puzzlement and concern spreading over her face. "You actually have *friends*?"

"Get your purse or your field pack, or whatever the hell it is you drag your shit around in and c'mon." Forrest ordered, freeing his legs from the picnic bench and marching off toward his hut.

"Where are we going?" Anne inquired, now that she realized he was serious and not just trying to put her off.

"Flying."

Credence Clearwater Revival's *Goin' up Around the Bend* blared in their headsets as the little plane wove through the treetops following the river below. Flying made Anne Sargent nervous. And flying in the tiny Zenair absolutely petrified her. But she couldn't let *him* see that. To allay her fears she concentrated on the job at hand—finding "his" herd.

Forrest rolled the little craft into a tight turn and watched her drop the binoculars into her lap to grip the plane's tubular frame. She held on so tight, he noticed, that she'd driven the blood from her fingers—a real "white knuckle" flyer. "You okay?" he asked on the intercom which automatically cut out the music.

Anne Sargent fumbled to find the mike button. "Fine," she strained to say as he eased back on the stick, loading on the Gs.

Forrest smiled thinly. *Yeah, right.* He moved the joystick to the left and rolled the wings level. The G loading returned to normal—1.0. "See anything?"

"No. Nothing so far," she said, swallowing as if she were trying to force a tennis ball down her throat. *One more maneuver like that and you'll bloody well get to see what I had for breakfast.* Sargent watched with interest as he checked his aeronautical chart. Her saliva glands were just starting to work again, secreting something other than sand and cotton. "Maybe we should try further upriver, toward the woodlands."

He looked at her. "Think so?"

She nodded. "If they were under pressure from poachers they might have headed for the safety of the forest. I've seen that happen before."

Forrest turned to follow the brown ribbon that snaked through the landscape below. Intent on the search, Anne forgot about most of her queasiness. The terrain changed from flat to hilly before turning into wooded highlands. As they followed the eastern branch of the Ewaso Ng'iro northward, into the Aberdare National Park, the elevation increased to nearly 3,000 feet. After passing over Lake Nakuru, they flew over the town of the same name where they landed at the airstrip to buy fuel and refreshments. The trip had taken over three hours.

Forrest took Anne aside and planned their afternoon search. His finger traced their proposed route on the chart as he spoke. "We'll turn west...pick up the western branch of the Ewaso Ng'iro...turn south...pass to the west of Narok, here...cross Lake Magadi and return to camp, the proverbial three-hour tour."

Her face grew tight at the thought of another flight. But she tilted her head, arched her eyebrows in a conciliatory way and sighed, "I think I can handle that."

"Good." Forrest replied. "Otherwise it's a long walk."

Minutes later they were off in a cloud of red dust.

An hour and a half went by along with a hundred miles of western Kenya. They spotted dozens of hippos and water birds, several herds of gazelle, but few elephants. As they flew south of Narok, Anne spotted the herd first—nine elephants in all, trotting across a hill-country clearing. "There's a rather sizable group."

Forrest didn't see them till they were almost past.

"Could be them," Forrest said as the herd passed under a wing which pointed almost vertically at the ground. "They look familiar but..." he racked the plane around in a hard reverse to the right, "there's too few of them and they're a long way from their normal habitat."

"Probably ran off because you threatened them with an airplane ride," Sargent grunted under the strain as they went from half a G to two-and-a-half in under a second.

Forrest nodded and smiled. He brought the ultralight around for another pass. "That's them," he exclaimed, excitement erupting in his voice. His tone changed suddenly. "Somebody's definitely missing...can't tell who, though." The elephants ran from the nasty buzz of the propeller, ears spread, trunks extended.

Anne had stopped trying to look. Her stomach was still out there somewhere, she thought, running alongside the plane.

"Look for a clear spot to set this little beauty down."

Forrest and the Zenair rolled out of the turn. Sargent's vestibular organs didn't. The color blanched from her face then returned in hues of gray and green. She poked her head out the door into the rushing wind. "Rrrrooowwf!" She coughed and retched into the slipstream, heaved again and jerked her head back inside gasping for breath. Her eyeballs rolled back under drooping lids.

Forrest looked at her. "Does that mean you didn't like the lunch?" he said with an almost straight face. His eyes went back to his search for a place to land.

Bingo.

He rolled the Zenair up on a wing and pointed the nose at a small clearing in the brush and trees.

Sargent felt the "down elevator" returning and heard the reduction in engine noise. The bottom of her stomach rose to the occasion once again. Even with her eyes closed, her head found its way out the door as the rest of her lunch made a U-turn on a one-way street.

With his throttle hand, Forrest grabbed her collar and yanked her head inside just in time to avoid a nasty slap from the tall weeds that brushed past the prop as the little craft bounced violently along the ground. In a moment, the engine had stopped and he was out of the plane and around to her side. Lunch, he saw, was now a streak down the side of the fuselage. Anne's uniform shirt rose in laborious breaths as she fought back lingering nausea.

Forrest suppressed a laugh. "You want me to call an ambulance or anything?"

Anne's eyes opened, uncovering an intense glare.

"Here," Forrest said in a more sympathetic gesture, "let me help you out."

"Go to hell," she snapped, jerking her forearm out of his hand. Gingerly, she eased herself out of the right seat and planted her wobbly feet onto the dry soil. Her head still reeled but she was beginning to come around. Her anger recovered first. "I'm going to the Transportation Ministry and have your bloody license revoked as soon as we get back."

"Well, you said you could 'handle' it." The edges of a smile cracked his face but was quickly replaced with a fake frown. "Look what you did to the side of my nice, clean airplane." He made it sound almost like whining.

"Good," she said before wiping her mouth and cheeks on his shirt sleeve.

Forrest looked down at the faint stain on his shirt and then at the vomit streak on the plane. They matched. His smile returned. "I'm not gonna buy you lunch ever again if you're just gonna waste it."

Sargent grabbed the binoculars off the floor and headed into the brush.

"Where are *you* going?"

"To find the bloody elephants," she snapped. "Where do you think?"

Forrest smiled again and started off after her.

It took 15 minutes of quiet stalking before they located the herd in the thick brush. The animals were still quite tense from their encounter with the roaring aluminum raptor. Forrest tested the wind and motioned for her to follow him on a flanking movement to a better vantage point.

When they reached a small bright clearing, the elephants filed off toward the river.

Sargent saw his frown. His aggravating humor and exuberance had suddenly drained away. "What's wrong?"

Forrest ignored her for a moment as he scanned the family.

"Roseanne's missing. Something's happened to Roseanne," he said, lowering the binoculars.

"Roseanne?"

"She's the matriarch...or was." He breathed audibly, his voice heavy. "Let's go."

They followed the family group down to the river's edge and took up a position downwind where they could observe without disturbing them. They'd had enough of that for one day, he said.

Forrest took a small spiral notebook out of his survival vest and took inventory.

"Poachers?" Anne asked.

He shrugged slightly as if he was suddenly too tired or too depressed to make a more demonstrative gesture.

"Who knows?" He scanned the family again with the field glasses as if he had made a mistake and just not seen her. But he knew in his heart that it was hard to misplace a five-ton animal with a uniquely broken tusk. "She was perfectly healthy the last time I saw her." Forrest lowered the glasses. "We've got to find her," he said as he led off in the direction of the plane.

"Today?" Anne asked looking at her watch and thinking about another two hours of combat maneuvers.

"Today."

Vultures in the trees had caught their attention and led them to the spot. Neither of them spoke a word during the short walk.

Forrest circled what was left of the carcass with leaden steps. They had found her only a mile down river. Roseanne had been dead for several days so there wasn't very much left of her, not enough left to interest anything but the vultures and insects. There was no positive proof that the remains belonged to the missing matriarch. But somehow, instinctively, Forrest knew it was her.

"Are you sure?" Anne asked from the invisible yet solid edge of the odor barrier.

He looked at her. "Yeah. I think so." There was a long uncomfortable pause. "I can't tell for sure. They took her tusks. The broken one was her trademark."

Rasping cries of dueling vultures interrupted the grimness. Anne startled. Her body jerked in a nervous spasm.

Without uttering a word, Forrest turned and followed the elephant tracks into the trees. There were many of them leading off in all directions. Anne followed silently, spooked by the shadowy veil of death that hung over the place.

Bones were everywhere. Most of them were elephant bones. Bleached white sculptures littered the dark ground under the forest canopy, each a tombstone marking an animal's final resting place. Most conspicuous were the skulls—monuments to the noblest of beasts. They came across dozens of them as they walked.

"Elephant graveyard," Forrest whispered respectfully as Anne came up next to him. "Every Sir Arthur Conan Doyle fan has heard about this."

"Mmm," she confirmed, wistfully. She turned her head, surveying the scene. "Despite the legends and folk tales, they really don't have a secret graveyard where they all go to die. The sick and injured simply seek out quiet, comfortable places in their final hours where they can die in peace—most often, heavy cover near water. That's why their bones are concentrated in certain areas."

Forrest nodded, a grim expression forming.

"I've seen a few of these places before," Anne continued, solemnly. "And I always get the same feeling—a mixture of sadness, respect and admiration. There's something awe inspiring about them, like when my father would take me to visit some of the great cathedrals. Yet this place is so sad...so very sad."

"'Specially when you know one of 'em, personally," Forrest added.

Anne produced a sorrowful frown as she nodded in agreement.

"Roseanne's death was anything but peaceful or dignified." Forrest played his eyes around the graveyard. Even to his untrained eye, there was ample evidence of poaching; small round holes in bones where none should have been; ribs and other bones shattered by bullets. His jaw tightened. Forrest suddenly brought his index finger to his lips. Ever the hunter, he sensed something she didn't. Their eyes met and he motioned for her to follow him back toward Roseanne's remains. With Anne in tow, he slipped through the grove as quietly as possible.

The scene that met their eyes caused them to stop abruptly. For a moment, they both held their breath.

Led by Oprah, now the most senior female and new matriarch, the family had made their way back down river. Silently, they drifted among the trees examining the bones. Particular attention was paid to the skulls.

Forrest and Sargent pulled themselves back against the trunk of a wide tree and watched without saying a word.

Two young females, perhaps eight-to-ten years of age, walked directly to Roseanne's body and stood motionless for a long moment. Gingerly, tenderly, almost lovingly, they passed their nimble snouts over her form sniffing and, occasionally, touching their fallen leader. One-by-one, the other family members drifted to the site, drawn by some invisible force.

Was it love, respect, admiration...grief that drew them here? Forrest couldn't decide.

Trunks extended from the forming semicircle, delicately examining the remains. A fifth elephant approached, picked up a loose clump of grass, and dropped it on the body. Another deposited a snout-full of dirt. Others followed suit, covering Roseanne's body with grass, sticks, branches and dry leaves. Still another elephant, a young male, dispersed a cluster of lingering vultures with a mock charge lest they defile their leader's corpse. He shook his head, watched the huge gray birds settle a few meters away, and returned to the ceremony.

Forrest's eyes turned to Anne's, his question unspoken: *Is this what I think it is?*

She understood. She turned her head back to the spectacle. "I've only seen this a few times," she said, her voice hushed.

"If I didn't know better," Forrest interjected. "I'd say we were witnessing a funeral."

"I quite agree." The faintest of smiles spread across her face. It was a sad, knowing smile, full of sympathy and admiration. Then she noticed something that shocked her. The same smile was on John's face, too. And, she noticed, his keen, cold, penetrating eyes had melted. They were moist with emotion. *Perhaps there's a heart in there, after all.*

CHAPTER-TWELVE

CONFLAGRATION *a: conflict*
b: a large disastrous fire

THE KAPJE SHIMMERED TWO MILES in the distance. A small hill, Forrest thought, although it looked more like the ruins of a castle whose walls had been reduced to a pile of boulders, the oldest granite rocks on Earth. It was one of many which dotted the otherwise featureless landscape. Kapje meant "little heads" in Swahili, he remembered reading, which seemed appropriate somehow. They were a lot like pimples or carbuncles on the plain's otherwise smooth face.

The Serengeti Plain, he reflected as he scanned the limitless horizon, a place steeped in legend, as vast and romantic as Africa itself. It looked bigger from the ground than it did from the air, and from the air, it looked immense. This'd be one helluva lawn if somebody had to cut it, he thought as he wiped the sweat off his forehead with the back of his hand. But then, he knew the place already had a lawn service; millions of animals whose sole purpose in life was processing grass.

Forrest's tired feet made him wish that he'd decided to fly. *Too bad there wasn't a more efficient way to hunt these guys.* He had left the Zenair nine miles behind him, hidden under a pile of brush and camo-netting at the base of a boulder mound. The plane, however small, would just attract too much attention in such a wide open area.

Heat, distance and age were catching up to him. He sat down in a patch of short grass at the top of a shallow rise. It felt good to stop. In Vietnam, his Ranger team could do twenty-plus miles a day if they had to. Now, at his age, every mile felt like twenty. He took a swig of water then brought out the Zeiss binoculars. The elephant herd he was paralleling was nearly a mile to the west but the optics brought them much closer.

Forrest scanned the undulating land, pausing to examine each object and feature. Some were clumps of grass or bushes or boulders. Some turned out to be hoofed animals grazing their way across the grassy sea. And some were predators, lions, wild dogs and hyenas who traveled along with their source of food. He scanned 360 degrees just to be sure he was the only human in the area. If he wasn't, he wanted to be sure that he was the spotter and not the spotee.

Smoke rose in the distant east. Grassfire from the looks of it, he thought. Columns of light gray smoke drifted high into the air before being flattened and thinned by upper altitude winds.

Forrest lifted his tired bones off the grass and reached down for the ERMA which was snugly resting in its cammo case. He had just gotten it back in service. After its stock had been damaged by the grenade he'd left as a booby-trap, a replacement stock from Colonel Grant had made it as good as new. He was glad to have it. The Barrett would have been far too heavy to lug the many miles he'd walked the past few days. Forrest slung the case over his shoulder and continued on toward the rocky hill in the distance. It would be a good place to rest, eat and maybe spend the night, he judged, if the herds slowed down a bit. Everything depended on which way the elephants went. He decided to make that decision when he got there. But just now, his feet and stomach were voting to stop.

****

It was the third day out and the seventh kapje he had climbed to observe the elephants. Forrest had put 27 new miles on his hiking boots. His thoughts turned to water and the limits human endurance would place on his mission. If something didn't happen soon, Forrest thought dejectedly, he'd have to turn back. He looked behind him, over the ground he had covered the previous day. There were other elephant herds he could monitor on his way back to the Zenair. Any one of them could be attacked at any time. He had no way of telling which one the ivory hunters would choose. It was all a giant crap-shoot; a matter of being in the right place at the right time. Therefore, staying with a particular herd wasn't necessary. And it was getting to the point where it was no longer smart.

Water wasn't a problem; at least not yet. There was plenty in his canteens but his supply wouldn't last long enough to get him back to the plane if he went much further north. Another day, he cautioned himself, and he wouldn't have any reserve water if the plane developed a mechanical problem he couldn't repair. *What if I have to hoof it out of here?* That was it, then. The decision was made. He would start back-tracking right after breakfast.

Henderson could've been wrong this time, Forrest thought. Photo analysis isn't an exact science after all. There was more guesswork required than most people thought, especially when the targets were as low-tech as these. Missile silos and motorized rifle regiments were one thing. Groups of men carrying small arms were quite another. Still, the "Peepergram" had said three camps near the northeastern border of the Serengeti National Park and Cynthia Marsh had confirmed that poachers were fairly active in the area. That was the best intelligence he was going to get unless some persecuted pachyderm decided to phone in a hot tip on his trunk phone. Forrest smiled at his own corn-ball humor. *Too much time alone in the bush, John.* Well, they could in a way, he reminded himself with a silent chuckle. At least they could alert each other over great distances using infrasound.

Forrest smiled behind the binoculars as he scanned the herds. Scientists had long ago noticed that wide-spread elephant groups simultaneously responded to mysterious stimuli both unseen and unheard. Some thought that the animals might be communicating telepathically—reading each other's thoughts or utilizing some capacity beyond memory and the five conventional senses. Whatever it was, the uncanny ability only added to the elephants' mystique. Then, in May 1984, Katharine Payne, a researcher observing Asian elephants in the Metro Washington Park Zoo in Portland, Oregon, "stumbled across" the first clue. When all the elephants in the enclosure suddenly froze, she noticed a sensation, a "palpable yet silent throbbing in the air like distant thunder." A pressure—something she felt rather than heard—accompanied the extremely faint rumbling from a large female. She also noticed a rippling motion in the elephant's forehead and realized that the animal was producing a weird sensation similar to one she had experienced as a child while standing next to the church pipe organ. It dawned on her that the elephant might be producing sound waves below the range of human hearing. Further investigation with sophisticated audio equipment proved her right. And since low-frequency sound energy can propagate over long distances, that explained how the animals could communicate with each other over many miles through woodland and grassland alike.

Forrest finished his peanut-butter-and-cracker breakfast and climbed down the rocky hill. Before setting off, he slipped a *James Taylor's Greatest Hits* CD in his Discman. *Walkin' Man* soothed his ears as he put one foot in front of the other in the knee high grass.

Moving in silent desperation
Keeping an eye on the Holy Land
A hypothetical destination.
Say who is this walking man?

He headed south, back toward the plane. It was six miles to the next kapje. A good milestone to set for himself and a good place to have lunch.

Walkin' man
Walkin' man walks
When another mans stops and talks
Walkin' man walks on by
Walks on by

Just before eleven o'clock, he settled down on top of a large boulder to scan the area. An elephant herd was close by flanked by several smaller families in the distance. Through his binoculars, Forrest checked out every object not readily identifiable with the naked eye. A dark object bounding crazily about in the high grass caught his eye. He turned the glasses toward it...focused...then laughed. A male Jackson's widow bird leaped and bounded spastically to attract a mate, its long tail feathers fluttered in the air like the streamers of an exotic Japanese kite.

After a moment Forrest moved the binoculars. A large herd of impala drifted to the northwest followed by a smaller herd of Thompson's gazelles. The antelope were on alert for a reason he had not yet determined. They definitely had seen something he hadn't—something threatening. Forrest panned the binoculars quickly, looking for predators.

There! A cheetah—a mother and two cubs.

She padded along pensively, trying to keep one eye on lunch and the other on her vulnerable kits.

Forrest saw that she was exceptionally gaunt. Her ribs were very prominent under her speckled coat. Probably *hasn't eaten in a while.* He could see the cheetah was torn between her cub's survival and her own—a tough choice for any mother. She stopped and scanned the surrounding terrain. Her gaze alternated between her cubs and her quarry. The gazelles were about to enter a patch of short grass ahead. Forrest could practically read her mind. She was planning her attack, calculating her chances and weighing the attempt against the risk of leaving her cubs exposed. She looked ahead and then back as the cubs approached. She had plenty of high grass in which to accelerate before she would burst into the clear. The Tommies would have little warning and by then, her speed would be over sixty miles per hour. She was the fastest thing on four feet but she couldn't sustain it for very long. Haul ass for one pass, Forrest thought with a smile—a twist on a standard fighter pilot's bromide.

The cheetah's cubs came up behind her and attempted to nurse. Annoyed, she stepped nervously away from them. There was no time for that now. Her alert eyes went back to the gazelles. A yearling fawn nudged at its mother's belly—a prime target—the Serengeti's version of fast food. The cheetah's eyes locked onto him. Her hind legs trembled in anticipation. Her tail and ears twitched as she coiled like a spring. In a flash she was off.

Forrest held his breath for her. She was going for it—she had to. In less than five seconds she had reached her top speed—better acceleration than his turbo Porsche.

"Go baby, go!" he whispered under his breath.

Her hind legs kicked up a small cloud of dust as she crashed through the edge of the high grass and broke to the right to cut off the fleeing Tommy. The mother gazelle quickly bounded ahead then cut 90 degrees to the left attempting to draw the cheetah off her fawn. The counter-measures had no effect. The cheetah was locked onto her target like a meat-seeking missile on a lead-pursuit intercept. Driven by hunger, she was not about to allow herself to be distracted. Her cub's survival depended on her skills.

As the distance between them closed, the young gazelle jinked and swerved in a desperate attempt to out-maneuver a high-performance predator he had no chance of out-running. The cheetah cut the corners like a defensive back, reaching out to trip the doomed fawn. Reach—miss. Another swipe. Reach—contact! The fawn went down and the cheetah slammed on the brakes in a cloud of dust that momentarily engulfed her and her prey. After a moment she emerged from the dust, her jaws tightly clamped around the gazelle's throat. Her lungs heaved as the fawn's limbs jerked in the final throes of suffocation.

Forrest heard himself let out a long breath. He noticed the mother gazelle a few meters away. Her soulful eyes wore a look of alarm that quickly changed to a look of defeat. It was no use, she saw. The death of one would mean life for three—arithmetic that held zero solace for the anguished mother.

Forrest turned his binoculars back to the cheetah. She was too exhausted to drag the kill back to her cubs. She dropped it on the ground and barked for them to join her. Then, for one brief peaceful moment in a land where life and death relentlessly chase each other, she sat down to catch her breath.

Forrest noticed that she seemed more nervous now than she had before the hunt. The reason soon became apparent. One of Nature's rules: *Just because you make a kill doesn't mean you get to keep it.*

Attracted by the commotion of the hunt, dozens of carnivores of all descriptions began to converge on the cheetah family and their hard-won meal. She stood, picked up the carcass and started to move toward Forrest's hill. She froze. Her tail went straight and began to twitch. *Something new had entered the picture. What?*

Forrest took the glasses away from his eyes and searched the base of the hill. *What does she see?* "Uh Oh."

Lions! Seven of them had emerged from their resting place among the boulders. Forrest knew that the cheetah was no match for the king of the beasts. They would kill her cubs and take her prize. They'd kill her, too, if they could catch her.

Forrest suddenly felt desperately sorry for her. *Time for more tough choices, lady—none of them good.* Forrest knew cheetah populations were in serious decline. The regal high-speed cats with permanent black tears were losing the battle for survival. Lions would instinctively kill cheetahs on sight without provocation. Eliminating the competition was the reason most scientists agreed upon. For the cheetah, it was reason enough when reasons didn't matter.

The mother cheetah arched her back and retreated trying to lead her cubs away from the fresh meat. But they were starving and did not realize the seriousness of the situation.

Forrest watched as the lions advanced. They displayed little anxiety. They were in complete control. They had a win-win situation developing and they knew it.

Normally determined not to interfere, Forrest had had enough. "Oh no you don't," he muttered to himself as he extracted the ERMA from its case. "She worked hard for her dinner. You guys get your own."

The lions were no more than 150 meters from his position and a mere 200 meters from the cheetahs when he cycled the bolt and flipped off the safety. A minor change in the scope's elevation adjustment compensated for the downhill bullet trajectory. Forrest steadied the crosshairs on the lead lion then moved the point-of-aim into the dirt two feet in front of her. He pulled the trigger. All of the animals jumped and turned at the sound of the shot. A fountain of dust spewed up in front of the lions, halting their advance. They hesitated for a second then moved ahead.

A second shot impacted near the lion's forelegs stinging her with flying dirt and pebbles. She cringed, looked around and veered from her line of advance.

The cheetah hovered over her two cubs which were startled by the thunderous noise. Only extreme hunger kept her from running away. She seemed to know the gunfire was not directed at her.

Forrest sensed that the cheetah realized he was trying to help her. "You guys get your own food," he heard himself shouting at the lions. "Don't be so damn lazy."

Another well-placed shot turned the lions back and they headed out into the high grass. Similarly, Forrest kept the hyenas at bay as the cheetah seized the gazelle carcass and dragged it into the concealment of the tall dry grass.

Forrest reloaded his rifle and leaned it against the boulder. He looked at his watch and then at the sun. *Plenty of daylight left. Plenty of time to make it to the next kapje. No point in staying here. Position's compromised now, anyway.*

He stood, picked up his rifle, inserted it into its drag bag and slowly made his way down the hill.

* * * *

"Mr. Henderson, Mr. Barber is here to see you."

Roselle's voice sounded tense, Henderson thought. He knew his secretary didn't like the man any more than he did. "Okay, send him in." *What does that little weasel want?*

Roy Barber strutted into the office and hovered at the edge of Henderson's desk. The short, white-haired man's rosy complexion shone at its maximum intensity accentuating his sharp nose and pale blue eyes. Everybody at Langley referred to him as the "white rat." It wasn't hard to understand why.

Henderson didn't bother to get up. "What can I do for you, Roy?" he asked, coolly. Leaning back in his chair, he made a steeple with his index fingers and rested his chin on it.

Barber tossed a folder onto the center of Henderson's desk. He misjudged the throw. The folder landed with a slap and slid off the edge. Henderson caught it just as it collided with his knees. "That the way you always treat classified material?"

Barber flushed at the admonition. "You running ops I don't know about?"

"Who wants to know?"

Barber folded his arms over his neatly pressed, tailor-made, light blue suit and lowered his chin. "In case you've forgotten, I'm acting deputy director. *I'm* supposed to know *everything* that's going on," he replied smugly. He stood fast, waiting for an answer.

Henderson let him wait. He opened the folder and scanned the perforated teletype paper. His heart skipped a beat when he recognized the conversation he'd had with Forrest. To his relief, NSA had only transcribed half the message. The bad news: it was his half. He hoped his discomfort didn't show.

"That conversation was routed from this building—within ID. I want to know who it is, and what op it's associated with," Barber insisted with a glare. Barber never swore, no matter how angry he became—a trait that really annoyed Henderson. He didn't trust anyone who didn't swear.

In the aftermath of the Director of Central Intelligence's "problems of a personal nature" and subsequent "extended vacation," the CIA had been subject to more political posturing than usual. High visibility voids in the hierarchy were like chum to a school of sharks. Think-tank civilians competed with retired generals and admirals for coveted director positions and the political fallout trickled down from there. Everybody who was anybody—the overeducated overachievers, Henderson called them—were making maximum effort to best their perceived rivals; back-stabbing and ass-kissing at its enlightened best. And Barber perceived, correctly, that his closest competition was Henderson. Especially since Henderson had been picked to brief the White House on the Somalia situation. To Henderson it was just a matter of being in the right place at the right time. Barber didn't see it that way. A combination of jealousy and paranoia consumed him. His fangs were out and he was out to sink them into his less qualified colleague.

"You know the rules, Roy—compartmentalization, need-to-know and all that." Henderson maintained his standard poker-faced spook look.

Barber knew, indeed. He had helped institute some of the safeguard procedures in the wake of the Aldrich Ames fiasco. Compartmentalized information structures within the intelligence community were designed to keep information from leaking out much like water-tight compartments on ships were designed to prevent water from leaking in. In either case, the principle was simple: a compromised compartment would contain the damage and prevent loss of the entire vessel.

"I expect a report in forty-eight hours."

"I'll see what I can do." The way Henderson said it, it sounded more like "go to hell."

Forrest heard the shots in the distance and sat up, his mosquito netting still clinging to his head. He didn't bother removing it. It camouflaged his face while he looked around. Another volley of gunfire brought his head around to the west where he saw a large heard of elephants running to the southeast across the plain. He ripped the mosquito netting off and brought his field glasses up just in time to see a large female roll over onto her side. Instinctively, Forrest reached for his rifle then hesitated. *Too far. Way too far.* The poachers were over a mile away.

Forrest scrambled to his knees and pulled on his survival vest. He slung the MP-5 over his shoulder and grabbed his rifle. Everything else was left behind as he quickly bounded down the rocky slope. When he got to the bottom he broke into a steady jog—a moderate, sustainable pace. He had a lot of ground to cover and didn't want to be too winded to shoot when he reached his rifle's maximum range.

More shots popped in the distance. As he ran, Forrest could hear the screams of the terrified elephants. He tightened his jaw and held his pace. His legs whipped against the knee-high grass.

From the top of the hill he had seen six men, four with guns. As he came to the top of a shallow rise, Forrest stopped to assess the situation. He dropped to his haunches and scanned with his binoculars. The poachers, he surmised, must have approached the elephants from the bottom of the deep depression that lay on the far side of the herd. He could see two elephant carcasses plainly and a portion of a third. The rest of the herd had scattered to the south, breaking up into small family groups of less than a dozen members. The gunfire ceased. Although he could estimate the distance, Forrest took a reading with the built-in laser range finder. *1,400 meters. Still too far.* He continued his advance.

Another very slight, down-sloping break in elevation lay two hundred meters ahead. Might be able to shoot from there, he thought. It had potential. Beyond that, there was six hundred meters of open ground between himself and the dead animals; all of it slightly downhill. It would be impossible to cross it without being seen.

Forrest dropped down to the prone position when he reached the rise. He brought the rifle up and scoped the targets. *Six men. One with an AK.* The rest had old bolt-action rifles. Three dead animals lay in tall grass at the crest of another shallow rise. The ground between himself and the target sloped down very slightly. Behind the targets, the ground fell off into the wide ravine before rising to another hill a mile or more in the distance. The nearest cover was an isolated cluster of acacias some two miles to the south. So much for concealment, he thought as he chambered a round, tightened the sling around his elbow and forearm and drew down on the man with the automatic weapon.

The wind was in his face now—about five knots and increasing as the sun came up. Definitely won't help the bullet get there, he thought. His first target was standing with his back to him. Then he turned to the side. "Settle down, dirtbag," he grumbled under his breath. "Lets have a little consideration here. It's gonna be tough enough to drop your ass at this range without you fidgeting around like that." The target presented his back again. "Good boy. That's more like it."

Forrest eased down on the trigger. The man moved just as the rifle went off.

"Ssshhit!"

Forrest knew it was a miss as soon as the bullet left the muzzle. As the round cracked by them, the men hit the ground.

"Shoulda crawled in closer, dammit," Forrest admonished himself for his overeagerness.

Deciding on his next move, he watched the poachers through his scope. They lay still in the high grass for a few minutes trying to figure out what was going on. Occasionally, Forrest could see heads twisting around and arms moving and pointing in nervous animation. One of the men rose to his knees then to a crouch. Staying low, the poacher scampered to the side of the nearest elephant carcass. He leaned against it, using its bulk for cover as he searched to the west for the hidden sniper.

"Wrong way, asshole." Forrest grunted a sardonic laugh as he brought the mil-dot reticle over the center of his target's back. "Over here." He watched the grass and the shimmer and added several clicks of elevation to the sight. He was determined to make this shot a good one.

BOOM! The sweet smell of gunsmoke drifted over his face. The poacher arched his back sharply and dropped to the ground. A solid hit.

The man with the AK-47 fired a long burst to the east then jumped and ran. Panic is contagious, Forrest thought as he watched the other men follow their comrade. He followed them through the scope as they took off toward the far ravine.

Forrest came to his feet and started off after them, straight toward the largest elephant. Its body would make a good shooting platform and provide cover. I'll lose 'em in the ravine for a few minutes, he saw, and take 'em when they come up the far side.

It took four minutes at a brisk trot for Forrest to reach the nearest elephant. Crumpled on its side, the body of the poacher lay next to it. Forrest kicked the dead poacher up against the elephant's huge belly and stepped up on it, using his body as a foot-stool.

The elephant, he noticed with renewed disgust, was a large pregnant female. Even with the poacher's body to stand on, he couldn't find a comfortable shooting position. Forrest stepped down and moved to her neck. He kneeled next to the elephant's throat and laid his rifle across her big flat ear. Much better, he thought.

Forrest caught his breath, made another sight-adjustment for the extra range and waited. The grass rustled in the breeze. Beads of sweat grew over his eyebrows. He could feel his heart pounding in his ears. He moved the scope back and fourth along the near crest below which the poachers had disappeared.

Where are they?

A movement caught his eye, then another. The poachers had spread out as they climbed the far side of the depression. Forrest took aim at the closest one. He was nearly out of range.

He squeezed off an extreme-range shot and hoped for the best. A puff of dust marked the bullet's impact in the dirt several meters behind the target. Forrest lowered the rifle and watched in frustration. Those guys were goners, he realized—well past his rifle's effective range.

What happened next stunned him.

Two of the five poachers stopped in their tracks and turned to look behind them. It suddenly dawned on them that by climbing the far slope they had brought themselves back into the shooter's field of view.

Forrest watched them stop and look. He started to pick his rifle up but waited. Two of the men looked at each other and ran back down the slope heading in his direction. The other men, unwilling to take their chances on the exposed hillside alone, followed a moment later. In a second, all had disappeared back into the depression.

"You gotta be shitting me!" Forrest couldn't believe his eyes. *What could those guys have been thinking? More importantly, what would they do next? Unpredictable targets are dangerous targets—even if they're stupid targets.*

He looked around, starting to think defensively. He checked the MP-5, thumbing the fire selector switch to full auto. *They might try to rush me. Maybe they realize I'm by myself.* He looked at the sun angle. It was still at his back. *Good.* The breeze was picking up now, he noticed, starting to bend the stalks of grass. It felt good on his hot, sweaty face.

Anxiously, Forrest looked left and right for the men to come up over the rise. He still wasn't sure what they would do. They could wait all day for him to leave or they could just move off under the cover of darkness. That thought reminded him he'd left his NVGs in his pack along with his water.

Things are going to shit in a hurry.

He gave a half second's thought to going over the ravine after them but instantly dismissed it as a stupid idea. They would have all the advantages. Retreat crossed his mind, but he would have to leave the cover of the elephants. And as usual, Mr. Murphy would probably bring the bad guys out of the ravine just when he turned his back. *Nah. Wait 'em out, John. They panicked pretty easily. They'll do something before long.*

Almost twenty minutes passed. There were no movements and aside from the rolling wind in the dry grass, no sounds.

Forrest kept his vigil. There was no way for them to flank him or get behind him without him noticing. Well, maybe in the tall grass, he considered, but it was a long way to crawl.

The breeze was up to a steady 10-to-12 knots now. And there was something odd about it. Forrest sniffed. *Smoke.*

An instant later, he saw the smoke rising in front of him. It was spreading out all across his front masking, his view of the ravine. Flames started to lick at the horizon. And, he saw, they were getting closer! The growing breeze was bringing it on fast—really fast!

Holy shit!

His brain rattled off options in adrenaline overdrive:

Run—Nope. It's moving too fast. Even if I could, they're probably using it to drive me—flush me out of my hole.

Stay—The building roar of the flames told him that he'd be cooked alive.

Can't run—can't stay.

The line of flame and smoke had grown into a roaring wall of fire—a conflagration that consumed everything in its path. He could hear the shouts of the men following it, waiting for him to break and run. When he did, Forrest realized, they'd cut him down.

Sit and cook or bolt and die. Terrific.

Forrest could feel the heat as the fiery wall marched ahead on the breeze.

Think fast pal, or you're gonna be a Quarterpounder—a well-done Quarterpounder.

His eyes went to the poacher's body lying in a heap against the elephant's belly.

Belly!

The heat had evaporated the sweat off of his forehead as he leaped to his left and drew his survival knife from its sheath. In cold weather survival school, he'd been taught how to use a deer's body to defeat the cold. *Temperature extremes are temperature extremes and insulation is insulation.* Forrest laid his rifle down and put both hands on the handle. "Sorry, lady," he muttered to the dead elephant, "this can't be helped." In rapid, repeated slashes, he plunged the blade into the soft mound of gray flesh. The flames were close now. He could hear the grass crackling as it burned on the other side of the carcass. Air drawn into the flames roared like a jet engine.

A mixture of fluid and blood ran from the huge wound he cut in the elephant's belly. With desperate strokes, he slashed at the edges of her swollen abdomen. Tissue tore and parted. Fluid gushed over him in a sudden flood. Entrails flopped out of the hole followed by something big—something heavy. Forrest recoiled at the sight—momentarily transfixed—a fetus, her unborn baby.

The gut-wrenching odor of burning flesh poured over the top of the huge beast. The fire was on him—consuming the skin on the elephant's back. *Get moving or you're fried chicken.*

Forrest jammed his rifle into the crevice where the edge of the elephant's belly met the ground then rolled the dead poacher over to cover the crack. He took a deep breath, cradled the MP-5 in his arms and inserted himself in the gaping abdominal cavity, feet first. His hands worked feverishly to cover the hole with large sections of intestines. He rolled himself up in a ball and waited like the stuffing in a giant turkey. He promised himself he would never—ever—eat Thanksgiving dinner again.

Smoke seeped inside the cavity along with the odor of burning hair and meat. Forrest gagged and choked back a cough. Acidic stomach contents gurgled at the top of his esophagus. The temperature was like the interior of a car parked too long in the Arizona sun. Blood and juices near the edge of the hole boiled and simmered in the heat. He heard muffled shouts outside—muted yet urgent. He couldn't make out what they were saying. Forrest clutched the submachine gun and held tight.

The wait was interminable. Pangs of claustrophobia and nausea were suppressed with pure willpower. His ears strained for any sounds. After a few minutes, he noticed the temperature had dropped a little. The juices still simmered, but not as vigorously as before. The flames had passed.

Slowly—very slowly, Forrest eased the entrails away from the gash. A fresh wave of seared flesh assaulted his nostrils. He made the hole a little larger—enough for him to peer outside.

The wall of flame had moved twenty meters beyond. The lower half of a man running in a crouch moved past the opening giving him a start. Forrest waited—counted to twenty and peered out again. The ground was charred and black. Ashes, black and gray, trickled down like snow. The man's legs appeared again—further away. He was still chasing the wall of fire, shouting at the others, asking if they had seen him, no doubt.

Forrest waited just a minute longer. *Don't blow it, now.* He could see two men in the narrow opening. Their attention was fixed on the wall of flame and what might lay beyond.

Time to move.

Forrest unplugged the hole and rolled out into the hot mud. His lungs spontaneously sucked in a chest full of fresh air—gloriously cool, sweet air. Pushing the MP-5 behind his back, he knelt, dragged the charred poacher's body off his rifle and leaped over the elephant's smoldering neck. After a second he stuck his head up and surveyed the scene.

Okay, where is everybody? Inventory the targets.

The wall of fire was fifty meters out and moving away rapidly. He could clearly see all five men. Spaced about ten- to-fifteen meters apart, they were spread out in a line that paralleled the advancing flames. From their body language it was clear that they had no clue as to his whereabouts.Forrest brought the MP-5 up and steadied it on the closest man. He let go a short controlled burst. The suppressor squelched the noise, reducing it to mere sputter relative to the roar of the flames. The man went down. No one else noticed. Forrest twisted slightly to his right. Another short burst. Then another. The next man went down.

He fired again. Three down.

The last two men were at the extreme ends of their original line, one hundred meters apart.

Forrest rested the MP-5 in its sling and picked up the ERMA. It was still warm to the touch but no worse for the wear. The scope was a little foggy. Otherwise, the poacher's body had insulated it well.

There were two targets left, one with an automatic weapon and one with a bolt-action Enfield .303. Forrest sighted on the man with the AK first. As he watched him through the scope, the poacher dropped to the ground, his assault rifle at the ready, his body oriented with his head toward Forrest's position.

Spotted his buddies.

Forrest twisted out several clicks of elevation and centered the crosshairs on the bridge of the poacher's nose. His shoulder absorbed his rifle's recoil. The top two thirds of the target's skull disappeared in a crimson mist.

Another shot rang out. A bullet thwacked into the elephant's thick hide. Forrest ducked. The last man had him spotted.

Forrest peeked over the top of the elephant. Another bullet cracked over his head. The poacher cycled the bolt on his ancient weapon and fired another shot without taking time to aim. It smacked into the elephant's body just to Forrest's right. He cycled the bolt and attempted to fire again. Nothing. In a panic, the last man dropped the rifle and ran for the ravine.

Empty, Forrest thought as he tracked him through the scope. "No problem, dirtbag. I've got one you can have."

Forrest couldn't stand himself. Hours later, the stench was still overwhelming. His usual stop at the weapons cache had been quickly followed by a stop at the river. A quick emersion and hard scrubbing had removed most of the dried blood, caked-on elephant tissue and body fluids. But without a good bar of soap to slice through the crusty slime, much of the fetor still permeated his body and clothing. His three-color BDUs would need several cycles in a downtown laundromat before they would again be tolerable.

The Zenair's engine sputtered a bit as he throttled it back for the landing. As usual, Forrest had changed clothes at the cache before going home but this time, he had brought his BDUs back with him, bundled up in one of his plastic garbage bags.

Cooling exhaust stacks ticked and pinged as he grabbed the bag and headed for his hootch. He looked around cautiously as he made his way through the trees at the end of the airstrip. Running into somebody was the last thing he wanted to do. His hair was matted and stiff, he reeked of spoiled meat and his skin felt like a glazed doughnut. Must look like hell, he thought as he rounded the corner of McCullen's hut.

"Ugh!" The plastic bag cushioned the collision. "Sorry, Doc. I didn't hear you coming."

With Forrest's steadying hand clamped on his upper arm, McCullen regained his balance. "Peeewww, lad. I'm surprised I didn't *smell* ya comin'." Exaggerated by his thick lenses, McCullen's wide gray eyes stared at the streaks of dried blood on Forrest's face and a dark blood clot clinging to his hair. "What in bloody hell happened to you?"

Groping for a quick answer, Forrest pushed past his flabbergasted friend. "Well Doc," he muttered, evasively as he continued on to his hut, "I guess you could say I was born again."

CHAPTER-THIRTEEN

TRAGEDY *a: the tragic element of drama, of literature generally, or of life.*
b: a lamentable, dreadful, or fatal event or affair.

OPRAH WATCHED FORREST, sniffing the air trying in vain to capture his scent. In the wake of Roseanne's death, they had ample reason to be frightened when any human drew near. Fear, he knew, was instinctive. Trust on the other hand, had to be learned and earned. And relearning it...well, that took a lot longer, didn't it? Maybe, over time, they could learn to trust him again. Maybe.

Images of Anne entered his thoughts. Maybe he could learn to trust women again. Maybe. Maybe not. Why should he? Outside of war, the most serious trouble he or any of his friends had ever encountered somehow had to do with a woman. And Anne Sargent seemed more than capable of ruining a man's day if not their life.

A trumpet downriver intruded on his thoughts. The young elephants moved into the river under Oprah's watchful eye. She was just like her older sister, he noticed. Only, Oprah was more friendly and social and spent more time looking after the welfare of the youngsters. Many of their mannerisms were the same, as well. Her rules were the same, too.

Roseanne had taught her well. The youngsters submerged in the soothing water then burst to the surface, squirting their backs with their trunks. Allomothers were in close attendance, making certain the preadolescents came to no harm. It was good training for them and it left the older elephants free to feed or manage the family's affairs.

Forrest noted the low sun as the elephants withdrew behind the brush covering the far bank. He decided it was time for him to follow suit. Stiffly, he lifted himself to his feet and made his way back to the Rover. An hour later he was returning to his campfire with an armful of wood when he froze. Forrest did a double-take, not trusting his tired eyes. Sitting in camp, flames dancing behind his silhouette, was the unmistakable outline of a man. He sat cross-legged on the ground five feet from the fire, his back to Forrest, as still as a bronze sculpture. The sudden apparition unnerved him. The intruder had somehow slipped right past his perimeter of trip flares!

Forrest thought about his Colt. Nestled in his survival vest, it was pressed against his belly by the load of wood. He considered his options: drop the wood, go for his gun and take the Clint Eastwood approach or execute a stealthy ambush.

Forrest eyed the man several minutes before deciding on the latter. The man had a calm presence about him. Forrest could feel it. Holding his bundle tightly, he silently circled the camp outside the firelight's flickering reach assessing his "guest" from the shadows. When Forrest reached a point directly across the fire from the man he paused again to watch him. Firelight reflected off his skin, revealing features as black shadows on a dark face. The whites of his eyes glowed eerily in the flickering light. Unblinking, they were fixed on the fire as if he were oblivious to its owner or his trespass. He didn't seem threatening and more importantly, he appeared to be alone.

What is this guy's story? he wondered. *Only one way to find out.* His eyes locked onto the new arrival, Forrest strode casually into the camp and dropped the wood on the ground next to the fire. At least now he would be able to get to the Anaconda if he needed it. Forrest wiped his hands on his vest to remove any clinging dirt and to reassess his weapon's position. Nonchalantly, he squatted, added new wood to the fire, stoked it, then lowered himself to his camp stool. "Staying for dinner?" he asked as if the man were an old friend, all the while scanning his body for weapons.

After a second their eyes met in a long silent stare. Neither of them blinked until the man shifted his eyes to the fire.

Forrest rose to his feet, walked to the Land Rover and unlocked the tailgate. He dragged a heavy cardboard box to the back of the vehicle. Holding a Mini Maglite in one hand, he took inventory of the cans inside, reading each label out loud. "Let's see. We've got corn...baked beans...pork 'n beans...string beans...beets...more corn—creamed corn this time..."

"The chili would be good," the guest interrupted, in a voice so calm it seemed to come from the night.

Forrest froze then snapped his head around toward the interloper. "I didn't say anything about chili," he said, incredulously.

Their eyes met, again.

No response.

Forrest picked up the next can and examined the label. *Damn! Chili!* He snapped his head around again, a wave of something unnerving tingling down his spine. The man hadn't moved, his attention fixed on the flames.

"Chili it is," Forrest announced, somehow knowing it wasn't necessary. He took out a can of corn, a personal favorite, closed the box and extracted another containing pots, pans, and camp utensils. Minutes later he was stirring the contents of each can into its own pot. Forrest spread the embers out on the ground and set a steel grate in place. "Here. You stir this one," Forrest said, handing the man a long clean stick which had been used previously for the same purpose. The man took it without a word and did as he was asked.

"Coffee?" Forrest asked putting a kettle of water on the fire.

"I prefer tea."

Forrest smiled wryly. "Oohh...Kay. Me too." He went to the Rover and brought back two ceramic mugs, a tea-bag label dangling from each on a flimsy white string. He handed one to the man, then settled onto his stool studying one of the damndest people he'd ever met. He was also one of the boniest men he'd ever seen—yet muscular and wiry, pronounced veins running along his forearms. He had a handsome face. Dressed in a three-piece suit, he could have easily passed for the TV sitcom character Benson. His hair, what there was of it, lay close to his scalp, traces of frost at the fringes. His clothes were barely passable as such. Tattered beyond the worst he'd seen on any beggar, his dark T-shirt—it was impossible to determine its original color—and long trousers bore the odor of stagnant water and mildew. His feet were bare and leathery.

"What's your name," Forrest asked in a probing yet friendly sort of way.

The man took a spoon and tested the chili. It was hot, judging from the steam it raised. "I am called Ruwizhu Rufira." His English, although broken and heavily accented, was surprisingly good, as good as Joseph's or any of the Kenyans in McCullen's camp. Like many Kenyans he had encountered, the stranger pronounced his TH sounds as a D. He looked up at Forrest, gesturing for him to share.

Forrest shook his head and smiled. He could see that Rufira was too proud to gulp the food yet was too famished not to. Forrest ate a few spoonfuls of his corn as he watched the chili disappear. "Well, my name is..."

"I know," Rufira interrupted in a matter-of-fact tone. He spoke between swallows without looking up.

Forrest drew back, his eyes dancing over the odd figure sitting at his fire. "Know what?"

"Who you are."

An incredulous smile broke over Forrest's face. *Okay pal, I'll play your game.* "So, what do you do?" he asked. He realized how silly that must have sounded but, at a loss for words, he couldn't think of anything else to say. And Rufira definitely wasn't holding up his end of the conversation.

Rufira scraped the pot vigorously before setting it aside. "I retrieve things." He looked at Forrest and saw the answer hadn't satisfied him. "I also tell people about the parts of their lives they have not yet experienced." His eyes dropped to Forrest's pot of corn like the family dog eyeing table scraps, then came back up. Forrest handed him his pot of corn with a smile then poured boiling water into their mugs. "What sort of things do you retrieve?"

"Dead tings," Rufira replied between gulps.

Forrest's look encouraged him to continue.

"During the dry season, when the rivers shrink to strings of ponds, I go into the ponds to retrieve dead goats, mostly. Sometimes dead people."

Forrest looked at him, his forehead knitting as if the story were just too incredible.

"When the people wash clothes or their dishes in the ponds, the crocs sometimes drag them away. Goats too."

Forrest nodded then raised an eyebrow. It was easy to understand why the average villager was less enthusiastic about wildlife than conservationists. "Why you?"

"Because the others, they are afraid of the crocs."

"You're not?"

"They cannot hurt me. My magic protects me."

Forrest did his best not to smile. He scratched his chin thoughtfully. "How...?"

"When the goats go to the ponds to drink, the crocs take them under to drown. Then they put them under logs or push them under ledges. They cannot eat them for a while, you see...not until they rot. Crocs, they cannot chew, you see. When a farmer lose a goat he call for me to bring it back while the meat, it is still good—while it can still be eaten."

Forrest listened, fascinated—a loose thought also reconsidering the chili's appeal. "And the crocs leave you alone?"

"My magic is very strong, you see. My father teach me. I enter the pool and spray water from my mouth. I sing to the crocs. Coo-coo," he demonstrated in low tones. "A magic song. It makes them unaware of my presence." Rufira sipped his tea. "If I bump into one, my herbs and spells, they protect me. The crocs, they shiver and become powerless. They flee."

"No shit?" Forrest commented with a skeptical chuckle, raising both eyebrows in amazement. "The farmer pays you for the dead goat?"

Rufira nodded. "Sometimes."

"Business should be pretty good about now," Forrest observed.

"I cannot find work during de rainy season."

Forrest was about to call the current dearth of rain to Rufira's attention but decided to let it drop—no sense confusing his "magic" with facts. "Why not?"

"They think I am a witch. When the rains come it brings lightening. The lightening kill people. People think lightening is the work of witches, you see. They become angry. Some like me have been stoned or burned."

"Hey, pal. I've met a few witches in my time—even married one. But I've never seen one who looks like you," Forrest joked.

Rufira continued eating, oblivious.

"I guess there's no Workmen's Comp or unemployment for that kinda thing, huh?"

Rufira looked at him vacantly.

"Never mind." Forrest poured more hot water into their mugs. The tea felt good going down. "What other job descriptions do ya have besides 'goat repo-man?'"

Rufira gave him the clueless look again, although he seemed to understand the intent of the question. "I keep elephants away from the crops. Elephants, they no like my magic."

"You hurt the elephants?" Forrest asked with a tone that suddenly bordered on threatening.

"No, I like the elephants. Like Baba Tembo, I protect the elephants. Farmers pay me to keep them away from their fields. I use my magic to chase away the elephants and the farmers, they are happy. The elephants no get shot, so the rangers and the elephants, they are happy, too. Baba Tembo, he very happy."

Forrest shrugged. "Baba Tembo? Who or what is Baba Tembo?"

The man drew back slightly and looked at him suspiciously as if Forrest had really confused him this time. "Baba wa Tembo is...how do you say?..Elephant Father...Father of the elephants."

Forrest nodded thoughtfully, though clueless.

"Baba Tembo kills poachers, you see. He leaves their pieces for people to find. He warn the poachers not to hurt his children. The dead men, they carry Baba Tembo's words back to their villages." One of Forrest's "death cards" materialized in the palm of Rufira's hand. "Big magic."

Forrest felt his pulse quicken. "Have you ever seen this Baba Tembo?"

Rufira shook his head. "Not until today." He gave Forrest a look that went right through him then returned his gaze to the fire as if it were the crystal ball from which his visions emanated.

Forrest felt the hair stand up on the back of his hands. *Remind me not to even think about playing poker with your ass, pal.*

Rufira read the American's face. "Elephants are my friends. Baba Tembo is the elephants' friend. So Baba Tembo, he is my friend. If there were no elephants, I could not use my magic to keep them away from the farms. I could not earn my way in life. Elephants are good. They too have much magic."

Forrest let out a breath and smiled. "Indeed." He started to pick up the empty pots and had a thought. "You still hungry?"

"No. But tomorrow..."

"Come with me."

The two men rose and Rufira followed Forrest to the Land Rover. Forrest dragged a rucksack out and sorted through several golf shirts and Dockers trousers. Rufira was easily two sizes smaller than Forrest but the clothes were a little snug on him, anyway. "Here," Forrest said, handing him the entire rucksack complete with two sets of clothes and a pair of Nikes.

"No. No. I cannot accept this. I work for things." Rufira stepped back and held his hands behind his back.

Forrest huffed a laugh. "Oh. Not a Democrat, I see."

Rufira gave him another confused look, but stood fast.

Forrest reached into his grocery box and stuck several cans and packages into the rucksack for good measure.

Rufira eyed the rucksack hanging in Forrest's hand but took another step back.

"Okay. Alright. C'mon over by the fire. I know what you can do for me."

Rufira followed obediently, almost robotic.

"Please," Forrest insisted, "sit down."

As they got settled, Forrest put the rucksack on the ground next to his enigmatic guest. He looked Rufira in the eye and folded his hands in his lap. "Tell me about the 'life I have not yet experienced.'"

Rufira returned the look. "Baba Tembo must be careful in Somalia. Much danger there."

Rufira penetrated deep into the American's eyes—right into his soul. "You have nothing to fear from me," he continued. "If I tell others your future, my magic will leave me. Baba Tembo is my friend. His secrets are safe with me."

Forrest sat quietly, staring back. Somehow he knew he could believe him, trust him. Rufira certainly believed in himself, he thought. And he had a work ethic. In any case he had no choice.

Rufira continued after a moment. "You seek a serpent who has brought you much pain. He will bring you much more—much more. He has someone you love—a young woman. And he will take another. You must not love a woman too much. Women bring pain."

"Well, your credibility rating just went up a few more points, pal," Forrest joked although there was a ring of truth about what he'd heard that was strangely unsettling. "Thanks for the warning."

"Where is the young woman?" Forrest asked, solemn and serious, now.

"In Tanzania. Where, I am not certain." Rufira's eyes glazed over as if he were traveling beyond himself. "If she dead, I know where she is. Her spirit would speak to me."

Forrest sensed the "reading" was concluded. No matter. None of it made any sense, anyway. Forrest smiled politely, dismissing everything the man said as illogical—except maybe the last comment. His eyes went to the rucksack triggering another thought. "Wait here a minute. I forgot something." Forrest jumped up and jogged to the Land Rover. Walking back carrying a can of Hormel Chili in either hand, he suddenly froze. Rufira and the rucksack had disappeared into the night.

****

Summoned by Joseph, Forrest ran to McCullen's hut thinking the worst. He expected to find the Scotsman laying face down on the floor. McCullen's inevitable heart attack was the first thing that came to mind when he heard that something was wrong with the Doctor. Forrest skidded to a stop two feet inside McCullen's open doorway. He paused at the entrance for a moment while his eyes made the adjustment from the brightness of the afternoon sun.

"I'm afraid it's very bad, John. Very bad, indeed," said a familiar female voice.

As his irises adjusted to the light, Forrest saw Malcolm McCullen was sitting on the edge of his cot, his chin resting on his chest. Anne Sargent stood next to McCullen holding a piece of paper.

"Is he sick?" Forrest's eyes went from McCullen to Sargent then back to McCullen. "Are you sick?" Forrest came to his friend's side resting his hand on McCullen's shoulder.

The Doctor didn't respond. He was despondent beyond reach. McCullen sat motionless with his hands clasped together in his lap.

"Would somebody please tell me what the hell is going on here?" Forrest demanded, looking up at Sargent. She handed him the piece of paper without saying a word. Forrest snatched it out of her fingers and brought it over to the light by the front door. He studied the message for a moment and looked back at Anne Sargent. "Who did this?"

"Poachers. Somalis, most likely," she answered, glumly. "They come across the border and take game outside the parks. Sometimes they venture *inside* the parks, as well."

"Are you sure?" Forrest asked, his mind racing now. This was a new line on poachers, one he had not previously considered. "Where do they go after they kill the animals?" he pressed.

"Most often they just take what they can carry and go back into Somalia."

"You mean they just stroll right into one of your national parks and you can't do anything about it? Don't your people have armed patrols? Where the hell were they?" Forrest's tone was venomous and accusatory.

Anne Sargent, overloaded by the rapid fire questions, simply sighed. "Now see here, John. The Ministry does all it can on a limited budget to protect these animals. There are over 12,000 square miles of savanna and bush in this country and we just don't have the money to hire and equip as many rangers as we need. You're acting like it's *my* fault."

"Well, whose fault *is* it, then?" Forrest blasted. He didn't know which made him angrier—the loss of the animals or his friend's suffering. "Now that they're dead, what does the government plan to do about it?"

"I'm afraid there's not much we can do unless we catch them in the act. As soon as they get what they came for, they make their way back over the border into Somalia where we can't touch them. They're like ghosts." Anne Sargent's tone was more defensive than apologetic. "They're brazen bastards, actually. The whole bloody lot." Her voice cracked under Forrest's third degree.

Forrest raised his eyebrows. "Are you people at least stepping up the guard on the ones that're left?"

"All of 'em, John," a new voice interrupted, a tired, defeated voice—an old man's voice.

Sargent and Forrest both looked at McCullen whose eyes remained fixed on the dark wooden floor.

"They killed *all* of 'em—every bloody last one. There are none left to guard! They were the last white rhinoceros in all of Kenya. And the bloody murderin' bastards killed every single one of 'em." McCullen spoke slowly and deliberately. It was the first time he had spoken since hearing the news. He got up slowly and walked over to a cabinet. He reached inside and retrieved a nearly full quart bottle of Glenlivet. Fumbling around on the counter top, he found a clean glass, poured himself several ounces and gulped it down. "Would you two mind taking your squabble outside?" McCullen asked the bottom of his glass. "I'm not in the mood to listen, just now."

Forrest and Sargent hesitated for a long tense moment then walked outside, shielding their eyes with their hands. Sargent led the way to the picnic table where she slumped onto one of the benches and rested her head in her hands.

"Were *they* in on it?" Forrest picked up the interrogation where he left off.

"Who?"

"The guards you had on duty."

"In on the poaching?"

"No! The Lindberg kidnapping! What the hell do you think?"

Sargent glared back. She could feel her chin quivering. "Impossible," she said weakly as if she weren't certain.

Forrest scoffed. "Don't tell me none of your guards has ever succumbed to the temptation. One rhino horn represents over two year's salary for those guys, ya know."

Sargent just stared back blankly, her eyes welling up. The government she represented had let Malcolm down. Her people had failed her one true friend.

When Forrest saw the tears, his contempt softened. The animals were dead and that was that. There was no bringing them back.

The tinkling of glasses brought Forrest's head around. McCullen was slowly making his way to the picnic table. He was clearly struggling to carry an emerald bottle, three glasses and what appeared to be a heavy photo album. Forrest rose to assist. He took the book and the bottle leaving McCullen to handle the rest. A moment later Malcolm poured some Scotch into each of their glasses. He had had quite a few already, effectively numbing the pain. His eyes were red and blurry, his speech a little slurred.

"Lady and gentleman. A toast to the end of life and the end of life's sufferin'." He raised his glass high, sloshing a little of the liquid on the table. It was met with the clink of two others raised in response. Forrest and Sargent politely took small swigs.

"I want to show you two youngsters one of my family albums." McCullen opened the binder and turned it around so all could see the pictures. Clumsy fingers slipped a bit as he tried to turn the pages. But he brushed away all offers of help with a wave of his hand. "This is the official photo record of all the animals in my rhino study group. The first few pages contain the pictures of some of Kenya's native white rhino taken before they were wiped out several years ago." McCullen flipped slowly and thoughtfully as if he were reflecting on the faces of long lost friends in his high school yearbook. Forrest saw many of the photos were yellow with age. Some of the images had faded badly. Each photo had names and dates marked next to them, two dates listed for each animal: the date they were born or their age when the study began and the date and age of each animal when they were found dead. "We use this book to identify animals when we study them out in the field and we also use it to help identify them when we find their bodies. None of the animals you see here are alive today. Most were killed by poachers." McCullen took another long gulp from the fresh glass he had poured. "It may interest you to know that in 1970, when we started keeping records on them, there were over sixty thousand black rhinos alive in east Africa. Today, there are less than three thousand. As for the white rhino, they haven't fared nearly as well. Outside of South Africa there are few, indeed. Maybe less than a thousand on the whole continent."

"What's the difference between a white and a black rhino?" Forrest inquired. "They look pretty similar to me."

"Well, laddy. There are several differences but the most notable is the face, or specifically the shape of the jaw." McCullen flipped to a photo of a black rhino and then compared it to one of the whites. "You'll notice the black has a narrow jaw with a protruding, dexterous upper lip. They're browsers, meaning they eat leaves and green stalks. They use their nimble lips to work around the sharp thorns. On the other hand, the white rhino is a grazer. He eats grasses almost exclusively. They work their way 'round the savanna munching as they go, consuming huge quantities. It doesn't take a biologist to notice that the white has a wide mouth suited more for grazing and chewing grasses." McCullen went on. "The term, white, has nothing at all to do with their coloring. It's actually a corruption of the Afrikaner word for wide."

"Will ya look at that! I'll be damned!" Forrest exclaimed as McCullen turned the page. A photo, a newer one, showed an armed guard actually leaning against the rump of one of the huge beasts while it fed. Other photos showed the guards playing with the animal's tail. The huge beast seemed to be paying no more attention to them than it did the oxpeckers that rode on their backs while feeding on the parasites attached to their thick hide. "Look how tame they are!" Forrest remarked. "I always thought they were cement-trucks with bad attitudes. Nothing you'd want to mess with."

"They certainly can be," McCullen replied, chuckling at the analogy. "These particular animals are not the usual variety you'd expect to encounter on the savanna, though. They're special... were special." His last thought sucked the smile off his face for a moment.

"These guys are more like two-ton lawn mowers with very expensive hood-ornaments."

Anne Sargent managed a small laugh.

"These animals were orphans raised by humans in South Africa and given to the Kenyan government as an attempt to reestablish the native species. They were around humans all their lives so they trusted them completely." McCullen paused for a moment to let a tinge of pain pass. "They were very tame indeed—just like big dogs. There were a total of nine," McCullen recalled, the grin leaving his face, again. "Three were killed last year and the rest were killed sometime in the last three days. Now there are, once again, no more white rhinoceros left in Kenya." On this somber note, McCullen poured himself another glass of scotch, then refilled the others.

"It's easy to see how you could become so attached to them. Judging by these photos, they were so tame you'd let your kids play with them." Forrest took a sip of his drink. He too, was starting to feel the effects of the Scotch.

"Why can't you guys just drug those bad boys, cut the horns off and they'll be useless to the poachers?" Forrest asked.

Sargent jumped to answer it. "That's been tried and it was a bust."

McCullen amplified. "The buggers hang out in pretty heavy brush a lot of the time for cover. So when the poachers are stalking them they often can't tell whether they have horns or not. They shoot them anyway."

"Jesus Tecumseh Sherman," Forrest exclaimed. "Assholes."

"It gets worse," Anne added.

Forrest's raised eyebrows asked: *How could that be?*

"We have testimony to the effect that they would shoot them in any case to cause the value of their existing stock to go up."

Forrest shook his head, welling up with rage.

"Now you see why we get so frustrated…" Anne started.

"…and I get so depressed," McCullen finished with a sigh as he rose to search his pockets for a cigarette, lit one and resumed his seat.

"Mmm." Forrest studied the photos of the guards leaning against their charges. Questions raced through his mind. And flying to eastern Kenya was the only way he was going to get answers.

"Malcolm. I'd like to fly out there and find out what happened." Forrest looked at the Scotsman who had stopped turning the pages and sat staring at the last set of photos. "Tomorrow. I'd like you to go with us." Forrest waited patiently for an answer.

"Us?" Anne asked, looking at Forrest, incredulously.

Forrest ignored her, staring instead at McCullen. He didn't want to push his friend. He knew the visit would be as painful as visiting his wife's grave.

"Well, lad, I don't think I'll go. You 'n Anne can learn a lot more if you go by yourselves. I'll only slow you down."

Sargent interjected. "I can't go, either. I have prior commitments. There's a canine distemper epidemic in the Mara's lions." She got up and walked toward her Land Rover.

Forrest rose. "I'd appreciate it if you would go there with me tomorrow," he called after her, following along. His tone had softened slightly. "Please. Those people won't talk to me but they might talk to you. I'll even drop you off in Nairobi."

Anne stopped abruptly and wheeled. "First off, my stomach hasn't completely recovered from the *last* time it went in an airplane with you. Secondly, the Kenya Wildlife Service doesn't need your help solving *their* problems. Thirdly, I have prior commitments and that's that."

Forrest felt a sudden flush of anger at the rebuke, yet didn't respond. Without a word, he turned, strode off, and disappeared into his hut.

McCullen walked up and patted Anne on the back, then hung on for stability.

"I know you like him, Malcolm. But I'm afraid you're quite alone there," she said in a quiet tone of exasperation.

"Well, he did say 'please,' my dear."

Anne shared a look with McCullen then turned her head to see where Forrest had gone. She gasped. Forrest emerged from his hut striding toward her, pistol in hand. She flinched and drew close to McCullen who stood as wide-eyed as she.

Forrest continued two steps past them, brought the massive Colt Anaconda up and fired. The right front tire of her Land Rover collapsed in a cloud of dust.

"Seems your vehicle just developed mechanical problems and *you* just had a change in plans," he said lowering the .44 magnum tire-killer to his side.

Unnerved but unyielding, Sargent's jaws tightened. "I have a spare and I'm perfectly capable of changing it myself."

Forrest eyed the spare tire mounted on the roof. Once again, he brought the Colt up and peered down its sights.

BOOM! Chunks of rubber flew into the air.

Sargent and McCullen stood frozen, jaws agape.

"Colt," he said with smug satisfaction. "The horsepower in firepower." His thin smile dissolved. "Right here. Oh-seven-hundred," he ordered, as she stomped off toward her hut. "Don't be late," he called after her, "or I'll come in after you. And I'm perfectly capable of dressing you, myself."

Amy Lee snapped awake with a start as she felt the presence of a woman hovering over her. Rough hemp cord bit into her wrists and bare ankles as she backed crablike into the corner of the hut in which she had been held captive for days—how many she could not tell with any certainty. As the fog began to clear from her brain, Amy scanned the crude, single-room hut in an effort to reorient herself. The musty odor of earth, wood and grass blended with the remnants of smoke and food as it invaded her nostrils.

The woman, the same one each time, had brought her food and some warm tea. Amy felt some degree of sympathy emanating from the thin woman with a dark, battered face, sad tentative smile and large eyes who had helped her wash her hair in the nearby stream the day before while under the watchful eye of two armed guards.

Though she'd had difficulty sleeping and eating, Amy had managed to gain back a pound or so. Owing to the availability of water, she had begun to recover from the effects of dehydration.

Amy slowly ate the food that the woman had prepared, savoring the flavor of cooked food so sorely missed during her long evasion. As she chewed, Amy studied the woman who was dressed in a mixture of traditional and western clothes.

Suddenly, the rising sound of approaching boots clumping across hard ground brought chills down her neck. She shared a frightened look with her hostess.

Oh God! It's him.

Fresh skeletons tented with torn hide were all that remained of some of the planet's most antique of mammals. Each carcass lay in a wide, dark stain alive with gnats and flies. Their guide, Hendrix Emerick, Meru National Park's lead ranger stopped the Land Rover. Forrest and Sargent got out, stopped and stared for a long moment. They paced around the area attempting to get a feel for what had transpired only four evenings ago.

"I'm glad Malcolm stayed back at the camp, John," Anne said walking behind him. "He wouldn't have wanted to see this. These rhinos were his last hope for a new start."

Forrest turned and gave her a blank look then put his eyes on Emerick, a beefy Brit with a ruddy complexion and very thin blonde hair. "I thought you people had armed guards out here. How'd the poachers get by them?"

Emerick puffed out his barrel chest defensively. "For every uniformed man out here, there are thousands of potential poachers. When they come across the border, they sometimes come in sizable numbers. And they come well armed. Just until a few months ago, most of my men carried Enfield rifles left over from the colonial days. Today we have two new G-3's. We are improving. But we can only put two- to-four men on guard at any one time; half armed with automatic weapons and half armed with the old guns. These poachers are frequently armed with automatic weapons and outnumber my men three- or four-to-one." Emerick paused for a moment to take a sip of water from a canteen. "Four days ago, my boys were rounding up the rhino to bring them into the night corral when they were ambushed. The boys put up a jolly-good fight but they were driven back in a fierce gun battle."

Forrest watched as Emerick's eyes went to one of his men's who looked at the ground.

"While some of the poachers kept my men pinned down," he continued, "the others killed the rhino and removed their horns. They kept my men on their faces until well after dark then escaped into the night."

"On foot," Forrest asked, "all the way to Somalia?" Forrest thought about his mysterious visitor Rufira and his warning about Somalia.

"Almost certainly."

"How many and what did they look like?"

"I'm not certain as to their number. Perhaps, six or eight I should think. The usual plunderers."

Forrest nodded then, without a word, began searching the ground for clues. Forrest walked in ever widening circles, his eyes fixed on the ground. He paused in a few places to examine several spent cartridge cases which he put in his pockets. Anne joined him. Emerick stood near the Rover watching Sargent and Forrest through the ribbon of smoke rising from his pipe.

Satisfied he had found all he needed, Forrest asked to see the rest of the animals. Over the next 30 minutes, Forrest walked the sites, looking for additional clues. Repeatedly, he picked up the brass casings which were, according to Emerick, ejected from guns used in the firefight between his guards and the poachers. Several times Forrest paused to ask Emerick where his men had been pinned down.

Emerick either shrugged or gestured vaguely. Forrest walked the designated areas examining footprints and spent cartridge casings. He found plenty of both.

Anne noticed Forrest's mood was becoming blacker and blacker. She, too, became increasingly depressed. Each rotting carcass represented a magnificent animal; huge docile creatures she had come to know on an almost personal level through her friend, Malcolm McCullen. These had been coddled animals who trusted their human custodians. Ultimately, it was their trust in man which had betrayed them. She watched Forrest kneel and rake the dirt with his fingertips.

"I've seen enough," Forrest said joining her near one of the carcasses.

"Me too," she muttered sadly. "Enough to last a lifetime."

They walked back to join Emerick at the Rover in silence. Without a word, Forrest helped Anne get into the back seat then climbed in the front.

Emerick was the first to break the heavy silence. "Satisfied?" he asked, evenly.

Forrest didn't look him in the eye. His eyes were locked straight ahead, staring off into space, his jaw set. "Yep."

A minute later, Emerick steered the Rover onto the dirt road which led back to the outpost. "Would you like to be dropped at your plane?"

"Yes, please," answered Anne who appeared to be exhausted by the ordeal. Emerick drove them back to Forrest's Cessna. He leaned inside, retrieved a chart from the glareshield and walked to Emerick's Rover.

"Hendrix, could you show me where you think those poachers' camps are?" Forrest asked with forced politeness. He unfolded it and laid it out on the hood of Emerick's Land Rover.

"Of course. Let's have a look." Emerick bent over the hood orienting himself with the chart's features. He studied the chart for a few minutes looking for key landmarks. "We've tracked the buggers to a camp here and one, here," he said pointing with a meaty finger to the Kenya-Somalia border.

Forrest marked the spots with a pencil. "Okay, thanks," he said refolding the chart along its original creases. "I'm ready when you are," he said looking at Sargent.

"Good-bye Anne. Nice to see you, as always." Emerick said squeezing her extended hand. "Pleasure to meet you, John. Come back again, anytime. We're always glad to lend a hand in your research." Emerick extended his hand and smiled a friendly, easy smile.

"I may be back sooner than you think." Forrest said clasping Emerick's huge paw. "Oh, and since you offered, there are a few things I'd still like to know."

"Quite so. What would that be?"

"Were any of your men killed in the ambush?"

"No."

"Any of 'em wounded?"

"No." Emerick's eyes narrowed. "Why do you ask?"

"How about the poachers? Any of 'em killed?"

"Well, I'm not certain..."

"Any of 'em wounded?"

Emerick hesitated for a second, taken aback by the rapid fire questions. "Not that I..."

"Doesn't that strike you as the least bit odd? Miraculous even?" Forrest's eyes went to the stainless-steel Rolex on Emerick's wrist.

Emerick didn't answer. He simply looked puzzled. His eyes sought out Anne's as if to ask what the hell's the story with this bloke?

"What are you driving at, John?" Sargent asked, running interference for Emerick.

"Never mind," Forrest said abruptly, sensing he had probed far enough. The question he wanted to ask most had to be left unasked. "We need to get going, Anne."

"Alright, then," Emerick said feeling a little uneasy. "'til next time, then."

"Good-bye Hendrix. I'll tell Allen you asked about him."

Minutes later he had the Cessna roaring down the airstrip, a cloud of red dust in its wake. Instead of turning to the west for the

Camp Uhura, Forrest rolled the airplane out on an easterly heading, toward Somalia.

"Where are you going, John?" Anne asked, raising her voice above the noise of the droning engine.

"I thought we'd have a look at the refugee camps on the border."

"Today?"

"Aren't you a KWS inspector?"

"Yes, but..."

"Then let's *inspect.*" Forrest shot her a contemptuous smile. He set the autopilot to hold heading and altitude and let out a long, pent-up, frustrated sigh. "Doesn't it bother you that a major firefight was *supposed* to have taken place between the Somali poachers and the guards and not *one* man was killed or even wounded?"

"Are you saying you would feel better about it if one of those men *had* been killed trying to save a rhino?"

"Now that you mention it, yes I would!"

"Really, John. How can you say something like that with a clear conscience?"

"Easy. Something stinks about this whole deal. You'd think four armed men could have put up enough of a fight to have at least *wounded* one poacher!"

She stared back blankly.

"Look at this!" Forrest removed cartridge after cartridge from his shirt and pants pockets. "Look at this one...this one...and this one. See anything odd?" Sargent looked but Forrest saw the "no clue light" in her eyes. "Okay, how about these?" Forrest took a half dozen of the brass casings and tossed them in her lap."

After a full minute she was still stumped. "I don't get it, John. They all look the same to me."

A satisfied smile appeared on Forrest's face. "Bingo! That's it," he responded with a slightly condescending tone.

"I'm sorry, John. I still..."

"Holy Inspector Clouseau, Batman!" Forrest exclaimed, slapping his hand down on top of the glare shield. "Say it again!"

"They're...all...the same," she whispered, quizzically.

"Right. They are all the same—AK-47 brass. Unless your guards picked up all *their* brass, and that's highly unlikely given their housekeeping habits, the bastards never fired a goddamned shot!" He searched her face for that brilliant light of revelation. It hadn't yet illuminated.

"I don't know anything about guns, John. Frankly, I hate the awful things!"

Forrest paused for a moment to control his temper. "Look," he said, realizing they had gotten off the subject. "There are only two- or- three possible scenarios that jive with the evidence. One, the guards were never there guarding the animals like they were supposed to be. Two, the guards ran as soon as they saw the poachers or three," he said holding up a third finger to illustrate his point, "the bastards were in on it and allowed the poachers to have at the rhinos."

"How can you think the guards would do such a thing?"

"Easy, lady! Think about it! One rhino horn is over two year's salary to those guys, remember? That's a powerful temptation to dangle in front of any man. Sooner or later, greed gets a grip on all but the most stalwart. The way I see it, they either chickened out or cashed in. Probably both. It's the only scenario that explains them not firing a single shot."

Anne grimaced. "I'd hate to think you're right." She fought off the idea that some of her own people could betray the very animals they were assigned to protect. But people were human, after all. And, she hated to admit, the concept of corrupt government officials was neither new nor unthinkable.

"Those trackers are probably following the poachers back to their camp for the pay-off. They'll hang out a few days to make it look good and then go back to the post, empty handed. But, their pockets will be full of shillings."

"You really think so?"

"I hope not. Like you, I'd like to have some faith in somebody. But this deal smells worse than those dead rhino. It sure as hell wouldn't be the first time government employees were found to be on the take. It's practically in their job description." He stopped short. "Present company excluded, I assume," he corrected.

Another annoyed glare. She found herself resenting Forrest for bursting her bubble and rubbing her face in the ugliness of a very plausible yet absolutely unacceptable explanation. Forrest spotted smoke ahead and checked their GPS position against the chart. "Ladies and gentlemen, fasten your seat-belts for landing. We're almost there."

Oh God, no! I thought he'd be gone for days!

Amy could tell from her captor's body language his mood was uglier than usual. His eyes were darker, his face tighter and his stumbling gait more menacing than normal. As he entered the crude hut's door he failed to duck low enough and banged his head against the upper opening, grunting angrily. It was at that moment Amy realized he was much more inebriated than he had been during previous drunken episodes which made him that much more dangerous.

Amy's caretaker sensed the same ominous signs. Reluctantly, she stood and faced the belligerent beast, contemptuously though cautiously keeping her distance.

Reflexively, the poacher's hands came to his head to cover the source of his pain. Leaning against the wall to steady himself, he clumsily rubbed his scalp and grimaced at the earthen floor. Acute discomfort crystallized his anger into rage.

Amy could feel the heat from the poacher's eyes as he lifted them from the floor and directed them at her. Though not aware of it, she drew herself into a defensive ball and pulled back against the wall, their eyes locked in frightful anticipation.

His faded green shirt was filthy with earth and stains. His body odor grew in her nostrils as he stumbled toward the cringing young woman who was willing herself an exit between the cracks in the woven-stick wall. His shadow grew over her as he bent down, grabbed her by an ankle and dragged her toward him.

Though bound at the wrists and ankles, Amy resisted, defiantly anchoring herself with a double-handed grip on a piece of the wall. She would not be taken easily.

Her struggle only amplified his anger. He grabbed both ankles in an attempt to lift her buttocks and lessen the friction with the dirt floor. Amy bucked like a nightmare rodeo mount kicking her feet as violently as she could. She clung to the wall with all her might. The attacker roared a series of grunts evoking much the same from the tenacious victim. Suddenly, the stick to which she was clinging snapped in two places, coming away cleanly from the wall. Amy tried to roll onto her stomach and secure another grip, but failed. After several seconds of struggling another idea came to her in a flash. She went completely limp, rolled onto her back and drew the stick close to her left hip in order to conceal it.

Her attacker paused, momentarily searched her face for an explanation, then dropped to his knees and tore her T-shirt from the collar to her navel exposing her chest. He paused again, searching her eyes for a reaction. He saw defiance in her eyes yet capitulation in her body language. A sinister smile crept across his face a he lowered himself further to attach his drooling mouth to her exposed breast.

At just the right moment Amy counterattacked. In a flash she jammed the splintered end of the hidden stick into the predator's right side striking him between the tenth and eleventh rib. The weapon inflicted great pain and knocked the wind out of him but was too thick and too blunt to penetrate anything vital.

As her attacker groaned in agony, Amy sat up abruptly and head-butted the foul bastard on the bridge of his nose, inflicting even more pain. He rolled off to his left landing on his back, momentarily stunned. Amy seized the advantage, rose to her knees and brought the stick above her head ready to finish the battle decisively. Her eyes flashed over the prostate body searching for a soft and vulnerable target. Propelled by adrenalin and rage, she replayed the self-defense advice her husband and uncles had repeated many times: "If and when you are able to win an advantage, *keep* the advantage and finish the job." Amy Lee Henderson-Forrest intended to follow that adage faithfully.

Her eyes fixed on the man's throat as she felt the muscles in her arms cocking for the strike.

A terrible shriek startled her and she felt a pair of hands grab her wrists and pull her over backward, slamming her back into the floor. As Amy lunged to regain an erect posture, the poacher's wife threw a leg over her, straddled her stomach and leaned forward pinning her wrists to the floor above her head.

"No!" the woman barked before lowering her voice to a terse whisper. "He is not much of a man but he is the only man I have. I won't let him harm you. And I cannot let you harm him."

The women's eyes remained locked for a very long moment before the wife felt the tension melt from Amy's arms.

Amy let out a loud sigh, venting the intense hostility of the encounter. This woman was no friend, certainly no benefactor, but Amy sensed she was someone who shared her plight—to a certain extent a captive not unlike herself. Amy wondered how many times the wife had been a victim of unspeakable abuse. For some unexplained reason—call it intuition—Amy sensed she could trust her as long as she did not force a serious division of loyalties. Whatever her motives, the woman had, after all, nursed her back to health, fed her, bathed her and treated the wounds obtained in her long ill-fated trek to freedom.

She would acquiesce.

For now.

"Hodding, I can't tell you why." Henderson said into his multi-buttoned STU phone's receiver. "I'm sorry. But I just can't." Henderson listened to the White House chief of staff cite a dozen reasons why it would be difficult if not impossible to set up the requested meeting. Frightening visions of FBI agents pushing past Roselle, handcuffs and search warrants in hand, danced in his head as he sank into his oversize leather chair. He wondered how long it would be until his second-worst nightmare became a reality.

"Look, Hodding, I need your help on this one. I know you're just doing your job running interference. But you're going to have to trust me on this one. I need a private meeting, soon. Very soon. I know she'll be interested and I know she'll be pissed when she finds out you wouldn't arrange it. Tell her it's urgent. Please, Hodding… Please."

CHAPTER-FOURTEEN

VERMIN

a: small common harmful or objectionable animals
b: birds or mammals that prey on game
c: *an offensive person*

THE REFUGEE CAMP EAST OF WAJIR, Kenya seemed like a scene from Dante's Inferno. Scores of people, reduced to leathery, skin-shrouded skeletons sat or lay out in the open all around the grounds. Extreme malnutrition had reduced them to less than human. Muscles, long suffering from lack of protein, had atrophied and withered away to the consistency of old rubber bands. Few had enough life left in them to stand. Some of the lucky ones who still had control of their faculties assisted in the care of those who didn't. Hemispherical huts constructed with any available scrap material were scattered about chaotically.

Upon arrival, their Cessna had been mobbed by starving people. Some of the children, running ahead of the rest, had narrowly avoided being chopped to pieces by the propeller as it spun to a stop at the top of a compression stroke. It took four Kenyan soldiers five minutes to move the crowd away from the airplane and back to the edge of the runway. Using their rifles like the sweeping arms of a gate, they moved several people at once. Forrest was confident the soldiers would keep the people away from the airplane but he took the key out of the magneto switch and locked the doors, just in case. Anne walked beside him as they entered the camp.

Insects filled the air, most a bumper crop of flies born in untreated sewage, animal carcasses and the putrid tissue of hastily buried corpses. As nature was ever the indifferent opportunist, what was famine for some became feast for others.

If there really was a Hell, Forrest thought, this must be it. He had seen a lot of carnage in Vietnam but never on this scale. He could see that Anne was visibly shaken by the spectacle. Thinking she was a doctor, some pawed at her, begging for help. Unable to understand much of what they were saying and completely unable to help, Sargent simply apologized with a dismissive shrug; an act often met with angry shouts and epithets.

"Dear God, this is awful, John!" her voice cracked. Anne studied his profile for a moment. He was visibly moved and disgusted. It dawned on her that John Forrest shielded a sensitive inner self with an abrasive exterior. Hardness and aggressiveness masked a great deal of pain. What on Earth could be its source?

Oblivious to her examination, his attention remained focused on the Somali refugees. He made note of the few, relatively healthy males who stared at him as they passed. Good health means that they're getting fed on a regular basis, he deduced. *But at who's expense?* Forrest glared back at them and continued on at a quickening pace. Absent common law and order, nature's laws—survival of the fittest—had taken over completely. Forrest looked behind him frequently to ensure none had decided to tag along. To a hungry mob, they would be a good target. Despite the heat, his survival vest and big Colt pistol felt reassuring.

Sargent scurried to catch up with him. His fast, determined pace had left her yards behind—too far for comfort. "I want to leave, John," she complained, coming along side.

"We just got here," he said out of the side of his mouth as he searched the crowds.

"What are you looking for?"

He noticed her struggling to keep up and slowed his pace—a little. "Not sure, exactly."

"Then how will you know when you've found it?"

"I'll know."

Just then, he noticed two young men who averted their eyes when they met his and ducked away behind two huts like scurrying rats. One wore a bright red shirt and a distinctive red- and-black baseball cap. The other was much less conspicuous in his darker clothes.

Bingo!

"Wait here." Forrest bolted off abruptly and followed the two men—boys, really—into a seemingly endless maze of huts.

Sensing they were being followed, the pair broke into a run and quickly reached the edge of the village. Forrest pulled up, watching them sprint away as they headed east toward the Somali border.

When the men discovered they were no longer being followed they slowed to a brisk walk, their heads turning frequently as they went.

Forrest watched them until they disappeared into the brush then turned about. Walking as fast as he could, he returned to the spot where he had left Anne. She was gone.

"Shit!" His mind raced with scenarios; almost all had unhappy endings. *Hope she had enough sense to go back to the plane and wait with the soldiers!* It took him nearly fifteen minutes to make a quick circuit of the greater camp before finding himself back at the airstrip.

"John!" a familiar voice shouted over the many voices and crying children. "Over here!" Anne was standing next to the Cessna in the company of two Kenyan soldiers.

Forrest trotted up to her and plowed to a halt, completely out of breath. "Where," he puffed, "the hell did you go? I told you to stay put!"

Anne was visibly shaken. "After you left me, I was mobbed by a group of women who were literally dragging me to examine their children. They still think I am a doctor."

"The doctor almost always comes in a small plane like yours, sah," one of the soldiers explained in excellent English. "They just will not believe that she is not a doctor."

"John, can we please go now?" Anne pleaded. She mopped her face with a handkerchief. Her face was flushed. Forrest couldn't tell if it was from heat or stress—or both.

"Okay, we're outta here."

Minutes later, Forrest had the Cessna's engine roaring as the little plane climbed five hundred feet above the ground leaving the horrid camp but few of its memories behind.

Anne noticed in an instant that her pilot had, once again, turned east instead of west. "You told me we were going back, straight away. Why are we headed east?"

Forrest dismissed her with a wave of his hand, a sort of never-mind gesture. "Get me some water out of the jug, will ya?" He shot her a quick glance out of the corner of his eye. She was staring at him. "Go ahead. Looks like you could use some too."

Just as she turned, she felt the airplane drop suddenly.

Forrest pushed the plane's nose down aggressively producing that gut-wrenching falling feeling associated with negative Gs. "Got 'em. Just ahead," he announced coldly through his headset as the prop snarled. He pushed the prop control and throttle to 25/25 in an effort to gain extra speed. Just ahead, the two boys had turned around and were walking back toward Kenya. "I guess they thought it was safe to turn back. Wrong!"

"Who? Where?" Anne groaned, holding onto the bottom of the seat to keep from floating out of it. Her eyes couldn't focus on landscape that rushed by in a blur.

"You'll see." His eyes were locked onto a tiny red shirt and a red hat, and he wasn't about to look away. "Hold on!" he warned, not noticing that she already was—a death grip with both hands.

With the airspeed indicator's needle rising near the top of the green operating arc, Forrest bore down on the two men who had not yet spotted the airplane diving out of the blinding afternoon sun. The instant the roaring prop noise reached their ears, they froze in their tracks. They had never seen a plane diving so low. Realizing that they were now targeted, the two boys broke and ran back to the east at the speed of fright.

"What are you doing?" Anne practically screamed into her microphone as the ground rushed up at them.

"I'm bird-dogging those two bastards." He pointed the nose of the plane straight at the bouncing red hat. The plane was a hundred feet above the ground and, if its course wasn't altered soon, three hundred feet from its point of impact. Out of the corner of his eye he could see her pushing her legs out straight, reflexively bracing for the crash she assumed was only seconds away.

Forrest pulled up with the landing gear less than two feet over their heads. The boys dove for the ground, face first. Gently, so as not to over stress the wings, Forrest pulled the nose ten degrees above the horizon and banked the plane hard to the left to keep the boys in sight. They jumped up and started running as fast as they could toward the Somali border. Dust, kicked up by the Cessna's wake, swirled about them.

Anne opened her eyes and looked up. "John, you might have killed them...and us too!" she scolded, her voice edging on hysteria.

"As long as they keep running, I'll leave 'em alone." Ahead, in the distance he spotted what looked like more refugee camps, only a lot smaller.

"What, besides scaring the absolute shit out of me, do you hope to accomplish?"

Forrest smiled and looked at her. He never thought he'd hear her say a four-letter word. She had to be stressed to the max. He thought for a moment before responding to her question. For a split-second, he wished he could tell her the truth. But, the less she knew, the better. "I'm just trying to scare two rats back into their hole." Forrest pointed at the camps about a mile-and-a-half in front of them. Marked by a wisp of smoke rising into the hazy sky, they appeared as little more than dark green blemishes amidst the desert scrub. "I think that's where your rhino poachers live. Just wanted to find out for sure," he explained as he pulled the Cessna up and turned toward Camp Uhura. "Other than that, there's not much we can do about it," he added as he made note of their position on the GPS. *For now, that is.*

Sargent gave him a long look as they climbed into the setting sun.

Forrest felt her eyes on him and turned. "What?"

Her eyes averted into a distant stare. "How can God let these things happen? Those beautiful animals and those poor wretched people, suffering so."

Forrest remained quiet for a long moment, his mind also revisiting the horrific scenes they had witnessed. Anger and frustration boiled over onto his tongue. "Well, if there is a God, he must be one sick son-of-a-bitch."

When Forrest returned to camp, he first took ten minutes to report his findings to Henderson. Included was a detailed description of the two young boys. Excluded was the young woman comment he'd heard from Rufira. No use in sending his friend on a useless search or exciting baseless hope with information derived from such a crazy source. Forrest shut down the data link and secured its components in their container. He took off his clothes and slipped inside the mosquito netting which hung from a hook above his cot. Forrest lay back in his bunk staring at the ceiling, his mind a kaleidoscope of the day's experiences. He was looking forward to getting intelligence on the Somali poachers, historically the worst in East Africa. And bringing Anne along, for all of its aggravations, had been worth it. The lady inspector, he reflected, had helped knock down a few political barriers. Maybe she's not that bad after all.

For the next hour, Henderson carefully studied the satellite images. He was looking for the telltale signs of human settlement. Clusters of hemispherical shelters resembling patchwork igloos punctuated the countryside. Just inside Kenya's eastern border with Somalia, Henderson counted over a dozen camps and temporary villages. Most were fairly conspicuous against the bleak semi-desert terrain. Some were official relief stations and feeding centers. Large tents, erected as clinics, displayed the red and white insignia of the International Red Cross on their roofs. Other camps were for refugees displaced by the continuing drought and fighting.

Henderson shook his head at their numbers. Drought and overpopulation had combined forces to put a merciless strain on both people and wildlife. But famine required more to accomplish its deadly work.

Enter politics. Political upheaval was the essential element. Warfare, however limited in scale, was the key ingredient in Africa's perennial stew of tragedy and misery. An old African saying summed it up nicely: "God makes drought. Man makes famine." War obviously accounted for much of the suffering. Less obvious, however, was the damage to tribal customs and a general breakdown of cultures and societies which had held people together for generations. Young men who operated tanks and technicals had never learned to farm and raise livestock. Some, who had tasted the power of organized gangs and abundant weaponry, earning large sums through robbery and extortion, would find it nearly impossible to return to the pastoral life of their fathers. Chewing kat, the habit-forming leaves and shoots of the *catha edulis* bush, and living the fast life of crime was much more alluring than the backbreaking tedium of agriculture. Without ancient survival skills and tribal culture supporting their infrastructure and ecosystem, they were doomed to be forever dependent on the political whims of other nations. And without Africa's exotic creatures to attract tourism, a tremendous opportunity to generate badly needed revenue was being destroyed as well. In a lawless land where every argument was settled with guns, Somalia, like many countries in Africa, was once again, staring into the abyss.

Forrest had been right, Henderson thought. He simply hadn't noticed them before. Located far away from the relief centers and government interference in Kenya were a few camps on the border just inside Somalia. Latitudes and longitudes of the individual camps had to be plotted on a map before their location made sense. International borders did not appear in reconnaissance photographs. Once he saw where the camps were, relative to the border, Henderson realized the significance of their position. Gangs could obtain food and water from the feeding stations and return to their strongholds across the border. Far from Mogadishu and the towns in the south, they would have little to fear from the well-intentioned but inadequate forces of the United Nations and the hollow-shell Somali government.

"Convenient little set up you have there, boys," Henderson thought aloud. Henderson leaned back in his chair for a moment and rotated his neck to relieve the cramped muscles. He returned his gaze to the map, his mind plotting positions and distances. After a moment, he searched his piles for a specific group of photos. One camp in particular caught his attention. In the satellite images, Henderson could see objects very similar to ones he had seen in Vietnam. Unlike the NVA, the Somalis, for some reason, appeared to have little appreciation of overhead imagery systems. Very little effort had been made to conceal their vehicles. Old cars, trucks, technicals and what looked like two old M-48 Patton tanks were parked about in plain sight.

And there was something else nagging at him: Forrest's verbal description of the poachers who had led him to this camp. His memory was too cloudy at the moment to put his finger on it but something about a red baseball cap kept calling to him from the fog.

The keyboard was too slow for a message this important. Written messages were appropriate for some purposes but sometimes, there was just no substitute for the nuances of the human voice and the spontaneity of conversation. Even with the occasional delay created by the encryption software, it was good to hear his best friend's voice.

Henderson sat in his black leather office chair with his feet propped up on the edge of an open drawer, the receiver of his STU phone again clamped between his ear and shoulder. The morning sun helped illuminate the black and white photos arranged in a classified file marked: CERTAIN THUNDER.

"Yeah, that's what I see. Two tanks, old American made stuff, and at least one APC. The rest are your garden-variety, commercially available, off-road vehicles. Some have gun mounts and some don't." Henderson shuffled the photos to be sure he hadn't missed anything.

Forrest made notes in a small notebook using the top of the SATCOM unit as a makeshift desk. "I couldn't get close enough to verify any of your imagery but I did see two camps just across the border. One was a click due north of the other. The two kids were making for the northern one when I broke off."

Satellite imagery was a marvelous intelligence tool but like any technical resource, it had its limitations. "I see what looks like big wooden frames in the northern camp, like the ones the bad guys use to cure their meat. All the hardware and most of the people are in the southern camp. Could you see any of that?" Henderson asked.

A short delay.

"No. I wasn't able to overfly the camps. I broke it off about two miles west. I did see some smoke coming from the northern camp so the rack theory makes sense."

Henderson continued to probe. "Tell me about the two you chased, again. Did they have any weapons or anything that looked military?"

"No. They looked just like any other teenage Somali boys. Common as dirt. So skinny they didn't even have shadows. Nothing unusual except their behavior and the red-and-black American baseball cap one was wearing. They were big time paranoid, though. Very jumpy. Bolted as soon as they saw me and the lady's uniform."

"Lady? Uniform?" the CIA man asked with a surge of interest usually reserved for office gossip.

Forrest noted the change in tone. "Forget it. It's not what you think."

"Just checking. Thought you might have malaria or something," Henderson snickered. "Besides, there is only *one* woman you should be looking for."

Forrest smiled at the last comment. "Don't worry, man. I'm definitely *not* looking for any female problems. They don't sell Midol over here."

Henderson chuckled. "That's 'cause we've used it all up at my house."

"Yeah, I bet." Forrest laughed and continued: "Anyway, those clowns were guilty about something. I'm sure it was them. I'd bet money on it. The clincher was the red baseball hat. It was definitely American. You don't see many of those things over here. Probably stole it from some tourist. Typical turd world vermin."

Henderson frowned. "Probably."

"The kids took off like spooked rabbits so I didn't get much of a look. But the red hat had some sort of emblem on the front. Maybe a sports team or something. The wardens said one of the poachers who did the rhinos had a red hat. It has to be the same guy. How many red, American baseball hats could there be in a place like this?"

Henderson didn't respond. His mind had just jumped into overdrive. Images of CNN video footage popped into his head.

"You still there?"

Henderson startled slightly. "Yeah. Yeah, I'm still here." *Could it be?*

"Thought I lost the signal again."

"No. I was just thinking about what you said. My gut tells me you're right about those guys. All the pieces fit. Looks like you stumbled onto one huge weapons cache, in any case. Maybe some of these guys do double duty. Sometimes they hunt animals and sometimes they hunt U.N. soldiers." Henderson rubbed the bridge of his nose where his reading lenses had left two pink dents.

"There's no way I can do these guys by myself. Too many of 'em. Too much firepower," Forrest hated to admit. He burned with both excitement and frustration. He wanted the bastards who'd killed the rhinos. A younger man might have gone in there and taken his chances. A younger Forrest might have. But that was the difference between an experienced soldier and a FNG (fucking new guy, as the Army referred to them). Experience and maturity didn't come easy. Each had its price. And knowing when to engage an enemy and when to avoid one were the basics of any military strategy. "Too bad we can't call in an arty strike or an Arc Light like in 'Nam."

"Yeah."

"Peeper?"

"Yeah?" He knew the tone in his friend's voice. There was a warning in it. It was the same tone Forrest always had when he came up with a ballsy idea to tackle a tough problem. "What?"

There was another long pause.

"We can't let those dirt-bags get away with all the shit they've done to our people," Forrest complained, his voice thick with frustration. "We've got to get 'em. We *have* to come up with some way of taking them out."

Henderson didn't answer. His mind was working overtime on the red hat his friend had mentioned, Somalia at large, and a thousand other things with which a top CIA official would normally concern himself—not to mention the NSA situation. It occurred to him to mention the intercepted conversation. It also occurred to him that an ELINT platform might be listening at that very moment. Henderson decided against it. Forrest had enough on his mind. *Wonder what's taking Schnafhorst so long to get me an appointment?*

"Hear me?" Forrest prodded.

"Hmm?...Yeah, pal. I hear ya. We'll get 'em. I don't know how, yet. But we'll get 'em."

"Thank you for seeing me, Mrs. Wilcox. Especially on such short notice." Henderson said quietly. He sat forward on the edge of his wing chair, too nervous to sit back and relax in its plush, flower-print upholstery.

"I'm not so busy that I can't find time for you, Mr. Henderson." The first lady said with that gracious smile that so charmed the American people. Attired in her dark blue Carlisle suit and crisp white blouse, she looked like any lady executive. Accordingly, her make-up was applied sparingly, her silver-gray hair perfectly coiffed. "It's nice to see the CIA doing something useful for a change."

Henderson gave a nervous laugh and let his eyes fall to the thick Persian carpet. How would he begin? How could he begin? He'd rehearsed this moment in his mind a thousand times. But it hadn't helped a bit. No matter how he strung the words he couldn't change the facts. How did you tell the First Lady of the United States—the President's wife, for Chrissakes—that a high-level intelligence officer—the son of one of her close friends—was conducting an unsanctioned paramilitary operation in a friendly foreign nation? Not to mention that your best friend—your accomplice—was assassinating elephant poachers and engaged in a manhunt for the foreign nationals who murdered his son and did God knows what with your daughter? And how did one justify the misuse of super-secret U.S. Government facilities to provide classified information to someone who no longer held a security clearance—never mind that the clearance required for such access was miles above any clearance the individual had ever held? At least it wasn't treason—or was it? No, clearly not. No one on his team would subvert U.S. interests, a thought which helped quell his nerves.

Henderson looked up and smiled, though sheepishly. He felt like a high school kid who was about to tell the meanest cop in town he'd somehow gotten his daughter pregnant. How did you do something like that? His eyes wandered the first lady's East Wing office, searching its traditional appointments for the courage to go on.

The stories he'd heard were true. Judging from the artwork, Abby Wilcox was an elephant fanatic. There were elephant figurines everywhere—dozens of them. The most impressive being the fifteen-inch Creart sculpture standing guard on the corner of her desk, its head and trunk raised in a defiant trumpet. Its detail was astonishing. "Magnificent fellow," he began with a nod.

"Mmm. Oh, yes. He's one of my favorites," she enthused, pleased that he'd noticed.

His eyes met hers, and he liked what he saw in them. He saw patience. Compassion. And he'd need all of that he could get. "Mrs. Wilcox..."

Her eyes said: "Go on." Her smile: "I won't bite."

Henderson drew his lips into a tight smile that vanished as soon as it formed. "It's terrible...what's happening to them, isn't it?"

"Oh, good heavens, yes. Disgusting." She winced, his reference to poaching clearly upsetting. Intuition told her that the handsome gentleman dressed in a black suit needed a jump-start. "I'm curious. What interest could the CIA possibly have in elephants?"

Henderson looked straight into her clear bright eyes and swallowed. "What would you say if someone...someone in the government...was doing something to put a big dent in elephant poaching...something dramatic?"

The first lady pursed her bottom lip as she considered the question. "I'd say that was a very good thing. How could it not be?" Her eyes asked for more information.

"What if that someone was doing something...uh...illegal in the process?" Henderson interlaced his fingers and squeezed until the tips went white.

Abby Wilcox took a thoughtful sip of tea and returned the cup to its saucer before setting it on the dark coffee table that stood between their matching wing chairs. "I suppose there are times when one does what one must—legalities be damned." Her eyes twinkled, a defiant little spark. "I'm not sure there's anything I wouldn't do to help friends in need." She leaned forward and poured more steaming liquid into each of their cups. "Just what is it that you're doing, Mr. Henderson?" she asked with a knowing smile and a look that penetrated right to the back of his skull.

Henderson's face blanched white then flushed with a tidal wave of blood. He felt himself turn ice cold. A timely sip of hot liquid couldn't quell the chill and he looked down at the carpet. Then he looked Abby Wilcox straight in the eye. "I'm bending at least half-a-dozen laws and probably fracturing a few more."

"But you're helping elephants? Right?"

There was that look, again. "Yes ma'am, indirectly. But it's a little more complicated than that. There's also a connection with poaching and the warlord who wiped out the U.N. convoy back in November. I promised the president I would find the people responsible. And…"

"I'm listening."

"Well..."

For the next fifteen minutes, the first lady sat spellbound, listening to the story, sipping her tea, emoting at the appropriate moments. Henderson was a good storyteller—she, a good listener, hanging on every word. At one point, he produced satellite photos from a folder marked "CLASSIFIED." Its tab read: FINAL TRUMPET. Mrs. Wilcox smiled when she noticed it.

"I was so sorry to hear about your daughter. I had no idea. I..."

"It's okay." Henderson dismissed her with a wan smile. "My wife and I...well...she's having a harder time coping with it than I am. Doing something about it is a form of therapy for me. But she hasn't had that benefit. I can't even tell her what I'm doing."

"So why are you telling me?"

"There's no one else to turn to...and you have a clearance."

Abby Wilcox leaned forward a few inches and looked the CIA man squarely in the eye. "What can I do to help?"

"Just offering to help is more help than you can possibly imagine."

"A man like you didn't come here looking for a shoulder to cry on. You're in trouble and you need high-power help. Don't you?"

Henderson looked at her. "I'm potentially in big trouble, ma'am. Big-time trouble. The operation is in imminent danger of discovery." He explained how NSA had intercepted their communications and how a probe by the CIA's Security Directorate could bring his world crashing down any day. "Given enough time, I think I can tie in mainstream objectives like the convoy massacre to give the overall operation legitimacy. The rest we can disavow—plausible denial and all that." The wan smile returned. "The immediate and most serious threat will come from within—from my own government. The rest, I think I can handle."

"So what do you want me to do?"

"Call off the dogs."

"How?"

"I need a presidential finding—White House sanction."

"What makes you think I can make that happen?"

"I know a make-it-happen person when I see one."

Abby Wilcox smiled, rose from her chair and walked to her desk, digesting everything she had heard. She paused for a moment, caressing the elephant sculpture's back affectionately. "You know, Mr. Henderson, we can never let there be a 'final trumpet.' We owe them that much. Their future is our children's heritage. And when people have the ability to act to protect those who can't protect themselves, ability becomes re-spon-sa-bility." The national matriarch turned and looked at the man from CIA.

"My husband has been in politics all his adult life—over forty years. And like it or not, me along with him." She gave Henderson another knowing smile, an honest smile. "To tell the truth, I've hated every minute of it. And I really don't care whether he wins the election or not. I just wanted to be a country lawyer's wife. Raise horses and babies and take care of the house." She rolled her eyes and gestured around the room. "Who would've thought someday I would be taking care of the most famous house in the world? Funny how things work out, isn't it?"

Henderson simply smiled while Mrs. Wilcox paused for a moment's reflection.

"Now that I'm here, I'm bound and determined to make a difference—make things a little better than they were when the last first lady occupied this office. I want to be more than just an occupant—I want an occupation. So that's what I do. That's my job. I make some things better whenever and wherever I can." She smiled humbly and shrugged. "At least I try.

"Richard Wilcox works twenty hours a day doing whatever it is that presidents do...for power, ego...money. God knows we have plenty of that. Can't even spend what we have. I honestly can't remember the last time I opened my purse to make a purchase. Everything I need just...appears! Wealth and power are amazing things, truly amazing. But wealth and power are reprehensible without responsibility. And the world's wealthiest and most powerful nation has a moral obligation to protect..." she gestured toward the elephant "...the world's disenfranchised and dispossessed from a world full of politics and politicians."

Steven Henry Henderson rose on legs much stronger than the ones that had brought him into the room and extended his hand. "Thank you, Mrs. Wilcox. I don't think Winston Churchill could have said it any better."

The CNN Pentagon Correspondent's office is located on the building's outer or E-ring room 2E772, just down the hall from the Pentagon Press Room. There, Willard "Bill" Haines sat at his desk, his back to the narrow room's windows, studying recent newspaper articles on Iraq, Iran, and the Somalia situation when the phone warbled for the first time in an hour. It had been an unusually quiet week at the U.S. military's nerve center. And he, along with the rest of his crew, eagerly awaited a new story. After all, correspondents and the soldiers on which they reported had a lot in common. Peace may have been their profession, but war was their business—bombs and bullets their bread and butter.

He snatched up the receiver on the first ring.

"Haines."

"Mr. Haines," said Steve Henderson almost in a whisper." My apologies. I can't give you my name. But my friends call me Peeper. I think we may be able to help each other." The Assistant Deputy Director put his index finger in his vacant ear as Amtrak announced the arrival of its 1:55 PM Metroliner. Union Station, a beautifully restored train terminal and shopping mall in central Washington, was bustling with travelers. And the ambient noise, though annoying, would mask his conversation well.

"What can I do for you...Peeper?" Haines asked, his interest piqued.

"Do you recall the ambush in Mogadishu in November? The one where the Somalis took out the U.N. convoy with the truck bomb?"

"Sure do." With that, the Dick van Patten look alike reached into a desk drawer, withdrew a steno pad, and began making notes.

"I seem to recall a video clip on the story. You guys got some footage of the detonation from a helicopter."

"That's right." Haines doodled a helicopter beneath the word Peeper.

"Didn't your camera man loose his baseball cap in the blast? A red cap. I seem to recall you used footage of it flying into the street to illustrate the power of the blast."

"Mmm, yeah. I think you're right. You have a pretty good memory." Haines doodled a baseball cap.

"I need a copy of the tape. Unedited, if possible."

Haines' pencil froze. "I don't know about that, Mr...er, Peeper. News film is proprietary. Same as a reporter's notes." He felt his nerves start to tingle.

"You'd be doing your country a great service, Mr. Haines." Henderson insisted more urgently.

"How so?"

Henderson thought a moment before replying. "The tape may contain the evidence we need to track down the perpetrators. We'd be very grateful for your help. And I might be able to set you up to scoop a great story in return."

There was a long uneasy silence on the other end of the line while Haines considered the request. "Well...I don't know. I can't help you. But if you'll standby a minute, I'll give you a number to call."

"That'll work."

Amy lay awake, her eyes closed, her face to the stick wall. She listened to the muffled voices behind her, trying her best to discern what was being said by the poacher and his wife in the dark. Some words were being spoken in English, some in Swahili.

Whenever the husband was in camp Amy was constantly on edge, never quite knowing when the next drunken attack would come. Since his last attempt at physical abuse had left him somewhat the worse for wear, he'd kept his distance perhaps out of respect for her defensive abilities and perhaps because his wife had come to her aid, as well. Or perhaps it was because his wife had threatened to tell the boss his prize was at risk for becoming damaged goods and far less marketable as a result of poor care. Maybe it was some combination of all those reasons. Whatever. As long as she was left alone speculation was pointless.

Amy could hear snippets of conversation, especially if there was a difference of opinion about one issue or another resulting in raised voices. During their most intense discussions Amy had learned that she was often the subject, especially of late. She strained hard when she picked up key words such as "American" which she had just overheard.

It was a male voice: "Shetani is making arrangements with his Middle East contacts to sell the American girl. He is disappointed that she is still so thin."

"She is naturally thin. There is only so much I can do," his wife explained with a defensive tone. "How long do we have?"

There was a pause while the monster did the arithmetic. "His shipper comes into Mombasa once a month. He wants her on the next shipment or the one to follow at the latest. You only have a few weeks."

"She is not an animal," the wife protested. "I cannot force her to gain weight or even to eat."

"Try harder. The sooner she is gone the sooner we can again have peace in my house."

A cold chill surged through Amy's body as she considered all of the announcement's ramifications. *Sold?! To Arabs!* Her mind raced through a thousand thoughts in seconds. It had never before occurred to her that, in the computer age, slavery was anything but chapters from a history textbook. She visualized herself crammed into the hold of some miserable ship awash in feces, vomit, disease and death just like in the 18th and 19th centuries. Those thoughts were dismissed as too awful to contemplate. *I'll kill myself first!*

The hemp rope biting into her wrists and ankles reminded her that she was, in reality, a prisoner, nevertheless. And, with almost constant surveillance, even suicide would be difficult. Though she had no idea what day it was or even what *time* of the day it was, it occurred to her, accompanied with a flood of bitter tears, it was now 1994! Acid began to burn her eyes. Knots of barbed wire twisted in her gut over the thought that she had missed Thanksgiving, Christmas and the New Year with her family and her husband. And that Nathan would never see another holiday—ever. She lapsed into a series of convulsive sobs so violent they were painful, then arrested them when she heard a loud noise.

She heard the monster lapse into a series of deep snores that rattled the stick walls. That was just enough to catalyze her tears into rage. *Get a grip, Amy! My father and uncles would let me have about two minutes of this before they slapped me across the face. Pity, especially the worst kind: self-pity, was debilitating. It often made the difference between life and death in survival and POW situations.*

She'd heard them talk about this poor guy and that stupid guy; about the dumb mistakes and the lessons learned from them; about the tough resolute bastards who'd made it out of Vietnam and the ones who hadn't. She remembered them saying that as time goes on and as POWs are moved to increasingly sophisticated confinement facilities their chances of escape diminish. She reminded herself she'd survived weeks in the African savanna. *And a river full of crocs, for God's sake!*

Amy wiped her eyes on the back of her bound, almost numb, forearms. *I'm going to be one of those "resolute bastards" who made it! I want my dad and Uncle John to be proud of me. I want Nathan to be proud of me. And, I'd rather be dead than disappoint them.*

After his driver had dropped him off in the Pentagon parking garage, Steve Henderson had taken the SECDEF's private elevator directly to his huge third-floor office. He was happy to see the Secretary had been joined by Admiral Small, the National Security Advisor, for their private meeting, as requested. "This'd better be good, Steve. We have a tee-time at the Congressional in forty minutes. You have ten," the Secretary of Defense, Mark Hudson, warned, demonstratively eyeing his watch. His half smile meant he was only half kidding. Preoccupied with his "sales pitch," Henderson had only just noticed the two men were not attired in their usual tailor-made business suits.

Henderson went directly to a television set positioned in front of a huge world map, just across the room from the SECDEF's massive desk. "If I may, sir," he said, inserting a video cassette in the attached VCR before he'd received permission. "This is the 'smoking gun' I alluded to."

"Please. By all means. You now have nine minutes." The SECDEF's smile had all but disappeared.

Henderson turned the TV on with a click and pushed PLAY. Seconds later, the image of armored cars, painted UN-white, appeared on the screen only to be obscured a second later by an enormous blast. As the tape was a copy of the original which had not been edited for broadcast, the audio was replete with helicopter noise and the muffled voice of the camera man. Henderson tweaked the volume down a bit to render it bearable.

"This part you've seen before, gentlemen," Henderson narrated as they watched a scene best forgotten. The picture went abruptly askew as the shock wave smacked the newscaster's helicopter.

"This part was also broadcast, but most people wouldn't remember it. The audio was edited out," Henderson went on.

The men watched as downtown Mogadishu reappeared in the picture just in time to catch the image of a red baseball cap fluttering to the ground, a muted, "Shit! My hat!" barely audible in the background. Several seconds of footage followed showing wrecked vehicles against a backdrop of smoke and gunfire.

"This is where the regular broadcast ended."

Next, they watched as a Somali kid, now wearing the captured red baseball cap, fired his AK-47 at UN troops as he bolted through Mogadishu's maze of broken streets. Shortly after the boy joined his accomplices in the back of a small pick-up truck, Henderson pushed STOP.

"Find the kid with the hat and we find the guys who did the ambush," Henderson said matter-of-factly, as if explaining the significance of the Rosetta Stone to high-school history students.

"Maybe," said Admiral Small.

"With all due respect, Admiral. More than 'maybe.' I'd venture to say a near certainty if he can be connected with a certain Somali warlord," Henderson countered. "The Ghuled clan has been high on our list of suspects from the start."

Admiral Small made a tight little smile. "Why do I get the feeling there's more to the story?"

Unimpressed, Secretary Hudson grew impatient with the guessing games. "Seven minutes, Mr. Henderson," he reminded, donning his golf cap. "If you're going to make a point, I suggest you get on with it. Frankly," he commented, "what I've seen so far doesn't exactly flush my bowl. If you found this kid and connected him to the bushwhackers I might be more inclined..."

"I already have, Mr. Secretary," Henderson interrupted. With that, he produced the CERTAIN THUNDER folder explaining that a reliable "asset" had seen the boy entering camps containing large caches of military vehicles and equipment. To clinch his presentation, Henderson walked them through the techniques used to identify the pickup truck in which the boys had escaped then produced astonishing high-resolution imagery which placed it in one of the camps. Henderson compared his satellite imagery with still frames from the video they had just seen. There were enough artifacts to establish a positive match. "Bang, gentlemen," said the CIA analyst, making a pistol with his fingers. "The gun doesn't get any smokier than that."

"Okay," said Admiral Small. "So what do you want us to do about it? Bear in mind, the military side of the house never wanted to get involved in this Somalia business in the first place. If it was up to General Clark, the only thing the Air Force'd be delivering would be napalm or rubbers."

Henderson saw the admiral and the SECDEF exchange looks. "Admiral, in the intelligence business, there's always reasonable doubt." He looked the national security advisor straight in the eye. "But, if you recall, it's an election year. And the president... Well, the race is fairly close according to the latest polls. Then there's the president's military record...or, more accurately, nonexistent military record. Suffice it to say that he's not exactly Audie Murphy, at least not as far as the electorate is concerned. You might also recall that being a military hero or at least being associated with military heroes has always helped presidents get elected. A few presidents were elected on their military records alone: Eisenhower, Grant, Washington... More recently, you'll remember what EL DORADO CANYON did for Ronald Reagan. Kicking Quadafi's ass made Reagan an overnight hero."

"You want us to attack this warlord to prove a point...make political points?" Secretary Hudson asked.

"Not me. But if you recall, President Wilcox said he 'wanted' the guys who destroyed that convoy. I thought he made that clear."

"I suppose he did, at that," Admiral Small agreed, trying to decide what his boss would say before being more committal. A sly smirk suddenly covered his face as he turned to the SECDEF. "Mark, you know what you call a Somali with a swollen toe?"

"I give up."

"A three wood."

The Secretary swallowed a laugh and looked toward his office door. "Be careful where you tell that joke, Walter. The political correctness police are everywhere these days." His smile fading, The SECDEF sat on the edge of his huge desk, now in somewhat less of a hurry to leave, his mind whirling with possibilities. "The idea does have merit, Mr. Henderson. Defense budgets are getting harder to defend than the country itself. But, it would take a while to move the required assets..."

"I've already talked to the Air Force," Henderson interjected, again way ahead of them. He removed another document from the CERTAIN THUNDER folder and explained. "We have a squadron of A-10s in Kuwait right now. Deploying them to Mogadishu would be very doable."

The SECDEF looked at Henderson then at his watch. "Damn Walter. We need to wiggle our asses, here." He jumped up and headed for the elevator. "I like it, Mr. Henderson," he said over his shoulder. "Put a plan together and call Melba tomorrow for an appointment." As the elevator doors started to close, the SECDEF stopped them with his hand. "Wait. Let me guess. You already have."

Forrest inventoried the contents of the latest air drop. Ten special .50 cal HEI rounds for the Light Fifty. Two UHF, hand held radios—one was a spare. "Whoa. Looky here," he told the noisy Bare-faced "Go Away Bird" observing from the safety of the baobab branches above his head. A small box contained four 12.7mm and four 14.5mm Soviet machine gun rounds. Forrest smiled when he read the note from Peeper:

> ...THE SOVIET MACHINE GUN ROUNDS ARE PACKED WITH SEMTEX. IF THE OPPORTUNITY PRESENTS ITSELF, YOU MAY WANT TO BOOBYTRAP SOME OF THE AAA PIECES...

"Might be fun, at that," he said, turning to the next piece of equipment—a box containing a new notebook computer for the satellite uplink. The accompanying note:

> ...INSTALL THE NEW NOTEBOOK IMMEDIATELY. I DISCOVERED OUR LINE HAS BEEN TAPPED BY NSA. BELIEVE I HAVE IT UNDER CONTROL BUT THIS NEW CRYPTO SHOULD CONSTIPATE THEIR COMPUTERS FOR QUITE A WHILE. IT'S AS BULLETPROOF AS IT GETS—A PGP ALGORITHM WITH A 64 BIT SESSION KEY...

"Whatever that means," Forrest muttered, shaking his head. He looked up at the brilliant white bird, which rather resembled a goblin with a coal-black face and a wild Moses-like beard and hairdo. The bird was noisy, voicing deep bleating calls and wild ringing chuckles, but a welcome companion, nevertheless. His visits made him miss his macaw.

Forrest set the notebook aside and opened a large manila envelope marked: MISSION INSTRUCTIONS. "Quiet now," Forrest scolded. "I've gotta concentrate, here." Leaning back against the empty shipping container which he would later bury near the others, Forrest stretched his legs and began to read.

CHAPTER-FIFTEEN

INTERDICTION *a: to forbid; prohibit*
b: steady bombardment of enemy positions, routes or supply and communications lines for the purpose of delaying, disorganizing or destroying his forces

TWO DOZEN AIR FORCE SECURITY POLICE stood guard in various sandbag bunkers erected on the huge concrete ramp that was the northeast parking area of Mogadishu International Airport. A mammoth, gray Lockheed C-141 Starlifter sat parked on the ramp next to six much smaller jet fighters. In the partial darkness, it assumed the appearance of a giant prehistoric bird with its high tail and great, drooping, anhedral wings. All the lights on the ramp had been turned out to make targeting more difficult for would-be snipers. Crews working by flashlight created an eerie scene as they prepared six warbirds for their morning mission.

Armorers went to work inspecting sixteen CBU-87 cluster weapons. Over seven feet long and sixteen inches in diameter, they resembled olive-drab hot water heaters with bulbous, black noses and four, stubby stabilizer fins. A two-inch-wide, yellow band painted near the nose indicated that they were packed with high explosive submunitions.

Other weapons specialists worked with machines used to load the A-10s' Gatling guns with 1,150 rounds of 30mm ammunition. As the ALS or automatic loading system machinery whirred and chattered, a combat mix of HEI (high-explosive incendiary) and API (armor-piercing incendiary) ammo, encased in white plastic sleeves, was extracted from huge rectangular ammo cans about the size of cigarette machines and fed into the bottom of the planes' fuselage where the rotating gun mechanism picked up the cannon shells and routed them into a cylindrical magazine tucked into the plane's belly. While the gun plumbers worked on two of the planes, two other crews used combination go-cart and fork-lift machines called "jammers" to raise the assembled cluster bombs from their trailers and attach them to the under-wing bomb racks. Four of the six airplanes were hung with four bombs each—two under each wing. The remaining A-10s received only a full load of cannon ammunition. They would be the mission spares or SAR (search and rescue) birds.

Inside the ops trailer, Major Eric "Hogger" Blaylock and his deployed contingent of five "hog-drivers" examined the unusual air tasking order which had been hand-delivered by the pilot of the C-141 in a sealed security pouch. It was written in a format more closely resembling a business letter than the usual teletyped message. He noticed, however, that despite its unique appearance, it did contain all of the essential information his pilots would need to conduct the mission. Included were maps and recent high-resolution photos of the targets—something of a luxury in the air-to-mud business. Major Phil "Hoser" Gray was the squadron's assistant operations officer. Standing six feet two inches tall, he and Blaylock had no difficulty plotting the target coordinates on the upper left corner of a large chart mounted on the trailer's back wall. When they noticed how close the target was to the Kenyan border they re-plotted it, just to be sure.

Captain Bob "Snot" Davies and Captain Jim "Zach" Czachorowski used a Dell laptop to compute the best delivery profiles for the cluster bombs. The eight-hundred-pound free-fall weapons were an ideal choice for antipersonnel-antiarmor missions. The A-10s' GAU-

8 30mm cannon would take care of any target requiring surgical elimination. Tanks, armored personnel carriers, trucks and even the walls of conventional buildings presented no particular problem to the gun's lethal stream of API and HEI projectiles. Fusing and delivery data was extracted from the computer and would be loaded by the pilots in the aircraft's LASTE computer-aided weapons aiming system.

Another pair of pilots, Major Brian "B-squared" Barnes and Captain John "J.C. the Teabag" Smith worked with another computer to calculate time and fuel consumption for their route to the target. J.C. eyed the results suspiciously. Things would have to go like clockwork, even with air-to-air refueling. The boys would have to have their shit packed as tight as a hundred-compression golf ball, he mused. Find the bad guys, blow their skinny asses into next week and RTB before the FUEL LOW light comes on. *It's gonna be tight.*

It had taken Forrest ten hours to hide the Zenair and hike into the target area. The last four hours found him walking in darkness with only starlight to illuminate his way. It was almost 23:00 when he arrived at his destination. He was beat—bone tired. Stopping to listen every few yards, he quietly approached the warlord's camp through the sparse brush. He was surprised that there were no barking dogs about. Maybe they eat 'em like the Vietnamese did, he thought. In their situation, these people would probably eat just about anything. Just as well, a yapping dog could ruin my whole night. Complacency and poor security would cost them—big time, he thought as he felt his way around two pickup trucks parked next to one of the old American made tanks. From the looks of it, the tank had not been moved in some time.

Parked along the other side of the tanks were two Somali technicals he had read about in the Nairobi papers and seen in the satellite photos. These two happened to be Toyota four-wheel-drive pickups which had seen much abuse. Soviet 12.7mm machine guns sat mounted on pedestals which were bolted to the corrugated steel beds. Loaded with full ammo belts, they were ready for immediate action. Forrest reached into a pouch in his vest and took out one of the booby-trapped rounds. He inserted it in the belt ten rounds from the chamber. In the darkness he grinned at the mental image of what that little invention would do to the next man to fire the guns.

Stacked in the corner of one of the truck beds were several two-and-a-half gallon gasoline cans and one, five-gallon can. In 3 minutes he had the big can resting atop the turret of the adjacent tank.

Forty-five minutes and several booby-trapped AAA guns later he was moving silently through the brush to the west. Forrest made his way five hundred meters across the semi-desert terrain to the spot where he had left his back pack and the Barrett Light Fifty. His position was at the top of a shallow rise surrounded by otherwise flat ground. He spent the next half-hour setting up three Claymore mines, putting the finishing touches on his sniper's hide and running his mental checklist. Everything was ready, he reassured himself. All that remained now was the hardest part…waiting.

"That's it, then. We're even." Steve Henderson struggled to hear over the roar of rain falling on the phone booth.

"Agreed. You did better than you promised—a lot better." Walker Riley, the President of CNN's international division, sat on the edge of his mattress in the master suite of his Buckhead mansion. His Mont Blanc pen wiggled furiously as he scribbled notes on the small pad parked on the nightstand next to his alarm clock. Its LED numerals read 1:11 AM.

What time was that in Somalia?

"Three, gimme an alpha check to the CP." Major Blaylock glanced at the distance and bearing readings on his HSI.

"Two-eighty-seven for forty-seven." The contact point, a navigational waypoint where they would contact the forward air controller who would direct their attacks, lay forty-seven miles ahead of them at a compass bearing of 287 degrees. Captain Bob Davies was number three in the formation of four A-10s. As number four, Czachorowski flew a line-abreast formation a mile off Snot's right wing and Gray flew the identical formation on Blaylock's wing as number two. The whole formation resembled a big square, called a battle box, which measured a mile on a side. Flying at an altitude of twenty-four thousand feet helped to conserve fuel.

"Target check," Blaylock commanded five minutes later. "Leader's 7.5"

In turn, each of the four pilots checked their engine instruments and weapons system switches then called out their fuel remaining to let their leader know who had the least amount of gas. In all four cockpits, the pilots armed their ALE-40 chaff and flare dispensers setting them to "program." Gloved fingers moved several switches and knobs on the weapons panel positioned above their left knee. They rotated the fusing selector switch to the proper option and rotated the release mode selector knob to SGL or single release. On this particular mission, a single bomb would be released with each activation of the red "pickle" button positioned at the top of the control stick. Another switch set the Gatling gun to fire at high rate or 4,000+ rounds per minute. Turning the "master arm" switch on last, the pilots supplied power to the entire weapons system. Several pairs of green "ready" lights illuminated in the postage stamp-sized station selector switches along with the faint green letters of the "gun ready" light. The system was now "hot"—the sum total of their Warthogs' awesome firepower at their disposal.

Images magnified by the high-power optics of Forrest's binoculars had an ethereal shimmer to them. Propped up on his elbows, Forrest watched the camps come to life. A few goats strained at the end of their tethers. Their mouths opened but their bleating was too far away to hear. Small, naked children emerged from the rickety huts following their mothers through the morning routine. A few small groups of women and young children fanned out from the camps gathering wood for the morning fires. Two of the groups started off in his direction and then, to his relief, veered off to the north.

The poacher's camp was quieter than the main camp. Big hunks of sooty black meat hung on wooden racks over fires that had burned out hours ago. The hairs on the back of his hands bristled when he noted two leopard skins stretched out on makeshift drying racks.

Interrupting that thought, the figure of a teenage boy emerged from the entrance of one of the huts. In his hand, Forrest noted the unmistakable shape of a Kalashnikov assault rifle. His interest was piqued when he noted the boy was wearing something familiar on his head. A quick adjustment of the binocular's focusing knob revealed a red and black baseball cap.

Forrest's nerves tingled with excitement as he followed the boy on his brisk, half mile walk to the clansmen's camp where he disappeared into one of the huts.

Forrest whispered to himself, "You get around, don't ya, kid. Looks like you were right, Peeper."

He waited intently for several minutes to see if the boy would reemerge. When that didn't happen, he turned his attention to other matters.

Just then, a faint sound in the brush, behind and to his left jolted his nerves. Instinctively, he froze and strained to focus every ounce of energy on the source. There it was again! Without turning his head, Forrest took his binoculars away from his eyes and ever-so-slowly lowered them to the mat. Straining his eyeballs to the extreme left of their sockets, he slowly turned his head toward the noise.

Shit!

Not ten feet away, the ghostly white eyes of a small child stared straight back into his—a little girl, frozen with fear. She held a few small sticks in the crooks of her arms. Forrest's right hand slid imperceptibly down his side as he felt for the MP-5.

Both Forrest and the girl flinched when they heard a woman call out from the brush. The little girl stood fast, her eyes transfixed on what must have been the strangest sight she had ever seen. Only the Brothers Grimm could have conjured up a moving bush with human eyes. The woman, probably her mother, called again. The little girl didn't move, she was too afraid.

Dammit-all, kid. GO!

The woman called again. She was closer although still out of sight in the shallow depression behind his position.

Great. Just great.

Forrest brought his finger up along the side of the trigger housing, straining to detect the mother's approach. No matter how innocent they were, he couldn't allow them to blow the lid off the mission. If the woman saw him and ran, she would return with half the camp.

"Hiisssssss!" Forrest made a sudden lunge in the girl's direction, spitting like a cornered cat.

She dropped the sticks and stumbled backwards a few steps. The little girl, still mesmerized by his appearance was, at once, fascinated and paralyzed with fear. Forrest gave some thought to crawling away to another hiding place but there was really no other place to which he could move without further exposing himself.

The woman's voice grew louder as she came closer. He could tell from the sound of it that the woman was becoming increasingly frantic.

Forrest flinched again when the woman's voice carried through the brush. She was very close. He slipped his finger through the trigger guard and brought his weapon around toward the sound of the approaching woman.

Her head appeared over the top of the bushes and then her upper torso. She called once again to the child who broke and ran the few steps to her side and wrapped her arms around her mother's knees. Although the woman spoke in a language he couldn't understand, Forrest could tell from her tone the little girl was getting a scolding for wandering off.

Forrest lay as still as he could, not daring to breathe. The MP-5 was pointed in their direction, his options diminishing by the second. *Don't look at me, lady! Don't look. I can't let you see me and live.*

Abruptly recalling the source of her fear, the little girl snapped her head around toward him, her eyes locked onto his. The woman immediately sensed her child's fear. Instinctively, she followed the direction of her daughter's stare. At first, she didn't see the figure lying on the ground a mere two meters away. It was like looking at a picture full of hidden objects—her mind had not yet separated the natural from the out-of-place. The camouflage was very effective at breaking up a sniper's outline and making him seem like part of his surroundings but it couldn't make him invisible. Then she noticed the eyes—the one thing he couldn't disguise.

The woman clutched her child close to her chest and shrieked.

That's it, Goddammit!

In a flash, Forrest snapped up the weapon and felt his finger applying pressure to the trigger. The momentum of the situation had taken over and he was no longer in control. Forrest felt as if he were standing on the edge of a tall building and was being drawn over the edge.

Sensing that she was about to die, the woman scooped the child up and ran. Forrest kept the weapon trained on her as she went. It would be a simple thing to drop them in mid-stride, his problem solved.

Damn!

Forrest drew his finger away from the trigger and let them go. A helpless feeling washed over him as he watched them run toward the poacher's camp. The woman tripped and stumbled a few times in her haste to get away from a man whose very presence she somehow understood meant certain death for her and her family.

Can't worry about this now. In a few minutes...What time is it? He glanced at his watch—ten minutes to go. A cold wave of dread passed through him. After laying the MP-5 on the mat, Forrest picked up his binoculars. The woman still had a fair distance to cover to the camp. Maybe there would be time before they came for him, but come they would.

While he waited for the inevitable, Forrest watched as a dozen women and children walked past his position, making their way westward toward the Kenyan border. Still unnerved by his close encounter, he watched all of them very carefully. Some passed off to his right as near as fifty meters but did not appear to notice him, though paranoia told him otherwise.

Forrest brought the glasses back to the poacher's camp just in time to see the woman and the little girl he had frightened disappear into one of the huts. He waited three painfully long minutes for something to happen. *Would they believe her—regard her story with enough credibility to check it out? Could they afford not to?* Only time would tell and time was running out.

Panning his binoculars from the poacher's camp at his eleven o'clock position to the warlord's camp at his one o'clock, Forrest noticed two women walking west with an infant and two small children. Lagging twenty meters behind, the upper torso of the boy with the red baseball cap appeared above the scattered brush, his assault rifle slung over his shoulder with a piece of rope.

Forrest, wrestling with impatience, waited until they were a quarter mile past his position before turning on his radio.

The woman and the little girl were still very much on his mind as he turned his glasses back to the poachers' camp and adjusted the focus knob. Although he was expecting it, the sight of the woman pointing out his position to three armed men gripped him with a twinge of anger. A conscience, he thought, is a liability in this line of work.

Where the hell are those fighters?

Forrest continued to watch the people in the poacher's camp. Three of the men fanned out, line abreast, cautiously moving in the direction the woman had indicated—directly toward him! They were still several hundred meters away.

"Damn! Damn! Damn!" Forrest pounded the butt of his fist into the dirt. The fighters weren't even here yet and he had already lost control of the situation. His fingers felt around for the MP-5 and the Claymore triggers just in case.

Forrest checked his watch for the tenth time in the last four minutes. In two minutes, it would be 09:00.

"Overkill, Overkill. Hogger One One," the pilot's voice crackled right on time.

Relief flushed through him. Forrest picked up the radio, held the mouthpiece close to his lips and pressed the transmit button. "Hogger—Overkill. Glad to see you guys!"

The A-10s approached from the east-southeast, out of the rising sun. His pulse quickened as he picked up the faint sound of jet engines.

"Overkill, authenticate mike-bravo."

Forrest glanced at the authenticator code card taped to the back of his radio.

"Zulu."

"Roger that, Overkill. You've got four hogs with wall-to-wall C-B-U and eleven hundred rounds of thirty mike-mike. We have two zero minutes playtime, max."

"Copy, Hogger. Proceed to the briefed target coordinates and set up an orbit at one five thousand. Call established. Target is low threat, as briefed."

"Hogger copies. Go trail."

He checked the progress of the three men approaching his position. In a few minutes he would be within range of their rifles. Forrest looked up to see the jets starting their circular orbit high over the camps.

"Okay, lead. Do you see the encampments directly below your position? They appear as clusters of huts with some vehicles scattered about." Forrest was certain that the fighter pilots would have no trouble picking the camps out of the desert scrub.

"In sight."

"There is a northern camp and a southern camp. The line that connects them runs north-south, parallel to the Kenyan border." Forrest released the transmit button and listened for Hogger's response amidst the radio's faint static.

"In sight."

"Okay, the distance between the two camps is about one click. We'll call that one unit."

"Roger."

Forrest picked up his binoculars and looked around the camps to see what was going on. He noticed that some of the men had come out of the huts in the southern camp and were staring up at the planes circling high overhead. Some of them had their hands raised like a visor to shade their eyes from the brilliant sunlight. None seemed to immediately appreciate the fact that they were in the center of a giant bull's-eye. They took no defensive action other than to stare up into the pale, blue sky. As Forrest watched, he could see more people emerging from the huts. He grimaced when he noticed that one of them was a woman holding an infant in her arms. He put the glasses on the three men who were searching for him. They too, had stopped for the moment and were looking skyward.

"From the two encampments, move your eyes due west about five units and you should see several larger camps and a small dirt airstrip."

After several seconds of hesitation, there was a response from the leader, "Tally-ho."

"Those are the friendlies."

"Roger."

"Move your eyes back to the bad guys and then look half a click west for a mirror flash." Forrest dropped his field glasses and felt around the front of his shirt for his signal mirror which hung around his neck on a nylon cord. Sighting through the hole in the glass, he caught the rays of the morning sun and aimed the reflection at the orbiting fighters. He wiggled the mirror around a little to insure that the reflected beam would have a better chance of catching the pilots' eyes.

"Tally-ho your flash," Blaylock announced.

"Roger. That's the FAC position. All your run-ins will be north-south or south-north. Repeat, north-south or south-north. Standby."

"Hogger copies."

So far-so good, Forrest thought. Time to kick the hornet's nest.

Forrest settled back down on the shooting mat and picked up the Light Fifty. He chambered a special incendiary round and removed the safety. A second later, he located the gas can sitting on top of the tank. Off to the left, he noticed two men readying one of the 14.5 mm machine guns. Some of them were beginning to catch on.

Forrest steadied the crosshairs on the base of the gas can.

BOOM!

The weapon thundered, sending the heavy bullet through the morning air toward its target. Less than a second later it tore through the gas can. A sharp booming sound reached his ears a moment after he saw the orange fireball expand, transforming itself into a mushroom cloud of angry black smoke. Forrest watched through the scope as men scurried for cover or to machine guns and rifles stashed in the various huts and vehicles situated around the camp. Thinking that they had dropped a bomb on them, some started firing up at the planes.

Forrest picked up the radio and laid the rifle down on the mat.

"Alright, Hogger. You see that smoke?"

"Roger the smoke!"

"Okay, that camp will be the first target. I need you to put down a line of strafe just to the east of the south target to shake 'em up a bit and to give the women and children a chance to make a run for it. Gimme one pass on that target and standby. Take care not to hit the target, just scare 'em a bit, first. Two, I need you to put down a line of strafe two hundred meters west of the north target. I've got bad guys in that area moving my way. How copy?"

"Understood," came Blaylock's reply. "One's in. Two, you take the north target."

"Two," Gray acknowledged.

Both pilots sent their jets into steep dives aiming their gun crosses per the FAC's instructions. Forrest watched as the lead jet bore down on the southern camp.

"You're cleared hot unless you hear otherwise, lead. I'm too busy down here to clear each pass. Aborts will be in the clear."

"Roger that."

The whine of the jets' engines increased in pitch and amplitude as they plunged toward the ground. A mile above him, Forrest saw the front of the lead fighter erupt in a thin trail of gray-white smoke. A second later, a roar that sounded like a cross between a ten-thousand-pound chain saw and the bellow of some primeval beast reached his ears. At the same instant, huge fountains of dirt shot twenty feet into the air on the far side of the south camp. The supersonic crackle of the bullet's high explosive warheads popped in the distance like a string of firecrackers. The second A-10 rolled in just as the first pulled off. A few seconds later, the blast of its cannon ripped up the dirt four hundred meters in front of him. A wall of dust and smoke billowed out of the ground as the rounds stitched the earth. As the dust settled, Forrest could see two of the three men running back toward their camp. A grin spread across his face.

Scanning with his binoculars, Forrest saw that all hell was breaking loose on the ground. Figures scrambled about, panicking amidst the noise, dust and confusion. He saw that the first pass from the fighters had had the desired effect. Immediately to the south, the few remaining women and small children were running west. To the north, he watched as the two men turned and also ran west, only a few meters behind the woman who was now carrying the little girl.

Forrest decided to let them go and turned his attention back to the camps. A cacophony of gunfire had erupted from various weapons. Streaks of tracer bullets zipped into the sky clawing for the circling warplanes. Using his scope, Forrest searched for the fighter's next targets. He saw two men jumping up on the Toyota pickups he had visited the previous night. The first one up pulled down on the back of the gun raising the barrel toward the sky. As he squeezed the triggers, a flash shot out of the back of the weapon spraying shards of hot metal into his face. Holding his hands over his eyes, the man tumbled backward over the side of the truck, disappearing from view. The man in the other truck leapt from its bed and took cover under its chassis. Forrest grinned at the sight. The steel truck body offered no more protection than a child would get from pulling the bedcovers over his head.

"If only Colonel Grant could see this!"

Forrest saw that the fighters had initiated evasive maneuvers, jinking to dodge streams of bullets coming up at them from the ground. Although their altitude kept them outside the range of the lighter weapons, the heavy machine guns could send bullets well above that height, albeit with little accuracy. Even so, the pilots still had to take the guns seriously. For every tracer round they could see there were five- to-ten rounds that were invisible. Bullets filled the air like hail falling upward.

Forrest picked up the radio. "Hogger, you're taking small arms fire from the southern camp! That's your next target. All the non-players seem to be clear, so let's put some shit on their heads to suppress those guns."

"Roger that! One's in," Blaylock's answered. He was anxious to return some of the steel the bad guys were throwing up at his fighters. "Two, set up for CBU. Three and four, you're cleared off for the other target."

The flight members acknowledged the instructions, in turn.

The lead fighter rolled off on its left wing and dove toward the ground. A few seconds later, Blaylock directed a deadly swarm of cannon shells at the pounding guns below. The stream of hurtling projectiles cut into the steel bodies of the two Toyotas reducing them to scrap metal in an instant. For the two gunners hiding underneath, it was like being processed in a fish cannery. They were sliced and diced and covered in metal in the blink of an eye.

There were still sounds of several heavy machine guns coming from the camp as the second fighter rolled in. Phil Gray steadied the bomb sight pipper just short of the longest stream of tracers and watched the lime-green altitude tape unwind on the right side of the heads up display. At 6,500 feet he punched the pickle button and pulled back hard on the stick, grunting heavily to ward off the effect of 6 Gs. With an audible clunk, the dispenser left its rack. A wire lanyard connecting the bomb to the rack pulled taut as it fell away tripping a spring-loaded latch which released the dispenser's extendable stabilizing fins. At the same time, two other steel wires were extracted, arming the radar-ranging proximity fuse that protruded from the bomb's nose which bounced a signal off the ground to measure its altitude. A few seconds later, the fuse sensed its preset 1,000 foot height-of-function and sent a signal to fire an explosive bolt, canting the bomb's fins. Performing like a propeller in reverse, the fins rapidly spun the bomb to a preselected RPM whereupon the fuse completed its function. After sensing a spin rate computed to symmetrically disperse the 202 bomblets packed inside, a fire signal went to the aluminum linear shaped charges built into the bomb's body. These explosive ribbons cut through the tactical munitions dispenser's aluminum case discarding the tail section and splitting the body longitudinally into three equal pieces. Suddenly set free to rain their man-made hell onto the enemy's heads, the bomblets poured outward like peas spewing from a spinning pod. The soda cans of explosive sprouted white fabric blossoms which stabilized them, pointing them at the ground, lethal end first. Their expanding pattern covered an area only slightly smaller than a football field. The bomblets detonated on contact, a shaped charge for maximum penetration of armor plate and a half-pound of cyclotol exploded symmetrically, hurling three hundred, 30 grain fragments of shrapnel in all directions. Finally, as a garnish for the lethal dish, pieces of white-hot zirconium added an incendiary effect, torching anything that would burn.

Forrest watched in fascination as flashes of white and orange danced around the ground, partially concealed inside reoccurring puffs of gray smoke and red dust. The noise was like the sound of rolling thunder that reechoes for several seconds beneath a summer storm. Regaining his composure after a second, he picked up the radio.

"Good hits, Two! I can still hear a fifty cal hammering away but I can't see him. That's some wicked shit you guys are dropping!" Forrest was almost breathless with excitement. "That ought to keep their heads down for a few minutes! Let's hit that northern camp with three and four."

Gray didn't respond to the radio call. He was distracted by the sounds of something pinging against his Hog's aluminum skin. He checked the instruments and warning lights for indications of a system failure. Everything appeared to be normal.

The third and fourth A-10s circled the northern target.

Payback time. "Let's put some CBU on that target, three!"

"Three's in, hot!" Snot called after a few seconds.

"You're cleared hot. Nail 'em good!"

Captain Davies sent his jet into a dive from the north, Zach setting up right behind him. A few seconds after Forrest saw the nose of the fighter point itself at the ground, he noticed two more men were attempting to run from the camp. Davies saw them also and adjusted his dive to put the green dot of the bomb sight just in front of them. Forrest watched the bomb come off the jet as Zach rolled in a half-minute behind Snot. Ten seconds later the two running figures were engulfed in a series of explosions that shook the ground. When the smoke and dust thinned, they were nowhere to be seen. They had been wiped off the face of the planet like a mosquito slapped off someone's skin.

"Shit hot, three! Four, hit the camp."

"Four's in."

"Cleared hot!"

Thirty seconds later the huts in the northern camp came apart under a shower of exploding death. All vestiges of human facilities were wiped out in a rolling tide of flash and thunder. The whine of Zach's climbing jet was barely noticeable in the din that reechoed across the landscape.

"Cleared re-attack, three. Let's clean 'em up!"

Davies called "in" as Captain Czachorowski pulled his Warthog back up into the hazy blue. A moment later, hundreds of bomblets struck the burning camp like marbles spilling from a jar.

No one could have lived through that! Forrest watched as Zach's jet pulled off from another pass. Another sheet of fire and thunder spread across the poacher's camp. There was a huge orange fireball as the gas tank of one of the trucks erupted in something military professionals called a secondary explosion. A moment later there was another. To an air-to-mud attack pilot, multiple secondaries were Christmas morning.

"Hogger, Overkill. Let's move the remaining ordnance back to the southern target. The north target has been neutralized." *More like totally-absofuckinglutely-obliterated!*

Forrest turned his attention once again to Ghuled's camp. The antiaircraft fire was having a rebirth of sorts as survivors of the first brief attack found their way back to their guns. Tracers were zipping back into the sky. Black puffs of diesel smoke erupted from the rear of one of the tanks as its engine roared to life. The tank lurched ahead then turned hard, rolling over the wreckage of the two Toyotas before plowing through a burning hut in an attempt to escape.

"Hogger, Overkill. We've got a mover!...Tank! Heading west toward my position. Take it out, ASAP!"

Blaylock called for a gun pass from the flight. He directed one and two to hit the mover and three and four to attack the stationary tank.

The man looking up from the command hatch at the top of the tank saw the lead fighter rolling in for its next attack. He dropped down inside the turret and closed the hatch behind him. Forrest snorted a laugh and shook his head. *Nice try, butt-crack. But it won't do you any good.*

Blaylock was well into his dive. He moved the pipper over the fleeing tank and then pulled the nose up slightly to give the target some lead. Blaylock pulled the trigger and felt the rumble of the gun firing just below his feet. He watched the wake of the supersonic projectiles cut through the air leaving a faintly visible shock wave trail. Spectacular flashes of white flame and molten steel, the pilots called "sparkles," marked the spot where several of the bullets, traveling at nearly 3,200 feet per second, struck the upper surfaces of the tank. In microseconds, the depleted uranium penetrators punched through three inches of low-carbon, steel armor like a fork through the side of a ripe melon. Tremendous forces of friction and compression super-heated the penetrators to 2,000 degrees as they bore through the turret's thinnest point. Emerging from the interior surface, the penetrators started to burn spontaneously when they came in contact with the relatively oxygen-rich atmosphere inside the crew compartment. Weapons engineers referred to this phenomenon as the pyrophoric effect. Victims would see it as hell's fire. Either way, the results were catastrophic to machinery and crew. The mortally wounded juggernaut came to a halt as black smoke poured out of the main gun's muzzle as well as holes created in the barrage.

Mesmerized by the spectacle of the burning tank, Forrest scarcely noticed new movement in the camp. Pieces of brush and dried vegetation fell away from the top of another armored vehicle as it rammed through the village, driving pell-mell toward the Kenyan border. If it made it that far, Forrest realized, he could not direct the fighters to follow.

Forrest recognized the vehicle as an old armored personnel carrier. Several men ran to climb inside as it picked up speed. A few made it through the rear troop hatch before it was slammed shut. Forrest dropped two of the remaining runners with his rifle, turning the others back toward the camp.

"Hogger, I need you to get some thirty mike-mike on that APC before it makes it into Kenya."

"Unable! Lead's not in position!"

The vehicle veered four hundred meters south of Forrest's position on a dead run to the west. Only a mile of desert remained between it and the border. Forrest tensed at the thought of some of the bushwhackers making it to safety. It was just then that he noticed the loud whine of a diving jet. The plane was arcing in a wide turn behind him to attack from the north. He looked around to see an A-10 swooping down low enough to kick up a trail of swirling dust. Another one followed half a mile behind the first.

"Three's in hot. Permission to fire!"

Forrest fumbled with the radio in the excitement. The jet's attack would take it right over his head. *Jesus Tecumseh Sherman!* Forrest gritted his teeth, covered his ears, and put his face in the dirt. "Take 'em, three!"

Snot's gun roared right over his head, deafening him for a moment. His ears rang from the terrific noise. Of the seventy rounds fired in the one-second burst, twenty-two tore into the target. The rest went a little long or short, plowing up the surrounding dirt. The bullets sliced through the aluminum and steel skin of the APC as if penetrating the sides of a cheap Styrofoam cooler. Its occupants were subjected to what amounted to a cruel science experiment where biology and physiology were no match for the indifferent forces of physics. The protection that the APC's thin armor provided them was completely psychological. Designed to protect squads of infantry from small arms, the M-113 was easy meat for the world's most efficient tank-killing machines. For all the good it did them against the awesome power of the A-10's cannon, they might as well have been inside an Osterizer. As the rounds passed through the sides and top of the vehicle, they shattered the metal walls in a phenomena called spalling. Like BBs passing through thick glass, the projectiles produced hundreds of metal fragments out of the vehicle's armor skin, multiplying their effects. Splintering shards of hot steel flailed around the APC's interior rendering its occupants the consistency of cat food before converting the vehicle's interior into a crematory when the armor piercing incendiary (API) rounds tore through the gas tanks. Those inside had learned, too late, that the last place you wanted to hide in the presence of a threatening A-10 was inside an APC.

"Beautiful, three!" Forrest shouted into his microphone. "Good shooting!"

Like the tank, the APC had been reduced to a burning hulk. Czachorowski, feeling a little disappointment, realized it would not be necessary for him to fire. He pulled up abruptly, banking to the left to join his leader as a renewed wave of antiaircraft fire erupted from the camp.

Forrest went back to business. "We've still got some triple-A firing from the camp. Let me know if you can see the remaining tank."

"Hogger has a tally."

"Okay. You'll be cleared in hot. Same restrictions. Flight lead control."

"Hogger copies."

As Forrest watched the "Hogs" circle to set up for their next attack, he recalled the words of an Iraqi officer captured during the Gulf War: Of all of the allied military aircraft, the A-10 was the single most recognizable warplane and the one most feared by his men. Now Forrest understood why.

Blaylock issued new instructions to the flight members. Davies and Czachorowski fell in line behind Gray as the four jets circled the target like a flock of marauding vultures. Blaylock rolled in from the north, looking for the remaining tank. It was obscured by the smoke and dust. At the last minute, Blaylock caught a glimpse of the tank through the smoke and fired. His finger took up the slack in the trigger turning on the gun camera and stabilizing the pipper over the target. Just as he did, he noticed one of the technicals spin out in the dirt and make a run for it to the west. It was too late to shift to the new target so he squeezed off a burst on the tank and pulled up from the dive. Sparkles amidst the smoke told him that his bullets had bit into something hard.

"Two, you got that truck?" Blaylock barked.

"Roger that. Two's got him." Gray was already well into his dive. His fangs were out and he wanted this target as a personal trophy. He pressed down to four thousand feet and shallowed his dive. He was just about to pull the trigger when the FAC screamed out the words a fighter pilot dreads most: "Two! Break left! Missile, missile, missile!"

Forrest watched as the telltale smoke trail of a shoulder launched SAM extended out of the camp, growing in length behind a short, slender missile. Its flight path was erratic and jerky as it guided on a corkscrew trajectory, homing on the hot parts of Gray's jet. Gray yanked back hard on the stick, rolling the fighter into the missile as he dove for the ground. He was attempting to make the missile turn a corner it simply couldn't hack. He pressed the red button on the right throttle to pump out flares which would decoy the missile's infrared seeker. Nothing happened. Unbeknownst to him, the chaff and flare system had been damaged in his first attack. The fast moving, fence-post size weapon closed the distance in a flash and rammed the starboard vertical stabilizer of the twin-tailed attack jet. Forrest watched in shock as the warhead blasted pieces of aluminum skin and fiberglass off the tail. The rudder separated and tumbled through the air. An instant later, the hidden ZPU-2 AAA gun opened up on the stricken plane as it descended to within two thousand feet of the surface. Several rounds pounded the plane's lower fuselage under the nose. Were it not for the titanium "bathtub" armor which surrounded the cockpit and vital flight controls, Gray would likely have taken a fatal hit. Still more 14.5 mm rounds tore into the left wing. One struck the leading edge of the wing where it joined with the fuselage. It was one of the few places where the lines of both hydraulic systems ran within a centimeter of each other. The lucky round severed both—the proverbial "Golden BB." For Gray's Warthog, it was like having both Achilles tendons cut simultaneously. Several warning lights came on inside the cockpit as the twenty-ton beast bled vital hydraulic fluid from its wound. Too low to recover with the manual reversion back-up system, Gray realized he had no time to nurse the doomed machine. He slammed his shoulders and helmet against the back-rest and reached for the two yellow handles next to his thighs. A sharp pull of the ejection handles blew the canopy and a second later, the Aces II ejection seat and pilot were propelled upward by a canon shell followed by a powerful rocket motor. Before Gray realized it, his parachute caught the air, jerking him out of the seat, leaving him dazed and dangling at the end of dozens of nylon shroud lines.

Forrest watched in silence as the pilot drifted toward the ground, some two hundred meters to the south. He flinched as the sound of an automatic rifle cracked behind him. A quick glance over his shoulder startled him. Less than a hundred meters away, Red Hat was doing his best to kill the helpless pilot.

These bastards love to shoot at Americans! Forrest pivoted in his position slowly and brought his rifle up to his shoulder. He centered the crosshairs over the boy's chest.

The boy inserted a new magazine and cycled the bolt.

"Don't do it, kid!" he hissed under his breath. "Put the gun down and run away. Run away!"

Red Hat brought his assault rifle to his shoulder.

Forrest squeezed the trigger and the boy was gone.

The A-10 pilot hit the ground and tumbled in the dust. His parachute canopy collapsed on top of him as two men from the camp ran toward him firing their rifles.

Gray twisted out of his parachute harness, jumped up and took off, running—away from his two pursuers—directly toward Forrest. Bullets whizzed over both of their heads as the pilot ran within five feet of the invisible sniper.

"Get down, goddammit!" Forrest barked.

It startled the already shaken pilot. He dropped to his knees at the sound of an American voice. Without thinking, Gray stuck his hands straight up in the air, surrendering to the talking bush. Two more rifle rounds zipped over their heads.

"On your face! Eat dirt!"

Glad to have made it that far and asking no questions, the pilot complied immediately, flopping down on his chest, his hands behind his head. Forrest took aim at the closest pursuer, dropping him easily. Wishing to escape the fate of the first, the second man dove to the ground. He blindly fired several rounds toward Forrest and the pilot hoping to get a lucky hit. Forrest lay quietly and told the pilot to do the same as he watched the A-10s dump the last of their lethal load on the last AAA gun. After what seemed like an eternity, the clansman rose up tentatively then moved forward in a crouch. Forrest reached for a small trigger switch whose electrical chord trailed off into the brush. The Somali came ahead gaining confidence by the meter. His eyes were wild with revenge and fear. He wanted blood—American blood. Forrest let the man approach to within twenty meters before throwing the switch. With the flick of his thumb, there was a thunderous concussion and the clansman disappeared in a plume of dust.

"What the hell was *that*?" Gray yelled, rolling over onto his back to see what happened.

"One of my 'Not Welcome' mats."

"Damn, man! What other cute shit do you have to play with?"

Forrest pulled his camouflaged cheeks into a wry grin.

"You must be the FAC," said Gray, crab-walking to the man who had just saved his life.

"Overkill," Forrest offered, extending his right hand, "Nice of you to drop in."

Gray grabbed the offered hand, shaking it with grateful vigor. "The name's Hoser. Looks like I owe you a beer."

"I'd kill for a good cold Michelob right about now."

Grays eyes went wide. "Shit, man. Looks like you already did!"

Forrest handed Gray a canteen then turned his attention to the battle.

Orbiting directly overhead, Blaylock had seen his wingman's chute and observed the smoke from the Claymore. "Overkill. Do you have our guy?"

"Roger that. But you can have him back. I don't want him."

At Gray's insistence, Forrest handed him the radio, "Hey pal, my ass's still only got one crack in it."

Blaylock chuckled to himself. He was relieved to hear his wingman was in one piece. "Overkill, Hogger's bingo. RTB. We're outta here to the east."

"Copy that. Standby for BDA and some pickup coordinates for your buddy."

After a hurried look at his map, Forrest read off the latitude and longitude of a point where the search and rescue helicopter could expect to extract their wingless wingman. He also listed the estimated number of vehicles and people destroyed in the attack. "Congratulations, gentlemen." Forrest added, dryly. "You guys just became the largest distributors of tank, vehicle, and gun parts in the country."

Forrest turned his eyes to the stranded pilot. "Whereas we just drastically lowered the population and the property values in this quaint little resort, I move we E 'n E outta here, post-haste."

Gray looked around at the roiling flames and billowing smoke. Ammunition of various calibers cooked off sporadically. Unaimed projectiles whizzed through the air like mad hornets. "I'll second that shit."

Forrest broke down his rifle, shouldered his backpack and started out with Gray following just behind. His course initially went east.

"I thought you said we were going south."

"We will in a minute. First, I wanna check that last shooter—see if he was carrying anything we can use."

Two minutes later, they located the Somali's body. He lay face down in a burgundy stain, his back blown out by the Claymore. Forrest picked up his weapon which he found was out of ammo. Then he noticed a gold ID bracelet on the man's right wrist. His heart raced when he read the inscription:

TO DAVID NCHOKO
COLLEGE GRADUATE - THE FIRST IN HIS PROUD FAMILY. KNOWLEDGE SETS YOU FREE. FREEDOM BRINGS YOU KNOWLEDGE. CONGRATULATIONS
- MAXWELL GRANT

Gray saw the look on Forrest's face. You know this guy, or something?"

"Or something," Forrest muttered, cryptically as he undid the clasp and shoved the bracelet in his pants pocket. He led the way as they reversed course to the west for several hundred feet where they came across the body of the young boy—more like pieces of a body—only the spinal chord connected the upper half to the pelvis and legs. Gray watched as Forrest picked up the red Bulldog hat, dusted it off and shoved it inside his rucksack. Both men stood for a moment surveying the crumpled body. The boy's thong sandals lay several inches away from his feet. He had literally been blown out of them by the mighty, fifty-caliber rifle.

"This one's just a youngster," Gray observed shaking his head. He gave Forrest an accusatory look. "You're cold, man. Did you have to waste a *kid*?"

Forrest felt an instant flush of anger that told in his voice, "Would it make any difference if I told you this kid was shooting at you while you were hanging in your chute?"

Gray's eyes went to the AK-47 lying in the dirt. A sheepish grimace developed. "Sorry man, you should've told me that before.... You know," he said, his voice acquiring a suddenly cheerier tone, "it's a good thing you wasted that little fucker!"

Forrest shook his head as he picked up the boy's AK-47 and handed it to Gray. "Here. Souvenir," he said disgustedly. He pointed at the fire selector lever on the side of the receiver. "Up is safe. Down is semi-auto. And the middle position is rock and roll."

As Forrest led off to the south he turned to speak a warning over his shoulder: "By the way, keep a sharp eye out. There's more than one kid with an AK in this neighborhood. And the little ones will kill'ya just as dead as the big ones."

CHAPTER-SIXTEEN

AFTERMATH *a: consequence, result*
b: the period following a usually ruinous event

FORREST LOOKED AT HIS WATCH. "They should be here soon. As soon as we see them coming, you move over to that clear spot and pop some smoke. Got one of your flares ready?"

"I'm set to pop." Gray removed a red-and-white signal flare from a bottom survival vest pocket and flipped off the orange plastic cap, then sat down on a rock.

"Better watch where you park your butt," Forrest cautioned, lowering his pack and drag-bag to the ground. "Puff'll take a bite out of it if you're not careful."

"Puff?" Gray asked between gulps of water. Tilting his head back, he drained the last of his survival kit's water cans.

"Last name's adder—as in puff adder. He's a big fat guy, about four feet long. Likes to sleep in the shade during the day. Packs enough hemotoxin to turn your ass into applesauce."

"How come they call 'em 'adders?' Seems like they specialize in *subtraction*," Hoser quipped as he scanned the ground intensely, before relaxing. It suddenly occurred to him that he would never see this man again. "Just who the hell are you, anyway? Where'd you learn to shoot like that?"

Forrest heard him but changed the subject. "You guys took out some real dirt-bags today."

"Yeah, but I lost my jet in the process."

"At least you're still breathing. And if the politically correct Air Force hasn't changed all that much since I flew fighters, in about two hours your buddies will have you and the life support techs totally shit-faced."

Captain Gray managed a laugh. "It hasn't changed *that* much."

"Good. Glad to hear it." Forrest smiled and focused his glasses on the eastern horizon. Two small dots appeared first followed 20 seconds later by another one, much lower to the ground. It wasn't long before he recognized the first two: A-10s. "What squadron are you guys in, anyway?

"104th Fighter Squadron, Maryland Air Guard."

"Mmm. National Guard guys get around these days. Long way from home."

"That we do and that we are."

The attack jets turned into each other and weaved across the path of a trailing aircraft, a large helicopter. Its blades slapped the air, the rhythmic whop-whop growing louder as it approached. The fighters, flying at twice the speed of the chopper, had to weave almost continuously to stay with it.

"Sounds like your ride's here," Forrest announced, turning on his radio.

Gray heard it too and stood up, sensing that he would not get an answer to his questions.

Forrest's radio crackled. "Overkill, Overkill. Sandy one-one. We're three minutes out."

"Roger that. Sandy. In sight. Heading's good. We're on your nose—about three miles. LZ's cold."

"Roger." The HH-60 pilot then asked Gray for his authenticator number followed by a personal question he'd written on his ISOPREP

SAR card. Only Gray would have the correct answer. The chopper crew had to be certain they were picking up the right man and not being sucked into an ambush by an enemy pretender.

Forrest motioned to Gray as the lead A-10 crossed behind the helicopter and then zoomed ahead of it, heading right at them. "Okay, Hoser, grab your shit and get down there. They'll be looking for that smoke."

Gray picked up his gear and extended his hand. "Thanks for the little nature walk and," he paused, "thanks for saving my ass back there, man. Thanks for everything."

"You saved my ass, too. We're even." Forrest gripped his hand firmly and smiled then nodded his head in the direction he wanted the fighter pilot to take.

Hoser descended the hill and entered the clearing. Seconds later, a stream of bright red smoke poured out of his signal flare and trailed off into the breeze. A shrill whine split the air as the Warthogs zoomed overhead and started a wide circle, ready to suppress anything that might threaten the survivor or the rescue helicopter.

"Sandy's tally-ho the smoke."

The HH-60 kicked up a cloud of dust in the clearing as the pilot maneuvered to a hover. Gently touching the ground, the wheels bobbled slightly as the machine settled on its struts. Major Eric Blaylock, grinning like he'd had a few already, leaned out of the side door waving one of the cold beers he had brought for his missing wingman.

Blinking his eyes in the blowing dust, Gray sprinted to the door, stopped and turned. Dust obscured his view as he turned to wave to a character whose name he had never learned. Too late. "Overkill" was gone.

"Atlanta won't mind spending ten thousand bucks an hour for *this* stuff." Brooks McKewen verbalized what Buddy Bates was thinking as the cameraman got everything on tape. "I wonder how Riley knew this was going down in advance."

"That's why they pay him the big bucks." Tony Assaf answered as he put the JetRanger in a shallow turn over the site, avoiding the numerous columns of smoke. Gray smoke from brush fires and smoldering huts mixed with the black smoke from burning tires, rubber, and fuel. Although he had seen devastation before, he had never witnessed anything quite like this.

"This just in," the attractive CNN news anchor with auburn hair and large, almond shaped brown eyes announced. "American, jet fighters have attacked and destroyed two guerilla camps in western Somalia. The camps were reported to be the stronghold of General Mohammed Ghuled, the renegade warlord who, according to government sources, was responsible for the ambush of U.N. peace-keeping forces in Mogadishu, last November. Seven American soldiers were killed in that attack.

"We warn you. The following video contains scenes which may be too graphic for sensitive viewers. Viewer discretion is advised. For more on the story we go now to our Pentagon correspondent, Willard Haines. Bill..."

If pictures are worth a thousand words, Henderson thought as he and the Secretary of Defense watched the broadcast in the SECDEF's office, then video tape is worth a million. The news video was everything they had hoped for. Better still was the follow-up file footage of the U.N. ambush—lest people forget. There was, however, one sour note:

"CNN has independent confirmation that one of the U.S. Air Force fighters participating in the raid was shot down by the camp's defenders. The pilot's condition is unknown. However, the CNN camera crew, who was the first to arrive at the scene, found an ejection seat and parachute." The video showed twin vertical stabilizers standing askew atop the blackened metal wreckage. Although slightly scorched, the letters "MD," painted in black, stood out against the overcast-gray paint. Rubber and plastic parts along with what remained of the fighter's fuel still burned, staining the air with thick black smoke.

The scene switched back to the Headline News desk in Atlanta. "In other news..."

CLICK.

"We got him out." The Secretary said offhandedly as he laid the remote control down on the thick glass which covered his desk. Henderson followed as the SECDEF, hands clasped behind his back, walked to the windows nearest the grandfather clock which stood in a corner of the spacious office.

Henderson, gazing out the windows, noticed how the steady rain trickled down a sheet of Mylar stretched over the windows to thwart laser eavesdropping.

"He's fine," Secretary Hudson continued. "Probably drinking too much beer with his squadron buddies, as we speak."

Henderson regarded him with an odd expression as this information was both pleasant and a surprise.

"Didn't you know?" the Secretary grinned, pleased to have aced-out the intelligence expert on a small but significant bit of news.

Henderson broke into a sheepish grin and shrugged. "Hell, Mr. Secretary, even the CIA can't know everything."

Forrest saw her coming through the spinning propeller's transparent disc. "Jesus Tecumseh Sherman," he moaned out loud, half hoping she would hear. "Don't they have leash laws in this country?"

He pulled the mixture control to the idle/cutoff position then switched the magnetos and master switches off. The blade spun to a stop not a second too soon. Anne Sargent was on him before he could completely extract himself from the cockpit.

"You wouldn't happen to know anything about *this* would you?" she asked his back, slapping his shoulder with a folded newspaper. It sounded more like an accusation than a question.

Forrest turned his head just enough to see her out of the corner of his eye, his jaw tight. His peripheral vision caught a glimpse of Malcom McCullen coming around the front of the plane—just in time. "Excuse me," Forrest ordered in a voice that really meant: get the hell out of the way.

Sargent jumped back as Forrest bodily moved her aside.

"Hey, Doc. How ya feeling?"

"Better, thanks. Where've ya been all this time?" The Scotsman smiled weakly, digging his hands into his pockets.

"Around."

"Around. Ha!...Somalia, most likely," Anne snapped out of the side of her mouth. "You still haven't answered my question." For the second time, she slapped the newspaper against him—this time against his chest.

Forrest snatched it out of her hands, too annoyed to tolerate a third assault.

"The Americans bombed two camps just across the border from Wajir. The same two camps you were so interested in. Rather coincidental, don't you think?"

McCullen looked at her, dumbfounded—completely out of the loop.

Forrest skimmed through the front-page story. To her disappointment he displayed no reaction.

"Well?"

"Well what?"

"What do you have to say about it?" Her haughtiness grated on Forrest's nerves.

Forrest looked past Sargent into McCullen's eyes. His reply, though directed at the lady inspector, was aimed at McCullen. "Oh, I don't know," he deadpanned. "Off hand, I'd say some damn fine fighter pilots exacted a little revenge for seven Americans and six white rhinos."

Marie Henderson, in the middle of dinner preparations, picked up the phone on the third ring. "Hello."

"Hello. Mrs. Henderson?" the vaguely familiar woman's voice asked.

"Yes." Sensing something unusual, Marie silently shushed her daughters who were loudly trading barbs as they helped their mother in the kitchen.

"This is Abby Wilcox calling," the woman said, politely. "May I speak to Mr. Henderson, please?"

Marie raised her eyebrows and shrugged in response to her daughters' inquisitive looks. "Okay. Hold on, please. I'll get him."

"Thank you."

After a moment, Steve Henderson came on the line while his wife returned to dinner preparations.

"Henderson."

"Hello, Mr. Henderson. Abby Wilcox."

"Oh, uh...hello, Mrs. Wilcox," he stammered. "How are you?" Henderson answered the quizzical stares of his wife and daughters with a knowing smile.

"Well, thank you." The first lady's voice warmed slightly now that she was talking to a familiar person. "I believe congratulations are in order."

"Well, ma'am. I appreciate the sentiment."

There was an awkward silence.

"Anyway, sorry to interrupt your dinner, but I just wanted to say I appreciate your efforts. And my best to your family."

"It was very kind of you to call, Mrs. Wilcox."

As they said their good-byes, Marie looked up from making salad and wiped her hands on a dishtowel. "Who was that?" she asked, pretending only moderate interest.

Henderson went to the refrigerator for a cold beer. "Oh, uh that was Mrs. Wilcox," he answered as casually as he could.

"Do I know her?"

Henderson laughed out loud. "Wilcox—Abby Wilcox. You know, as in the First Lady of the United States."

The daughters looked at each other then at their father. "Yeah, right Dad."

"How do you *stand* that man, Malcolm?" Anne Sargent groused as she and Dr. McCullen strolled through the camp toward the holding pen, Hoover trotting along just behind.

McCullen turned up a corner of his mouth. "He's not so bad

when you get to know him, my dear. In fact, I rather like havin' him around." His eyes twinkled as he talked.

Sargent frowned and kicked at the dirt. "Well, that makes one of us, I'm afraid." She stopped abruptly with a thought, clamping her hands on her hips. "Did you know that he's an atheist—a *heathen*?"

Hoover seized the opportunity, his probing trunk frisking her pockets for treats.

McCullen pursed his lips thoughtfully, then grinned at the baby elephant. "Best be careful, laddy. She's feelin' a might feisty t'day. She'll likely tie your little hose in a knot." He patted the elephant's head and gave him a peanut which promptly disappeared into his drooling mouth.

Hoover rocked his head from side to side, probing anew, this time through McCullen's pockets.

Anne's frown melted into a smile and she stroked Hoover's wiry hair. "That's the problem around here. Too many men—too much bloody testosterone. You're all ganging up against me, lately."

One of Joseph's brothers met them at the entrance to Hoover's pen with a fresh bottle and a blanket. With a little coaxing and teasing, they all went inside.

"Mind you now, religion is an abstract concept, my dear. You can't always judge what's in a man's heart by what's on the tip of his tongue. All people see the world differently. Who's to say which among us has all the right answers?" McCullen continued. "He's a good man in his own way. John gets things done around here. Everybody likes him. Hoover likes him." McCullen looked over his glasses at her. "You're the only one who seems'ta be havin' a bit of a cramp."

Sargent jammed her hands into the pockets of her uniform shorts and leaned against the log wall. "He's the most irritating man I've ever met. He's rude, vulgar, insensitive, callous, stupid..."

"...compassionate, unselfish, intelligent, brave..." McCullen countered. "He insisted that I treat a wounded elephant out in the bush. Then he stayed out there with her for days, makin' sure she healed up, alright. He found little Hoover out there in the bush and..."

"...drove us all to distraction, getting him back here," Anne interjected.

McCullen smiled. "That he did. But saving this little creature was not the act of a callous man...was it, now?"

Sargent's eyes met the Scotsman's and dropped. She knew he was right, but wasn't quite ready to admit it. Therefore, she exercised her prerogative as a woman—she changed the subject. "What do you know about him?"

McCullen looked at her and shrugged. "Not a lot, come'ta think of it."

"I thought you just said he was okay, 'once you get to know him.'"

McCullen rolled his eyes and gave her another disarming smile. "There's lots'a different ways'ta 'know' someone, my dear."

"You know perfectly well what I mean, Malcolm." Her hands found her hips, again. "How did he end up in your camp?"

"I got a letter one day...from Colonel Grant. It said that one John Forrest would be arriving on a date certain and asked that I extend him whatever assistance he required. The letter explained he was a graduate student working on his Master's. And when the Colonel asks a favor...well, you don't say no to the man who provides most of your funding."

Sargent looked at him. "He's no researcher. That I can tell you."

"Give him time. I'm sure we can remedy that problem. All he needs is a little guidance."

"Please, Malcolm. That's a bit like saying that all Adolf Hitler needed was a little guidance." She glanced at him then turned her head back to the baby. "Why would Colonel Grant spend all that money—two airplanes, a new Land Rover, computers, and Lord knows what else—on a man with so little formal training?" She looked back at the elephant. "*Hoover* could do a better thesis."

McCullen smiled. "Maybe. But then Hoover has inside information."

Sargent managed a smile. "What about his background?"

"He used to be an airline captain. Lost his job, I think he said. The airline went bankrupt or something. He was a military pilot before that."

"What about family? Is he married—children?" She thought a moment. "God, I hope not. Nobody deserves that."

"He mentioned a wife at one time, I think—in the past tense. He said something about a divorce, now that'ya mention it. I don't remember, now. We were havin' a few whiskeys at the time. And... well..." He gave Anne a sheepish smile, she responding with a look of disapproval.

"He's a wee bit quiet when it comes to personal matters. He has a picture of his son in his hut. But, he never talks about him. I get the feelin' they might have problems between them. Lots'o fathers have conflicts with their sons 'till they grow up a bit. Anyway, it's none'a my business. I probably shouldn't have said this much." McCullen folded his arms across his chest. He watched Joseph lie down next to Hoover who was about to take a nap. Baby elephants, he knew, required almost constant tactile contact and reassurance, their emotional health being directly linked with their physical health. With a nod of his head, McCullen led Anne out of the holding pen and down the path toward their huts.

"Does he ever talk about women? Wife? Girlfriend? What he likes—what he doesn't like."

McCullen sighed, sensing he had somehow gotten onto an uncomfortable subject. It was then, for the first time, he realized that Anne might really be a lonely woman—husband or no. That makes two lonely people, he thought. "Oh, now you're really gettin' into..." McCullen interrupted himself. "He's comin' to the ball next week. Why don't you ask him yourself?"

Presidential Findings are used to justify and authorize various government operations in a timely manner without having to deal with Congress. Sometimes presidents find themselves in a position where they have to act first and seek congressional approval later; business-as-usual on Capital Hill.

Henderson read the document over three more times to ensure it covered his butt from every conceivable angle—if such a thing were possible. He had already asked Roselle to make two copies; one for his office safe and one for his personal safety-deposit box in a Leesburg bank. His eyes went down the pages finally coming to a stop at the bold signature—the most important autograph he'd ever received. "That oughtta do it," he breathed just as his secretary poked her head through his door, her face wearing a big meaningful grin.

"Steve. Roy Barber's here," she said in taunting, sing-songy voice.

Henderson smiled—his first confident smile in weeks. "Send him in."

"Oh shit! I almost forgot. Thanks for the souvenirs," Henderson exclaimed into his office STU phone, suddenly remembering the most recent addition to his trophy case. A DHL shipment had come from Nairobi just 3 days after the A-10 interdiction mission. He rotated his desk chair to face the full-sized china cabinet, which lined the wall opposite his large mahogany desk. It contained mementos collected over a long career in military and government intelligence operations. The cabinet's florescent light gave the red Georgia Bulldog cap a purplish hue. "Midas was particularly impressed with his trinket. He also added his thanks. I thought the man was gonna bust out crying, or something. He must've really liked that kid. Thanks again from both of us."

"All in a days work, pal," Forrest said in a soft delivery reserved for close friends. "And no," he added in a sympathetic tone, "nothing new about Amy. Sorry, man."

Malcolm McCullen had to practically threaten him to get him to go. But go he did, griping all the way. Forrest made it clear he was only going because the Doc couldn't drive himself and Joseph was too busy taking care of the growing collection of orphans.

Each year, McCullen had explained, the Kenya Wildlife Service sponsored a ball, inviting the country's entire scientific community.

Every researcher, conservationist, and naturalist was encouraged to attend in order to foster greater awareness and cooperation, and promote the sharing of information among scientists and government officials. An evening of dining, dancing, and hob-knobing would be followed by a week of meetings and seminars designed to address East Africa's most critical wildlife concerns. Oh, just great, Forrest had thought with a sigh of disgust, imagining what the ball would be like: a funeral with hors d'oeuvres and live music. He visualized a bunch of pasty-faced, bearded, eco-nerds overly fond of speaking twenty-dollar words from a long-dead language.

A white taxi with a horizontal yellow stripe deposited him in front of the Norfolk Hotel a full hour after the appointed time. After consulting a bellman for directions, Forrest made his way down carpeted corridors through which he was sure Ernest Hemingway had once passed. The hotel was old, one of Nairobi's oldest, his CIA friend had told him. Henderson had also mentioned that the Norfolk's bar had once, during the Cold War era, been well known among the world's intelligence operatives as a great place to pass information. Admiring the building's charm, Forrest rounded a corner, searching for the ballroom entrance. Terminal homing was aided, in part, by the muffled music of a small band playing tunes even Dick Clark wouldn't recognize.

There were probably two hundred people in attendance, he assessed as he scanned the room looking for a familiar face in a room full of unfamiliar faces. Spotting an inviting out-of-the-way corner in which to get lost, Forrest moved to his right, working his way around clusters of people alternately engaged in serious intellectual conversation or jocular banter. He started to take a vacant seat at one of the many round tables draped with white linen tablecloths when Doc McCullen grabbed his arm from behind.

"Ah, there'ya are, laddy. Where've ya been?"

Busted. Shit! "I...uh...took my time getting here, Doc. Didn't think there was any rush."

"Aye, but you're wrong, Johnny me lad." McCullen's eyes went wide and serious for a second then yielded to a cheery smile. "We've got lots'a people to meet and you've already wasted a whole bleedin' hour."

Maybe, but you sure as hell haven't. McCullen's red dimples were already two shades brighter than they'd been that afternoon. Forrest rolled his eyes and smiled, realizing full well he was on the Scotsman's turf and any protests would be futile.

"How 'bout a drink, lad. Loosen'ya up a wee bit," McCullen offered, nodding his head toward the bar positioned at the end of the room.

"Okay, Doc. You win." Forrest laughed. "Lead on."

Forrest and McCullen stood facing the bar, patiently waiting to capture a bartender's attention. McCullen gulped down the remainder of his drink making maximum room for a fresh one.

"Would the Venerated Order of Chauvinist Pigs allow you two gentlemen to accept a drink from a lady?" came a voice from behind.

Forrest turned to behold the face of a woman—a beautiful woman—one he didn't recognize, though there was something vaguely familiar about her. She looked like a celebrity at a Hollywood party—absolutely stunning.

A pair of sparkling green eyes stared back at him, enjoying his look of blank astonishment.

"Ah, Anne," McCullen exclaimed, squeezing her bare arm with ice-cold fingers. "You've really outdone yourself t'night, lass." He stepped back to take her all in. His glazed gray eyes twinkled through his eyeglasses' thick lenses. "You look absolutely ravishin'." His mischievous smile accentuated his alcohol-reddened dimples.

"Anne?" Forrest gasped in a hoarse whisper. He shot a look at McCullen who beamed confirmation, then looked back at Anne, staring in disbelief. Impulsively, he extended his hand to greet her, subconsciously wanting to touch her just to make sure his eyes weren't deceiving him.

Her smile waned somewhat as she let him take her hand. It was soft and moist with a touch of lotion, the palm cool to the touch. The intoxicating scent of her perfume filled the space between them.

Part of her was annoyed that he hadn't recognized her or somehow thought her incapable of beauty. Another part was afraid that he might not approve or worse, not notice or react at all.

Her eyes followed his as they moved over her body starting at her shoulder-length light brown hair recklessly teased and moussed to give it a wind-blown look of abandon.

Forrest felt a tingle as his face flushed warm. He never knew she had such tresses; they had always been tucked into her uniform baseball cap. She stared back for a moment as his eyes met hers—strangely exotic eyes he had never seen before.

Nervously, she looked away as his eyes continued to the plunging neckline of her black silk evening dress. There they lingered for a long moment at seductively sculptured cleavage which channeled into the shimmering fabric.

He had never really noticed her ample breasts before. They had always been hidden under the pockets of ill-fitting uniform shirts like a well-kept family secret. Oozing past her tiny waist, the slinky fabric curved over slender hips before terminating at ankles covered in sheer, black nylons. Long, delicate legs tapered into black satin pumps complete with tastefully seductive spike heels.

Gravity held Forrest's gaze to the floor while more mysterious forces halted his breathing.

"He acts like he hasn't seen a woman for months," Anne sighed, half-smiling, half-frowning. Giving McCullen a sideways glance, she was uncertain how to judge Forrest's reaction.

Forrest's pleading eyes tore themselves away from Anne for a moment, searching McCullen's face for reassurance. "Well, I haven't..." Then realizing how that sounded—however truthful—his eyes darted back and forth between the two.

McCullen laughed.

Anne frowned.

Forrest grimaced. "Hell. You know what I mean."

The bartender came to the rescue with a timely interruption. "May I get you something?"

Forrest seized the opportunity to recover, giving Anne a sheepish smile.

Anne, inwardly pleased to have one-upped the difficult American, addressed the barman directly: "A scotch, please, a chardonnay and..." looking at Forrest, "...hemlock for this one."

"Canadian Club," Forrest translated over his shoulder, unable to take his eyes off Anne. "Make it a double."

The bartender served them promptly followed by a toast delivered by Forrest. He raised his glass. "To...uh...what's the Latin for foot-in-mouth disease?"

"That would be 'John,'" she answered coolly, touching her glass to theirs. Clearly, she was enjoying the results of her bold fashion experiment and having John Forrest off balance for a change.

"Touche." Forrest gulped his drink with a painful frown while the others sipped and shared a mirthful look.

McCullen followed up quickly with a corollary. "To beauty and the beasts."

Forrest smiled while Anne blushed. "Here, here," he echoed.

Clink.

"I'm glad you two came," Anne said, addressing both men but clearly directing her remark to Forrest. She lowered her eyes timorously then looked up. "So, what do you think?" she asked, striking a model's pose, half afraid of the answer.

Forrest looked at her, his smile all but vanishing. "I think if you weren't a government official they'd have to arrest you for disturbing the peace."

Anne cocked her head and narrowed one eye. "Was that a compliment?"

Forrest simply smiled.

"Indeed, lass. You look lovely." McCullen beamed. Suddenly, his eyes shifted, his smile partially falling away. "Uh oh."

"Good evening Doctor McCullen. You're looking rather well this evening," a thin, medium height man commented, walking up to the group.

Forrest studied the new arrival who, for some indefinable reason, seemed threatening. His smile was more a sneer; his platitudes more like veiled taunts. His wire-brush shock of pure white hair contrasted strongly with a dark tan and the vacant blue eyes of a vulture. Forrest looked to see Anne's smile dissolve completely. Her discomfort was palpable. Forrest felt a surge as his defenses went on yellow alert.

"Allen," Anne began, delicately. "I'd like you to meet John Forrest. He's the field researcher who's been working out of Malcolm's camp these past months."

"Indeed?" Windridge extended his hand.

Forrest saw the man's eyes darken. He clasped the vulture's hand very firmly, deliberately just below the threshold of pain.

"John," Anne continued, "This is my husband, Allen Windridge, Director of the Kenya Wildlife Service."

Forrest felt Windridge's grip tighten as if accepting a challenge—which was, after a fashion, how he intended it.

"So, this is the cowboy you're always complaining about. The 'ill-mannered American,'" Windridge sneered, slightly slurring his words.

Until that instant, Forrest hadn't realized that the man was drunk. "Me?" he laughed for Anne's benefit. "Oh, what's a mother to do?" He shrugged and took a gulp of his drink, all the while eyeing Windridge over the top of his glass.

Anne looked at Forrest apologetically.

Windridge smirked, obviously enjoying his wife's discomfort. "Aren't you going to buy me a drink, my dear?"

"No. I thought you were going to...Remember what you..."

"...promised?" Windridge huffed. "Well, if you can dress like a tart and buy *other* men drinks, I think you can buy one for your beloved husband. Don't you?" He paused for a moment polling the faces for reactions.

McCullen looked to see the hurt look on Anne's face.

Forrest felt the rubber band in his gut make another knot.

"Well then, I'll buy myself one." Windridge pushed past his wife to the bar, almost knocking her down, then slapped his hand on its polished surface. "Bartender! Another Scotch for me, please."

Forrest felt himself reaching deep for patience.

Windridge turned unsteadily, smiling as only an arrogant drunk could. "Oh forgive me. Talk about ill-mannered." He spun back to the bar. "Another round for my wife and her friends, as well."

The bartender beat his last record for promptness, Forrest noted. *Probably to get rid of this asshole as quickly as possible.*

Windridge handed Forrest and McCullen their drinks, getting them reversed, then took a sip of his own while he waited for Anne's wine.

Forrest set his glass on the bar and shared a look with McCullen.

Forrest: *This fuckin' guy is definitely pushing his luck.*

McCullen: *Keep your tarts, laddy. He's baitin' you, he is.*

Windridge slapped a crumpled wad of shillings on the bar, then executed a wobbly turn with Anne's chardonnay. He took a step toward her then stopped, a defiant sneer spreading across his face. With his eyes locked onto his wife's, he demonstratively began pouring her drink on the floor between her feet, splattering her shoes.

"Allen!" she gasped, jumping back a step, her eyes welling up with tears. "What on Earth..?"

Forrest had seen enough. He clamped his hand over Windridge's wrist, folding his right arm behind his back into a hammer lock while simultaneously seizing the offender in a half-Nelson with his left. "I think your party's over, pal," he growled in his ear. Forrest forced Windridge forward by lifting his arm toward the base of his neck. The wine glass tumbled out of his fingers, shattering on the floor. "How 'bout we go for a walk."

Anne and McCullen moved aside as the astonished crowd parted, making room for Forrest and Anne's crimson-faced husband.

Windridge struggled until Forrest's tightening grip sent a knee-buckling wave of pain through his shoulder. He gasped in agony, doubling over at the waist.

"I asked you to dance, asshole," Forrest hissed. "So I'll lead if you don't mind."

The music stopped momentarily as Forrest disappeared into the corridor. Minutes later, Forrest ushered Windridge outside where he stuffed him into a waiting taxi. Forrest tightened the hammer lock momentarily before letting his escort go with a shove. When

Windridge made a clumsy move for the open door Forrest unleashed a swift punch to his jaw, shutting off his lights for the night, the Englishman passing out on the back seat. "Remember, now. For your safety, keep your arms and legs inside until the ride comes to a complete stop."

Forrest pulled Windridge's wallet from his inside jacket pocket and dropped it on the cab's front seat, smiled at the nonplussed driver, then dropped a generous fold of bills into the driver's lap. "Take him home. His address is in his wallet." He slammed the door and watched the leaf-green taxi disappear into the Nairobi traffic.

Forrest returned to the main ballroom to find McCullen alone at the bar.

"You didn't hurt him, did'ya, lad?"

Forrest straightened his jacket as he responded, noting the looks from some of the guests. "Nothing his health plan won't cover."

The bartender came immediately. "This one's on the house, sir," he offered with a wink and a smile. "What'll it be?"

"Beer," Forrest grunted. "American beer." He turned to face McCullen. "Where'd Anne go?"

"To the privy, I think." McCullen looked past Forrest and smiled. "Cynthia, my dear. So good to see you."

Forrest turned to see Cynthia Marsh approaching along with Diane Chernik. "Evening ladies."

"No one said anything about entertainment, tonight," Chernik chuckled while eyeing Forrest. "Everyone okay?"

"Just one wine glass killed-in-action...so far, anyway," Forrest responded with trademark understatement and a half smile. It was just then that Forrest noticed a rotund black man he recognized—the police commissioner—studying him from across the room.

Marsh turned to McCullen, her eyes darkening. "I'm afraid Amboseli has suffered a more serious loss. Hunters killed another one of my best bulls. M-10 this time."

McCullen grimaced and grasped her hands sympathetically. "I'm dreadfully sorry. Any idea who did it?"

"Word is Morgan Richards…again. He was seen in the area recently with a wealthy German client," Chernik explained.

"Mmm," Marsh added. "And Minister Mboto has been avoiding me all night. I think he's afraid I'll ambush *him.*" Marsh gave McCullen a wry smile. "He's probably right. Tanzania is still waffling on their border hunting policy and he knows I'm not happy about it."

"You'll get your chance to embarrass him this week in front of God and everybody. I'll make sure you get the floor for a time," McCullen promised.

"Oh there will be a blue stink raised about this one," Marsh said in her most determined voice. "Remember, I have media connections and *they* need tourist dollars."

Forrest, his blood up for a fight, locked onto the conversation. "Isn't that Richards the same butt-crack you told me about when we visited your camp?"

"Probably. He's the worst," Marsh answered.

"Have you ever visited the guy—explained the far-reaching damage he's causing?"

Marsh sighed. "He won't give us the time of day. It's useless."

McCullen interjected: "He's even shot out their tires on at least one occasion."

Forrest gave the Doc a surprised look. "You've got to be…" he began then hesitated, realizing the ladies might not appreciate his lexicon of military expressions. "So how does one get in touch with this infamous great white hunter?"

"Oh, he has a brochure and a Nairobi phone number." It was Chernik. "Why?"

"Maybe someone needs to have a serious talk with him."

"It won't do any good, I promise you. He's a first-class scofflaw and quite the bully," Marsh scoffed.

Forrest made a faint grin. "Maybe. But I can be pretty charming and persuasive, sometimes."

Marsh smiled warmly dismissing his comment.

Chernik, scanning the room, spotted another political target. "Whoops. Gotta go," she blurted, grabbing Marsh by the upper arm. "We've got ears to bend."

"Bye ladies," said McCullen. "Good luck to'ya, now." He watched them disappear into the throng.

"Doc, I'm gonna get a little fresh air," Forrest announced nodding toward a veranda which beckoned from beyond a pair of French doors. "Too much smoke in here."

"Of course, lad. I see some Zambian friends I need to speak with, anyway."

Forrest walked out onto a veranda which ran the length of the hotel. The sound of traffic murmured beyond the grounds' lush foliage. He leaned forward, placing his hands on the ornate concrete railing, lost in thought. It had been weeks since he'd arrived in Africa—weeks since a gang of poachers had slaughtered his son and snatched his new daughter-in-law and taken her who knows where and done who knows what with her. And what did he have to show for it? Fucking zip! Sure, he'd turned a few poachers into vulture chow, and probably created a few more "Depends" users with his psy-ops campaign. But he wasn't a bit closer to finding the ones who'd devastated his kids' lives. The Kenyan police were as worthless as wet toilet paper and the KWS Director, he now realized, was a waste of gravity, too.

"Jesus Tecumseh Sherman," he whispered a groan to the warm Nairobi night.

He felt a cool, delicate hand settle onto his and turned to look.

"I thought you didn't believe in Him," Anne Sargent said in a very tired, very distant voice.

Forrest sighed. "I do take the name in vain every now and then. Just like most *good* Christians I know."

"What other Commandments do you break?"

"Most of 'em at one time or another—some, more than once."

Anne smiled, too tired to react and somehow past caring. An awkward silence hung in the air for a long moment. "Thank you," she whispered out of nowhere.

Forrest looked at her curiously then realized what she meant. "He do that often?"

"Not at first." She looked away, lifted her hand and nervously picked at a cuticle.

He saw her eyes look into the past. They sparkled in the night like her diamond necklace.

She looked at Forrest. "The doorman said you put him in a taxi."

"Friends don't let friends drive drunk."

She smiled.

"You're not going home tonight, are you?" Forrest asked, concerned.

"No, I've taken a room."

"Good idea."

"And you?" she asked.

"Got one at the Hilton—the Doc and I."

"Mmm."

They shared a long, awkward look.

"Well, then," she said, finally. "It's been a long evening—and a stressful one, at that. I think it's time to say good night."

Forrest touched her arm. "Good night, Anne." His smile gained warmth. "And you really *do* look stunning tonight."

There was a moment's awkward silence as they shared weak smiles. Forrest exaggerated a look at his watch. "I'll give the Doc a few more minutes. Then I'll carry him home and tuck him in."

She smiled and turned to go. "Take good care of that dear old man. He's rather special you know?"

"I know."

Allen Windridge strode boldly into the office of the Kenya Police Commissioner, a sullen look on a gaunt face battered by alcohol and fatigue. Without so much as a word or pleasantry, he slammed the office door behind him and pulled a chair close to the Commissioner's desk.

Commissioner Afande, a large man with an equally large round head looked up to see an angry though familiar face. "You appear troubled, Allen." His fuzzy white hair contrasted sharply against skin as black as a rubber tire. A small pronounced diastema in an otherwise sparkling collection of porcelain white teeth peaked through his weak yet polite smile.

Windridge plopped his slender frame down heavily with a painful grunt. Leaning against the end of the desk, his eyes closed against the pain of an industrial strength hangover, Windridge heaved a long sigh.

The Commissioner regarded Windridge warily, the faintest hint of a knowing smile creeping across his face. "Sit down, Allen," he said with a twinge of sarcasm. His white shirt collar was stained at the edge, turning it a yellow brown.

Windridge, dressed in uniform green khakis, put his hand to his forehead and glared at Afande from beneath long feminine fingers. "Please, Simon. I'm in no humor for you today."

Afande's smile doubled in size. "Would you like a drink, then?" he asked without meaning it.

Windridge lifted his head from his hand and looked at the Commissioner. "Actually, I'd like a favor."

"What can I do for the KWS Director, today?"

"I'd like you to do a background check on someone—one of the researchers. An American. A wazungu," Windridge said, his haughty nasal inflection giving the word its full derogatory weight—rich, arrogant whites. Although most of the Kenyan Police were white, former British soldiers who had often served in India, most of the high offices were occupied by blacks who, try as they might, never strayed far from their undercurrent of resentment toward whites. Windridge, although unable to break through this ebony ceiling erected after Kenyan independence from the British Empire, was a wily dog who played the game of anti-white politics as though he meant it.

The Commissioner's smile faded. He took a pen from his desk and made a note on a pad of paper lying among piles of folders and forms. "What's his name...I assume it's your dance partner from last evening."

Windridge nodded and winced. "Forrest. John Forrest."

Commissioner Afande scribbled the name then brought his hand to a chin which, at first glance, would have otherwise gone unnoticed.

"Something wrong?"

Afande looked up, his eyes searching the ceiling for something.

"I don't know. There is something familiar about that name, and the face though I can't quite place it."

Windridge looked at the Police Commissioner curiously. "Well, I'd like it to be a lot more familiar by this time next week. Check immigration, aviation records, motor vehicles, everything," Windridge snapped. Then remembering his place, added: "Please."

SMACK! The monster's backhand knocked his wife across the hut and flat on her back. He lunged forward for a follow-up only to be intercepted by Amy who threw herself over the prostrate figure, her back to the attacker to absorb the expected blows. The enraged husband grabbed Amy by the hair and began to pull her off his wife when a large dark hand clamped his arm firmly at the bicep.

"No. The merchandise is already damaged beyond selling at a good price." It was Mpika, there to conduct an inspection.

Despite the intervention, the monster gave the American girl an angry shove, tossing her onto the dirt floor. They shared glares for a long moment.

Mpika studied his property carefully, a look of disgust firmly planted on his very dark face. Blood-shot eyes as black as coals dissected Amy's anatomy, part-by-part.

Amy looked horrible. Her hunger strike had her bones poking out in all the wrong places. Though she was careful to eat enough to stay relatively healthy, she ate far fewer calories than required to maintain her weight. She was emaciated. Her face was gaunt and grey, her eyes dark and sunken. Over the last several days she had deliberately smeared dirt from the floor and ash from the fire pit onto her visible skin. Her clothes, mostly borrowed from the wife, were as disheveled and filthy as if she lived under a shanty-town bridge. She had tangled her normally beautiful blond hair into a tussled rat's nest complete with interwoven fibers of grass and flakes of leaves. If she were a car, even a junk yard would think twice about taking her.

Mpika turned his piercing look on his lieutenant who drew back. "Come with me," he commanded in a low growl, before stepping out through the entrance into the blinding sunlight.

After the men had left, Amy crab-walked back to Sarah, whose name she had only learned in the last few days. She put her fingers to the cut on her head and noticed the blood trickling from her lower lip.

Sarah pulled away from her in a flash of anger. "Leave me, girl! Leave me!" she hissed. There was pain in her eyes and a dash of fear. "You see what your defiance has caused?" The voice was forceful, bitter and on the verge of tears though Amy could tell that after years of abuse she was well beyond and probably incapable of tears.

Amy slowly crawled back to her space in the room. With her she took a combination of satisfaction for the small victory she'd won accompanied with a sense of guilt that someone else was paying the price.

"And what brings you down here, today, Inspector Sargent," John Forrest said with a friendly yet uncertain smile as Anne climbed out of her Land Rover. He looked her over carefully, as if he were meeting her for the first time. Yep. Just like the last time I saw her in camp, he thought, still unable to make the connection between Anne, the belle-of-the-ball, and Inspector Sargent, the supreme ball-buster of the Kenya Wildlife Service. A weird feeling suddenly came over him. It was as if the "other" woman was somehow a dream.

She halted for a moment next to her Rover, clutching a large document pouch and a loose-leaf binder over her chest, not quite able to look him in the eye at first lest he see the vulnerabilities beneath the official uniform. "Hello, John," she said with the weakest of smiles. "I was on my way down to Namanga to meet with some of my Tanzanian counterparts. I thought I'd stop in to see how Malcolm is recovering."

Forrest grinned while hiding his vague disappointment at not being the reason for her visit. "He's still got a pulse, last time I checked." There was something different about her, he noticed. She looked the same, dressed the same...but the edge was gone. She seemed...softer, somehow.

"And a good mornin' to you, darlin'," McCullen sang as he walked up to greet his surrogate daughter with a fatherly hug. "Did I hear'ya say you were headin' for Tanzania?"

"Cynthia Marsh asked me to meet with some of the Tanzanian wildlife people to see if there isn't something we can do to stop the slaughter of migrating elephants until their government gets around to banning hunting altogether."

"You think they ever will, lass?" McCullen asked already certain of the answer.

"Who knows? But we have to try something." She opened the folder then produced a series of documents and newspaper articles pertaining to poaching and big game hunting.

One headline, in particular caught Forrest's eye: *BABA TEMBO STALKS THE MARA* - Three poachers found dead. "What's this one all about?" he asked.

"Hmm...oh that. I'm afraid Baba Tembo has been quite busy of late. It means father of the elephants, or elephant father." Her eyes went to the article then to his. "It seems that there is a hunter out there in the bush—a murderer would be more accurate. He kills poachers, mutilates their bodies, and leaves a warning for the survivors. Quite gruesome, actually. But, oddly enough, very effective. The Masai say it's Baba Tembo...protecting his children. I've heard reports that even moran are afraid to venture very far. And none of them want to spear an elephant."

"Moran? What's that?" Forrest asked. "Anything like a moron?" A smile crept in.

"Masai warriors, lad," McCullen interjected, grimacing at his bad joke. "The boys have to kill a dangerous animal to prove their manhood—a rite of passage."

"I see. *Very* manly. Just like I said...morons. What does killing an elephant prove?" Forrest asked, rhetorically. He noticed the photo album under her arm. "What's that?"

"Police photos of poachers who operate on the border."

The hairs on the back of Forrest's hands stood up. "Can I have a look?"

"I suppose." She handed it to him.

Anne and McCullen chatted while Forrest scanned the plastic-covered pages. He flipped through page after page of two-by-two black-and-white photos before stopping, his eyes sticking on a familiar face. *Mpika, Philip M.* the caption read along with other statistics: *six feet two, one hundred seventy-two pounds, DOB 8 December, 1954, five arrests for poaching and trafficking in illegal goods, assault on a park ranger, attempted murder...*

"Who's this character?" Forrest blurted without realizing he had interrupted a conversation. "Oh...excuse me."

"That's alright," Anne responded. "I'm not familiar with many of them—just some of the worst. Those we see over and over...Which one?"

Forrest poked a finger in the man's face.

"Oh him." She looked up at Forrest. "One of the worst, that one." Sargent grimaced. "He always seems to slip through our grasp—always gets off with little or no punishment."

"You know anything about him?"

"Just what I've heard at a few of his hearings. He's Tanzanian. Walks with a limp...he was wounded in Angola or injured by a lion—I can't remember which." Her voice trailed off as she searched her memory. "Oh...he's got quite an interesting physical abnormality—very rare." She smiled, proud of her recall. "A bifid tongue. My husband told me about it."

"A what?" Forrest asked, squinting his eyes.

"A bifid tongue. It's genetic, actually. You see, as the fetus develops, the tongue starts out as a forked organ with two separate halves. Over time, the halves fuse together leaving that little crease down the center." She stuck out her tongue to demonstrate then snapped it back in like the bird in a coo-coo clock.

Forrest snorted and smiled. It wasn't like her to be so animated, he thought. Maybe she's starting to loosen up a little.

"Mpika has a forked tongue—like a snake. His halves never completely fused. The Masai call him Shetani—The Serpent—in the Biblical sense. They're scared to death of him. No one will ever testify against him in court. It wouldn't surprise me at all to see him in Namanga, today." She gave Forrest a look. "Why do you ask?"

"Just curious." Forrest shrugged, trying to downplay his intense interest. *Jesus Tecumseh Sherman. Anne had this information all along! Is this just too ironic or what?* He snapped the binder closed and handed it back to her. "He had the most interesting face of the bunch."

"Indeed."

"When are you leaving?"

"Straight away. The meeting is scheduled for this afternoon."

"Can I come along?" He asked, smiling at the way she pronounced the word scheduled—with a soft SH. Then he added: "You can drive if you like," after noting her look of trepidation.

She looked at McCullen for a moment, considering the proposal. "Alright then." Anne continued talking to McCullen while Forrest bounded off to get his survival vest and camera.

Two hours and a hundred kilometers of unpaved road later, they pulled into the little village of Namanga. It was little more than a collection of dilapidated commercial enterprises straddling the main road between Nairobi and Arusha. Forrest noted concrete block buildings with shingle roofs nestled among the hills that surrounded the official border crossing point. The tallest structure was a twelve-meter-high water tank standing on four steel legs. Only the main street was paved, tar and gravel from the looks of it, the rest a mixture of dirt and gravel. All were in typically poor condition. Their Land Rover passed a red-and-white Caltex petrol station, a market with interior and exterior displays of produce and food stuffs, and a bar; an evil looking little place with a dirt parking lot, badly weathered paint and a dirty ring of hand prints lining an entrance open to the road's thirsty travelers. Western music blasted through the doorway drawing the attention of anyone who hadn't first noticed the signs. All sorts of people roamed the streets, mostly native men dressed in Western style clothes. Loud T-shirts, Levis, denim jackets and Reebok sneakers were common.

It had to be the limp, he would later reflect, which first caught his attention. "Slow down," Forrest ordered suddenly, spotting a small knot of men heading into the bar. One wore a black hat with a leopard-skin headband and walked with a noticeable limp. Forrest felt his heart leap into his throat. His head jerked forward as Anne hit the brakes hard; their dusty screech drawing the attention of the men who instinctively turned to look. *Son of a bitch!* Forrest's mind screamed when he saw the face of the man wearing a red bandanna. Another familiar face bore a long flesh-colored scar which traversed his left cheek, terminating just below a vacant dead-white eye. *Son of a bitch!* Forrest's hands tingled as if he had just touched a high voltage line with wet fingers. "Stop here," he said evenly, choking back an urge to shout.

"What?" Anne failed to notice the faces, so focused was her attention on the street and its unpredictable hazards.

"Stop here," he repeated with a calmer voice so as not to arouse her curiosity.

"Well, alright then," Anne said with some confusion in her voice. "But the border checkpoint is just ahead," she added, pointing to a tiny sand-colored stucco shack no larger than a telephone booth. A red-and-white steel gate extended across the road just in front of it. "I'm to meet my people there," she turned to say to a now vacant seat.

Forrest leaned in the window as the Rover ground to a stop. "I'll meet you at the market when you're finished."

"But I thought you wanted to meet..."

He cut her off. "Watch my stuff," he barked over his shoulder as he strode away at a pace just short of a jog.

Completely confused, Anne continued ahead, parking next to the guard shack where she greeted three men wearing the uniform of Tanzanian game wardens. She didn't notice Forrest disappear into the bar.

It took a moment for his eyes to adjust to the dim light. It took somewhat longer for his nose to adjust to the odor, a bouquet of rancid beer, cigarette smoke, BO and urine. At first, the patrons appeared but as silhouettes edged with artificial light reflected from behind the bar and sunlight from two tiny windows. After a moment, he watched four men, one with a dark safari hat take a seat at a table near the back of the dirt-floor establishment.

Calm down, John...What would the General do?...He'd make time...

Think things over...He'd order... "A beer," he said in a voice so tranquil he wasn't sure it was his. "Nataka tuska baridi," he repeated in Swahili, one of the few phrases he knew.

The bartender, his eyes glowering with the resentment reserved for wazungu, moved on stubborn legs to a cooler before producing a tall, amber bottle of Tusker. Forrest returned the look, slapping down a bill which would easily cover the price of six beers. His eyes went back to his prey, his mind at work on a plan. Trying not to be too obvious, Forrest alternately studied the men at the back table and the other patrons, sizing them all up. Though none appeared threatening, his was the only white face in the bar. *And I left my Colt and my knife with Anne!* Fifteen minutes later, he swigged his second bottle of Tusker as he watched a man exit through the back door. A small sign just above it said choo—toilet. An idea hit his brain just as the first bottle of beer landed in his bladder. Forrest set the bottle down and ventured through the rear exit.

Forrest strode quickly across the back alley and eased inside the choo, repelled by a stench which held him back like a strong undertow at the beach. Half the flies and all the shit in Africa must be at the bottom of that trench, he thought, choking on his own breath. Like an Army field latrine, it had a long wooden bench constructed with two-by-sixes spaced far enough apart that you could either sit or stand if your aim was good enough. Puddles of amber liquid and sections of damp wood indicated that the average marksmanship was well below average. Forrest lifted the knee-high "seat" which he saw was hinged at the back. Below, a shiny surface punctuated with dark objects reflected the dim sunlight which squeezed in between cracks in the walls. Must be six feet deep, he guessed as he let the lid drop with a heavy clunk.

As Forrest was taking care of his own pressing business, it became apparent that there wasn't a piece of toilet paper to be seen. He shook his head and shuddered as he zipped his fly. "What...how do they...?" He started to ask the squadrons of flies which buzzed about in the semi-darkness. "Never mind. I don't want to know," he muttered as he turned to leave. Ducking his head, Forrest noticed the entrance had a wooden door which was held open by a three-foot two-by-four.

He re-crossed the alley quickly and resumed his place at the bar. Forrest looked past his upturned bottle to see that his "friends" were still there—still enjoying themselves. Just then, one of the men got up from the table and walked past him on his way to the choo. Forrest deliberately looked away, instead watching the man in the cracked mirror as he went by. Dead Eye Dick, he thought, matching the man's face with his mental mug-shot. *Sure as hell.* Forrest felt his blood rise and took a deep breath. He delayed for a few seconds, took another swig of beer, belched, then, bottle in hand, followed the man to·the latrine.

He was at the far end facing the bench when Forrest entered the outhouse, shutting the wooden door behind him. Forrest shoved the two-by-four in place to prevent someone from walking in on them then took his place at the bench as if preparing to relieve himself. Instead, he took his beer bottle by its long neck and waited, mentally rehearsing his moves. A second later, he heard the man's stream trickle to a stop. Forrest took a deep breath as the man went behind him for the door.

In a flash, Forrest shattered the bottle on the bench, wheeled and thrust it into the man's throat before he could react. His victim started to resist until the sharp glass sliced through the outer layer of skin.

"Simama, dirt-ball!" Forrest growled, tightening his grip on the man's arm—driving it into a hammer lock. "Speak English?" he hissed.

Dead Eye grunted in pain. "Yes...a little bit...Ughh!...I have no money."

"I don't want your money." Forrest pinned Dead Eye against the door and shifted his weight to hold him there. "The man you're with—the one with the hat—what's his name?"

"He has all the money. He is my bossman."

"I don't want his money, either. I want his *name!*" Forrest tightened the hold to emphasize his point.

"Ughh!... He is Mpika."

"Mpika?"

"Ndio...yes."

"They call him Shetani?"

Forrest felt the man draw a short breath.

"Does he owe you money?" he gasped.

"I've got the weapon, asshole, that means I ask the questions. Where does he live?"

"Half a day's drive...southeast."

Forrest reached to his back pocket for his map with his free hand. He tossed it onto the bench. "Show me."

"I cannot unfold the paper with one hand."

"If you can see with one eye you can work with one hand...Do it," Forrest growled, bending the man over the bench, "or I'll cut your good eye out and make you eat it." Forrest braced himself for treachery as the man slowly did as he was told. It took a few minutes but he succeeded. Forrest felt his face flush with anger as he spotted a familiar diamond ring on the man's pinky.

"There," he grunted. "In the hills near the border."

"Show me...Wapi?...Put your finger there."

The man's right index finger touched the spot—a valley which ran between the hills southeast of Tsavo National Park—much further south than he had searched thus far. The diamond sparkled in a ray of light which squeezed through a crack in the wall.

Forrest burned the image into his memory. "You sure?"

"Yes."

Forrest dug the bottle a little deeper into the man's skin. "You're a fucking poacher...aren't you?" He felt the man tense.

"Tafadhali...Please." Dead Eye, sensing a possible opening, shifted to a new tact. "We have much ivory...we can share it with you...I will take you..."

"You killed a wazungu boy...in Tsavo...last year...you and your marafiki." Forrest felt the man stiffen. He braced himself and continued in a whisper. "I saw you there...You cut him down with your rifles."

The man shook his head.

Forrest saw the guilty look in his good eye. "You captured a girl, didn't you?"

Another shake of the head.

"No? Then whose ring is that? Where'd you get it? Zales? 47th Street?"

Dead Eye stiffened and resisted. His eyes widened in fear.

Forrest let the glass penetrate a little deeper.

Dead Eye winced as he felt the warmth of his blood trickle down his neck.

"You have her there, don't you, motherfucker?" Forrest growled, tightening his hammerlock to the point where it began to tear the rotator cuff.

Dead Eye cried out, then nodded mechanically, twice.

"That boy was my son. The girl is his wife," Forrest hissed like a coiled snake. "And that ring belongs on *her* finger."

Dead Eye tried to lunge, shoving his weight into Forrest who kicked his feet out from under him and lifted his arm with a sickening crunch as the shoulder popped out of its socket.

"Ahhhh—gukkkk!" he screamed, then went silent as Forrest shoved the broken bottle through his larynx then raked the jagged edge across his carotid artery, jugular vein, and windpipe, traversing from ear to ear down to the bone. Dead Eye struggled, gasped and gurgled for a moment before falling limp.

Forrest listened to see if anyone was coming. His heart pounded against his sternum like a trapped animal trying to escape.

Nothing—just the throbbing music and the sound of a truck horn.

Forrest dropped the bottle into the latrine then stuck his map into his waistband. He paused to listen as he slid Amy's ring off the poacher's finger and slipped it into his pocket. Holding Dead Eye by the belt with one hand, he raised the bench and lifted the body over the side, letting it drop into the goop with a thick splash. He dropped the lid, yanked the door open and peered out into the alley. A scurrying rat was the only movement. Forrest checked himself for blood. There was none on his clothes—just a little on his hands, which he wiped on his socks then lowered his trouser legs to cover them. Careful to see that no one saw him leave the outhouse, he walked calmly down the alley toward the market where Anne would be waiting—he hoped. He came around a pile of discarded cardboard boxes to see her Rover sitting out front and she somewhere inside. He leaned against the fender and waited for her to appear, which she did after some minutes.

“Oh, there you are,” she said with a curious smile.

He smiled back as a bead of sweat trickled down his forehead and dripped off his nose.

“I searched the entire market for you. Where were you?” she asked, climbing back into the Rover.

Forrest looked across the parking lot to see Mpika and one of his men emerge from the bar looking up and down the street. “I was in the bar for a few minutes.”

“The bar? What for?”

“I had to use the restroom.”

CHAPTER-SEVENTEEN

STALKER *a: one who pursues or hunts game or quarry*
b: one who proceeds in a stealthy or deliberate manner

"YES I'D LIKE TO BOOK A FULL MONTH," Henderson told the woman on the other end of the telephone line. "Well, I'm not too familiar with African hunts. I thought you could suggest the best time to come." Henderson scribbled notes on a legal pad as he listened to the woman's comments. "Okay...Uh-hu...Dry season, of course...sure... Right. I understand."

"What about the month of January, then?...Oh, it's booked. Damn...Uh-hu...Okay, how about February?...Aw. I should have called earlier...I see. A year in advance...Wow. Popular guy. Ha ha."

Henderson laid his pencil down on his desk and studied the plastic-covered calendar in his checkbook cover. "Well, may I suggest something, then? I own my own business and I can leave on fairly short notice if need be. Would it be possible to put myself on a waiting list in case someone cancels? Oh, okay...good...No, that would be fine. I don't mind joining a party as a single. It's a great way to make new friends...Ha ha. You're right. That makes sense. It might be easier to fill in, at that."

Henderson laid the calendar down. "Okay. Why don't you tell me when Mr. Richards is scheduled to start his hunts and I'll compare it with my schedule and we'll see what we can work out."

He picked up his gold Cross pencil and positioned his hand over the pad. "I'm ready. Go ahead."

Henderson scribbled. "Okay...okay...yeah. Got it."

"And where are those going to be?...Tanzania...Wait, how do you spell that?...G-R-U-M-E-T-I...Grumeti River. Okay...good."

He laid his pencil down again and moved the receiver to the opposite ear.

"Okay...Yes. I've hunted big game before...No. Just in North America...Yes, I've been looking forward to doing the "big five" for years...Right. No I heard about Mr. Richards through a friend of a friend."

"Steve," his wife called.

"Excuse me," Henderson said before cupping his hand over the mouthpiece.

"Dinner's ready."

"Okay. Coming," he called back.

Henderson winced and continued with the woman on the phone. "Sorry...I've got to go...Oh yeah, sure. Of course. I thought I gave it to you: Stein. Yes. S-T-E-I-N...Stein. First name's Frank...."

They really weren't horses at all, Forrest recalled. Actually, they were artiodactyls, cloven-hoofed ungulates; more closely related to pigs and deer than to horses. Hippopotamus was the name given to them by the Greeks whose first encounter with the curious animals had preceded his by nearly 3,000 years. Over the centuries, Hippo Potamos—Greek for river horse—had become hippopotamus, or more correctly, *Hippopotamus amphibious*—*H. amphibius* for short. Although they seemed out of place with their environment, they were actually perfectly suited for it. Hippopotamus life revolved around water. They slept, fought, mated and gave birth in it. And, like most of nature's other creatures, they gave something back. Their feces fertilized the aquatic flora which, in turn, supported fish and other river inhabitants. Without them, the rivers would be largely sterile.

Forrest lingered at the edge of the high bank cut into the earth by an abrupt curve in Tanzania's Grumeti river. Below, a large congregation—perhaps 30-to-40 animals—clogged the deepest water doing what hippos do best…sleep. A sputtering, gasping sound accompanied a huge head breaking the water's surface. Its wheel barrow sized mouth yawned. Forrest couldn't tell for certain, but judging from the animal's bulk and the greatly elongated, razor-sharp lower canines, it appeared to be an adult male. The great, fleshy trap door hinged shut, ears wiggled, nostrils hissed and the head disappeared below the murky surface. Over the next several minutes, other animals surfaced to breathe before returning to their waterbeds.

Forrest's vantage point, the top of a sheer sandy precipice which fell off into deep water, allowed him to see across the river into the swamp and mud flats that lay on the other side. There, several more hippo groups wallowed in the thick mud like fat ladies in a health spa. Their bloated, disproportionate figures and rubbery skin gave them the look of cartoon characters or inflatable plastic toys. In this case though, looks were deceiving. The three-ton animals were anything but playthings. Every year, hippos killed more people in Africa than any other animal. Usually the result of people in small boats venturing too close to young calves only to have angry mothers react with drive-by drownings.

Fascinated by the spectacle, Forrest decided to take a break from his reconnaissance. He backed into the concealment of a leafy thicket growing at the edge of the cliff and sat down to take it all in. Up river, he noticed long stretches of muddy beach where a few young males cavorted in mock combat that would train them for the serious mating competition that came with maturity. Elsewhere, along the thin strands of palm-lined mud and sand, large, mature bulls stood guard over their territories frisking itinerant females and showing trespassers the exit. Aside from the occasional hippo-fight or courtship ritual that resembled fighting, the scene was one of riverine tranquility.

In a few hours that would change. The hippos, McCullen had said, would become more active at night when their stubby legs would take them several miles away from the river in search of forage. No problem, Forrest thought. By then, he hoped to be a few miles away, himself.

For twenty thousand bucks a head, they *ought* to get a champagne breakfast, Forrest thought as he sat perched in a tall acacia tree watching them eat. Morgan Richards and his clients were camped nearly a hundred meters to the south at the edge of a long steep bluff that ran for several miles along the Grumeti river. Richards, Forrest realized, had chosen a very strategic location. His camp was on the north side of the river that formed the border between The Serengeti National Park and neighboring Mara Province. On one side of the river the animals were protected. On Richards' side they were fair game. Trouble was nobody had told the animals about the arrangement.

Forrest scanned the camp, gathering intel and generally sizing up his quarry. A tall black steward, impeccably dressed in a crisp khaki safari shirt and matching shorts, served hot tea to an equally well-attired party of wealthy Brits. Richards and two "gentlemen" with George Hamilton tans, silk ascots and silver-gray hair, grinned and laughed silently at some inaudible joke. The two clients, Forrest saw, had brought their wives along on their little African adventure. He assumed they were wives, because the men paid a great deal more attention to each other than they did to the women. And the ladies, it seemed, were content to be ignored. They sipped their tea out of china cups and cackled about silly things that probably had nothing to do with the upcoming hunt. They too, were dressed to the nines. Cotton blouses and khaki shorts looked very nice with their knee-high white socks and brand-new hiking boots. Tan pith helmets with pleated white cotton hat-bands accentuated the safari chic.

"I say, aren't we just too fashionable," Forrest muttered sarcastically in his most uncomplimentary British accent. "Dressed to kill, are we?"

Four hours after midnight is the time when most people settle into their soundest sleep. It's also the best time to launch attacks, conduct reconnaissance or perpetrate simple cat-burglary.

Backlight from Forrest's night vision goggles glowed faint green against his eye sockets as he circled the camp checking for sentries. He made note of any object that could make noise or impede his movement. Everything was pretty much as he expected. Three Land Rovers were parked side-by-side next to a duce-and-half, ladder-back truck. The camp fire and gas lanterns had long since died out. The only sounds, other than his breathing, were a chorus of night insects and distant noises of the African night.

He moved deliberately and silently among the vehicles like a panther, placing small, explosive charges between gas tanks and steel frames. Each device had a small radio receiver which would activate five minutes after Forrest switched it on. When that happened, he would be well back and under cover just in case one of the devices malfunctioned and detonated when it went active. *Queer electrons or queertrons, pilots called them.*

The explosives would serve a dual purpose: First, they could act as a diversion if he was discovered and help screen his escape. Second, Forrest planned to disable the vehicles as he egressed at the conclusion of the mission.

Disable, he thought, with a smile. *Spookspeak for 'blow the living shit out of something.'*

When his luminous dive watch showed ten minutes had passed, he doubled the arming interval, just in case. Forrest moved next to the guest tents and listened. Heavy labored breathing and an occasional snore told him it was safe to proceed. Then again, he reminded himself, "safe" was a relative term.

He poked the MP-5's muzzle through the overlap in the mosquito netting and followed it through. Inside, he froze...listened...and scanned. No changes.

Forrest moved over the matted floor searching for places valuables might be kept. The whole situation was reminiscent of the snatch-and-grab missions his Ranger team had performed in Vietnam. On orders from battalion command, they had sometimes kidnapped communist political figures and brought them back for interrogation. Sometimes, accompanied by CIA agents, they had picked up select individuals, interrogated them at length and then executed them. They were people who had "done the same and worse" to village chiefs, town mayors and their families, according to the spooks. Forrest never knew for sure, never trusted the spooks and never liked the missions although he had twice been sent out to assassinate similar people with his rifle. Once, he had been successful and once the target didn't show. "Part of winning their hearts and minds," the officers and intel people had said. Back then, who knew? To an eighteen-year-old PFC, it was all in a day's work and he was just following orders. Today, in retrospect, he saw it all as an incredible waste.

Forrest slowly and quietly unzipped a money belt that had been carelessly hung from the tent pole. Behind a thick wad of Kenyan shillings and British pound notes, he found two passports.

Bingo.

The hunting party hadn't traveled very far. It wasn't necessary. Their quarry had been considerate enough to come to them. Urged onward by thirst and drawn by the river, a herd of Grevy's zebra had wandered into the boganis situated a mile from Richards' camp. Stands of tall trees and patches of dense undergrowth complicated the otherwise uncomplicated landscape.

Two of the striped stallions, Forrest saw through his binoculars, were magnificent specimens. They were hard at work defending their mares from other interested males.

Grunts from a small herd of cape buffalo also carried through the brush and tall grass. Only one or two at a time were visible in the dense cover. From his vantage point, Forrest couldn't tell which herd the hunters were stalking. Capes, he knew, were one of the "big five." They, along with lion, leopard, elephant and rhinoceros, comprised the grand slam of African big-game trophy hunting. Therefore, the dangerous beasts seemed the most likely target. But rich people, he'd learned, intoxicated with new thrills, were often silly, frivolous people. And that made them unpredictable. Having a lot of money somehow seemed to relieve them of accountability to rules, laws, conscience and sometimes common sense. Hunting was not a problem, he reminded himself, as long as certain sportsman's rules were adhered to. First, the animals couldn't be threatened or endangered. Second, the hunter had to observe proper hunting etiquette and respect the land. Third, the animal had to be dispatched quickly and mercifully. If you ate the animal, used all of its parts, then you were a legitimate hunter in his book. But, Forrest thought, if you hunted just for bragging rights, picture taking and taxidermy, and left the animal to rot, you were a pariah and an embarrassment to all true outdoorsmen. And, he added, you were a pathetic excuse for a human being.

The ladies waited at the edge of the brush while Richards and his "great white hunters" moved to the far edge of the clearing to see what the trackers had found.

Cape buffalo are one of Africa's most dangerous species, entirely capable of killing everything from lions to humans. Their temperament is just as dark as their hide. And, just now, the droopy-horned, black-eyed cattle from hell concerned him more than the humans and their big-bore, custom-made bush guns.

Forrest held his silenced weapon at the ready as he maneuvered through the brush, its magazine loaded with 9mm Hydra Shock ammunition for maximum stopping power. The fire selector switch was set on semi-auto: one shot for every pull of the trigger. Every few meters, he stopped and listened. The air was full of sounds: buffalo grunts, zebra brays, occasional bird-calls and wind in the trees. The human hunters, as expected, were silent, completely unaware that there was another hunter stalking the bush.

He came to a break in the brush and froze. Forrest caught a glimpse of the native trackers hunkered down in a small clearing under the trees. Their attention was fixed on something in the brush—something he couldn't see. Just then, Morgan Richards came up and crouched in the grass next to his clients. Subtle arm and hand movements indicated the position of the trophy animals. Forrest watched the professional hunter trickle a handful of fine dust through his finger tips to test the wind. After a few minute's consultation, Richards motioned for his clients to come forward where he very quietly brought them up to speed and gave them their instructions. Using his powerful binoculars, Forrest brought himself right into their huddle. When the trackers got up and split off from the hunters, he knew their plan almost as well as they did.

Morgan Richards moved ahead through the brush followed closely by one of the Brits, his friend, and two of the four trackers. Richards had sent the other two trackers ahead to scout the buffalo. He carried a .577 Nitro Express double-barreled rifle slung over his shoulder leaving his hands free to use his binoculars and give signals. The client, carrying a beautifully finished .375 H & H, matched paces with Richards. They were heading into the light brush surrounding a grassy bogani; straight for the herd of zebra that Forrest had seen earlier.

As he suspected, Forrest saw the hunters single out one of the stallions.

Think you brought enough gun for a little circus pony, Sir Lancelot? Forrest shook his head and took a deep breath.

On Richards' signal, the designated shooter moved ahead followed closely by his guide and his friend who acted as camera-man with a 35mm SLR.

Forrest thought about his own rifle for a moment before dismissing the idea. He wanted badly to intervene. But to do so at this point would unravel his plan. There were too many of them, just now. Before he could act, he had to cut the party down to size. And he had to do it in a certain order for maximum effect.

From his position, fifty meters to their right, Forrest watched in frustration as the shooter rose from a crouch and sighted on the target zebra. The animal was only one hundred meters distant, an easy shot for even a novice hunter. His friend cautiously moved up with the camera snapping off frame after frame. The ladies, about ten meters back, crouched low in the brush holding their ears.

The thunder clap of the high-powered rifle echoed across the clearing as the zebra staggered, ran a few steps and dropped. The shooter stood for a moment in a thin wisp of smoke before Richards urged him ahead with a jubilant shout.

Forrest watched as the party went through a ritual of poses for the camera. Then, as if the senseless killing wasn't bad enough, the hunters stood by slapping each other on the back for 30 minutes as Richard's men skinned the animal and displayed the souvenir hide for another round of photos. Forrest watched, aghast, when the entire group casually walked off to join the other two trackers at the edge of the clearing. The dead zebra, valued only for its hide, was left to the nature's clean-up detail.

John Ruger Forrest, bile at the back of his mouth, slipped off quietly to wait at a place he had chosen along the trail that led back to their camp.

Forrest watched from a thick cluster of palms that stood at the edge of the trail. The two skinners strolled lazily toward their camp where they would cure the prized hide. Conversation mixed with laughter and cigarette smoke followed them along. And although smoking was certainly hazardous to their health, it would not be their cause of death.

The heavy thud of two shots rolled through the brush startling the vultures who had gathered to attend to the zebra. About a mile away, Forrest judged. Maybe less. *Sounds like they got their buffalo.* He homed in on their direction and set out at a quick jog.

* * * *

"Bloody hell," Richards exclaimed, angrily. "What's gotten into those boys?" He and his four clients stopped short, taken aback by the sight of the abandoned zebra pelt laying on the trail.

Richards came ahead, his face flushed with a combination of anger and embarrassment. "Very sorry about this. It's not like my people to..." He gasped as he lifted the black-and-white skin. One of the skinners lay underneath as if he were asleep. Richards knew immediately that he wasn't. He leaned forward and retrieved something from the skinner's forehead.

One of the women choked on an urge to scream. Their husbands moved them back and turned them away.

One of them came forward after a moment, wearing a look of puzzlement and concern. "Is he dead?"

"Quite," Richards remarked, glibly, preoccupied with curious marks left in the dirt. Long, shallow ruts, two of them, ran off in parallel toward the thick trees that lined the river bank.

"What in God's name...?" the client asked.

Richards held up his hand and scanned the woods. He broke open the breech of his rifle, checked to see that it was loaded with two live rounds, and snapped it shut with a crisp click.

"Go back to the buffalo and get the rest of my boys. Tell them to get their bloody arses back to camp, straight away."

"What about...?"

"Nigel," Richards interrupted, curtly, turning his eyes to the man comforting the two women. "Take the ladies directly back to camp," he ordered with icy calmness. "Don't stop for anything."

The man did as he was told, leading the ladies in a wide circle around the dead skinner. He glanced at the body and then at the striped hide as they passed. It suddenly seemed a ghastly thing—no longer something to be prized.

"But..." the remaining man started to protest.

"Go." Richards' cold blue eyes told him there was no time for argument. He watched to see his client disappear down the trail.

The professional hunter was suddenly alone in the brush. He felt his throat go dry. His breathing became shallow. He felt someone's eyes burning into him. *Who? Why?*

Of course, he'd been unnerved before, he reminded himself, frozen in the brush sweating out the charge of a buffalo or an elephant. But that was different. He could deal with animals. They were almost predictable. Richards looked at the object he'd lifted off the skinner's forehead—a plastic business card. He had heard stories of the man who roamed the countryside assassinating poachers and terrorizing hunters. Baba Tembo, the boys called him; they almost wouldn't come with him—not like them, a'tall. His friend, Allen Windridge, had shown him a card just like the one he now held in his hand. *So now it's my turn.*

Richards rose from his crouch and moved off following the drag marks. Wherever the trail led, he was sure he would find his missing man. The thought of what else he might find rose a sweat on his upper lip. It suddenly occurred to him that he should be more afraid than he was. After all, he was now the one being hunted. But, to his surprise, he felt oddly composed. The stalker was less a threat, he rationalized, and more a...challenge.

He moved ahead, setting one foot deliberately in front of the other, as silently as a leopard. His eyes scanned the terrain ahead. His heavy rifle led the way deeper into the thick trees. Occasionally he stopped, scanned and listened before proceeding ahead. The underbrush became thicker, indicating a natural edge to the woodland. The drag marks terminated abruptly. He stopped again before proceeding on. There was no more sign. Richards felt a sudden twinge of fear. *Which way, now?*

"I say, old man," a voice mocked. "Did you lose someone?" it taunted.

Richards froze, crouched and spun around bringing his rifle up to his shoulder. His eyes struggled to find the source in the mottled splashes of light that danced among the dark leaves and shadows. His heart raced.

There was an infinitely long silence. Long enough for his mind to start playing tricks on him. "Where are you?" he whispered to himself. *"Where?"*

"Oh look, Morgan. Here he is," the voice said, tauntingly.

Behind that big tree.

Branches snapped as the object rushed toward him. Leaves rustled, flew and settled into the dark shadows.

Richards fired one barrel into the onrushing outline of a man.

It continued onward, picking up speed through the whipping branches; cutting through the hazy shafts of sunlight.

Richards fired again, then recoiled, recognizing the distorted face and bulging eyes of his skinner only three feet from his own. He came on faster, several strands of dark cord wrapped around his neck.

A noose!

Richards brought his rifle up to cushion the blow. Instinctively, at the moment of impact, he flinched, turned his head aside and closed his eyes. Branches swept his safari hat from his head as he tumbled backward. Dark turned to light. He opened his eyes to see blue sky above—trees rising above him. His fingers left his rifle and clutched desperately at his sides for a branch or a limb. Flailing in circles, his hands found only air. His feet bicycled in space trying to recapture his balance. His back hit flat with a concussive smack, knocking the wind out of him. Blue sky went dark green, murky and wet as the river swallowed him. Something big—powerful—pounded him hard! Huge, rubbery jaws clamped around his chest and squeezed. His lungs burned—ribs cracked. The world went black.

The dirty water churned green, gray and brown 30 feet below his feet. Forrest watched from the edge of the high bank as hippo backs and heads broke the surface in a violent melee. Brown-tinted bubbles erupted where Richards had impacted the water. There was no sign of him.

Forrest's eyes were drawn to the light-colored object that lay on the ground beneath the feet of the dark limp body that swayed gently at the end of the OD nylon cord. He picked it up and dusted it off. It was Richards' hat.

His eyes went back to the water below. The hippos had calmed down a bit, he saw, although all heads seemed to be above the surface. Most eyes were on him, assessing the potential threat.

Just then, a large female close ashore, opened her mouth wide unleashing a long, anguished bellow.

Forrest stared at her for a moment and smiled. "It's okay now, darlin'. Nobody's gonna hurt you. Like Yogi says, it's all over when the fat lady sings."

"My God, Nigel, did you hear that?" his wife asked from inside their tent, her voice very shaky as if on the verge of tears. Two rifle reports reechoed like thunder in the distance. The look in her eyes was a mixture of fear and hope—mostly fear. She hadn't been too keen on the idea of a trip to Africa in the first place, what with the savage humans and even more savage beasts roaming about. Then there were the discomforts and diseases: malaria, cholera, bilharzia, sleeping sickness and those new horrifying, incurable viruses. Every mosquito bite had her in a cold sweat. She'd hardly eaten a thing since leaving the hotel. In the last week, she'd lost seven pounds. And now this. The bandits had taken their money and killed one of their skinners. *I told you this would happen*, she started to remind him for the eleventh time, but didn't. If she had been in charge, they'd be on their way to Nairobi right now and to hell with their belongings—well, most of them.

The tall, thin Englishman ignored her, turning his head in the direction of the two shots. "I bloody well hope Morgan got him." The wealthy businessman listened intently. After a moment, he returned to packing his gear. "Hopefully, he'll return soon."

His wife, a petit woman whose doelike, perpetually worried eyes stared at him beneath light brown bangs, hesitated for a moment, trying to decide if she shared her husband's optimism.

The other woman, whose once blonde, now silver, pageboy haircut framed a face lined with worry, stared apprehensively down the trail.

Her husband, Michael, had still not returned with the two trackers. Normally a quiet reserved woman by nature, she was reaching the limits of her patience.

"Now ladies," Nigel said in a reassuring voice, "we needn't worry. Richards is a good man. I'm sure he has everything under control. Let's finish packing, shall we?" He hefted a large aluminum camera case and started off toward one of the Land Rovers wondering whether he believed himself.

"If everything's under control, why are we packing?" his wife asked in a tone that indicated her fear was fermenting into anger.

Nigel stopped short, closed his eyes for a second and then turned, "Because, dear," he replied with a forced calm that helped hide his own fears. "We have a *dead* man here and we will have to report this whole ugly affair to the authorities. That will likely muddy-up things for a few days." He sat the camera case down, extracted a handkerchief from his pocket and wiped his forehead and eyeglass lenses, before returning the wrinkled linen to his right rear pocket. "Don't despair, my dear," he added as an afterthought, "after this matter has been disposed of, we can return and pick up where we left off."

"Ha." It wasn't a laugh. There were tears mixed in. "You and Michael can if you like. Constance and I are taking the first flight back to London."

Nigel sighed heavily and reached for his camera case.

"It's Michael!" his wife shrilled.

All heads turned to the trail. Michael Worthington half-ran, half-stumbled the last few yards into camp, his expensive rifle almost dragging the ground at the end of his jellylike arm. His breath came in heaves.

His wife ran to him as he sank to the ground at the base of a high tree. She knelt and fussed over him as Nigel approached.

"Good to see you, ol' man," *Very* good, he didn't say. "Where are the two boys?"

Worthington gasped, raised his head and looked at him. "Unavoidably...detained, I'm afraid," he said between labored breaths. He read the confused look on their faces and saw the question in

Nigel's eyes. "Two...two shots apiece, I should think."

"They're dead?" his wife gasped.

He nodded. "'Fraid so, luv."

Nigel's head snapped around, his vacant stare directed into the forest where he had last seen Richards. His optimism suddenly plummeted. His thoughts whirled. There was no good reason for bandits to kill the trackers and leave the zebra skin...*a diversion? Why?* "Michael, do you feel up to watching the trail?"

He swallowed and nodded, again.

"Right, then. Keep an eye out for Richards and whoever else might be out there." Nigel's voice quivered. "Ladies, let's hurry with the rest of the packing. Take only the essentials. We'll come back with the police for the rest."

Everyone scattered.

"I want to be ready to leave as soon as Richards returns." *If he returns.*

When Forrest reached the brush at the edge of the camp, the cooks and camp boys were scurrying about packing vehicles. The pampered women, not so crisp and serene as before, struggled to load their personal belongings into the back of the Rovers. One of the husbands assisted, more or less supervising the operation, while the other watched the trail.

Forrest could hear bickering over what to leave and what to take. After enduring what had to be the most frightening experience of their lives, their nerves were probably stretched to the limit, he assessed. He saw that they were stumbling all over themselves in their haste.

"Mimba," the sentry shouted over his shoulder at one of the camp boys, "don't forget my skin."

One of the women, apparently the sentry's wife, stopped abruptly on a return trip from the Rover. "You can't be serious, Michael."

The other Englishman turned his head and listened.

"After we've come all this way and worked this hard to get that damned hide, I'm not about to abandon it," he whined before turning his eyes back to the trail. "The bloody thing cost me 40,000 pounds. It's coming with us."

"Now see here, Michael," the second Englishman intervened, "there isn't time for all that."

Michael turned and glared at Nigel's wife. "If she has time for all her undergarments and frills, and you have time for all of your precious camera gear, I have time for *that.*"

Forrest watched as the other man, escorted by his wife, approach his friend. Forrest used the distraction to ease through the brush toward the tree where the sentry was posted. As he neared the trunk, he retrieved the small transmitter from his pocket and switched it on. A red LED lit up. His thumb flipped the safety cover up and settled over the firing switch. He steadied himself, mentally choreographed his moves and took a deep breath.

In one simultaneous motion, Forrest grabbed the rifle barrel that stuck out past the tree with his left hand and pressed the button with the right.

A bright flash preceded a thunderous boom. Forrest snatched the rifle away from its owner and sprang from behind the tree.

Pandemonium swept through the camp. Porters and cooks ran for cover. The Brits hit the ground. They flinched with each sharp secondary explosion as pockets of fuel burst into flame.

When Nigel turned to check on his friend, he saw the thick black muzzle of a submachine gun jammed into Michael's cheek. The weapon, he saw, was held in the gloved hand of a man in a camouflaged commando suit. He started to push himself up.

"Very slowly, ol' boy," Forrest said.

The women turned at the sound of a strange man's voice. Michael's wife screamed. The camp boys saw what was happening and scattered into the brush.

"Please, ma'am." A faux wince contorted Forrest's face amidst the loud pyrotechnics. "All that noise hurts my ears."

Nigel spoke. "Richards?"

Forrest looked him straight in the eye. "He won't be joining us, I'm afraid. It seems he dropped in on some of the local ladies; decided to go for a little swim."

"What happened to the other man?" Constance asked stiffly.

"He hung around to watch."

"I see," she said with widening eyes and a growing, confused frown.

Forrest smiled malevolently.

Nigel sat up in the dirt and brushed his shirt off. He glanced at the automatic weapon planted against his friend's head then looked into the commando's eyes. "What do you intend to do with us?"

"Nothing."

"Then what do you want?"

Forrest didn't answer for a moment as he stared into each of their eyes for effect. "I want you to leave here; leave Africa; never come back and never hunt another animal."

"And you'll let us go?" one of the women asked, a mixture of hope, relief and anxiety in her voice.

Forrest shifted his eyes to her and said nothing.

"What do we tell the police?" Nigel asked.

Forrest reached into one of his vest pockets and extracted four passports which he fanned out like a hand of playing cards. "I know who you are and I know where you live. You'll say the right things."

"You *murdered* four men!" Constance chided.

Forrest stared at her, his eyes like lasers. "I wasn't keeping score."

She looked away.

"I hunted them down just like they hunted helpless animals, often in violation of Kenyan law. I can hunt you down, too, if that's what you want. Now, you know how it feels. Unlike you, my intention was to capture the hired help—tie them up and take 'em out of play. They chose to put up a fight and lost. So be it. Bottom line, I came here to protect the animals that are left. And I'll do whatever it takes to make that happen."

"But they're just *animals*, we're human beings," Constance continued, shifting her eyes back to his.

"*Real* human beings have more regard for their fellow creatures. My good man, Michael here, shot that zebra and left him to rot just so he could hang his skin in his office and brag to his friends at some goddamned cocktail party about how he conquered the wild beasts of Africa." Forrest gave the MP-5 a sudden shove to emphasize his point.

Michael grunted.

"Didn't ya, Mike."

Michael grunted again. "Yes."

"That wasn't the act of an intelligent, classy human being, was it, Mikey? Wasn't very sportsmanlike, was it?" Forrest gave the weapon another shove.

"No."

Forrest stared ominously. "Now that I've made my point, let me make another. You've got five minutes," he glanced at his watch, "to get as far away as you can. Take whatever water you need and a little food."

Forrest looked into each of their eyes. "After that, all bets are off—safeties too," he added, lifting his weapon to clarify his message.

"How do we get back to Nairobi? You've destroyed our vehicles," Constance whined.

"A little walk will give you a chance to commune with nature—get close to the animals—let them get close to you. That's what you came here for wasn't it?"

"But..."

Forrest glanced at his watch, again. "Now you've got four minutes."

His stereo headphones drowned out the engine noise as the Zenair headed southeast along the Kenya/Tanzania border. Mick Jagger was at full grunt, his guttural sounds and pounding music driving the pilot's fingers and toes into rhythmic accompaniment on the rudder pedals and flight controls.

"Ohhhhh, whose to blame..." Forrest sang along to the Rolling Stones, thankful the prop noise prevented the wildebeest grazing below from hearing just how bad his voice was.

"That giiiiirrl's just insane..."

His voice stopped abruptly as he spotted three armed men, wearing civilian clothes, running for the cover of a grove of acacias, two of them carrying an elephant tusk between them. Forrest whipped the plane into a hard turn to the right as he strained to keep them in sight. They were running full out, he saw as he dove on them from an altitude of a thousand feet. They dropped the tusk and dug in hard, their pumping legs and flying heels kicking up the dust. The engine whined as the little plane picked up speed.

Forrest reached behind the passenger seat and pulled a plastic pail forward which he placed on the seat next to him. It was full of home-made flechettes he had fashioned from finishing nails with cotton balls glued to the heads. Stick and rudder movements duplicated his quarry's changes in course as they headed for the cover of the tree canopy a few hundred meters ahead.

"You Maasai guys sure can run," he commented as *Nineteenth Nervous Breakdown* faded in his headset. "Well this oughtta let the air outta your tires."

At one hundred feet and maximum airspeed, Forrest pulled back on the stick and poured the contents of the bucket out the left door. Five hundred darts weather-vaned into the wind as their cotton tails spread like dandelion seeds on a summer breeze and zipped toward the ground.

The trailing man couldn't help himself. He turned his head to locate the marauding plane just as the first steel dart buried itself in his right eyeball, followed closely by five others which penetrated various parts of his anatomy. While none of the wounds were fatal, he fell flat on his face in a cloud of dust, writhing in agony.

The leaders ducked sharply as Forrest snapped the plane into a hard turn just above their heads and pulled for the sky. He looked back over his shoulder to see them veer and run hard for the trees leaving their companion behind. By the time he had the little dive-bomber turned around the poachers had ducked under their sheltering limbs and disappeared from sight.

As Forrest throttled back at the top of his climb, a new rhythm began in his headset: the intro to the Rolling Stones' *Sympathy for the Devil.*

Please allow me to introduce myself...
I'm a man of wealth and taste...
I've been around for a long, long year...
Sold many a man's soul to fate...

Forrest leveled the Zenair off and started an orbit to see if he could locate their hiding place. It didn't really much matter, he decided. It's hard to hide from fire in a bale of hay. He reached into the small compartment behind his seat and produced two Mason jars half filled with gasoline. Resting securely beneath their metal caps sat two M-67 fragmentation grenades, their pins pulled. The glass sides of their containers held their safety handles in place. Forrest squeezed the first device between his thighs as he reached for a second which he held in his left hand while he flew with his right.

Pleased to meet you...
Won't you guess my name...
But what's puzzling you...
Is the nature of my game...

He put the plane into a shallow dive then banked it to the left to orbit the cluster of trees. At just the right moment, he flung the first jar at the ground followed a few seconds later by the second.

I rode a tank...
In a general's rank...
When the blitzkrieg raged...
And the bodies stank...

He watched the first glittering orb disappear into the tree canopy followed by the second. A few seconds later, a bright flash was followed by an expanding fireball cloaked in thick black smoke. He heard the dull thump of the explosion through the music and then another. Paper-dry brush ignited at the first hint of heat, hungry flames expanding rapidly through the brush and dry leaves.

In seconds the entire cluster had become a giant torch.

Just as every cop's a criminal...
And all the sinners - saints...

Forrest pulled up and widened the circle. His eyes scanned the ground for...*there*!

One of the men, his clothes and skin ablaze, ran from the inferno and fell into a blazing heap, lighting off three small grass fires.

Forrest orbited for a few minutes before turning to the southeast, toward Amboseli. The other man never reappeared.

Pleased to meet you...
Won't you guess my name...
But what's puzzling you...
Is the nature of my game...

* * * *

Cynthia Marsh and Diane Chernik returned to their camp in a good mood. One of their young elephants' mothers had just given birth to a healthy young male and everyone was doing well. So often burdened by tragedy, their spirits welcomed a little good news.

"I think this calls for a celebration, don't you?" Cynthia asked as they walked toward their tents.

Diane, a great lover of the vine's fruits, responded without hesitation. "Definitely!" She split off to walk to her tent as Cynthia headed toward the camp kitchen.

Marsh noticed something lying on the picnic table and changed course to investigate. It was a hat, she saw as she drew nearer—a man's hat. Somehow, it looked vaguely familiar. But it was a just a safari hat, not at all uncommon in East Africa. Her curiosity piqued, she picked it up uncovering a large fold of Kenyan shillings carefully wrapped in a rubber band. Also tucked under the band was a piece of paper upon which, she saw after unfolding it, there was a handwritten note:

A CONTRIBUTION FOR THE CAUSE

Just then, Diane Chernik walked up with a dark-green bottle and two goblets. She noticed the perplexed look on Cynthia's face. "What's up?" she inquired, setting the wine bottle down on the table. Then she noticed the money. "What's this?" she asked with a note of astonishment.

Cynthia shrugged and looked at Diane, handing her the note. "Their must be twenty-thousand shillings in this wad."

"My Lord!" Chernik gasped. "From whom?"

"Don't know," Marsh replied, as perplexed as her colleague. She turned the hat over to examine its interior where she noticed a name penned beneath the crown: MORGAN RICHARDS. She looked up at Diane who was thumbing the heavy fold of bills. "Are you ready for this?"

CHAPTER-EIGHTEEN

REVELATIONS *a: acts of revealing or disclosure*
b: things revealed not before realized

"I THOUGHT THAT name sounded familiar," Police Commissioner Afande went on. "And when my investigator brought me his file I remembered why." Afande lifted his eyes, looking right through Windridge in a far-off stare.

Windridge waited for the Commissioner to collect his thoughts.

"He visited me some weeks ago; he and another American. Quite disrespectful, actually. His son and daughter-in-law were murdered in Tsavo by poachers, it would seem."

Windridge sat back at this bit of news. "That so?" he asked feigning ignorance but curious to know what Afande knew and more importantly what he didn't. "May I see the file?"

Afande handed it over hesitantly. After all, controlling such information was his source of power and he was instinctively reluctant to allow access to others.

Windridge scanned the pages quickly, as if the Commissioner

might change his mind at any moment. It suddenly occurred to him that he hadn't seen any of the KWS paperwork on Forrest, something he would remedy straight away.

While Windridge read on, Afande pulled another folder from his top desk drawer and flipped through the contents. "Your man Forrest was an airline pilot for several years," he announced. "It would seem that his airline went bankrupt last year, as well. Just about the same time his son and daughter-in-law were murdered. Rather bad luck, I'd say."

Windridge, intrigued by the new information, lowered his file and listened. Realizing that there was *another* file—one he apparently wasn't privileged to see—he felt a twinge of anger.

"This is somewhat confusing," Afande said, thinking aloud as he scanned the document. "The background check mentions service in the U.S. Army. But...oh, I see. He joined the Army first, then went to college before joining the U.S. Air Force."

"What did he do?"

"Hmm?"

"In the Army."

"It doesn't say, specifically. But it does mention being assigned to a Ranger battalion in Vietnam."

Windridge gave the Commissioner a blank look. He was unfamiliar with American military organizations. "Ranger?"

"Some sort of special forces unit, I believe. Similar to your British SAS."

"Hmm." Windridge's mind reeled. His men had often said that whoever this "Baba Tembo" was, he was a skilled soldier. "Special Forces, indeed," he repeated in a voice burdened with thought. Some things were beginning to make sense.

As it turned out, the satellite imagery Henderson had downlinked to him was well worth the wait. Two nights later, an overflight using the Cessna's FLIR system gave Forrest an idea how many people he could expect to encounter when he entered the camp. It also gave him a better idea as to the camp's layout. High altitude daylight photography yielded more details as to buildings, topography, roads, fences and other essential elements of information.

Three days later, with these photos in his back pack along with a few day's provisions, Forrest hid the Zenair at the edge of a clearing and set out through the woodlands covering the hills which straddled the Kenya-Tanzania border southeast of Mount Kilimanjaro. He elected to leave his rifle hidden near the plane, instead substituting his H&K MP-5SD submachine-gun and Canon EOS 35mm camera upgraded with a Canon EF 300mm USM super-telephoto lens. This would be a reconnaissance probe and he would use his MP-5 only in self-defense. In any case, judging from the size of Shetani's camp and the number of vehicles he saw in the satellite photos, there would be too many men to take on by himself—even at long range.

Forrest scanned its layout through his binoculars making note of every building, every vehicle and every person who came into view. He spent the next few hours alternately scanning, photographing and sketching the camp's layout on a steno pad. The camp had a permanent look to it—more like a small village. He counted five huts complete with thatched roofs and stick walls. On the opposite end of the camp, Forrest spotted two tanker trucks which appeared to be the type used to transport gasoline. One was attended by a crew of four men who looked to be loading pieces of ivory into the...tank? Could that be? He adjusted the focus knob for a better look. What would have been the tank's aft bulkhead was folded up like a hatch, hinged at the top revealing an inner chamber two-thirds the size of the outer tank. His camera clicked quietly as he snapped a few frames. Minutes later Forrest finished filming as the men completed their loading, lowered the hatch and bolted it into place.

Son of a bitch! A secret compartment!

Forrest set the camera down and made a note of the truck's tag number then rolled over to take a drink of water. "Wonder where that stuff's going?" he asked the trees. "Sure would be nice to go after the end-users."

After a moment he rolled back to the prone position and continued his reconnaissance. The field glasses revealed a small stream meandering through the camp from north to south running parallel to a narrow dirt road. A shrieking monkey brought his binoculars back to the near end of the camp where there stood clusters of boxes...no...cages, he saw after a moment...constructed of wire and wood. Though he was too far away to see exactly what they contained, he could make out dozens of birds, monkeys and other small animals including a pen for highly endangered leopard tortoises.

"You bastards've just about cornered the whole illegal wildlife market, here," Forrest muttered to himself. "When I'm finished with you, *you'll* be the ones calling the SPCA...Society for the Prevention of Cruelty to Assholes."

Forrest studied the huts through the binoculars. *Wonder where they keep Amy? I wonder if she's still here or even alive.* He released a frustrated sigh and dismissed thoughts he didn't want to think.

As Forrest surveyed the camp looking for Shetani, he thought he heard an odd sound. He lowered his binoculars and cocked his head to listen. The hills could play tricks on you—collecting sound in one place and projecting it to another. It was more like a pulsing throb. But what...a helicopter! Suddenly, he could hear the distinct clatter of its blades as it rounded a nearby hill.

A familiar figure emerged from one of the huts and gazed skyward. "'Bout time you showed up," Forrest whispered to the tall, lean man with a black safari hat.

The sound of the helicopter shifted—changing direction—instead of fading in the distance as Forrest expected.

It's circling the camp! He looked up to catch a glimpse of it through the branches.

Could this be a raid?

His eyes went back to Mpika who, judging from his body-language, appeared to be completely unfazed. The wiry man, whose skin was as black as his hat, folded his arms across his chest and leaned back against his hut, lighting a cigarette. "Well, if it is, he sure as hell isn't worried."

Forrest heard the chopper slow as it moved toward the clearing then settled to the ground amidst a cloud of dust and blowing debris. He watched Mpika grab the brim of his hat and lower his head against the windstorm. A second later the blade noise abated leaving only the high-pitched whine of a turbine. Forrest watched as Mpika sauntered over to the machine as casually as you please—just like he was expecting them.

Forrest shifted the binoculars to the helicopter—a Bell JetRanger—with... *Hmm*! Kenyan fin-flash on the side of the fuselage, Forrest saw, next to its registration number. The figure in the observer's seat hung his headset before emerging into the sunlight. Forrest sucked a breath and held it, his fingers frantically working the focus knob. "You gotta be shitting me!" he exclaimed in a hoarse whisper, momentarily forgetting himself when he saw the face.

Shetani limped into Forrest's field of view, transferring his cigarette to his left hand before shaking the passenger's hand with his right. Forrest dropped the binoculars, quickly focused the camera then snapped off a few shots. "Does your wife know where you are?"

The shutter clunked as Forrest repeatedly focused and fired. The man removed his baseball hat revealing a shock of pure white hair capping a thin angular face. Allen Windridge wiped his brow with a handkerchief then stuffed it into a rear pocket while carrying on an animated conversation with The Serpent. "What is the Director of the Kenya Wildlife Service doing in Tanzania chit-chatting with its most notorious poacher like they're members of the same cricket club?" he muttered.

Forrest lowered the camera and checked to see how much film remained. Satisfied that he had a few more shots on the roll, he brought it back up to his eye and twisted the focus ring just in time to see something emerge from Mpika's pocket—a small object about the size of a pack of cigarettes. Forrest couldn't quite make out what it was until a small gust from the whirling blades blew several pieces of paper onto the ground just as the object was changing hands. Judging from the way both men lunged to capture them and their familiar shape... "*Money. A whole wad of it.*"

Forrest's fingers flew over the shutter release and cocking lever.

Suddenly the whole encounter made sense. "Well now—isn't this a Kodak moment."

"What would *you* do?" Forrest asked, chewing his steak gingerly, trying not to burn his tongue on the sizzling hot beef.

Grizzly Adams leaned across the table, bracing himself on his elbows, his utensils poised in either hand. "You say the guy's the *head* of the goddamn wildlife department?" he whispered, looking around the landmark restaurant to see if anyone reacted to his question. Like themselves, the Carnivore's other diners were too busy enjoying the vast selection of exotic meats to notice a pair of Western tourists among many.

Forrest nodded, sawing off another hunk of his rib-eye steak. He was much too finicky a diner to try any of the dozens of exotic meats featured on the menu.

"I'd turn the sonofabitch in, then," Adams concluded before settling back into his chair, chewing a mouthful of ostrich.

Forrest shook his head emphatically as his eyes came up from his plate. "Can't."

"Why?" Adams asked incredulously, waiting for Forrest to finish chewing.

"It's more complicated than that," Forrest said with his mouth still half full.

Adams raised his eyebrows. "What's so complicated about turning a corrupt government official into the police? You caught him red handed and you've got it all on film! What more do you need?"

Forrest regarded him for a moment then went back to his plate. "Like I said, it's more complicated than that. There are political considerations for starters. And, two; I've gotta get Amy outta there first—make sure she's safe." He pushed his vegetables around with his knife then inserted a forkful into his mouth. As he chewed, he glanced around to ensure no one was listening to their conversation.

"When have *you* ever worried about politics?" Adams laughed, sipping his beer. "The Thumper I know always does things balls out; the 'kill everybody-let God sort 'em out approach.'" Adams stifled a belch then set his glass down on the table. A knowing smile clung to his face as he studied Forrest for a moment. He sensed his friend was being a tad evasive. But, Adams remembered, that was typical behavior for a man who, for months, hadn't told even his best friends he had split up with his wife of twelve years. Forrest's clam was especially tight when it came to women.

"Wait a minute...I smell a woman here." Grizz squinted his eyes, looking at the man who sat across the table from him, enjoying his first good meal in a week.

Forrest looked up, took a sip of his beer, then cut himself another bite of steak. He deliberately ignored his friend's gambit, his eyes glued to his plate.

"That's it," Adams laughed. "I knew it!" he slapped the table hard enough to draw looks. Adams lowered his head and whispered. "Who is it?" A "caught-your-buddy-doing-something-embarrassing" grin clung to his large round face.

Forrest swallowed before answering. "Who said anything about a woman?" he asked evenly.

Adams wasn't buying it though he knew his friend didn't have a lot of patience with the opposite sex. "Alright. If it's not a woman then what is it?"

Forrest looked at him.

Adams smiled. "Well..."

Forrest put his fork down and wiped his mouth. He took his time answering. "First, I can't just go turning in a government official. Most of 'em are just as corrupt as he is and you can't tell who's who without a scorecard. Second, if I approach anybody, they'll know who I am and what I'm about. I can't risk that—can't trust *anybody.* I can't even tell his wife!"

"Why not? From what you tell me, it would be a good payback for the *both* of 'em."

Forrest closed his eyes and shook his head. "No way." He started counting reasons on his fingers. "A: she'd want to know *how* I know, B: she'd never believe me, C: if she did believe me, she's just the type to confront her husband which could be hazardous to her health, Amy's health and my operation." Forrest sighed, clearly vexed by the new developments.

Adams nodded thoughtfully.

"And...where was I? Oh yeah." He held up three more fingers of his left hand touching the middle one with the index finger of his right. "D: I can't risk having word get back to Windridge. If he doesn't have me arrested he might try to have me knocked off... which is what I would do if I were him. They do that sort of thing in this part of the world, in case you hadn't heard. E: he might even hurt Doc McCullen—maybe figure he's in on it somehow," a thought which had just occurred to him. "Finally, if I turn him in it'll disgrace his wife—people would naturally think his wife at least *knew* about it and they might even think she was an accomplice." Forrest guzzled more of his beer. "She might be something of a bitch but she deserves better than that," he added under his breath.

Adams smiled. "See. I knew it. A woman."

Forrest glared at him.

"Thought you swore off on women, man!"

Forrest rolled his linen napkin up in a ball and plopped it on the table. "I don't remember swearing off dessert," he replied, changing the subject. He raised his hand to summon their waiter who was dressed in black slacks and a crisp, white shirt with black bowtie. A wide-brimmed straw hat accented his full-length blue-and-white striped bib apron. The men asked for a pair of dessert menus then ordered, finishing their beers while the bus-boy cleared the table. After he departed, Forrest leaned forward and gave Adams two canisters of undeveloped 35mm film. "Get this to Peeper as soon as you get back to the States. Have him keep the negatives and a set of prints in a safe place. Tell him to include two sets of prints in my next air drop. They'll come in handy when I get set to take out the camp."

Adams nodded as he jammed the film deep into his pants pockets.

"One more thing," Forrest added. "The scumbag we're targeting uses a couple of old gas trucks to smuggle ivory and rhino horn out of his camp. I want to know where they go and what route they take. I could follow them in the airplane but they might spot me and worse, it would take longer than my fuel would allow. Ask him if there's any way his technical people can come up with a couple of satellite transponders—small jobs like the ones the researchers use to track large animals. We can use 'em to track the trucks to their final destination."

Adams scribbled some notes on a cocktail napkin as a waiter went by hefting a huge hunk of glistening brown meet skewered on a traditional Masai sword.

"Oh, another thing. Tell Peeper to get me some intel on the assholes who buy that stuff. I need to know who the dealers are, where they store it and ship it and how? You know what I mean."

"I thought you just wanted to get the guys who fucked with the kids and get out," Adams commented with some surprise.

Forrest looked at him as the waiter arrived with their Carnivore Cheesecakes, the restaurant's most popular dessert. "I do." He waited for the waiter to leave then continued. "But like I said, the problem's a lot more complicated and a lot bigger than I thought." He looked around and lowered his voice. "I'll get the guys who did Nathan soon enough. Now that I know who they are and where they live and where Amy is—*hope* Amy is, he corrected—their asses are mine. In the meantime, I want some good to come out of this operation. In this case collateral damage is a *good* thing."

"You might be biting off more than you can chew," Adams warned as his second forkful melted in his mouth.

"Maybe." Forrest shrugged. "But this has become more than just some pissed-off father out to avenge his son and rescue his daughter-in-law."

Adams watched their table's candlelight dance in Forrest's eyes. It was hard to tell if the fire was inside or out.

"Oh, we'll have our revenge, Peeper and I," Forrest continued. "I swear we will. But it won't end there. It can't. Revenge may be sweet, my friend. But simple revenge is no longer enough."

Forrest stopped for a moment to listen, the sound of an engine in the distance his center of focus. He gently set one foot down after the other, creeping ahead through the brush. Peeper had told him there was a large gathering of elephants in the area, very close to a camp which had all the earmarks of a poacher's camp. And although he had already located the poachers who had killed Nathan and made an example of a high-profile profiteer, he couldn't resist Cynthia Marsh's unspoken cry for help—the call to save Africa's most noble children from her most gifted. This last mission would be just for them—something to do until he had all of the logistics in place to take on Shetani's camp.

Coming to the edge of the brush dashed his hopes. His enthusiasm settled to its knees along with his tired frame. Two hundred meters ahead, Forrest could see the tops of men's heads and the top of their pickup truck protruding above an expanse of dry grass which stretched before him like a field of summer wheat, the gray domes of two dead elephant carcasses looming nearby. His stomach soured with disgust as he counted targets and assessed potential shooting positions.

A lone umbrella acacia stood fifty meters ahead and to his left, its canopy hovering over swaying stalks of golden straw. A last-resort position, he thought glumly as he lowered his equipment to the ground. It might work. But it would be a dangerous gambit. "So what's new?" he asked himself as he extracted his rifle, climbing rope, and a pair of Claymore mines. Fifteen minutes later, after backtracking along the animal path which had brought him to the clearing, Forrest made his way through the waist-high finger grasses toward the lone acacia then pulled himself up into its waiting arms. After catching his breath and making himself as steady as he could, he brought the ERMA's muzzle to bear on the busy butchers.

Five of them, he counted. Two hundred yards—maybe two-fifty. Within range of their AKs, he reminded himself; a thought which suddenly made the ten-inch limbs on which he rested seem as flimsy as willow boughs. "It'll have to do," he muttered to himself as he selected his first target and pulled the rifle into his shoulder.

One man brandished a Kalashnikov, Forrest saw as he studied the men through his scope. The others were preoccupied with the task of chopping away an elephant's face to get at the base of its tusks. After five minutes of twisting, prying, and cutting, the first length of ivory came free. Forrest saw two men move to either end of the tusk, drop to their knees and prepare to lift—a prelude to opportunity. His eye followed the two men as they lifted opposite ends of the big tusk and carried it toward the open tailgate. His fingertip compressed against the machined grooves of the trigger as he anticipated their movements. Like a machine programmed for the most efficient kill, Forrest waited for just the right moment. In a multi-target environment the first shot was the most important. As the man carrying the base of the tusk began to circle the man holding the tip, Forrest realized that, for an instant, they would line up as they maneuvered their heavy load into the truck. As the edge of the closest man's shoulder touched the outline of the furthest man, Forrest pulled the trigger. The bullet parted the air, reaching the center of the near man's back just as his body came into alignment with his partner's. It plowed through his torso, burst through his chest and plunged into his partner's neck. The blood-splattered length of ivory dropped to the ground a split-second before its crumbling supporters.

Instantly, the others scrambled for cover. The top of a man's head appeared behind the steel sidewall of the pickup. Magnified by the optics, the man's dusty boots were plainly visible just below the truck's bottom.

"You've got a lot of faith in Japanese steel don't ya, asshole." Forrest moved the crosshairs to the near wall of the truck bed and aligned them with a spot halfway between the man's head and his boots. The rifle recoiled as it sent another .338 projectile on a ballistic arc. In the blink of an eye, the bullet cut through the sides of the truck before boring into flesh.

"That's three," he whispered to himself, already looking for his next target. Forrest knew it would be just a mater of minutes until they spotted his position. By then, he hoped, it would be too late.

Forrest moved the scope rapidly, trying to locate the other two men. Thirty seconds' search proved fruitless. They had disappeared into the high grass. His hands tingled at the thought. Quickly, he jerked the scope around hoping to spot movement in the grass.

Nothing.

Not good.

He lowered his trigger hand to feel for the rope as he continued the search. Opposing parts of his brain debated his options—bail out or stay put. Forrest safed the rifle and took a strain on the rope just as the first rounds cut into the surrounding wood, showering him with leaves and splintered bark. He froze. A long second burst exploded the wood near his head, filling his eyes with grit.

"Huuhh!" A round ripped into his side, knocking the wind out him. He momentarily lost his grip and struggled to keep himself from falling. His rifle tumbled out his hands and fell into the grass. Sharp pain shot through his body as he tried to take a breath. His right side was on fire. Mustering all of his reserve strength, Forrest slid awkwardly down the rope and dropped into the grass. He gnashed his teeth as he sucked in short, searing breaths. He felt himself losing consciousness when an exalted shout brought him back.

They're coming! Move or die, his brain screamed.

Forrest rose to all fours and pointed himself at the thorny cover. Grass rustling behind him urged him ahead. He stumbled as he ran, staggering from side to side, grass crashing under his leaden feet. A burst whizzed over his head, clearing his vision for a moment. He spotted the path just twenty meters ahead.

"Gotta make it," he huffed. "Gotta make it!"

Another shout from behind. He dared not look.

Keep going, man!

Forrest zigged to his right, falling on his face near his gear. Bullets cracked through the air just above his head as he winced, breathed, and stumbled on. Another burst. Branches exploded all around him as he rounded another corner, searching frantically for... *there*!

He sucked in an excruciating breath and leaped over the almost invisible strand of trip wire. Pain exploded through his body as his feet slammed into the ground, wobbly legs sending him around yet another corner. His vision grew fuzzy with exhaustion.

Forrest cut right and threw himself under a bush. Thorns dug into his shoulders as he pulled himself into a ball. Tears rolled down his cheeks with each vicious lung-full of air. He tensed and strained to listen over his own wheezing.

He heard voices then flinched with the sound of a sharp concussion.

Claymore.

Forrest froze for what seemed like an hour, his breathing finally giving way to the sound of his pounding heart. His throat burned, his lungs ached, and his rib cage felt as if someone were tightening a coil of barbed wire around it. He took a long breath, grit his teeth and passed out.

"He's probably kickin' back right about now. Waitin' for me to arrive and show him how it's done." Frank Zito speared his sly grin with the soggy butt of his trademark cigar. Yellowed teeth clamped down, preventing its escape.

"I don't know 'bout that, Zit," Henderson countered warily. "He contacted me just 2 days ago for more target intel." Henderson set his beer down on the wooden table with an authoritative clunk.

"When's he want me?"

"As soon as you can get there. When might that be?" It sounded more urgent than he would have liked under other less personal circumstances.

Zito removed the cigar and set it on the table next to his mug. Henderson looked at it as if it were a dead rat. Zito lifted his mug, hesitating with a thought. "Two weeks, yet. I've got some leave comin'. But, I've got a class about to graduate." Zito took a long pull from his mug, wiped his mustache with the back of his hand then reinserted his cigar.

Two fucking weeks! Amy might not be alive in two weeks! She might not be alive now! Henderson's eyes said what he wouldn't. "Okay. I'll let Thumper know. He's counting on you."

"Not to worry, my man. Tell Thumper the cavalry's on its way."

Not soon enough for me.

* * * *

Forrest lay under the thorn bush for several minutes, trying to collect his wits, a process Forrest begun by replaying the attack in his mind. It suddenly occurred to him that his pursuers might still be out there—still searching for him in the dense thicket. His body tensed again at the thought. Yet everything seemed quiet, very quiet—only the rustling of leaves intruding on the anxious silence.

Forrest strained for sounds as his left hand moved to investigate his wound. Trembling fingers probed the damp warmth of his BDU shirt then jerked back as their pressure took his breath. He felt a tear in his shirt surrounded by a circle of slippery wetness. Extracting his fingers, he saw they were coated in a viscous, crimson basting. Forrest took as deep a breath as pain would allow. His lungs sounded clear—no telltale rumbling—no indication of internal bleeding. Additional probing, however unpleasant, revealed his wound to be superficial. The bullet hadn't penetrated the thoracic cavity. But, given the level of pain, it had cracked a rib. And cracked ribs could be life-threatening if splintered bone were to penetrate a lung.

The weary casualty lifted himself from the dirt, fighting back acute pain as he rose. After several minutes he made his way back to the spot where his boobytrap had finished the job he started almost an hour ago. Cut down by the waiting Claymore anti-personnel mine, the mutilated remains of the two poachers lay sprawled near the trail. Forrest hesitated there for a moment, reassuring himself that they were no longer a threat. At least, he reminded himself, he'd had the foresight to set up some security; a back-up plan that had likely saved his life.

For the next forty minutes, Forrest set about on rubbery legs gathering his equipment, alternately working, resting and recovering from bouts of severe pain.

I'm in no shape to walk back to the plane, he thought before remembering the poacher's vehicle. Driving it would be risky, he considered. He would certainly be a lot more visible. But after weighing the risks, he decided in favor of driving. An hour later, after a short but miserable ride, he took a last look at the abandoned Toyota as he pushed the Zenair's throttle full forward for takeoff.

It seemed as though he would never get there. The joystick wiggled a ghostly dance, driven by the autopilot servos. Pain and near exhaustion had long ago driven him to relinquish control and shove the Zenair's throttle to the firewall, lashing the engine's eighty-five horses with a taste of the whip.

Forrest nodded off several times only to be prodded awake by the raging fire burning in his side. Through hooded eyelids, he noticed the hundreds of wildebeests grazing below. The ponderous creatures seemed to be moving across the ground faster than his plane. He caught himself looking at the airspeed indicator obsessively, willing its needle further around the dial.

"Come on baby, just a few more knots," he gasped through clenched teeth.

Lake Magadi appeared ahead through the haze. It lay just below the horizon, alluring, soft and serene, like a waterbed; like heaven. His eyes found the dark smudge of fever trees marking the camp... then the runway. His right hand found the throttle, pulling it slowly back to idle. The engine seemed to sputter a sigh of relief as it let gravity do some of the work of maintaining airspeed. Without being fully aware of it, Forrest's hands took control of the plane, relieving the faithful autopilot, guiding the little craft onto the short brown scar in the grass it called home.

Lacerated muscles and protesting ribs screamed at him as he gingerly applied the brakes, bringing the bird to a dusty stop at the end of the strip. Fingers operating completely on habit somehow found the mixture...the mags...the master…the door latch...then his lap belt. Forrest tried to lift himself out of the seat but found he didn't have the strength. He sat back, closed his eyes, and heaved an excruciating sigh.

"John...John. Are you alright?" It was Joseph's soothing voice, clouded with concern. He and his oldest kids had jogged to the strip when they heard the approaching plane. "Are you hurt?"

Forrest's eyes opened a crack.

Joseph's welcome face wore a troubled scowl. His eyes darted over Forrest's desert-color BDUs stopping at the blood.

There was no hiding it, now, Forrest thought as the camp boss took off to find help leaving his children to stare at the strange camouflaged face which looked more like a frog's. They would *all* know. They would finally know the truth. He took another painful breath and passed out.

Something cold and wet slid over Forrest's face stirring him awake. His eyes opened to see an unwelcome face, however pretty. And he especially didn't like the look he got in return. He tried to sit up but a piercing pain pulled his head back to his pillow. His eyes darted around the room—his room, taking note of his gear: his back pack, his rifle wrapped in camouflaged burlap, his blood-stained BDUs. His eyes came back to Anne's. They burned right through him.

He heard a noise—footsteps—and turned his head to locate their source. Doc McCullen entered his bedroom, his grave look giving way to a smile when he saw Forrest was awake.

"So. When are you planning to turn me in?" Forrest asked matter-of-factly, as if it somehow didn't matter anymore.

Anne Sargent set her water bowl and washcloth on the floor then rose from her chair.

"Ah, lad. Don't you be worryin' 'bout..."

Anne cut McCullen off with a look then faced Forrest. "As soon as you're well enough to ride to Nairobi," she declared with an acidity he hadn't heard in a while. Abruptly, she walked out of the hut to get fresh water.

Forrest's eyes searched McCullen's for concurrence. The old man blanched. His eyes lowered, shoulders shrugged. What could he do?

"What in God's name put'ya up to it, lad?" McCullen asked, walking to the side of Forrest's cot and taking a seat in the chair.

"They killed my son—and they're holding my daughter-in-law if she's still alive."

"What?" McCullen gasped. "Who?"

"Poachers."

"Where?"

"Tsavo...last year."

"Dear God, lad. Those were *your* kids?" His eyes went even wider.

"My son and his new bride."

"What were they doin' down there?" McCullen asked, leaning closer, his eyes fully dilated behind his thick glasses. He sat spellbound for the next few minutes as Forrest related the unabridged version of the story, minus the involvement of Colonel Grant, the CIA and his Army buddies.

"I'm so sorry, laddy. I didn't know."

"You weren't supposed to know."

"If Anne knew all the facts I'm sure she'd have a change of heart."

Forrest shook his head. "She knows too much already."

McCullen sighed.

"Doc. I want your word on that."

McCullen looked at him and changed the subject. "Do'ya think you can sit up? I need'ta change your dressin' 'n tape your ribs."

Forrest sat on the edge of his cot, his feet on the floor. For the first time he noticed the bandage taped to his right side. "When did you put that on?"

"I didn't."

Forrest looked at him, incredulously.

"Anne did."

Forrest's eyes narrowed. It was then that he noticed he was in his underwear, a pair of BVDs and a T-shirt—a *clean* set. "You let her?"

"I'm afraid there's no *lettin'* that woman, lad. She does what she wants. Besides, it took her and Joseph, both, to move you. You ain't as light as'ya look."

"And she ain't as shy as *she* looks," Forrest muttered.

McCullen eased the bandage off and examined the wound.

"What's the story?" Forrest grumbled.

"I think you'll live." He probed the edges of the wound with his fingers then applied a generous portion of antiseptic gel. "It's a flesh wound. And the bullet cracked a rib. On palpitation there was no crepitus. So I just put a few stitches in the gash. Not a pretty job, mind ya, but you should heal up nicely, I think."

After applying a new bandage, McCullen asked Forrest to lean forward slightly as he wrapped his torso with a length of rolled gauze. "Now for the tricky part," McCullen announced, producing a roll of wide adhesive tape.

"Take a breath and hold it. We need to make this tight."

Forrest did as he was told then braced himself as McCullen began the procedure.

"You're lucky...that rib, not to mention that bloody bullet, didn't puncture your lung, lad," McCullen observed, his speech intermittently broken by grunts of exertion. "You almost landed yourself in the hospital."

"Ugh!...and forego the pleasure of your...yeow! God*damm*it, Doc", Forrest gasped. "...of your state-of-the-art...medical treatment."

McCullen chuckled. "It's the least I can do for you after all you've done." McCullen's attention remained fixed on his work as he snipped off the nearly empty spool. "How many do you suppose you've killed?" The doctor smoothed the end of the white tape into the rest of the wrappings then stood for a moment, assessing his work. He shared a confused look with his patient. "Those murderin' bastard poachers, I mean."

"I don't know for sure, Doc—two or three dozen—maybe more. I wasn't keeping score."

"Well lad, whatever the count, it's not enough. If I was a tougher man—a younger man—I'd like to kill a few of the mothers myself."

Forrest smiled at McCullen fondly. "You're tough enough, Doc. You're just not *mean* enough."

McCullen nodded at the left-handed compliment. "The police couldn't help you?"

"We tried that. They're a waste of gravity. Feckless government bureaucrats won't do anything about it."

McCullen smiled sympathetically.

Anne Sargent strode into the hut. She had been standing on the porch for a moment, listening. Her glare burned into him. "We 'feckless bureaucrats' may not be able to stop all the poaching but at least we don't stoop to breaking the law. And we bloody well don't stoop to murder!"

Forrest retreated for a moment and then responded in a quiet, even tone—his voice almost a whisper, "I don't see it as murder, exactly. I prefer to characterize it as justice served."

Anne folded her arms across her chest. "Well, I assure you the court will see it somewhat differently."

Forrest rolled his eyes and looked at his backpack. "Well, your royal high-ass, I think there's maybe something *you* need to see differently." He glanced at McCullen who raised an eyebrow. "When you march your little high-and-mighty ass into police headquarters there's something you should take with you. In my backpack there's a manila envelope. Get it."

She looked at him with a mixture of defiance and curiosity.

"Go on. Get it."

Anne went to the pack and fumbled through its contents before extracting the requested article. She held it up for Forrest to see.

"That's it." Forrest gave the envelope a nod. "Open it."

She did as she was instructed, her fingers flipping through the two-dozen 8 x 10 color photos expertly blown up and enhanced at CIA. Her eyes tracked over the glossy surfaces, examining each detail. Her brow wrinkled, her breathing all but ceasing as she absorbed the significance of what she saw.

McCullen looked at Forrest, a puzzled expression glued to his face.

"In case you don't recognize the guy taking money from the Serpent, it's your darling husband."

Anne refused to look up.

"The dirtbag *paying* the bribe is his good pal, Mpika—Shetani—the worst low-life, poacher in East Africa. His mug shot's in your book, if you recall."

McCullen's mouth dropped open. He sank down on the end of Forrest's cot. Two shocks in twenty-four hours were two too many.

"The police should have their hands full, don't you think?" Forrest asked, rhetorically. "Unless *they're* in on it, too. In this shit-hole of a country when you say government corruption you're being redundant."

Anne shoved the photos back into their envelope without looking up, a thousand thoughts flashing through her mind. She shot a look at Forrest then at McCullen whose mouth snapped shut in advance of a dry swallow. She spun about, tucked the envelope under her arm and stormed out, leaving a ringing silence in her wake.

Anne Sargent waited in a side chair positioned next to the branch manager's oversized mahogany desk. Her legs crossed at the knee, she impatiently bounced her foot as she looked at her watch. Allen would be home in less than an hour, she reminded herself. And his records which, at the moment, lay next to the manager's computer terminal, needed to be returned to his desk drawer well before then.

Anne watched as the computer screen reflected in the distinguished looking woman's large round eyeglasses, the image flickering as she paged through the file. Mrs. Maple, a long time acquaintance, was sixty-ish, barely wrinkled, and well maintained. Her dark blue suit was as impeccable as it was conservative. Although she was pleasant enough, her demeanor was always stoic and serious—all business. As it should be, Anne mused, for someone you trusted with your life's savings.

"Hmm. I see several accounts." Mrs. Maple poked her finger at the screen in a descending fashion. "I count six," she intoned in a most dignified British accent. The bank was old-world ornate; marble and mahogany abounded. A computer monitor seemed an anachronism in such a formal office constructed during a time when the British Empire spanned the globe.

Six! Anne felt a pang of anxiety as she pressed her investigation, hoping it didn't show. "Mmm? Oh yes. We seem to have misplaced our most recent statements. Could I please have the balances?" she stammered, all the while hoping that her husband would not have taken precautions to prevent such snooping.

"Very well, but it might take a moment."

They exchanged polite smiles as Mrs. Maple tilted her head back and peered at the keyboard through her bifocals. Slow but deft fingers pecked away as Anne's heart raced—ten beats per keystroke. Finally, the branch manager began dictating while Anne scribbled account numbers and balances onto a note-pad.

"Oh, by the way," the woman commented in a rather sympathetic voice, "my condolences on the death of your aunt."

Anne's frown betrayed her confusion. For a second she stared blankly at the woman who, fortunately, was too thoroughly engrossed in her task to accurately interpret her expression.

"Your husband told me how much you thought of her. She must have shared your feelings," she offered with a knowing smile as she handed Anne a slip of paper showing a six-digit figure next to an unfamiliar account number.

"Mmm...Yes," Anne agreed with a nervous chuckle, though both of her parents had been only children. She didn't *have* any aunts—none that she knew of, anyway. "We were very close," Anne lied then grew quiet, her heart rate doubling as she considered the implications. She did some quick arithmetic to discover the accounts totaled nearly two-hundred-thousand pounds! *My God, all this money! And why would he have it all in joint accounts unless...unless he did it to help hide it, or...implicate me if it were discovered.* Anne took a long quivering breath, held it, then let it out slowly.

"Mrs. Maple." *Should I or shouldn't I? Should I or shouldn't I?*

"Yes?" the woman answered with a flat smile that made Anne more nervous than she already was.

"I'd like to have you cut a check for one hundred fifty thousand pounds." Anne scribbled her sister's full name on her slip of paper and turned it around so Mrs. Maple could read it. "Make it out to her, please," she added with a note of confidence she only wished she felt.

The branch manager dutifully went back to the keyboard and began transferring the appropriate amounts into one account.

Anne's thoughts ricocheted in four different directions at once. John was right, she admitted to herself with the greatest reluctance. *There was no other explanation—none which reconciled with the facts. And that certainly explained the new car and some of the other extravagances.* Anne chastened herself to think that Allen had always been such a good money manager. *How stupid of me.*

Mrs. Maple rolled a blank draft into her typewriter then methodically pounded the keys, slowing down to carefully count the zeros.

Anne watched over her shoulder. She had never seen so much money—not on an instrument bearing her name, at least! She watched as Mrs. Maple rolled the completed form out of the typewriter and laid it on her desk for review.

Anne looked the check over then tucked it into her tiny purse. "Thank you ever so much for your assistance, Mrs. Maple," Anne said gratefully though nervously, rising to leave. She looked at her watch again and almost gasped. "Have a pleasant day," she said over her shoulder as she hurried off across the lobby, her heels echoing in the labyrinth building.

Once outside, Anne's fingers moved quickly, automatically starting her Land Rover's engine and jamming it into gear. She checked her watch as she waited for a wave of heavy traffic to pass, mentally calculating the driving time to the post office, the time waiting in line, and then the drive home. The decision came to a simple choice: do I turn left or right? Right would take her directly home with enough time to put the records back just as she had found them. Left would take her past the Nairobi post office but make getting home very tight, a thought she weighed against holding onto the check and maybe losing it—or losing her nerve. Anne took a deep breath and swallowed hard, reaching deep for the elusive answer. *Left or right?* A rude horn scolded her to get moving. She looked in the mirror, releasing the breath she didn't realize she'd been holding, waved her hand apologetically and pulled out into the street. With a blink of the directional signal, she turned.

Left.

A mounting pile of freshly turned earth grew on both sides of the hole as Amy dug furiously at the floor where it met the hut's stick wall. The hour before had been spent slicing through her wrist bindings using a broken piece of glass she'd found near the camp's crude outdoor latrine. Once her hands were free, the knots of her ankle rope had been simple to negotiate.

She was alone in the hut. Sarah and her husband had left her to go for supplies which they did every few weeks. That usually took several hours given the camp's distance from anything resembling civilization. The rest of the men were busy working on the tanker truck or tending to the creatures they'd captured for sale in the illegal pet trade.

The only guard remaining was one of Mpika's flunkies, an unmotivated idiot who, along with others like him, did most of the grunt work around the camp. He sat outside the hut, back against the sticks, chain smoking cigarettes and occasionally talking nonsense with some of the few women and children who wandered by. The only time he moved was when he had to urinate or follow the shade of the trees and the hut's roof around the wall, sort of like a human sundial. Predictably, around dusk, he would wind up on the far side, napping between attacks of the relentless flies.

In her escape-plan risk assessment Amy had been quite circumspect, a trait she inherited from her father. Prudently, despite the fact that the "sundial" probably had the IQ of a hamster, she had not underestimated the threat he represented. His sinister-looking assault rifle was never far away from his side. He wasn't so stupid that he didn't know how to pull a trigger. And being intellectually challenged made him more likely to be dispossessed of responsibility; hence, more prone to foolish temptations like an attractive, young, vulnerable female over whom he had absolute power when no one else was around. Apparently Sarah shared the same impression of the man as Amy. She had adamantly forbade the sundial to enter the hut for any reason—an instruction he apparently took very seriously. He was to guard the entrance—nothing more.

Amy dug as vigorously as her limited stamina and the blunt stick she was using would allow. Momentarily she would pause to listen and check the position of her guard's shadow where it blocked the penetration of sunlight between the sticks. Her tunnel was well over a foot deep and growing. If she heard a noise, she would quickly pull her sleeping mat over the excavation and lie on top of it, feigning a nap.

Two hours and two migrations of the sundial later, Amy's route to freedom was nearly complete. It was small. But, she judged, it would allow her to wriggle out beneath the wall and make a dash for the heavy cover surrounding the camp.

One more benefit, at least, of having starved myself for so long.

Before exiting, Amy crawled to the far side of the hut and gazed outside. Nothing seemed out of the norm. A long listen from behind her guard's position revealed long, heavy breathing—the rhythm of sleep.

Good!

As Amy started her head and arms through the trench her heart began to pound in her chest. She rolled onto her back to better judge the clearance from the bottoms of the sticks. This is when she knew she would be the most vulnerable—half in and half out, struggling to free herself from the confined space.

Getting through the opening took longer than she thought, adding to the anxiety. Finally, after a few more minutes' work, only her lower legs remained beneath the wall as she sat up and looked around before making a run for the brush.

Nobody around. Excellent!

Amy extracted her feet, brought them underneath her and started a crouched walk toward the shadows of the heavy vegetation, her head twisting rapidly from side to side scanning for people. The sound of someone calling out to a co-worker rang her alarm bells and she broke into an all-out sprint for cover which stood only a few meters ahead. She never looked back, focusing instead on the myriad branches and thorns impeding her progress.

As she plunged into the shadows a feeling of elation began to displace the burden of terror and dread. She actually began to feel lighter—a metaphysical buoyancy at the thought of freedom! With great agility she wove through the bushes, breaking their grip on her tattered clothes and tender skin. Her heart quickened with elation as she saw the brush thinning ahead, just before—*it*—stopped her blood pump cold in mid-beat.

Her gasp was deep and audible, loud enough she was sure it had been heard back in the camp.

Only 10 feet in front of her stood a dark ribbon of death. A young *Naja* had reared up with two-thirds of its four-foot length erect above the ground. It was drawn to the camp by the rodents subsisting off the byproducts of human activity, its favorite prey.

Both the human and the serpent were frozen in fear, both watching with the utmost intensity for the other's next move.

Amy's eyes shifted for microseconds looking for a way around the threat. Although she didn't know what sort of snake it was and at the moment couldn't have cared less, its long, narrow hood and olive-grey scales told her it was a deadly cobra. However, she had no way of knowing that this particular species had special defensive talents.

Another shout from a human behind her compounded her tension. Afraid of being overtaken, Amy lunged impulsively to her right, heading for another opening in the brush. At that instant the highly strung cobra fired a secret weapon evolved to keep it from being trampled by the large, hoofed animals which shared its habitat.

It spit. Venom. Reptilian mace.

And it did so with remarkable accuracy aimed at its target's eyes. Only the extreme range and Amy's sudden move degraded the result. Although the main stream missed her face, a droplet caught her in the left eye crippling her with intense, searing pain. Despite above-average self control, she couldn't help herself. She screamed in agony.

In seconds, Mpika, the sundial and other men from the camp host were upon her. In seconds, three shots rang out, killing the spitting cobra followed by two more shots ending the sundial's pathetic existence. In seconds, she was thrown over someone's shoulder and carried back to camp—back to prison.

Moments later she found herself writhing on the ground outside her hut having copious amounts of water flushed through her eyes and any hope of escape flushed from her heart.

Aberdeen Proving Ground is an old U.S. Army post situated about an hour's drive up Route 40 from downtown Baltimore. On any given day, area residents are treated to thunderous booms which carry for miles down Chesapeake Bay, a byproduct of the many weapons and explosives tested at the facility.

Henderson's white Chevy Celebrity took him past the mile or so of restored if obsolete tanks arranged in a permanent convoy along the grassy median of the post's four-lane main entrance road. He followed it past the golf course and the Ordnance Museum to an unremarkable white building, circa 1940, located a block east of the airfield. "Dr. Pyro," an old friend who had begun his career as a U.S. Army demolition expert, was waiting for him just inside. Now in his late forties, a wiry man with an ultra-close buzz cut and clear penetrating eyes, Ron Henry was the man to see if you wanted something to go boom in just the right way, at just the right time, with just the right results.

After exchanging the usual pleasantries and catching up on family, friends and politics, Henry offered Henderson coffee which he politely refused, explaining that he was already as wired as a pinball machine. The two men sat at a government-issue gray-topped table in Henry's shop office discussing the latest challenge to Dr. Pyro's unique talents.

"Basically, your operator's got a pretty good idea." Henry commented with a smile which fell somewhere between surprise and admiration. "Pretty kinky—even for me." Henry poured over the numerous sketches lying on the table between them. His eyes returned to a drawing of an elephant tusk, bored-out on the thick end to accommodate a two- to-four-foot length of three-quarter-inch copper water pipe. The pipe, like a manicotti noodle, would be stuffed with plastic explosive packed around a piece of copper wire running the length of its axis, like a coaxial cable. Both ends of the pipe would be capped-off with one end housing a timer, battery, capacitor and an initiator. Wired into the circuit would be a mercury switch similar to the ones used in older household thermostats. Once the timer armed the circuit after a few days had elapsed, motion would trigger the initiator, setting off a high-order detonation. Another version of the device, minus the mercury switch, would be triggered when a saw blade sliced through the ivory and the imbedded pipe. A steel ban-saw blade contacting both the pipe and the inner wire would complete the firing circuit setting off a powerful blast. Pretty simple and quite lethal, Henry saw at a glance.

"Very kinky," Dr. Pyro repeated. "This guy works for you, I take it?"

"Sort of," Henderson replied with a wry smile. "And I've heard him called lots'a things, but 'kinky' is a new one."

Henderson listened on the secure phone line with a rising tide of frustration and apprehension. "So when do you think you'll be able to do the grab?"

"Doc said a couple weeks," Forrest explained with a mixture of shame and a good measure of his own frustration. "When I can take half a breath without feeling like a steak knife is stuck in my side, I'll move."

"Okay."

Forrest could hear the despair in his best friend's voice. He felt a pang of guilt for attempting the extra mission before Amy was secure. "I'll do my best to assess her situation when I install the transponders you sent. We'll have her back at home real soon. I promise."

"I know you will. But it won't be soon enough for Marie and me."

"Sorry, pal. Just too many actors and too many guns to take on by myself. I'll try to do it sooner if you want to come and help." Forrest's offer was sincere.

"I can't. I was lucky to get away with what I've done so far. I'll never get away with visiting a foreign country. Especially now. The Company requires us to disclose all foreign travel," Henderson sighed. "Otherwise, you couldn't keep me from being there."

"I feel you, man. Don't worry. We'll handle it. But then, that's what friends are for."

CHAPTER-NINETEEN

HIJACK *a: to subject to extortion or swindling*
b: to commandeer an airplane in flight
c: to steal by stopping a vehicle on the highway

IT HAD BEEN 13 DAYS since he'd been shot. And though still sensitive to direct pressure, Forrest's wound had healed well. He'd been lucky, he thought, as he scanned Mpika's camp through his Litton Gen III night vision goggles. His last skirmish could have ended his mission or, he reminded himself, his life.

A glance at the luminous face of his dive watch told him it was nearly 03:00. Everyone should be at the low point in their sleep cycle.

He turned his head slowly, examining every detail for signs of life. NVGs were a marvelous aid, he considered, a lot better than the early starlight scopes he'd used in Vietnam. Although the goggles gave everything a ghostly lime-green hue, they illuminated all but the darkest shadows with an image that was crystal clear. Ambient light entering the 4x objective lens was focused onto a photocathode which converted visible light into a stream of electrons. Those electrons, in turn, collided with the sides of gallium arsenide-coated fiber optic tubes bundled in a micro-channel plate exciting more electrons—rather like a cue-ball breaking a rack whose individual balls went on to strike still more racks. Thus, the electron stream was intensified many thousands of times before being reconverted by a phosphor screen back into visible light which was then focused by another lens onto the wearer's eye. Light amplifiers sensitive through the visible light spectrum and into the near infra-red revealed body heat in much the same way a pit viper locates its prey. Appropriate, Forrest thought as he crawled along the open ground to the rear of three gasoline trucks parked under an overhanging tree canopy.

Forrest stopped every few meters, MP-5 cradled in his forearms in case he stumbled into a sentry...or a barking dog. He didn't like the idea of killing an animal. After all, it would just be doing what dogs are "paid" to do. But, in the dark, they were his enemy's eyes and ears.

Fifteen minutes later, he slid beneath the nearest truck and paused to listen. The smell of oil-fouled dirt invaded his nostrils as he slowly turned from side-to-side. The goggles wouldn't focus closely enough to see objects at arm's length so he pulled them off and inserted them into his backpack.

Forrest lay still for several minutes, allowing his eyes to adjust to the darkness. Most of his work would be accomplished by feel, moving the transponders into place on the vehicles' frames and securing them in place with olive-drab duct tape. He felt along the bottom of the first truck, his fingers searching for a ledge along a box beam which would both hide and support the small plastic device. Finding one, Forrest armed it with the flick of a weather-proof rubberized switch and taped it securely into place. To better disguise it in the unlikely event anyone were to crawl underneath the truck to perform maintenance, he splashed a few handfuls of dirt onto the tape and smeared it in.

It took another ten minutes to install the tiny device on the other vehicles.

As Forrest stowed his gear and extracted the NVGs, a sudden, faint noise startled him. He froze and strained to listen. There were sounds of footsteps and muted voices—female voices behind him. Very slowly, he rolled onto his back then onto his left side to better view the source.

He saw two women—one limping—no, hobbled—walking ahead of another, toward something which appeared to be a latrine of some sort. Though dressed more like a local, he was able to discern, despite the green hue of the NVGs, that the woman was white. A surge of adrenaline shot through his torso like a bolt of high voltage. *Amy!*

His mind reeled with options including taking out the woman and grabbing Amy. Those plans were canceled, however, when he noticed a man partially dressed and armed with an AK walking slowly behind them. *Security.*

Forrest watched as the women apparently took care of business while the man smoked. Then Amy led the way, plodding along head down, back to the third hut from the stream bed. The reason for her awkward gait became apparent—a rope tied to both ankles to prevent running.

Dammit! Forrest fought with his instincts. He thought better of a snatch and grab when he considered Amy might be too debilitated to keep up with him in what would surely be a haul-ass escape and hell-bent run to his hidden plane with armed hunters in impassioned pursuit.

Well, he thought, at least I'm positive she's alive and I know exactly where she's kept. That's something.

Ten very long minutes later he crawled into the comforting undergrowth surrounding the camp where he stopped to catch his breath and take a long drink.

Before moving off into the darkness, Forrest scanned the camp one last time. By now, the tiny beacons were transmitting their position to a ring of satellites orbiting high in the night sky. And his best friend would soon get some very exciting though mixed news.

* * * *

"We've got a mover," Steve Henderson told John Forrest two days later across thousands of miles of space. "Been traveling east for about an hour."

"Mombasa?" Forrest asked, already assuming the answer.

"Probably."

"Okay. We're on the way."

By the time they had arrived at the Mombasa airport, Forrest had thoroughly briefed his "commando team" on all aspects of their plan. While Forrest tied down the Cessna, McCullen and Joseph made arrangements to hire a taxi, which arrived surprisingly fast. Several large bills and the promise of more assured their driver's complete cooperation in what must have seemed a very unusual request from a very unusual trio. His orders: "Just drive around until we tell you to stop."

For ninety minutes, they cruised the streets along the waterfront searching for their objective, passing warehouses, shops and bars frequented by truckers, dock-workers and merchant seamen. Like any waterfront city, Mombasa had its share of drunks, prostitutes, and other unsavory characters, all of which made McCullen decidedly uncomfortable. The driver, he assumed with a great deal of embarrassment, probably thinks we're looking for tainted women. If he only knew, McCullen agonized. It's much worse than that.

It was nearly eight PM when Forrest caught sight of the truck. Two blocks east of them, it appeared to be slowing for the stop signs posted on every corner.

"Driver," Forrest said, casually so as not to give away their game. "Pull over here."

The man complied instantly, gratefully accepting a wad of shillings and twenty American dollars with a toothy smile.

Forrest scanned the street as his two accomplices emerged from the vehicle. Music, heavy with bass, pounded the air from a bar across the street; an establishment, McCullen noticed after adjusting his glasses, one wouldn't venture into unless well armed and well inoculated.

"Follow me," Forrest ordered, leading them into a dark shadow half way down the block. He drew his Colt, checked the cylinders, and snapped it closed. "Okay, Doc. You're on."

McCullen regarded the approaching truck warily.

Forrest could feel his apprehension. "C'mon, Doc. I didn't say you had to throw yourself under the wheels, or anything. Just get him to stop. Go on now," he added with an easy shove before the geriatric guerilla-fighter could change his mind. "It's Oscar night."

McCullen moved out into the street, emerging from the shadows into a pool of light cast by a lonely street lamp. As if on cue, he began staggering about as if he were all but embalmed.

Forrest and Joseph watched the act for a moment then shifted their eyes to the gasoline truck which slowed with a screech of its brakes. Suddenly, McCullen stumbled directly into its path.

Jesus, Doc! That's pretty damn convincing. For a moment Forrest thought it might be a heart attack! *Wouldn't that be great timing?*

The driver hit his brakes even harder, locking up the rear wheels. As the truck ground to a halt, McCullen put out his arm, supporting himself on its front grille.

"Hey! Old man," the driver shouted, opening his door. "Get out of the way or I'll kill you, you old fool."

"I'll do all the killing around here, thank you," Forrest growled after yanking the driver's door open and jamming the Colt's stainless steel barrel into the driver's sweaty cheek so hard he could feel the man's teeth. The sound of a cocking hammer made the driver go limp. "Slide over, or you'll never need to brush and floss again."

Joseph pulled open the passenger door and climbed inside the cab. He produced a zip-tie with which he bound their victim's hands behind his back. A strip of speed tape stretched over Yumba's mouth precluded any distress calls while McCullen climbed onto the bench seat between Forrest and their prisoner. "How'd I do?" the Scotsman asked with a twinkle in his eye.

Forrest snorted. "Good, Doc. Almost too damn good."

The prisoner began to struggle when he realized he'd been had. A hard rap on the head with the Anaconda's barrel solved that problem.

"Shove his ass on the floor," Forrest commanded, handing the heavy revolver to Joseph. With grinding gears and a lurch, Forrest turned the truck around, destination: the airport. The plan called for Forrest to fly the Cessna 185 home where McCullen and Joseph would meet him several hours later with the captured vehicle and its original driver. Their guest came around shortly before they reached the Cessna's parking place.

Forrest addressed the prisoner through Joseph who translated: "We need to borrow your truck. Play your cards right and you'll get to see home again in a few days. Give us trouble and Joseph, there, will skin you out just like one of those leopard pelts you've got hidden in the back. Understand?"

"Umeelewa?" Joseph repeated, thrusting the pistol into the man's nose.

Yumba nodded vigorously.

Forrest addressed McCullen: "For the record, Doc, the only reason I acquiesced is because his face is not on my son's video tape. Otherwise his teeth and the rest of his face would be spread all over the taxiway."

McCullen smiled and gave a small nod. "I appreciate the concession, lad. I just don't want to be an accessory to murder."

"Don't worry. I wasn't planning on you being an accessory."

"Thank you."

"I was gonna let *you* pull the trigger," Forrest followed up with a sinister chuckle.

"Well, thank you for the opportunity, John. But, no thanks. I wouldn't want to deprive you of the satisfaction."

Good, Forrest thought, with a single nod, wishing he hadn't promised the Doc he wouldn't kill the sonofabitch in the first place.

* * * *

Installing Dr. Pyro's "pipe bombs" in the ivory they had seized had taken a day longer than they thought. Like a lot of things in life, it was more complicated than anticipated, especially since they had to take extra pains not to become part of the landscape. After the last tusk was loaded in the fuel truck's secret compartment, McCullen, Joseph and Forrest along with the captured driver who, surprised and grateful to not only be spared but treated well as their prisoner, shared a hearty meal and several beers before falling into their beds, dead tired.

Forrest had just finished signing on to the satellite when a text message flashed across the screen:

> WED. 1904Z THUMPER: YOUR SHIP JUST CAME IN. TRY NOT TO BE AT THE AIRPORT.

After a quick acknowledgement, Forrest broke down the SATCOM unit, stored it under his bunk and went to find Joseph.

The street was much busier than last time, Forrest noted as they drove toward the docks in the Serpent's gasoline tanker. People, bathed in the garish glow of neon, jammed the sidewalk in front of the same loud bar he and Joseph remembered from their last visit. Forrest felt Joseph let off the gas as they rolled through the pool of electric blue light flooding the street. "Don't slow down," Forrest breathed as they nervously scanned the shadows.

A stumbling drunk caught their eye, making their hearts skip a beat.

"Keep moving. Don't stop," Forrest prodded his driver whose shirt was already soaked with perspiration. Wary as a cornered cat, Forrest leaned forward to ensure that the drunk reappeared in the side-view mirror.

As the crowd thinned, Joseph pressed down on the gas pedal, bringing the truck back up to the posted speed limit of forty kilometers per hour.

Forrest, dressed in black, pointed a Maglite at the satellite photograph and counted the streets. A moment later: "Turn left… here."

The transmission groaned as Joseph downshifted and applied the brakes which protested with a loud squeal.

"Okay. Stop here." Forrest scanned the 8 X 10 photo one more time. "This is it. I'm getting out here," he said in a hushed voice, already feeling the tension. He pulled on a black silk balaclava, rolling it down over his face, exposing only his eyes and the bridge of his nose—an opening his NVGs would soon cover. "Remember everything I told you?"

Joseph nodded, afraid to speak.

"Just tell 'em the truck broke down last week and you just got it fixed," Forrest repeated for the third time, more for his reassurance than Joseph's. "Your boss heard they were in port and sent you to deliver the shipment. "Alright?"

More nods.

"Take this clown with you and don't let him say anything," Forrest stated evenly, holding up the MP-5 for Yumba to see. He waited a moment while Joseph made the translation with a considerably more threatening tone than originally imparted.

The driver nodded vigorously and smiled excessively.

"Don't worry. If anything goes wrong," Forrest assured him with a demonstrative slap applied to the MP-5's composite forestock, "I'll be just a few feet away, covering you with this."

To be sure, the man's appearance was something of a surprise, the captain decided, stroking his black beard with hard fingers battered by years of exposure to sun, salt water and hard labor. But his story did have a certain ring of truth and it had happened before. Captain Sabah recognized the truck and the other man well enough having seen it so often on other nighttime rendezvous. And from its outward appearance it was certainly plausible that it could have suffered a serious malfunction. Mechanical things did break down, occasionally, did they not? As a mariner, these were maladies with which he was all too familiar. And as a master—owner of his own vessel—the expense of such mishaps was a constant burden for which he alone was responsible.

He had seen the envious look in his men's eyes when the stranger handed him a plump fold of bills as what?..an apology?..a gesture of goodwill?

Captain Sabah smiled inwardly as dark, weary eyes watched the intelligent few among his crew who had stayed aboard and were now loading his most valuable cargo of the voyage. Indeed, the stranger was a welcome sight, as was his money. And the money these goods would bring would take care of his many needs. His sails were in need of repair as was the rigging only recently damaged in a nasty ocean squall.

"One moment," he commanded as a large tusk was brought aboard. "Put it down."

Sabah lowered himself to one knee, letting his hand run the length of a particularly beautiful piece—one so rarely seen these days. Even fingers as cracked and calloused as his could admire the texture of eighty pounds of white gold. His greedy side wondered what had happened to its twin. Damaged, perhaps. Or perhaps Mpika had decided to keep it for himself—a thought which gave him pause. Perhaps that was not such a bad idea. After all, as master, did he not deserve a larger share than the rest? "Wrap this piece in canvas," he ordered his most trusted mate. "Put it in the bilge beneath my cabin."

"That went better than I thought," Forrest told Joseph and McCullen as he climbed into the waiting gasoline truck after securing their prisoner in the cargo compartment.

"And look at all the money he paid for the ivory," Joseph exclaimed proudly handing Forrest a very thick wad of bills.

Forrest waved his hand at it and shared a smile with McCullen. "Split it up among the camp families. You've earned it."

Joseph beamed and nodded appreciatively, shoving the money into a pocket.

"Now let's ditch this piece'a-shit." Forrest scanned the street leading to the dock looking for a deserted place to stop. He spotted one just ahead, next to an old warehouse where the lighting was particularly dim. "Pull over. Here."

The brakes groaned as the old tanker came to its final stop. Joseph set the brake, shut off the engine and extracted the keys.

"I'll take those, Joseph," the man in black ordered as he stowed his MP-5 in his backpack and extracted an odd-looking slab of putty and a spool of wire. "Pull the hood release." With a metallic clunk, the hood popped open as Forrest reached the front of the truck. Joseph soon joined him. "Keep an eye out," Forrest cautioned.

Joseph looked around nervously. But curiosity pulled his eyes back to follow Forrest's hands. He watched them deftly remove a spark plug lead and wrap the naked end of one of a pair of wires around the tip of the plug before replacing its cap. The other wire was quickly secured to a solid ground where the negative battery cable was bolted to the engine block.

Forrest took great pains to conceal the wires as much as possible as he routed them beneath the engine. It took only two minutes to connect the blasting cap, conceal the charge and close the hood.

As Forrest arrived at the passenger door, McCullen reminded him of their agreement concerning the prisoner.

"Okay, Doc. You and Joseph drag him up here."

McCullen complied promptly and kept a lookout as Forrest and Joseph cut the zip-ties binding Yumba's wrists.

Forrest turned the driver so his left pants pocket was blocked from McCullen and Joseph's view. Deftly, he slipped the truck keys in the man's pocket and went back to unwrapping the prisoner's wrists.

"Joseph," Forrest commanded, drawing a generous amount of money from his pocket and flopping it in Yumba's hand. "Tell this piece'a butt-cheese he's free to go."

"Are you going to let him take the truck?" McCullen asked. "How's he supposed to get home?"

"He's not. If he goes back home," Forrest explained, "his boss will probably do what I wanted to do in the first place after our man, here, spills his guts on what happened and describes who did it."

"I hadn't thought about that," McCullen sighed.

Forrest turned to Joseph. "Tell Richard Petty to walk up the street, get drunk, get laid, and get lost—in that order." And as an afterthought he added with an extended finger in Yumba's face: "Warn him not to touch the truck. In its present condition it's quite the death trap."

Anne Sargent-Windridge rubbed her tired, tear-reddened eyes as she mentally reviewed her list of preparations. Several boxes and bags were packed and the Land Rover had plenty of petrol—enough to get her to Malcom's camp, at least. She shivered under the breeze stirred by the ceiling fans as she reread the letter she had written to her husband before laying it on his desk next to his bank statements and the photographs Forrest had taken of him with Mpika:

> ALLEN. I AM LEAVING YOU. THE EVIDENCE ON THIS DESK IS REASON ENOUGH, I SHOULD THINK. IF YOU FOLLOW ME OR ATTEMPT TO HARM ME, REST ASSURED THAT COPIES OF EVERYTHING HAVE BEEN SENT TO MY FAMILY IN ENGLAND WITH INSTRUCTIONS TO GIVE THEM TO THE AUTHORITIES.

"Ya look awful, I'm sorry to say." Malcom McCullen put his arms around his "adopted daughter" and gave her a long, reassuring hug.

"I'm afraid I agree." Anne let her arms hang limp with nervous exhaustion for a moment before locking them around McCullen's waist. They stood in the late morning sun for several minutes without another word. Then: "I've left Allen," she blurted before looking up. The look in McCullen's eyes told her further explanation was unnecessary as she started to sob uncontrollably.

Everyone in the factory was too busy to notice as Henry Poon walked outside with his entourage, a business associate from Paris, his warehouse manager and two bodyguards. Most donned sunglasses against the bright sunlight reflecting off the concrete pier and an ivory-colored Mercedes sedan parked at the edge of the dock which gleamed to the point of florescence.

"The new shipment is most satisfactory, Ying," Poon told the manager of Building 65A, a Chinese man chosen because no foul-smelling Arabs could be trusted with an operation as important as this. "Captain Sabah did well." *Although he was nearly two weeks late.* And because he was late, most of the goods had already been loaded onto ships bound for China and Japan by the time Poon arrived.

Poon's bodyguards scanned the fences and the rooftops of the surrounding buildings warily, constantly alert for anyone who might have more than a passing interest in their employer. Tight security was a must in this part of the world where hazards seemed as limitless as Poon's wealth. Everyone was a potential threat. In such an atmosphere, typical precautions ranged from the armored Mercedes 560 that waited with its engine running to the Uzi submachine guns, which hung from straps inside their suit jackets.

"With your permission, I will extend your compliments," Ying offered with a slight bow from the waist. His tight smile and submissive demeanor concealed the fact that he and the dhow captain had long been skimming the shipments as added incentive. But such was the nature of any business where no records were kept, was it not?

Flanked by two huge men, each more than twice his size, Poon walked to his waiting automobile. As he slid to the center of the rear seat where he waited while his bodyguards sat on either side, a faceless worker, one of two-dozen drones just like him, pushed an elephant tusk toward his ban-saw's whining blade. The Mercedes' heavy doors slammed shut followed by the reassuring click of their electric locks.

The laborer eased the tusk into the blade, pausing but a moment to wipe the ivory dust from his glasses. Holding the piece steady, he resumed the cut without noticing the copper flecks mixing with the ivory dust on the steel support table. Adding a little pressure, he moved the tusk forward a millimeter at a time. The sharp blade sliced easily through the soft pipe and embedded Semtex before making contact with a copper wire.

His life ended in a flash he would never see and a thunderous roar he would never hear. Pieces of his body were flung away at over three thousand feet per second, becoming part of the growing wave of flame and detritus propelled outward by the expanding gases.

Overhead doors which opened to the dock acted as a funnel channeling the explosion's full fury at the automobile which had paused but a second too long at water's edge. The shock wave slammed against the Mercedes rolling it over the side of the pier where it landed on its roof in five meters of murky water. Steel plate and heavy bulletproof glass dragged the car to the bottom where it settled into the mud. As water rushed into the dark chamber, the bodyguards struggled frantically with the electric locks which, along with the rest of the electrical system, had shorted out and were now useless. If panic hadn't completely overtaken the vehicle's owner, he might have had time to consider that at $250,000, his custom-built automobile had just become the world's most expensive coffin.

The tea, though a little bitter for her taste, felt good, her second cup more soothing than the first. Anne looked off toward the rhino pens where Joseph and two of his six children emerged with Hoover. Porkahontas and Spike, Forrest's names for the orphaned baby warthogs he'd found in the bush, trotted along behind them as they made their way toward the picnic table.

"What do you think Allen will do now?" McCullen asked in an attempt to assess the consequences of Anne's bold move.

"I don't know." Her eyes came back to meet his squarely. "I

honestly don't." A weak sarcastic laugh came along with a shake of her head. "Everything I thought I understood was really a lie. Allen, John, the government. Everything. All lies."

"Well now. Certainly not everything."

She paused then smiled, extending her hand across the table to affectionately caress his. "Everything except you."

McCullen chuckled dismissively, patting her hand. "In John's case, at least the lie has its good points and good intentions."

"Mmm." She smiled. "I suppose." She looked affectionately at Hoover as they passed on their way to their mud bath. "Does John have any children?"

McCullen looked at her in a funny sort of way. "He used to," slipped out of his mouth before he could think of a more direct answer.

Anne scrunched her forehead. "Used to?"

McCullen set his mug down with a sigh. *She had to know.* "They killed his only son."

Anne's eyes narrowed. "What? Who? Whose son?"

McCullen pulled his head back. "You didn't know, did you?"

"What on Earth are you talking about?"

"Poachers...in Tsavo...last year. They murdered his son and kidnapped his new bride."

"John's new bride?"

"No, his *son's* new bride. They were here on their honeymoon—on safari."

Anne looked off in the distance searching her memory for the event. "I remember something about a young American couple...on their honeymoon, now that you mention it. I think that's what made it stick in my mind." She paused and her chin dropped as the news finally sunk in. "They were *John's* kids?"

"Aye, that they were."

"Oh my God!" Anne gasped. "No wonder...why didn't he tell me?"

McCullen gave her a wry cloying smile. "Oh, I can think of a few reasons. Besides, you didn't give the poor man a chance before you went tearin' outta here like a banshee."

"What reasons?" Anne looked genuinely astonished.

"You know what reasons." McCullen laughed. "First, he didn't tell *anybody* about it. Not even me. Secondly, you're the government, or at least you represent the government. To trust you would be dangerous—no, foolish, more correctly. And third...well you do come across as being a little implacable, sometimes."

Shock melted into shame. Her eyes went to the table while she worked on that thought.

McCullen noticed the change in her. She was a much better listener than before. "When he first came to find out what happened to his kids, the police gave him the run around. He saw straight away that they never would have solved the crime on their own so he became a little frustrated, to say the least. And you know how he gets when he gets frustrated."

Along the longitude of fifty-six degrees east, the sun was two hours lower than in Nairobi and about to plunge into the sea two points off the starboard bow. Captain Sabah paused for a moment to let the orange glow of sunset bathe his face one last time before he went below. After a three-day stay in Abu Dhabi to rest his crew and replenish his supplies, Sabah had set sail for Yemen; specifically the port city of Al Hudaydah. With port calls in Al Mukalla, and Adan, the voyage would take ten days. A long trip, to be sure, but one which would yield him and his crew an enormous profit.

He heard his first mate telling the evening watch to ensure that all loose equipment was stowed or lashed down. They were expecting something of a blow during this, the fourth night of their voyage, and the seas would be as high as any they had encountered in a month. Even now the swells made standing difficult as the captain moved about in his cabin making preparations for sleep.

Hidden in a compartment below decks sat an entire crate full of rhino horn; the best of the lot. Much too good for Poon and the flat-faced orientals he so despised and distrusted. They would bring a handsome price in Yemen's capital city of San'a where a wholesaler who sold them to carvers would only be too eager to lay his hands on them.

And then there was the eighty-pound tusk which lay in the bilge just below his cabin. It too, would bring a handsome price, especially in today's black market, and especially in one piece. Much more than it would after Poon's men had sawed it into little blocks in their sweltering warehouse.

Sabah felt the vessel come about on a starboard tack as he tallied the profits in his head. No, he decided, the ivory money he would keep for himself. There was no point in sharing it with his crew as was the custom. His men would only squander it on satanic vices and foolish pleasures. He, on the other hand, would put it aside for a new vessel, perhaps a much larger one. Yes, a marvelous idea!

Captain Sabah's mind traveled far into the future, designing his new dhow, dreaming about new contracts with bigger shippers while another "brain"—a tiny, digital brain at work two meters below his feet—concluded its programmed task. After days on duty, the countdown timer embedded in the trophy piece of ivory finally ticked to zero. Instantly, batteries began transferring their stored energy to a whining capacitor which, at full charge, would be capable of exciting the attached blasting cap and plastic explosive. That took only three minutes. The ship's plunging bow sent a slippery glob of mercury to the cold end of the glass tube in which it was trapped. Contacts on the hot end waited for its return where it would complete the firing circuit. As the ship pitched bow up, the quick silver lived up to its nickname, slithering in a flash to the hot end of the switch. The faint electrical spark inside the tube was duplicated a billion-fold as the entire stern of the wooden ship disintegrated, scattering flotsam and flame for a hundred meters over the black waters of the India Ocean.

"Speak of the devil." Anne said flatly.

Anne and Doc McCullen watched as Forrest walked through the trees from the airstrip carrying a small bag.

Doc McCullen broke the ice. "Where've ya been, lad?"

Forrest stopped, put his foot up on McCullen's bench and looked at the Scotsman. "The Cessna needed an oil change. I took it to Nairobi." He shifted his eyes to Anne. "What, no cops? Or did they get lost on the way?"

"I didn't bring the police." Anne said, so quietly it was as if she were afraid to speak.

"I know," Forrest said icily. "I checked. You didn't think I'd just land and let some holier-than-thou woman and a bunch'a idiot cops grab me, do you?"

"How did you know I was here?"

"I saw your Land Rover. You always park it in the same place."

McCullen thought it was a good time to intercede. "John."

Forrest looked at him expectantly.

"Anne left her husband."

Forrest shifted back to Anne Sargent. "Good. Better now than *after* he makes the newspaper."

Tamotsu Murasaki awoke early, dressed and walked past his studio to a bench in his favorite part of his garden where his wife had left his newspaper just as she had every morning for the past twenty-three years. The coolness of the stone penetrated his robe after a moment as he sat absorbing the peaceful energy of the garden's rocks and lush vegetation. Morning was his favorite time of day—the most tranquil—the most pure. A good day began with a good morning, he often told himself.

His wife brought him a cup of tea as he opened the paper to the front page where disturbing headlines blared: EXPLOSION ROCKS OSAKA FACTORY. Murasaki set his cup down without looking only to find that, in his moment of distraction, he had missed the bench completely, leaving his cup to topple to the ground. He felt the warm liquid splash over his sandals as his eyes continued down the column:

Osaka. Wednesday. Late Tuesday, a powerful blast severely damaged the Tokunaga factory, killing five and injuring twenty-one. The explosion occurred on the lower floors of the building where hanko and other products are manufactured. Police have labeled the explosion as "suspicious" and are still investigating...

Murasaki put the paper down and gazed off into space. Those poor people, he thought. I warned Tokunaga. I asked him to stop using ivory. Perhaps now he will listen.

"What do you mean, 'makes the newspaper?'" Anne Sargent asked.

"Sooner or later, he's gonna get caught," Forrest answered in a round-about way. "He can't get away with it forever. Somebody's gonna screw somebody else and the whole thing is going to come apart." Forrest, finally realizing he was in no danger of arrest, sat down next to McCullen. "That's the way it usually happens. Greed begets more greed. And thems that gets too greedy, gets caught...or gets dead." Forrest's stare made Anne lower her eyes.

"Don't tell me you told him," Forrest probed.

Anne looked up. "Of course, I did." Her eyes went to McCullen for approval and came away disappointed.

"Bad move."

"Why? I found more evidence, as well. Bank accounts...in both names." She checked the faces for reactions. McCullen, she saw, didn't quite get it. "Joint accounts helped him hide the income. He told the bank it was an inheritance from my aunt."

"It also implicated you as a conspirator. Nice guy," Forrest commented sarcastically.

"Now you know why I left him."

McCullen's face flushed with anger. "Indeed, lass. You can't go on livin' with a man like that. There's not a day that goes by that I don't worry about you."

"You don't think that's the end of it, do you?" Forrest interjected.

Anne took a breath and drew back. She looked away to find an answer. "I won't turn him in. I think he knows that. But I told him I would if anything happened to me. I also took a substantial part of the money and sent it to my sister in London for safe keeping." Her eyes went to McCullen. "I have the photos and bank statements in the Rover."

Forrest, shaking his head, sensed new danger. "You may have stepped on a snake's tail without first stepping on its head."

Allen Windridge left his Kenyan pilot standing near their government helicopter as he walked with Mpika toward a secluded spot under the shade of his camp's tall trees. Things were going badly for both of them and each felt the other's tension. Windridge had with him two newspapers containing articles about the terrorist incidents in the Middle and Far East. The attacks on their foreign markets were certainly not good for business but that was far from the worst of it.

"It seems someone has targeted us, Windridge," Mpika said with a voice clouded with anger.

"So it would seem." Windridge extracted a package of cigarettes from a shirt pocket and offered one to his accomplice and business partner.

"Whoever they are, they are very good at what they do. People with professional training." Mpika let a string of ashes flutter to the ground as he pointed to the spot where two of his three gasoline trucks used to be parked. "Someone blew up one of my trucks in Mombasa a few days ago. Killed one of my best men. At first, I thought it may have been someone attempting to take over my business. I was almost certain one of my drivers was involved until he was killed in the bombing."

Windridge recalled reading about the incident in the paper but hadn't associated it with his Tanzanian partner. "That was *your* truck?"

Mpika nodded as he took a puff then plucked a bit of tobacco from the tip of his malformed tongue.

Though he had seen it before, Windridge couldn't help but stare.The organ really did resemble a snake's tongue. No wonder his men were afraid of him. "I think I know who's behind it."

Mpika's expression changed. "You know who did it?"

"Mmm hmm. I think so. One is an American. An ex-soldier. Special Forces, I think—the sort who's been trained to blow up trucks and shoot people at long ranges. And," he added with an ominous tone, "he's got motive."

"Motive?"

Windridge gave him a hard, disapproving look. "You killed his son and my pilot says you have his daughter-in-law."

Mpika regarded him oddly—it was a mixture of apprehension and surprise.

"Indeed. And I told you to get rid of the girl."

Mpika looked away into the trees for a long moment, analyzing this new bit of disturbing information. "I was going to sell her in Yemen. But she was skin-and-bones. I decided to fatten her up a bit before I shipped her."

"Don't tell me she's still here?"

"Come," Mpika said glumly. He led the Brit toward his accomplice's hut. Inside, lay a white woman, asleep on a mat.

"Jesus-bloody-Christ," Windridge hissed, grabbing The Serpent by the shirt and slamming him into a wall. "What in bleeding hell are you thinking?"

Mpika shoved back hard. "She is worth thousands in Yemen."

Windridge brushed away his arm. "Then bloody well *sell* her. Now! I can't cover for this!"

"I have to make new shipping arrangements," Mpika muttered, lowering his eyes. "My shipper in Mombasa has not responded to my messages."

"I don't care what it takes, get rid of her. Straight away."

"And what of her father?"

"Organize a party, find him and kill him. We have no choice. He must be stopped before he stops us. If I were him, I would never rest until my children were avenged."

"Why can't you arrest him and see to it that he doesn't arrive in Nairobi?" Mpika countered.

"It's not quite that simple." Windridge hesitated before continuing, not quite sure how to put it. "My wife may be with him." He felt a twinge as The Serpent's narrowing eyes bored a hole right through him.

"What do you mean?"

"She left me." Windridge left it at that, hoping the meaning was as implicit as it was painful. In any event, he didn't want to admit it aloud. That would require that he first admit it to himself.

"To *be* with him?"

"Don't know, precisely. I don't think she's romantically involved with him if that's what you mean. I don't think she even *likes* the man. She always talked as if she despised him."

"Always? Then she talked of him often?" Mpika took a last drag from his cigarette and flicked the butt to the ground.

Windridge cocked his head to one side. "Fairly often."

"That's your answer, then."

Windridge's brows went up and he looked away for a moment, considering the concept before dismissing it. But then there was the old man she liked so much. That could explain it, he told himself, though he wasn't certain. He thought of the banquet—what he could remember of it—and how the American had been so quick to come to her rescue. *Could it be?*

"I can see you have your doubts, Windridge."

The Englishman's face flushed with equal parts of embarrassment and anger. No man liked having his wife's infidelity rubbed in his face—especially by scum. He swallowed it. "We have more pressing problems than that. This American is dismantling our entire enterprise," Windridge groused. He looked down at a passing rhinoceros beetle and then, with a sudden angry grimace, crushed it with the sole of his boot. His eyes came back up with a sadistic smile. "There's more."

"What could be worse?"

"He's been to your camp," he told him with a certain amount of pleasure. Windridge let that one sink in for a moment before adding: "He has photographs of the two of us together." He paused again. This sort of news was best delivered in small doses. "My wife has copies."

Mpika looked at Windridge blankly for a long time trying to decide if this vulture-faced white man was more an asset or a liability.

"But, photos are worthless without witnesses," Windridge told him—something he had learned over the years during one of his many trips to court.

"Does he know we have the girl, here?"

"I don't know, but I don't think so. He would have already killed you if he did."

"The American—this Baba Tembo—is wanted for murder, is he not?"

"As yet, there hasn't been a warrant issued. But that's a mere formality. The army and the police have been looking for the person or persons responsible for some months, now."

Mpika's black eyes glimmered like polished onyx. "Then you have the legal right to detain him as a suspect, do you not?" His mouth twisted into a sinister grin. "Take some policemen to the camp and arrest him for murder. Then, on the return to Nairobi, shoot him when he tries to escape."

The Serpent had the Englishman's full attention. "That still leaves my wife and the old man. Dealing with them might be a little dicey. The doctor is a very well respected member of the scientific community."

"Every problem has a solution," Mpika declared, clarifying his point by dragging his hand across his throat like a knife.

Windridge shuddered at the poacher's cold-blooded nature and ventured a self-assessment. Admittedly he was ambitious—corrupt, perhaps. Perhaps a bit greedy, as well. But he was no savage.

"Do you have any idea where he might be found?" Mpika asked, clearly formulating a back-up plan.

"If he is not in Dr. McCullen's camp, he might be found by the Ewaso Ng'iro. Anne says he goes there often to be with the elephants. Find the elephants and you find *him*, I should think."

Mpika looked at him with a sly smile. "What if we find your wife with him?"

Windridge felt a flush of hot-faced temper as he pictured the two of them together. Savage or not, there were certain things which were just intolerable. "What would you do if it were your wife?"

CHAPTER-TWENTY

RHAPSODY *a: a highly emotional utterance*
b: a highly emotional literary work
c: effusively rapturous or extravagant discourse

ANNE'S HANDS TREMBLED as they went through the desk drawers in the home office she shared with her husband. "Please be here," she whispered to herself with an urgent, quivering voice, cursing herself for overlooking something so important. It had been well over a year since she had last used her passport. But she could have sworn she had last seen it in one of these drawers.

"Come on. Where are you?" she moaned, violently slamming one drawer and yanking open another. "Please, please, *please* be here. You *have* to be here." Her fingers probed recklessly, shoving aside envelopes, bills, statements and other desk drawer detritus looking for that familiar official pamphlet. She lifted two checkbooks and froze at the sound of a closing door.

"Hhhuu!" She jerked her hand back and turned her head to focus on the sound. She thought she had heard the door leading from the carport into the kitchen. She looked at her watch. Allen wasn't due home for at least three hours. *Could it be...?* She thought about calling her housekeeper's name then decided against it.

She heard the tinkling of glasses and a kitchen cabinet close. *Oh God! Allen.* She froze. Her heart pounded in her ears so loud it seemed she couldn't hear a thing above its hammering. Rapid-fire thoughts raced across her brain: freeze, hide, flee. She ruled out the last option. She would have to cross the living room at the foot of the stairs then skirt the kitchen on her way to the carport which was the closest exit. She remembered that Allen normally came into the office to check his mail before retiring to the lanai with his evening drink. People, after all, like animals, were slaves to habit. Her forearms tingled at the thought. She slid the center drawer open and felt for the letter opener—a suitable weapon.

RING! She almost exploded out of her skin.

The telephone rang a second time. She heard him lift the kitchen extension.

"Yes," Allen's voice echoed in the huge kitchen. "Yes Commissioner," she heard him saying with some concern.

Anne was dying to know what he was saying to that sloth of a man. Judging from his tone it was something important.

"Have you tried visiting their camp?" Windridge asked the receiver. "That's where Forrest has been living."

Anne's heart skipped a beat. Her eyes went to the telephone sitting on the desk. A voice told her not to pick it up though another voiced screamed: *do it!* A blossoming thought moved her eyes to the answering machine. Her finger hovered above it for a moment. She swallowed hard and pushed the "RECORD" button. A red light emitting diode flickered in synch with her husband's voice as the cassette spools began to turn. For a second she wondered if he might have heard something on the line—something that might give her away. Her grip tightened on the letter opener as she strained to listen to her husband's voice.

"That's right," she heard him say, "the American. I think it's time we arrested him."

Anne gasped. She felt a chill. Her mind raced with a surge of adrenalin. Suddenly, fleeing seemed like the best option, however impossible. Without a way out she realized she was trapped.

"I'll back them up in my helicopter," Windridge offered. "How many men can you give me?"

Her eyes were locked on the answering machine. The red light flickered with the answer.

"Alright, then. Tomorrow will have to do. I'll come down straight away to help you coordinate the details."

Anne heard him hang up and felt a new wave of fear. Would he come into the office before leaving? She crawled under the desk and pulled the chair in behind her when she heard him set his glass down. She heard footsteps on the tile. They stopped...then continued toward the office. She felt as if she might throw up. She could hear his leather shoes creaking as he approached. A second later, she heard the water closet door next to the office close then the sound of a liquid stream hitting the toilet. It suddenly occurred to her she was holding her breath. Anne released a long breath and crawled from beneath the desk as quietly as she could. She almost ran across the living room then hesitated, her eyes going back to the checkbooks lying at the bottom of the desk drawer. Quickly, her hands shaking visibly, she lifted the checkbooks and...there! She snatched the passport up as she heard the toilet flushing. She started for the door again, then spun around and popped the cassette tape out of the answering machine.

"He knows it's you, John." Anne told him before shifting her eyes to McCullen who stood by in silence, a grave look on his face. He looked more ashen than usual.

"How do you know?" Forrest asked.

"He mentioned you by name. Here," she said, handing him the cassette tape she had taken from the answering machine. "It's all on tape."

They walked to Forrest's hut where they listened to the tape on Forrest's Walkman. The corruption went higher and deeper than they ever thought possible. Forrest's eyes shifted to McCullen then back to Anne. He was more concerned about them than he was about himself, especially McCullen. Forrest was a visitor and could always leave. McCullen was a permanent party and would have to deal with the aftermath. Anne, he could take with him. The old man would have to stay and profess ignorance—and do it convincingly. He hoped his age and professional standing would help protect him. But given the situation and the twisted personalities with which they were dealing, there was no way to predict the doctor's fate. "This is it, then. Game over," he said solemnly.

McCullen returned Forrest's forlorn look with one of his own. He had hoped this day would never come.

"Doc, get Joseph," Forrest commanded, softly. "We're gonna need some help packing up some of my equipment. We'll put most of it in the Land Rover. Anne will drive it to my camp on the Ewaso Ng'iro. I'll put some stuff in the Cessna and fly out to join her. But we need to get moving."

Without saying a word, McCullen turned and walked off toward Hoover's pen to find Joseph.

Anne looked at Forrest. "John, I'm worried about him. He's not up to this sort of thing. Too much stress."

"Do you think your husband would hurt him?"

The answer came quickly as if she were sure of it. "I don't think so. But, then, I never dreamed Allen was involved in criminal activity. I thought I knew him; knew his limits. Now I'm not so sure." Anne sighed. "I'm not sure about anything." Her eyes began to fill before she fought it off.

Forrest put his hand on her shoulder reassuringly while he considered a thought. Political problems were best dealt with by the media—the written word was a silver bullet when it came to defeating corruption. "Do you have any friends at any of the newspapers?"

Anne looked off into space. "I have quite a good friend, a woman who does articles about wildlife issues."

"Can you get her to come down here and just sort of be here when Windridge and the cops arrive? A journalist might make them a little more cautious when it comes to strong-arm tactics."

"Hmm. Maybe. I could drive to the Mara ranger station and call her."

"Okay. Get going! Take your Rover. By the time you get back, we'll have everything packed in mine."

"How many times does this make?" Frank Zito's wife sighed with a voice more disgusted than fatigued.

"How many times for what?" Zito asked, preoccupied with his checklist. He lined through four items neatly penned on a steno pad before turning to look at Mrs. Z, the name the neighborhood kids had assigned her.

She stuffed a dozen sets of BVDs into the top of an Army-issue duffel bag, the old pro's luggage of choice. "How many times have I helped you pack your gear?" she repeated.

"Hell if I know." He ran his pencil down the list, pausing over a line near the bottom. "A couple dozen, I guess."

"You might be right." He itemized the adventures aloud. "Four shooting wars and at least one deployment every other year for thirty years."

"I'll be glad when you retire. I'm looking forward to a life of our own. No more kids. No more Army. No more packing."

"Me too, darlin'." He patronized her though he wasn't sure he really liked the sound of the R-word. He feared no enemies except the ones who marched to time's relentless drumbeat.

"How long will you be gone this time?"

"Coupla weeks. Maybe three. It's just a vacation. And Thumper needs my help."

She'd been around long enough to know a lie when she heard one. "Since when do you pack your BDUs for a vacation?"

Malcolm McCullen and the reporter from the *Narobi Nation* stood on the former's front porch sipping coffee when the helicopter touched down on the dirt airstrip.

Minutes later, two government vehicles pulled into camp, each manned with four uniformed policeman. They fanned out as if by prearranged plan and began a systematic search of each of the camp's cabins. The squad leader, a sergeant, reported to Windridge as he strode briskly up to McCullen. "They are not here, sah."

"You searched everywhere?"

"Yes, sah. Every building."

Windridge turned his eyes to the woman standing next to the old man. She was a short woman with smooth, mocha skin and bright clear eyes, about the same height as McCullen "I don't believe we've met," he said with the thinnest of smiles.

"You have a short memory, Mr. Windridge. We've met on several occasions but as I recall you were a bit under the weather on most of them." She smiled politely and extended her hand. "Bettie Loibooki. I'm a reporter for the *Nation.* I've written several articles, flattering articles as I recall, about you and your wife and the successes of your conservation programs."

Windridge smiled and gave a tacit nod of thanks. "Dr. McCullen, do you know the whereabouts of your American guest?"

"I believe he's with your wife, Allen," a statement he delivered with an intentional barb. "They're out in the bush somewhere, doing work on his research project. They didn't tell me where they were goin' or when they'd be back."

Windridge locked eyes with the Scotsman for a long moment.

"Sah," the police sergeant announced. "They are not here. We've searched everywhere."

McCullen saw his jaw tighten.

"Aright then," Windridge barked over his shoulder. "Assemble your men. We're returning to Nairobi."

"By now every policeman in Kenya will be looking for you," Anne Sargent-Windridge said to her American companion as they sat in his Land Rover watching their elephants bathing along the banks of the Ewaso Ng'iro river.

"Let's hope they're no better at finding us than they were at catching the bastards who killed my son," Forrest grumbled.

She looked away, concentrating on the gathering of God's most magnificent land animals just across the river. A blaring trumpet split the air.

Schwarzkopf, the immense old bull who dominated the region, was circling the herd, sampling the air and droppings for signs of a fertile female.

"Shouldn't you be making plans to leave the country?" Anne asked. "It's just a matter of time before they find you."

"I'll be leaving soon."

"Why not now?"

"I haven't finished what I came here to do."

She looked at him. That sounded ominous but she decided against asking for specifics. "How long until you are finished?"

"Not much longer. I'm waiting for a friend to join me. Then we'll settle our accounts and be on our way."

"An Army friend?"

"Yep. That's the only kind I've got left."

"Oh, I don't know. I think you've got a good friend in Malcolm. That dear old man thinks very highly of you."

Forrest glanced at her and smiled, then turned his attention back to the elephants.

"Then there's me," she said, deliberately not looking his way.

Forrest continued to look straight ahead, pretending not to hear. After a moment's thought, he smiled to himself and turned. "I thought you hated me."

Anne looked at him with the faintest of smiles. "Not that much."

Forrest snorted a laugh. "Well, uh...thanks...I guess."

"You're welcome...I guess."

Forrest's smile widened for a second then faded as he watched the elephants. Schwarzkopf had discovered Dolly was in estrus. He had become noticeably more agitated, sniffing her with great interest. Oprah, the new matriarch, kept her distance along with the rest of the girls. When it came to the dating game her charges were on their own. The big bull had developed a huge erection which occasionally dragged on the ground, emitting an almost constant flow of urine—a sure sign of musth.

Forrest stole a glance at Anne for a moment to see if she had noticed what was going on across the river. From the tracking movements of her eyes, he could see that she hadn't missed a thing. *She never does.*

"So, what do you think?" Forrest ventured, delighting in making her feel uncomfortable. "Is he gonna get lucky?"

Anne didn't miss a beat. "I believe it's a foregone conclusion," she responded dryly.

Forrest smiled again at her flat, clinical reaction. Dolly moved off again as if the mammoth brute were bothering her. "I think she just told him, 'not tonight, honey, I've got a trunk-ache.' She doesn't seem very interested."

"Oh, she's interested, alright. She's just being very subtle about it. Very lady-like."

Forrest gave Anne a curious smile that went unnoticed, then looked back to the family.

Dolly trotted off again, stopped, then began toying with a big stick.

"I don't know," Forrest commented. "Subtle's one thing. Disinterested is another."

"You men are so stupid. Can't you see that she's only playing hard to get?"

Forrest gave her an incredulous smile. "You can tell all that from way over here?"

Anne shook her head. "If she were *genuinely* disinterested, she wouldn't let him anywhere near her. The females are very picky about those with whom they mate. They will reject all of the other mature bulls for hours, even days, allowing only the biggest and most mature males to copulate."

"See. I always knew size mattered," Forrest joked. "You women always lie about that."

"That's so we don't permanently damage your pathetic little egos." Anne displayed the thinnest of smiles but he could tell she wasn't joking.

"On behalf of all the pathetic male egos out there, I thank you for sparing us. Rejection is devastating enough without you picking on our penises, too." Forrest watched Schwarzkopf get behind Dolly and rise up on his rear legs. His fire hose-size penis seemed to take on a life of its own. He guided it, independent of his body movements, from below and behind into her vagina. Dolly, though inexperienced, was a patient partner who seemed to know exactly what to do. She held perfectly still, her trunk dangling limply to the ground. Schwarzkopf loomed over her as he rested his front feet on her back. It appeared his body mass would surely crush the much smaller elephant, but he supported most of his weight on his own hind legs. After a brief coupling, his penis fell away and smacked the ground. Following several more couplings, the huge male walked to the edge of the woods and defecated while the rest of the family, led by Thelma and Louise, rushed to Dolly's side to touch and sniff her amidst agitated vocalizations.

"Now this part I recognize," Forrest joked. "He goes off to smoke a cigarette and the girls talk about it on the phone for a few hours."

Anne restrained a knowing smile. "It's getting late. We'd better head back to camp. I'd like to wash up before dinner."

Forrest wiped his face on his sleeve. "Yeah, I'm feeling a little flushed myself."

He started the engine and drove the Land Rover through the dense thicket and into a meadow of tall grasses. Off to their left they noticed a small pride of lions lounging under the shade of a beautiful wide fig tree. A large male with a full mane sat panting in the heat as a large female began rubbing against him like a domestic cat would against its owner's legs.

Forrest pointed the affair out to Anne with an impish grin. "Will you look at that. Somebody must've put something in the water or something. *Everybody's* getting frisky around here. The poor guy's been hard at work all day making fries and shakes down at McAntelope King, and now he's home trying to read the paper and she's pushing herself in his face."

Anne smiled, closed her eyes tightly and shook her head.

Forrest coughed a laugh and drove on.

The sun had fallen into the tops of the trees growing along a branch of the Ewaso Ng'iro where, during the dry season, the waters ran shallow and mute. Forrest had selected the site for its proximity to Oprah's family and its heavy tree cover—better to hide his camp from aerial surveillance. He had hidden the Cessna under the trees and enhanced its cover with cammo netting and a few well-placed branches cut from the thick brush. Similarly, he had erected a tent for Anne which, along with the Land Rover, he had hidden in a notch cut into an equally dense thicket. The arrangement did, however, afford a nice view of the setting sun and the river a few steps beyond its flaps.

After preparing a fire pit and gathering wood, Forrest backtracked shirtless along the river to the Cessna to retrieve some of his gear. Minutes later, he was returning to camp when he abruptly halted in his tracks. His eyes were transfixed on a scene which struck him in the pit of his stomach like a blow from a fist. The vegetation growing along the shallow bank thinned for a few meters revealing the exquisite silhouetted form of a nearly-naked woman standing resplendent in a shimmering pool of water turned molten gold by the afternoon sun. Forrest froze—almost dropping his gear.

Wearing only panties and a thin layer of soapy lather, Anne stood knee-deep in a quiet pool ten meters from shore. As she lifted her arms to run her fingers through long, dark tresses heavy with water and shampoo, she arched her back, lifting her full bare breasts into the sun's caress. A lathery stream oozed down her chest flowing between her breasts, the creamy liquid dripping from her nipples. Her profile stance accentuated her curves revealing a lean, hard belly that tapered into long perfect legs that melted into the mirror surface.

It had been a long time since Forrest had seen such a sight. It was riveting. Unable to help himself, Forrest tuned out the rest of the world, shutting out all of its sounds and smells. Time stood still, his vision tunneled, blinding him to all else. Reality, for the moment, was limited to a stunning image suspended above the dark ripples it formed in the shimmering lagoon.

Suddenly something caught his eye. A small, swirling eddy altered the mirror-like surface a few feet behind her. There it was again, this time closer. Something akin to the rough bark of a swollen log broke the surface then submerged. Suddenly it registered, snapping Forrest out of his spell. He dropped his gear and, in a single leap, cleared the brush growing along the bank. As his feet shattered the liquid surface to find the sandy bottom, he broke into a dead run.

A shout rose at the back of his throat, turned into a scream but was swallowed by a gasp for air. His legs crashed through water that with each step became deeper and more the viscosity of molasses.

Startled by the splash of legs bounding through the water, Anne turned to look just as Forrest slammed into her, sweeping her up in his arms. Thinking the worst, she squirmed and struggled to break his hold as he propelled her toward the deep sand mounded at the base of the river's far bank. Reaching it, he stumbled forward, falling on top of her, covering her body with his own. Anne managed to pull her arms free enough to pound him with her fists, striking quick hard blows to his shoulders and back.

Forrest, taken aback for a second, suddenly realized what she must think. "Stop it!" he shouted. Rolling off her, he grabbed her by the hair at the nape of her neck, pulling her head abruptly upright. "Look!" he roared.

Anne stared on in wide-eyed horror as the snout of a huge crocodile lunged out of the water, its menacing mouth agape as it pursued them onto the beach. As she rolled over to scramble toward the steep earthen bank behind them, Forrest grabbed a nearby piece of driftwood and wheeled. The croc was a monster, sixteen feet if he was an inch, weighing at least a thousand pounds. It came on like a small tank, its armor-plated body plowing through the sand, jaws open like the business end of a limb chipper.

Forrest leapt to the side, narrowly avoiding the snapping jaws as he brought the heavy limb down like a sledge, pounding squarely on the reptile's head. Hissing and flashing jaws studded with rows of jagged white spikes thrashed and counterattacked as Forrest dodged them to deliver repeated blows just behind the prehistoric monster's eyes. Its eyelids blinked with each impact. It turned and lunged at Forrest's legs only to snap the air and spraying sand kicked up by its thrashing tail. The bludgeoning continued for nearly a minute before the creature whipped its tail onto the beach and retreated into the safety of the river.

Forrest gasped for breath. He stumbled backwards on rubbery legs and dropped the club. For a moment he stooped over trying to catch his wind before collapsing onto the sand next to Anne. He lay on his back for a time, eyes fixed on the clouds, his chest heaving laboriously.

Anne settled next to him and searched his eyes for a moment. "I thought..."

"Thought what?" he interrupted, a trace of frustration straining his voice. His eyes locked onto hers.

"Well, I suppose you know what I thought." She smiled sheepishly. "It's a good thing you happened to..."

He put a finger to her lips. "No..." He paused then released a pent-up breath. "...it's a good thing I happen to love you or I would have let him eat your prickly ass."

Her breathing froze for a moment, her eyes welling up with emotion. Flushed with a mixture of erupting feelings, Anne threw herself into his arms. Their lips collided, probing tongues fenced with each other between stolen gasps and hungry breaths. Their bodies writhed in the sand.

John kissed her deeply—a kiss she wanted to last forever. His muscular arms surrounded her, holding her, pulling her into him. His fingers slid down her back and over her firm buns which he squeezed tightly. He found the flimsy wet fabric clinging to her bottom and tore it away in a single motion.

She gasped and felt her body tighten.

Forrest rose to his feet, undid his pants and flung them to the side before kneeling next to her. He reached for her and she came willingly, both bodies reclining.

She rolled into him, lifting a knee across his hip. She drew his groin into her delighting in the hardness she felt pressing between her legs.

He felt her sweet wetness. Electricity shot through his body at the realization she was so ready for him. He thrust his hips into her, taking her slowly and deeply. Their cathartic passion consumed them, shutting out the entire world for a few precious moments. Clad only in a coating of sand and the warmth of their love they satiated their passion and consummated a once inconceivable relationship.

"Cleanliness is a virtue you know," Anne told him as she splashed river water onto herself, this time from a five-gallon plastic bucket Forrest had filled for her after first carefully checking the river for reptilian attack submarines.

"Well, I'd say three baths makes you pretty virtuous, then," Forrest commented over his shoulder as he washed the aluminum dishes. Their dinner had been delicious for a camp meal. He'd made his trademark chili and even baked bread in a Dutch oven buried in the glowing embers of their campfire. She had contributed the wine—one of two bottles of chardonnay she'd liberated from her husband's private stock.

"I love baths," she declared with a voice so relaxed it sounded like a sigh. "The hotter the better. It boils away all of the impurities." She approached the campfire, vigorously toweling her hair then froze with a thought. "If a married woman makes love to a man other than her husband, she really can't be very virtuous. Can she?"

Forrest turned around, looked at her for a second, then picked up the wash-bucket and poured the dishwater onto the ground. "Your marriage was over months, maybe years ago."

"Not legally; and not in the eyes of God." Dressed only in one of Forrest's khaki shirts, she plopped down on a camp chair and gazed into the fire. Her eyes remained fixed on the flames as she repeatedly passed a comb through her damp hair many times beyond necessity.

"You're the one who has to live in your skin. And you're the only one who knows all the circumstances. So I wouldn't be too hard on myself if I were you."

Anne shook her head. "You wouldn't understand. You're not a Christian."

Forrest studied her eyes for a moment before speaking. "Well I guess that's it, then." He hadn't enough energy left to argue arcane points of theology.

She looked up with a blank expression. "What do you mean?"

"Looks like you're going to burn in hell along with the rest of us sinners," he said cynically. He poured some chardonnay into a coffee cup and handed it to Anne, then poured another for himself.

"Well, here's to a *slow* burn, at least." He raised his cup and waited, hoping she would catch the double entendre. His eyes twinkled, a smirk turning up the corners of his mouth.

She looked at him for a moment before returning the smile and the look. "One shouldn't joke about things like that," she cautioned as she sipped her wine.

Forrest looked at her curiously then drank. "One shouldn't be so serious about everything," he said after swallowing. "Life's too short to brood."

"You brood about your son."

He looked away and became quiet for a moment. "Not really. My definition of brooding is sitting around all day feeling sorry for yourself. Sure, I feel pain every time I think about him. I'll miss him the rest of my life. But I'm not going to let it paralyze me. I'm doing something about it." Forrest sat down on his campstool and studied a giant wall of cumulonimbus clouds building to the west. He watched the evanescent glow of lightning veiled within the blue-white sculptures but heard no thunder.

"Lusting after revenge may get you killed. Is it worth it?" She swallowed the last of her wine whereupon Forrest refilled her cup.

It was a beautiful, peaceful evening—his most pleasant since coming to Africa—and the wine was beginning to work its magic.

"Of course it's worth it. Defending one's honor is always worth it. It may be the only thing really worth dying for—that and freedom."

"Is that what you were doing when you nearly broke Allen's arm at the ball—defending my honor?"

Forrest responded with a small shrug. "Maybe. I should've broken his neck. I don't like it when people bully those weaker than themselves."

An elephant trumpet blared down-river.

"Like them?" she asked.

Forrest shrugged, again. "Even though they're the biggest and baddest, they really don't bother anybody who doesn't bother them first. They take care of each other, take care of each other's children, and they respect seniority. Even when they're fighting over cows the bulls rarely injure or kill each other, at least not intentionally. That's more than I can say about humans."

Anne nodded and sipped her wine. It felt wonderful going down—at once cool and warm. She felt her face flush. She rose. "I'm going to freshen up a bit." With that, she disappeared into the tent and pulled the flaps closed behind her. Once inside, she lit four thick candles and sat down in front of a shaving mirror to begin the transformation from beautiful to breathtaking.

Forrest went about the process of cleaning up the camp, stowing gear and tending to equipment. When he'd finished, one special task remained.

Twenty minutes later, Anne emerged from the tent to find Forrest enjoying the last of the wine. She stood just outside the tent dressed in a translucent white blouse and short black skirt. Her face was radiant, illuminated by the firelight's glow.

He felt gooseflesh rising on his forearms. He stood up slowly, went to her and kissed her on her glossy red lips. He pulled back to let his eyes dart over her face. Only one word passed his lips: "Stunning," he whispered as he held her in a gentle embrace for a long scintillating moment. "Come over here. I have something for you."

She looked at him curiously as he led her by the hand to her camp chair. A small package was on the seat "gift-wrapped" in newspaper and decorated with wild flowers he'd found growing along the water's edge.

"What's this?" she whispered with a fractured laugh.

"It's for you."

She looked at him with softening eyes for a moment before curiosity got the best of her. She peeled the paper away revealing a small amber bottle. Perfume.

"Obsession," he announced. "My favorite."

She looked at him with the faintest of smiles as she removed the cap and dabbed some on her wrist which she brought under her nose. "Mmm. Wonderful!"

Forrest smiled at her.

"I love it." She touched his arm lightly with her fingers. "Thank you."

They shared a look before the gentle rumble of thunder and a gathering wind drove them inside the tent.

"John, I've got a bad feeling about this." She settled onto the cot, her thoughts coming back to their situation.

"Bad feeling about what? We've already…"

"No, silly not about that." A smile came and went. "You've hurt some very powerful people—ruthless people. They won't let this rest. You should leave the country immediately."

He sat down next to her and put his arm around her shoulders. "I have a plan."

"A plan is just a list of things God is going to change," she countered with a grim look.

Forrest gave her a small patronizing smile. "Don't worry. I have an old friend due into Nairobi soon. He and I will take care of business then E & E."

"E and E?" Anne asked.

"Escape and evade—as in get the hell outta here."

Anne nodded understanding. "An Army friend?"

"Those are the best kind, especially for what we've got to do. Of all the people in the world I'd want covering my six, it's Zit."

Anne stroked his forearm, ran her nails through the fuzz. "Covering your six?"

"Watching my back."

"Oh, *that* six." Anne looked Forrest in the eye. "If you seek Him out, put His light at your twelve, He will cover your six every minute of the day."

Forrest gave her another of those patronizing smiles. "Converting me will take too long. I'm hopeless."

"No one is hopeless in His eyes. But you may be right about how long it would take. No matter, He has all the time there is."

"You'll have plenty of time for a lost cause, too," Forrest countered dismissively. "I'm taking you with me."

"I was hoping you'd say that." Anne slipped out from under his arm and removed a small gold cross from around her neck. "This is for you." She smiled and fastened the delicate chain around his neck, then silenced his protests by pressing her fingertips against his lips. "You're a good man at heart, John Forrest; tragic, confused, chauvinistic, and infuriating perhaps—but a good man, nevertheless. Maybe there's enough room in that black little heart for God to find his way in. Besides, with the kinds of things you do, you'll need all the protection you can get."

"I don't qualify. I've broken all ten commandments. Multiple counts."

"It doesn't work that way. It's not about your record. It's about His grace."

"Well in that case we can get away with breaking the same one over again, right?"

She looked away and smiled, suddenly a little uncomfortable.

He studied her face then turned her chin with his fingers, pulled her to him, taking her in a powerful kiss. Their lips parted and she closed her eyes as he unbuttoned her blouse and slipped it off her tanned shoulders. She did the same for him then flung his shirt across the tent. Candlelight flickered in her eyes as he laid her down gently onto the cot and held her there with a long, lingering kiss. His fingers caressed her calf then slid lightly along her thigh. Traveling upward, they disappeared beneath her skirt to find the dampness where her smooth legs met.

Moths, frenzied by the flame, beat themselves against the mosquito netting as the remnants of their clothes found their way to the floor. Rising wind and rolling thunder drowned their breathy voices. And for the first time in two years it began to rain.

CHAPTER-TWENTY ONE

FUGUE

a: a polyphonic musical composition in which one or two themes are repeated or imitated by successively entering voices or passages

b: a disturbed state of consciousness in which the one affected performs acts of which he is conscious but on recovery has no recollection

"WAKE UP! WAKE UP, JOHN!" Anne Sargent shook her leaden partner vigorously. Forrest came around slowly, his brain numbed by too much chardonnay and too little sleep. "What?" His eyes still closed, he sat up and rubbed his throbbing head. Wine hangovers are the worst, thought a man who, of late, was unaccustomed to such self-inflicted infirmaries. Then it hit him...*sounds...screams and gunfire... coming from down river.*

"John!" she called to his back as he bolted out of bed and balanced on one leg as he pulled on his pants. "They're killing them," she cried. They shared a look that electrified the air between them.

Anne's feet hit the matted floor as Forrest put his arms through sleeves of a cotton shirt as wrinkled as a crumpled beer can. He looked up just as her butt disappeared inside her uniform shorts. "Where do you think you're going?" he growled.

"I'm going to do something about it," she snapped without

hesitation.

Forrest pulled on his boots. "And just what do you think *you're* gonna do...give 'em a yeast infection?" He turned, looked her hard in the eye and pointed an adamant finger in her face. "You're stayin' put!" he ordered as he rose and blew through the tent's mosquito netting. Then he paused, summoned back by the defiance he'd read in her eyes. He wheeled and pointed his finger at her through the screen. "I mean it. Stay here."

Anne finished buttoning her shirt and glared back. She set her jaw, swallowing a futile response as Forrest spun about and broke into a dead run for his hidden airplane.

His heart pounded in his chest as he kicked up the loose damp soil. He heard the trumpets and wails of huge beasts in great distress. In seconds, the camouflaged plane appeared a few meters ahead. He slid to a halt then ripped aside the cammo-netting and snapped open the door. A distant burst from an AK-47 shattered the air as his fingers pulled the cover off the baggage compartment extender where his rifles were hidden. Sweat burned his eyes as he pulled the ERMA out of its case and slung his survival vest over his shoulders. Still more gunfire echoed down river as he turned to run back to the camp. The ammo in his vest pounded against his chest with each footfall, slamming in synch with his stride and drumming heart.

"Oh no!" he gasped, pulling up abruptly. His eyes swept the camp as still more shots cracked further ahead. "God-*damn*-it!" he raged to a vacant tent and indifferent trees. Anne and the Land Rover were gone. Forrest heard a burst of machine gun fire and felt his limbs go cold. "Anne!" he anguished under his breath. It was difficult to estimate through the trees, but the gunfire seemed to be nearly a mile away—a long distance to cover without the Land Rover. *Never get there in time!*

Forrest darted across the camp, grabbed his coil of climbing rope and took off down river as fast as his legs would propel him. After four minutes' hard run, he ground to a halt, his lungs heaving for breath.

Two distinct shots rocked the trees. *Close.* He knew that sound. *Coups de grace.* The sort of shot delivered to the head in order to finish off a victim.

He thought to run then reconsidered it. Bullets are faster than feet, he thought, looking up into the trees. He was overcome with a wave of dread. His right hand found the ribs that still ached as a result of his last arboreal expedition.

Quickly, he set the rifle down and prepared his rope, which he sailed over a high limb on the first try. Forrest slung the rifle over his back and pulled himself up. Once up in the tree, he repeated the procedure, pulling himself still higher for a better view. The trees thinned somewhat along the river revealing an open grassy bogani and the carcass of dead elephant. Forrest braced himself against the trunk, uncapped the rifle's scope and began scanning the terrain. Deep in the shadows, he saw his Land Rover, its doors open. Anne was nowhere to be seen.

As he panned his rifle, Forrest caught sight of two elephants running across another clearing two hundred meters to the right of the Rover. Shots erupted just behind them. Forrest cycled the bolt and flipped off the safety just as two armed men emerged. He took aim on the trailing man and dropped him with a well placed shot straight through his "boiler room." Forrest cycled the bolt in a flash and heard the spent casing pinging as it tumbled through the branches. Before he could steady his rifle, the lead man swung his weapon, blindly firing at the sound of Forrest's rifle. Rounds cracked and buzzed through the trees showering leaves onto the soft ground as the man plunged into the brush and disappeared.

Two more men flashed through the clearing and took cover behind the trunks of two mature trees. Forrest took aim on them and waited for a well-defined target.

A head peered around one tree. The man's eyes scanned the treetops as Forrest centered the crosshairs over a point between the bright white orbs and squeezed. BOOM! The head snapped back and vanished.

Gunfire rattled in the brush as the poachers returned fire. This time, they had a good fix on his position. Two-dozen rounds cut through his treetop hide clipping branches and raining leaves and bits of bark onto his head. *Time to take the elevator.* Just as Forrest gripped his climbing rope and took up the slack in preparation to descend, a second volley peppered the tree. One round cut through a three-inch limb above his head partially severing it. Buckling at the point of impact, it swung downward like a huge baseball bat striking Forrest a glancing blow to the side of his head. He saw a bright flash and felt his legs buckle before his vision went black. Tumbling from the tree, he bounced off the leafy extremities of a lower branch, which broke his fall. He landed flat on his back, unconscious in a dense thicket.

"Sir," a soft, accented feminine voice called. "Sir. Fasten your seat belt, please," the pretty, blond Swiss Air flight attendant urged. Pleasant though it was, it was more an order than a request. "We will be landing in Nairobi in twenty minutes."

Frank Zito sat up and rubbed his bald scalp then his crusty eyes. For a man used to going into combat in the back of a C-130, or worse, the plush 767-300ER was a pleasant change. He looked out at the strange brown landscape gliding beneath his small window then glanced at his watch. He felt a vague excitement—the sort of feeling an old soldier gets when arriving at a new base—in a new theater of operations—to fight a new war.

Mpika peered around a tree just in time to see two of his men empty their magazines at the sniper hidden in the trees. The bursts were well aimed, he saw, knocking their target off his perch. His heart leaped at the thought of killing the American who had caused him so many hardships of late.

"Finish him!" he shouted after his men who quickly searched their pockets for full magazines. "Go! Go!"

Mpika stepped from behind the tree and prepared to advance when rifle shots exploded behind him.

* * * *

Ranger Ben Otieno, the officer in charge, lowered his rifle and ordered his Masai rangers to cease fire as the poachers across the river crouched and scurried off into the shadows. He signaled his team to move then halted thirty meters ahead, their advance blocked by the rushing waters of the Ewaso Ng'iro river which had swelled in last night's torrential rains.

Otieno took cover behind a log as the two squads exchanged volleys, driving the poachers into a hasty retreat.

A bright ray of afternoon sunshine penetrated the tree canopy to find Forrest's eyelids, stirring him awake. Badly shaken, he lay in the dirt and matted leaves beneath a large, leafy bush holding his head in an attempt to quell the pain. Nearby, a family of curious baboons sat at the base of an acacia tree eyeing him warily as he suddenly remembered how he came to be lying on the ground. "Anne!" he moaned, sitting up with a start.

Ignoring the pain from several minor injuries and his inflamed ribs, Forrest pulled himself to his feet, steadying himself against the trunk of the tree from which he had fallen. Baby baboons clung to their mothers' necks as they nervously backed off a few paces, poised to beat a hasty retreat in the presence of a human who was acting more strangely than most.

Rubbery legs supported him for a full five minutes while Forrest rested his back against the bark and listened for signs of danger. Buzzing insects accompanied the chatter of a few gregarious birds and the occasional bark of an anxious baboon. Otherwise, there was only an ominous silence.

Forrest noted the low sun and looked at his watch. "Damn!" He'd been out of it for hours! Memories of the morning's events were coming back in short, frightening, instant-replays. He remembered the defiant look on Anne's face. "I told you to stay put!" he hissed, admonishing her image. "Why didn't she listen?" he anguished.

Still groggy, it took another five minutes to find his rifle. He checked it for damage, blew dirt off the lenses and action then leaned it against a tree. Before setting off to find Anne, he pulled his climbing rope out of the tree, coiled it and poked his head through its center.

Forrest crept ahead wishing he'd brought the MP-5 or at least the Colt, both of which were better suited for a close-in fight than his rifle. The brush opened up slowly before him giving way to a grassy area lined by tall graceful trunks that supported dark sprawling canopies. Forrest studied the shadows carefully before moving into the open then slipped into the darkness on the other side of the clearing. The river whispered in the background as Forrest himself became a shadow, blending with the darkness like a spirit of the forest. After ten minutes of stealthy stop-and-go progress, Forrest came across the first of four mutilated elephant carcasses. He smelled them long before he saw them. His legs went stiff with dread. "Schwarzkopf," he whispered to himself with a gritty voice. The huge animal lay on his side as if he were sleeping. A few meters away lay another carcass, a large cow, her tusks also intact, her vacant eyes staring into nothingness.

"Ohhhh no!" His heart sank when he saw the large identifying tear in her ear. "Oprah." Forrest walked up next to her, shooing away the first foursome in a growing crowd of vultures. He laid his hand on her back, grimaced and turned his head away. "I'm sorry, lady. I should've been here for you."

He studied the ground near her body. He was sure he'd dropped a bad guy in the vicinity. *Where was he, now?* Drag marks and a blood trail told the story. They'd taken the body with them, just like Charlie used to do. *But where?*

Forrest came across two more carcasses under the trees: Custer, a mature male who had lost his tail to a pride of lions as a cub, and Rosie, Oprah's younger sister, a round female who was always eating.

"Sons of bitches!" he growled in disgust.

It suddenly occurred to Forrest that the poachers hadn't finished their business. But despite his fears to the contrary, they were not waiting in ambush. *Why? Probably assumed they'd killed me when they saw my ass tumble out of that tree.*

Throwing caution aside, he plunged ahead through the thicket searching for signs of Anne and the Land Rover. Where could she be? What could they have done with her? Answers to that last question were too awful to contemplate. He raced past a fly-covered pool of blood and more drag marks. *Theirs or hers?* What he wouldn't give to see her now—hold her again. If only he could have the morning to live over.

"Anne!" he bellowed at the top of his lungs, no longer caring that he might give away his position. He stood motionless for a moment, begging the mute trees to hear her voice. He ran another two-hundred meters along the river and stopped, falling to his knees in a small pool of light. He gasped for breath, almost in tears as he looked up at a little piece of sky peeking through the canopy. His hand went to the little cross hanging from his neck. "God, please help me find her," he anguished. Forrest jammed the butt of his rifle into the dirt and leaned forward, bracing himself on the barrel with both hands.

His eyes came back down to the ground to find tracks left by two separate sets of tires. One set appeared to be the familiar track of his Rover, the other made by a truck judging from the width of them. Both led off down river and disappeared into the woods. That had to be it, then. They'd taken her with them. *Better be alive!* "I'm coming for you, lady," he shouted down the trail. *And for Chrissakes keep your mouth shut. Don't provoke the bastards.* Another thought suddenly occurred to him as he turned back toward the camp and the plane he would use to pursue them: At least he hadn't found her body, so there was always hope.

Ranger Ben Otieno's five-man Masai ranger team was frustrated at not being able to find a suitable ford across the Ewaso Ng'iro. The previous night's storm had turned the river into a raging torrent. And as they had so many times before, this gang of poachers had eluded them.

Otieno stood on the bank of the river, canteen in hand, as his men rested under the shade of a tree. Pursuit on foot was useless, he realized. Their best course of action would be to return to their vehicle and cross down river at the bridge where they might be able to pick up the poachers' trail before a passing shower washed it away. He replaced his canteen's plastic cap then returned it to the pouch clipped to his web belt as he turned to rouse his weary men.

Trees and grassland rushed beneath the Cessna's wings as its prop pulled the craft through the warm air thick with new moisture. Forrest wove through the treetops, his head swinging left and right, his keen eyes scouring the terrain for any signs of the poachers and their prisoner. Once or twice, he'd pulled the plane around in a hard three-sixty thinking his eyes had caught a glimpse of something beneath the trees only to be disappointed on his second pass.

The Cessna roared on, its propeller and engine set for maximum forward speed. Miles of grass and trees streamed by, punctuated by bounding antelope startled by the sudden appearance of a winged monster buzzing just above their heads. The *Immaculate Contraption* chased its shadow along the ground crossing and re-crossing the wandering river and its bordering woodlands. Off to the left, Forrest saw the trees give way to nearly a mile of grass and small shrubs where he spotted the bent-grass wheel-tracks left by two vehicles. Forrest yanked the plane to the left to follow them until they once again disappeared into the trees. On the far side of the grove the tracks reemerged. He followed them for nearly a kilometer before realizing there was now only one set!

The prop roared as Forrest whipped the plane around to revisit the woodland he'd just passed. He circled multiple times before detecting a glint of light reflecting off something shiny, something metallic. He felt his chest tighten as he pulled the throttle back to idle, bled off airspeed, and lowered the flaps for landing. Minutes later the Cessna bounced in the grass and gradually came to a stop.

A small cloud of grass clippings churned up by the propeller had not fully dispersed before Forrest emerged, MP-5 in hand. He stood and listened for a moment before bounding off through the grass toward the trees. Once into their shadows he moved ahead quickly but carefully, leery of stumbling into a trap.

Forrest crept circuitously toward the point where he'd seen a reflection through the treetops. A few meters ahead he heard something move in the shadows and froze. *Footsteps? Had he heard something or merely sensed it?* He felt his fingers tighten on the forestock. He detected something—a presence—behind him. The hair stood up on the back of his arms. He wheeled and spurted a short burst into a thick tree trunk he'd just passed.

"Cap'n!" a soft voice called out from behind the trunk.

Forrest couldn't believe his ears. The voice sounded vaguely familiar.

"Don't shoot, Cap'n." The muffled voice urged.

Forrest steadied the submachine gun on the tree which already bore fresh bullet scars in its bark. "Show yourself," he barked. "Hands first."

Movement at the bottom of the tree surprised him. Sneakers. His finger eased up on the trigger. A tall, dark man emerged from behind the trunk, his eyes staring blankly at the man who'd almost killed him. *Rufira. The witch!*

"She is just ahead, Cap'n."

Forrest felt a chill run down the back of his neck. His face reflected his confusion.

"The woman is there. Follow me," he said devoid of emotion and walked off into the shadows.

Forrest swallowed and did as he was instructed.

After several minutes the pair entered an area beneath the trees where the brush parted. Forrest's Land Rover sat in the center, oddly shiny in the light which trickled from above. The place was silent, cool, foreboding. Forrest stepped ahead and froze, the MP-5 poised to fire. He warily checked the perimeter, though he somehow knew there was no longer a threat.

Forrest's eyes went back to the Rover. Another chill surged through him. "Is she...?" He turned. Rufira was gone. He let out a long nervous breath and returned his attention to the Rover.

The clearing was deathly silent. Even the wind seemed to be

holding its breath as he moved up next to the vehicle. He peered through the glass checking the interior. The front seats were a mess, papers, maps, and leaves were strewn everywhere. The floors were covered with dirt.

His eyes shifted to the back seat where he saw a blanket which appeared to be covering something. Forrest sucked in a deep breath and held it. Trembling fingers pulled the back door open.

At the near end of the seat he saw the top of Anne's head. He started to reach for the blanket then pulled his hand back. He softly called her name.

"Anne."

No response.

"Anne," he repeated in an anxious whisper.

Forrest lifted the blanket away from her face. "Noooooo!" came the cry of an anguished soul. He recoiled in horror at the sight. Anne's lifeless eyes stared at the roof. He tore the blanket away and dropped the MP-5 on the ground. Her nude body was covered with scratches and bruises. Dried blood covered the upholstery under her buttocks and the skin of her thighs. Forrest sank to his knees, resting his heavy head against the side of the seat.

An eternity passed before his legs found the strength to lift him. He stood grim-faced as he passed his fingers through her hair then closed her vacant eyes—those beautiful green eyes. His dam of control ruptured, loosing a flood of torment down his cheeks.

His eyes went to her chest where a large rhinoceros horn rested, its pointed end caked with a blackened crust of dried blood. Beneath it lay a blood-spattered photograph—one he recognized—the one he had taken of Windridge in Mpika's camp. Forrest studied it for a moment then went to her bloody thighs and bruised neck. "Motherfucker!" he growled. Only one man would be callous enough to leave such a calling card and arrogant enough to leave one as valuable as this.

"Shetani," Forrest hissed through clenched teeth. He tightened his fists and looked to the southeast. Forrest coughed up some phlegm and forcefully spit into the dirt.

He turned back to Anne, his hand coming up to the little gold cross hanging around his neck. "God should have protected you instead of me." He stroked her cold cheek with the backs of his fingers and smiled. Tears dripped on her chest. "I love you, lady." He bent forward and kissed her cool forehead.

Forrest stood silently for a moment gazing at her face. Then he suddenly sucked in a deep breath, steeling himself to the searing pain. Tenderly he rolled her body in the blanket and left it on the seat. He closed the back door and picked up the MP-5 then checked the vehicle over once more—carefully this time. It wasn't until then that he saw it had a flat tire and realized it was the reason they'd stopped here. He opened the front door and found that despite the disarray, the keys were still in the ignition. It took only a short time to change the tire.

As he drove back to his Cessna, visions of the previous night raced through his mind before turning to what lay ahead.

Malcolm McCullen met Forrest at the airstrip soon after he landed. The sight of Forrest holding Anne's body wrapped in a blanket chilled him to the bone. "Dear God, lad," he gasped. "What happened?"

"Not now, Doc," Forrest grunted, his eyes staring off into space, avoiding eye contact. "Not now," he repeated more softly than before. He led the doctor back into the camp, walking directly to Anne's hut. Laboriously, he climbed the stairs and went inside where he laid his precious bundle on the cot. He stood in silence for some time before brushing his fingertips along the blanket. "Good-bye, lady," he whispered. "I wish we'd had more time...and not wasted the time we had."

He turned to see McCullen standing in the doorway. They shared a long, blury look before Forrest walked past him out into the bright sunlight. McCullen followed in stunned silence. Forrest walked slowly toward his hut allowing the doctor to catch up. "They killed her, Doc." He felt McCullen bristle and took three more steps. "It's my fault."

"Hold on, lad." McCullen grabbed his arm. The grip was amazingly strong. "Who killed her?"

Forrest stopped and turned, a tear rolled down his cheek and dripped onto his shirt. "The same bunch of poachers who killed my son."

"Why?"

Forrest pulled the blood-stained photo from his top pocket and handed it to McCullen. "They attacked Oprah's family. Anne ran off to stop them when I went to my plane to get my rifle. I think they were sent to kill both of us."

McCullen looked at the photo and stopped breathing. "Her husband was here looking for both of you. The police were with him."

Forrest turned and continued walking. "It was just a question of time. What did you tell 'em?"

"I played dumb. I told 'em I didn't know where you two went." McCullen's eyes were filling, hands trembling.

Forrest turned away to consider this new bit of information. "Well, somebody did."

"What now?" McCullen asked nervously. His whole world seemed to be unraveling by the minute.

Forrest sensed his fear and put a hand on his shoulder. "Now I finish what I came here to do in the first place." Forrest started up the steps to his hut and called behind him. "Can you ask Joseph to come help me pack? Tell him to bring his kids," he commanded softly, beginning to get a grip.

"Alright then," was the soft reply.

Forrest went through his belongings packing the minimum he needed. Minutes later Joseph and two of his sons arrived to help. They spent twenty minutes loading the Zenair with anything the police might think incriminating, beginning with the satellite communications unit and the ERMA sniper-rifle. Not that it mattered, anymore but Forrest didn't want to leave sensitive equipment behind, especially if it might implicate McCullen, Grant, or the U.S. Government in any way.

After the Zenair was loaded, Forrest donned his parachute, telling his helpers he would be right back.

One of the boys, the youngest, asked: "Can I go for a ride?"

Forrest, who would have laughed and complied under other circumstances, did manage a smile. "Not this time, little man." With that, he climbed into the tiny machine, started the engine and took off. Ten minutes later, he leveled off over the camp at an altitude of five thousand feet, turned the aircraft toward the Indian Ocean and set the auto pilot.

Joseph and his sons watched aghast as Forrest leaped out of the airplane and fell a thousand feet before opening his parachute. The children cackled with glee when the first sky-diver they had ever seen spiraled down gracefully and flared the solid-black square-rig canopy to a soft landing on the airstrip. They all watched in fascination while Forrest spent the next twenty minutes repacking the chute before putting it in the Cessna.

The older boy asked the inevitable question. "Who is flying the plane, Bwana John?"

"George."

"George?"

"That's the name we give the autopilot," Forrest explained.

"Autopilot?"

"Later, my son," Joseph interrupted, sensing a need to end the interrogation. "We have work to do."

The group returned to Forrest's hut where they assisted with the rest of the packing. All that remained was some of his personal gear which the boys, ages eleven and eight, eyed with great curiosity and a certain amount of envy.

Forrest read their faces. "Gentlemen," Forrest said with sentiment. "I think this is good-bye. It's time for me to go." Forrest shared a sad look with Joseph and left it at that. "I have something for all of you." Joseph's expression said, 'no' but the children became excited. To the youngest, Forrest presented his Sony Discman and several CDs. The boy squealed with delight when the American put the headphones over his ears and cranked it up. For the older boy who appeared quite jealous of his brother's prize, Forrest had something as well. "Michael, I know you've wanted this for a long time. You'll be a man soon. And this is a man's tool. Use it carefully." With that, Forrest presented him with his Gerber survival knife and scabbard. "Your father will show you how to use it so you don't carve up your friends." Forrest looked at Joseph who seemed very uncomfortable with all of it. Joseph was clearly torn between refusing the generosity and disappointing his boys. Forrest sensed he was about to protest and cut him off. "And for you my good friend," he said to Joseph, "I have something very special."

The tall Masai man searched his eyes.

"Do you remember where we camped when we darted that little elephant, the one with the wire wrapped around her leg?"

"Yes."

"I need you to fly out there with me."

"When?"

"Right now. I'll meet you at the plane."

Joseph and sons took off for the airstrip while Forrest scribbled a note, stuffed it into an envelope and went to find the Doctor. His first guess was correct, McCullen was sitting in Anne's hut staring at her corpse. When Forrest placed his hand on the old man's shoulder he saw a tear splash on the floor among a dozen others. Forrest placed the note, addressed to Allen Windridge on her blanket then knelt down on the floor next to McCullen's chair. There was a long moment of silence.

"You were like a father to her," Forrest said, softly. "She loved you very much."

McCullen sobbed silently then spoke: "Some father I am," he said with a great deal of effort. "A good father," he managed between sobs, "protects his children." A second later, after realizing what he'd said, McCullen turned his head to face Forrest. He wiped his cheeks with the back of his hands. "I'm sorry, lad. I didn't mean..."

Forrest, who was on the verge of tears, himself, cut him off. "It's okay, Doc. I know what you meant. We can't protect our children all the time. And we sure as hell can't protect them from themselves.

But I could have done a better job this time." Forrest's eyes dropped to the floor.

McCullen partially regained his composure and gripped Forrest by the forearms.

Forrest, really struggling for control, looked up and the two men searched each other's eyes then shared a long, intense hug.

McCullen pushed Forest to arms length, shook him and gave him the strongest smile he could manage. "Now get out there and finish what you've started."

It was nearly dark when Joseph and Forrest finished packing the tent and other gear into the Land Rover. It had been a much more painful exercise than Forrest anticipated. Seeing her clothes, her hat, the candles and the little bottle of perfume he'd given her made it almost unbearable. Funny, he thought, how in a world of huge problems and serious undertakings it was always the little, insignificant things that meant so much in the end. And, he reflected, it was weird how those little sentiments could bring an otherwise invincible man to his knees.

Having Joseph there had helped. It gave him a reason to be strong. He couldn't break down in front of a man who had come to expect stalwart leadership. Forrest left a pile of food stuffs under the trees for the man who had helped him find Anne. When they were finished Forrest turned to Joseph and said his good-byes. As the American "father of the elephants" turned to walk to his plane, Joseph called after him. "What shall I do with the Rover when I get it back to camp?"

Forrest turned and said with a half smile: "Whatever you want, my friend. It's yours now."

The director of the Kenya Wildlife Service had apparently taken him seriously, McCullen thought as the helicopter landed on the near end of the camp's airstrip some two hours after their telephone conversation.

Windridge was out of his seat and walking full stride well before the pilot could shut the engine down. "Where is she?" he snapped at a gentleman who was far more upset than the new widower. Windridge might have walked right over Malcolm McCullen had the elder man not stepped aside.

"We put her in her hut," McCullen said to her husband's back as the pair made their way to the row of living quarters standing near the camp's center. Windridge strode directly to the guest cottage where he swept aside the mosquito netting McCullen had drawn about his dear departed friend. He stood silently for a moment before leaning over and picking up the envelope with his name on it. He read with clenched teeth.

> SHE WAS TOO GOOD FOR EITHER OF US.
> WHEN YOU COME FOR ME BRING A
> BODY BAG IN YOUR SIZE.

Windridge turned and slapped the note into McCullen's chest.

"Where is he?" Windridge demanded abruptly. He saw McCullen's eyes go wide at the confrontation.

McCullen shrugged. "He's gone. Cleared out."

Windridge pushed past the old man, down the steps and turned left. Two minutes later her pounded up the steps and kicked open the door to Forrest's old hut. All of the American's belongings were gone. Windridge backed out of the hut, confronting a browbeaten McCullen. "Our business is far from finished," he warned. "Aiding and abetting a murderer is a serious crime."

"You're late, goddammit," Zito groused with a smile as he opened the hotel room door late that same evening.

"So sue me," Forrest muttered walking past him into the double room Zito had reserved at the Nairobi Hilton.

Zito pulled back, immediately sensing something was wrong. He went to get Forrest a beer from the mini-fridge. Forrest had just landed on the sofa when Zito put a cold TUSKER on the end table at his elbow. He twisted the top off his own bottle and plopped down in an upholstered chair positioned next to the television.

"You wanna tell me about it?" Zito asked evenly, after taking a gulp then ripping a long shameless belch.

Forrest looked up from the floor then turned to open his beer which he consumed in one long continuous drink. "Got another one?"

Zito, who hadn't seen Forrest do anything quite like that since some of their buddies were killed in Vietnam, half-smiled and raised his eyebrows. It took only a second to retrieve another bottle from the fridge and twist off the top.

Forrest took a smaller gulp this time and leaned forward, holding the bottle between his legs as he looked at the floor.

Zito regarded him curiously then leaned back and frowned. He let a full five minutes pass before breaking the silence. "I was worried about you, man. It's not like you to be late. You're one of the few men I know who's as dependable as daylight."

Forrest didn't respond. It was almost as if he hadn't heard a word his friend said. Instead, he continued to burn a hole in the carpet. Thunder rumbled outside as a steady rain pelted the windows.

Zito finished his beer and got himself another. "Don't tell me you've lost your nerve after I came all this way to help you."

Forrest looked up. "I lost a good woman, today, Zit. And I said good-bye to some good friends—some *damn* good friends." He took another sip from his bottle. "All in all, I'd say it was a pretty fucking bad day. But I guaran-goddamn-tee you I haven't lost my nerve."

"A woman?" Zito asked, never really thinking it possible for Forrest to back down from a fight. He'd certainly never done it before. And besides, if the stories about his great, great, great uncle, the Confederate general, were even half true, big, brass balls were fruit which grew plentifully on the Forrest family tree.

Forrest dismissed the question with a wave. A few more beers would have to go down before he could begin to talk about it. To that end, he gulped down the rest of number two and held his hand out for number three.

Zito complied promptly and sat back as a wry smile crept across his face. He knew his friend couldn't be rushed and didn't attempt it. No way. Besides, he didn't want to be the only drunk at the party. He watched Forrest open his third beer, shifted gears and changed subjects. "So what's the plan? I know you have one. Other than me, of course, you are the scariest, most diabolical, calculating motherfucker I know. You don't shit, shower or shave without a plan."

Forrest looked into his eyes with a penetrating stare. "Tomorrow morning we receive an air drop from Grizz. Then we go splatter a few dozen despicable assholes desperately deserving of it and rescue Amy. Questions?"

A huge grin erupted on Zito's face as he stood, clinked his bottle against Forrest's, gulped the rest of his beer then exclaimed: "Now *that* sounds like my idea of a vacation!"

CHAPTER-TWENTY TWO

MANHUNT *a: an organized and usually intensive hunt for a person, especially one charged with a crime*

"SO WHADAYA THINK?" Zito asked his friend as they scanned Mpika's sleeping camp with their NVGs. All had been quiet for hours, the only movement had been a man who'd ventured outside his hut to relieve himself.

"Let's stick with plan A," Forrest whispered. "The classic L-shaped ambush. You take the fuel truck and the long side of the L. When you light up the place, I'll slip into the back of Amy's hut, grab her and we'll take the short side of the L around back." He held his watch up in front of his face to examine its luminous hands. "Let's circumcise our watches. I'm coming up on zero two three two in twenty seconds."

"Okay."

"Ready...ready...hack," Forrest announced with a cadence while Zito hit the appropriate button on his Casio digital at the appropriate instant. "Plan on being in position at 04:00. Remember, Amy's in the third hootch over and, if we get separated, we'll rendezvous at the plane at dawn."

"Got it," Zito responded, eager to get to work. Most professional soldiers and law enforcement officers were reticent to admit, at least in public, that they *lived* for the day when they could cancel all of some bad guy's future appointments. Frank Zito was no exception and nowhere near ready for his imminent retirement. He'd 'rather cut throats with a Kabar than grass with a Briggs-and-Stratton,' he'd told his commanding officer. But the Army had its rules—no exceptions. Another chance to "get it on" kept him smiling as he soundlessly made his way down the ditch, setting up eight M18A1 Claymore antipersonnel mines whose concave inner radii faced him and convex surfaces did as the embossed letters instructed: FRONT TOWARD ENEMY.

When he reached the end of the ditch, his pack was nearly empty, except for a little water and a lot of ammo. He looked back at his work. He'd made two rows as he went—one positioned slightly behind the other, each device laterally spaced about eight feet from the next. Most were aimed more or less at the first two huts and the open space between them and the fuel truck, poised to cut down all who dared stand before them and taste their wrath. The remaining three devices planted at the end of the line, were angled to cover the gas truck. These were critical. They would launch the initial and perhaps most lethal blast, when nearly everyone would be baited to the spot by the next little goodie in his bag of tricks.

Zito pulled his NVGs down over his eyes and scanned the camp before exiting the ditch and sliding beneath the truck, the last of Mpika's smuggler specials. It took only a minute to position a block of plastique and arm its radio-activated detonator. After one more scan, he reentered the ditch and worked his way back down the line of mines, wiring them in two separate circuits as he went—a pyrotechnic one-two punch of sorts. What the first string didn't kill, the second one would.

* * * *

Forrest's assignment was a bit more complicated than that of his partner. Though he would have to place a smaller number of Claymores than Zit, his work was more intricate—covering the exits and their escape route—two narrow pathways that led through dense undergrowth up a steep slope and over the low ridge which backed the small, wooded village.

To prevent bad guys from leaking through the trees, Forrest had come up with an innovative idea—an explosive fence—a concept similar to an electrified fence, only pyrotechnic and lethal. Dr. Pyro, by way of Henderson and Adams, had provided a number of the devices based on Forrest's design. Forrest moved about in the darkness stringing ten-foot lengths of det-cord at waist level between trees. One end was wrapped around a tree and the other, looped and fitted with a blasting cap, was held in place by a clothespin that doubled as a switch. Anyone running into the trees would snag the wire pulling it out of the clothespin which would spring closed, completing the firing circuit. Though Dr. Pyro hadn't tested it thoroughly, the characteristics of primer-cord detonations were somewhat fickle and therefore, predictably unpredictable. Forrest had been told he could expect varying results. If a man were running fast enough at the time of impact, the cord would partially wrap around his waist. When the clothespin snapped closed, the blast could cut him in half. Or it might merely stun him, though it would certainly make major alterations to his wardrobe. Each device was powered by a 9-volt battery and a capacitor which, like a camera's strobe unit, would build and store a charge until triggered. Forrest rigged five such devices and wired eight Claymores in two rows along the base of the L-shaped ambush configuration before retiring to his position.

He checked his MP-5, pulled off his night vision goggles (the bright fireworks would gain them down severely, making them useless in the initial attack) then got a radio check with his partner who sat out of sight behind a tree on the other side of the ditch.

"Zit. Thumper," he whispered into his headset's boom-microphone.

"Gooood mooooooorning, Taaan-za-n*i*a!" came the enthusiastic though muffled response. "Got you five-by-five."

"Same." Forrest took a deep breath and looked at his watch. It was nearly 04:00. "All set?"

"Lets boogie."

"Roger. Don't forget…" Forrest cautioned, with a small tight voice. "Don't rush the choreography. And don't kill Mpika unless you have to. I've got plans for him."

"Yes dear."

"And don't direct any fire at the third hut until I call with Amy in tow.

"Yes dear."

"Fuck you."

"Yes dear."

Forrest smiled at the comeback. "Okay, let's light 'em up," he ordered, making himself as small as he could behind a tree.

The blast echoed through the hills, the fireball illuminating the camp like daylight. Splattering gasoline torched the nearby brush and the lower branches of overhanging trees, expanding the inferno well beyond the fuel truck. Forrest could feel the radiant heat fifty meters away.

"Here they come," Zito transmitted. "You want I should call nine-one-one?" he joked.

Forrest watched the huts, his hand on his M57 Claymore clackers. "For them or us?" he radioed back.

Three men emerged from two huts, clad only in trousers. As predicted, they ran toward the fire shouting in Swahili. More stumbled out of their houses in various stages of dress. Forrest watched Mpika's hut intently until The Serpent appeared at the door, pulling on his pants. "Serpent's in his hole. Last hootch on the right, closest to me."

"Got him." The leader didn't seem very agitated. He took his time getting dressed, letting his men run to extinguish the fire. He was either very wily or very lazy, Zito thought. Zito's eyes went back to the men who had begun throwing water on a hut near the burning truck. It was too late to save the truck, they realized. A group of six had gathered to form a bucket brigade, drawing water from the drainage ditch then passing it along where it was ultimately splashed on a thatched roof alive with flame.

"Time for the first cut?" Zito asked.

Forrest shifted his eyes from Mpika to the fire brigade. "Give it a minute," he cautioned as two more men ran to join the effort. "We want a higher body count. I'm heading for Amy's hootch."

"Roger that."

As he made his way through the foliage, Forrest's eyes went back to Mpika who stood in his front door watching the firefighters assault a hopeless task. Forrest noticed something in his hand—the barrel of an AK. "I think Shetani's on to us. He's got a weapon," Forrest advised.

Zito looked to the leader's hut and confirmed Forrest's sighting. "Roger that."

Forrest, MP-5 at the ready, reached the flimsy back wall of Amy's hut and without hesitation kicked a hole in the brittle wood. Another kick and he had a hole big enough to wiggle inside. Once in, he pulled his NVGs down over his eyes and scanned the room. Quietly, on the balls of his feet, he crept forward looking for his daughter-in-law.

Amy was sitting up, alert and staring at the door, her hands tied behind her back. Although she couldn't make out who it was she had a feeling…"Uncle John?" she whispered.

"You bet, honey. Who else would it be?"

"My hands are tied," she stated, standing up and turning around.

Forrest lifted his NVGs and made quick work of the cord with his boot knife then jerked his submachine gun up high to make room for the spontaneous hug which followed.

"When I heard the explosion, I knew it was you. I knew you would come," she whispered, squeezing as hard as she could. "What took you so long?" she added.

"We weren't sure you were alive for starters. Not until your dad saw your lake-o-gram."

"Oh, thank God!" she gasped.

"C'mon, honey," he urged. "We're not out of the shit, yet."

Just as they turned Forrest caught a glimpse of a human silhouette back-lit by the fire. He swung violently, catching the figure's cheek with his elbow knocking it down. When he raised the muzzle of his MP-5 to administer the coup-de-grace Amy grabbed the barrel and pulled it high.

"No. She was nice to me, actually. A lot nicer than her husband."

Until then Forrest hadn't realized it was a woman. "Mmm," he grunted. "Let's go before we get more visitors."

"You have one of those for me?" Amy asked, gesturing at Forrest's dull black submachine-gun.

Forrest laughed and extracted the Anaconda from his shoulder holster. "That's a lotta gun," he cautioned.

"Have you forgotten whose daughter-in-law I am?" Her voice caught in her throat. "I'm a lotta girl," she said, dismissing the reminder of Nathan and heading for the front door.

Forrest grabbed her arm. "No. This way. Back door. There's some nasty shit waiting out front."

"There's no back door," she announced, freezing in place.

"There is now. I remodeled the place on my way in."

Forrest made his way through the hole first, cleared the area with the NVGs then gestured for Amy. They moved quickly to Forrest's original position where they settled in behind a big tree.

Mpika was still in place watching the fire brigade from his steps.

"We're clear," he announced into his mike.

"Shit hot." A moment's hesitation, then: "We…?"

"Roger that."

Zito grinned and glanced toward the big tree hiding his friends. The sound of footsteps to his immediate front caught his attention. Zito looked back just in time to see that one of the firemen had spotted his line of Claymores. A man crouched next to one of his mines, fingering the wire and detonator. *Fuck!* The man turned to shout something but never got it all out.

"Fire in the hole...ass-hole." Zito's thumb came down on the trigger twice unleashing 700 steel balls belched outward in a tooth-rattling roar. Everyone and everything disappeared in a cloud of dust and smoke. When it cleared, there was no one standing. The front wall of the burning hootch had collapsed as had the front of the hut next door.

Forrest checked Mpika's doorway. Gone. *Shit.* "Serpent's gone," he growled into his microphone. Two men, one with clothes aflame, and a woman ran from the second hut, its roof totally engulfed in flames. One of them sporadically fired a rifle as he went, covering their escape. They were running right at him, unaware of what lay in their path. For an instant he hesitated.

"Now that's what I call a real hot dresser," Forrest muttered, watching the panicked man run into the brush to his right. He turned his attention to the remaining couple. Professional, civilized warriors didn't kill women if they were noncombatants. But, he reminded himself in the time it took to draw a breath: *Nobody cut Anne any slack.* Forrest flipped the wire bail out of his Claymore clacker and cut them down, simultaneously smashing the side wall of Mpika's hut. A second later, he heard one of the Claymores he'd set along a rear trail thump sharply. A second, more urgent crack told him the first of the det-cord clotheslines had snagged another frightened runner as well.

"Good heavens," Amy exclaimed, confused by the widespread pyrotechnics. "How many men did you bring with you?"

"Just our 'Army of one,' your uncle Zit."

"Uncle Z? He's here?"

"Figured that's all we'd need for this op."

Directly across from Zito, someone let go a burst from an AK-47 through an opening in the wall. Zito located the source, leveled his M-79 grenade launcher and fired. A ringing thump was answered with a thunderous boom. Further such skirmishing was systematically eliminated with accurately placed grenades.

Forrest interrupted Zito's fun with a radio call. "Blow your last string on my call."

"Roge." Zito hunkered down behind his tree and waited.

"I'm moving to cover the rear." Forrest moved to his right, Amy in tow, one tree at a time until he had a full view of the backs of the burning huts. "Hit it." He flinched when a staccato blast peeled back the fronts of the huts, launching flaming debris over their roofs. "Put a grenade into the Serpent's hut and fall back to my position," Forrest ordered.

His answer was a tympanic thump and a boom, followed by the sound of legs crashing through the brush—two sets of legs.

To his left, Zito caught sight of a man and a woman racing into the darkness. He swung his MP-5 to fire but they disappeared before he could.

"Two players escaping stage left. Want me to pursue?"

"No," Forrest snapped. "We can use the publicity." Forrest's voice suddenly became urgent. "I've got two movers over here! Snake's on the move. Get back here!"

"On the way."

Forrest heard Zito coming and directed him to his hiding spot. The flames were beginning to diminish as he knelt down next to Forrest. A burst of rifle fire splintered the tree trunk near Forrest's head, driving them into the dirt. "Two of 'em," Forrest told his friend. "Goggles on. We'll flush 'em out."

Zito peeked around the tree, examining the woods through his NVGs.

"Pop a grenade into the top of that tree," Forrest suggested. "The biggest one at one o'clock."

Zito shoved a grenade into the launcher's breech and locked it closed. THUMP! BLAM! A limb and several branches crashed to the ground. A man broke and ran a few paces before hitting a length of det-cord. He went down in a flash of thunder, his detached arms thrashing in the leaves and dirt.

Forrest allowed the spectacle to occupy his attention for a moment then glanced at Amy who didn't bat an eye. He noticed another moving object, a warm one. It moved cautiously—tentatively—limping away from their position, deeper into the trees like a green ghost. Forrest tapped Zito on the shoulder and pointed in its direction. "Mover. Limping. It's him. You circle left. I'll go right." They parted and drifted into the darkness one careful step at a time. "Watch the boobytraps," Forrest cautioned. "They don't discriminate."

Zito moved further left, pausing to listen and scan the green patterns of light. He put one foot in front of the other, testing each footfall for noise-making debris.

Forrest did likewise, ducking under one of his own clotheslines before pausing behind a tree. Smoke from the smoldering fires drifted through the trees restricting his vision. His head twisted left with the snap of a distant stick. He swallowed hard and moved ahead. "He's moving again." Forrest turned his head to Amy. "Stay here and stay low. I'll come back for you."

Forrest caught a glimpse of his friend moving quickly ahead before he disappeared behind a tree. He duplicated the move in an attempt to sandwich the poacher between them.

Zito lost sight of their quarry and rushed ahead, the rustle of leaves revealing his position to a man accustomed to lying in wait.

Mpika pulled back into some bushes, allowing his pursuer to pass twenty meters beyond his hiding place.

Ten meters further along, Zito froze, scanning the brush.

Mpika slowly brought his rifle up and laid the invisible steel sights over Zito's silhouette. He squeezed the trigger, pumping out his last two rounds. POP-POP. The man went down.

Forrest recognized the weapon's sound. *AK!* "Zit!...Zit! You okay? Zit. Goddammit! Answer me!" he whispered tersely into his microphone.

No answer.

Forrest moved in the direction of the shots a few meters at a time, freezing to listen in between.

Mpika pulled back against the tree and waited. Setting his empty weapon down, he pulled his knife and hugged the bark. He strained to listen for the American who would almost certainly come to his friend's aid.

Forrest crept ahead, his MP-5 protruding in front of him. His heart skipped a beat when he saw the crumpled body of his friend just ahead. His first instinct was to rush to him. But wisdom and experience held him back. *He's bait!*

Forrest froze, examining each tree and bush. Nothing. He felt around on the ground for something, anything, an object to hurl into the bushes to make noise. His fingers came upon a stick which he flung into a bush growing five meters to his eleven o'clock.

Mpika flinched at the sound of movement...close...just on the other side of his tree! He pulled back, moving in slow motion, a millimeter at a time. His bare left foot came down as would a sloth's onto some leaves, then his right foot onto something odd. WHAM! He gasped and leaped ahead, something rubbery fell off his foot. The pain was ferocious. *Snake!*

Forrest saw him stagger and sent a short burst into his lower legs, knocking them out from under him. Mpika went down with a thud. In a flash Forrest was on him, planting his knee into his chest, the muzzle of his submachine gun into his forehead, pinning him to the ground. A swift move knocked the knife out of Mpika's hand before he could react. Forrest felt him struggle against the weight and answered it with a hard right cross to the jaw, delivering every ounce of weight he could with the blow.

Mpika fell limp.

Forrest cinched two zip-ties around his wrists and ankles, effectively immobilizing his victim while he attended to Zito. His fingers found a strong carotid pulse and regular breathing. Forrest breathed a sigh of his own as his friend came around when a trickle of water was poured over his face.

Zito sat up with a groan and rested his throbbing head in his hands. His right hand went to his ear then came down wet with a warm slipperiness.

"You okay?" Forrest asked with more concern than his tone revealed.

"Mmm...think so," Zito responded with a grunt, pulling his NVGs off his head. *Ain't dead and ain't paralyzed but it sure stings like hell. And the ringing in my right ear...* "Yeah, I'm fine," he added a moment later.

Forrest pulled out his Maglite and played the beam over his friend's face, then the rest of his head. A bullet had cut a ragged notch in the top of his right ear which bled as head wounds are prone to do—profusely. He followed the blood to the side of his neck where he saw a clean gash in the epidermis—a grazing bullet wound. *A half an inch to the left and the consequences would have been quite different.* "Don't see anything life threatening," he said flatly. "But your modeling career is over."

Zito felt the top of his ear with his fingers.

"Flesh wounds. One to your ear and one to your neck," Forrest summarized. "Can you stand up?"

"I told ya I'm fine." Frank Zito gathered his legs beneath him and lifted himself to his feet. He wavered for a moment, more wobbly than he thought.

"Can you walk?" Forrest asked, careful not to be too patronizing. Zito had an economy-size ego and a temper to match.

"If I can stand, I can walk," his buddy groused in his signature raspy voice. "You get the sumbitch?"

Forrest gestured toward Mpika. "Over there. Sleeping."

"Musta walked right past the fucker. He hit me from behind."

"Let's move him back into the camp and get you bandaged up."

Unseen behind them, a figure converged on their position, then hesitated a moment before raising a weapon. Hidden in the shadows, the figure steadied the rifle on his target.

BOOM!

Zito and Forrest hit the ground and rolled to level their weapons on the assailant before realizing the prostrate figure was no longer a threat.

"Good thing I was here to rescue you guys," Amy taunted, moving forward from the shadows, lowering Forrest's powerful pistol next to her thigh.

"No shit, honey," Zito exclaimed with an astonished smile then exchanged a flabbergasted look with Forrest. He stepped forward and gave her a big hug. "Damn glad to see you, honey. Your father will be, too."

"Let's not be planning the party just yet," Forrest interrupted. "Let's mop up this mess and get the hell outta Dodge."

Amy knelt next to the body of the man she had dispatched. It was her "keeper's" husband. She shuddered for a moment as she looked into his lifeless eyes. Black emotions drained out of her, freed by the opportunity for revenge. She suddenly felt hollow, completely empty. Strangely, she felt no remorse for the man who had helped make her life a living hell since she had been captured.

"You OK?" Forrest whispered consolingly as he gently retrieved the Colt from her hand and holstered it in his vest.

Amy hesitated then rose and turned to look at him with a strained smile. "Whatever OK is, I don't think I'll ever be that way again."

"At least you can still shoot!" Zito commented with a dismissive laugh as he looked up from examining the dead man's body. "No shit, little girl. Center of mass."

Zito and Forrest exchanged thin smiles as Forrest gave Amy a one arm hug.

Amy massaged her right wrist with the left then did an exaggerated yawn as she tilted her head from side to side to clear her ears. "That pistol is a monster. Kicks like an NFL punter and *trashed* my ears."

"Hurt that asshole a lot worse than you, little girl," Zito cackled, clearly enjoying the moment.

"It's not like he didn't have it coming," she muttered with a last glance at the body.

"We need to get a move on," Forrest advised as he slung his sub-gun over his shoulder and removed his belt. He bent over Mpika's body looping the belt around his wrists. Then, using it as a leash, he began dragging the unconscious poacher through the brush. Zito led the way, checking for survivors, one of which he dispatched with a short burst to the head. Eight minutes later, Forrest let Mpika's arms drop in the center of the camp and retrieved his belt. Then he and Zito went through the camp making sure no one presented a threat. A few judicious three-round bursts of 9mm removed all doubts.

The sun was just beginning to tint the horizon when Forrest sat his friend down to bandage his wounds. After applying cream antiseptic from a tube, Forrest wrapped Zito's head and neck with a roll of gauze he retrieved from their medical kit.

"How much is missing?" the patient asked as Forrest tore off a piece of adhesive tape.

"Top ten percent," Forrest assessed. "Maybe fifteen. Nobody's gonna confuse you with Yoda, if that's what you're worried about. Then, again..."

"Kiss my ass."

"Hmpf. Now that you're feeling better, how 'bout you get the video camera and set it up while I stake this bastard out like a pup-tent."

When they were finished, the sky had brightened enough to film all of the captured animals before he and Amy released them from their cages. Some, in sad shape, had to be nursed with fresh water and what food they could find. Some, they found, were beyond even that, the hidden costs of the illegal pet trade. They worked most of the morning until Forrest stood shaking his head as the last of the tortoises lumbered off into the deepening shade of the surrounding trees. I hope they make it, he thought, wondering if their treatment during captivity had weakened them to the point where, even though they were free, they might still be serving a death sentence.

"Yes, Colonel. That is correct. A light airplane. A Cessna," Windridge explained to the commander of the Kenya Air Defense Interceptor Squadron. He waited for the man on the other end of the telephone line to scribble the information down. "Its pilot is a fugitive. He's wanted for murder...several as a matter of fact. He's also involved in international drug trafficking and poaching. Informants tell us he has been sighted in southeastern Kenya, somewhere along the Tanzania border. I'm coordinating with the Tsavo Rangers and the Tanzanian authorities to aid in the arrest." Windridge waited for a moment at the colonel's request. From the sound of it, someone had interrupted him for something or another.

After a moment, the officer apologized then asked: "So, how can we help, Mr. Windridge?"

"I'd like you to put your fighters on alert to shoot him down if he attempts to escape by air. He must not be allowed to leave the country. We are taking off immediately by helicopter to join in the search."

"I see." The colonel liked the sound of it. He hadn't had the chance to attack a real target in years. And this might be the last opportunity of his career. He would have to check with his superiors but Windridge had already told him the Defense Minister had given his approval. The more he considered it, the more appealing the mission became. He turned and barked an order for someone to bring him the day's schedule. "I will make the arrangements, Mr. Windridge. My people will be standing by for your call."

It was early afternoon when Zito and Forrest had begun persuading their prisoner to talk. And it was late afternoon when they finished. Mpika lay on the ground in the center of the camp, as naked as the day he was born. For the best part of two hours the two Americans had inflicted unendurable agony on a man already suffering from painful gunshot wounds to the lower legs and the bite of a puff adder to his right foot.

Amy had been assigned the task of caring for some of the captured animals who were too weak to release. Then she had spent some time attending to the woman Forrest had knocked unconscious in Amy's hootch.

Forrest looked down at the insensible form lying in a puddle of mud formed when buckets of water had been splashed in Mpika's face. When he had passed out as hot coals were dropped onto his stomach to sizzle their way into tender flesh, he'd been brought back, coughing and sputtering, to endure the pain all over again, time after time until he admitted to every crime and named all of his conspirators including the current Director of the Kenya Wildlife Service and counterparts in the Tanzanian government. To men who lusted for revenge, Shetani's screams were music to their ears. But the real objective, however satisfying the method, was the videotaped confession. It painted a horrific picture of the havoc power, money and greed could wreak upon creatures who knew nothing of such things, only their terrible consequences.

They had it all now, footage of Mpika's pitiful inventory of captured birds and reptiles along with piles of ivory, skins, and horn. They had the Serpent's admission he'd committed the most heinous murder of a government official with the knowledge and consent of her husband, an admission forthcoming when Zito had stood up on the monster's shattered shinbone to hear it crack beneath an anguished scream.

"That about do it?" Zito asked, bringing Forrest back from his numbing trance.

"Hmm?"

"That it?" Zito repeated, laying his hand on his friend's shoulder. He knew the moment had to be hard for him—coming face-to-face with the demon who'd haunted his every thought all these months. And now to end it—end the quest—to come back from an altered consciousness and adjust to living among normal people in a conventional world governed by the rule of law and abandon a world where the only rule was "whatever it takes." "You're gonna finish him, now, right?"

Forrest hadn't taken his eyes off him—the wretch who'd shattered his life. "He's already finished," he declared quietly. "The adder started it. Let the vultures finish it."

Zito's mouth dropped open. "Ain't you gonna *waste* the sonofabitch?"

Forrest turned and looked at his friend with cold eyes. "Too easy... let him die slow and hard."

Their prisoner suddenly coughed, capturing their attention. The Serpent began laughing, a weak hysterical laugh broken by coughs and gasps. "She liked it," he taunted. "The bitch took the tips of our horns very well. Ha, ha, ha, ha...cough...cough."

Zito ceased the taunting with a swift kick to the side of Mpika's head. Without another word he stomped over to the pile of ivory where he found a long, straight tusk with a particularly sharp point. Then, returning to straddle Mpika whose limbs were each tethered to a wooden stake, he raised the tusk to waist level. "If she liked that, then you're gonna *love* this, douche-bag." With that he plunged the tusk into the poacher's chest, crushing his pounding heart.

A moment of heavy silence passed before Forrest commented just above a whisper: "You always were a heart breaker, Zit."

"He is evil personified." It was a somber female voice—behind them.

Zito and Forrest turned to see Amy staring at Mpika's body. They shared a guilty look then turned to attend to one last chore. They moved quickly, dousing what was left of the huts, cages, and contraband with gasoline then touching it off with the last string of Claymores. Crackling flames raked at the sky as fire and billowing smoke consumed the products of mankind's most shameful enterprise.

"Lets go," Forrest said, cocking his head in the direction of his airplane. "I want to get to Lunga Lunga early."

CHAPTER-TWENTY THREE

EXFILTRATION *a: extraction*
b: to exit through enemy lines

FORTY MINUTES LATER, they boarded the *Immaculate Contraption.* Zito stowed their gear as Forrest cranked the engine and lowered the flaps for takeoff. Three minutes later, he coaxed the bouncing bird through the grass and into the air where, hanging on a snarling prop, she clawed her way into the evening sky.

They were barely above the treetops when machine gun fire bit into the wing covering their heads, splintering the right rear Plexiglass window and jamming the bellcrank, which through a cable, connected the flaps to their operating handle.

"Jesus Tecumseh Sherman!" Forrest shouted. His hands fought for control as his eyes searched for signs of damage.

Zito's head snapped around to search for the source. "Helicopter! Five o'clock," he exclaimed as he reached for his MP-5. "He's all over us like a bad sunburn. Friends of yours?" He leaned out of the window to return fire, only to find that the foldout window was in his way.

"No problem," Forrest yelled, as he banked the Cessna hard to the left. "We can out run him." He reached to the long handle positioned between the seats and attempted to lower it to the floor. It wouldn't budge. Two more rounds impacted the right wingtip. "Correction," Forrest groused. "Flaps are stuck down. This is max speed."

Zito gave Forrest a concerned look before Forrest yelled: "Blast the fuckers! Keep 'em off our ass until I come up with a plan B."

Zito attempted another shot, but again, the foldout side window got in the way as the two aircraft cut and weaved through the tops of the trees.

Forrest saw Zito struggling. "Jettison the door," he shouted as he stomped on the right rudder pedal so the flying metal would clear the tail. "Red handle."

Zito reached for it and yanked, snapping his hand back as it popped free at the hinges with a rush of air. The structure struck the right flap before tumbling past the trailing helicopter which jinked to avoid a collision. Zito followed up with several short bursts from his submachine gun.

Forrest reversed the turn, rolling the aircraft hard to the left before jettisoning his own door. He looked back to track his pursuers. Their identity was no surprise. *Windridge.* The helicopter was so close the Director's face was clearly recognizable. The JetRanger slid to its right, giving the white-haired left-seater a shot with his FN-FAL. Forrest saw faint puffs of smoke erupt from the barrel as bullets whizzed by his door. One round pinged through the aluminum wing. *If one hits a flight control cable, we're done.* Forrest let go of the yoke for a second to slip his arms through the straps of his parachute and cinch up the straps. He instructed Zito to do the same then realized Amy didn't have one. He rolled the aircraft hard right then rolled level in order to give Zito a shot while denying Windridge the same opportunity. "Coming up on the right!" he shouted over the engine noise.

Zito was ready. He leaned through the door hosing the chopper's exposed belly with a long raking burst.

Windridge and the pilot both flinched.

"Got a piece of 'em that time," Zito roared as he pulled himself inside the door, ejected an empty magazine and jammed home another. "Little girl, grab another mag out of my bag."

"Hope it was a big piece," Forrest grunted, turning hard in his seat for a glance at the helicopter.

And so it went for the next fifteen minutes, an eternity considering most combat dogfights last only three or four minutes. Each time Windridge would bring his rifle to bear, Forrest would pull the Cessna up and to the right forcing the chopper pilot to do the same. Then Forrest would immediately reverse the turn and dive for the treetops.

Frustrated that he couldn't get a shot and worried that he would lose the light plane in the coming darkness, Windridge transmitted a coded message on a prearranged frequency.

Colonel Mgomo and his wingman, the operations officer, had been in their offices when the call came in from the squadron command post. In minutes they had donned their parachutes and ridden in the back of a crew van to their waiting Northrop, F-5E Tiger II fighters. Their plane captains strapped them in as they each started a pair of General Electric J-85 engines and went through the after start checklist.

Four minutes later, they lowered their canopies in unison, taxied onto Laikipia Air Base's main runway and lifted their roaring fighters into a crimson-gold African sky on the blue-white plumes of their afterburners. In 90 seconds they had accelerated through the sound barrier, their needle-nosed jets heading to the south.

"Turn! Turn!" Windridge shouted into his boom mike as the Cessna veered hard to the right. "Cut him off and give me another shot, dammit!"

Blades clattered as the pilot banked the helicopter rapidly to the right and pressed down on the right pedal, pulling inside the slower plane's turn. Once the tail of the American's plane cleared his door, Windridge pointed his rifle through his sliding window and cut loose.

On Zito's call, Forrest rolled the Cessna hard left then pulled up to spoil the Brit's shot. In air combat, a stationary target is a dead target, so Forrest kept maneuvering as violently as his low airspeed would allow. He couldn't get behind the helicopter. That wasn't possible under the circumstances. It had all the advantages of maneuver and speed. With frozen flaps and restricted speed, even vertical moves were denied him against a foe whose vertical performance was normally much more limited. His only hope was holding his own in a defensive battle where victory lay not so much in winning as it did in not losing. In such an engagement, one mistake was all you got.

"A *good* pilot would have gotten us out of this shit by now," Zito shouted over his shoulder as he watched the JetRanger disappear behind their tail.

Forrest rolled the Cessna up on its side and pulled back on the yoke until the airplane ran out of speed. He let the nose drop and rolled hard to the left hoping to drop below Windridge's range of motion before he could reverse and pull up on the pilot's side of the helicopter. "A *good* rifleman would have nailed that bastard by now," Forrest shouted back. The Cessna reached maximum speed before Forrest hauled back on the yoke. "He's coming up on your side. Be ready."

Zito turned in his seat and steadied his subgun in the door. He held down on the trigger, spitting out a stream of brass as the helicopter flashed through his narrow window of opportunity. "Hard left," he yelled, reaching for another magazine offered by Amy as the helicopter reversed its turn on Forrest's blind side.

Forrest did as he was told, burying the nose as low as he dared given their perilously low altitude.

"Bloody hell!" Windridge screamed at his pilot. "Get down there!" He poked his rifle through the narrow opening and waited for the Cessna to stabilize. As it did, he led its flight-path a little and squeezed.

PING. PING. TWANG. A fusillade of bullets cut through the Cessna's skin, punching holes in the wings, fuselage and windshield. Instruments exploded as four rounds found their way through the cabin roof.

"Shit, Zit," Forrest cursed. "You gotta do something about..." A glance at his friend choked off his appeal. "Zit?...Zit!"

Amy howled in anguish.

Supersonic flight in a modern fighter was surprisingly placid, Colonel Mbomo reminded himself. His only sensation of speed came from zipping past towering cumulus clouds and the telltale needle on the face of his airspeed indicator.

Mbomo turned up his gunsight's rheostat and activated his radar. He checked his present position against his chart and noted the distance to the target area: 150 miles.

Forrest grabbed Zito by the shoulder and pulled him toward the center of the plane. Fixed and glassy, his eyes stared blankly at the roof of the plane. Forrest pressed his fingers into his friend's neck. No carotid pulse. No respiration. He felt suddenly awash in a huge wave of despair. Two best friends in a week...it was more than a man could take...more than any man should *have* to take. The ground rushed beneath the plane. Treetops whizzed by. Anguish boiled over into anger. Forrest swallowed hard and closed his friend's eyes, then pulled his shoulder harness tight to keep him from flopping around during hard turns.

Forrest turned to see Amy sobbing as she loaded a fresh magazine into Zito's MP-5. "Hang on, honey."

He yanked and banked the Cessna blindly trying to avoid further damage. The prop wailed as he pushed the engine to its limits. "Hold together, baby." *Just a matter of time before the plane or I take a fatal hit.* Every piece of Plexiglass in the *Contraption* was perforated or shattered. *How the hell I'm not hit I'll never know,* a thought which brought his fingers to the cross Anne had hung around his neck. *Lord, if you're really up there, now would be a good time for a little intervention.* For a brief second, the beleaguered pilot felt a warm rush surge through him. A thought he somehow knew wasn't his own came to the front of his mind: *He's got your six, John.* Although he knew better he could have sworn the thought sounded like Anne's voice. Forrest felt some of the stress melting.

Forrest startled back from the mental excursion to take stock of the situation. For a moment it seemed he'd been gone for a while. His eyes moved around the cockpit first checking engine instruments then fuel gauges. Running a little hot, he noticed, but that couldn't be helped. *Plenty gas. Maybe I can run those bastards out of gas. The chopper's got to be low if it came all the way from Nairobi.*

Another torrent of bullets slammed into the valiant craft. Forrest ducked instinctively though he knew it wouldn't do any good. He pulled hard on the control wheel and banked sharply to the right to dodge another assault. It was then that he realized the last attack had changed his latest strategy. Precious fuel streamed from at least seven holes in the right tank. A single hole streamed fuel from the left. *Time for plan C.*

Forrest pulled back on the yoke to begin a weaving climb. He glanced back at Amy to see her wrapping a strip of cloth around her bloody forearm.

"Is it bad?"

Amy tied off the bandage knot with her teeth. "I'm OK. Just don't crash this thing looking at me." She jammed a fresh magazine in Zito's MP-5 and leaned forward for an opportunity to shoot.

Forrest turned in his seat. It would soon be time to abandon ship. And for that he would need as much altitude as he could get.

The fuzzy coastline of the Indian Ocean was now discernable through the F-5E's windshield. Towering cumulus clouds lined the shore just inland from the water's edge. Colonel Mbomo pulled the throttles aft of the detent—out of afterburner and into military power. He let the nose drop slightly as the fighter bled speed. In a few seconds it would reenter subsonic flight.

The colonel instructed his wingman to move to a fluid trail position a half-mile or more to his rear where he could maneuver freely and aid in spotting their quarry without fear of running into the leader. He set the radar to scan ahead at a 20 mile range and adjusted the elevation control lower.

"Helicopter Kilo Alpha Kilo," he called into the microphone built into his oxygen mask. "Your fighters are ninety north. Say your position and situation. Over."

Slowly, the altimeter climbed, its needles indicating twenty-three hundred feet. The VSI (vertical speed indicator) read a hair over three hundred feet per minute, Forrest saw. A tortuous climb rate to be sure, but it would have to do.

Forrest looked over his shoulder to see the helicopter still parked at his six o'clock almost as if it were on a tether. His eyes came back to the instrument panel, lingering for a second on the fuel gauges. The right tank was almost empty and the left, still leaking fuel, might not last long enough to make the little coastal airfield at Lunga Lunga—the place he'd coordinated for his rendezvous with Grizzly Adams. It was only thirty miles ahead, but under the circumstances it might as well have been thirty-thousand. Forrest was ready to bail out of the Cessna but he decided to wait until the last possible moment. The wait would be risky but the alternatives were worse. Like every decision in life, this one had its pluses and minuses. If they bailed early, they would never make the rendezvous on time. And that would present a whole new set of problems to fugitives on the run with absolutely no equipment, no food and water, and no way to contact friendlies. Then there was the virtual certainty that Windridge would shoot them in their chutes or beat them to the ground where he could nail them when they touched down. Well, that was it then. The air battle had degenerated into a waiting game—a game of move and counter move. It had all come down to a question of which machine would run out of fuel first or which pilot would make the first mistake.

As the JetRanger moved to its right, Forrest pulled the Cessna into a hard right turn, cutting the helicopter off before reversing into a violent diving turn to the left, narrowly missing an invisible stream of lead.

As the plane came level with its adversary, the Kenyan pilot pushed down hard on the right pedal yawing the nose to the right far enough for Windridge to get another quick shot. Spent brass bounced off the inside of the windshield before tinkling to the floor to join a growing pile in the chin bubble as the rifle jumped in Windridge's hands.

Another swarm of lead tore through the Cessna's roof, crashing into the instrument panel. "Jesus Tecumseh Sherman!" Forrest roared as he flinched then shoved forward on the controls sending the nose down hard enough to float his gear above the floor. He turned around in the seat just in time to see the helicopter rise out of sight above the wing. A glimpse of his climbing rope among his equipment inspired an idea—a last-ditch desperate idea.

Colonel Mbomo allowed his jet to slow to 375 knots as he descended through fifteen thousand feet. He brought his flight around a billowing cloud, came back to his original intercept heading and peeked into his radar scope. The system showed four targets within its 20 mile range. Two, near the outer edge of the scope, were rather close together and appeared to be moving as a flight, just like a pair of fighters only much slower. *Probably them.*

"Possible target," he announced to his wingman. "Twelve o'clock for seventeen miles."

"Two concurs."

The veteran American-trained pilot called Windridge for a situation update and asked for a description of their target. Shooting down the wrong airplane this close to the Tanzanian border could create an international incident and cost him his wings.

"Master arm, on," the leader commanded.

"Two. Switches green."

* * * *

Forrest snapped his head around to see that the helicopter was close—so close he could see Windridge's animated gestures as he directed his pilot into position for another shot. "Gimme that coil of rope," he shouted above the noise.

Amy ripped off another burst at the menacing chopper before turning to comply.

Forrest stretched to take the coil from Amy. Grunting with exertion, he laid it on Zito's lap.

As Windridge lifted his rifle, Forrest began a scissors maneuver; a rhythmic weave across the helicopter's flight path which its pilot copied. Forrest varied the rhythm to keep his pursuer out of phase. Flying the Cessna with his left hand, Forrest insured the coil was loose enough to unravel easily. He watched over his shoulder as the chopper settled into a predictable weave. Only one chance to get this right, he reminded himself as he waited for just the right moment.

"Okay. Okay," he muttered to himself. "Ready. Ready...*now*!" Forrest pulled up abruptly and heaved the coil through his open door just as the helicopter moved directly astern. The coil unwound in the slipstream as it flew back into the JetRanger's windshield startling its occupants before sliding up into the rotor system where it wrapped itself around the mast. In the blink of an eye the rope tightened enough to bend the pitch-change links connecting the transmission to the rotorhead leaving the pilot no semblance of control. Forrest could see the panicked look on their faces as the pilot struggled with the cyclic. Forrest banked hard to the right and watched as the doomed chopper's nose dropped hard to starboard in a death spiral for the ground. A minute later, it began to come apart as the air-loads collapsed the tail boom which flew into the whirling main rotor blades, twisting them like fried bacon. Flailing wreckage tumbled for a full minute before blossoming into a fireball as it hit the ground almost three thousand feet below.

"Breaking up is hard to do," Forrest grumbled acerbically as he rolled back to the left and leveled off at thirty-five hundred feet. He slumped in the seat and took a deep breath, his first since the fight began. He held it for nearly half a minute before letting it out. His eyes were drawn to his friend whose original bandage was now soaked in blood. There was just no time to grieve, and in his heart, he knew Zito would be angry if he did. He looked away and searched the cockpit for his GPS receiver.

"Did they crash?" Amy yelled, unable to see exactly what had happened.

"Crashed aaand burned, honey. They're fried chicken. Are you OK?"

Amy bent over and put her head in her hands. "I think I'm gonna puke."

Forrest turned back and checked his instruments. The ones that still functioned revealed a very sick engine about to get real quiet for lack of something to drink. He reached for his hand-held GPS. "Well lady," he said to his badly wounded Cessna. "Where the hell are we?"

While the GPS resolved its position, Forrest checked his chart. Though he was well ahead of schedule for the rendezvous, it was imperative to determine his position and get back on course. Ahead he saw the lights of a small town near the coast as he ran his fingertip over the chart reconciling the visible geography to the graphics. *Damn if we haven't drifted back into Tanzania.* "That makes those lights Tanga," Forrest told himself. He toggled the GPS for a "go-to" course to Lunga Lunga which lay just north of the Kenya-Tanzania border, corrected his heading and set the auto pilot to hold it. *Could be worse. At least that still works.*

Forrest leaned back in the seat, turned his eyes to Zito and his retching daughter-in-law and let out a long deep sigh.

"Two's got a visual. Eleven thirty, eight miles," the wingman called. At age thirty-four, his eyes were better than those of his flight lead.

Though tiny, the light airplane was fairly easy to see, it's gleaming white paint contrasted brightly against the darkening terrain blanketed in the underlying terminator.

"Lead's tally-ho. Go combat trail." Colonel Mbomo had already seen the fire from what he assumed was the wreckage of the helicopter. It had to be, given the fact that its pilot could no longer be raised on the radio. The sight was disturbing. The towering column of black smoke marked at least two graves. And now there would be no last minute clearance to fire from a government authority. But no matter, he'd already received it and the downed chopper was all the justification he would need. "We'll take him down the starboard side for a positive ID."

"Two," his wingman acknowledged.

The F-5s bore down on the hapless Cessna from behind and above giving its pilot little chance of spotting them before it was too late. They covered the last three miles in less than thirty seconds, watching as the high-winged craft flashed by on the right as if it were standing still.

"That's him," lead confirmed. "Go to guns."

"Roger, guns."

The flight turned north and slowed to three hundred knots. Three miles of air separated them from their target as they reversed the turn to reacquire their target. The leader attempted a radar lock which failed owing to the target's size, tail-on aspect and too little time to stabilize his approach. No lead computing sight and no ranging, Mbomo reminded himself with a grimace. With a fixed sight and a closure rate of two hundred knots, it would be an extremely difficult shot, rather like a paper-boy trying to hit a townhouse porch from an Indy car. Undaunted, he bore down on the bright speck which grew bigger by the second. At an estimated slant range of 1,000 feet he steadied the pipper and squeezed the trigger. Twin 20mm canons rattled in the fighter's nose pumping a short burst of high-explosive incendiary rounds at the defenseless target.

* * * *

Tracer rounds burned through the air, streaking past the side window, startling Forrest. He snapped his head around in time to see the lead fighter whiz by. "Shit! It's worse. Windridge called the cavalry."

He realized it wouldn't take long for the pilots to correct their error and set up for another attack. *If they don't get us on this pass they sure as hell won't miss on the third.* He watched as number two circled behind his leader as they zoomed north to set up for another pass.

Forrest turned to Amy. "Honey, we've got a problem."

"What?" she responded weakly, wiping her mouth with the back of her hand. "*Another* problem?"

"Come on, Amy. We've gotta get Zit out of his seat and then you need to put on his chute."

"What?"

"Get it together, now. I can't move him by myself."

Forrest looked back to see the fighters lining up for another pass. He banked and pulled hard to the right ducking the Cessna into a towering cumulus cloud.

Amy and Forrest lifted Zito's body out of the seat and Amy dragged it into the back. Struggling to stay on her feet in the swirling turbulence, she slipped into the seat and pulled the parachute harness over her shoulders.

"Are we going to have to use these?"

Forrest turned the control wheel hard to the left to level the airplane as they popped out of the cloud in a steep bank. He looked back to locate the fighters. "Depends on how hard you want to hit the ground."

"Good Lord, Uncle John. I've never jumped before."

"No problem, honey. Gravity and I will do all the work." Forrest reached into the back of the plane and popped the video tape out of the camcorder. Although justice had been amply served with respect to Allen Windridge, the tape would still prove instrumental in clearing Doc McCullen of any complicity or wrongdoing. He stuffed the cassette into his BDU shirt and unfastened his seat belt as the lead fighter started into his turn. Forrest turned to Zito. "Good-bye, pal. Your family is now my personal responsibility."

Forrest set the auto pilot to hold heading and altitude then turned in the seat to face the open door and looked aft past the tail. The fighters were about three miles back, commencing their attack. Forrest stepped out onto the landing gear, and motioned for Amy to come to him. As she came chest-to-chest with him he fastened their harnesses together at the chest strap with a carabineer, put her arms around his waist, steadied himself, then dropped away. With Amy's back toward the ground, he entered a classic spread-eagle free-fall position to get well clear of the plane before it was destroyed.

On any other occasion, he would have enjoyed the thirty-second drop. The circumstances and the extra burden made that impossible.

Forrest unsnapped the carabineer and grabbed for Amy's rip-cord. Her eyes, filled with dread, met his for the briefest moment before he yanked the cord and pushed her away. He watched with relief as she rushed above his head when her canopy grabbed the air.

Seconds later, he reached back with his right hand and yanked his own rip-cord at what appeared to be a thousand feet above the ground—the lower the better to avoid detection from above or below. Rattling fabric and a gentle tug told him the canopy was open. A quick look told him there were no malfunctions and another found Amy floating earthward a hundred feet above him. He watched overhead as the Cessna droned out to sea. Seconds later the fighters roared by, their guns spitting death. The third of three streams of tracers found their mark. A fireball consumed the little bird as the right wing snapped off sending it tumbling into the black waters of the Indian Ocean. Forrest felt a tremendous sadness overtake him as the little craft which had served him so faithfully for so many months carried the body of one his closest friends to a watery grave.

* * * *

Grizzly Adams looked at his watch: 19:30. Thumper, Zit and their precious package should be in the air by now, he reckoned. Two hours to rendezvous time...forty minutes to get there if the winds aren't too bad, he mused. *Hope those two boneheads aren't late. A plane this big and this noisy won't be easy to hide for long on some little po-dunk airfield.*

He turned to watch the Somalis finish their off-load of medical supplies and bottled water as his co-pilot stood by smoking a cigarette.

"That is correct," Colonel Mbomo transmitted to the Laikipia Air Base command post. "Target aircraft was destroyed." *And I've got the gun-camera film to prove it.* "No survivors." In a more urgent voice he added: "Believe a government helicopter crashed in the vicinity. Recommend you launch search and rescue. Standby for the coordinates..."

Floating in peaceful silence, John Forrest drifted under his soot-black canopy in the cool night air..His head was still reeling from the violent dogfight and the loss of Frank Zito. It seemed surreal to be, one minute, fighting for your life and the next, walking on air—a stunning contrast.

Thunder from a dissipating coastal storm rumbled in the distance as the smell of rain and seawater filled his nose. Now that he'd had a chance to get his bearings, he discovered he was a lot closer to the coast than he first thought. The lights of Tanga twinkled a mere four miles in the distance. And what looked to be the runway lights of its small airport gleamed some two miles closer! With only five hundred feet of air under his feet, he took a mental bearing on the runway as he prepared to meet the ground.

So busy was he trying to fix his position, he'd neglected to select a decent landing site. Looking between his feet at the last minute, he saw the gray wooden spears of a dead snag reaching up to impale him and violently yanked down on a steering line just in time to avoid becoming a Forrest-kabob. The nearby thorn-bush however, was huge and worse, unavoidable. Flying skills were for naught, now. He merely bent his knees, flared to the maximum to reduce his ground speed, and hoped for the best. Five or six branches grabbed at his legs as he crashed through the top of the bush to tumble ass-over-elbows in an area of loose earth—a lucky landing from a very unlucky approach.

Forrest stood up quickly, shucked his parachute harness and dusted himself off. Amy landed nearby with a thud. She lay for a moment dazed by the abrupt stop at the bottom of the ride.

Forrest reached her in seconds. "Can you walk outta here?" he asked as he helped her shuck her harness and checked her for injuries.

"How far?"

"A mile or so. Maybe two."

She sighed. "I think so."

"Atta girl." Forrest took a deep breath to clear his head and looked at his watch: 19:30. Two hours to rendezvous time. "Shit. That does it," he griped, kicking at the backpack. "Thirty miles to Lunga Lunga and two hours to get there. Might as well be two goddamn years," he muttered. *Brutal math. Never do it without wheels or wings.* He began what was to be a long frustrated sigh then sucked it back. *Givin' up easy's not your style, John. There's an airfield two miles that way. And where there's an airport there are airplanes. Maybe you can 'borrow' one.* Their boots spitting dirt, he and Amy took off running into the gathering darkness.

It took forty minutes to make it to the perimeter fence and another ten to mount it and jog to the hangars standing on the south side of the runway. Amy and Forrest leaned against a rusting steel building, catching their breath as he listened for possible threats. Unlike

American or European airports where entire empires had been built around security, there seemed to be little standing between him and the ten-or-so light airplanes and helicopters parked on the dimly lit ramp.

Forrest moved to the front of the hangar, careful to remain within the darkest shadows. From his new vantage point, he assessed the prospects. Two Cessnas, a twin-engine Piper Aztec, a Beechcraft Baron, three helicopters, and seven aircraft he didn't recognize—probably foreign. The twins were the best bet, he figured. If you could get past the door, you didn't need a key for the mags.

He dropped to his knees and peered around the corner. He looked down the broad expanse of the hangar's sliding doors and saw another helicopter parked by itself in front of a second hangar. Otherwise, the place seemed deserted.

"Wait here," he whispered.

Forrest checked again, in every direction, before sprinting across the ramp to the door of the Aztec. As he reached for the latch he pulled his hand back. "Jesus Tecumseh Sherman," he hissed. *Never mind.* The right engine was minus a propeller. Apparently it had been removed for maintenance.

Entering the Baron was easy. It was unlocked. But a flip of the master switch yielded zip. The battery was either dead or missing. Either way, it wasn't going anywhere anytime soon.

The Cessnas were next. But like the twins, they were unserviceable as well. "What *is* this—a stinking bone-yard?" he fumed. Forrest leaned against the Cessna 172 for a moment, wiped his face on his camouflaged sleeve and contemplated his next move. He looked at his watch. Fifty-four minutes to pick-up. Fifty-four minutes until their flight to freedom left the Lunga Lunga airstrip. Forrest looked around. That left the helicopters. Only one problem: aside from a few flights he'd made with Adams in Vietnam where his friend had let him handle the controls, he had no formal training in rotorcraft. He still remembered the first lesson which had brought Adams great amusement at Forrest's expense and he'd discovered hovering only *looked* easy. Worse, those minimal yet focused training sessions had occurred over twenty years ago.

Just then, a barking dog interrupted his musings. Forrest dropped to his knees and scanned the ramp. Footsteps echoed off the hangar doors to find his ears. A second later, he saw the feet producing them. Two men and a dog were walking toward him, though they had not yet reached the lone helicopter which sat silhouetted against stanchion lights over a hundred meters to his left. Forrest edged back to the Baron, climbed inside and closed the door. Minutes later, the guards passed behind his hiding place and continued down the ramp where they disappeared around the corner of a third hangar. Forrest popped open the door, listened for a moment and darted back into the alley between the hangars where Amy waited. He paused there for a minute, trying to decide what to do next.

Another bark made the decision for him. They were coming back. One man lagged behind the other, zipping his fly. Forrest and Amy pulled back to the front corner of the hangar where he would wait for them to pass. But like everything else that had occurred since he and Zito had left the Serpent's camp, this one didn't go as planned. The men stopped, tied the dog's leash to an electrical conduit and broke out smokes.

Forrest grit his teeth and checked his watch. "For Christ's sake. You guys are starting to piss me off." He eyed the guards then looked past them at the helicopters parked on the ramp. It would take time to untie the blades, slip inside, then figure out how to start it. Time. *When you don't have any, you have to make some.* Thumping the side of the hangar got the dog's attention. It barked viciously and tugged at its leash as Forrest, seeing that the guards were coming to investigate, grabbed Amy's hand and ran the length of the hangar and rounded the far corner. Without so much as a look behind them, they bolted straight out onto the ramp where he climbed inside the closest Bell JetRanger leaving Amy to stand watch outside. He froze as flashlight beams played around the hangar wall and ramp. After a moment, he began breathing again as the guards continued along the opposite side of the hangars and disappeared from sight. "Let's get moving, John," he whispered to himself. Forrest squinted in the dim light until he had located the ship's battery switch on the overhead panel. Flipping it on just as he'd seen Colonel Grant's pilot do when they had their ranch tour, he moved his eyes to the instrument console, where he located the guarded "fuel valve" switch just in front of his left knee. He raised the red cover and flipped it to the "closed" position.

Forrest carefully checked the ramp once more before climbing out. Quickly, he located a rubber-coated button on the side of the fuselage, pressed and held it until a large puddle of fuel had expanded across the tarmac. He released the switch, then without hesitation, removed his cigarette lighter from a BDU pocket and ignited the fuel. As the flames spread with a whoosh, Forrest and Amy took off running toward the helicopters parked at the far end of the ramp. Bypassing an Astar 350, Forrest halted abruptly next to another JetRanger's tail-rotor, where he instructed Amy to untie the blade restraint and toss it aside while he took care of the main rotor blade tie down.

"Do you know how to fly one of these things, uncle John?" Amy asked, climbing through the left front door.

"I'm not certified in choppers, if that's what you mean."

Amy gave him a nervous look as she felt for the shoulder harnesses behind her back. "You didn't answer my question."

"Your Uncle Grizz gave me a *few* lessons in Vietnam," Forest stated with a confidence he certainly didn't feel.

"A few lessons? Vietnam?"

His return scowl abated further interrogation.

As Amy buckled in, Forrest shoved all of the overhead switches forward, and jammed his right thumb down on the starter button. The engine whined to life as he snapped the throttle to idle and waited for it to wind up to speed. When it seemed that the turbine would stay lit, Forrest slowly cranked the throttle to full open and waited for the rotor RPM to reach 100 percent. It maxed out at 98 percent. "Close enough," he muttered, slowly lifting up on the collective control. "Uh oh." He looked down the ramp to see the flames engulfing the other machine. The guards were dealing with it, wheeling a large fire bottle into place when they heard his rotor noise. One came running behind the dog—a German Shepherd—who dragged its leash across the concrete.

As the dog ran beneath the rotorwash, its fur ruffling in the blast, its handler reached to his side and drew his pistol. The dog, whose deep barking was drowned out by the roar of the rotorblades, dropped away as Forrest picked the machine up to a wobbly hover and moved it forward, toward the hangar. The machine was barely under control. The dog ran along beneath the skids as Forrest saw the guard raise the pistol and take aim. Novice helicopter pilot or not, he pushed down hard on the right pedal sweeping the guard off his feet with the tail boom. The man rolled on the ground as the snarling tail rotor passed just over his head. After turning one hundred and eighty degrees, Forrest stabilized the machine and cringed as the guard found his feet and raised his revolver at the pilot's side window. Reflexively, Forrest moved the cyclic toward his assailant, attempting to knock him off his feet with the skid. The steel tube caught him square across the chest knocking him backwards, his arms flailing for balance. An instant before his head would have met the concrete, the guard hooked his arms around the skid tube and hung on.

"Give it up, asshole!" Forrest shouted without effect in the din. "This damn thing isn't worth your life."

Amy cringed at the sight, unable to distinguish between the dangers of the guard's weapon or her father-in-law's flying.

Still struggling to hold on with his left arm, the guard raised his pistol, leveled it towards Forrest's window and pulled the hammer back.

"Look out Uncle John!" Amy yelped.

Forrest didn't give him a chance to fire. First he jammed his foot into the right pedal, then the left, alternately whirling the helicopter in opposite directions. Centrifugal force lifted his passenger's legs as his body weight increased under the G-loading. He couldn't both shoot and hold on, so the gun was quickly dropped in favor of a better grip. During the wild ride, his hands growing ever more slippery with sweat, he began to lose his grip. Forrest watched as one of them popped free. Instantly, Forrest reversed his turn with hard right pedal and a strong pull on the collective. The JetRanger swung wildly to the right, flinging the terrified man into the closed hanger doors where he impacted heavily and slid to the concrete like a bag of fertilizer.

As the other guard ran to help his colleague, Forrest spun the helicopter's nose toward the runway, eased aft on the cyclic after gaining some speed and climbed into the night. A look over his shoulder revealed several flashing lights. Police and fire trucks, he assumed, as the city lights thinned before giving way to the blackness of uninhabited terrain.

Most of the coastal storms had dissipated or drifted out to sea he noticed as he gained altitude—a small but welcome break after an incredible ordeal. In the dim light of a rising new moon, Forrest picked up the shoreline and followed it north across the Kenyan border. Twenty miles to go, he estimated looking at his watch. He pulled the collective up a bit, increasing the torque to almost 90 percent. A little tough on the transmission, he thought. But who gives a shit? It's a rental.

Forrest, his shirt soaked in sweat, had the machine "bent over," as Adams used to say—pounding along at maximum forward speed.

"Grizz, if there was ever a night for you to be late, it's this one."

"Where are we going?" Amy asked.

"Lunga-Lunga International."

Amy thought that over for a moment having no clue where it was. "Is there an international airport in Lunga-Lunga?"

"There is tonight, honey. We're flying Air Grizz to Germany."

Amy gave an amazed look in response.

Minutes later, the dirt airstrip whipped by on his left before he noticed it. There were no lights and no buildings, just a gray scar in a sea of black.

Forrest lowered the collective to the floor and compensated with right pedal as the machine yawed to the left. He held back on the cyclic allowing the machine to slow as he pulled it around into a hard right turn. He dropped down to eight hundred feet and seventy knots and began a wide circle to reconnoiter the strip for obstacles. There was little wind, so Forrest made an approach from east to west, turning the landing light on at he last minute with a flip of his left thumb. *Whoa baby!* He overshot the center of the strip by about fifty meters, got the machine under control and hovered back to a wide area next to a darkened shack. *Deserted. Perfect!* Owing to Forrest's lack of experience and the JetRanger's control sensitivity, he wobbled a bit as he felt for the ground. The landing was firm and sloppy but acceptable. With an audible sigh of relief he bottomed the collective and gave Amy a grin glowing with nervous pride.

After shutting down the turbine engine, Forrest alighted, helped Amy out and looked around.

"I can't believe you got us here in one piece," Amy half-teased.

"I just said I wasn't certified. Didn't say I couldn't fly the damn thing."

"Well I'm not getting back in that thing with you until you are certified," she chided lightheartedly.

"Oh yeah?" Forrest raised his eyebrows and asked: "Then what's your plan B if we've missed our ride?"

Amy looked away, then at the helicopter, folding her arms across her chest with a sigh. *Hadn't thought about that.*

Forrest smiled inwardly as he scanned the darkness. The night was warm and silent and for the first time Forrest realized how much he was perspiring. He looked at his watch: 21:36. *Where is the Grizz?* Paranoia began creeping into his thoughts. Had he landed on the wrong airstrip? Had something happened to Adams? Though once he was hoping his friend would be late, he now began to worry. Had Grizz come and gone?

Forrest walked out into the center of the runway and strained to listen. The only sounds were produced by ocean waves and amorous insects. He thought he heard something...like the familiar drone of the L-100's Allison turboprops. Then it was gone. "Must be hearing things."

He looked at his watch. 21:41. "Damn, man. This isn't like you!" Suddenly, a blinding bank of white lights bathed him in painful brilliance. A fraction of a second later, the deafening roar of a mammoth airplane drove him to the ground as it passed just ten feet over his head. Forrest closed his eyes to the stinging sand blown about by four huge props as it bounced onto the ground and reversed its engines, grinding to a halt at the far end of the short strip.

Grizz!

Forrest, once again cloaked in darkness, remembered his prayer spoken under dire circumstances. He looked across the airstrip to see Amy bathed in the approaching landing lights. She stood next to the borrowed helicopter, applauding the L-100's arrival. It occurred to him a debt was still owed. He bowed his head and said a simple silent prayer. *God, I don't know the ROE for prayers. Anne never covered that part. And, I don't know how we got here. That little plane was pretty buggered-up. I guess you held it together. And me flying that helicopter, if you could call it flying…well, that was sort of miraculous, too, I suppose. I guess you were really flying both of 'em, now that I think about it. Anyway, thanks for saving our asses.*

His eyes came back up to Amy who was animatedly clapping her hands together and waving amidst the growing howl of the huge propellers.

God, you've got three great people with you now. His emotions caught in his throat for a moment. *Well, two, anyway. I'll never understand why you took them, especially ZIT. Why anybody would want him…* He allowed himself a half smile. *We would take them all back in a heartbeat, even Zit. But, now that you've got 'em, please love them as much as we do and take care of them. Tell my son I'll take good care of his wife and get her home safe. Amen. PS: I'm sorry I called you a sick son-of-a-bitch.*

Minutes later, the noisy transport taxied to a stop as the landing lights picked up a familiar figure waving his hands, a young woman in tow. The flight engineer opened the forward door as Adams climbed down the ladder to greet his friend who was both elated and irritated. Adams took Forrest's hand in his great paw and slapped him on the back.

"Where the hell have you been?" Forrest snapped, tersely, no longer able to control his emotions. "I didn't think you were coming," he groused though he wasn't the least bit ungrateful.

Adams' broad grin dimmed slightly. He saw that his friend was shaken, noticing flecks of blood splattered on his face and uniform. He could only wonder whose it was. "Sorry man. We had a little trouble at our off-load point." He gave Amy a long bear hug before realizing someone was missing. "Where's Zit?"

Forrest looked into his large friend's eyes for a long time then shifted them to the dark ocean. "He's taken his last flight."

EPILOGUE

VERO BEACH, FLORIDA – SEVEN DAYS AFTER EXTRACTION

"SEE YOU SOON," Forrest promised as he waved to Steve Henderson and his sweet wife, Marie, from the end of his driveway.

"Thanks for the warning," Henderson called as they pulled away in their rented Lincoln Town Car on their way to the Melbourne Airport.

Just then Henderson hit the brakes. "By the way, Griz called to ask if we'd like to go hunting in a few weeks. What do ya think?"

Forrest's eyes dropped to the pavement for a moment. "Nah. Tell him no, thanks. I've kinda lost my taste for it." His eyes came back up and a weak smile crossed his face. "But if he wants to go fishing, I'm in."

"Okay. I understand. I'll tell him," Henderson responded with a sympathetic smile. Without further discourse, he ran the window up and pulled away.

Forrest watched and waived to Amy and the other Henderson daughters as the luxury car rounded a landscaped island and disappeared behind its lush tropical foliage. He walked beneath overhanging oak limbs draped with resurrection fern and blooming wild orchids for which the Orchid Island was named. He traversed his driveway and the winding sidewalk then entered the house through massive, twin, rosewood doors. Though burdened by persistent sadness, he was glad to be home—glad to be back in paradise—glad everything was over.

Frank Zito's memorial service, from which he had just returned with the Hendersons, had been a military affair held at Ft. Benning, Georgia. There had been hardly a dry eye among the large gathering of family and friends as the U.S. Army paid tribute as only the Army could to one of its most decorated and colorful veterans.

Forrest's proudest moment, however, came afterwards when he took Zit's wife aside as people grazed on the impressive spread of home-made dishes family members had prepared for the occasion. Her dark brown eyes had filled with tears when he produced a letter addressed to her from Maxwell Grant. Forrest said: "Your family has lost its father and I'm a father who's lost his family. I promised Zit I would look after you and the kids until you find someone better suited for the job."

She smiled and hugged him then looked him in the eye. "They don't come any better than you, John Forrest." Then she read the letter twice, rereading the part explaining the purpose of the enclosed check made out to Mrs. Francis I. Zito in the amount of four hundred thousand dollars:

> *...So that a burden may be lifted from a hero's family. This should cover college and living expenses for you and your children. Should you require anything more, you need only call.*
>
> *With lasting gratitude and highest esteem,*
> *Maxwell T. Grant, Colonel, US Army, Retired*

Forrest had already read the letter. After all, he had called the Colonel the day after he had arrived back in the United States through Miami and asked him to help Zito's family. And Grant, a man of integrity, had been true to his word. Then, being a big man from a state whose citizens pride themselves on living large, he'd come through in a big way.

Ralph, his blue-and-gold macaw, greeted him with a low throaty gurgling sound as he entered his office. He gave the playful bird an affectionate scratch while scanning the contents of a package Henderson had given him. Also strewn across his desk were dozens of newspaper and magazine articles pertaining to events surrounding his mission including the articles the CIA had planted in the Far Eastern press warning Chinese and Japanese consumers about the hazards of consuming animal products—especially rhino horn. Quite a number of the clippings were from African publications which had followed the exploits of Baba Tembo who, Henderson had told him, was reported to have been killed in a plane crash. The most recent articles covered the scandalous aftermath surrounding the deaths of Kenyan government officials and their embarrassing connection to the poaching industry.

His hands left Ralph's head and went to a letter which, judging by its similarity to the one Zito's wife had received, had to be from Colonel Grant. He opened it and read the Colonel's redundant congratulations on the success of his mission and condolences for his loss. Two additional enclosures were both unexpected and stunning. The first was a check payable to John Ruger Forrest for fifteen thousand dollars for, as the note explained:

> *...your first month's salary as the head of my aviation department. Your first month, by the way, is to be spent as a paid vacation, so that you may relax, recover, and get your affairs in order.*
>
> *Rest well, my friend, I have big plans for you.*

"Mmm, Ralph, my boy. That sounds pretty interesting, doesn't it?" Forrest muttered without looking up. "Looks like only one of us has clipped wings, after all." The macaw uttered something in response then retrieved a sunflower seed from his cup.

The second enclosure was a slip of paper bearing the logo of his bank. "Holy shit!" Forrest gasped as he read the notice:

> *...Congratulations. Your mortgage loan obligation has been*

satisfied in full. Thank you for financing with Harbor Federal. Should your future plans...

"Damn!" He read the notice over at least six times. Forrest shook his head and gave Ralph a smile. "Well pal," he announced, laying the notice down on his desk. "You've got to hand it to the Colonel. He definitely knows how to make you an offer you can't refuse."

Beneath the pile of mail, he noticed the edge of a VHS video tape cassette. Attached to its vinyl cover was an envelope addressed to him in the familiar hand of Malcolm McCullen. Forrest pushed everything aside, eagerly tearing into the envelope with his letter opener.

...I can't tell you how relieved I was to hear that you were still alive. Like everyone else, I was certain you had been killed when the Immaculate Contraption was shot down over the Indian Ocean.

Things are going pretty well, considering. Hoover, Spike and Porkahontas said to say hello and to tell you that all are doing well though they, along with the camp's children, aren't having nearly as much fun now that you're gone. By the way, I told Joseph that you were still alive and in good health. I hope you don't mind. Don't worry, he was very relieved and agreed to keep that bit of information a secret. He hasn't even told his wife. With all the rain we're getting, he spends a lot of time washing his new Land Rover. On a more somber note, I thought you, of all people, would like to see the video tape of Anne's funeral. She and her husband were laid to rest in a small cemetary outside her father's school. That's all for now. I'm doing well. The police seem to have lost interest in me, of late. But you know how that goes. I've quit smoking, or at least I'm trying. Though the Scotch intake seems to have increased somewhat under the circumstances. I guess a man of many vices must choose his poisons. Please take care of yourself and stay in touch. And thank you, once again for all that you've done for the animals, Joseph and me.

Fondly,
MM

Forrest swallowed hard. His hand reached out to give Ralph a pet then eyed the video cassette as if might explode. He picked it up, looked at it for a moment then opened a drawer, dropped it inside, and shoved it closed.

CHYULU HILLS, KENYA – TEN DAYS AFTER EXTRACTION

"Forward fifty. Down fifty," the crew chief of the HH-60 Black Hawk helicopter called into his headset as he eyed the LZ through his night vision goggles. The powerful helicopter eased downward and forward a few feet at a time in the inky blackness of an overcast Kenyan night.

"Forward thirty. Down twenty," the crew chief continued as he hung out of the open doorway just behind the cockpit. "About five left, sir."

"Roger. Five left," the pilot responded, easing the cyclic a nudge to the left so smoothly its effects were imperceptible to the rest of the crew. Using his crew's calls as confirmation for his own assessments, he eased back on the cyclic and tugged on the collective as the powerful machine lowered itself onto the edge of a small, shallow lake fifty meters from a huge gnarled baobab tree. The tail-wheel touched an instant before the main gear, whereupon a team of four Navy SEALs disembarked to secure a perimeter around the chopper. Their mission: retrieve a cache of special weapons and equipment from the interior of a huge baobab tree and drop it into the Indian Ocean on the way back to the ship. Of course, like all such peacetime missions conducted within the borders of a friendly foreign nation, its code name and purpose were top secret, and after debriefing, it would never be discussed again.

MERU NATIONAL PARK, KENYA – SIX MONTHS AFTER EXTRACTION

"Careful now lads." Malcolm McCullen urged with a hint of a laugh in his voice, so great was his joy that almost nothing could spoil this moment. "You don't want to hurt them now after they've come all this way."

And a long way they had come, indeed; 1,800 miles from South Africa, who had presented them to Kenya as a gift, and all the way back from oblivion. Their transportation expenses had been funded by the African Wildlife Fund and Friends of Animals, one of many such projects ongoing around the world. McCullen beamed as the first of three pairs of white rhino were off-loaded from the back of a special carry truck and released in Meru National Park, which was once populated by hundreds of the often placid, sometimes ornery beasts. Just a year ago the population was zero, he remembered. In a few hours it would be six. A humble but auspicious beginning, McCullen thought as the second animal, a beautiful female, was prodded down a ramp into a special corral where they would be observed and fed for a few days before being released into the wild.

Park Warden, Hendrix Emerick, climbed to join McCullen on a catwalk from which they could observe the new arrivals. "What do you think, doctor? They are beautiful, are they not?"

McCullen smiled but eyed the Englishman suspiciously. There was something in the man's eyes he didn't like.

THE WHITE HOUSE, WASHINGTON, D.C. – THIRTEEN MONTHS AFTER EXTRACTION

Newly elected for his second term, President Wilcox looked on admiringly as the First Lady, Abby Wilcox, was sworn in as the honorary chairperson of the African Wildlife Fund. The Rose Garden was at its botanical best. Resplendent flowers, which included more than the namesake roses, were at their spring peak. The clear, blue sky was bright and fresh, a harbinger of a cool spring in a city where the seasons sometimes leaped directly from winter into summer.

Among the crowd of friends and dignitaries was a familiar face. Steven Henry Henderson stood off to the side behind the press corps so as not to appear in any photos, watching as the chairman of the AWF presented Abby Wilcox with a plaque, a gavel and a bronze statuette of an African elephant.

After a short round of applause, she stepped to the podium, opening her speech with the usual remarks, careful to mention as many names as she thought reasonable. Her eyes searched the crowd as she spoke, falling on many familiar faces before coming to rest on one she had invited, personally.

Without skipping a beat, the intensity of her smile increased just enough to let the man from the CIA know his presence was acknowledged and appreciated.

"...Though, we have come far in the battle to save the world's wildlife, there is still much to do. Many among us today have already given their all in every sense of the word. On behalf of the Wilcox administration, the African Wildlife Fund, and the United States government, I thank you from the bottom of my heart." Her eyes fixed on Henderson who responded with an imperceptible nod and smile. "I pledge to you that I will champion this fight with all that's in me for as long as it takes."

CIA HEADQUARTERS, LANGLEY, VIRGINIA – EIGHTEEN MONTHS AFTER EXTRACTION

Henderson had never seen the White Rat's face so flushed as he did that fall morning. He was absolutely livid that he'd been aced-out for the DDI's slot at CIA—the great Roy Barber, Harvard Graduate from Grosse Pointe, Michigan—passed over. Unthinkable as it was, it had happened. And he would never quite get over it.

Henderson stood between the podium and his proud wife Marie as the newly appointed Director Central Intelligence, Richard Morgan, a slight, clear-eyed graduate from Baltimore's Loyola College, made the announcement to CIA employees, mostly department heads and supervisors, in the main building's foyer. Of course, the White House had had some influence on the decision. But everyone present knew he had made it on his own. Mentors, like degrees, were earned after all. You had to perform to be noticed.

The ceremony was over in minutes. After all there was work to do. The eyes and ears of democracy never slept—*could* never sleep. For, as it was once said: eternal vigilance was the price of freedom.

VERO BEACH, FLORIDA – TWENTY-TWO MONTHS AFTER EXTRACTION

Ralph leaned forward watching Forrest's every move as his "father" opened the mail box to find a special envelope among otherwise unremarkable mail.

"Hey, pal!" Forrest exclaimed upon seeing the familiar handwriting, Kenyan stamps, and postmark. "Looks like we've got a letter from Malcolm McCullen."

The macaw leaned further forward in hopes of getting some mail of his own.

Forrest handed him a letter—as good a use for junk mail as he'd yet discovered—which Ralph promptly shredded with a beak entirely capable of removing a human finger. The playful bird especially enjoyed trashing brightly colored envelopes with cellophane address windows. They made a cool crunching noise which he found fascinating. Forrest carefully sliced open the one from Doc McCullen. A broad smile cracked his face as he leafed through a small stack of snapshots that, judging from the date electronically recorded in the lower right hand corner, the doctor had taken during the past few weeks. The first few depicted Joseph and his family and another caught Joseph and the boys washing the family's Land Rover. Three photos had been taken of McCullen and Kenya's new white rhinos.

Forrest held the photos aside for a moment as he scanned the enclosed letter:

Dear John,

Glad all is well with you. I'm still off the cigarettes though I do miss them after a belt-or-two of Scotch. Joseph sends his regards. As you can see by the photos, he and the family are doing fine.

I miss the company and the good conversation, though I must admit my stress level is down quite a bit since you were here. Never a dull moment with you about. The white rhinos were a gift from the South African government. Two of the three females we received are now pregnant and we should soon know the joy of the first Kenyan birth of a white rhinoceros in nearly a decade!

Speaking of births, I thought you would enjoy a picture of your new 'granddaughter.'

Forrest flipped through the photos until he came to one of an elephant cow standing next to her new baby, an adorable little female. He studied the picture for a moment before he realized who the mother was... "Dolly! Ha! I'll be damned!" Then it struck him that Schwarzkopf had to be the father and that he and Anne had witnessed the act of conception. One of those pangs hit him in the gut as he read:

...I thought you'd be pleased to know that all of the surviving members of the family group are doing well. Three of the cows including Thelma and Louise were pregnant the last time I checked on them. Poaching is down significantly, thanks to your efforts and those of the new KWS director—a first-rate chap.

And by the way, John—about that new calf… I named her Anne.

...IT NEVER WILL, AS LONG AS IVORY IS CONSIDERED TO BE MORE VALUABLE THAN AN ELEPHANT'S LIFE AND WHITE GOLD IS COVETED OR SOLD.

UNDER CONSTRUCTION

"FOR DEAR LIFE"

Karl Lenker's next hit novel

Jardin Michaels, a TV news helicopter pilot with a prominent television station in Atlanta, Georgia, is shot four times during a convenience store robbery. As he floats out of his body in a near death experience, he views the chaotic aftermath of his brush with mortality. Important clues as to the identity of the robbers who shot him are seared into his memory. After an audience and life review with God in heaven (he assumes), Jardin, formerly a devout atheist, is sent back to resume his Earthly existence until "he has done something of significance with his life."

After he recovers from his wounds and fights to regain his flight status, the bright and resilient young aviator embarks on a quest to identify the thugs who shot him and left him for dead. Along the way, a diverse cast of characters are encountered amongst the colorful and determined Atlanta Police homicide detectives known as the "Hat Squad." To the astonishment of the professionally skeptical detectives who interview him in his hospital room, Jardin is able to recall vivid details of the incident which were not recorded on the store's surveillance video and could not have been seen from anywhere except the store's ceiling.

Instrumental in his mission turned obsession are Georgia Life Flight heroic EMS helicopter crews who helped save his life as well as members of his own news organization. While Jardin is convalescing, he falls in love with the beautiful and worldly flight nurse who went beyond protocol during his "Golden Hour." For reasons even she can't understand, Jan Valderas follows up with almost daily visits to Jardin's bedside where she talks to him and reads to him while he is in a coma.

With everyone's help and hampered by the edict from the Almighty, Himself, that he cannot "harm the soul of another" or he is not allowed to return to God's presence, Jardin sets out to hunt them down and bring them to justice—God's way. INSPIRED BY A TRUE STORY

green press
INITIATIVE

Karl Lenker and TriMark Press are committed to preserving ancient forests and natural resources. We elected to print *Final Trumpet* on 30% postconsumer recycled paper, processed chlorine-free. As a result, for this printing, we have saved:

7 Trees (40' tall and 6-8" diameter)
2,499 Gallons of Wastewater
5 million BTUs of Total Energy
321 Pounds of Solid Waste
602 Pounds of Greenhouse Gases

Karl Lenker and TriMark Press made this paper choice because our printer, Thomson-Shore, Inc., is a member of Green Press Initiative, a nonprofit program dedicated to supporting authors, publishers, and suppliers in their efforts to reduce their use of fiber obtained from endangered forests.

For more information, visit www.greenpressinitiative.org

Environmental impact estimates were made using the Environmental Defense Paper Calculator. For more information visit: www.edf.org/papercalculator

Some proceeds from the sale of this book will be donated to select organizations dedicated to saving elephants and other endangered species around the world.

If you would like to help, please contact TaleWinds Press at:
help@talewindspress.com

About the Author

Karl Lenker, Lieutenant Colonel, USAF, retired fighter pilot, combat veteran (Bosnia), has logged over 29,000 hours in the air. Action is his middle name. Others write about on-the-edge adventures ...Karl Lenker lives them. Though recently retired from piloting Boeing jets around the world for Delta Air Lines, he now flies life-saving, EMS rescue missions, chases offshore race boats for TV, does television and movie shoots or explores central Florida swamps—all in helicopters.When he feels the need to back off a bit, he races his 930 Turbo Porsche, cruises A1A down the Florida coast on his Harley Davidson or flies his own airplane.

Final Trumpet is his debut novel. A portion of the proceeds from this book will be donated to organizations committed to protecting elephants around the world.

Karl's next novel, FOR DEAR LIFE, is now under construction.